D1239968

FIGHTING THROUGH LOVE AND WAR

T.G. RICHARDS

To the readers, no matter how you identify.

You are unbreakable.

PART I

THE OPENING ACT

OCTOBER, 1917

FRIEDA

FIGHTING THROUGH LOVE AND WAR

FIRST IMPRESSIONS

What's before me is absolutely nothing like what my mind painted.

It grabbed its paint buckets, swished its brushes once or twice. The buckets tipped, splashed, and spilled in soggy puddles and shades at my feet. Plenty of things happen in the art of getting lost in the world and its madness, diving into the unknown not knowing what it'll hold. Just like an artist dabbing away at a canvas, unaware of what maelstrom they'll create.

The paint drying at my feet is the murky brown of dark and disgusting mud. The canvas is slathered in layers of the chaotic mess on its fine cotton. The paint tears at it, eating it away, spreading the plague of death through a battle of pigments.

Except, instead of viewing it as an abstract piece of art, imagine the canvas as Europe, the varying browns and blacks resembling the armies sweeping in with their disastrous dominion over the lands, fighting in the war that strips the world in two.

Wars are melodramas built for the viewing of wealthy, cigar-smoking upper class men sipping whisky and playing poker with human lives in lavish houses. They're for the devil perched upon their shoulder. The devil that whispers deceptions and orders of destruction in their ears. Each lie morphs each man into something new. They shed their skin for scales. The fangs appear. The horns sprout. The tongue yearns for a taste of blood. After that, there's no going back.

The Western Front is a picture of madness and everything that's evil: The very birthplace of the Devil's patrons.

I came under the impression that it would look like the images depicted on the posters that wave in the wind back home. There were mascots and bold letters that jumped out and crawled under your skin, rolling hills and cloudy skies; a slice of a dystopian paradise. Although, what's presented to me is nothing more than a graveyard; a town wrecked by war with collapsing buildings, smoke settling upon the skyline in tendrils and plumes.

The walkways and alleyways are inhabited by soldiers dressed in battle-stained uniforms. They scurry through the streets like a nest of disturbed wild mice in a kitchen: wheeling wagons, driving trucks, building up or repairing walls, digging through debris, and queuing up to receive their rations. The men are exhausted, their cheeks hollowed out, uniform sagging from their frames as if they themselves have turned into scarecrows, stuffing themselves with straw to give the illusion that they're still human. Ghastly shadows concocted of missed sleep lie under their sockets on their gaunt, hardened faces. A myriad of them are phantoms, shells of who they used to be before the bells of war rang out.

The cold, drab weather has my core shivering as I walk through the decaying town. There's the occasional dull murmur of soldiers and the clopping of hooves as horses trot by, all seemingly unaware of my presence, taking me in as another member of their colony.

I draw my worn coat tighter, shivering profusely from the icy breeze that stings my cheeks and bites my hands. I attempt to ungracefully move my ungloved fingers to fix the strap of my satchel that digs into my shoulder, nearly tripping over the uneven chunks of broken brick.

Despite this miserable example of a day, a smile slips onto my face as I walk with my head held high. It feels so criminally good to be walking the streets of St Mihiel after so many months of hard work developing my faux persona, creating a false identity, and training to reach where I am now.

My next move is to find the mysterious Lieutenant Colonel and head off to the war on the front lines. Finding him shouldn't prove much of a challenge. Except for the fact that all the men around me are identically dressed with caps tipped over their faces, busy chatting amongst themselves as they work. Their superiors bark orders with the powerful tang of smoke and grime sitting heavily in the air.

I take another quick glance at what I can see over the many heads of newly enlisted men of all ages and backgrounds. Shuffling through the crowd, I begin running my hands through my unevenly chopped brown hair—the results of trying to trim it myself are still painstakingly obvious.

My first attempt at pushing to the front of the crowd results in abruptly bumping shoulders with a man passing by with a small, leather-bound book in his grip.

Both of us go spiraling. His lips part with a gasp of surprise as his hands clutch tight to his book like it's a lifeline. Under his cap, his eyes widen to become the size of dinner plates from such an unexpected jostle. He's caught in a state of shock, a flurry of alarm.

I catch a glimpse of his finger wedged between once-open pages. A lucky save, really. If he hadn't sandwiched his finger between those pages, he'd have more of a dilemma than bumping into a stranger as he reads while walking.

"I'm so sorry!" The apologies spill like a leaky faucet. I stick out a hand to help him up, but he declines and gets up on his own, unhurt. "I didn't mean to trip you, sir! If there's anything I can do to make up for it, I—"

"Save your breath! It's alright!" His voice is a deep grumble, one marked by a stubborn youth. He tucks his book under his arm. "*I'm* sorry. I should watch where I'm going. The fault is mine."

I suspect I'm goggling at him too long for his liking. His head inclines sharply to the side, questioning brows taut at my presumably adrift expression. "I'm sorry, are you okay?"

"I'm lost." My reply is far too flat. Just when I think his head can't incline any farther, it becomes acute, almost like an owl observing its surroundings. "I was trying to find Lieutenant Colonel Sallinger's regiment—"

"Sallinger, you say?" He flashes me a grin and thrusts his chin forward with pride, his cap falling back to reveal his face. "Quite a coincidence that you bumped into me. I know exactly where the Lieutenant Colonel is."

If I met him in another setting, another life, my jaw would be on the floor from just the sight of him. It takes everything in me to hold down my shock.

The mystery bookworm I bumped into by accident looks like the type of man people all over the country would fall head over heels for.

He's attractive, but not to the point where his attractiveness is blinding. To be brutally honest, I'd just say he's a little more than average. He sports a storm of thick black hair that curls and sticks up in all sorts of angles—a rather brilliantly untamed, ruggish bedhead. Strong hazel eyes that would shine magnificently in the sunlight compliment the small, faint blemishes and moles that dot his skin. His complexion is of a warm olive with a faint blush to his cheeks. His smile is heartbreakingly crooked but welcoming all the same, and makes me want to drop dead and stare.

"I'm part of his regiment, as a matter of fact. You'll follow me, yes?"

My nerves fizz beneath my skin; jolts of electricity that spark with nervousness. "Thank heavens, I thought I'd be lost forever out here. You see, I've just come off the boat and have been wandering aimlessly with a group of men who are as equally lost as I am."

"Well, of course," he shrugs, "it's extremely easy to get lost here, so please refrain from wandering too far."

I keep my distance. "I'd imagine. I'll try not to."

His eyes dig under my skin as he observes me. "Also, just a tip: Don't get caught in any barbed wire. It kills."

"I'll keep that in mind." I fiddle with the straps of my bag, eyes to the floor, as he continues to take me in. I hate when people do that; look at me like I'm some complicated code they must decipher. Perhaps I hate being acknowledged. Perhaps I'm not used to it. Hell, maybe I hate eye contact all together.

"So, mystery bookworm, what's your name?" I ask, trying desperately not to stutter.

Did I ask too soon?

Am I being too assertive?

Did I really just call him a *mystery bookworm?* For God's sake—

"Oh." He takes a small half-step back, the smile not vanishing off his lips, quirking *up* at the dreadful nickname. "I'm sorry, I was walking a bit too close. This mysterious bookworm's name is Marshall. What about you, stranger?"

"Frederic." I rebound almost too fast, announcing my chosen name. My voice is too dry, too choked to sound as laid-back as I'd aimed to appear.

His name—*Marshall*—it sounds familiar, but I can't place my finger on it.

A hand emerges from his pockets with scars and questionable burn marks running all over its palms and knuckles. Hesitantly, it presents itself in front of me for me to shake as we walk. His hands are warm, fingers of the long and square sort, save for his thumb. It's boldly round and clubbed; a rare gene, but it holds firm against my thin and awkward grip.

"Welcome to the club, Frederic. May I call you Fred? Just for short?"

I shrug, replying gruffly, "I don't see why I should stop you."

"Amazing." His shoulders slouch, exchanging their tension for comfort in my presence as he cracks another smooth grin. "It's a pleasure to make your acquaintance, Fred."

My anxious thoughts intrude on the even flow of my calm mind. No one here knows that my name isn't Frederic Charleston, who is merely my chosen identity, purely made of lies and deception. I mustn't let anyone know, or else I'll be put in jail. I'll put mine and my family name to shame. In future generations, when my descendants ask their parents who the 'man' Frederic Charleston was, they'll reprimand them and tell them to shut their mouths from the shame of being related to me.

"Fred? Earth to Fred!" Marshall's hand is waving in front of my face.

I snap back into reality like a whip's been slashed across my back. "Oh, sorry."

"Everything okay up there? You're a bit dazed."

"I didn't sleep that much on the way here. It's the nerves. I tend to overthink."

I sneak another glance at him. He's not much taller than I am, probably by a few inches. His cheeks and nose have turned red from the cold, and he appears quite relaxed but uptight at the same time.

What is he thinking?

What is he thinking of *me?*

I shouldn't be so overwhelmed. I've gone to great lengths to prove an authentic disguise: cutting my own hair, wearing as many layers as I could find, mimicking the men in the street's body language and dialect, eating large quantities and working out to desperately gain some sort of muscle mass.

"So, where do you hail from, Fred?" His hands tighten around his book as he continues our conversation; small talk to fight the silence. He's awfully good at it, I must admit.

"Seattle," I reply, asking before I forget, "What about you?"

"Good old Philly," he responds, with that ongoing, never-ending smile of his. I'm starting to suspect it's a filler for the tension that buzzes like an electrical wire between us—a bandage for an already damaged impression that I've created.

I attempt to smile back, which only has him smiling brighter. He must be putting in a lot of effort in handling me when in truth, he's dreading our interactions, our short and sparse words. Every word I mumble must be pointless to him. As soon as we find Sallinger, I predict he's going over how he's going to escape from my dull company.

As we stumble over the rubble path that leads to what I presume is a campsite, Marshall's back straightens when we turn the corner. There's the clinking of metal and the sound of men yelling at each other while busy at work. Maids and nurses giggle and spy on the soldiers who've stripped themselves of their tunics, who are doing their washing, either in singlets or nothing at all. The commotion rings in my ears, and I have to tell myself to look away in embarrassment, ashamed of seeing men in such a fashion.

Marshall seems to be used to it, but senses my repulsion, giving me another piece of advice that slithers its way into my ears. My palms dig into my eyes to block out what I've just witnessed. "You'll get a lot of *that* here: lots of pretty women looking for a man to steal away for the night. Stay close so we don't lose each other. Don't mess with the French that are nearby, either. My pals and I accidentally spilled water on them during the winter and they stole my buddy Ed's rations during the night."

I give him a simple bob of the head. Silent, but affirmative.

"It's quite good advice, actually. They're little yippers, just like their French Bulldogs."

I can't help but throw my head back and laugh. His own laugh is stifled at the back of his throat, shrinking to a satisfied '*hmph'* with the victory of wiping the frown off my face.

When he halts, he counts down the seconds to speak, folding his hands behind his back, standing straight as a pin as he addresses the man standing with his back to us. His shoulders are decked with chevrons and epaulets; the mark of an authoritative figure.

"Lieutenant Colonel, sir!" Marshall yelps, saluting. "We have a new recruit. Private Frederic—I'm sorry, what's your name?"

"Sir," I stiffen into a salute, the man's gaze swiveling to me, "I'm Private Charleston. I arrived here this evening, appointed to serve your regiment. It's my great duty to serve you."

His glare is like steel, wrinkled with lines of age at the corners of his eyes. Clearing his throat, he returns my greeting with an equally steely reply. "Welcome, Private Charleston. I see that Private Clark has done well in guiding you here. My best advice is to stay around him, as he knows his way quite well around these parts. You two should get ready for supper. It's nearly time. Say, Private Clark, we should start up a business for you to guide lost soldiers around the Front like a sheepdog on a farm. How does that sound?"

"You amuse me, sir." Marshall barks out a cold laugh. "I expect a thorough and large income annually. It's a high-paying job, if I do say so myself."

Sallinger huffs and stalks off with a simple turn of his heel.

Once out of earshot, I whisper to Marshall, "Is he usually that blunt?"

"Most of the higher-ups here are like that. It's their job. They can't be soft. You better get used to it. Also, another thing: Never disobey your superiors. The punishments are brutal. They don't give a damn if your life depends on it. They'll shoot holes through you without a single care in the world."

I cringe at the thought of what *punishments* Marshall is specifying.

My heart almost leaps out of my chest as a loud voice breaks through the still air.

"Ey, fellas!" A man laughs, an entourage trailing him close behind, with a proud air. "The park ranger is back!"

His gang stalks in front of us, blocking our path, getting much too close for my liking. Their leader, a fair-haired, scrawny man, just a few inches shorter than Marshall, snickers and closes the gap between the two of us.

His breath is stale and disgustingly bitter. I try not to breathe it in. "New meat, are you?"

Marshall pushes himself forward, his chin raised high, holding a threatening glare. "Do I have to remind you again of when you first came along? I had to search for you all night under Sallinger's orders because you got lost in the women's tents, Private Sawyers. Did you really get lost? Or did you follow your primal instincts and let what's in your pants guide you? I could never imagine you anywhere that isn't up a woman's skirts."

The man's pale brows knit together. "You're cold as always, Private Clark. Anyway, we'll leave you alone for now." He hesitates before he turns back to poke another jab at me. "Enjoy your new toy while he lasts."

"Sod off, will you? Right before I slam you to a pulp in the rubble?" The threat grates out in a growl, Marshall's fist clenched in a warning.

Taking no chances, they take off, laughing like rabid hyenas while Marshall rolls his eyes, clearly unamused. "Don't mind them. They're a bunch of insolent clowns with no moral sense."

Shortly after, we make our way towards a large, beige tent made of stretched canvas. His head pokes out of the entrance as he curls his index finger in a beckoning motion. "You're not just going to stand outside while I give you a tour of your new home, are you?"

With a gulp, I push the flaps back.

Inside the tent, it's small, yet adequate. In the far left corner is a dark bedroll with a briefcase at the foot of it, lying half open with an extra pair of breeches peeking out of the corner. A grooming kit sits innocently atop the traveling case, and a crate acts as a nightstand beside the head of the roll. Resting atop the crate is a journal with a beaten cover and a small inkwell with a pen lying in anticipation, waiting to be used.

Marshall gestures to the right of the tent with a grand sweep of his arm. "That space is all yours. We're roommates now, my friend. What's mine is yours. I must warn you, though. The bedrolls aren't as comfortable as they look."

"Thank you." I set my satchel down on the floor and get to setting up and unpacking. In the meantime, he polishes the toes of his boots. He's squinting at a small wrist watch to read the time.

"Wow, time flies. It's suppertime."

"Already?" I gasp, as he fumbles with a comb and makes an attempt to brush down his bedhead. "But we just got here!"

"Yes, as I've said: Time flies on the Front. I hope you don't mind, but I dine with a few friends...I hate being lonely. My mates are quite friendly and accommodating. Once they meet you, they'll be all over you."

"These are the people you were mentioning before?"

"Indeed. We'll stop by their tents and pick them up." Marshall opens the tent's flaps awkwardly. "Ask them about the French if you really want to. The story is obscenely horrific and will leave you crying on the floor with a belly full of laughter."

I follow him to an identical tent, where he opens the flap just a little, pokes his head inside and chuckles, "Having an evening nap are we, Corporal Surry? It's suppertime!"

There's a grumble from inside the tent, and out comes a man with a small amount of the recognizable and common stubble on his chin. His hair is similar to a mop, some getting in his eyes. Their colors are equally enchanting: one is of a pale, grayish blue while the other is a tawny brown with a slice of dark green near the bottom of his iris.

"Damn you. Could you stop yelling? The Ottoman Empire and their *dead* can hear you jabbering away."

"It was enough to wake you. Also, I'm excited to announce that I have a new friend I'd like you to meet."

"Who is it? Let me guess: another woman you've drunkenly asked to dinner that you've finally gotten in touch with since last winter's banquet? Good luck sneaking her in. I applaud you."

"How dare you make such perverted assumptions about me, Edward! I'd like you to meet Frederic Charleston. He came in just this evening. Fred, this is Edward Surry, but he doesn't mind if you call him Ed."

Ed's face remains soft from fatigue. He manages a wan smile. "Yes, call me *Ed* if it pleases you, as Marshall's rewarded me with the nickname. It's a pleasure to meet you, always a pleasure to meet newcomers."

"A pleasure to meet you," I echo and reach to shake his hand. It's of the coarse-palms-and-bitten-nails sort. On his left ring finger is a band of gold, a wedding ring.

Marshall snorts to himself. "No need to be so bitter, Ed. Fred, no need to be so uptight. Just relax. Shall we meet Lester at dinner?"

Ed rolls his shoulders to get rid of his cricks and aches. With a crack, he grunts, "You're that hungry, are you? Let me wake up first."

"You can wake up on the way. C'mon, the cold will wake you up nice and quick."

"The very thing I was trying to escape before *someone* woke me up!"

"If you'd slept any longer, you would've missed supper!"

Ed releases a half-suppressed, bitter chortle. He grips Marshall's shoulder to slow his heavy pacing. "You're so persistent, so *loud.* You want to get there first because when we first came here, we were the last to get anything. I couldn't care less, but I don't want you getting the grumps because of an empty stomach. The other side of you without food is simply nasty."

We reach what appears to be the mess hall when Marshall breaks into a sprint toward the growing line. He taps a man furiously on the shoulder, their rushed conversation audible once we come closer.

"Seriously, Marshall," the man whines. "I can't believe you made another one of your millions of friends."

"*Awww,*" Marshall claps him on the back with a cocky grin, "I'm not that popular. I don't have *that* many friends."

"Indeed not, when you're literally a tourist guide."

Ed taps me on the arm and points. "That's Lester McDouglas: another companion of ours. If you're friends with Marshall, you'll find more people walking alongside him each day. It's getting hard to keep track of how many he's picked up."

With dark eyes and sandy blond hair, Lester McDouglas has almost the same ruggish look as Marshall. On his bottom lip sprouts a moderate amount of stubble. In the rare event that he smiles, his eyes twinkle— much more approachable than his perpetual scowl. His hair is just past his ears, thin and easily-manageable. When he shakes my hand, his eyes, though he comes off as friendly, dig into mine. I guess I'll always feel like I'm in the eye of a hidden-away predator while I'm here—however long that may be.

We lazily sit down after grabbing corned beef and biscuits, plus some ham that's been donated by a small cottage in the mountainside who farm pigs. Marshall complains that it's too salty, so he slides it to Lester and Ed to share.

"You're throwing away perfectly good rations, Marshall. You don't want to starve this fall." Lester pushes the rations back to him, Marshall's bottom lid twitching at the sight of it. "You lost a lot of weight while you had bronchitis. You barely ate anything. It's time to get it back."

"I don't have much of an appetite. Besides, I can't have too many salty things, it'll make me dehydrated. That's not good when there's not much drinking water here."

After a few scrapes of forks against cans, Sallinger stands and rings a small bell, signaling for silence.

"May I have your attention? We have a special package from our lovely people back home. Enjoy the beer that's recently been shipped in. As always, a warm welcome to all the new troops that have settled on our tables today. Thank you."

The hall erupts into cheers and a deafening amount of whistling. I remain still and silent as Marshall itches behind his ear like he's still in deep thought, his fingers tapping intently on the table. He groans against the noise, dipping his head and curling his lip.

After dinner, they hand out bubbling glasses of beer. Marshall pushes his glass away, his face shriveling in disgust at the golden liquid. He then turns to me as I hesitantly observe mine.

"You've never drunk this before, I presume?" he asks.

I shake my head. "No, never. How'd you know?"

Marshall tips a dark brow. "You're hesitating. Why don't you try it to see if you like it?"

I take a small sip. The bitter taste fills my mouth before I hurriedly spit it back into the glass and gag, spluttering.

"I know, I don't like it either." Marshall chuckles as Ed and Lester drink together, content and chattering away with mugs in hand. He hands me my cup of water and watches as I chug it down.

"How do people drink this? It tastes like piss!"

Marshall shrugs, unfazed by my sudden curse. "It has a rather peculiar taste, beer. I like to think that most men drink it to...well...lose themselves for a bit. Or just to fit in, to conform."

I lean on the table, resting my jaw on my hand. At the bored gesture, Marshall sighs. "But, you're rather different, aren't you, Fred?"

His eyes turn dark with skepticality.

Did he accidentally see through my façade?

Did I slip up somehow?

Panic surges through my body as my nerves set themselves unmercifully alight.

"You're zoning out a lot," he remarks. "Probably didn't hear a word I was saying."

"Oh? I heard everything you were saying, Marshall."

His eyes move from me to around the room while he absorbs the chaotic commotion of men drinking themselves silly. He remains disinterested, only wincing whenever a loud clang against a wooden table rings out.

Whenever the noise rises, so does the pressure of his *tap-tap-tapp*ing fingers against the tabletop. His rhythm matches my hammering pulse that nails itself unforgivingly through my pulsating heart.

* * *

Marshall and the rest of his friends walk together later that night. They're chattering about, by the sound of it, the air force and the new privates that came in this morning, just like I did earlier this evening.

Ed turns to his tent where, to my surprise, Lester camps with him. Ed's eyes shine brighter in the dark. The light of the lamps' wavering flames refract off of his brilliantly-colored irises as they flick between the both of us. "You get some real rest tonight, okay? I don't want you staying up being all paranoid again. You too, Fred. Hard labor is upon you at first light."

"We won't stay up past our bedtime, Mother." Marshall yawns, dramatizing it with a wave of his hand. "I know for a fact I'm going to collapse as soon as my body hits the floor."

With a pat on the back from Lester, a kiss on the cheek and muttered words from Ed, Marshall grins and sets off to our tent, leaving them to retire.

I burrow under my blankets and make an attempt to get comfortable while Marshall unwinds. Another gaping yawn escapes while he plays with the buttons of his trenchcoat. Off it slides from his frame before he folds it neatly on a chair and takes off his cap. He then smooths his hair down and cleans his teeth, climbing onto his bedroll, turning his back to the wall and writing in the small black journal.

"What're you writing?" I move onto my side, his pen pausing when he hears my question.

"Information," Marshall says. "If I die, I want my family to read my entries and see how cruel the war is since the government doesn't allow any bad news through their mailing systems."

"Your family? Who do you have in your family? Your mother? Your father?"

A sad slump appears in his shoulders. "My mother died when I was eleven."

"Oh, I'm so sorry." I cringe at my ignorance, asking a sensitive question like that when we've only known each other for only a few hours.

"It's alright." He unleashes another heartbreaking, grieving smile. "She's in a better place now. My father is a retired soldier. My sister is training to become a volunteer nurse while my brother is in Italy."

"Why did he retire, your father?" I ask...and curse myself. Another dense question to ask someone I've just met.

"When he returned from the Front, he kept saying that his friend, Sergeant Major Joyce, had died brutally in a burning old factory in Verdun. The building was engulfed by the fire. They couldn't find his body: it had burned to a crisp after the fire was put out, burned alive, I presume. He saved my father's life when only one of them could get out alive. Father's mental state was terrible afterwards, so he retired. I pity Mr Joyce's family, honestly. His wife and child loved him to shreds. I can't imagine what it's like to lose your father to such a tragedy, you know?"

This brings multiple tingles of shock to my spine.

His father—no, it couldn't be.

The casket: black with white lillies on the top, *Papa*-sized. Another box housing a soul, another loved one turning away to the light.

He faded away along with his French intonations, his expressions of *mon petit fille* and *mon amour* across his lips with his enchanting smile. When I see him in my dreams, I can't catch him before he disappears. No matter how fast I run, he always finds a way to escape.

The air stills in my chest as my pulse roars in my ears.

It's all too much to handle, all too much to swallow down.

Sitting before me is Cooper Clark's son.

His son.

The boy that's bred and born with his blood: the blood of the man my father died saving.

It's like a chaotic comedy show, a cruel joke: a boy, motherless. A child, fatherless. They find each other by sheer coincidence with the knowledge that one of their parents saved the other so they wouldn't end up as an orphan. As tragic and innocent as it sounds, it's nowhere near.

I was right about war. It rips people apart while it tries to mend them back together. It tears families, lovers, and friends apart all under the lie that they're trying to bring peace to the world.

What they're doing isn't for the people, but for political gain, a fantasy of their conceited ideas.

When he first died, I resented his actions, for leaving a vulnerable mother with her child all alone without a man in their life to lead them. Now, all I feel is a swell of shock.

He didn't die without a second thought, but with the heart of a lion and that remarkable, selfless stroke that roared through his blood. What he did was noble, foreseeing the future. Without their father, Marshall and his family would end up at the lowest of the low without their father to light the way.

My head starts to spin. I have to close my eyes against the swimming of my senses. I slump against my bedding, shutting out the rushes of adrenaline that pass with my sudden surprise.

My voice is small, weak. "I'm going to bed. Please don't stay up too late, okay?"

All that comes back is the shifting of Marshall's body, his journal propped against one knee with dark stains on his fingers. His face creases with his smile.

"Don't worry about me. I'll manage." He sets his journal down, closing the cap of his inkwell. "I'll get as much shut eye as I can. Goodnight, Fred."

2

OVER THE LINE

A freezing cold draught blows into the tent as my eyes flutter open with sleep crust scratching at their corners. I could barely sleep last night, since I was so on edge about the war with thoughts swirling inside my head of what would happen if I were to let something slide, something I didn't want everyone to see, to know.

My tired eyes venture over to Marshall, who's managed to stretch out on his stomach. His face is slumped against his pillow with his lips slightly parted. His lashes flutter, eyes moving rapidly behind their lids as he dreams, brows pulling themselves into one dark line on his forehead.

On my wristwatch, I read that it's quarter past three. With a full head of bedhead, I sit up and reach to brush out my short locks and attempt to detangle them.

The sound of Marshall awakening hits my ears before he sits up and rubs his eyes. They lazily scan the tent and land on me. "What're you doing up so early?"

"I couldn't sleep." The answer is daunting, but it's enough for him to question me no further. His tired voice—a grumble, just warming and waking up—shouldn't be so jarring. I make an attempt to swallow the thoughts down before he yawns.

"If you're not sleeping, I'm not going to either."

"Why's that?"

Marshall's expression darkens. He runs a hand through his hair. "Ever since I came here in July, I've had the growing suspicion that a spy is among us. Maybe not a spy, but someone that's out to get us. I can't sleep without the constant worry of getting hurt. It's merely a theory, but it's enough for me to lie awake and ponder. As you were falling asleep, I heard someone howling."

"Howling?"

"Yes. What I thought was a pained howl was just a bunch of drunkards having a good time with the leftover beer. That's what I saw when I investigated."

"Marshall, there are no spies here. No one's going to hurt you."

"You don't know that for certain."

Before I can disagree, an explosion blasts through the morning air.

Marshall's eyes widen. There's a sudden panic rising from deep within them that flashes bright like lightning. He quickly combs his hair down, grabs his coat, buttons it up, and loads his gun that's in the corner of the room, packing his webbings with ammunition and supplies.

"What was that?" I snap over the racket.

"An attack from the enemy—shells—I know that sound from anywhere. Let's go!"

"I can't fight! I don't have a gun."

"Use my spare!" he yells. "Please tell me you know how to use the thing."

"Perfectly well!" I shout back as Marshall handles me a rifle. "How many guns do you even own?"

He pulls on some black leather gloves, racing out of the tent, rifle in hand. "That's out of the question!"

We both sprint out into the open, skidding to a stop as Marshall pulls someone back by the shoulder and yelps at them, "Where's Sallinger's regiment?"

"Darn, I don't know!" he yelps back in a Southern accent, Marshall cursing under his breath. He then spots Ed running with his hair messily tied back and follows suit. I struggle to not lose them in the crowd as they trot on ahead to their stations.

This is war. The mice are no longer building a home, but protecting it from the enemy, a hungry cat just waiting to catch one of them between its jaws.

Out comes the Devil with his horns, his tail swishing maliciously as his patrons transform into monsters. Their teeth draw back into dangerous snarls as they bark orders, shout and thrash around to get to their places. It's a horribly conducted orchestra as we slow to a heavy jog when the bombs return. Ed is the first to almost lose his footing, leaning back against a dirt wall to regain his balance as a shockwave echoes through the earth.

"Corporal Surry! Over here!"

Ed glowers and tips his helmet forward to protect his eyes. He then swerves around and beckons us through the bunkers towards the rest of the men of the regiment, the blast of guns shaking the ground beneath our feet. We trudge through mud and rainwater dropping down from the bare trees. Men dig holes in the trenches, ducking to cover themselves from the shrapnel and shells.

It's an absolute shitshow down here as the battle reaches its first crescendo. It's obvious that this won't be the last.

"Stay undercover! Dig!" Sallinger's calls crack through the air as we all duck inside the bunker, a shockwave sending Marshall tripping over his own two feet and rising with a mud stain across his cheek.

A bomb ends up exploding nearby. The yelling only grows louder.

"On my whistle, we run!" Sallinger yelps.

There's a mumbling of the words 'yes sir' that rushes through the regiment. Marshall and Ed reach to grip each other's hands, their foreheads touching, murmuring an exchange of prayers. They then share a tight, quick hug before they load their guns and grab hold of the rungs of the ladder.

"We have to run over the trench?" I gasp.

Marshall and Ed's eyes are wide. They know how thick the potential for death is around here.

Running straight towards the enemy. What a terribly sick idea.

"Follow us! Don't get lost, or it's the end of the line for you!" Ed shouts. A pang identifies itself in my stomach when he kisses the golden band on his ring finger as Marshall hurriedly crosses himself, angling his glare towards the sky.

The whistle blows a shrill and deafening battle cry.

Bouncing off his heels, Marshall hauls himself up the ladder, Ed following close behind on his right. I'm not as fast, but fast enough to see Marshall slip and fall from a shockwave, grunting as he falls on his back. His rifle skitters away from him on the rotting wooden boards.

It takes a few fleeting moments for him to get back on his feet, a shallow tear of skin on his face slowly turning redder with blood by the second. He fastens his helmet back on and races to retrieve his gun from Ed's grip.

Lester then bursts in with his rifle, pulling us down from the ladder, yelling over the noise, "You guys have all your limbs still attached?"

Fighter planes fly ahead in a triangular formation with their roaring engines blazing through the sky. I attempt to aim my gun at them, but Marshall tears down my arms.

"What the bloody hell are you doing? They're ours!" Anger and distress show on his face, his blood still staining his cheek a deep red as blood dribbles down his chin. The planes drop the first of their bombs, exploding on the ground below as he raises a hand to wipe at the wound hurriedly.

We run through the trenches with the shaking earth under our feet, ducking underneath the lip of the trench. I'm pressed tight between Marshall and Lester's shoulders. They're busy taking ammunition from Marshall's spare rounds, plus a swig of water.

Bombs are now being set up. Shells blast from machine guns and pepper the air. Marshall's wiping his cheek as someone hands him a mask along with Ed, Lester, and myself. He slides it on, helping me as Ed and Lester pull on their own.

The bombs are loud against my eardrums, slightly muffled by the mask as a white-yellow fog forms.

"What in the world is that?" I start to panic as Marshall ducks to his knees.

"They must've released the gas," he answers, pointing at Ed and Lester. "Get down! Chlorine gas, isn't it?"

"Aye, sir!" Ed calls back. A pungent odor fills the air as the four of us remain as still as stone on the ground.

The bombs are set off yet again and explode faster than the ones before.

Something sharp hits my shoulder, and I cry out in pain. Marshall dives to push me lower under the clouds of gas, shoving me against the planks with a loud thud.

His gloved hands grip me tight. "Are you okay?"

"Fine." I level my gaze with his as he lets go, slumping against the wall with a pained groan. "Marsh—"

"I'm fine, I'm fine." He waves away my worry. "Just in pain from my fall. I'll have a small bruise. Stay low until the gas clears up. Don't take off your mask. If you do, Death may as well welcome you with open arms."

* * *

I end up leaving the battle that lasted from dawn till dusk with a cut on my forearm and a ruthless pain in my shoulder.

When I slump on a chair in the tent, exhausted, with a bandaged arm, I watch Marshall as he bandages a scar along his chest and wrist. His torso and limbs are thin but graciously long with a small amount of muscle; the probable result of hard labor. I wonder how long it took him to get so tall while he's still so young.

I'm snapped out of my thoughts as he hands me a canteen full of water. "Here. It does you no good to be dehydrated."

I take it from him gratefully.

His sigh is wary, exhausted. "I'm sorry for snapping at you out there."

"Are you kidding me? I'd rather you be tough and teach me how to survive rather than make the decision to treat me like a child."

I hand him the canteen as he buttons up his freshly washed and dried tunic. He fetches a wan smile.

"How's that shoulder holding up?"

I wince, mumbling back, "Not so great."

"I should take you to the medics if that's the case." He offers a scarred hand. "Shall we?"

While Marshall walks me to the medics, he occupies me with a lively conversation about *The Adventures of Huckleberry Finn* and how he thoroughly enjoyed it as a child when I bring up the question of the book he was so concentrated on yesterday. He helps me laugh again with butterflies in my stomach. Then he leaves, his fading footsteps sparking a bone-deep emptiness.

A medic comes to examine my wounds and sits me down. He inspects my shoulder for any broken bones, and I wince yet again, inhaling through gritted teeth and a clenched jaw.

He pauses before he examines it any further. "Can I see your wound up a bit closer, Private?"

Panic buzzes through me.

This may as well be the end.

I give way to a nod.

Then, he unbuttons my tunic to have a closer and more thorough look. "What is this? You've...you've bound your chest...My god! You're..."

I glare at the ground, ashamed. *Not a woman,* I tell him internally. *Not entirely.*

He buttons up my tunic and glares into the deepest depths of my eyes. His previous warmth has been obliterated, replaced by an unforgiving cold stare, as if I've transformed into a hideous beast.

Not a girl. Only partially.

"I'll have to take you to Sallinger!"

I'm close to tears as his hand clamps around my shoulder, forces me to stand, and walks me over with an inescapable force. While Marshall helps Ed bandage his ankle, he hears the commotion and inclines his head. I hurriedly look away and whimper two simple words, unable to meet his innocent, inquiring gaze.

I'm sorry.

The medic yaps out the Lieutenant Colonel's name once he reaches the outside of his tent. "Lieutenant Colonel?"

Sallinger answers, clearly disturbed, "Yes, medic? Is that you?"

He tugs me along, causing me to whimper. His hand grabs me tighter by my sore shoulder, forcing me into a chair. I shake uncontrollably and sit across from Sallinger, hands clenched in fists upon its arms.

The medic glares at the both of us, his eyes scanning the room, digging into my skin. "Sir, I believe you have a mishap with one of your troops."

"What does this have to do with Private Charleston?" Sallinger presses the spectacles that rest on the tip of his nose just a little bit higher, pushing aside the thick tome of paper resting on his makeshift desk made of an unused crate.

"They aren't Frederic Charleston."

Sallinger blinks up at him. "I beg your pardon?"

The medic perches himself on the head of my rickety chair. He's ravished by the damage he's causing and the methodic curl of the evil words on his tongue. "That's right. This person is not Frederic Charleston, sir."

Sallinger doesn't shift, doesn't show any sign of unease. His face is marble; cracked with age, yet it remains unfractured. His tongue skirts over his top two teeth, taking this all in at a measured pace.

"What is your name?" He leans forward, gazing at me with an interested sheen in his eye.

I take a deep breath, stealing too much air for my constricting lungs' liking. I'm shaky with fear. "My name, sir...My name is Frieda Joyce."

The corner of his mouth tips into a knowing smirk. "Joyce...I've heard that name before...Ah! Your father was a soldier, was he not?"

"Yes, sir. Sergeant Major Frank Joyce."

Sallinger's smirk turns into a sad, remembering smile. He slips momentarily into the past—whatever he remembers of my father, whatever connections he had.

"Why have you decided to endure all the trouble of getting here? I hope it isn't to try and find him because you don't believe his death certificate."

"No," I curl my fingers inward so hard my knuckles turn white, "because I wanted to fight, Lieutenant Colonel. I wanted to fight, chip in some service to our great nation, just like my father."

"Why didn't you become a nurse instead of a soldier?"

"I wanted to help with our victory. Being a medic doesn't fascinate me as much as having a legacy of fighting for our freedom. I paid all the funds for the training camp out of my own allowance just to get here, sir. Being an enlisted personnel will satisfy me, if you don't have any objections."

The medic glares. "What are you going to do? Are you sending them home? Are you going to shoot them? They're clearly a bad omen!"

"Silence!" Sallinger's command snaps the tension of the air in half. "They're a tolerable and noble soldier, coming a long way to pay us the greatest debt they could ever offer, their life, for a good cause. Their father was equally as noble and loyal while he was alive. I don't see an issue with them being here. As long as they don't cause too much trouble, they will stay. You have one chance. Don't make me regret this."

Letting out a shuddering breath, I flash him a stiff smile. "Thank you, sir."

He dips his head, acknowledged, without returning my grin. "But before you depart, I need your *real* information."

"Of course."

The medic storms out after he stomps his foot, dismissed and dissatisfied with the verdict.

"So," Sallinger reaches for a pen and paper, "your name was Frieda Joyce, right?"

"Yes. My middle name is Sarah."

"Are you still eighteen, or did you lie about your age, too?"

"Indeed," I reply. *Ouch.* "My birthday's the nineteenth of January, 1899."

"Brilliant. The only thing that was changed was your name and gender. Alright, stay out of trouble. You're dismissed."

I stand and salute. "Thank you, sir. I'll be sure to never disappoint you."

Sallinger takes me in before I turn away, with a slow blink. "You won't. I know that for a fact. Your father was the same as you."

With another curt bow, I turn the corner, only to knock into someone's chest.

When I step back, Marshall stands before me.

His face is stretched in a dreadful mix of shock and disbelief, jaw slackened, agape and fumbling, groping for words.

"You're not Frederick?" His voice is strangely winded. His chest heaves.

"You heard? Why do you sound like you've run a marathon?" I ask.

"Are you really Frank Joyce's child?" He creeps closer, his face paling. "Is it true?"

It's too hard to hold eye contact. "You didn't have to run after me."

"Oh my god." Marshall continues to struggle at grasping for the right words. "Frieda? The one who always dressed in dark dresses no matter what the event and visited us almost every holiday?"

"You remember me?"

"Of course I remember you!" Marshall's frown ceases. "Great heavens, you've grown."

"And you're alright with me...being…you know...not a woman—well, partially, but not wholly, if you know what I mean—"

His face relaxes into a smile, an unusually excited one that makes his eyes crinkle with his newfound discovery, the truth that the identity of Frederic Charleston has been buried six feet underground. A nobody takes his place. "I don't see a problem with it."

"Huh, I expected you to turn back in shame now that you know."

Marshall shakes his head. "I wouldn't turn my back on a friend. Come, walk with me."

There's another awkward silence between the two of us, Marshall making an attempt to break it. "So, Frieda, I never got a chance to fully meet you, and I'll say that you have a pretty name." I can't find a way to hide my bashfulness as he draws nearer. "I still like you, Fred, or Frieda, whatever you want to be called, I will call you by it. Geez, I gotta start calling you Fri, Freddy, Fr—"

"Frieda will do." I cut him off, a beam still etched on my face. He flashes a returning simper and, somehow, an adoring haze appears in his eyes. "And I'm fine with 'she,' and 'they.'"

"Okie dokie. Since we're friends and all," Marshall shrugs, his hands in his pockets, "I like learning people's birthdays. He said you were born in January?"

"Mm, the nineteenth. 1899." He's digging for his notebook, itching to write it down. "Let me guess how old you are: nineteen?"

"You are so close," he whimpers.

"Eighteen?"

"Gosh, if only." He laughs. "I turned twenty last May."

"I was so far away. What day?"

"The twenty-first, but I'll happily look younger, if that's what people are into nowadays."

"I'm sure you'll be able to pull that off," I tease. He lets the compliment sink in with a cocky and proud roll of his shoulders.

* * *

Tonight, it's cold in the trench. I'm shivering hard without my blanket. So hard that I can't feel my hands anymore as the temperature continues its suicidal nosedive. My teeth start to chatter as more and more chills freeze me to my bones.

At the sound of my whimper, Marshall shuffles. I take it he's a light sleeper, susceptible to awakening even from the slightest whistle or bang that reaches his ears.

"Cold?" he asks, his voice croaking, eyes weighed down from sleep. It doesn't take long to notice that he's also shivering under his blanket.

The reply surfs across a cloud of warm air that plumes from my lips. "A little."

"Lies," he argues. "You're shaking a lot more than just *a little.*"

24

His arms spread out wide, a welcoming walkway toward him, toward a source of warmth. His eyes glitter at me with hope. On the inside, he seems to be praying to some powerful god that I accept his offer.

"You said you were cold, didn't you?"

"I'm not so sure. I've never—"

"Frieda," Marshall's tone has turned dangerous, warning me, "I'm not going to do anything you're thinking of. All I'm doing is trying to keep you warm. If you aren't warm at all by the early hours of the morning, you'll get sick and die."

"I'm fine!" I whisper. Another shiver creeps across my skin.

His gaze flickers at my reply, arms dropping to his sides. "Sorry, I worry too much."

"I do too."

"I don't want to worry about my friends dying while I'm here, and I—"

"It's quite alright. Calm yourself. It's the same for me."

Marshall steals one last longing glance at me before he turns his back; a silent gesture that probably means 'I trust you' in his vocabulary. It's a subtle change from resting with his back up against the wall. He's finally letting his protective barrier crumble in my presence.

I lie awake for a minute before the shivers bite into my core. I make an attempt to roll closer to him, absorbing his warmth, hungry to feel it creep across my body. He's nearly asleep when my elbow knocks against his back.

He lets out a yelp, and his lids snap open. "You took my advice, did you? It's either that or the fact that you're a paid hitman trying to kill me in my sleep."

"Why would I be a hitman?"

Marshall shrugs, sleep dragging him down. Soon enough, I also feel the pull. "Some people are what we don't expect them to be, I've learned. They put on masks and like to play charades."

Marshall, asleep, has warmth generating off of him as his back expands against mine with each breath. I lay my head on the wooden boards, inhaling the night air and his strong but wafting smell: dirt, soap, and coffee.

It's strange, I've known him vaguely for such a long time, but trust him as if we've been friends for years.

My head pains me at the thought, remembering how my father always talked of a mysterious boy called 'Marshall Clark,' who he joked would end up taking me away if his brother didn't beat him to it. I saw Marshall once at a gathering when I was about ten. He hated socialization, but now, he's a social butterfly, acting as a tour guide for men he barely knows.

Then, my heart lurches and startles me awake, beating in my ears. A wave of dizziness washes over me before the giddiness comes. My hand bangs against my mouth to stop the scream threatening to escape.

I try to suppress my feelings and shove them down. But, with a hiss that escapes my mouth and a queasy flip of my stomach, they keep growing.

And growing.

3

THE SECOND BATTLE

It's been about five weeks since my first experience with trench warfare.

The weather has gotten harsher, and the rumors have flown far and wide to announce that I am, in fact, Frank Joyce's child. It's giving me a headache, having to answer all their questions, all their queries. Most of them have been about what he was like, how he was as a father, and our relationship, nothing about the fact that I myself am non-conforming; fluid in a way that I feel comfortable being feminine, or nothing at all. I've taken that announcement into my own hands, telling those who seem interested, who accept it or have no problem with it. Most choose not to acknowledge it, either from the fact that their views are either backward or they simply don't care.

But I still get the more-than-often individuals who spit at my feet and call my bloodline pretentious, or complain that I have an inflated ego because I came here under an alias. I receive a lot of mixed opinions about my father's legacy and his service to the war. He was famous among the troops, I hear, and took great care in making sure all plans were in order whenever he assisted or led a unit into battle.

Marshall tails me most of the time when someone wants to ask me questions, get to know me better, and often watches me from afar. Whispers have been traveling, that we're indulging in a secret, raging love affair behind closed doors. Marshall himself gets defensive and dismisses it flatly every time it's brought up. Just the thought of such an illicit theory only riles me up—both from nervousness and disgust at the fact that some weasels can't stop burrowing further and further into holes of lies for entertainment.

But, although the rumors place a scar on my heart that never heals, the feelings still beat with no complaints through my veins.

With every smile, every exchange of words, every glance, my heart falls to pieces no matter how hard I try to glue it back together. He's broken it, turned it into fragments that stream across the floor, a mess that he can't even see. He dances across it, bathes in his own blood from when they snag on his skin, all with the graciousness of a gentleman.

His laugh: a jingle of pleasant little bells.

His smile: a tiny slice of paradise.

His voice: possessing the same beautiful and melodic elements of a crooner.

Good God, my feelings for this boy are turning me into a poetic mess. I'll crumble to the ground the next time he compliments or teases me.

* * *

My eyes open against the sun and a cold draught flitting through the folds of the tent's entrance. Marshall is back to his usual: sleeping deeply in the corner of the tent on his stomach.

I get up and ready, fixing my puttees and belt, clipping on the food rations I have in a small pouch, digging up extra ammunition to load my rifle with. I do up the collar button of my tunic before I step out of the tent, Marshall stirring at my careful movements, an audible yawn escaping him as he rises.

It's recently rained. Though the smell is heavenly, everything is soaked by rainwater. There's mud and puddles all across the ground.

Marshall steps out, fully ready. He stretches, gritting his teeth as a bone in his back cracks. He shakes out his shoulders, painful, stiff, clearing his throat and rubbing his eyes, standing straight.

"You got up before me again, early bird." He's particularly close to me. I take a tiny, cautious step back before he offers a hand. "Shall we go to breakfast?"

With no hands held, we walk to the mess hall with people staring, whispering. Marshall keeps up with his usual somber expression, his head held high.

I keep my head down. Marshall's hand fastens on my shoulder to power me forward.

I wince when my name is called.

With little to no hesitation, Marshall rolls his eyes and grimaces. We pick up the pace to get to the mess hall. Somehow, I'm capable of keeping up with him and those long legs of his.

Something is whispered, and a group of men break into laughter.

He's about to snap back with a snarky response when there's a bang in the distance, a crash that makes everyone stand on edge. There's the deadly drone of the German planes that fly up ahead; dark birds of prey and a bad omen.

There's another bang and more collective gasps. Marshall's hand grips my shoulder tighter. The pain is faint, yet clear.

"Well, I'm ready to shoot some planes out of the sky like they're ducks in hunting season."

Then, almost on cue, machine guns being loaded with bullets rumble not far off in the distance.

We race back to the tent to grab our guns. Mine slips from my grip when I trip, my chin knocking against the hard ground. Before I can retrieve the rifle, someone swipes it away from me.

"Hey! Give that back!" I yell over the protestful ringing of my ears.

The soldier, Andrew, snickers. "Sorry, Joyce. Survival of the fittest. Go home already!"

I hiss at this remark, scoring a solid kick to his shins and spit on his boots. He curses and drops the gun at his feet. I scramble to retrieve it and hurry along with the rest of the regiment.

Upon the many metal-covered heads of soldiers, Marshall is jogging fast with his rifle in hand, index finger curled around the trigger, hurried pants escaping him. He has on those godforsaken leather gloves again and a dark glare. I skid around the corner to tail him. His eyes briefly scan over his shoulder as he pushes his way through the bustling trench, the ground shaking beneath us.

Puffing and slumping against the dirt wall, Marshall's wet helmet drips from the storm into his eyes, wetting his dark lashes. They tilt upward to narrow at the sky as the planes, with their menacing wings, roar up ahead. One man fires up at them, no coughing or sputtering of an engine present, Marshall spilling out a long line of profanity.

"We need to shoot those planes down." Marshall ducks under the ladder, teeth gnashing together. A nearby shockwave nearly causes him to lose his balance. "We need to stop them from—"

"We don't."

At my flat reply, his nostrils flare and his brows knit incredibly tight together. "Pardon?"

It all comes out in a lecture—one I never thought I'd be capable of giving with such assertiveness. "The planes. That's for the air force to take care of. Is that our problem? No, of course not. We're the army. Don't waste a perfectly good bullet on a rusty machine when, as it crawls inside a man's chest, it does real, irreversible damage."

Marshall pauses, his grip still tight on the trigger. I know I've gotten through to him when he gives me a snarky grin.

"I like how you think," he comments. "Just pray we don't get one in ours instead. Where's Edward? Lester?"

"They're here." I brace myself against the ladder, my teeth chattering uncontrollably. My heart is going a million miles an hour. I struggle to let any air inside my lungs.

"Oi," his other hand is back on my shoulder, "you okay there?"

"Just breathless." I swallow, wincing as another shockwave ripples across the battlefield. Dirt is ejected from the ground and sprays into the trench in pellets.

Marshall flinches when lightning flashes against the gray sky, another roll of thunder following close behind.

The whistle blows. Marshall hesitates before he climbs up the ladder to shoot. Unlike any other time, he doesn't pray before he wedges his boot on the highest rung he can reach, grabbing hold of the topmost one. He hoists himself over in a swift, singular motion.

I climb as fast as I can, firing at anything that moves in the enemy trenches. The guns are loud. The world around me is a blur. Marshall props himself on one knee, firing a round which meets the bodies of men who lie unaware of their fate only after he sets back off running.

Another shockwave rattles us about. My foot gets caught on a fallen, gnarling tree root, slamming me down on my chest upon the dirt with a sickening crack that shoots up my leg.

With a fist slamming into the hard earth from the pain, a body falls just inches away. The man's eyes are wide, his body writhing as he struggles to breathe, gasps for air, for life.

Digging my nails into my palms, I lie still and make the attempt to shut out the dying man's noises, his cries for help, the squelching of flesh, and the oozing of warm blood as it leaks onto his hands from a wound in his chest, dribbling from his mouth when he grows still.

The acidic taste of spit up is in my throat. His eyes remain wide open, staring, unseeing, as I let out a horrified cry, covering my mouth. My stomach squeezes in on itself. The need to throw up grows. The pain throbs through my foot.

Someone screams my name from some yards—no, feet away.

That someone yelps out a prayer and dives to the ground. Bombs crash down, creating craters as the man lands beside me on his back, letting out a howl, obstructing my view of the other man's corpse. I cup my ears against the commotion. My teeth bite into my lower lip and draw blood.

Beside me, his helmet lies askew, his chin tipped to the sky. His teeth clench whistling out a strangled groan. His black hair is covered in dust, face caked with mud.

Marshall is beside me in a crumpled heap, coughing up brown-tinged spit that dribbles down his chin.

"Marshall?" The realization comes out in a gasp. Another shot of pain blasts through my lower limbs. "You're—"

"I looked back and you weren't there. I had to find you—"

He's interrupted by a weak thud to the chest from my fist.

"Are you mad?" I scream, my voice hoarse in my dry throat. "Do you have a death wish? You should've kept running! God *damnit,* Marshall! You nearly killed yourself running back here!"

30

"Would there be any less of a potential for death if I kept running forward?" He coughs out the witty response, choking on his words and saliva. He's able to raise his head by an inch. "Death at every angle."

"And what're you going to do about it? My whole leg is probably twisted!"

"I don't know, haul you back to safety? Get you to a medic?" he whines. His body goes slack. head hitting the floor.

Medics are approaching with stretchers ready to carry our weight. Marshall's breathing becomes uneven as he struggles against the pain tearing through him. He's fading away, growing faint. He attempts to look around, but his eyes end up creeping to the back of his sockets.

He shuts down beside me.

"Marshall, come on." I reach to shake his shoulder, swat him across the face, check under his nose to see if he's still breathing, squeeze his upper arm hard enough to inflict pain. Anything to gain a response, demanding, with more urgency, "Marshall, *get up.*"

Arms clamp down on me as I call out, "He's not breathing! He's not breathing! Help him, not me!"

I'm piled fast on a stretcher. The medics kneel down to examine his doll-like body; still as a corpse. They put their finger under his nose, check his pulse, and nod at the other medic, who sighs with relief and grabs his legs, the other hoisting him up under the arms. More turn up to lift our stretchers and carry us away from the scene.

Marshall, minutes into the trip, is still out cold.

He's a dead weight. A bag of muscle and bone. His skin is waxy with an unhealthy pallor. His head of thick black hair, covered in mud, lolls to the side. I want to bring him back to life, see the color return to his face, warm blood pooling under his skin, those hazel eyes flitting open, that boyish grin returning to his lips as he cracks a joke about his evident near-death experience.

Teams of medics hurry along with their work, but Marshall's team works even quicker to place him on an unoccupied bed next to mine. Four men are on him, one kneeling and holding a bottle of salts before his nose, another banging his knees with a hammer and shining a penlight in his eyes to check his reflexes. A scribe scratches down notes, digging into his collar to retrieve his identity tag, jotting down the numbers engraved upon its metal surface.

When he awakens, a doctor takes his side, asking him questions. Barely alert, he's either nodding or shaking his head and taking small sips out of a mug. He grimaces occasionally at the nurses' work to turn him onto his stomach to check his spine. He grips the sides of the bed and yelps when the doctor presses his fingers down on his lower vertebrates.

"Stop it! It hurts! It hurts! It hurts!" he howls, his mug of water shattering on the floor when he knocks it with a hand that attempts to grip the side of the nightstand, visible tears in his eyes. The doctors continue to press along his back nonetheless. "It hurts! Please stop it!"

Despite his cries for help, the doctor shoves needles under his skin — probably full of painkillers or something of the sort.

They pull his tunic over his back, Marshall turning, showing a face full of tears and eyes that are a puffy, disturbing red. It hurts to see those beautiful eyes cry like that. The same eyes that smiled at me earlier this morning.

His cries of pain quiet down as the drugs kick in. When grows still once more, a medic slides a thin pillow under his head and a blanket over his shoulders.

* * *

Marshall doesn't move again until the sky turns dark, where his eyes flutter open. With a groan, he balls his hanging hands into fists.

"Jesus, Mary and Joseph..." he starts, only to be interrupted with another bout of pain. "How long have I been out?"

It's hard to answer. My last words to him before he passed out were a series of scoldings.

"Quite a while." I manage to coax the words out. He hisses with discomfort. "They were going to give you more painkillers, but you were still out. They might come back now that you're conscious."

"They better not," Marshall replies, groggy. "I've been drugged up enough."

"Look, I..."

I'm interrupted when he lets out another whine.

"Carry on. Don't mind me, your hero, dying before you as you send me to Heaven with your elegant words."

"Please take me seriously this time."

"My bad. Go on."

"I'm sorry for...you know, what I said back there." Another wave of pain shoots up my leg. "I feel horrible for screaming."

"No," Marshall points at me, "you're fine. It's on me. You're right. It was a witless thing for me to do. This isn't the drugs speaking, by the way. I was so worried when I saw you lying there. I wasn't thinking."

Silence. Conversation over. Everything broken is fixed.

I turn my gaze away from him, but feel the tapping of his fingertips against my knee moments later.

"Hey." He's poking me right on the joint, pressing harder and harder each time. "Please don't dwell on it. It won't do you any good. It happened. Look forward. We survived an assault together. We nearly died, but we're still here. I'm honestly glad you reprimanded me."

I cast a look his way. He emits another hiss and a string of swears. His cheek slumps against the pillows, hand dropping back to the side, dangling off the edge of the cot.

"These painkillers really do make you feel woozy." His remark is enough to break the silence. It takes a lot to shove down my laughter. "Seriously, I'm about to go under again. They may as well give me a moose tranquilizer while they're at it."

4

LIAR VERSUS LIAR

The damage done to my leg is a twisted ankle, plus a shallow gash that's opened the skin of my calf to just below my knee. At least that's what the nurses said, when they examined me from head to toe early the next morning behind a curtain.

Over the next six weeks of recovery, Marshall's been discharged with a bruised back, bandages lining his torso. He's not the happiest man in the room, itching uncontrollably under his uniform.

Despite his discomfort, he's eagerly taken up the responsibility of smuggling food and gossip that the soldiers eat up like wolves in the mess hall.

Amongst his ravaged burglary, he proudly stole the short term nickname of the 'Food Racoon': the product of his adventures and scouting missions to retrieve double the amount of food; rations fit for two men. He pokes his head around the corner with his hands full and his nose high, trodding in like a proud hound showing off his catch during the hunting season.

During our dinner for two, he interests me with various stories of his childhood and the days before the war, which produces a nasty lonely feeling in my gut that never fades, never changes. It's an ugly churning of bile that sloshes against my stomach's walls. I could've had the potential to know him and his charming presence even before the war broke out.

We met a few times before, but it was always either a quick 'hello, how are you' or a brief mention during a conversation. He wasn't the proudest teenager, nor the most social. Now, he laps up the attention from his friends and has turned himself into a people pleaser. His selflessness is strong, as it makes my heart skip an unhealthy amount of times. He pushes my feelings down the stairs with enough force to send me flying.

I keep wallowing in the waters of my emotions, working things out as I go, even if it gets challenging. Each time I ponder, each time I take another step forward, I always want to dive into the deep end and declare that I am, in fact, enchanted.

But like everything else, feelings must be accounted for one step at a time.

* * *

I'm picking at my bandages when a Southern accent, sugary-sweet with false kindness, calls for my attention.

"Private Joyce, please don't pick at the bandages. You'll give yourself an infection. Anyway, you're free to go. Keep the wound clean and take it easy."

"Already? Wow, time flies." I slide off the cot and reach for my boots that remain in a heap on the floor with my puttees. "Thank you for your service, Miss. I'll forever be in your debt."

Before I'm able to reach for my left boot, a hand clamps over my upper arm, squeezing tight. Nails dig into my skin.

"Hey! What do you think you're—"

"You foolish child," she curses, her breath warm near my ear. "I'm surprised you haven't died from sepsis with all that picking around of yours. I'll drink to the day you finally lose your footing. You're a disgrace. Tell Private Clark that he isn't any better with his rent boy aura." She unclamps my arm, still holding on to her taunting glare. Her smile is icy, her sneer cold. "Just give up already, Joyce. Even with him as your lucky charm, you'll make it nowhere besides the gates of Hell."

My jaw snaps shut before I make matters worse. I turn to go.

Marshall's waiting patiently outside, his foot tapping against the ground, deep in thought. He perks up upon my entry. "Well? All fixed?"

My shrug comes first. "All patched up."

He pats me on the shoulder with a preposterously glad grin. "Great! It's been so lonely without you. We've missed you. All of us have."

I let out a smile—a real smile. One that hasn't been painted on my face since before my father died. One that doesn't serve to mask the unpleasant feelings crawling under my skin.

He makes me feel this new feeling. An extraordinarily new feeling I've only ever felt once before in my life so fleetingly. He sends tingles up my spine when he talks, each time he sets a gentle hand or his warm eyes upon me.

"Are you feeling okay?" I ask him, taking note that he's rather jumpy beside me.

He shuffles from one foot to another with his hands in his pockets, providing me a short answer. "Yeah, as always."

I furrow my brow, causing him to flinch under my gaze.

"You're quite rigid today." I elbow him, careful not to hurt his back. "Are you ill?"

"Ow! I'm not sick!" His gaze lowers to his boots. A thin veil of sweat forms along his brow.

"What's wrong?" I bump him a little harder. He jumps back from the force.

His jaw is set. "Nothing! I swear, it's nothing."

I know a liar when I see one.

We enter the mess hall, Marshall's irises now the shade of dark, bitter coffee. No light refracts off them, even though the hall is brightly lit. People stare, whispering and gossiping behind their hands in hushed voices as we make our way through the crowds. His head remains high. He appears untouchable, unfazed by his name spilling off their tongues.

Let them stare, Marshall instructed me when the rumors started to fly. *Don't give them a reaction. Don't let them gain the satisfaction of seeing you fall.*

With a wave and a rushed handshake, Marshall and I settle at a table with more of his friends I've met along the way. They became frequent visitors in the tent as I was recovering. It didn't take a lot to warm up to them, which I'm thankful for. They took no second chances in accepting me as one of their groupies, their packmate inside a wolf's den.

Social hierarchy comes in strides with this pack, as it does with many others. Of course, Marshall isn't the boss. Ed handles that powerful status with style, keeping the group stable on their axis. Often, Marshall challenges him for the role, but it always ends in a scuffle; Ed licking his claws clean, Marshall running with his tail between his legs, a scar or two etched into him.

"Hey, you two!" Chip's loud, louder than the commotion around us.

Now, Chip isn't his real name, simply a nickname held in place by the chip of his front tooth that can be seen when he smiles. *Charlie's* hair is swept neatly back from his face in pin-straight locks like dark blades of grass in comparison to Lester, who sits beside him with his dirty blond curls.

"Looks like we've got our Frieda back!" Chip exclaims.

"Chip, please have a little respect for our friend." Marshall ruffles his hair, sitting next to him. "What're we playing here? Blackjack?"

"We were just finishing. If this was any sort of gambling, I'd be screwed to no end." Chip pushes his battered playing cards back at Lester, who thumps them against the table into a neat pile, setting them back into a box in his pocket.

"You poor boy. Perhaps I could win you some chips by seducing our dealer?" Marshall winks. "I'm told I'm a charmer. I could act as a lapdog for a few gambles."

"No way in hell are you sitting your arse on me, Clark." Lester glares over the table, Marshall emitting a somewhat sinister chuckle from deep within his throat. "On a more serious and less *vulgar* note, those Germans think they can invade us now? Not on my watch!"

As a heartfelt discussion assembles itself, the chefs call that the rations are ready to be distributed: undercooked, hard meat and frozen vegetables.

I don't care how it tastes. I'm practically starving and wolfing it down in such a feral way that my mother would reprimand and smack me to Heaven and back if she were here.

I start drinking the bitter-tasting water. After swallowing down every last drop, my stomach growls. It demands me to feed it more than what's available, grumbling in protest as a dull ache forms.

Beside me, Marshall avoids tasting the corned beef at all costs as he hurriedly empties the can, downing the last of it with water out of his canteen.

"This food has gotten utterly disgusting," comments Lester. "It's hardly edible; no taste."

"Since when has it ever been good?" Chip pushes his vegetables away with an air of distaste. "I've lost so much weight since I've been here."

"Everyone has." I lean over the table, chewing at my lip. "They're basically feeding us dog food."

Marshall wipes the corners of his mouth. "Amen. But we must remain thankful that we're actually being fed tonight."

Our discussion is interrupted as the doors swing open.

A cold current chills the hall, Lester cursing once it reaches our table, brow twitching with vague annoyance. "Git's late."

Ed, his hair whisked back by the wind, skids to a stop to get his rations and plonks himself down beside Marshall as Chip murmurs to Lester, "*There's* a lap he can gladly sit his arse upon—"

"Woah, woah, woah!" Marshall slams a scarred hand on the table. "I was kidding! I was kidding!"

"What's this?" Ed gives Marshall a quizzical glance as he peels back the lid of his beef, winter and fall eyes flickering with questions.

"Marshall was planning to master the art of seduction during our game of Blackjack," Lester drawls. "I'm afraid I'll have to pass. He's too much of a yapper."

"Woof," Marshall replies with his signature smirk, flying back into a panicked stammer. "But I was kidding! I would never—"

"Of course," Ed replies, "if I were a lonesome bachelor, I'd personally pay Marshall Clark to sit like a parrot on my shoulder, with a large sum of money. Lest we forget, my bachelor days are over and our man has his eyes set elsewhere."

"Edward!" Marshall hisses. "Lest we forget, I merely *jest*. No need to out me like that!"

Childish laughter and boyish teases roll across the table. Ed resumes his role as the alpha male, the mediator. His warmth radiates as Marshall ducks his crestfallen face into his hands.

"Please, let's not torment Marshall anymore about his romantic adventures, for that's his own issue to solve." Ed pats him on the back, Marshall letting out a pained sob at his touch and murmuring a line of 'oh god' with a few more incoherent words targeted at Ed, the sentence finishing with 'right there.'

My heart skips a beat as he pushes him away. It doesn't take me long to piece together the puzzle.

His rigidity. His added attention towards me. Ed's taunts and his response.

Obviously.

Sliding hints right under my nose, Edward was trying to provoke him to make a move. It all adds up to one simple answer, one simple solution.

Damnit, Ed, I curse inwardly and I clench my hands into fists. *Sly as a fox.*

I gulp hurriedly to hide my reaction and my rushing feelings; both joy, both fear, accelerating my heart inside my chest.

Raising my eyes once I gain the confidence I so desperately need, I stare right into the face of Marshall Clark, the man dead set on winning my heart.

* * *

After dinner, I'm pulled back by a forceful hand on my shoulder.

"Bet you like that, Joyce. First you're trying to squeeze in with the men. Then you decide to stick with him and his halfwitted friends."

I pull away, knowing immediately who it is from their familiar sneer. "Shut up, Andrew."

Behind me, he scoffs. "Don't think you can shove this conversation away. We both know you've fallen in love with the imbecile. Even the gossipers know their rumors are coming true. I must warn you. He's reckless, a landslide of problems and emotional outbursts. If you hang about, you'll only get hurt."

"So be it. Why do you care?" I snap and push him away when he draws nearer. His laugh chimes in my ears as he shoves me horrendously hard against the wall, my back slamming against the bricks as his talons grip my bruised shoulder. His breath stinks of tobacco as he watches me writhe beneath him.

"Who said *you* could fight? This war is no place for you! You're just a lovesick puppy waiting for a man to notice you!" His grin widens as he digs his nails deeper into my shoulder, taunting me. "Has society lost their heads nowadays? Why don't you pack up and go home, rid us of your ominous presence? Go back on your seldom journey of finding your next man to—"

My leg moves before my brain does.

My foot lands square in his abdomen, though his groin would be a far better landing pad and would bring more satisfactory results.

The force of my kick alone is enough to send him bending over, slinging an arm over his stomach, grunting in pain, crying out, "You bitch! Just you wait until I get my hands on you—"

Before I can escape, a captain wheels the corner and peels us off each other.

With explosive yelps of profanity from Andrew, we're dragged by our collars to Sallinger's tent, where he listens to the captain's recount before he asks us to tell our side of the story.

The energy of the tent is the same as what it would be in a courtroom. Everyone watches as you give your testimony, waiting for you to fall and say something they can use against you.

"He then grabbed my shoulder," I feel small in my chair as I point to my bruised shoulder, still throbbing from Andrew's vicious grip, "pinned me against the wall and told me to go home, that I shouldn't be here. I kicked him, sir, in self defense, as I should've."

Andrew's story is far worse as he plays his cards. He's a cunning cheater. "She approached me, sir. She threatened to kill me if I ever approached Private Clark, threatened to shoot twelve rounds through me if I ever laid a hand on him. You know what she and Clark's relationship is, right, sir? They have an affair—"

"Objection, if I may?" My blood roars in my ears. I point an accusing finger at him. "There is *nothing* between Private Clark and I. How dare you bring an innocent man into this? He has *nothing* to do with your testimony of lies!"

"Nothing between you, you say?" Andrew's eyes scan me as a smirk plays along his lips. "Yet, you still defend him. What a terrible liar she is, sir. Wouldn't you agree?"

Sallinger grimaces, considering his options. His broad shoulders are tight as he whispers into the captain's ear. He issues a grave sigh as I babble, making struggling sounds, trying to protest, trying to find a way out of this.

"Private Joyce," his fingers thrum against his desk, "when Private Sawyers approached you, you were alone? No other men or women were around to witness this?"

"I was alone." I clasp my hands together as my throat tightens. "He approached me straight after dinner, sir."

"Lair," Andrew sneers. "You approached me."

"Silence, Sawyers." Sallinger's glare sweeps across to him. "I did not ask you to speak."

"Sir, if I may, she's lying! You wouldn't believe someone who falsified her identity to get here, would you?" Andrew speaks as though he's spitting venom. "She was able to lie into this mess, now she's trying to lie her way out of it! She is not to be trusted!"

Sallinger sighs. "I'm afraid you have a point."

"Sallinger, if I may add," I stand up straight, landing a death stare at Andrew, "Sawyers, your name was? He's built himself a throne of lies. He's sitting proudly upon it right in front of you. I may have made a mistake, I confess, but I'm being nothing but truthful. *You're* making a drastic mistake by trusting this fabulist and helping him build his chair higher for his royal behind to sit!"

"Ouch." Andrew sniffs at my insults. "And what about you, Joyce? How many lies have you told? Surely your total is higher than mine, is it not?"

"If I may add—" I raise my voice, but I'm sorely interrupted.

"Private Joyce, I mentioned before that if *anything* happened, you'd be dismissed—" Sallinger starts.

"Sir, this isn't fair!" I lean forward, my cries all too desperate. "This is unjust!"

"I'm sorry to announce that you'll have to be decommissioned. You're guilty, Ms Joyce: of lying about your identity, your relationship with other troops, and utilizing that tactic to escape your fate which you knew was coming. You surely can't be trusted."

My pulse instantly drops. "Sir, please—"

"Pack your bags. You must leave by tomorrow. Is that understood?"

I've lost so sorely, so bitterly, to another liar. Another thieving *liar*.

"Yes, sir. I will."

Once dismissed, I wrap my arms around myself, against the cold winds.

A hand slinks around my shoulders. The struggle to get away, to run, is all too real as Andrew's lips brush my ear.

"I'm sorry, starlet," he whispers, wicked through and through. "I'm afraid your little games are over and your time's up. Perhaps your boy can make this night worth remembering, hm?"

He has the nerve to kiss my cheek before he stalks away. I'm about to crumble to my knees before a warm hand replaces the cold one on my shoulder from behind, startling me.

Marshall's cheeks are a rosy red against the cold, his collar popped up against the whistling winds. "There you are! I was looking for you. You see, Ed found some booze he brought from home and suggested we try some. What do you say?"

Perhaps your boy can make this night worth remembering?

Oh, how his words still sting.

When I don't reply, his smile wilts and withers. "Is something wrong? Is something bothering you?"

It all pours out in a disgusting, acidic mess.

"Andrew decided to get himself involved in a fight with me to set me off my rocker. He told Sallinger I was a liar to get him on his side and to believe him, to send me away. After all my hard work to get here, I have to go home back to *her*. I'm ruined!"

I break down into tears. Marshall's swift to curse Andrew's name. "Your mother? Is there something going on between you two?"

Wildly, I shake my head, repeating 'no' over and over again. Marshall brings me into an embrace I shouldn't be sharing, though it takes everything in me not to pull away.

"Frieda, please. You don't need to hide it from me. I want to help."

"No, Marshall, no. There's nothing you can do."

"What's going on?" He kneels before me, his eyes finding mine and watching my every move. "Talk to me."

I pick at my sleeves. "It was just a small disagreement..."

"Please don't lie to me." He doesn't look away. He doesn't budge.

I unbutton the cuffs of my sleeves through my tear-blurred vision. I roll them up to show him the myriad of bruises and scars that line my wrists.

"I"—after waiting for me to say it's okay, he runs his fingers delicately over my skin—"Frieda, did she—
"

"She hits me, Marshall. That's why I don't want to go home!" I shout. I don't care who hears anymore. "Ever since *Papa* died, she's hit me! Again and again! Do anything! Please don't let me go back to her!"

As I reach for his forearms to steady myself. I trip, landing square against his chest. He wraps his arms around me when I squirm. He's about to let go when I grow rigid, but wraps me closer when I don't try to wriggle out of his embrace.

Even without looking at him, I know he's searching for a sign of hope, scanning me up and down. "I shouldn't have asked."

"It's fine. It's *fine*. I'm the one to blame. It's all my fault."

I stand there in his arms, my shoulders heaving with my ragged breaths. Marshall steadies me when I slump too far forward. "It hurts me to see you so upset. Andrew and your mother deserve to perish. Both of them will go to Hell. They'll both pay for what they've done to you. None of this is your fault."

His hand rubs my back so delicately it hurts with just the lightest brush. Dear lord, he's slammed with so much sympathy that he treats me like glass that's bound to break. Perhaps today I've finally shattered and he's trying to piece all the jagged shards back together.

I make a sorrowful attempt to peel myself off of him. "I have to go."

Marshall hesitates before his arms loosen their grip. "I don't want to let go."

"I know. I don't either."

Marshall lets in a shaky breath. "Well, I'll miss you. Would you do the noble favor of writing to me? I don't want to lose touch with such a remarkable person."

Another move of his infatuated mind. It sounds too much like a fantasy: a scrawny, young soldier in love with someone unfairly excluded by society.

Marshall Clark and Frieda Joyce: two totally different planets orbiting each other, two stars looking to collide as one draws near, desperate, while the other pushes back, afraid.

"Of course." My answer brings a hopeful light into his eyes. "Perhaps you'll bring me a shred of joy?"

"Hah, I'll try my best. Would you mind giving me your address?" Marshall reaches for his journal and a pen where I write my address for him in small, scrawled handwriting.

During the process, I catch him as leans in. Looking up, his face is awfully close. So close that I can make out the small light freckles that dot his cheeks and the details of his hazel irises. His lashes are wet with tears.

After those long hours of agony in the medical tent, I never wanted to see him cry ever again. But here he is before me with eyes preparing to sob themselves dry.

"I'll miss you so much." His voice is trembling as his lips move, unsure of what words to shape before they choke out, "I don't know how I'll live."

I pat his shoulder briskly. "I'll miss you too. You'll live. I'm easily replaced."

"You're not. You're memorable. You don't see it, but I do."

"You'll be surprised by how replaceable I am. You have your other friends to talk to. You'll be fine without me. It'll be like I was never even here."

"It won't. It never will be. I regret not knowing you fully until now. Trust me when I say you're truly remarkable. Someone like you would never be easy to replace."

My scowl disappears as his warm breath spreads across my cheeks. His voice is low, a comforting murmur as he stows his journal back in his pocket. "Do you need help packing?"

I shake my head, turning my face away from him. "I'm alright, thank you."

Marshall steps back with a miserably reluctant half-step. His eyes never leave, even when he starts to walk away. "As always, my friend."

Finally letting the extra set of tears fall, the world around me collapses as I make my way back to the tent to pack.

A million thoughts fly through my head as I stuff my belongings into my father's bag, hugging his shirts tight to my chest, folding them. They remain two sizes too big. I feel far too small when I wear them, as they still feel like they belong to someone else. Like the too-big sleeves, the bagginess of the fabric, there's nothing that can fill the space he's left behind. If only he could see me now, a disgrace to our family name. The news and the gossip will spread like wildfire. I'll be forced to bow my head in shame each time I walk through the streets, never moving up in life. The boys can move on without me, as everyone else does.

Ed, with his two-colored eyes.

Lester, teasing his clanmates as if he's a concerned uncle.

Charlie, whistling through the gap in his mouth.

Last but not least, Marshall...*Marshall*.

His name is a siren continuously issuing a storm warning inside my head. One that echoes across the valleys of my mind with his laughter. It's embarrassing how emotional I get when I see him striding my way. I nearly cry each time he says my name. His personality is contagious; the happiness and joy he radiates and the warmth in his eyes makes me want to scream.

To stop myself from screaming, I screw my eyes shut and snap up the satchel, leaning over it as each limb in my body shakes and shudders with fear and sorrow.

* * *

Marshall takes my hands in his at the docks to calm me down, waiting for the boat to arrive. Nothing about the atmosphere around us sparks anything close to happiness or joy. It's all empty space, silence, everything dead and barren in the fog of the morning. The sun has barely risen over the horizon, an icy breeze digging under my uniform.

I angle my gaze over at him as he sits on the bench beside me. He's as bedraggled and dazed as I am while he stares out at the horizon and over the water. His eyes shine in the glare of the sunrise glimmering through the fog, his gaze steady, watching every ripple, every churn of the waters below.

"Do you still have my address?" I ask as another gust of wind blows.

Marshall doesn't look at me, but dips his head as a simple indicator that he does, stowed safely away within the pages of his journal. He shuffles closer, so close that his shoulder brushes mine. Like me, he's shaking, terrified of parting, of letting go.

"You know you look like your father, right?" Marshall's eyes watch over the horizon. "I met him quite a few times before the war."

"Of course." I shrug off his compliment. The dismissal doesn't come with much ease. "I hear it all the time. I don't like the thought of looking like a dead person. That's all I'll ever be."

"Oh?" Marshall wraps his arms around his shivering torso. "I, for one, think you're more than just a lookalike, as you say."

I fold my legs over one another. "What do you see in me?"

"I see you as different. A smart individual who has the guts to come out here to fight with nothing but bravery. Not many would do that, would they?"

"None would."

"One did, and she did an awfully good job." Marshall brushes his hair out of his face. "You're a daredevil, too. I dig those."

"Like what? What makes you say that?"

"People who take risks excite me." He's content to reply. His eyes meet mine with a bright spark in them. "People who don't take risks once in a while are who I deem as boring. They lead boring lives, boring jobs, boring families. Boredom as a whole fits their persona. Those who take risks are simply eccentric. How can you live your life and not take any risks?"

"I don't know." I pick anxiously at my cuticles. "Fear could be one reason why they don't."

"Alas, fear can also be a reason why they take risks."

The boat reaches the dock and anchors itself while it waits for people to board before Marshall can explain his reasoning. I stand and grab my things while he watches me leave.

"I guess this is it." Tears spike at the back of my eyes. "Please stay alive for me."

He buckles under my request, his face laced with an expression I can't wrap my head around as he gives me a slip of paper with the regiment's address printed on it. Likewise, we share the same talent of masking our feelings, letting them become undefined, blurring the lines of one's perception. "I'll try my hardest. I'm brilliant when it comes to keeping promises."

With cold hands, he reaches to embrace me, hold me tight.

I don't want to let go of him. I don't want the distance to stretch between us.

His hand is tight around mine, pulling me back, eyes glassy. "Please listen to me."

"Make it quick."

The ship blows its horn, telling me it's time to go.

Fumbling with his words, he's racking his brain for something to say and how to express it. It hurts to pull myself out of his grip, to watch him as he crumples with words that remain unsaid.

"I'm sorry. I have to leave. Whatever you want to say, don't hesitate to write to me. There's nothing stopping you."

Hurrying along and handing over my ticket, Marshall shouts my name, sending tingles up my spine.

When I whirl around to face him, he's standing at the edge of the docks, shouting, cupping his hands to project his voice, strained and cracking. He's leaning over the railing, eyes alight with desperation as he yells shamelessly, "I love you! I love you! *I love you*! I am truly captivated by you! Head over heels in love with you! I know it sounds unreal, but it's true! Remember to take care of yourself: eat your fill, take baths, clean your teeth, keep hydrated, take supplements if needed and stay healthy for me, okay? Write to me as soon as you can!"

My face is frozen in shock. Once again, this is another move by his infatuated mind. I take it Ed's teasing provoked something inside of him. He's taken it upon himself to profess his feelings then and there, unprepared, throwing himself into battle against his heart and fear of rejection. I have to admire him for his strength and determination to declare such emotions without it being scripted or even being the slightest bit ready.

This time, it's either do or die. A saddened smile crosses my lips as he awaits his answer.

"I will, I swear! It's kind of surreal, but I love you too!"

Marshall's face is stricken with shock before he hides his victorious smile behind his hands as he raises them again to shout, "You're going to miss your boat!"

"Oh, right," I mumble before shouting back, "Goodbye!"

As I climb inside, Marshall waves frantically before the doors lock shut. The last glimpse of him I get is of his hands over his heart before he turns away, head dipped. His fingers run through his hair. He knocks a fist against the side of his head once, cupping his mouth in his palms to hide his sobs that're carried away by the wind.

* * *

If I were to ask someone the first thing that came to their mind about Seattle, I'd wager nearly everyone I ask will say the rain.

Of course, today, it pours. The clouds up above show no mercy for the flooding gutters; little rivers on the sides of the road that flow fast as I mope on by. Horses whinny as the convertible carriages lift their roofs to protect their clients riding in expensive silks.

What a terrible day to hire a convertible carriage. Do people even read the forecasts anymore in a city such as this? With the unpredictable weather, the patterns are nearly indiscernible. I know I shouldn't be talking. It's hypocritical of me to say so when I myself refused to purchase an umbrella from a stand at the docks for my stroll back home.

The suburban streets, unlike any other time, are dead quiet against the rain thundering down. The lights are on inside houses, some windows daring to be cracked open to let the heavy, wondrous scent in. The fumes of an open fireplace are thick in the air. I don't stop to let it swallow my lungs as I pass by.

Through the storm, I'm a specter returning from long years of hardship. The sensation of being back home aches in my bones, and I finally catch a grip on how badly my flesh sags with my fast-decreasing weight. I paid it no mind whilst in the trenches, but seeing the ladies as they stream by with cheeks full of rogue, plump with liveliness makes me look gangly and gaunt in comparison.

Wrapping my thin coat tighter, I fasten my pace as men smoking cigarettes on their porch call out furiously disgusting things to me. I fight every instinct to call back to them as another yells for me to 'get down' on him.

Such vulgar words from such a well-groomed gentleman.

When he starts making smooching noises, I almost flip the switch. I greet him with a rude hand gesture before I storm off, not bothering to acknowledge the guffawing that comes from my profanity.

Once again, my mind runs in circles, reliving the morning on the docks.

It's obvious Marshall isn't one to handle people leaving his side all that easily. I'd wager it's the aftermath brought from his mother passing away. The feeling that he's failed and lost his grip on yet another loved one must be unbearable.

I hesitate before I climb up the steps to knock on the light-toned door of my home, regretting doing so. Silence hangs in the air for a few intolerable moments before a fair-haired woman with pale eyes, my mother, opens the door.

When she sees me, her lips purse before she speaks the first few words she's ever uttered to me in weeks.

"Oh, it's you."

So, this is how she addresses me. No 'hello, where have you been?'. No rushed questions or frets. Instead, she drags me inside by the collar.

Her face is shriveled in disgust. "You smell like a sewer rat! What did you do? Roll in mud?"

"I nearly died on No Man's Land." Despite being a good few inches taller than her, I still can't bring myself to look at her. I fear that she'll smack me for thinking I could ever meet her glare. "You could at least play the part of a good mother and start crying about my return. Try it out someday. I'm sure you'll be the perfect actress."

She tuts, erupting into a bitter guffaw. "How coincidental! Your father died there too! It would be hysterical if you died the same way he did."

I turn away without uttering a word before she can see the tears springing from my eyes. It's been not even a minute since I've returned and she's already picking and pulling me apart. Already do I long to be back in Europe, waist-deep in mud and gore with the adrenaline brought by a battle coursing through my veins. I'd much rather hold the weight of a good hunting rifle than an embroidering needle in my hands.

Heels clamber down the steps and stop at the landing.

A girl is decked in a lengthy high-collared green dress with her hair pulled tight in a high bun under a dark hairnet. She's blonde and around my age. Her fair skin is almost as pale as a ghost's with light pink lips to match. Gray dull eyes smothered with a light touch of khol stare back, inspecting me from crown to toe.

"Who is this rat?" Her voice is of a higher octave than mine, her accent hinting she hails from somewhere in England.

My mother smirks. "This *rat,* Irene, I say with regret, is your step-sibling, Frieda. She's the child of my late husband, Mr Joyce. Frieda, this is Irene. She's from Yorkshire, all the way in the United Kingdom."

So, I was right.

I develop a wicked smile. "So, you found another man to bore. Not new news when it comes to you, *Mother.*"

Not exhibiting her insulted air, she tuts. "So, hanging around young boys has developed your foul tongue further?"

"Seems so." I glare over at Irene. My eyes catch hers, burning her, charring the hem of her precious skirt.

I was mentally preparing myself for this moment. The moment my mother grabs me by the shoulder, whispering deathly remarks into my ear that gnaw at my insides, demanding a response.

"Your father was too obsessed with the army. I'm not surprised he died. I'm also not surprised you've fallen in his footsteps."

"And to think you used to love him. You used to love me," I spit, challenging her sneer. "I won't be surprised if you end up throwing this girl out if her father dies. Speaking of whom, who's my step-father?"

"Mr Fitzroy South; a prestigious businessman in charge of a winery."

I laugh coldly. "Sounds posh."

The door to the study—my father's study—opens as a man wearing square-framed glasses and a navy blue waistcoat stumbles out. He certainly looks the part for a man in charge of a winery with his expensive air. When his eyes land on me, they crease into a welcoming smile. I don't hand him the victory of returning it.

"Rose, you didn't tell me we'd be having visitors! I've heard of you. You must be Fiala?"

He too has the ridiculous Yorkshire accent. It curdles my blood and makes it run cold.

"Frieda," I correct him in a monotone voice. I cringe at the name, knowing it was chosen by my mother. It was beautiful, angelic to hear, once upon a time. Now it's insufferable to hear it echoing across the walls of this house.

I now glare at my mother, knowing she's easily replaced her family like broken jewelry.

"No one can replace my father, Rose *South.* No one. You may think that he was some sort of military addict, but I think he was a brilliant man. These people cannot replace my family. I'm not counting you as my family either. You can marry as many men as you like, get as many step-children as you wish, but they will never be counted as family. I am the heir to my father's legacy, and I'm a Joyce with pride. I am not surrendering my good name to these *imposters.* He died to protect an innocent man from death; a selfless act that only he could think of at a time like that with little to no time to ponder. Can you shed just a drop of grievance for him?"

Mother remains unaffected, holding her head so apathetically high. "Such strong words from the one I so adored and brought into this world. You've grown into such a *remarkable* young adult. You really do have your father's strength, his stubbornness, his self-righteousness. It's a blessing to see it in full bloom."

I glare before I stalk upstairs, dodging a handshake from Fitzroy and an insult from Irene as I open the door to my room, still thankfully occupied with my belongings, and slam the door shut.

Throwing my bag on my bed, I observe that the white pillows I made look like my sleeping figure have been disarranged, the covers pulled back in a hurry, presumably by my mother once she found out I ran away. On my desk and gathering dust sit *Anne of Green Gables* and *Little Women*; books I don't feel like indulging in just yet.

Putting my clothes back in my drawers, I change into a high-collared blouse and dark skirt and reach for a picture framed of me and my father when I was younger that sits atop the dresser. I lie back down with it against my chest, tears flowing down my cheeks. Floods of memories are coming back of what happened in this house, memories too precious to let go of.

I look for the fountain pen on my desk in a hurry along with some parchment I can make out through my blurred vision.

I feel like writing to Marshall, but what should I say?

I get up, the rain still waging a war outside. Sitting down at my desk, I load my pen with ink and start writing.

Dearest Friend,

It's been so terrible since I came home. I haven't been here for even a full hour and I've already been tormented. I utterly despise it here. It was much better when my father was around, as the house was brighter. I was happier. Get this, I've come home to a step family. Marshall, a step family. My mother somehow married herself off while I was away! Can you believe the woman?

Besides that, I miss you a lot. Excruciatingly a lot. I know, it sounds odd when I haven't seen you for the past eight days, and I'm sorry I left you so distraught so quickly. I want to hold and comfort you.

I feel terrible, knowing you're dealing with such challenging emotions I myself supplied with my abrupt departure.

Please update me on the war. I'm interested to know what's been going on. I beg you to give me updates on how you're doing, too, or else I'll start stressing and seem as though I've lost my mind. Tell Ed, Chip, and Lester I said hello. I miss you all, and I love each of you dearly. The four of you are the family I long to have, but have lacked for a very long time. I have to suffer with my new step-father and step-sister that I would never call family in a million years. I'd much rather be back with you fine boys, goofing off in a trench somewhere, despite death lurking at every turn.

I'm sorry I can't write that much. I will attempt to write more.

I miss you dearly,

Frieda

PS: Do you favor pocket watches? Also, please get more into detail on the proclamation you made on the dock: That you loved me. I want to work it out and take it to the next step with you. Let's talk it through. I figured it all out at dinner when Ed asked that we stop teasing you about your love life. You're a terrible liar. It simply makes me guffaw. You're adorable when you get so flimsy and embarrassed.

After I proofread it, I seal it inside an envelope.

I wonder, how am I going to deliver it?

My mother would gut me alive if she knew I was delivering mail back to the Front, ripping the letter I so artfully crafted right in front of me.

If times haven't changed, I still have the role of retrieving the evening post from the letterbox out front. If I'm able to sneak to the postbox down the road, I'm sure I'll be able to smuggle the letter inside before I go back down in the morning to check the post.

Writing the return address on the back and the Front's mailing address on the front, I hide the envelope inside my skirt pocket, a mischievous bout of laughter bubbling within me.

* * *

"Oi, Rat!"

Before me stands Irene at the door of my room. She's leaning against the doorframe, refusing to enter, as if a dangerous beast lurks within.

"Could you knock? My name is Frieda, by the way." I snap my book shut, setting it aside on my nightstand. "What is it?"

"Mother says it's time to get the post." She tucks a loose strand of hair behind her ear as I stand eagerly at attention.

"Already on it."

Making my way out the room, I jump over Irene's foot that's laid out and waiting to trip me. "Oh, Irene. Don't start thinking I was born yesterday."

She glares and reaches to throw a spare inkwell from my desk by the door at me. I dodge quickly to the side. It shatters on the wooden floor in the hall.

I turn to sneer, "I thought you were smarter than that. That's also your problem to take care of. Be careful not to get the ink on those rich hands of yours. It'll stain."

I prance outside to the letterbox, opening the latch to grab the multiple envelopes and the scroll of newspaper from the mailbox. The yard remains empty and the curtains shut tight across the windows.

With no one to see me, now's my chance.

I sprint through the rain with my skirt weighing me down to the mailbox on the corner of the road. Hurriedly, I push the letter inside and hoot, sending a victorious fist into the air, sprinting back to the house.

My damp hands shake with the prolonged excitement of living dangerously as I hand Fitzroy the newspaper.

"Thank you, my love," he says, and the acrid stench of vomit threatens to rise in my throat.

I'm scared to lie to him when he notices my chest heaving, my ink-stained hands.

Unfortunately, he's caught me red-handed.

"Smuggling mail to your accomplice, hm?" He winks over his newspaper. "I did that a lot when I was your age. Don't worry, it'll be our little secret."

When I trod back upstairs, I laugh to myself. It's unbelievable how easy this action of smuggling letters can seem. Perhaps I like Fitzroy now that he's keeping quiet about my crime, but it doesn't stop the suspicion that he'll be telling my mother about it sooner or later.

Time will reveal all, I tell myself. *Time will reveal all.*

Perhaps I'll give him a chance.

* * *

Dinner is one of the absolute worst things in the world when you're at the table with Irene.

She keeps making every topic about her, always talking about herself and herself only, boasting how she was a 'straight A' student when she was enrolled at school back in Yorkshire. During her shameless bragging, I fidget with my food and give her the death stare over the salt and pepper grinders. Hearing her speak has made me lose my appetite along with my mother's bland and poisonous cooking.

Irene kicks my ankle under the table. A sly look on her face appears. I clamp my jaw shut to stop myself from screaming bloody murder.

I lean back on my chair, gagging and setting my silverware down. "Have you tried putting rosemary on the lamb? It's bland."

My mother dabs at her mouth with the corner of her napkin. "As much as I despise just looking at you now, I want you to be successful in life. No, I won't. It'll make you gain weight."

This woman believes nonsense.

"Jesus Christ! I'm so starved that you can see my rib cage!" My cheeks flush with a burning red blush.

"You wouldn't be so gaunt if you didn't follow your father's ideals or have his impetuous, arrogant air to your personality. It would be much simpler if you didn't have his bad genetic streak. The Joyce family is a coven of nutcases."

"Yet, you married into them." My hand clenches into a fist and grips tight at my skirt beneath the table. "You had a child with one of them. You had *me*. How could you talk of your in-laws so carelessly?"

"*Ex* in-laws, must I correct you, dear child. After *he* left, after he didn't listen to my pleas to stay behind—"

"He was *conscripted* just like Mr Mellison, Mr Davis, Mr—"

"And he chose to comply!" she yells, Fitzroy reaching to steady her.

"Utter nonsense!" I snap back. "He didn't have a choice!"

"Of course! The wicked streak is tying you to him! You truly are your father's kin! I wouldn't be surprised if you don't find a suitor and become the biggest bitch of the brothel! Perhaps they'll house you and enjoy their time with a pretty young thing with a head full of lunacy! I should've sent you to a shrink, an alienist, for that little warped mind of yours! Shall we? I shall arrange for a car in the morning—"

I've had enough.

My chest heaves. My cheeks burn. I scrape my chair back and slam my palms against the table.

"Have you no regard for individuals other than yourself? You are truly the most callous and cruel woman I've ever laid eyes on in my entire life. I don't care how unbecoming my outburst is right now. It's making you mad, isn't it? You only see a failure of a masterpiece you yourself tried putting together to make money off of instead of the child you raised crumbling apart right in front of you!"

I can't stop the words from escaping as my heart pounds. It's getting harder with each passing second to obstruct the tears, to stop them from falling. "You, of all people, my *mother*; the person I should be looking up to is the person I run in fear from. Where did the mother I knew go? What monster crawled into her skin and is having fun playing her part? My head, filled with lunacy? I understand where you're coming from, but it's all *your* lunacy that floods my thoughts and fuels my fears! I…"

I start to break down, babbling, lost for words. Try as hard as I may, but my tongue grows numb in my mouth. My tears smudge the smallest amount of kohl I put on my lids to look the slightest bit more presentable. I make an attempt to sew the threads of a sentence together before I finally break.

Fitzroy is the first to move and reach for my arm, but I shrink away from him as his gray eyes wash over me.

"Please." The words come out as fragile as glass. "Please don't touch me."

"Are you ill?"

"She's begging for attention, Fitz," Mother growls over her wine glass. "Let her have a sook. She'll be back on her rotten feet soon enough."

"Hush, Rose. Let me handle her. You've done enough damage to the poor thing already."

I'm frozen, caught like a deer in headlights. It's like my soul's left my body, examining the room for a place to run, to hide. I want to crumple in on myself and the tightness of my chest.

Fitzroy offers his arm as he strides over to my side of the table. Irene sneers as I take another step back.

"Come. Let us sit outside for a while. I won't hurt you, I promise. Come along."

"Fitzr—"

"*Rose*," he warns. She shrinks back. "Come with me. Let's get you some air."

As if on autopilot, I accept his offer. I have to get away. I have to get away from her.

The next thing I know, I'm seated on the stairs of the front porch near one of the flower bushes. My eyes are wide. My hands reach to cover my mouth. I rap my knuckles against the inside of my wrist, my leg jogging beneath my skirt.

"I take it this isn't the first time you two have had a disagreement?" Fitzroy's the first to break the silence, carefully sitting beside me. "Mind if I sit here?"

"You don't understand."

"Tell me, then." He picks at the lint on his pant leg and shivers from the cold breeze. "Tell me what happened."

"You...You don't understand..." I can't bring myself to look at him. "Ever since—"

"Deep breaths, my dear." He's about to press a hand on my back, but hesitates. "Deep breaths."

"Ever since *P-Papa* died...she's hit me..." I don't break my eyes away from the ground. "M-Mother's scary when she h-hits me...I'm terrified of her..."

"I'm sorry, I—"

I put a palm up to block his pity. "Don't. Don't you dare say those words. I don't need your pity. I'm going straight...straight to bed."

I bolt up before he can say anything more, running up the stairs to slam my door shut.

It takes a great deal of pacing to drown out my thoughts and to calm my breathing. I try writing another letter to Marshall, but he shouldn't be concerned about me, so I rip it to shreds. Words better left unsaid are sliced to pieces. It somehow helps me get my energy out before I wash my face, splashing it with cold water in the bathroom basin. I wipe off my eye makeup, trying to avoid looking at the disgusting puffy and red face staring back at me in the mirror.

When *Papa* was still alive, he called these attacks *tidal waves*. He always used a boat example where I was sailing in one of those little escape boats found on cruises through a dark ocean. Whenever I grew uneasy, the boat rocked as a tidal wave washed me off course. He told me I had to find a way to stay afloat when the boat sank, when it diverged, as the hull filled with water.

I presume now that he didn't want to call the illness I have what the doctor called it, most likely didn't want to face its true form.

The doctor said it was something to do with my nerves, some sort of panophobia: an anxiety disorder of sorts.

Because it's certainly not neurasthenia. She has more...a lot of anxiety. A multitude of fears that something terrible will happen. A constantly recurring dread.

How the health system has failed me: sending me off without any treatment, leaving me to suffer.

The house is quiet as I tip-toe back to my room. I change out of my day clothes and put them inside the drawer that's the lowest on my dresser. I slide into some comfortable pajamas that consist of a silk gown and slippers, tighten my robe's strings around my waist and bring a book into my lap.

When I get into bed, it's so peculiar to not have Marshall here next to me with the scratching of his pen and his soft snoring. As I close my eyes, falling asleep, I catch myself thinking of him again as his face melts into my dreams.

He sits by the window: soldier's uniform, dark hair and all as he cradles a flute of red wine and leans against the glass. His silhouette blends in with the glass as he smiles and stands, setting the wine down on the sill, reaching to waltz me around the room in my nightgown.

Does he dream of me too?

What acts of virtue does he commit? What sins?

I'm yet to uncover what occurs inside the subconscious valleys of his dreams.

If only, for one night, he'd waltz me around the room like the carefree couple we desire to be, holding each other close.

His dark curls frame his face as he dips me. The melodic tune hovering in the air fades away as his eyes glint down at me in the moonlight. They wander over my face, my figure, taking me in one slow step at a time.

His boyish grin shapes his lips as his arms tighten around my waist. When he pulls me into his chest, he doesn't let go, but ducks his head so that his eyes are level with mine.

"*Mon amour.*" Hearing him speak French is oddly exciting, but the delicate language doesn't suit the deep rumble of his voice. "*Je t'aime, mon amour.*"

"*Je t'aime aussi,*" I reply quickly. "You learned French for me?"

"I'd do anything for you," he says. "Anything for you, Frieda. I'd die for you."

"Surely you wouldn't."

"You underestimate me." His grate is too unnatural, too out of place, as all things are in dreams. "I could show you the entire world and you'd still underestimate my abilities."

"Show me the entire world. Take me wherever. I'm sure that wherever we go, it'll be beautiful."

5

The Response

In the following week of havoc and griping from my mother, I wake up before the sun rises.

It's still dark outside. A chilling breeze wafts through an open window. I open my eyes, my comforter providing all the warmth I need as the birds chirp their morning numbers. I haven't heard this exact sound in weeks, and Marshall's snoring is gone, leaving the room to feel empty.

I should go get the post. It's about the time when the postman comes to the mailbox. I'm too impatient to wait until later for my response.

I yawn, stretching and sitting up. I would hear Marshall mutter a good morning if he were here, but he isn't, fighting on foreign lands, foreign lines, while I'm on the other side of the world.

I get out of bed and throw on a blouse under a knitted sweater and a plaited walking skirt with dark pantyhose and short heels. Upon sliding my other heel on, I'm reminded of how much I hate these shoes, so I ditch them and put on my boots that don't squeeze in my toes and guarantee that I'll still walk at fifty.

I creep down the stairs into the silent hallway. Fitzroy's faint snoring—probably sleeping in *Papa*'s old spot—comes from upstairs. The idea of *him* lying there in *his* spot infuriates me as I grab my key, unbeknownst to my mother that I have it hidden away in a false-bottom drawer, and click open the door. I quietly snap it closed behind me, trying to avoid its creaks running through the house.

Strolling through the autumn sunrise, I get to the mailbox, pulling out envelopes. Some are addressed to my mother, some to Irene. My excitement turns into painful anxiety, but I shuffle farther through the pile. That's when I find it.

I let out a joyous squeak when I read the small, cursive handwriting belonging to him. His handwriting remains neater than mine. He has a hand that prints letters with a beautiful swoop to them. They're much better than my disgraceful, scrawling cursive that includes smudges coming from being left-handed. I have to stop myself from screaming when I see that he's even put a love heart next to my name on the address.

Frieda S. Joyce, it reads. I'm relieved he got the address correct.

My address.

I speed walk back inside, lock the door, drop the other envelopes on the kitchen counter, and run up the stairs. I sit in my squishy desk chair, unfold it haphazardly to read:

Dearest Frieda,

How glad am I to get your letter! Most people in the trenches usually don't get their mail received, nor do they get them delivered for weeks on end. Some don't even reach their destinations at all. It would be a miracle if this one got to you. If it did, we shall celebrate. I've shown the boys this letter. Ed and Chip and Lester miss you dearly. Each one of them laughed when they were mentioned. They were all rather joyous after they heard their names.

The tent's lonely without you. I miss your company to an extreme where I want to start sobbing all over again. It feels like you've been gone for a year already, and your bedroll still smells like you. It's the scent I breathe in every night when I go to sleep and in the morning when I wake. It fills the air like perfume straight out the bottle.

I'm sorry, I can't write that much. There's a lot going on with promotions and assault organizations. But you have asked for me to get into further detail of what you call my 'proclamation.' I understand it was quite sudden, but I felt it was the right time to say it, as there's a slim chance we may not see each other again—do or die, really—so I decided to announce it on the docks.

Frieda, the truth is that over the weeks I've known you—possibly years, since our fathers introduced us to each other—I'm not able to take my eyes off you. I know, it sounds like a bunch of rubbish coming from my mouth, but it's come to the point where I can't stop thinking about you, even if I try so desperately hard. I can't keep you off my mind. You have me by the neck, up against the wall with your presence in my life. I can't stand the idea of not being by your side. It's painful, Freddy!

Reading that you want to take it to the next step with me is what makes me happy—truly overjoyed. Do you feel the same as I do? Do you feel affection for a man such as myself? Though you want to continue this relationship, I must warn you: I'm a sensitive young man and have a longing for affection, as I enjoy relationships with communication and extra attention. I'll return the same qualities to you in full. It's in my nature to want to satisfy mine as well as my partner's needs.

If you ever get the privilege to return here, I've got something to show you. Perhaps during Christmas, if we get a break, we can do something together, like an outing, most likely? A date? Would that be what you call a first date? I'll have to look into that matter beforehand.

With all my love to give to such a remarkable, irreplaceable person,

Private M. Clark

I catch myself squealing as I read the final post and post-post scripts he's managed to squeeze in.

P.S: Yes, I do favor pocket watches. Preferably gold, since silver is overrated. Also, there are rumors that I'm going to be promoted to corporal. Do you think I've got a shot at it? It's very unlikely for a person like me to be promoted. I believe that I'm nothing but air.

PPS: Quick to solve mysteries, you are. Quick as a whip. I know, my frequent embarrassment is a dead giveaway—it's nowhere near adorable. It's downright annoying how flimsy I get! I rarely fall in love. It's been years since I last did. I thought I became incapable of such feelings, so let's fall together.

I hold the letter tight to my chest, the paper crushed under the pressure of my hands. With a victorious laugh, I jump around the room and set the letter on my nightstand, flopping back down on my bed as I start hooting.

The door opens. Irene walks in on my rush of euphoria.

"What in the world?"

I continue to smile like a vulnerable drunken maiden at a bar downtown as I sit up and take a long breath in. "Yes?"

Irene hesitates before answering. "Uh, breakfast is ready."

"Uh-huh." I stretch my arms, yawning. "No good mornings? That's fine."

Irene walks out of the room and closes the door to leave me to freshen up. I feel courageous enough to open the window and let in a morning breeze as I think of the watch I'll get Marshall the next time I go to the market. It would probably be the early afternoon there, since Italy is a few hours ahead of America. I wonder what he's doing right now.

I walk downstairs, fully dressed with my hair brushed back. It's far too short to be pinned back; a hastily chopped pixie cut that I adorn with a pale hair ribbon.

My joy is soon disturbed by Irene, who glares at me from across the room. "Don't think you can scare me what you have up your sleeve."

"What do you mean?" I ask.

"You can't scare me with your stories of war. It's hard to scare someone like me."

"Your rich bloodline needn't be concerned with the tragedies of war. They have too much money to fight with already. Much more than the lives already lost."

Irene only folds her arms, jutting out her chin with pride. "Is that so? Would you like some, rat? I could write you a loan, but I don't want your grimy hands ruining my riches."

"Say that again when you break another inkwell." I strut into the dining room, running my fingers over the head of one of the elegant wooden dining chairs, the one my father called his own. "If you're not careful, that won't be the only thing soiling your bread. It'll burn it, too."

Before Irene can retort, Fitzroy scuffs into the room with his dressing robe wrapped loosely around his pajama-clad frame.

"Good morning!" He smiles, pushing his glasses farther up the bridge of his nose. My mother follows in a long, elegant red day dress, her hair done up tight.

With a glare, she sits next to Fitzroy. Irene follows suit.

I pull a sick grin and sit in my father's chair, which only makes my mother's glare intensify. I fold my legs over each other and set one of my elbows on the chair arm.

"What's for breakfast, dear?" Mother gazes over at Fitzroy, her glare still made of steel as she runs a hand through his hair, a disguised attempt at ruffling my feathers.

"I decided to make waffles." Fitzroy sets a plate on the table with a truly heartfelt grin and offers me a coffee, but I shake my head. But I do take a waffle and start eating, my stomach telling me not to eat so much after eating barely anything at all for weeks. It's obviously shrunk from the rations, grumbling after almost every swallow I take.

Eat your fill. His voice is in my ears, overpowering all my other thoughts. My legs start to shake. My arms grow stiff. *Stay healthy for me.*

I bring my head into my hands, a polite giggle chirping from my mother's lips as Fitzroy leans forward to ask, "Is there something wrong?"

"Nothing...nothing..." I gulp and try to hold myself together. The anxiety writhes inside of me as the flashbacks crash in upon a large tidal wave.

I stare deadpan at the tablecloth as more visions of Marshall come into focus: of his laugh as he pushes back the curtains of the tent with a tray of food, singing improvised lyrics about it as he walks in, the same scolding voice forcing me to eat more than my stomach can handle. He says something about getting better quicker and having more strength. It's also the soothing coo of his voice as he calms down from a panic attack I have over the loud bangs of gunmen practicing their shooting. I thought we were under attack as he reassured me and held me in his arms until I fell asleep.

I blink back into the future, Fitzroy leaning over me, pressing his hand against my forehead.

"You're sweating, but you don't seem to have a temperature." His brow furrows, and I feel dizzy.

I stand hurriedly, pushing him out the way. I make for the door with my name echoing across the walls.

I run down the street, past the morning traffic. My vision blurs, but I keep running, never braking, never halting, as my only signal is to run like my life depends on it.

On my whistle, we run! Sallinger ordered over the unforgiving gunfire.

Don't get lost, or it's the end of the line for you! Ed shouted louder.

I'm already lost. I've already walked the line.

You're guilty, Ms Joyce. You surely can't be trusted. Sallinger slammed down the gavel as a lie became his truth.

I'm afraid your little games are over and your time's up. One of Andrew's disgusting teases. They never stop circling like vultures inside my head. I'm trapped in its center. In the eye of the storm. The only way out is to run.

Tears sting my eyes as I reach the cemetery, puffing through the open gates and down the rows of erected graves. I find wild daffodils growing along the way and take them to a particular grave, sitting on the clipped grass, tucking my knees to my chest like a child.

"I'm back, *Papa.*" I set the daffodils on the headstone and let the tears run free while my chest heaves.

"It's getting hard again. I wish you were here to help me like you always were. If only you stayed home or came back earlier, or if this damned war didn't happen, you'd still be here to help me."

* * *

I stroll through town, clearing my head as kids play in the morning sun. It's a lovely morning. The weather's nice and mildly warm for an autumn day. Flower shops have their stalls sitting outside with colorful flowers in vases, florists watering them with all their grace and poise. I can't help but stop and sniff them, their scent intoxicatingly sweet when it reaches my nose. Tulips have a strong smell; one I quite like.

I open the door to the bookshop that's next door. Books usually clear my head with their papery feel, their musty, old smell. If the world didn't have books, I wouldn't know how to live. It's easy to get lost in a good book and its worlds that you don't need to buy a ticket to access.

I used to come here all the time when my mother's abuse was too much for me. It was a safe haven, and still is to this day. The staff here are as friendly as the day I left, climbing ladders to pile books on shelves. One of the old men waves at me from the top of his ladder as I pass by, waving back.

I head to the Bestsellers section, picking up a thick tome of works by Sir Arthur Conan Doyle. His book, *The Hound of The Baskervilles,* is what introduced me to him, and I'm keen to read more.

I sit in one of the chairs by the window and open the book to the first page. Marshall recommended Doyle to me along with a few other authors like Arthur Rimbaud, who I've read in French and Fyodor Dosteyevsky, who I have long awaited to read. Marshall has a refined, mature taste in literature. He's read, apparently, the majority of Jane Austen's novels in their entirety.

The church bells ring outside, as it's Sunday today. The records on the turntable in the corner still play.

Placing the book back on its shelf, I exit the shop, sagging my shoulders in the morning sun.

* * *

One month later, many letters have been fluently exchanged.

Our relationship is growing rapidly to the point where we're able to call each other sweet little pet names. For example, he's taken to calling me 'little love.' I've been calling him, by his reluctant permission, 'Marsh.' He writes that it'll only be me who'll be able to call him that, ever. Also, he's been nothing but the sweetest gentleman in his letters. His writing is able to mimic and carry that same presence he possesses outside the worlds of his words.

This morning I run to the mailbox and retrieve the usual set of envelopes. There's two this time, addressed to me, which is odd.

I cock my head, put the rest on the bench in the front yard, and unfold the first one. The first is a heartfelt letter from Marshall, the second is something I didn't expect to happen at all.

Ms Joyce,

It is my great privilege to inform you that I have decided to recommission you back into my regiment after a long period of consideration. Private Sawyers is a man who tends to over-exaggerate, and there were many holes in his account of what happened. You may be here as soon as possible.

I must warn you. The next time a mishap like this happens, there will be no second chances. I do not have the time to play courtrooms and act as the judge of whether you should stay or not.

Kind Regards,

Lt. Col. Robert Sallinger

My eyes are wide as my hands go numb.

Part of me wants to go back, but the other tells me to stay here.

But who would I be if I stayed here? I'd probably be wondering if my friends are still alive, only hearing from them in letters or in articles. My life would be completely under my mother's vain control. I don't want that. It's not my life.

I don't stand on the sidelines and watch.

I am not my mother's puppet with strings for her to pull.

I am no one's puppet.

I fetch my uniform out of its drawer and slide it back on, the comforting weight of the wool against my frame. I've washed it thoroughly of dirt and grit, sewn up any rips or holes. It looks as good as when I first wore it.

This is Frieda Joyce: the next-of-kin of one of the most high-class sergeant majors in the army. Not in dresses that my mother wears, the fancy hats with peacock feathers on the sides, the heavy-as-a-paperweight earrings, no pointy shoes or heels that suffocate my circulation. I'm an independent individual: one that doesn't follow rules, laid out by my mother, like a housemaid. One that doesn't back down from a challenge, that fights for what she believes is right. I don't abide by a path decided for me by someone else. That's a waste of life. A waste of potential.

On my dresser, my father's cap sits before the mirror, staring me down with its intimidating crest of the army and its surrounding burnt fabric.

Is it telling me of something that's yet to come?

I pick it off my dresser and peer at it. The fabric is worn from wear and frayed at the edges. I'm thankful it was saved after he died. My mother was about to burn it, but I stole it from the pile of his belongings she was going to throw away along with a few of his journals and clothes: one of the things I was able to save before the flames ate them away. It's one of the last things owned by my real father with the fading photos of us I keep inside it. It shows a fifteen year old me standing with my father on the beach with our toes in the sand. His smile in the picture deeply pierces my heart, making his death hurt even more each time I look at these photos and recall the memories they hold.

I hold the hat tight to my chest, swallowing back a grieving sob before I stow it away into my desk drawer, protecting it from my mother's prying eyes and the flames of the hearth.

"I'll make you proud, *Papa*. I promise," I whisper as I close the drawer, something moving outside in the front yard.

A man strolls across the rose garden lining the pathway to the house, a military cap over his head, a soldier's uniform polished to the point that no speck of dust remains, a satchel at his side. His hands hold onto a map and an address stuck in his journal as his head ducks to read the number on the mailbox, nodding and strolling up to the stairs of the veranda before the front door.

No.

It can't be him. My eyes are playing tricks on me. I rub them hard, waiting for the hallucination to vanish.

Nothing changes. He's still standing on the veranda. I'm quick to press my face against the window pane to watch Marshall's hand reach for the doorbell, the sound booming through the house over my racing heart.

6

NEWS AND COFFEE

The ringing resonates through the house. My mother opens the door before I can even travel down the first set of stairs. I pack my satchel: thermos, food rations, plus the pocket watch I bought at the market earlier this month for Marshall to wind up.

"I'm sorry, ma'am, but Lieutenant Colonel Sallinger ordered me to collect Private Joyce."

"I give you no right!" She closes the door on his hand as he tries to stop it from slamming shut. He grunts in pain as the wood squeezes his knuckles.

"Please, Mrs Joyce, haven't we met before? It's me, Marshall Clark." He fetches a pained smile. "Cooper Clark's son?"

My mother pushes the door farther down on his hand, causing him to whimper. "Indeed we have, and it's Mrs *South* to you."

"Mrs *South*, my apologies, may I please retrieve your child? She's requested in the field."

"I said that I gave you no right to take her away!"

I creep downstairs to see Marshall clearer through the crack of the door, distressed, with his hand wedged tight. He has a new shallow gash under his eye, which doesn't look that bad compared to the bandage wrapped around his wrist under his sleeve.

"Marshall, it's fine. I'll go. Stop badgering the poor woman. It's no use. Mother, please, I've got to go." I cringe at Marshall's fingers that have started to turn purple. "Please release Private Clark from the door. His fingers are turning deathly dark."

Instead of releasing him completely, she grabs him by the tie and snaps, "I have said it before and I will say it again. You have no right to take my child away from me. You and your father are men I can't trust!"

"Say that to my brother. It would be more fitting." Marshall raises his hands in a surrender, flexing his wounded fingers. "You can trust me. I'm unarmed. Also, I'm under specific orders, and if I fail those orders, I'll be fired. If I'm fired, I have nowhere to go."

"Back to your father," my mother says, her grip tightening, "back to where the hell you came from, boy!"

"Mother!" I shout sharply.

Marshall's gaze darkens. His voice dips to a low, threatening rumble. "I must underline that I'm under specific *legal* orders. Ms Joyce has been requested to return to her post and serve in the war to aid our country. I have her consent to leave dangling right in front of you on a stick. She's right here, ready and waiting to go. I've come to collect my partner. After, that will be all. Now, if you may please release and excuse us, we'll be out of your hair as soon as possible."

My mother releases him, letting him adjust his tie and lapels. I scamper outside with my bag as she slams the door shut.

"To hell with you, Marshall Clark. If she dies, make sure it's the most painful death possible! The Joyce family deserve a dramatic, show-stopping finale!"

There's silence as the door locks. We're standing together, uneasy, on the doorstep.

I fiddle with a loose lock of my short hair. "I can't believe you just did that."

Marshall shrugs, flexing his fingers which now have a wedgemark along his knuckles, blue bruises forming. "I was more worried that I wouldn't have any fingers by the time we were through. You'd have to lend me a hand to get out of here."

My laughter bubbles warmly in my chest. I reach to wrap my arms around him. "I missed you."

"I missed you too," he says. "Hey, you stopped things from getting out of hand."

"Stop it!" I shriek, issuing a jab to his side, making my way out of the garden before he can think of any more hand puns.

I follow him to the harbor, children and other passers-by staring at our uniforms. Marshall slows his pace. He's made a new discovery.

It's a coffee shop. The gas lamps hanging from the ceiling illuminate the inside as the flower beds sitting on the front sill attract pollinating insects. Behind Marshall's eyes, his brain is ticking away, at work with an idea, his brow arched in thought. His face softens into a smile once he reaches a conclusion.

"I don't recall ever taking you on a date." He snickers, tilting his head towards the coffee shop. "I *did* promise one in one of my letters, did I not? Shall we?"

"Marshall, we don't have ti—"

He cuts me off, speaking over me. "The ship doesn't depart until this evening. We have time."

"But Marshall—"

"Frieda—"

"We don't—"

"We have time!" He barks out a laugh. "I promise you, we have time! We're wasting it by arguing. Please, let's enjoy ourselves before we get back."

I groan, rolling my eyes. "Fine. I hate being late. You're too persuasive."

He loops his arm through mine and walks me to the cafe. "To persuade you even more, we have five days to get to France from here."

"Five?" I echo.

"Five days on a boat." Marshall sighs, opening the door to the shop, whispering in my ear, "Did I ever tell you that you're cute when you're mad? Your ears and cheeks turn red."

"Shut up." I grit my teeth. "Your eyebrow twitches when you're angry. It freaks me out."

When we're seated, I'm itching to ask Marshall what's been happening. He hasn't been very descriptive in his letters as of late. Maybe to avoid government officials from drawing their thick black markers through information prone to being stolen by the enemy?

"So, what's been happening?" I ask.

Marshall ticks off the events on each of his fingers. "There were about fifty crashes on the Front. One had the plane hit the ground nose first. Another one beheaded its pilot. One had both pilots blasted to bits. There were many others that happened. And, I hate to tell you this, but someone we know became a casualty."

I expect something horribly wrong when he leans forward on his elbows. Ed. Lester. George. Chip...Something could've happened to them. Something irreversible. Something terrible.

Marshall reaches to grip my hands, squeezing them tight, announcing, "Chip passed."

I'm almost rendered speechless. "How?"

"He died from illness; pneumonia. There was a small outbreak not long ago."

A part of my heart falls away at the news. "I'm so sorry, Marshall."

Marshall's shoulders slump as he dips his head. "You needn't apologize. It isn't your fault. Life is cruel. War is cruel. That's all there is to it."

The drinks come; Marshall's coffee and my tea. He handles the bill as I thank him for taking me, which brings a new crooked smile to his lips.

The clear blue Seattle sky shines through the windows as the birds tweet away. Squirrels climb hurriedly up nearby trees. I don't understand how they can live such perfect lives while humans are at each other's throats waiting to draw blood.

"So," Marshall raises his mug, pulling me out of my thoughts, "what's been happening with you? Besides with your family, of course."

"I found a bunch of old books in a thrift shop and read all of them in one night."

Marshall giggles as he sips his coffee, the strong scent wafting to my nose. I tense all over again as he sets his cup back down upon its saucer.

"Come on! I know, I'm terrible at communicating! I'm too awkward for this!"

Marshall waves a lazy hand. "It's not that. I knew you enjoyed reading, but I didn't expect you to enjoy it *that* much. How often do you read?"

"Very often." My cheeks redden as Marshall smiles wider.

"I read quite often too, actually. I find Doyle's works to be one of my many favorites, as you know."

"Doyle is good. I read one of his books." I drink my tea. "I favor Charlotte Brontë."

"Oh! That's brilliant!" His eyes sparkle as he gasps. "She's one of my favorites, too!"

"Also..." I reach into my pocket, handing him the pocket watch. It's a nice gold one that isn't too large or heavy to carry. With a bigger smile, he takes it. "This is for you. For being my guide in battle."

"Frieda, it's beautiful." Marshall starts examining it, rubbing his thumb over the engravings on the lid. His smile falters not long after. "You didn't have to."

"I wanted to. I saw it and thought it would suit you perfectly."

"I'm sorry, I usually don't get such high quality gifts and I don't think I deserve—"

"*Shhhhh!*" I put a finger to his lips. He grips his cup tighter. "Don't mention it. It's a gift from me to you."

Marshall finds his smile again, his skin paling, probably becoming a little giddy. With another chortle, he brings his cup up to his lips, trying to hide the blush that spreads as soon as his face gets its color back.

"A-anyway..." Marshall accepts the watch. I catch him calculating something on his fingers, watching the clock on the wall, adjusting the time on his watch. "I've just set it to Belgian time. Do you notice anything different?"

"The scars on your face?"

"Nope."

"You've lost weight?"

"Try again."

"Your eye bags have disappeared, making you appear more youthful?"

"No," Marshall winks shamelessly, "but that's quite flattering."

He takes off his cap, running a hand through his hair, hinting it to me proudly. His curls no longer tumble down to his brow, but to the middle of his forehead.

"You cut your hair?" I gasp.

"Ed did it for me." Marshall sets his cap on the table next to the salt and pepper shakers. "He was a hairdresser before he went to war, so he saw I had a lot of split ends and managed to tame my abyss of hair. My fringe was in my eyes. I could barely see, even with hair gel."

I pour myself more tea out of the small pot. "He did a good job."

Marshall's grin vanishes. His eyes narrow in thought at the floor.

"Is something wrong?"

"I'm just thinking..." He snaps his fingers. "That's right! You missed an epic fight between two privates. We were part of it."

"No way!"

"Yes! We were caught in the midst of things, so we joined in because George wanted to. We tried to stop him, but we ended up looking like we were fighting, too. I have no idea what their fight was about, but it was eventful."

"And what the hell happened to you?"

"You see this?" He points to the scar scabbing near his eye, his scarred hands pale in the sunlight. "Got the daylights knocked out of me."

With a nervous laugh, I nearly spill my tea. "Are you okay?"

"I lost a few brain cells, but that doesn't matter. I'm fine." He taps his temple. "Thick skull. It's not like I had any brain cells to begin with."

"I could never imagine you getting into a fight."

"Must I remind you, it was *George* who got us into that mess." Marshall moans, cupping his mug with a dorkish grin. "Now my devilishly handsome aura is ruined by one simple brawl."

* * *

Marshall fiddles with the tickets in his pockets, handing them to security before we board and lugs his bag over his shoulder. We probably look like a strange, out of place couple as he opens our cabin door, putting his bag in the corner, lying upon one of the beds. He breathes in the boat's perfumed air as his gaze hardens at the light comforter below him, the sunset pouring through the window and lighting half his face so that all I see are shadows and angles.

"Marshall?" I place my satchel at the foot of my bed, sitting upon it with my legs dangling off the edge. "Are you alright?"

"I…" Marshall jumps at the jolt of the boat setting sail. "I have a fear of boats, actually. It was hard getting here without having multiple meltdowns a day."

"I'm here for you."

70

"It's like you're scared of nothing." He picks at his bandages, pulling his sleeve over them hurriedly.

"I'm actually scared of a lot of things: spiders, sometimes the dark, being alone without someone to guide me...I'm scared of the world. Everything poses a threat to me."

"Then I'm damned scared we're going to sink at any moment and I'm going to drown. Cold water freezes your muscles and makes you tired easily. Hypothermia doesn't sound like an enjoyable way to go."

"We're not going to drown, I promise," I say. The horn blows and Seattle recedes into the distance as we depart. "I bet you the captain has years and years of training."

Marshall reaches into his bag, grabbing a leather-bound book. I can't quite see what it is, but then he grabs a pen, propping the book against his knee.

Of course. His journal.

"Writing helps me unwind." He pauses. "It's not like I'm any good at it, though."

"I'm sure you are." I sit cross-legged and watch him flick through pages dotted with ink; paragraph after paragraph of his own thoughts poured on them. If that isn't commitment, I wouldn't know what it is.

"I mean, my handwriting is fine. It's just that I'm not the creative type, nor can I write very well."

"In your letters, I think you proved that wrong." I shuffle through my case, opening one of my books, the slim, cracked spine soft against my fingers. I thumb my way through to where I left off.

His brow flicks upward. So do his eyes for a split second. He's still tense as he dips his pen and continues to write, setting his inkwell atop the windowsill. The sight of it all eerily mirrors him in my dreams with his glass of wine, sitting up against the window, cradling an object delicately in his hands.

* * *

Marshall refuses to eat dinner, complaining of a churning stomach, only eating after I coax a bread roll with some butter and a bowl of peas into him. He's been lying in bed atop the covers since then, trying to soothe his upset stomach. He was retching in the bathroom earlier, dry heaving with nothing coming out, miserable, leaning over the toilet bowl with me rubbing his back and setting a rag to his forehead to stop his sweating. I searched the cabinets for anti-nausea pills, but none came. He refused to be brought any by one of the stewards.

The boat rocks, presumably reaching choppy waters, sending Marshall shocked upright with his face paling.

"We're going to die." Marshall's gasping, clutching his chest in panic.

"Marshall—" I start.

"We're going to die, Frieda." Marshall's hands close over his throat, gasping for air. "Oh God, I'm dying. I can't breathe."

"Marshall," I raise my voice over his frenzied wheezing, "come to me."

Marshall's wide eyes only stare back at me, his chest rapidly rising and falling as he descends further into fear. "I don't want to die, Frieda. Not like this."

"We're going through rough waters, nothing dangerous." I beckon him closer. "Come to me."

Marshall shakily crawls over. I bring him into a hug the moment he's within my reach. He's sweating horrendously, awfully pale as he holds onto me.

"Are you hot? You're sweating."

"No."

Trying to nuzzle closer, his whole body shakes in my arms. He's fragile, shaking like a leaf in the wind, threatened by the news that at any given moment, it'll be blown away.

"Tell me," I run my hand through his hair, fingers lost in his thick locks, "how brave were you to get on this boat?"

"I had to," he mumbles, reaching for my hand, clasping it in his own. Even his palms are sweaty. "I had no other choice."

"Still," I reach to wipe his forehead, "if I were you, I wouldn't even set foot on the dock."

Marshall looks up at me with red and puffy eyes. "But you're not scared of a damned boat."

"I know, but you were brave enough to accept that you had to travel by boat."

"Sallinger made me."

"That's still accepting it," I disagree. He groans and rests his head on my shoulder. "You did it, soldier."

"If we're not careful, my stomach would like to intrude on our affections by serving up a brilliantly tangy liquid called hydrochloric acid."

"Do you have to—"

"No, no." His shaking subsides, resolving to minute tremors. "I need to rest."

"You could stay here if you don't feel right."

"No, I'll go. I have the bed over there." He pulls away. His face remains pale as he settles under the comforter of the neighboring bed, turning his back away from me until the boat rocks again.

Marshall shrieks, bolting upright once more. He turns to face me with a crease in his brows. "The ocean and this boat are bullies."

I burst into a laughing fit as he stands and stomps his foot on the ground, an upheaval of childish laughter escaping him. "Ah-hah! You don't like that do you? Huh?"

I hide my laughter behind my pillow as he sits on his bed, untucking the comforter, taking off his puttees and boots. "Stop stalking me! A man taking his shoes off isn't appealing at all. Unless you find it appealing?"

"I'm trying to sleep, for your information." I turn over when his dull footsteps tiptoe over to my side of the room, his shadow setting over me. "Let me sleep!"

"I came over to say goodnight! Is it that much of a crime?"

I poke my tongue out at him playfully. "Stop it."

After teasing and tickling me, his laughter subsides as his lids droop tiredly, fighting to stay awake. He bends down, hesitantly dipping to kiss my cheek delicately. "Goodnight, sleep well."

"Goodnight. I love you so much."

"I love you too." He takes my chin in his hands, looking down at me with an urgency in his eyes. "Will you make me a promise?"

"Of course," I reply. "Why the sudden request?"

"There's a war outside, but that doesn't stop the fact there may also be a war going on inside our heads. It's inevitable." He strokes my cheek with his thumb. "It's more of a compromise. In order to love, honesty is the key. I...I liked how honest we were about our fears—well, mainly my fear of boats—you get it. I want to be more open. If you're struggling, Frieda, please don't hide it from me. You know I'd listen to your worries regardless of the issue. If you'd do the same for me, I'd appreciate that. Our heads are a dark place, turning darker when we refuse to let in a little bit of light. Tell me all your worries, and I'll do my best to open up about mine. Promise?"

The question on his face hurts me on the inside, but his vulnerability makes me proud of the fact that he's brave enough to show it in the first place.

"I promise."

"Great." He kisses me quickly on the forehead. "We have a long journey ahead of us back to Hell. I wouldn't do it with anyone else other than you."

* * *

After five days of travel, we're back.

Funnily enough, there's a clear blue sky in Seattle and fog setting over Belgium. It must be from the rapid gunfire that's lasted for days on end and the smoke of the bombs that dent the earth.

As if we weren't shaken enough from the amount of travel we've endured and the number of freakouts Marshall's had, we trample through the wet, murky trenches. It's certainly quieter than the last time I was here. No soldiers sing their happy songs, none laugh at each other's jokes. They only murmur amongst themselves as we lug our tired bodies past them.

Through the fog, Sallinger stalks. His broad, bulky shoulders are stiff against the cold, his leg slowing him down in a visible limp as his eyes screw up against the wind. Salt-and-pepper hair lies in a mess under his cap as his badges clink together on his breast pocket over his heart. He's covered in all sorts of new wounds. Just the look of him is enough to frighten me.

As he draws near, I pause, jaw clenched. I'm fearful of what I should say after I forced down his hostile, parting words.

You surely can't be trusted.

It still stings as though they've only been said yesterday.

Sallinger halts. Marshall and I straighten to salute.

"Private Clark, thank you for returning in time with Private Joyce. It's great to have you back. I'd like a short word with the both of you."

We trail behind Sallinger in the fog. I'm the one that dawdles behind, my shudders setting deep within my bones as Marshall reaches for my hand, gazing at me. He delivers an encouraging nod as we step inside Sallinger's tent. The chair where I delivered my verdict, where I witnessed my lies being used against me, still remains.

Sallinger sits, opening a cracked leather notebook, motioning for us to sit. I refuse to sit in the same chair for another trial, another denouncement, but Andrew's chair isn't any better. Marshall removes his cap, thick brows furrowed. I try to peer over Sallinger's notes, but it's pointless, as the handwriting is too tiny to make out, too scribbled and scrawled across the page for it to be legible.

A prayer to the heavens for boys and their handwriting.

"Private Clark?" His eyes land on Marshall.

He doesn't show any sign of fear, though the air is thick with it, wafting around us, accompanied by the sickly scent of smoke.

"Yes, sir?" Marshall clasps his hands in his lap, his eyes dull, lifeless, as his mouth moves, detached from his deadpan expression.

Sallinger fumbles through his drawers and slides something across the desk towards us with slips of brown paper to match.

Certificates.

A muscle feathers in Marshall's jaw. He scans the paper, and when I follow along, I can only make out one sentence through the boldly printed font.

Know ye, that reposing special trust and confidence in the fidelity and abilities of Private Marshall A. Clark, I do hereby appoint him Corporal.

On the other:

Know ye, that reposing special trust and confidence in the fidelity and abilities of Private Frieda S. Joyce, I do hereby appoint ~~him~~ her Corporal.

That's all I'm able to read before Sallinger steals my attention away from the page.

"It should come as no surprise to you that I've put forward a request to promote you both." His gaze is cold as ice as it flicks from the epaulets, chevrons, and certificates sitting before us. He pushes them farther forward. "You've done quite a lot for our army, and we're short on NCOs at the moment. I thought you two were the most suitable for the job. Though, Ms Joyce, I understand this comes as a shock for you. Your father was a noble man, and I've seen through the holes of Private Sawyers's account of what happened. You two possess a strong partnership, and I would be glad if you two were to demonstrate that in full out on the field."

Marshall stands to salute. I follow his lead cautiously. Despite thinking I'm back on Sallinger's good side, I may never know where I lie with his scowl that permanently creases his lips.

Sallinger dips his head, saluting back, dismissing and returning us out into the cold, clasping our certificates, chevrons, and epaulets with matching looks of shock.

Marshall tugs on his collar. "Much more work for us, then. We'll be up all night sewing."

Out of nowhere, a pair of men jump and pull us into a crumpled heap on the ground. Marshall lands on his back with his legs kicking up in the air as Lester and Ed clobber all over him.

"Christ, Lester. You didn't need to kill them!" Ed swats him over the head and ties back the hair escaping from his updo, turning to me, breathless. "Marshall told us he'd be going to Seattle to pick you up, and here you are! We were shocked enough to know you left us, but welcome back to Hell. Nothing's changed. Nothing's come and gone besides mass genocide and bad omens."

"I see you two have been promoted." Lester smacks Ed on the back. "Promoted too soon. Digging an early grave, you are."

"Lester," Ed whispers sharply. "Why must you darken the mood on such great news?"

"It's fine, leave him be." Marshall picks at the bandage on his arm. "We should head down to the field before Sallinger questions where his new corporals are."

"We should," says Lester. "I heard there's going to be a raid on the Austrian side with some of the new tanks coming in. Muscular beasts, they are. It's unfortunate, they don't stand a chance with their own tanks that malfunction to no avail."

Marshall replies, "The more advantages we have, the better."

As we stroll through the grimy rows of tents, the storm clouds draw nearer. The stench of death thickens around us as the mud sloshes over the soles of our feet, rotting the boards of the walkways.

We're about to enter our tent to unpack when a voice calls, "Corporal Joyce, ma'am! So sorry to interrupt, but I was sent to alert you that you'll assist the sergeant with hauling in supplies from St Mihiel. The sergeant is waiting by the mess hall!"

Even after five days trapped in a boat cabin, it seems I can never afford to catch a break.

"Understood. Tell him I'll be there in a moment."

7

Target Practice

The bangs of guns are loud in my ears as I enter the range. Extra wooden boards are propped up against a brick wall under a pale canvas canopy. Ed said Marshall had gone to practice shooting targets to pass the time.

My feet are aching and sore from carrying my weight and a multitude of boxes and heavy canisters, plus from the walk back as I stroll past the many men handling their guns like prized possessions. One or two whistle as I pass by, and I fight every impulse to kick their shins before another gunshot rings across the range. The bullet chips away at the board's lower end. Its marksman lets out a grunt of disapproval.

"Bit too low there, Clark." He's talking to himself, eyes narrowed against the sun as he reloads his rifle in one swift motion, observing his shot.

"Good aim you have there." I whistle once I'm within earshot. "I'm sorry if I disturbed you."

Turning the safety back on, his only response is to give me a lax smile. "Not at all. It's not every day I'll be blessed with such a remarkable individual's presence."

"Give your flirtations a rest." I groan as he sets his rifle on the ground with care. "You know they worked, so why bother?"

"Fine." He titters. "So, how was it?"

"If I find one word other than *boring* to describe the great adventure I just embarked on, I'll tell you."

"How about *dull* or *uninteresting*? *Unstimulating* also sounds like a pretty good word."

"You get what I mean, don't you?" I step just the slightest bit back for the sun to get out of my eyes. "It was one of the most painful workloads I've ever had to do."

"So you came to watch a man shoot to relieve the boredom?" He gasps. "How scandalous!"

"You're going to be the death of me someday with all your—"

"Corporal Clark!" a voice calls. "I hope I'm not interrupting anything too personal."

The teasing shine in his eyes vanishes as he addresses the person calling on him. "First Lieutenant Wilham, not at all. What brings you here?"

"Supposedly, there's going to be an invasion at dawn. We need you on the night watch from ten to three at the hillside."

Marshall curses under his breath, answering briskly. "I shall be there at ten on the dot, sir."

As the first lieutenant departs, Marshall runs his hands through his hair, letting out an exasperated noise of anger. "I won't get any sleep tonight."

"You could've said no."

He dismisses my attempts at consoling him. "I can't. Superior's orders."

"But look at you, getting called to go on a night patrol. That proves they trust you and that your aim is superior."

"It's not that great." Marshall fusses with a stray string of the chevrons sewn hastily into his sleeves as he stands; the same set of stitches were sewn into mine when I couldn't even fit the thread through the eye of the needle. When we were given time to unpack, he volunteered to sew them for me and endure the suffering of slipping needles that occasionally pricked his fingers.

"My real question is how I didn't have to teach you the basics of how to fire a gun."

"My father." I grin wide with a twinge of grief dulling my pride. "He taught me how to protect my family before he went to war."

"That's really…" Marshall takes his gun and slings it over his shoulder with a huff, his lips smoothing into a smile. "If I'm going on a night watch, I better practice. I'm going to shoot some more. You can watch if you'd like."

"I could use some practice."

Marshall's eyes flicker with a dark, intrigued interest. "Alright, let's see how good you've gotten."

"Is that a challenge?"

His eyes flash dangerously, smile widening. He hands me the firearm. "Perhaps so."

As he steps back, I arrange myself and aim at the target, turning the safety mode off.

Marshall immediately shakes his head.

"Did I do something wrong already?"

Marshall's now shifted into tutor mode: blunt and cold, standing straight as a pin. "Bend your knees. It'll stop the recoil from knocking you as far back when you fire."

As I adjust my positioning, Marshall remains close by to check, his eyes on my hands.

"Much better. Now, try to shoot the target."

"You're just teaching me the basics again. Better?"

"Better, but don't look so squished. You're shooting the enemy. Look more…carefree, like handling a firearm your second nature, as horrible as it sounds. Remember, you have a gun. Let the enemy know not to mess with you."

"Is there ever a time where your head isn't full of flirtations to experiment with?"

Marshall puts a finger to his lips. "Don't you dare talk back to your teacher."

I swallow and adjust my position once more. Marshall gives me the briefest nod, melting back into tutor mode. His gaze sticks to my back. "You know what to do: aim, let the bullet find its home. Let it burrow deep into the target."

I push down on the trigger, the familiar feeling of knockback threatening to tear me down. The gun's bang blasts in my ears, the gownpowder's acrid stench in my nose when the bullet releases itself.

Marshall steps forward and shields his eyes against the sun, squinting to see where the bullet lands. With a steely grin, he places a hand on his hip and points.

"Did I do well?"

He puts a hand on my shoulder. "You shot it where the thigh would be. No instant death, but if you puncture their femoral artery, they're a goner. If you don't, it'll trip them up and slow them down."

Handling the cold rifle with care, putting the safety back on, I give it back to him, only for him to turn it back off. "But this is something that would knock them off their feet."

He shoots, his bullet lodging into the top of the target, the very place where a head would be on a body. It shakes me to my core, witnessing his marksman's aim in action, right before my eyes.

"There we go. You don't have to do that all the time, but it's enough to send a warning to those waiting to catch you."

He puts the safety back on, watching the others shoot. His cheery smile is put back into place, his tutor mode wiped away. "You'll get better over time if you keep practicing. I'd say you're pretty good already."

* * *

Ed's reading a letter from his wife back in Pennsylvania, chuckling as he turns the paper over to the other side. He leans on the log nearest to the fire and folds his legs at the knees as he reads.

Marshall's buttoning up his coat and dusting it off from a day full of work and firing practice. His eyes are bright by the firelight, his cheeks hollow and his frame growing gaunt. He's obviously gotten skinnier, leaner, as the war draws out all of his energy.

Ed finishes reading and folds the letter carefully into his pocket. He gives Marshall a shake of the head. "You have dust on your back, Marshall."

"Where?" Marshall attempts to look at his own back, straining his neck, obviously struggling.

"Here. Stop embarrassing yourself." Ed stands to dust him off, patting him down as clouds of dust rise from his coat.

Meanwhile, the cold droughts blowing by cause a shiver to bite deep into my bones. I rub my hands together in a weak attempt to keep warm as the boys squabble. Ed assures Marshall there's no more dust, and once he wheels around, he gives Marshall a loud smack of his haunches with a lecture to keep clean for his own good.

Like a wounded dog, Marshall scampers back to his place beside me, rubbing his behind and cursing at Ed. "You didn't have to smack me!"

"I knocked some sense into you."

"Some hand you've got there," Marshall teases. "I suspect there'll be a questionable bruise there by tomorrow."

"I didn't even slap you that hard." Ed leans on his knees.

"I don't think you understand the meaning of the word *hard*." Marshall slowly and carefully sits himself down, cursing as his teeth grit with pain. "I can barely walk straight. Don't you laugh at me!"

Ed hides his smile behind his hand as Marshall snarls one last curse at him, taking in my shivering figure.

"You look to be the slightest bit cold."

"A little bit, yes," I answer.

Despite his recent tirade of curses and cusses at Ed, his gaze remains steady. His shoulder brushes mine, and the strong smell of coffee returns.

"Did you drink coffee recently?" I reach to fix his collar, his chin raised.

"If I'm to stay awake for a great deal of the night, what else would I do? It's just one cup: no sugar, no milk. It felt like I was doing hard drugs just swallowing it."

"Fair point." I rest my head on his shoulder as Ed begins a new letter. His pen moves quickly along the paper of his notebook.

Its faint scratching itches against my ears as Marshall leans in to whisper, "Ed writes to his wife nearly every day. I'm surprised at how many letters he's sent: seventeen so far."

"*Seventeen?*" When he shuffles closer, he proceeds to lean his cheek atop my head. His arm wraps around me. "You're kidding!"

"No, I'm serious. We have to catch up."

"Who is his wife, anyway?"

"Alice Surry, from Boston. She's pregnant. I can't imagine how much stress they're under."

"Hopefully this all clears up soon. But my question is why you two enlisted?"

"Pardon?"

"Why did you two enlist?"

"I enlisted because, when I was in a dark place, I was sick of sitting around doing nothing. With all these men out there having the time of their lives and coming home with such courageous stories, I wanted in on it. Ed followed me because his family insisted on him going, as they forced him to enlist before his conscription papers came, just because they wanted recognition and a reputation from putting their son in the war. Also, they wanted to mooch off of Ed's wages."

"Wow." I close my eyes against the wind, yawning. "Compared to you two, I don't think my reasoning would stand a chance."

He huffs a half-suppressed breath of amusement and ruffles my hair when he sees me growing tired. "That story's for another day. I think it's time for someone to go to bed."

I don't argue. He reaches to lift me in his arms, my own looped around his neck with his hands supporting my thighs. He calls to Ed, "It's past someone's bedtime. I'm going to tuck this little one in."

Ed pauses in writing his letter. "Fine by me. What time are you even going to be on patrol?"

"They said to meet at ten. I'll most likely be out until three or four."

"Fine." Ed resumes his writing, pen poised in thought, thinking of how to start a new sentence to the one he loves. "Stay safe, okay? Goodnight, Frieda."

"Goodnight, Ed," I mumble, resting my cheek on Marshall's shoulder, his epaulet strap digging into my face. He takes it as a signal to carry me to the tent. His arms are shaking from either the cold or my weight, and I feel guilty for making him suffer through either burden. "You can put me down if I'm too heavy."

"No, I won't," he replies. "You'd collapse as soon as I set you down."

"Fair call." I set my chin upon his clavicle, Ed's tent shrinking as we venture farther away.

He ducks to enter through the entrance of our tent and bends down to set me on the floor before he prepares my quarters for bed. He tucks me in the bedroll and fixes the blankets, giving me a caring smile.

"All comfortable?" A gentle hand sweeps the stray hairs sticking to my forehead out of my eyes.

"So tired...You didn't have to—"

"Shush, you were practically going to fall asleep on me on the way back."

I moan tiredly, "I don't deserve you."

"Once again, shush. I have to leave soon."

Marshall stands, and I make a poor attempt to grab at his ankle.

"Please stay, just for a while." My voice quakes, pleading. "Please, Marshall, please?"

His mouth opens to speak, hesitating, looking for words, replying with, "I have to go. I'll come back. I promise."

"You promise?"

"I promise." He takes his webbings and fastens them across his chest with a grimace at the weight of them. He loads the buttoned pockets with ammunition, rations, and a canteen, casting one last look my way. He bends down to stroke my cheek, the action there and gone in almost an instant. "Sleep well."

His footsteps fade as he closes the tent flaps behind him, giving me one last reluctant glance. Once he's out of sight, I light a gas lamp, rummaging through Marshall's satchel. Carefully casting aside his journal, ink, and pens, I find what I'm looking for.

Books.

It's the only way I can entertain myself when I make my decision to wait for him. Observing the paperbacks he's brought with him, he has some poetry by T.S Elliot and *Anna Karenina*; a rather thick tome in comparison to the slim volume that accompanies it. I take out *Anna Karenina*, cracking open the cover against my thighs, running my hands over the cracked spine, crushed against the pressure of many, many rereads with his name in his swirling font on the front page on a bookplate with the Latin words *Ex Librus* etched into it. It's a gorgeous bookplate, the ink dry after many years of it being in his ownership.

When I turn the page, his font is scrawled neatly on its edges, underlining and annotating lines he's either found interesting or wanted to define. His passion takes me elsewhere. His little remarks take my mind off his absence while I have his thoughts here in front of me, manifested in written form inside a book he and I both clearly enjoy.

I continue my reading, my stomach hurting from laughing at Marshall's annotations. My eyes grow heavy. I tilt my head back.

What was once a small dozing off becomes being asleep for hours.

* * *

My eyes stay closed, but my body awakens to someone entering the tent.

Whoever decided to stroll inside is careful not to disturb anything around them, almost fox-like with almost-silent footsteps as their owner strays closer.

The sounds of layers being shed and the *plonk* of webbings on the floor reach my ears. Feet scuffle to reach for the book in my lap, their owner releasing a *hmph* of amusement.

"Only made it up to chapter eight, huh? Fast reader. But, of course, sleep defeated you."

His feet scuffle some more, the sound of a gun being unloaded clicking dully in my ears.

Out of instinct, my eyes flit open.

Before me, Marshall's unloading his rifle. His eyes meet mine, blinking back. "I didn't mean to wake you! Go back to sleep."

I give him no reply as he neatly folds his tunic, places it on his satchel, and settles down on his own bedroll, blowing out the oil lamp that provides the dull light inside the tent. His eyes close as his arms pillow his head.

I prod his side. "Marshall?"

"Mmhm?" His eyes open, groggy from sleep deprivation. "What's the matter?"

"Thanks for lending me your book."

A snicker emerges. "You stole it, but no worries. As long as you didn't read my journal."

"I didn't. I swear it to you."

Clearing his throat, he moves closer, his fingers brushing mine; cold and bare, shivering.

I poke him again. "You're so bad at hiding things."

"How so?"

"Do you remember when we slept next to each other that night?"

"You slept as still as a rock the entire night. I thought you were dead."

"So, you remember?"

"Yes, because I didn't want you to fall ill."

I spread my arms out. Marshall's mouth opens in surprise. "Wait—"

"You're cold, aren't you?"

Marshall shrugs. "I don't know. Am I?"

"Stop lying to me."

Marshall turns onto his stomach, grunting. "I don't know if I'm cold or not cold."

"Just come here!" I make an attempt to drag him over, but he pushes my hands away.

"Fine! Fine!" He shuffles over so that his head rests millimeters from mine. "Better?"

"You're the most mischievous person on the planet sometimes." I yawn, covering my mouth. "But I can deal with it."

"Are you sure about that?"

"We'll see." I get comfortable beside him as he closes his eyes, a humored snort escaping from his nose. I ask him something, my mouth acting faster than my brain.

His eyes open at the question. "Pardon?"

"I asked you: What's Philadelphia like?"

"Why do you want to know all of a sudden?"

"I'm curious. Late night thoughts. I would like to know more about the mystery land the mysterious bookworm comes from."

"I see." Marshall settles deeper into his blankets, his shoulder brushing mine. "I haven't actually thought about home for a long time. Where should I start?"

"I don't know. With your neighborhood?"

"Well," his smile lights up the dark, "I live in the neighborhood of East Falls; a nice little house by the river called the Schuylkill. It's a pretty green area, and ducks fly over to the river to swim nearly every afternoon. When I wake up in my room in the morning, I have a brilliant view of the river, the trees, and the trail people walk on out the window. I would then get dressed, go downstairs, check the mailbox for any reply from Beasley University about my acceptance letter. I'd go for a walk down the trail after that to clear my head, maybe sit on the porch in the backyard and read for the afternoon if the weather is nice enough. If not, the study will work."

He takes a break, covering his mouth when he yawns. "Ed recently moved from Pittsburgh with his wife. They currently live in Society Hill, which is one of the oldest neighborhoods in all of Philadelphia. He's just under half an hour's ride away. There's this really good café not far from East Falls, too. They serve delicious eggs on sourdough toast. I'd love to take you."

"I think I remember my father taking me one time. We were in your living room, the one with the big fireplace?"

"That's the one. I'm surprised you remember."

"Yes, and you came downstairs half an hour late with ink stains on your hands and the meanest of glares?"

"I don't really remember much of my teenage hormones. It's been a long time since then. Wait, how old were you?"

"About thirteen?"

Marshall snorts. "I must've been fifteen then. I was a very angry teenager. I remember thinking of you as just another person who would come and go in my life."

"And now?"

He shuffles even closer, broad chest rising and falling with each breath. "Look where I am now." His exhales are warm against my neck. "I made the mistake of waiting to meet you. I was unsure if I wanted to, because I thought I had no time to meet with anybody, nor did I want to."

"You were pretty introverted."

"No, actually, I was anxious." Marshall lays his head closer to mine, gazing at me through dark lashes. His eyes are closing, but he refuses to nod off to sleep. "I used to walk away from social interactions so much that my father would yell at me: 'I should've brought you up better! Come on, Marshall, say hello to our guests!' Like that did anything. I stayed in my room, studying."

"You seem very dedicated to your studies."

"I had to get my brain ready for university. I studied almost every day, and I got better at long division. That was my weak spot in math. I can do it perfectly now. I didn't want anyone to break my stride. I wanted to get the best grades so I could become successful in life."

I rub at my itching bottom lid. "What about your family?"

"My family? I'm a middle child. I have an older brother—he's twenty-three—and a younger sister. She's sixteen, nearly seventeen. I think you and her will get along just fine."

"Where is she now? And your brother?"

"Alistair's fighting in Italy. Edith's at home taking care of Father."

"I was supposed to have a sibling, but they were a miscarriage just days after the first trimester."

At this, he wraps me closer. "I'm so sorry."

"It's okay. That was years ago. I was still extremely young."

Another warm exhale plumes from his lips. He checks his watch. "I say we hit the hay. We need as much rest as we can get."

"Are you a bit warmer now?"

"Much more, yes." He closes his eyes, murmuring a goodnight, falling deep asleep.

I force my eyes to close, attempting to fall asleep as he moves deeper into his dreams: lashes fluttering, lips pursing, and brows creasing.

Careful not to wake him, I step outside as the sun rises in the distance. There's the faint glow and a curl of smoke from a campfire in the distance. Lester has lit his fire, sitting by it, his head in his hands. Marshall informed me earlier that he prays every morning, as he's an orthodox Jew who owes his life to the ones he believes are up above.

In the morning silence, his rushed prayer is audible as he reaches to read from what I wager is a copy of the *Siddur*, which is of a brilliant navy blue clutched dearly in his hands, closing it softly, issuing a brief 'amen' to close his prayer.

8

THE AUSTRIAN INVASION

"Marshall!" I shake Marshall harshly by the shoulders, only to be answered by a groan, protesting my commands to awaken. "They're serving breakfast soon! It's time to get up."

"Let me sleep some more…" He turns his back on me, blindly swatting my hands away. He lets out a frustrated and disturbed moan. "Please, five more minutes. We can reach a compromise."

"No compromises. You can sleep more tonight. Get up. I don't want you to starve."

"Fine, fine." He sits up, squinting. He rubs away sleep residue from the corners of his eyes. As he pouts tiredly, he stretches his arms over his head as his back cracks. "I'm up."

"Slept well?" I hand him his coat and tunic, grabbing his comb, brushing the teeth through his hair, a whimper arising when they snag onto a knot. Teasing it away, he relaxes against my grip as he buttons his tunic tight.

Marshall's speech is slurred. "I don't know. It would be nice if I could sleep all day. I only got about two or three hours."

"Better than nothing. Gosh, Marshall, when was the last time you grabbed a grooming kit?" I exclaim as my hand scratches along his stubble. "Trim those sideburns or lord, help me."

"I'm thinking of going all out Blackbeard." He reaches to stroke his chin in thought as I comb his hair to the side. "What do you think? If that doesn't work out, perhaps I could fancy a mustache and become the next Charlie Chaplin?"

"Please, before you make a grave mistake, burn that idea out of your mind. Charlie Chaplin's mustache is a Charlie Chaplin exclusive."

"If not Charlie Chaplin, then perhaps I'd be devilishly handsome in a chin strap?"

"Heavens no."

Placing his comb back with the rest of his accessories, he kneels to grab an almost-empty cologne bottle, spritzing the inside of his collar, tipping his cap over his head after he cleans his teeth. He pulls the belt of his trench coat tighter once he stands and slides on his gloves. With a thread of curses to the morning sun, he emerges outside with tired eyes still droopy from sleep.

With heavy regret, we begin our journey to the mess hall with Andrew Sawyers lingering not far behind us, smirking so wide for the simple expression to be considered as displaced with an uncanny amount of mischief. Far too much of it in the ungodly hours of the morning. The spread of his shoulders is slumped with teasing glee as the toes of his boots wedge between rocks, making small squeaking noises of leather and rubber soles while he walks.

Marshall huffs a bothered sigh, complaining about his night watch, how the cold made his fingers turn blue, how he forgot his gloves and nearly burned himself trying to warm them by the fire. Now I see the red skin along his fingertips in the waxing morning light.

Andrew falls into step beside Marshall, shoving his hands in his pockets. With a grunt, Marshall walks just the slightest bit faster, sniffing his nose inattentively in the air.

"*Corporal* Marshall Clark!" calls the forever-vexing Andrew with a content shrug of the shoulders when he notices Marshall stiffening. "Beautiful morning, isn't it?"

It's hard not to ignore his eyes crawling up my back as he wets his lips, eagerly waiting for one of us to face him, to react. Marshall's nose wrinkles, but he keeps walking, uttering no witty response.

Andrew's footsteps only grow faster to catch up to our harried pace. "Oi, Pidge! What're you even doing, hanging around this flirt? I should tell you about the magical month of June—"

At this, Marshall wheels around, stomping his foot on the gravel. His expression is unreadable, a stale poker face. Andrew continues to infuriate him, satisfied with his response. "You surely remember last summer, don't you, Clark? You must think about it every night before you go to sleep; getting so jittery about how pleasurable it was."

Marshall swears under his breath. He ushers Andrew no outburst, controlling himself as he grits out an equally stale reply instead. "Yes, simply delectable. The flowers were in full bloom. Daisies, were they not?"

Andrew's perplexed as Marshall turns his back to him. A muscle jumps in Marshall's cheek as he grabs me by my arm. "Just keep walking."

"What was—"

"Don't even mention it," he whispers bluntly. "It never happened."

Ed files through the crowd, spreading his arms when he finds us. "There you two are! We were waiting. I take it, someone slept in?"

"Dreadfully so," Marshall says. Ed reaches to pull him into a teasing hug. He pushes him away. "Please don't touch me."

"What's the matter? Slept on the wrong side?"

"Nothing," he answers. "Now get off of me."

"It was Andrew." I hear him groan irritably when I answer. "He was talking about—"

"Shush about that, won't you?" Marshall raises his voice, hissing. Ed tuts and braces his hands on Marshall's shoulders. "I'm sorry, I shouldn't have yelled at you, but please, don't go any further."

Ed kneads his fingers through Marshall's arms, making an attempt to relieve his tension. "Marshall, what did I tell you about Andrew?"

"Let go of me."

"I told you that he's just looking for ways to get to you. I'm not letting go of you in case you have an unsightly outburst."

Marshall's shoulders slump. A growl rumbles deep within his throat.

Ed lets Marshall go after making sure that he's calmed down. "Seriously, try not to let him get to you. If you're in this irate mood for the entire day just from what someone said to you, then it'll do you no good."

Marshall's death stare is just as sharp as a knife.

We enter the mess hall, retrieving our rations and sitting down. Marshall's nose wrinkles once more in repulsive disgust. "Bloody hell. They don't add milk to their coffee."

"That's a shame." I pat his shoulder before I sit carefully next to him.

He's glaring at Andrew as his hand fastens itself around the handle of his metal mug, shaking horrendously as his anger builds up inside him. "I'm going to kill him. One day, I'll get the pleasure of shooting holes through him and watch that rat shrivel before me."

"No," I start lecturing him, far too much like a strict mother, "behave yourself. Seethe with rage at a later time."

After a few seconds that render Ed and I breathless, he slowly takes a deep breath in, calmly spreading butter atop his toast, eyes remaining glued on Andrew as he gains control over his impulses.

There's a bang as Lester sits down, cursing, making Marshall laugh dryly as he takes a bite out of his toast. "You need to be more careful, Lester."

Lester points an accusing finger at him as he reaches for his mug. "So do you, klutz."

"You're both klutzes," Ed quips.

"If you get me drunk, then I'm the klutziest of the klutzes." Marshall butters his other slice of toast, cringing at its burnt bottom. "But if you have me carry ten school books at a time like high school did, then *boom*: I'm always a klutz."

"So, you're admitting that you're clumsier than me?" Lester drinks out of his mug, swirling his dark coffee.

"I confess," Marshall takes a bite of his burnt toast, "that I'm the clumsiest of them all."

Leaving them to their bickering, I stare at my food, not feeling too hungry.

As Ed and Lester laugh together, Marshall looks at my plate. "You're not eating?"

"I'm not hungry."

"Are you nervous about anything?"

"Not in particular."

"Please eat a little something," he pleads. I shake my head before he asks, "Not for me?"

All I do is shrug my shoulders, a part of him shattering at my response. "I don't feel hungry."

"You need to eat." The apprehension and fear in his voice is loud and clear as he pleads with more urgency. "Please, one piece of toast, at least?"

It hurts me to see him so desperate to get me to swallow even a crumb of food, something to keep me going. "I've lost my appetite."

"But you still have to eat something." Marshall presses a piece of toast in front of me. "Will this suffice?"

Instead of toast, I take some crackers. They're stale, but Marshall nods with his success. "Have some beef, please."

I take small mouthfuls of beef. He breathes a sigh of relief and glares at something.

I follow his gaze. Andrew is staring right at us, grinning from ear to ear.

"I'll kill him one day, I swear." His eyes don't leave Andrew's face. He raises his mug to his lips.

"Calm yourself." I stand, taking his hand. "Walk with me."

The disgruntled Marshall follows me outside, where a loud crash sounds in the distance.

A cloud of smoke spreads across the sky, the air around us doused in its bitter stink.

We freeze, Marshall's hand tensing around mine as soldiers spew out of the mess hall in a frenzied tirade. His hand tightens as another bang crashes when the second bomb lands.

With little to no hesitation, we set off to grab our rifles from our tent under the booming shockwaves of bombs and machine guns.

His eyes, cold, calculating, look from one face to another as we pass through the trenches, barking for soldiers hanging off the walls to move out of our way, shouldering past them, even bumping them with the butt of his rifle as shrapnel splinters the dirt walls. There's a bout of yelling not far from where we're hiding. Some men are praying, holding their arms tight to their chest, hugging themselves to comfort their shaking limbs and racing minds from the storm of the war. They're covered in soil, coughing out dust from their poisoned lungs as they shiver in the little holes they've dug to protect themselves from the enemy.

The booming of gunfire and explosions die down. Yelps of pain echo in the distance. The only noise that breaks the short duration of silence is the roar of aircraft above. They come like a swarm of wasps, their wings spread wide, soaring high through the storm that lashes at them.

A bolt of lightning lights the sky, sending a plane down.

The drill sergeant's hands tighten around his whistle, ordering that the waves are to be organized. His voice, calling men to attention, is enough to send a sudden chill down my spine as he starts ordering us into sections, for death to hit us immediately with its unforgiving aim.

9

The Spy

The trenches are alive with men shouting orders at each other once each of them see the plane fall out of the sky. Its engine sputters as it dies. Once it collides with the ground, the dead trees and their skeletons of branches and roots catch fire. The pungent smell of the smoke rising in tendrils sends my head spinning.

"If that damned whistle blows now," Marshall hisses, glancing at his pocket watch, "I'm going to shoot myself."

"Why would they blow it in the middle of gunfire? That's suicide." I nearly trip from a shockwave that spews dirt into my hair.

Marshall's eyes whip around to look at me. "They did once."

His hands grip the ladder tight as his nervous breaths escape from his lips. He may look ready to fight, a soldier, loyal to his country, but on the inside, he's a scared little kid who doesn't want to die young. I'm sure everyone else is like that here; all nails and teeth clawing each other down. A never ending battle for survival until all is quiet is on the Western Front, the strongest fighters still standing.

Now he's on his toes, oddly not alarmed by the shrieks of shells plummeting to the earth. His glare has gotten to be so solid that it can cut through metal, just like the shrill sound of the whistle that tells us to run.

Without hesitation, we haul ourselves over the ladder, Marshall reaching to pull me up with his rifle at the ready, shooting at anything moving on the other side, barking for me to stay close.

Something isn't right with my rifle. It's firing fine, making the noise a gun should. Nothing is broken, nothing has changed. Each time I shoot, the regular plume of smoke appears and fades in seconds.

As I trip from yet another shockwave, a folded note falls out of my pocket.

I unfold the paper and try my best at reading the writing that's etched into the parchment.

Joyce,

Like my present? All of your ammunition is now made of blanks. I'm sorry, starlet. This time, you won't be able to play again.

Enjoy. I'll see you on the other side.

−Andrew

My mouth fills with mud when I fall. Marshall, yet again, is running back to help me up. I couldn't care less as my blood sings with anger coursing through my veins.

"What's wrong? Are you hurt?" Hands prod me everywhere, searching for any scratches, any wounds. "Did you get shot?"

I simply shove the parchment in his face, letting him read it. His voice lowers to resume its deathly grate as he chews at his lip. No light enters his eyes as he crumples the paper under his fist.

"That bastard."

I scan the land around me, making out Andrew's light hair among the men hiding behind a broken tank from the gunfire. Once the guns cease their fire, I take the risk of charging towards him. Marshall follows close behind, readying his rifle, stalking the menace like a wolf hunting its prey; eyes dark and hidden under an even darker fringe. He's bloodthirsty, ready to fire once the order's been sent. He's ready to kill the vermin who continues to cower behind the tank's body while shells ping at its metal.

"Sawyers!" I snarl.

Andrew turns and rolls his eyes. "Damn, you've come to thank me?"

My glare is stone cold as Marshall steps beside me, gun at the ready as a smirk plays on Andrew's lips. "What in the name of God goes through your head when you start mixing blanks with my ammunition?"

When the whistle blows for the next wave to go over, he releases a snicker. His accent is different, cold— *European.*

"Just doing my job, giving the enemy fewer troops to eliminate one step at a time."

Marshall's face stretches in horror as Andrew launches himself at him, kicking him to the floor and off his feet, his rifle skittering away and out of reach. The both of them are a flurry of bodies, a snarling heap as the smack of Andrew's knuckles cracks through the air. Marshall's chin juts upward from the force as a cry of pain escapes him. He lands a swipe of his nails, almost catlike, across Andrew's forehead, narrowly missing his eyes, Andrew yowling from the sharp pain.

With all his hatred, Marshall wouldn't hesitate to take another swipe, this time gouging his eyes out, blinding him.

Andrew's still on top of him, Marshall baring his teeth. He draws an arm back to send a hard fist flying at Andrew's nose. When his grip loosens, Marshall makes an attempt to stand, Andrew grabbing him by his hair, throwing him back down to the ground, slamming a foot into his stomach before he spits on him. The blood dribbling from his nose mixes with his expelled saliva.

"You son of a bitch!" Marshall manages to get on his knees once Andrew stands, prepping a pistol after he wipes his nose, making an attempt to stop the stream of blood, ignoring Marshall's insults.

"I'm sorry I have to do this to you, Marshall. We were such good friends. Alas, this is the end."

Marshall's eyes are blazing with anger, challenging and staring straight ahead. "Shut up! Curse the day you were born! Go on, shoot me. Or are you too scared that I'll catch you first? Because I'd do it over and over again. I'd grab you by the hair and smack your head against this very tank until you cry at my feet to put an end to your filthy misery. I wouldn't even care if I ever go to prison. I'd bathe in your blood and set your corpse on fire to celebrate my victory."

Andrew releases a guffaw, loud, fizzing with menace. "Perhaps you'd like to take those words back? Your bravado is lacking."

"My bravado? Lacking?" Marshall spits on his boots, barking out a horridly bitter chuckle through snarling teeth. "I have to laugh. I've been waiting for this day since I was eleven. So, here we are. Go on, *Andrew*, if that's who you really are. Shoot me!"

"Wait!" I take a daring step forward, Marshall's eyes growing sickeningly wide. "Shoot me instead. Leave him. I'm the one who deserves to die."

Marshall snaps, "If I die at his hands, don't you *dare* follow me."

"You won't." I take another step forward. Marshall freezes as I close the distance. I nudge my head towards his rifle which lies within an arm's length away from him. Not taking any chances to ask what the hell I'm up to, his eyes slide from horror to understanding, sneaking to reach for the rifle. "Go on, Andrew, let him live. It's me you want, isn't it? You teased me on my first day, assaulted me, lied to get me away from here, taking away another root of joy from me. What more could you possibly want other than to eliminate me?"

A cold stare.

A bang of another bomb.

Marshall's fingers are inches away from his rifle as Andrew raises his pistol.

"My darling, you have no idea."

It all happens so quickly.

Before I know it, Andrew's gun fires, a state of confusion crossing Marshall's face as his hands fly reflexively to his arm, pulling them hurriedly away, sticky and red with fresh blood.

His scream is piercing, earsplitting, as the heat of the bullet burns into his flesh. Hurriedly, he reaches into his webbings with his unwounded arm, possibly searching for gauze, bandages, or even a tourniquet. He's shouting, howling until his throat is red and raw.

Panic surges through me at the sight of his wound and the blood quickly wetting his sleeve. Though, I'm frozen in my spot, fearful to run to him and meet a bullet to my side.

"I'll kill you," he blindly snarls, coming back with nothing. "You swine, I'll kill you!"

My brain works fast with Marshall's life on the line. I try to look at my alternatives as Andrew lowers his gun to observe the damage.

"What a show by a soldier with actor potential!" He turns callously to Marshall. "What was it you were saying about letting my bullet ring true? I missed. Care to let me take a second shot?"

Marshall turns feral as he clutches his upper arm, yowling dangerously up at him.

"That's a lot of blood." Andrew snickers, cruel with mocking sympathy. "Just six liters waiting to be lost. It hurts, doesn't it? Damn, I missed your vitals by a mile, but the sepsis and the blood loss will make it even more enjoyable to watch you die. Now, shall I give you the name of your killer before I shoot your accomplice? Yes? Andrej Johannes. Nice to meet you, Corporal Clark."

"In my father's name and everything holy..." Marshall applies more pressure to his wound. His hand stains a deeper shade of crimson. He's already starting to blanch. "I won't die. If I do, take me in. Let my face be the one you see in your dreams for many nights to come."

Andrew—or Andrej—laughs. "Save your breath. Threatening me will get you nowhere."

Not taking any second chances, I race to grab Marshall's dropped gun lying in the mud, face hot, nerves zapping.

Before Andrej can react, I pull back on the bolt, locking a bullet in place.

Screaming bloody murder, a single shot rings out.

Blood spurts from Andrew's chest, pooling down his shirt front.

Uttering a gasp, his pistol clangs to his feet as he drops to his knees, clutching his chest. Blood dribbles down his chin and neck, staining his teeth and tongue red. Though I would love to see my tormentor in pain, his eyes frighten me, his damaged lungs rattling for air as he falls onto his front.

In a spreading pool of his own blood, there's no chance of going back. He's reached the end of the line, of all his living days, lifeless before my eyes; a marionette cut from its strings.

The spy is dead.

Stained in blood spatters, I lower the rifle with shaking arms and take in what I've done, vomit churning in my gut, shock settling in as I swallow back a scream. It isn't until Marshall whimpers beside me that I'm summoned back to the present, back to his voice mumbling one single word.

Tourniquet.

Reaching deep into his webbings, I manage to come across the beige strap, working with fumbling hands to put it below the wound, Marshall snapping at me to put it above it to slow the rush of blood. He's growing pale, faint, not taking much notice of the fresh corpse only inches away.

The medics rush over, tripping over older bodies, pulling me away to examine Marshall. There's a struggling yelp of pain from him as another medic leans over him to haul an arm over his shoulder. The other medic wraps his wound in bandages. I take my eyes away from the sight of it all: the blood oozing through bandages, the deathly pallor of his face as he fades in and out of consciousness.

Something warm drips down my own arm as I tail the medics who haul him onto a saddle. Not wanting to lose Marshall in the thicket of the aftermath and damage done by the assault, I chase after the stallion as it trots to the medic tents while I fold back my sleeves.

My arm has suffered a shallow cut from falling. I probably snagged it on a twig or something sharp. While I begin wrapping bandages around the cut, he's loaded onto a hospital cot as a nurse undoes the tourniquet, unwraps the bandages, and sets to work, prying the bullet out with a set of metal tweezers. His screams erupt once more as nurses hold his flailing limbs down. The bullet is removed. The wound is cleaned with stitches to follow as the suture needle dips and pulls his skin back together, as if he were merely a doll that's fallen apart. His arm is then bandaged and put in a sling, his exhausted body lying still in the cot.

Now that Marshall's screams have died down and the whole procedure is over, he lies flat on his back, staring at the ceiling. When I reach to grip his hand, he spooks, gasping and fearful.

"*Shh*," I hush him, "it's just me, just me."

Once his eyes settle upon me, he parts his lips to let out a minute cry. "It hurts...God, it hurts."

With a pained whimper, he reaches for my hand. "Rest," I say. "Don't move."

"Am I going to die, Freddy?" His eyes are elsewhere, staring at me, but elsewhere; the gaze of a terrified little kid facing the danger right in front of him. "Am I going to die?"

A muscle in my jaw jumps. I start debating whether I should lie and say no or tell him the truth. Either way, both answers will hurt him. One more, one less. I don't want to cause him more grief than what he's gone through in a single day.

"I...I don't know." His eyes remain wide open, staring at me while still far away. His forehead is damp with sweat, and I scoot my chair closer to wipe it away with the edge of my sleeve. "We just have to pray. You're in the best of hands at the moment."

"Sepsis. Infection. If the wound reopens..." He stirs, panicking. "I'll—"

"No, no. Don't think about that now." His grip tightens on my hand as his mind ticks away with thoughts. Behind his eyes, he's constructing all the many imaginative outcomes just from one single bullethole. I smooth his dampened fringe as his eyes threaten to break into tears.

Footsteps pound across the floor. Ed skids to a stop beside Marshall's cot, caked with mud, brown gunk under his fingernails and between the webbings of his hands.

"God, Marshall, what happened?"

"Damned spy...decided to shoot me," Marshall replies, choked by fear. "Andrew...was the spy."

"Just wait until I—"

"Don't worry, he's long gone," I interrupt. "I—he got killed in a crossfire."

Eyeing me suspiciously, Ed nods, taking it all in, gripping Marshall's other hand.

"The gunfire's stopping." He traces a thumb over Marshall's knuckles, tenderly watching as he closes his eyes against his touch. "I guess that was all for today. Another job well done. We survived."

"I'm dying," Marshall says.

"You're not." Ed bends over him. "Did the bullet hit deep?"

"Tore some muscle...apparently," Marshall replies with his eyes closed. "I feel so light."

"Well, it's not every day you get shot in the arm, is it?" Ed pulls the blanket up to his chin and tucks him in tight. "Why don't you rest?"

"You're going to go away."

"Who said I was?" Ed strokes his cheek. "I promise, we'll try our hardest to be back when you wake up."

Defeated, he sighs. "Damn you and your calming words."

When Marshall finally falls asleep, work begins.

Ed and I are on cleanup duty, and at lunch, when Marshall's spot at the table is empty, Ed tells Lester the news, making him promise that he'll visit him later.

* * *

The sun is behind the trees when I make my way back to camp, limbs creaking in protest with every step as I march forward. Lightning flashes up ahead as I walk into the medic tent, the rain spitting down on the roof upon my entry. A new man in the corner rocks himself back and forth, chewing his lip as he goes. There's another who spits ugly insults at me as I pass.

They don't stop me strolling to the furthest bed, where Marshall remains lying on his back, still as a rock. He's still tucked under the blanket, just as we left him hours before. He's still starkly pale, still horribly blanched as his body repairs itself. In sleep, his bottom jaw hangs slightly open as a scarred hand rests upon his blanketed stomach.

I sit beside his wounded person, running a soft hand through his hair. His eyes fly open, pupils dilating to balance their intake of light and shock. He startles, but calms when his gaze focuses on my face.

"Feeling any better?" I wipe the sweat from his forehead as he emits a groan.

With his cheeks stained with tears, he mopes. "It hasn't stopped hurting."

"That's unfortunate. Have they given you painkillers?"

He shakes his head. "No. They said they wouldn't work with this amount of pain."

"Not even just to calm it?"

"It would be useless."

"Have you gotten any rest by any chance?" My hand resumes its stroking of his hair.

"No."

"Let me tuck you in."

"I'm not a child," he argues.

"No, but it'll help you sleep better."

"Come, rest with me." He pats a free, small space on the bed with pleading eyes. "It's so lonely here." Reluctantly, I reject his offer.

"I'm sorry. I have to go on night watch." I hug my coat tight against the winds that blow against my back from an opening in the tent, rising gooseflesh under my uniform.

His gaze drops as he feebly reaches for my hand, shaking as he pulls it to his lips.

"I almost forgot." He cradles my fingers, kissing my palm. "What I wanted to say...What you did back there," another kiss, "was...It was...I'm too tired to think of a word."

"Is it good, what you're thinking?"

"All good things," he grins tiredly, "all good things. You saved me, Frieda. You saved *us*. If you hadn't...if you hadn't shot...we'd be...we'd be…"

Dead. Two wilted lovers lying side by side.

I don't need to finish the sentence to know what he's thinking.

"I know." I hold his hands in mine, clasping them tight. "Don't think about it too much."

"What I was trying to say was...thank you." He squints as more pain gushes through his body.

"Don't thank me." I lean over him, our eyes meeting; green and hazel, a forest of colors.

"Why shouldn't I?" He's fading back into sleep, one side of his mouth turning upward into a grin. "You saved my life."

"I was only paying you back for when you saved mine."

"My dear," he makes an attempt to shuffle closer, but his discomfort stops him, "you're far too humble...far too modest. You could save me from a burning building, save me from falling off a cliff and still say those words. It makes my heart explode."

"Even while on a hospital bed, you're flirting."

"You know it." His eyes close again, blissfully aware that he's safe here with me. "You know I'll always find a way to give you a bit of an adrenaline rush, right?"

"Are you sure they didn't give you anything?"

"Positive." He's nodding off, falling asleep. "You can't deny my feelings of gratitude, nor can you deny my feelings about you. When the heart speaks, it speaks true. My heart is just writing out song lyrics...lyrics I just don't know how to fluctuate yet...how to orchestrate them. But I know they're all about you, and I'd like to perform for you one day the beautiful symphony they shall create."

* * *

Marshall's days in the medic tent stretch on with agony riding strong through his body. He's often three shades paler, the gorgeous warm undertones of his skin bleached out as he's left to dry. He's grown out a stubble that desperately needs shaving and possesses a lax, deflated air as his injury takes its toll.

The nightmares don't stop tonight. They've fazed me all day as I worked, and I've had enough of sleeping on my lonesome without some amount of comfort, some reassurance that I'm not losing my mind after all the blood that spills at my feet in my mind's eye.

I know what I'm doing is selfish, that with every silent footfall, I'm committing some sort of crime.

It's awfully cold out for a November evening, a cold that creeps deep into my bones and turns their very marrow to ice. When the winds make my eyes tear up, I send a curse out to break the silence.

A light is still on in the tent as I carefully pull back the flaps. I make sure to close them behind me to keep in the overwhelming heat of a furnace burning nearby. It thaws my joints, melting each little icicle in all my crevices. I emit a groan of delight as the warmth spreads.

He's sitting upright in bed, arm in a sling, finally freshly shaven. "Look at you, sneaking in here to meet a man in the middle of the night. Also, without an arrangement for a tryst? Wow."

"It's not even after ten." My eyes sweep the tent to find it empty of nurses. "Where is everyone?"

"Gone out to help with unpacking supplies or something like that." He stands and sneaks over with equally soft footfalls. He presses a finger to his lips. "You may want to keep your volume at a low. We have some light sleepers among us."

"You make me coming over here more sinful than it should be."

"Was it originally?" He dodges a light swat to the cheek with a crooked grin.

"You're horrible sometimes. Do you know that?" I stiffen at his amused chuckle.

He shushes my rising voice. "Well? What *did* you come here for?"

"Couldn't sleep," I mumble.

His grin fades, his eyes search my face. Recognition flickers behind them. Quick as ever to deduce that something's off.

"What's the matter? There's something bothering you more than your inability to sleep."

"Bad dreams," the words escape, "recurring bad dreams."

He remains still, quiet in the heavy silence, beckoning me closer. "Why don't you sit down? Unless, you don't want to talk about it?"

"That's why I came here." I make my way to the chair at his cot's side, the wood squeaking under my weight. He sits atop his mattress and rests his chin on his hand. "Ever since...*that* happened, I've been having bad dreams of the same thing over and over again."

"So you've come to talk to me about it? I'm glad you trust me. How long have these dreams been occurring?"

"A week? A week and a bit? I'm not too sure." I have to dip my eyes away. His concern wounds me. "But they're the most abysmal things my mind can conjure. They have me shaking each time I wake up."

He doesn't acknowledge my shaking hands, my stiff back. "If you're comfortable sharing, what're these dreams about?"

"A floor covered in blood, like, an ankle-deep, unending lake of blood." He himself freezes at the image. "I'm not sure if it's my brain trying to cope with some sort of trauma—I'm bad at psychological terminology, but the bodies of men who've harmed me in some way are floating in blood. There's Andrew...he's the one who dunks my head under and drowns me…" It hurts to push the next few words out, but I have to do it. I have to be rid of the secret. "And you."

He blinks. "Me?"

"I assure you—"

"Have I done something to upset you? If I have—"

"Please, will you just listen?" The request wasn't supposed to come out as a command, but he obeys it nonetheless. "I assure you, you've done absolutely nothing to harm or hurt me in the slightest. But somehow, you're there even if you yourself have done nothing wrong. The two of you morph into devils and surround me until I wake up."

He struggles to grasp at the right words. "I...it must be terrifying to go through that every night, and I'm sorry it has to burden you like that. I'm just making sure, are you—"

"Sure that you've done nothing to upset me? One hundred percent." My eyes travel to his slinged arm. "Well, perhaps the sight of you being shot is involved. I'm not too sure."

He pauses before making the next move, patting the space beside him on the bed.

"I can't—"

His eyes glitter in the dark. "I don't mind."

"I understand this is a lot to take in. I don't deserve—"

"My pity? I'm not pitying you. I'm simply offering a hug to convey my solace." A hand rests on my shoulder. "Unless you don't want that. Whatever works for you."

"I just needed someone to talk to." I meet his eyes and hold their stare. "Thank you, Marshall. Really, it means a lot."

"Don't thank me for such a simple favor." He winks and lets go of me. "Now, why don't you stay here tonight?"

"I think I'll take my leave." I stand hurriedly. He's struck by surprise at my refusal. "I don't want to inconvenience you and your recovery."

"You'd do nothing of the sort, but it's your choice entirely. It's not my business to force you into anything." He reaches for my hand, brushing a thumb over my knuckles. "You'll be alright?"

"I'll try."

"That's what I like to hear." He hesitantly applies a chaste kiss to my carpals. "Please rest well. Goodnight."

Leaving the tent and its warmth for the cold outside, I sneak one last look at him from over my shoulder as he dives under the covers, a whimper of pain expelling itself from his mouth. It's all the evidence I need to come to one final answer that puts some of the tremors of my heart to rest.

Monsters never feel pain, nor do they offer compassion, unless they want to lure in their prey. No jaws of sharp teeth or pointy claws were waiting for me. No sinister gleam shone in his eyes.

Marshall Clark is perfectly human, tainted ever so slightly by the war and its violence. He wears a suit of armor made of metal to soak up all the damage, remaining pure at heart. No monster is using his skin to grow close to his next target, where he plans on cutting me open and playing with my entrails in the shadows.

That doesn't stop the possibility of him transforming at any given time into another bloodthirsty beast. Yet, I don't imagine that happening anytime soon with that mind of steel nestled inside his skull.

* * *

The winter snow comes early this year.

Each night, I still sleep in the tent alone and cling tight to myself as I move in and out of dreams. The nightmares still wrap themselves in the darkness inside my head; flashes of colors and bright lights as blood swallows my feet, corpses drowned in the horrible, metallic liquid that swamps my senses.

His dark hair is slick with it as he lies on his back, practically bathing in it as the other's pale hair is now a deep, crusting red as he licks the liquid hungrily off of his lips with a gaping hole in his chest. I swear I saw horns sprout from his skull once or twice, fangs growing from his gums as the other rises, eyeing me callously with a grin tugging at his mouth.

I step outside as snow blankets the grass in a layer of pure white. It's about ankle deep and freezes my toes nestled in my boots and thick socks. Inside the medic tent, Marshall's getting his sling taken off after weeks of being stuck in recovery. As he strikes up a chipper conversation with the nurse, she *tsks* in disbelief that he's yapping his mouth off after going through so much agony as she unravels his bandages. His wound is clean and scabbed over, almost fully healed.

Once discharged, he creeps outside, gasping as his boots sink into the snow with an impressionable crunch.

"Ah!" He stops himself from letting the swears out, cutting himself off. "I wasn't expecting the snow to be too deep. But *this*...this is *deep.*"

His nose and cheeks turn red after so many weeks of staying pale, stained and irritated by tears, the cold turning his exhales into transparent clouds as he walks by my side. When the silence sets in, I wheel around and call out to him, mild anxiety arising when he doesn't answer back.

Did he get taken away by one of Andrej's henchmen?

Was he kidnapped?

Something thuds against the back of my neck, my shoulders hitching upon reflex as freezing cold snow slides under my tunic and across my skin.

Marshall's clutching his stomach with contagious laughter, the remains of a freshly-made snowball melting upon his gloved hands.

I see what he's done. There's a hole in the snow that he's dug out to make a snowball to throw at me.

I roll my eyes, bending to gather some snow in my hands and throw it at him as he attempts to avoid his coming fate. He ends up tripping and falling on his unwounded side, snow spraying from his crash landing.

"Cold!" Marshall wails, sitting up with snow sticking to his uniform. "Too cold!"

He kicks snow up in my face, causing some to get caught in my eyebrows and lashes. He's filled with complete joy, laughing his backside off as he recovers and brushes the snow that hangs onto him. I throw a second snowball, spraying it across his uniform, getting it in his face and hair.

"You want to play at that, huh?" He starts towards me, his hands out in front, fingers wiggling threateningly.

I screech as Marshall picks me up off the ground, hauling me over his shoulder like a sack of potatoes.

"Put me down!" I half-laugh, half-scream.

Marshall pretends to drop me, making me squeak as he catches me again. He's laughing a terrible lot now. He stops once he gets a snowball to the face out of nowhere.

I catch sight of Ed, who's wheezing his amusement in and out as Marshall's hair now has specks of white in it, looking like a dandruff explosion.

He shakes his head in joking disapproval. "Goddammit, Ed. I thought I could trust you."

Marshall gently puts me down and dusts his hair of snow. Next, he gets tackled to the ground by Ed. The men start flailing their limbs and squealing like children as they tumble in the snow, spraying white flakes in their wake.

Ed screams at Marshall when his back slams against the ground, a wounded laugh booming in his chest as he swats at him.

"*Gerroff*!" Marshall slaps him on the back before he crawls on top to pin him, hooting with victory. Ed claps him on the side of his thigh and curses his name.

"Get off me, you brute." Ed rises to his elbows. Marshall doesn't budge. "You weigh almost a hundred tonnes."

Marshall only chuckles down at him, pulling himself up and off. "Most people say I'm light as a feather."

"Maybe they don't want to hurt your feelings."

Marshall's astonished face is priceless.

* * *

Breakfast consists of the usual set of biscuits and canned bully beef with the new exception of overcooked eggs. We make sure to call dibs on the table furthest away from the doors, which doesn't help much, as the cold winds still have much room to travel, coming for us as soon as we sit down.

"I heard that the third platoon is coming later today," comments the gruff voice of George next to me.

Private George Wellins, brother of Charlie 'Chip' Wellins, is a tall man with the build of a boulder. Eight years senior to his younger brother, his eyes are sunken with age despite him being only thirty. His mousy dark brown hair is a military cut confined to his scalp. It accentuates his high cheekbones, giving them more attention as they stand out pointedly on his face. On his top lip sits a neatly-shaven mustache that quivers when he speaks.

As Ed leads the pack with Marshall as second in command, George is the father figure of the bunch of horrendously loud boys as they squabble and bicker. He was on the front line for quite some time with the miracle of not going over, digging out passageways underground.

"Are they?" I ask, Marshall stiffening by my side. He leans in to hear George better.

"Yes. They're coming to help fight the Germans."

Marshall *tsks* and lifts his canteen to his lips. "My brother will be among them."

"Your brother?" George inquires.

Marshall's eyes, at the thought of him, are as cold as ice over the rim of his canteen.

"Alistair Clark: the most annoying and selfish person I've ever met. Living under the same roof as him has made the last twenty years of my life a living hell."

"Is he older or younger?" I ask.

Marshall scoots closer, fetching a murderous glare. "Regrettably older by four years."

"That's a shame." George sighs. "I take it you don't have a great relationship with him?"

"As long as he doesn't bother me, I don't bother him. He's just air-headed and a real goon. He parties at his lady friend's house and doesn't come back till the early hours of the morning. In the past, before his marriage, he had a new girlfriend almost every month. He was and still is a real gambler when it comes to making mischief at the dinner table. He's a carbon copy of my aunt. It's truly distressing."

"Sounds like my cousin," I reply.

"I'm glad I'm not the only one who suffers." He swings an arm around my shoulders, his eyes scanning me to make sure what he's doing is okay. When I don't shrug him off, he stays put.

"I'm relieved that I'm not the only one who suffers the wrath of a party animal."

"Oh," he moans, "and you think I'm any better?"

"I think you're a gentleman."

Marshall turns to George, who blinks back at him in return. His frown is replaced with a silly grin.

"Yes, I'm glad you think that. Here's a lesson for you, dove." He swirls his canteen, most likely for dramatic effect. "Gentlemen, as high and mighty, as polite and generous as they may seem, can turn into immoral beings who are deathly sinful."

"He speaks from experience," George teases with a wink.

"Shut up, George." Marshall taps his fingers against his knee, voice lowered. "Basically, how do you know I'm any better than my brother? Sure, I may seem like a gentleman. You've never seen me drunk. You've never seen me—"

"I see you for who you are now. Don't think of trying to change that."

"You're so pure," he rubs my shoulder tenderly with a sheepish chortle, "so innocent."

A smirk lines my mouth. "But how are you when drunk? I'm interested."

Marshall's dorkish grin fades, his face paling. "Oh."

"What? Is it bad?"

"Well, no. I—"

"Flirty drunk," George comments. When Marshall glares at him, he quickly adds, "He can surely hold his liquor, though. No doubt about it."

"I'm sure it's priceless." I titter. "I'd love to see it happen."

"You would *not*," Marshall counters. "I'll turn into a catastrophe right before your eyes."

I elbow him playfully. "A beautiful catastrophe, I must add."

He opens his mouth to speak, but the words die before they reach his lips. He's the color of a wild rose. I feel his heart quickening in his chest. His leg jogs faster under the table.

"I take back what I said about you being pure, Frieda." He draws me closer, whispering in my ear with his lips teasingly close, "Perhaps you'll enlighten me one way or another?"

With my brow twitching, I glare at him. "You're utterly a handful, you know that?"

He feigns flattery through a sigh. "Is that a good thing?"

"Whatever you like to classify it as." I poke his cheek and lower my voice so only he can hear, gripping him by the tie. "Being bad feels good in some circumstances."

"Oh," Marshall gasps, his hand flying over his mouth, "*oh,* Frieda, oh! No!"

George is struggling to hold in his laughter. "Ah, yes. Lover's quarrel. Let the best flirt win."

"Giving up so easily, Clark?" I poke him again. "You're being out-flirted. Your amorosities are getting the best of you. Did it hurt when you were dropped out of an angel's arms? Do you need me to kiss your wounds better?"

"I think, George," Marshall removes his hand to reveal a knowing smirk, "that the winner has already been decided by a longshot."

10

HELLO, BROTHER

Marshall starts a campfire outside the tent by the time I emerge with my coat. I start buttoning it up to fit nice and snug against my frame, fixing the crooked collar as Marshall polishes his rifle. He looks up upon my entry, envying my attire as his eyes reflect the bright light of the fire.

Since our flirting battle in the mess hall, his cheeks still haven't lost their warm rouge. He still hasn't conceded, still hasn't accepted his losses.

"You look warm," he remarks, slowly rubbing the barrel of his rifle with a harsh cloth, attentive to the marks of dust and grit sticking to the firearm's wood and metal body. When I sit down next to him, he inspects the gun's barrel once more for dust or grit.

A bang erupts from miles away, catching me off guard as I jump into his arms. Marshall's rifle drops with a clang to the floor, him screeching and breathing a sigh of relief as the safety mode stays on.

His chuckle rumbles in his chest as he hugs me close. "Got scared, huh?"

"That bang—"

"Just testing the new machine guns." He pinches my cheek and cradles me against his chest. "It's alright. I won't let anything hurt you."

"Your rifle..."

"It'll be fine. It's gone through worse." He sets me back down and he picks his rifle up off the ground to resume cleaning it.

I settle with my knees tucked against my chest, the bangs loud as they pepper the air. Marshall still polishes his gun, unaffected by the noise. He sings to himself calmly, his voice carrying me away with the rhythmic movement of his cloth swathing against the barrel as he works away. Snow starts to fall, and commotion arises far closer than the machine guns.

Marshall's eyes take themselves off his rifle. He hears it, too. His eyes narrow to focus on the flock of soldiers in the distance.

"That's the platoon. They're here," Marshall mutters. He cracks his knuckles, slinging his rifle over his shoulder as he stands, stuffing his cleaning cloth in his pocket.

As we walk on over, I overhear Sallinger talking with the captain: arms folded respectfully behind him, hands clasped, cuffs embroidered in gold, as he listens to his fellow Lieutenant Colonel.

"You got my letter, sir." Sallinger is as stiff as a board when he looks up at the captain, who has to be about a head taller than him. His smile is hidden under his mustache as Sallinger greets him.

Marshall mutters in my ear, "That's Captain Addington. My god, that's really him!"

"I haven't heard of him."

"I didn't expect you to." He stiffens as the captain's eyes land on us from over Sallinger's shoulder. "Come, let's go greet him."

We march over, standing beside Sallinger in a silence that makes me want to squirm. Sallinger acknowledges our sudden appearance and dips his head. "Oh, Captain Addington, these are my two new corporals."

Addington scans the both of us up and down. "A pleasant greeting to you, Corporals...?"

"Joyce." The hairs on the back of my neck stand on end. I get a lot of mixed reactions whenever I introduce myself, but his reaction is rather neutral as his gaze lingers.

"Clark." Marshall struggles to share the same pleasantries as us. His eyes are elsewhere, glaring at a youthful, black-haired man that steps into view with a smirk on his lips. He returns Marshall's glare, his eyes a great blue, colder than Marshall's, that burn like fire.

"Brother, we meet again," says the man. He lets the words waver in the air, basking in the stiffness that they bring. "Surely you've been holding up okay?"

"As a matter of fact, I have, *Brother*," Marshall snipes through clenched teeth.

Alistair's smirking mouth produces a low, entertained chuckle. His eyes swivel to me, digging into my skin, unlike his brother's warm eyes.

Marshall bristles, the brow twitch I'd mentioned weeks before returning. "Leave them out of this."

Alistair takes a daring step closer. "Joyce, how is he treating you?"

I don't answer, not buying into his taunts.

Marshall's hand clasps mine as he bows curtly, stopping me. "Excuse us, sirs, we must be off. We have errands to run. Come along, Frieda," Marshall's words are monotone, "let's get back to the tent."

Marshall, stone-faced and cold, drags me away from the men who start to crowd around us, watching it all play out. Once out of earshot, Marshall lets go of me and kicks a fallen tree stump, howling in pain as his foot collides with it, and curses Alistair's name along with other long lines of profanity that spill from his lips.

"Marshall! Stop! You'll hurt yourself!" I pull him away from the stump by the arm and cup his face in my hands. His jaw is clenched from the pain and anger that spits out searing flames behind his irises.

He curses, "Son of a bitch—"

"Pull yourself together." I stare deep into his eyes, holding his gaze as he pants, swallowing back swears as the last of his outburst exits. He dips his head, still panting as his fringe catches in his eyes.

"I'm sorry," he puffs. "He just...He gets on my nerves...a lot. I get so angry at him for the things that come out of his mouth. I was so scared he'd say something that would be used against us. I was scared that I was going to lose you."

"You're not." His pants die down, into slow and measured breaths. "Please believe me. Nothing could take me away."

"I do, I really do. I got so scared—"

"You don't need to be." A pause. "He's your brother, Marshall. You know his methods, how he riles you up. Don't let him get to you."

Marshall's hands snake up my arms to grip them. His throat bobs as he looks for the words to say. He's shivering, his eyes downcast.

"Marshall, you're shaking. Are you cold?"

"No."

A lie.

I reach for his lapels, buttoning them when he lets go of me. He inhales a shaky breath and starts fiddling with the straps of his webbings, staring at the platoon hammering flint blocks in the ground for their tents. Alistair is chatting away with his comrades as he sets himself up.

"Don't tell me you're thinking of committing fratricide," I say.

"As much as I loathe him, I wouldn't be able to pull the trigger."

The crunching of snow comes closer as a sergeant appears before us. "Corporal Clark, Corporal Joyce. You're needed at the front line. Major's orders."

"Understood, sir." His voice is grave and grating. When the sergeant leaves, he turns back to me. "Well, come on. Are we going to be standing here all day?"

"As much as I'd like to, no."

As we make our way through the trenches, body bags are being piled along the wooden floorboards. The need to gag fills me as an arm grips me around the waist, making me jump.

"Hey, hey! Just me!" Marshall puts a hand over my mouth to stop me from screaming. "You were about to step on the corpses."

Looking down, my blood runs cold. A blackened hand sticks out from under a white sheet, bony, inhuman. The need to heave is overpowering.

"Marshall? His hands...they're..."

"Black, I know." He puts his light hands over my shoulders, pushing me along as he directs me away from the corpses, lecturing me like I'm a child. "Shortly after we die, we start to grow pale, cold, brittle, and finally, we bruise. He's reached that stage; *livor mortis*, I think it's called. He's been dead for quite a long time. I'm afraid you'll be seeing various stages of death and decomposition as you move along. In wars, death is inevitable. Now, if your stomach's settled, let's keep moving."

"Why is he like that? What happened here?" My stomach flips as I swallow back vomit. "Besides...because of...why...why is he...so dark?"

Marshall explains things delicately to prevent me becoming more upset. "There was a cold front a few days ago. I suspect, by the looks of things, it was too cold for him. Most likely, he died from hypothermia as his hands have gained frostbite."

He directs my gaze away, walking on the side of the corpses, careful not to step on any with a mindful avoidance. He grimaces every once and a while at the sickly-sweet stench hovering in the air.

"That's why I told you to huddle with me that night." He's staring straight ahead at a wagon being loaded with fresh cadavers. "I didn't want you to expire the same way he did."

He's right. Death is inevitable. When it comes to conflict, leaving without a dollop of it is inescapable.

With nothing else to say, we find the major, who acknowledges us upon our arrival.

"We're going to attempt to get into the enemy trenches in one hour," he explains. "This is an absolutely critical move to get right, or else they'll overtake us."

"Yes, sir." Marshall's voice is beside me, echoing, distant.

As the major turns his back, my vision sways. His hands return to my shoulders to steady me, keeping me close, wheeling me around to face him. Before I can open my mouth, he interrupts me and puts a finger to my lips. "*Shh.*"

Marshall himself looks like he's going to burst. Over the noise of the major ordering others around, his eyes lock on me, shutting everything out except his gaze. We take each other in: cold, tired, desperate to survive, to live on.

I whimper. "I can't do it. I can't do it anymore."

Marshall nods slowly, his grip on my shoulders tightening. "I understand, but we have to. We're forced to fight whether we like it or not."

"I wish it were different. I wish this world were different."

"And what would this world be like if it were different?"

"Freedom. None of this. Just eternal peace."

"In that world, I hope that I still have you."

"You do."

He inches closer. "It wouldn't be the same if I didn't have you." He takes my shaking hand and presses it against his lips. "Stay strong for me. We'll get through this."

Our return to the front line involves moments of silence, clearing the way for body collectors with their stretches and the bittersweet stench of death clogging my nose. It's stronger near the entrance, I find, where most of the bodies are left to decompose as they wait to be loaded into a truck (not a very flattering sight, I must add). The acrid reek of bloating bodies was enough to give me a headache that pounds on all sides of my cranium.

There's not much snow as we venture farther into the trench, most of it shoved aside to promise no slipping hazards. But, it's freezing, enough for me to impulsively stuff my hands deep within my pockets, but have them come back out for my arms to hug my coat closer to my body, to trap the weak waves of warmth I'm able to create.

Marshall's exhales spread in frosted clouds as he frantically writes in his journal, his shoulders shaking as he signs off, placing the book in his pocket, mumbling to himself, "I love you, Mother, Father, Edith, Alistair, if it be damned."

The ground shakes. Explosions rattle around us. They all make me jump no matter how close or far away they land. Despite all the havoc, Marshall prays silently, screwing his eyes tighter with every loud noise. The whistle blows an ear-splitting shriek as men scream and haul themselves over the trench into action.

Men all around me are falling one by one.

Bang. Bang. Bang.

Their guns fall from their hands. Their bodies crash back into the trench, wounded or dead.

Shells and debris ricochet along the walls. I pull my metal cap down over my brow to protect my head from being harmed. Once the dust clears, my eyes dart across the narrow walkways of the trench. Marshall is nowhere to be seen.

Right on time, he clamps a bracing hand on my shoulder. But, his grip is too harsh, too rough to be him. When I catch its true owner, I shrink away.

I take a step back, gasping.

"Joyce!" Alistair exclaims. "I knew it was you!"

"What're you planning, Alistair?" Another shockwave sends me crashing against the wall, Alistair reaching to catch me before I drop to the floor.

"Absolutely nothing."

I steady myself as another bomb explodes around ten miles away. "Marshall!" I wheeze, choking on smoke. "Where is he?"

"Marshall's fine. He's on the other side of the trench. He's alive for now."

"They're going to send him over—"

"No, they're—"

"They're going to send him to the enemy. Why didn't he tell me?"

"He couldn't, I hate to break it to you. He was pulled aside and had no time. I saw him running at full speed through the trench like a madman."

"I have to get to him! Which way did he go?"

"Left, but—"

Without another word, I take off, pushing relentlessly through mobs of men, dancing over fresh and stale corpses blocking the way. He's nowhere to be seen, to be found. I push on, Alistair calling after me, over the bombs that whistle through the air.

I'm stopped, dragged back, Alistair's hand clamped around my wrist.

"Let me go!" I yelp.

"Don't you realize that what you're doing is dangerous?" He pleads at me behind his blue eyes. "Please, Frieda—"

"What if I don't care anymore? He's your brother, Alistair! Your blood! You should be as batshit scared as me! Do you not care for his safety?"

"Superior's orders, Joyce," Alistair commands. "It wasn't his choice to be sent over. It never was, it never will be. This is your choice to die by running through the trenches like a madman. The main lesson of survival here, Corporal, is you don't move unless you're ordered to. We're merely pawns in a game of chess. Don't you dare make assumptions of how much I care for my little brother, because I'd never forgive myself if his corpse ever lands on one of those stretchers, rotting away in those damned body bags lying out there in the open." I make an attempt to break away, but Alistair snarls. "Don't you dare try to escape me, Joyce. Don't even think about moving. That's an order from your superior."

The whistle blows.

I nearly fall apart at the thought of it now being too late to save him. His brother's eyes never leave my face as mine search the ones of the many men climbing over the top.

"I don't see him," I tell Alistair. His gaze is still ferocious with, surprisingly, brotherly love. "Alistair, I'm...I'm so sorry—"

"Don't." His reply is curt. "Don't jinx it. He always finds a way out"

Smoke rises in the distance. Alistair lets go of me, my wrist throbbing with the pain of his tight grip.

When the planes fly over in their triangular formation, another blast rings in my ears. The man hurtling forward at full speed through the walkway trips, his right shoulder banging into the wall. He collapses at my feet, tripping me over as well. The pressure of his body weight is applied along my front, strong hands shaking my collar as I scream my throat red raw at the surprise attack.

"Frieda, look at me," he demands, shaking me harder to gain my attention.

My screams reduce to ugly sobs, but I still can't stop. "Please don't hurt me! I swear, I'll do anything...Anything!"

He lowers his face down to mine, his voice changing to be of the same level of authority as a general. He cups my face in his hands for me to focus on him. I squint my eyes shut to avoid looking at him, who only tightens his hold. "Jesus Christ, Corporal Joyce. *Look at me!*"

His command jolts me to attention, my eyes shooting up to look at him.

He's staring down at me, holding my gaze through hardened eyes, his body straddling mine to reduce my struggling as he pins my legs to the floor. His face is crusted with dirt, dry blood staining and appearing in flecks upon his cheeks.

"What the hell are you doing here?" Marshall yells over the noise, jumping as an explosion bangs nearby, shrapnel flying across the trench. His head dips to dodge the flying pieces of metal and wood. "Were you trying to find me? You'd have killed yourself if you'd gotten any farther!"

"I didn't see you leave. I was worried. I thought you were going over. I thought you died!"

His appalled eyes flicker with anger a moment longer before they soften just a little. He watches Alistair turn on his heel before he returns to me. "I'm right here, aren't I?"

A lieutenant passes by in a sprint, his feet booming across the floorboards, yelping to a nearby drill sergeant, "Twenty minutes left of the assault, sir!"

"Send them over the top again, Lieutenant!" he replies.

Hurriedly, Marshall pulls me off the ground, his hard glare returning, crying out as another bomb lands, shaking the ground, sending me smack-bang into the wall. His chin smacks against the top of my head, his foot wedging itself awkwardly in between my legs as his chest thuds into mine.

Gasping for air, blood comes in beads across his bottom lip from teeth marks, staining his teeth red before he spits over his shoulder. His heart is beating frantically inside his chest.

Pressing his fingers to his lips, he pulls them away and curses. "Give me a break. Give me a bloody break." He peels himself off of me, shaking.

A major strolls through the crowds, tapping him on the shoulder from behind.

"Corporal Clark," the major hands Marshall a silver whistle, "at 13:20, you are to blow this whistle. No hesitation. You know the consequences. You have five minutes to meet me at the front of the trench."

Marshall stares at the whistle like it's a weapon. I'm frozen as his eyes flicker with a million emotions at a time.

He stuffs the whistle into his pocket, checking the time, not telling me what it is. He doesn't hesitate to cup my face again, eyes alive with urgency. "I need you to promise me something."

"Promise you what?"

"Survive, Frieda. Survive."

"Survive?"

"Yes, Frieda, survive. *Promise me.* Promise me you'll survive. Fight as well as you can. Shoot as far as you can, even if it nearly kills you. Hide when under fire. Anything to keep you alive. Please promise me. I'll do the same."

"I promise." I take no second thoughts. The urgency of the moment overrides any chances of logical thinking. "You'll come back for me, won't you?"

The urgency only grows, ticks up the dial. "I'll try."

He looks at his watch, stepping back.

"I have to go. Major's orders. Remember, fight the best you goddamn can."

"Until we meet again?" I reach my hand out for him to shake.

Hesitantly, he reaches to shake it with a firm grip. "Until we meet again."

On his heel, he turns away, breaking all contact. Once he's out of sight, I brace a hand on the ladder, muttering a prayer for his survival.

"Fight the best you can, Clark. If you die, I'll never forgive you."

I shield my eyes against the debris that spray my way, loading my rifle to shoot and hold it tight as I turn the safety mode off. The shrill screech of the whistle is weak against the explosions as I imagine Marshall blowing his lungs out reluctantly with his lips against the silver mouthpiece.

The yelling only gets louder.

Men fall.

They rise.

They run over the front line.

In the haze, I find Marshall screaming out commands. He ducks under the lip of the trench. The mask in his hands is enough to tell me what to do as more blasts sound close by, knocking me to my knees.

The wind howls overhead, gas hissing out of their tanks in clear, white clouds. I slide on my mask, taking in steady breaths, checking if it's safe to make my way back to my station.

When I peek around the corner, he's sprinting, eyes wild, mask over his face. His shoulders slump as he rests against the wall, hyperventilating uncontrollably. The gas cloud creeps closer, swallowing him hungrily up to his knees, continuing to rise. His chest convulses with a dry cough as he stumbles.

A scream erupts from his throat as the cloud swallows him whole. He rushes away from it, tripping and panting blindly in front of me and resting against the wall. He's gasping for air, yanking his gloves off of his hands. When the gloves come off, they're bleeding, his burnt skin an angry, irritated red.

"I promised," he pants through the pain, "I promised."

"Marshall! Your hands!"

"I'm—"

He's cut off by an explosion.

I'm knocked yet again off my feet onto the floor next to him. With great effort, I push myself up onto my elbows before Marshall orders me to stay down when dirt and rock threateningly spray over us. He's pouring water over his hands when a cry blasts through the air, the bombs and guns quieting.

"Lay down your weapons!" cries the major. "This assault is now over!"

Marshall's panting hard, almost breathless. He doesn't move a muscle, little gasps of pain escaping his lips. He turns to me, scanning my body. "Are you okay?"

"You should be asking that to yourself." I stand, looping an arm through his. "Up, up!"

Marshall groans and slings an arm around my shoulders. He has to bend down to meet my height as he leans on me. His limbs sag, exhausted from another survived assault. Another battle he's waged on through.

"The first thing you're going to do when we get back is wash this uniform of yours and rest."

"What about you?" Marshall grunts.

"I'm not the one who got trapped in a gas cloud."

"Fair, but you still need to clean up." Marshall coughs, a bleeding, blistered hand over his mouth.

Once we reach the tent, I help him take off his webbings and rifle, stripping him of his coat to hang it on a nearby chair. When he pulls his mask off, I ruffle his hair softly. "Good job, soldier. Off to the bathhouse you go. You reek of male body odor and trench warfare."

He replies in kind, smiling wanly, "You wouldn't have me either way. Perhaps I could sell the fragrance and make millions?"

"Shush. Stop dawdling. Those wounds need to be washed and dressed as soon as possible."

Heeding my words, Marshall stalks off, the sound of his boots against rubble fading as I change out of my uniform, washing it and putting it out to dry as I scrub at my skin furiously and bandage up any open wounds. I douse myself with water and wet my hair, shaking it dry, toweling it and brushing the short locks back from my face.

Half an hour later, a tired voice sounds at the entrance to the tent.

"Knock, knock?"

"Are you bathed, Mr Clark?"

"Yep."

"Then you may come in once I just get these last few buttons."

"I'll be patient."

After I button up my tunic, I call to him, "You may come in now."

"I even got myself bandaged up." He climbs inside, fixing his undershirt, his tunic hanging shamelessly over his forearm. "I went to see the nurses after I bathed to look at my wounds. Look. They bandaged me up like a mummy!"

He wiggles his hands at me. His palms are covered in white gauze while the bandages on his fingers scratch as he waggles them. He raises his shirt teasingly to give me a preview of a bandaged torso.

"Wow, you truly do look like a mummy. How many rolls did they use on you? Also, if this is your sick and twisted way of bragging about your body, I'm not interested."

"I'd say a whole roll. This isn't half as bad as the burns on my chest. They're like a line of ants—no, cobwebs. Who'll marry me now with all these marks on me?"

"I'm sure anyone would love to get a chance with you and that gorgeous face."

Marshall runs his bandaged fingers over his jaw, grinning. He knows all too well how to stir up trouble. "So much for not being interested."

I'm quick to shut him down. "Even when in pain, you manage to crack a smile."

"I try, with a lot of perseverance." He pulls his suspenders over his shoulders and slides on his tunic. He does it all too agonizingly slow, continuing to tease me with a humorous glint in his eye, avoiding my disapproving glare.

"Is there ever a time where you're not an absolute tease?"

"Perhaps, but there's none that I can think of." He lies next to me on his side as I read the letter I received from my cousin. He yawns, getting comfortable with his bandaged hand brushing against mine.

There's a peaceful silence between the two of us before he opens his mouth again. I'm expecting another tease, another boyish jab, but he doesn't move to poke fun at me.

"I've learned to smile even when I'm sad. It tricks me into thinking I'm happy. Emotions are tricky things, and I think it's time to go to bed. We have a busy day ahead of us."

I fold the letter in my pocket and settle next to him, turning to watch his eyes close as he props his satchel up behind his head, using it as a pillow.

"Goodnight, Marshall." I yawn.

In the darkness, he shuffles closer. Still side-on, he reaches for my hand and clutches it momentarily. "Goodnight, Frieda."

The rain comes as my eyelids close. I start to toss and turn as thunder rolls on ahead, Marshall bolting upright with my ruckus. "Oi, I'm trying to sleep here!"

"Remember all the fears I listed on the boat?" I don't wait for him to nod, for recognition to slide across his features. "Above all, one of my greatest fears is thunderstorms."

He settles back down and beckons for me to creep closer. "Come, I'll protect you."

Gratefully, I close the distance between us, but hesitate halfway. As the thunder crashes outside, the storm inside my head pours with uncertainty.

Instead of letting his arms embrace me, I reach for his hand, entwining my fingers.

My own uncertainty refracts upon the furrow of his brow. "Did I do—"

"No." I shuffle the slightest bit closer. "You didn't do anything wrong. We're okay. This is okay."

His fingers wrap themselves tighter. Without an explanation, he counters my words against the boom and clash of the storm belting against the tent. "You're right. We're okay. We'll be okay."

* * *

I awaken early the next morning, blinking and waiting for my surroundings to come into focus.

My eyes land on the wall of the tent. I've turned over in my sleep with my back facing him, my hands empty of his. When I turn onto my other side, his bedding is empty, cold, made up. I take it he's off on some early-morning errand somewhere, hopefully keeping warm and healthy in the fast-approaching winter.

Once dressed and out of the tent, I take a morning walk, finding one of the privates I made friends with while we helped with the supplies from my first assignment as a corporal.

"Morning, Jeremy."

The private, Jeremy, turns and gives me a tired smile as his tent mate throws more logs into the fire. "Morning. How do you do?"

"Just fine, just fine. How about you?"

"About the same, really." He watches as more wood is fed to the crackling flames.

"That's good. Look, I hope I don't disturb you when I ask where Corporal Clark ran off to?"

"Oh, him? He went with Sallinger to negotiate battle plans over at the General Headquarters a few miles away. He's acting as an escort."

"I see." I yawn, stretching my arms. "When did he leave?"

"Early morning. He's been gone since four. I saw him marching beside Sallinger. The journey to HQ and back on foot is rumored to be a horrendous one."

The cracking of footsteps across the gravel path is behind me as a deep and tired chortle rises from their owner's throat. "I'm right here. Be glad I come when I'm called."

Jeremy tenses at the sight of Marshall, whose hands are stuffed in the pockets of his coat. "Good morning, Corporal. I hope the walk wasn't too much for you."

"Morning," Marshall says. "The walk was nice for the first few minutes before my feet started killing me. Countless times I have a rock nearly stab me."

"That's a shame," Jeremy says. "It's good to see you back safe."

"As to you. Rest well for today." Marshall continues walking, waiting for me to follow. When I'm back by his side, he starts up. "You were looking for me, weren't you?"

"Good deduction. Yes, I was."

"You must really like me. I've only been gone for a matter of hours and here you are, pestering people for my location."

"Is that bad?"

"Bad? No, it's rather...what's a word to describe it?" The tips of his lips curl into a good-natured smile. "Adorable. Yes, that's it. It's rather adorable that you get so concerned about my whereabouts."

"I can't help it when you suddenly disappear during the night."

"I'm here, aren't I? It was Sallinger's offer to sneak around with him."

"Well, tell me."

His brow flicks up. "About what, my dear?"

"How was it? The conference?"

"I was suffering," he sighs, "and almost completely ignored. There was French, Russian, and whatever other languages can be spoken in Europe being thrown around. A little bit of Portuguese and Siamese were in the mix, too. I couldn't hear much over the Russian general, who was deafeningly loud. I'm so happy to be out of there. Even our own general was terrifying. I stole most of the biscuits on offer, too. Quite delicious, I must say."

"How so?"

"The biscuits?"

"No, the general."

"For one thing, he's tall. Another thing, he gave me the side eye around three times as he spoke. Even Sallinger was on edge."

In the mess hall, we sit and eat. I only pick at my food, my stomach turning with visions of the corpses in their body bags, lying on the rotting floorboards.

"Come on Frieda, you need to eat," Marshall encourages me, poking my shoulder.

I take a bite, eating devastatingly slow. Marshall nearly chokes, as he's eating much faster than I am. He swallows, barely touching the potatoes on his plate, complaining that they're undercooked.

Sallinger's voice cuts through the lively chatter of the mess hall. He rings a bell to get our attention. "Good morning, all. I would like to have your attention for a few moments, as the General has an announcement."

Marshall slumps against the table, his chin resting on his forearms, pushing his rations away, whispering, "Here's the special announcement we were talking about for three hours."

There's a widespread wave of whispering that circulates around the hall as the General steps forward, decked in gold.

Damn. Marshall was right when he said he was intimidating.

"Good morning to you all. Following the meeting I had this morning with Lieutenant Colonel Sallinger, I've come to announce that there's going to be a gathering going on at the Le Havre town hall near the English Channel. The French want to thank us for our service here in their country."

There's excited whistling and whooping of some men nearby. Marshall only *tsks* at their rambunctiousness.

The General appears to do the same, waiting until they quieten. "Now, gentlemen, you need to be dressed in your uniforms and look *sharp*. I mean it. No uncleanness will be tolerated. Get those uniforms washed and sewn up, hair slicked back nicely, facial hair neatly groomed. For nurses and others," he throws an accusing glare at me that turns my insides out, "skirts or suits of your own, if you please. Thank you. Continue with your breakfast."

The chatter recommences. I let out a disoriented groan, bringing my hands up to cover my face. "Despite being a ballerina for seven years, I can't even dance."

Marshall snorts. "I could teach you."

"Not in a million years!" I hiss. "You'd humiliate me on the first step!"

Marshall waves off an incoming laughing fit. "I'd say I'm quite a passive dance instructor, as I *am* a winner of five dance competitions and taught my sister how to dance. My dance partner threw a fit and said she had enough before she slammed the door on our instructor. I've been searching for a dance partner ever since, but the war got in the way."

"There's no way I'm going to join you in competition."

"No need. I'm quitting anyway. But, for social gatherings, there is no excuse for you to be a wallflower, as it's expected of an individual of this era to know how to dance."

"You're really into this, aren't you?"

Marshall shrugs. "I'd like to help save you from awkward outcomes in the future. I'll teach you how to dance."

"Fine. Enjoy your suffering while it lasts."

"I've been through worse." He shoulders me playfully. "My sister kept stepping on my toes with nearly every step."

"I'll be much, much worse."

"No, I'm sure of it. If you've been a ballerina, you have an idea of footwork and posture, plus following timing and counting. It's just conjoining two steps of a pair and working in sync."

"That's a very poetic way to put it."

"Oh, but it's true." Marshall tidies his scraps as he continues explaining. "You'll get the hang of it, I'm sure."

"Geez, I wish." I glare at his smiling face. Yes, it's crystal clear he's enjoying this.

"Why the long face?" He leans in. "Why look so sad when you'll get to dance with your handsome lad over here, hm?"

"A bit conceited, don't you think?"

His giggle sends my stomach plummeting. I roll my eyes to the high heavens. "You aren't afraid to admit it, though."

"No, I'm afraid not."

II

Dress Shopping, Le Havre

The streets of Rouen are far cozier than the towns I've seen near the Western Front. It's small, in the northern region of Normandy, with houses and shops that stand close together, the walkways made of cobble, signs hanging overhead. It carries the same mystic energy of a town found in fantasy novels; the ones that take your breath away as you venture farther into its streets.

Upon our journey through the north of France to the small commune of Le Havre, this is our first and only stop, but also a sight for travelers and wanderers who pass through its splendid architecture.

This morning, I don't take in any of it.

Marshall's having a fantastic time window shopping with his arm looped through mine, taking in the sights and sounds as his nose sniffs the air like an eager pooch. I'd be laughing my lungs breathless if I were in a better mood, if we were here for the sole purpose of tourism. He's busy telling me about a coffee shop he saw as we were walking, and when he gains only an 'uh-huh' and 'mm-hm,' he falls quiet.

Turning another corner, he follows a map he collected from a tourist guide a while back. I see now that he's brilliant with locations, with maps; a skill much needed on the battlefield.

He presses a hand on mine. "Are you mad at me?"

"No? If you didn't know already, it's hard to be mad at you."

"Most people say I'm annoying. So, no, I didn't know that."

"I wish we weren't here to go dress shopping. It makes me uncomfortable. Just the idea of undressing and putting on clothes that might not even fit behind a mere curtain...no."

"Understandable." He nods along and listens to me complain, uninterrupted, before he finds the sign of the 'high-quality' tailor he badgered the tourist guide for. After trying and failing to communicate in English, he resorted to having me translate for him to grab its address.

He opens the door. A bell triggered by a tripwire rings, far too loud for my ears. He stands in the doorframe, his arm outstretched to keep the door open.

"After you, my love," he bows.

Inside the shop, rolls of fabric are kept on shelves near the varnished counter, a doorway leading to a basement. On display are mannequins in fur coats for the winter and hats on racks. Marshall marvels specifically at a black velvet bowler on one of the mannequin's heads.

"Hey, Frieda." He points to one of the cotton duster coats: a dark shade of brown with matching buttons on the front. There's a small half-cloak across the shoulders. "Do you see me in one of these?"

"Very cowboy themed." I grimace. "You're far better with padded shoulders than a cloak."

Upon the arrival of new customers, feet clamber up the steps of the basement: the tailor with a pin cushion strapped to his wrist. His cheeks are adorned with bushy and graying sideburns over a round face, his stomach bulging under a midnight blue vest.

"Apologies. I was mending a coat...had some frayed edges that needed looking at." His French accent curls off of his tongue. "Good day. What can I do for you two?"

Marshall gulps. "*Bonjour, monsieur...*I don't speak French. I don't mean to offend you."

"No offense taken," replies the tailor in English, as I feign interest in one of the bright evening gowns. "How may I assist you?"

"We're here to purchase an evening dress for my dear who's here with me today. There's a gathering coming up and we'd like to have a browse of your shop, please. If it doesn't hurt, I also have a few scars on this coat of mine that need healing."

His head bobs eagerly, outstretching an arm to him. "Of course, of course! Anything for a man of honor such as yourself. If you'd just give it here. I recognize your accent. American, yes?"

Marshall loosens the belt around his waist, folding his coat and handing it to the tailor with care. "Right on, and thank you. We really appreciate you helping us."

"I've had a lot of English customers come along, but not many Americans. There's no need to thank me. Right this way."

With a beckoning hand, he leads us to the back of the store where he takes my measurements while Marshall cowers when he comes across the feminine garments and corsets on display, earning a snicker from me as a measuring tape tightens around my waist.

When the tailor disappears into the many rows and racks of attire, I lean against the wall as Marshall investigates with utter confusion etched into his face. "How—how do people wear these?" He takes a step back from a white corset on a mannequin. "Don't they crush your inner organs? Where does your digestive tract go? Your rib cage? Where does *everything* go?"

"Organ crushing corsets are myths, my dear. Everything is still there. It shouldn't hurt you if it's properly fitted. Just imagine being stuffed in a barrel for hours straight. That's how tight it is."

He crinkles his nose. "Must be satisfactory, taking it off at the end of the day."

"To make you more scared, some want such a defined hourglass figure that they tighten it to the point that they become winded."

He whines and shrinks onto a nearby footrest, head in hands. "Just when I thought today's beauty standards weren't outlandish enough!"

When the tailor returns, he hands me dresses on their hooks. Most of them have a dark and cool tone that he says will compliment my pale skin and make my freckles stand out.

When it was just my mother and I after my father left for war, she had always made me wear the brightest dresses. They had the most ridiculous designs, the most ridiculous palettes, just because she thought that me donning a black or gray frock would make me seem like I was attending a funeral instead of an afternoon tea party.

I despised her opinion and the bright pink, red, green, and yellows she made me wear. I'm more of a black-and-white person, as wearing shades makes me feel less exposed and calm.

Just the mere action of trying on dresses makes my skin itch.

Beauty is pain is still etched into my mind. *In order to find a suitor, you must be a beautiful flower; attractive and bold. As the flower wilts and wrinkles, the less attractiveness it holds.*

My teeth sink into my bottom lip when I hang the dresses up on a peg, steadying my thoughts as I sit to unwrap my puttees, sliding off my boots.

But there are dark flowers, I think, *that blossom in the dark. The finest of suitors have to cross valleys to experience their beauty.*

Outside my thoughts, there's polite laughter as the tailor compliments Marshall's coat when he hands it back to him, Marshall praising him for his neat stitching. "So, are you and your young friend married?"

"Married? I'm flattered. No. We still have a very newfound love. Perhaps I should tell others that we're married to merely confuse them."

Once the tailor leaves us, I ask from behind the curtain, "I need you to play the role of a brutally honest fashion critic, alright?"

"Alright. Lay it on me."

I walk out in the first dress I've been given: a vermillion frock. It produces a scratchy feeling against my wrists with its lace gloves. The fabric is tight around my figure, and I can't take a full step forward in the skirt.

Marshall's nose crinkles in distaste, not liking it either. He's lounging in an armchair, leaning back on his elbows with a men's fashion magazine on his knee. He clicks his tongue. "Oh, honey, *no!*"

"Doesn't look too comfortable, does it?" I ask.

"It definitely shows off your figure, but it looks itchy. Says evening dress, screams 'I'm going to ditch this gathering and go clubbing instead.'"

"Thank you for your honesty." I turn back into the dressing room.

I reappear with the second dress. It's a duckling yellow with silly little frills on the hem, skirt, and sleeves. With the matching elbow-length gloves, the whole outfit feels horrendous.

"Are you trying to audition as the star on top of a Christmas tree or one of the ducklings from *The Ugly Duckling*?"

The insult makes me laugh. "I know, right? With that duster coat, we'd be the perfect pair."

"Stop trying to make me feel bad about that horrid decision while you're standing there dressed like a dandelion. The yellow is hurting my eyes just from looking at you."

"You're *ruthless*, Marshall."

"'Brutally honest fashion critic,' you said." He winks.

"I didn't expect you to insult me out of these dresses."

He only grins. "I'm trying to make you laugh. At least give me some closure here. Next one, if you may."

This is the third dress: a Prussian blue evening dress. It's not too exotic in design, unlike the others, though its neckline is a little bit low for my liking and shows off a small amount of cleavage. Its sleeves are sheer and reach to my elbows. Small, silver, elegant, and embroidered patterns are stitched on the waist. The skirt reaches down to my ankle. The heels on my feet are black and thin, small matching black bows on each shoe at the toe.

Shrugging my shoulders at my reflection, I step out for Marshall to insult me yet again.

When he sees me, his eyes widen as his jaw drops. He's at a loss, trying to find something to say, something to point out.

"Why are you looking at me like that?" I ask, shrinking under his goggling eyes.

Marshall tenses. "It's nothing."

"Well?"

He only stares, not saying a word.

"What? Does it look so bad that it's rendered you speechless? Aren't you going to burn me again with an insult?"

"No! It's...wow," he gasps, "it's beautiful. It suits you. Give us a twirl."

I spin on the spot. He stands and sets the magazine aside. "How do you feel about it? That's what matters."

"Comfortable, for one thing." I catch him staring, chewing his lip. "What's that look for?"

"Just taking it all in." He scans me once more, nodding to himself. "I'm a huge fan of the skirt."

I shy away from his compliments. "I like it."

"I love it. It suits your frame, your aesthetic. It suits you, Frieda. You and only you."

"You're flirting."

"No I'm not." He takes a step forward, raising my chin with his fingers. "I can't see anyone else standing before me in that dress. I can imagine us stealing the night away with it. Despite my liking of it, I want you to be brutally honest on how you like it yourself. Don't let me decide for you."

"I already said I liked it. I'm glad you agree with me."

"You've got it wrong." His eyes wander over the dress again. "I don't like it, I love it. I adore it."

As I pay for the dress and thank the tailor for his assistance in, somehow, good spirits, Marshall's waiting outside. "If you're not careful, that dress might steal my breath away."

"Like the corsets?" I tease.

"Oh, please, not the corsets!" he moans. "Truly, when I saw that dress, the air just suddenly whooshed out of my lungs."

* * *

Ed is sitting in front of the fire as the sky darkens and the stars twinkle while the day grows old. The night is young as he reads another slip of parchment by the firelight, folding it neatly before he gazes up at Marshall.

"Where did you get the blanket?" Ed asks.

"This? My sister gave it to me before I went to war. Just a little going-away gift." Marshall smiles lovingly at the white and blue woolen blanket over his shoulders like a cloak. "She knitted it herself."

I close my eyes against the wind, exhausted. My eyelids droop as Marshall sits in between us. He peers over his shoulder, sees me slump, and pulls the blanket over me.

"But it's your sister's." I take the blanket off carefully, but he stops me.

"I don't think she'd mind me sharing it. Now sleep."

Ed's soft humming plays in my ears as Marshall asks him, "Any interesting news?"

Ed answers, "Nothing much. Cousin Murray's come over from Delaware and is helping look after the house while I'm away. I wish I could see her again. The poor woman is enduring so much. I shouldn't have left. No one deserves to suffer like her."

"I'm sure she'll be fine. She's a strong woman. Be glad that your cousin is there to help."

"He won't be there for long. Goddamnit, if only I could see her." He slams his fist against his knee, stuffing her letter in his pocket.

Marshall swings an arm around Ed. "I know, I know. We'll go back one day."

"And when is that? A week? Five years? Fifteen years?"

"I don't know, but I hope it's soon." Marshall runs a hand affectionately through Ed's hair.

"Marshall, you're squishing me," Ed grumbles as Marshall hugs him close to his chest. His arms are wrapped around his back with one of his hands stroking his long hair.

"My sincerest apologies," Marshall loosens his grip, "is this better?"

"Mm," Ed mumbles. "I feel terrible that I'm not there."

I stumble over, hesitant to join in. Ed's melting into Marshall's arms, his head resting under his chin. Not knowing if I'll be able to fit myself in, I lay a reassuring hand on his shoulder.

"Thank you, the both of you." Ed wipes at the corners of his eyes, reaching to grab both of our hands. He flashes us both a shaky smile, his wedding ring digging into my fingers as he squeezes my hand momentarily.

When Ed's hand slips from mine, I watch as Marshall comforts him, hushes his frets and dabs at his tear-stricken face as Ed stares into space.

Seemingly not needed, I retreat into the tent, listening to their conversation as I get ready for bed. There's a stutter, a laugh, a snort, and a sniffle. I take it Marshall's telling another one of his jokes to cheer him up and take his mind off of his wife's loneliness. I feel guilty for the bitter and jealous weight in my gut.

I have no one to turn to. They're either abusive, substitutes for lost family members, or too far away for me to reach them. Most of my family lives far away, the peace they live with, the connection I desire so much, is out of my reach.

Marshall has his father, his siblings. Edward has his wife. I have no one.

I screw my eyes shut against the thoughts. I shouldn't be letting them crawl inside me when one of my friends is suffering just inches away. I tire myself while trying to stop the feelings, anything to stop the thoughts from pursuing inside my head. I'm unaware of the silence outside as a hand brushes the hair out of my face.

Not knowing who it is, I flinch, wild and alert.

"Woah, woah! Steady now!" Marshall's bending over me. "It's just me."

My eyes adjust to the darkness. He's turned the lamps down low, a shadow cast over his face outlines his jaw and the hollows of his eyes as he watches over me. The wind whistles, singing through the trees as it blows, the crunching of footfalls across the snow outside in the distance.

"Did I scare you?"

"It's dark." I fail to hide the tremors in my voice. He sits beside me. "You were a shadow in the corner of my eye."

"Now you know I'm not just a shadow." He sits, cross-legged. When I don't say anything else, he asks, "Is something wrong?"

"Do I have to be honest?" I bury myself deeper into my bedroll. Marshall's deep in thought before he walks over to his side of the tent, bringing his own bedroll over next to mine, leaving space between us as he settles.

He grunts as he throws a loose twig over his shoulder, cursing it with annoyance, "Preferably, yes."

"You don't need to hear me after dealing with Ed."

"Who says I don't?"

"I do."

He gives me a glance as he lays beside me. "I say otherwise. Remember the promise we made?"

"Not for something like this."

"If it's bothering you so much that you feel like you should keep it from me, it'll help if you let it out. I promise I won't tell anyone."

"Fine, because I know you won't leave me alone until I do." I flinch when he moves closer, taking his sister's blanket and setting it over the both of us. "But your sister...That blanket was made for you..."

"I'm merely loaning it," he says. "Now, talk to me."

"I really don't know where to start, what to say." I look away from his observing eyes. "When you two were talking, I just had a moment of realization."

"What was that?"

"That he has his wife, you have your father...I have no one back home to turn to. No family, no friends, no one."

He watches me as I duck away from his gaze. "What if I said to you that you do, in fact, have someone?"

"I don't."

"Silly goose," he pokes me on the nose, "you have me, Ed, George, even Lester, despite how begrudging he can get. We're your family. Not all families need to be blood-related. Love has no boundaries."

"No one at home—"

"Look," he props himself up on his elbows, "not all family members have to be right in front of you, living in the same home. They can be everywhere. Family comes, family goes. People live, they die, they walk into your life, and they walk out of it. Families can do that, too. Even if they're your blood, you don't have to deem them as family. Family is who you're comfortable around, where you feel the safest. You feel comfortable and safe around us, don't you?"

"I do."

"There you go. You have us. We're your family, where you belong."

"How do you do that?"

"Do what?" He blinks. "Did I say something wrong?"

"How do you know how to comfort me, all of you? Dammit, Marshall, you're making me cry."

"Hey, come here." He throws an arm around me, brushing my fringe out of the way when it gets in my eyes. "I can't imagine how hard it is to feel this way. Please remember what I told you. You still have us."

"But you said you'll leave..." My eyes are wide, fearful. "You'll leave! You said that family leaves."

"I forgot to say that not all family leaves." His body heat merges with mine as he pulls me close. "You can't possibly imagine how much I want to stay with you. We could sail across the Atlantic, move to São Vicente—random choice, by the way—and I'd never go home again. But why would I want to go home when my home is with you?"

With no interruptions, he coos, tucking me in tighter with Edith's blanket. "I assure you: We may travel far, we may go elsewhere, but we'll always come back together. Do you know why? No matter how far they travel, no matter how far away they are, family doesn't move in our heart. They stick. It's hard to loosen the bonds of those we love, because they're set in stone."

* * *

A couple weeks later, it's the morning of the gathering as I open my eyes. It's dawn outside, the sun not yet awakened to bring light to the new day.

Christmas was a truly spectacular event, a highlight of this most troubling year. Marshall was treated to some gin by the medics, refusing to drink it and sending it back with a thank you note tied on the bottle's neck. There was gin in the eggnog he had been mailed from his father while he got even drunker off of the chocolate sent from the townspeople as a gift, which had liquor inside their centers.

Ed had gotten intoxicated off of the leftover gin Marshall rejected, resulting in the both of them having a drunken scuffle in the snow and a fast paced, frenzied waltz to the music playing on the radio before we had to leave two days after for Le Havre. We've been traveling by train for this event; a long and hard journey through France.

In the traveling tent, Marshall's still sleeping. He barely got any sleep the night before due to the splitting aches and pains of his hangover. He turns over onto his stomach, his face buried in his pillow, messy hair sticking up. He's muttering incoherent things in his sleep.

I sit up and shake the hair out of my eyes. Marshall's waking up as I comb it down and out of its knotted state. He groans against the cold and digs deeper into his bedding. When the whistle blows for us to wake up, Marshall's falling back asleep.

"Marshall," I crouch down and poke him, "come on, sleepyhead. Time to rise and start the day."

He pushes my hand away. "No."

"Come on, today's the day."

"I'll get up when it's time."

"How unproductive of you." I continue poking him. "Come on, get up."

"Fine, fine." He brushes me away. "I'll be up soon."

"No, right now."

"*Fine.*"

He sits up and curses at the cold. As he hurries to ready himself, he stretches, bending down to touch his toes with yet another of his signature back cracks. He's taken to committing to a morning routine of stretching, as he says that it helps his mind sharpen for the day and also helps loosen the pain of his tired limbs from all the hard work they make us do.

"How do you get up so early so easily? You don't even look tired!" he marvels as he shakes out a sore leg.

"I am. I'm just more awake than you."

"Fair enough." He continues stretching his arms as Ed pokes his head through the entrance.

"Morning!" he calls and slips inside. He hands a cup of something warm to both of us. "Coffee and tea from the residents. I do hope you like chamomile, Frieda. I already had one. Seriously, you *have* to try it."

"I love chamomile. You didn't have to." I take the steaming plastic cup, grateful for its warmth that spreads through my palms.

"It would be nice to see Paris, don't you think?" Marshall takes his coffee gingerly, drawing in a small trying sip, going back for more.

"That's miles away," Ed says.

"If we can make it fast enough, we can see it."

Ed shakes his head in denial. "I wouldn't think so."

"Aw." Marshall takes another long sip of his coffee. "I really want to see Paris."

"You will one day." Ed pats his shoulder. "Who knows, maybe they'll treat us after tonight?"

"Doubt it," Marshall says. "It's not within walking distance. To try and catch a train would be impossible."

When we step out of the tent, Lester is there to greet us and shrugs his coat over his shoulders with a tired smile.

"Good morning, lads. Is that coffee I smell?"

Marshall raises his cup. "Indeed it is."

"Look at this. One of the nurses who came along has sewn the massive hole in my sleeve for free! Look at how well she's done it!" He holds out one of his sleeves.

"I must say that that's better than I'll ever do." I run a hand down the stitches planted tight into the wool.

"I can't even sew," Marshall grumbles.

"Say, it's a free day today. Let's grab breakfast from one of the restaurants in Le Havre. Is George coming?"

Ed answers, "No, unfortunately—"

"Oi, you gits! What're you doing, going out without your old man?" George calls as he jogs over. "I was cleared for today. We can go on an adventure together."

"Yes, but see, we have a problem," Lester says. "None of us speak French."

"Actually," I step forward, "I do."

"How fluent are you?" George asks.

"I've spoken French since I was five. So, pretty fluent, I guess."

"You *guess*?" Lester gasps.

"I'm just joking. We'll be fine." I dismiss his blabbering. "But really, since I was five—"

"We get it. No need to brag." Lester clutches his stomach as it produces a loud rumble. "Now that we have that established, let's go. Maybe we can score some crêpes."

"Sounds great. Chocolate would be sublime." Ed fixes his collar. "Also, Lester, this is the perfect time to try and find a girl."

Lester only scoffs.

Marshall offers me his arm, grinning as he holds his coffee cup in his other hand. "Beautiful day, isn't it? Why don't you walk with me?"

I accept. "It's winter. But, for once, the sun is shining."

Marshall's hair glistens under the sun's weak rays. "It truly is. I never thought I'd see a clear sky ever again."

"Me neither." The faint smell of coffee wavers as he takes a shorter sip and observes the town we stride past. Lester, George, and Ed follow closely behind, conjuring up a lively conversation about tonight between the three of them.

"Your father was French, wasn't he?" Marshall observes the window of a jewelry shop.

"Yes, he was from Lyon."

"Lyon," Marshall echoes. "What made him move?"

"My grandmother is from Seattle, like me. Apparently she was studying abroad in Lyon when she met my grandfather who was studying English as his undergraduate, as he wanted to work in America. Obviously, they fell in love, had my father, and moved back to Seattle when he was three."

"Interesting," Marshall comments. "My mother was from Ponce, in Puerto Rico. She moved to Philadelphia for a better shot at living. She and my father were neighbors, surprisingly. It was apparently tough to get my grandmother's blessing for their marriage. My father fought with every tooth and nail to get a single ring on her finger. They both did."

"I'm glad they met," I tease. "If they didn't, we wouldn't have you."

"And that makes me jealous," he takes a haughty sip of coffee, "that another man would be walking beside you instead of me. He wouldn't know anything about treating anyone fairly. *Sigh,* men these days."

"Speak for yourself," I quip.

"*Some* men these days. I'm an exception." He reaches to pet a plump tortoiseshell cat perched on a fencepost, having it cower away when his hand meets its whiskers.

"Hey, lovebirds! We found a place with some cheap crêpes!" George calls.

Marshall giggles, eyes shining. "Well, who's hungry?"

"Come on, we can't wait all day!" Lester yelps.

Marshall takes off after throwing his now-empty cup into a nearby trash can.

132

I shout after him, "You're not coming?"

"I'll catch up with you. I want to have a look at a shop nearby."

"Whatever you do, don't get lost."

I walk inside the cafe to find that the boys have gotten a table and are pouring themselves glasses of water, laughing in friendly conversation.

"I thought you wanted me to translate, gentlemen." I reach to pull out a chair, but Ed stands and does it for me just when I thought he couldn't be any more polite.

George eyes his menu. "We got impatient. The waitress spoke good English."

Lester kicks George under the table as I sit down, taking my cap off. "We got *hungry,* George. Stop being so polite! The menus are in French, so, please help us."

We order: strawberry chocolate, vanilla, bananas and caramel, chocolate, and one with whipped cream and strawberries for Marshall, who's still regrettably absent.

"Where's Marshall?" Lester questions, pouring more water for the table. "I swear he was with you a minute ago."

"You just realized he wasn't with us?" George inclines his head questioningly.

"He said he wanted to check out a shop close by." I bring my face into my hands. "I hope he isn't lost. He knows barely any French. He's hopeless here."

A few minutes later, the bell over the door rings. The man himself stumbles in with a small paper bag dangling from his fingers.

"I hope I'm not too late." Marshall takes his cap off, hurriedly sitting across from me and next to George. "I bought chocolate."

"With what money?" Ed pours him a glass of water.

He freezes. "About that—"

"You didn't steal it, did you?"

"Let me explain." Marshall thanks him and takes a sip. "The lady at the front desk saw that I was a struggling American and enlisted man. So, she gave me a discount. It cost me zero francs."

"Don't tell me you bribed her." Ed glares. "You'll receive a smack to the face and the behind if you did."

"Bribe? No. She saw my uniform. When I came up to pay, she shook her head and told me with a heavy French accent to take what I wanted. I tried to reason with her and give her my money, but she denied it and thanked me for my service. Bless her soul."

With a sigh of relief from Ed, the crêpes arrive.

Marshall leans his chin on his hands. "I take it you ordered all of this?"

"*Oui.*" I grab my knife and fork. "I didn't forget about you. I ordered you something, too."

"Thank you, my darling." Marshall dips his head in thanks as I tingle at the name he's called me. No matter how many times he says it, it still makes my heart faulty. Then, he glares at the rest of the boys who mimic him mockingly. "Gentlemen, thank our translator at the table. How very rude of you not to. Without her, you'd all be starving."

Ed peers over his plate. "I already did, but I'll thank her again. Thanks, Frieda."

Lester waves. "*Merci,* Frieda."

George gives me a small smile. "Yes, thank you, Frieda."

"You're all very welcome," I reply.

Marshall chuckles to himself happily, the happiest I've seen him in months. It must be the fresh air, the new environment. He leans in and gives me the largest smile a man could ever muster. "How're the crêpes?"

"Brilliant, thanks. What about yours? I didn't know if that's what you wanted."

"You're kidding," Marshall gestures to his plate, "these are amazing, thank you very much."

I don't hide my satisfied grin, his happy, radiant energy swallowing me in its sugary sweetness. "I'm glad."

He leans closer, offering me a wink. "I bought chocolates for just the two of us to share. Assorted, nothing special."

"You have quite the sweet tooth, don't you?"

His fingers trace the patterns on the tablecloth slowly, suggestively, teasing. My grip on my fork tightens. "Not really. Just a small treat."

"Marshall! Always obnoxiously flirting!" Lester hisses over the rim of his cup.

"Jealous are we?" Marshall shoots back.

"Shut it!" Lester stuffs his mouth full of crêpes to keep himself from biting Marshall's head off. Marshall, meanwhile, breathes an amused *hmph* with a smirk. He finishes his food, puts his knife and fork neatly together on the plate, and dabs the corners of his mouth with his napkin.

"So, everyone, once we finish up and pay, what else shall we do today?"

"Go window shopping," George offers.

"Go to the beach," says Lester.

"Take a walk around town," adds Ed.

"My God, one at a time." Marshall leans on the table. "You lot are just as excited as elementary school children."

"Don't blame us." Lester snickers. "We have all the time in the world today to be ourselves. Don't you feel the same?"

"I do, I do."

"Hypocrite, I tell you!" Lester slams his palm against the table.

When it all calms down, I add to the conversation, "Whatever you gentlemen are up for, I'm not too fussy to comply. It's France. We're decommissioned for the time being. We're free. Let's enjoy our time here while it lasts."

12

The Event

After a fun day of running around Le Havre like young, wild, and free teenagers, Marshall opens the box of chocolates back in the tent while we prepare for tonight's gathering. One by one, they disappear. We pop out one after another. I let him have all the orange ones, as I despise them. He lets me have the strawberry ones, as he complains that they're too sweet and leave an undesirable tang on his tongue.

With a glance over my shoulder, I get the dress out of its bag.

"I..." I trail off. Marshall looks up as he cracks open his grooming kit. "I need to get changed."

Silently, Marshall closes the tent tightly shut, standing outside and waiting. I beckon him inside in my dress after I take a look at myself to make sure everything's in place.

When he's permitted to come back inside, he finds me pulling my hair out of its small updo, letting it cascade down to my ears.

"You're going with your hair like that, are you?" Marshall picks up a comb as I sit down upon a stool. He grabs his coat and begins smoothing its wool out over his lap with his hands, checking for wrinkles, placing it delicately on a chair and getting to work with his hair.

"No, I'm styling it." I look away to give him some privacy to peel the bandages off his fingers and examine his wounds that have healed up quite nicely over the passing weeks.

With some struggling and brushing my short locks into different styles, I part each side at my hairline and let my curls form around my face. They should be okay for tonight. With short hair, I don't have many options.

Marshall seems to agree with my styling choice, as his eyes linger on me, biting his lip as he reaches for a red-ribboned medal to pin on the front of his tunic. He's ultimately lost, observant, as I smooth out the matching blue wrist-length gloves the tailor said would compliment the dress.

It's embarrassing to be this dressed up, odd to let the masculine uniform rest for just one night. I've grown used to my breeches scratching against my skin, growing out of the weight of a skirt holding me down. I'm yet again contained, back in a state of dress only my mother would approve of. Even though Marshall and the tailor said the dress suited me, I still feel trapped behind a suffocating layer of femininity. It's never looked good on me.

I regret not bringing any sort of makeup with me, as I didn't see it necessary. The nurses most likely wouldn't let me borrow any to hide my sunken eyes, my chapped lips. Instead, I pinch my cheeks to bring color to them.

Hands go over my shoulders. Marshall bends to whisper in my ear, "How do you feel?"

I answer back dully, "On display."

"Let me just say that I think you look beautiful," he breathes against my ear. "You chose this dress. She didn't. This was your intellectual choice to wear this dress, to own it. It's not hers, but *yours*."

He lets go of me as I stand, pulling up my skirts so they don't get dirt-stained or muddy. "I'll be ready when you are."

"Let me make my hair look as pretty as you." Marshall bends back down to his grooming kit, picking up a jar of hair gel and another comb. Slathering its teeth with gel, he brushes it through his hair and slicks it back. When he turns to me, his hair is unnaturally flat compared with what I'm used to: the boyish locks that shape his face, the ruthless curls I could spend days running my hands through. He combs back his fringe, his pale forehead possessing freckles I never knew he had. He has a mole near his hairline and a scar cracking the skin of his temple.

Ridding his hands of gel, he disposes of the soiled bandages and hesitates with his roll of gauze. "Should I wear gloves or not?" He holds up his leather gloves for me to consider it for him. "I don't want to frighten anyone."

"No," I dismiss his worries, "you'll be fine without them."

"So be it." He repacks his gloves. "Bare hands it is."

When he stands at full height, I almost fall over my own feet.

His boyish curls are gone, settled down for the night. His cheekbones are sharp as he stands proud, sensing my wonder, letting my eyes travel. He's still wearing the same uniform, the same crooked smile, but he looks too much like he's aged a whole year around the calendar.

"What have you done with Marshall Clark?"

"What do you mean?" He takes a small step toward me. "I'm still me. Just because I've gelled my hair down doesn't mean I'm a totally new person."

"It's different to what I'm used to."

"Is that a good thing?" His eyes gleam, eager for an answer.

"I'll take it." I can't stop staring at him, can't divert my gaze.

"I'm glad." He offers me his hand, scabs of old blisters lining the insides of his palms and the backs of his hands. Still the same hand: rough from hard labor, wounded from war. "Shall we depart, my dear?"

After a bout of hesitation, I take his hand, my other lifting my skirts to keep them from becoming soiled. I almost shrink away from the eyes of many men staring us down as we march past, my eyes attracted to the floor like a magnet.

The whispers are rising again, the rumors, the loverboy and his mistress on full display, the man hungry and brimming with lustful desire. All rumors have been classified untrue. Yet, they still stick sharply to me like thumbtacks.

I'm deep in thought with my fingers clutching the corner of my skirt, a gloved hand squeezed in his bare one. The nurses went into town earlier this week to buy their own dresses, all glamorously lined up, staring and muttering behind their hands as we stroll past.

I don't sense him drawing closer. I don't pick up his warm breath against the cold air until he pulls me back into reality.

"Eyes up, my dear," he whispers encouragingly. "Tonight's the night to be yourself. Chin up, eyes up. Show them Frieda Joyce, who defied the laws of men."

Swallowing, I train my eyes to look straight ahead, at the crowd of soldiers and nurses. Most soldiers are goggling at the nurses' dresses, chuckling away as the magic and excitement of the night sparkles through the air.

Once we find our crowd, Ed scans us when we approach. He's braided his hair and gelled down the stray locks that try to escape. His eyes survey us with the corner of his mouth lifted upward, amused. "You've cleaned up nicely."

"Didn't we?" Marshall's grip on me relaxes. "I admit, it gave my heart a little bit of a rush walking this magnificent darling over here."

"Always flirting." I sigh. "Your handsomeness tonight is intimidating."

Ed rolls his eyes and points an accusing finger at Marshall. "I'm also surprised to see you've actually done something to your hair, sir. No sign of your boyish flamboyance tonight?"

"I gelled it back." Marshall runs a prideful hand over it. "I'm just hoping it'll stay down the whole night. You, sir, are dashing, as always."

"Hush," Ed retorts. "All I did was comb my mane back."

As they bicker at each other, I zone out, overhearing the nurses' gossip behind us.

Noticing that my gaze lies elsewhere, Marshall stiffens beside me. "Ed, are they talking about me again?"

"I think so?" Ed leans in to whisper to me, clothes scented faintly of spiced cologne, "Since Marshall is supposedly the equivalent to a mens' fashion magazine model to these women, they're probably going wild about his new hairstyle."

"Ed, you flatter me." Marshall grins wearily. "I'm nothing in comparison. I must say, they need to step up their game." I shoulder him moderately hard, making him gasp. "Not you, Frieda! Your standards are completely fine!"

The women behind us laugh. Marshall casts a dangerous glance over his shoulder, and a collection of whimpers and gasps become audible. His forehead wrinkles in frustration as he pulls his glare away.

We set foot into the town hall, hand in hand with Ed walking beside Marshall, hands in his pockets. The stars are starting to creep out from behind the trees, the townspeople saluting and cheering as we make our appearance.

It's all too overwhelming.

Marshall's hand tenses around mine as the flags are raised and both anthems are played by the band in the corner. Sallinger presents a speech dedicated to the mayor who's in attendance, a translator relaying his words in another language I can understand just fine, though it takes double the amount of time to get through.

Once the welcoming ceremony ends and the crowd disperses, Marshall asks, "Shall we try to find something to eat?"

"Yes, but shall we find Ed first before we move out?"

He looks around briefly before pointing. "There he is."

Ed, lost in the crowd, maneuvers his way apathetically through women trying to grab a hold of him. A scowl is on his face as he reaches the confectionary and beverage tables, brings back a flute of champagne for himself, and holds it fondly in his hand.

"Already indulging in alcohol?" Marshall asks.

"While we're here, why shouldn't we?" Ed tugs at his collar nervously. "It's so crowded here."

Marshall shrugs. "I wouldn't start drinking too quickly. You don't want to get drunk and dance right into someone, do you?"

Ed glares. "I don't plan on dancing with anyone."

I whisper in Marshall's ear, "Just like Mr Darcy."

He snorts at this, a wicked grin appearing on his face. "Exactly what I was thinking."

The waltzing begins. I cower away from the dancefloor and stand stiffly beside him as I make out George and Lester among the crowd, waltzing away to the music with cheery women in their arms. I'm shaking. My legs feel like jelly as I watch them. It's a fast paced waltz; far too fast for me to learn.

Marshall slides a steady hand around my waist. "We can sit this one out. It's too fast-paced for a beginner."

He sounds reassuring in one half of my mind, but mocking in the other. I look away from him when he steps closer and clasp my hands together; a meek attempt to remain stable with every shake and shudder that threatens to make me lose my balance.

"We could always practice in another room. Follow me." Marshall whisks me away from the ballroom, taking me into a separate corridor. Immediately, a cold sweat rises and dampens my brow. My lungs constrict with many nervous flutters.

He shuts the doors, drowning out the noise of the ballroom behind their thick wooden bodies, heel tapping against the polished floor as he rolls his shoulders. There he is again, back in tutor mode. But this time, he's softer, more emotive than when teaching me how to handle firearms. He looks onward with excitement, eagerness to teach and welcome me to a part of his world.

"So, how to waltz, you ask? It's fairly easy."

I take a cautious and unsure step back. "What if I fall?"

"If you fall, I'll catch you. Nice and swift." Marshall closes the space between us and steps closer. "I'll go easy on you, I promise. I'm not a strict dance instructor."

"I can't imagine you yelling at me if I take a wrong step."

Marshall presses on, careful. "The first thing you want to do is get the beat correct. Here, I'll show you."

He starts with a step to the left, taking two steps on the spot to count the beat and steps to the right to do the same.

"It's the same thing if you want to go forwards or backwards." He demonstrates. I watch his feet move. I haven't seen him dance yet, but he must be just like a swan on a lake, as graceful as a skater on ice. "Also, when you dance, when you move forward or backward, you do the opposite action to your partner. If you're moving side to side, your right will be their left."

I gulp as I make an attempt to follow his lead, his mutters of *one, two, three* drilling in my ears.

"Good, good. Keep your steps in time with the beat. Count in your head if it helps you keep time. If you wanted me to spin you, we'd have to keep the beat then, too."

"Too hard!"

"No spins yet." Marshall grins, enjoying his teachings. "Now, if you're ready, we'll put the placement of the leader and follower's hands into effect."

"Is it anything—"

"No, not hard, nothing uncomfortable. This part's easy. If you just give me permission to touch you...I don't want to make you uneasy."

"Permission granted."

"Great. So, you place your left hand by my right shoulder. Your right hand stays on top of my left—no lacing together of fingers, Frieda, that's it. Keep your right hand right there, your arm just like that: nice and planted."

"Are you sure?"

"Perfectly sure. Absolutely." He adjusts himself to fit in my worried grip. "Now, my right hand will go right here." His hand moves to my shoulder blade, holding me soft and firm.

The warmth of his hands is enough to make my head spin. "We're awfully close."

His face softens at the remark. "As dance partners should be."

"I'm sorry. I've never danced before. That was pretty obvious of me to say."

"No, it's fine. That's why I'm teaching you, repaying you. You taught me how to open up about my feelings, let me into your world, so now I'm letting you into a sliver of mine." When I incline my head questioningly, he adds, "I feel lucky, you know, being your first dance partner and all." Cutting the silence that follows, he slips back into teaching mode. "Anyways, if you ever feel your partner's hand on anything other than your shoulder blade, that's incorrect. Also, the taller partner leads. The shorter partner follows. When I step forward with my left foot, where do you step?"

"Backward on the right?"

"Perfect." Marshall steps forward, grinning as another delightful-sounding waltz vibrates off the walls with its sweet tune. "Remember to do the remaining two beats on the spot!"

When I'm ready, he waltzes me around slowly, a few stumbles occuring before it starts to get easier to keep up with him. I'm less frustrated, less afraid of messing things up. His brows are pulled tight in concentration, watching our feet move across the floor beneath us. He stumbles himself as I trip, leaning forward to catch me.

"See? I've got you." He speaks so pleasantly quiet, as if I'm the only one he wants to hear him. "Just as I said: nice and swift. Congratulations. You've just learned how to dance."

My stomach fills with the killer butterflies when he lets go of me as the music stops and walks over to the doors, pushing down on the handles. "We should head back before the boys wonder what we've been doing. I'm feeling slightly woozy from the lack of water I'm consuming."

"Sure."

He opens the door. The muffled music grows louder and surrounds me as I shuffle beside him, who basks in its noise. We spot Ed with Lester and George in another corner, fast and secretive words flying from one man's lips to another.

"Gentlemen." Marshall pours himself a glass of iced water infused with lemons from a pitcher, taking steady sips from it. "What're we discussing so secretly?"

"Where were you two?" Lester asks over his plate of chocolate cake.

"I was teaching my beloved how to dance," Marshall replies proudly. "She learns fast, and hopefully we'll join in on the next waltz."

"He was a surprisingly good teacher." Laughter from the other side of the room washes over the crowd, threatening to drown out my words. "I apologize if I fall."

With a friendly giggle, he waves a lazy hand. "No problem. Just make it graceful."

"Marshall, you're too mean!" George hisses.

"I'm merely teasing, George. You, on the other hand…"

"Don't even start," Lester warns.

A fair-haired girl makes her way toward us. Curtseying in front of them, she bends a little too far forward to make use of showing off her most valuable assets in her peach-colored dress made of a low neckline, one dreadfully lower than mine. It kills me to see the look that crosses Marshall's face. He catches himself staring and averts his gaze away from her chest to her face in shame. She notices and speaks in a thick French accent, pulling and teasing her hair along with her enticing drawl.

From what I know, Ed and George are married, decent gentlemen, as they divert their attention. Marshall and Lester are bachelors, Marshall nodding along and forcing himself to look at her, obviously uninterested, ignoring her antics. Lester presses up against his arm, cowering away.

The girl hands him a folded slip of paper from the pockets of her dress, Marshall pushing it back into her clutches.

She tries to bribe him with alcohol, chocolates, cakes, and money. "You can come visit me, sir."

All he does is shake his head with a stiff smile. "I'm sorry, ma'am. I have important plans elsewhere. I'd die if I missed them with my special someone."

Special someone. The words rile me up, my heart beating faster as he nurtures the words on his tongue, taking his time to bask in their sticky-sweetness.

"Maybe they won't mind?"

"I promise you, they will." Marshall glances over at me, momentarily holding my watchful gaze. "They'll have me hung, drawn, and quartered before I even get the chance to think of an alibi."

"Just for one night?"

"I decline." He presses the folded paper back into her hands when she offers it again. "Are you married or in a relationship, perchance?"

My jaw hardens and my hands curl into fists.

No answer.

"When you are, you have to learn that being unfaithful is a felony, a string of murders upon each of the things that keep you and your partner together. The more you commit the crime, the more evidence you have that can be used against you in the court that is your partner's heart." The girl blabbers, but Marshall puts up a silencing hand. "It's quite a salacious request that I must decline. Enjoy your night, Miss."

Stone cold, he turns away, the girl rushing away and shouldering her failure to entice him.

Lester is goggling at him, jaw hanging open. "I can't believe you just did that."

Marshall gives me a challenging grin, the one that he lets out when he knows that he's achieved something. It's the grin that's crossed his face countless times in my company. A wink. Another wink that may very well be my undoing. "I know where my loyalties lie."

"What was she even trying to give you?" I inquire.

"An invitation to a steamy night with a mystery maiden." His teeth work at his bottom lip. "I'd rather spend my nights elsewhere."

"Romantic," Lester teases.

"Quite literally," Marshall snaps, "in my study, reading a book."

"I take it that nightlife isn't one of your greatest interests?" I ask.

"Not so much." He drains the last of his water from his cup, setting it aside. "To have one isn't one of my priorities."

On the stage, the band are flicking through their music books. When the silky tune of the string band hums, the beat is easily counted as a waltz, along with pairs lining up to dance.

"But one of my priorities is getting a certain someone to dance with me." His eyes glitter at the thought.

Standing before me, his eyes lock with mine, a swaggering smile plastered across his lips as he bends in a deep bow, channeling all of his movements with a grand effort of grace. If it weren't for the soldier's tunic or the scars along his hands, I'd mistake him for that of royalty. His hand lies outstretched with his offer.

"My precious darling," his brows raise as hope paints his face, "will you give me the pleasure of having this dance?"

Hesitantly, I take his hand. "I may."

"That's the spirit." He flashes me an encouraging grin as he escorts me to the dance floor. His other hand returns to my shoulder blade, cautious as ever when he adjusts his arm to suit his comfort.

When my hand situates itself upon his arm, he mutters to me, "Remember what I taught you?"

"I sure hope so."

"Remember, if you fall, I'll catch you," he teases. "Not that you will, but just in case."

"You're terrible, you know that?"

"Terribly amusing? You don't have to tell me for me to know that." When the rest of the pairs begin to dance, Marshall nods at me to follow his lead. "Also, please refrain from stepping on my toes. Remember the placement of your feet."

"Will do."

Gently, he sways me. Time slows as he holds me in his arms, the music merely an echo in the background as I concentrate on my footwork, Marshall whispering the beat's steady rhythm to me to keep me in check. It's almost like a heartbeat.

One, two, three. One, two, three.

Pivot, step, step. Pivot, step, step.

His hands remain firm as he graciously maneuvers me around the dancefloor against the rising, falling pitch of the string instruments. I swear I get lost once or twice just from the mere sound of it caressing my ears. I don't take notice until later that Marshall's stopped counting, the silence hanging comfortably between us, an unspoken peace held in our hands.

Soon enough, he breaks it. "Doing okay?"

For once, I can give him a straight answer without contemplating what else to say. "Just fine."

"Good," his eyes shine the tiniest bit brighter, "because you've been brilliant so far."

I struggle to find the right words yet again, which only gets him to chortle affectionately. "That's great."

"Besides that, are you enjoying yourself?"

"Dancing isn't as bad as I thought. Are you?"

He *hmphs* his amusement. "I'm having a ball. I think I know what the highlight of my night is."

"What is it?"

"Dancing with you." He leans in momentarily as he pivots to the right, my skirt swishing in response to his pull. "It's like living in a dream. I hope I never wake up."

"I actually had a dream about this a few months back."

"Did you?" he inquires, his brow rising inquisitively. "Was I the prince of your dreams?"

"What a conceited assumption." I roll my eyes. "Of course you were."

"I was hoping I was." He leans closer as the music dies, halts and brings my hand to his lips, brushing them against my gloved knuckles. "It's been a pleasure to dance with you. I feel so special being your first waltz partner."

"You're so good at it."

"Hush, I'm just an amateur."

"How many competitions have you won?"

"Say, five?"

"'Amateur.' *Psh*, please."

Not bothering to argue back, he surveys the room. The brightness of his eyes ceases. "Oh, no. The ladies are looking again."

"Go dance with them if you really want to."

"They'll get all over me. I don't want that."

"Oh? Be a good boy and dance. You don't have to stick around me the entire night."

"But what if I want to?" Marshall asks. "I might dance, I'm just not sure about the nurses here with us. They've been all over me since Christmas Eve!"

"I find it humorous that a man is scared of women flocking all over him. Usually he would charm them with his good looks and run straight into their reach."

"I don't feel like becoming a social butterfly tonight."

"Are you sure? I don't mind you dancing with others beside me. When you want to branch out, don't hesitate."

"Completely sure," he replies, peering at the large window nearby. The snow silently and calmly drifts past its panes as that comfortable silence settles between us again. "Do you think they're trying to find suitors tonight?"

"Huh?" I whip my head up to look at him.

"If I were a French lady at a party with American men, I wouldn't hesitate in trying to salvage a taste of their country."

"Scandalous." I lean on the table that sits between us. He's leaning with his arm on the wood, relaxed, at ease. "Perhaps that's why that woman came up to you?"

"No, she just thought I was beddable and wanted to use me to satisfy herself with expectations that I'd do the same. A one night stand, they call it."

"You wouldn't."

"Of course not. What would we be achieving out of it? Besides pleasure and pain, what's beyond that? Nothing. No love, no trust. Just pastime and dirt on our family names."

"I take it you're a very morally driven man."

"Not so much. I just know what I want to do with my life and what's best."

"Perhaps you're more selfless while upholding the morals of a gentleman."

He knows it's not a question. "Perhaps so."

Out of the corner of my eye, I catch his hand creeping across the table to reach for mine, just inches away. His face slides into a grin, the specific one that comes when he's thinking up a mischievous storm. "We should sneak out."

"Just when you were talking about doing what's best. Also, that'd be breaking the rules."

"It would be fun!" Marshall leans closer. "We can live like renegades for just one night! We could go to a bar, order a few drinks and run through town."

If the laws of physics could be defied, my brows would rise higher than the ceiling. "So much for possessing the morals of a gentleman."

Among the crowd, Ed straightens his collar as he emerges, hands rid of his previous champagne glass. "There you two are. Sallinger wanted to speak with you, Marshall."

"Me?" Marshall blinks in unsuspecting surprise.

"Yes, you. Who else?" Ed clucks. "Go on. He's waiting by the band."

Marshall saunters off, pushing through the crowd. Ed takes his place when he disappears.

"How're you enjoying yourself?"

"For once, I'm having fun."

With a clearing of his throat, he asks, "He taught you to dance, didn't he?"

"He did."

"He's apparently a good teacher. Patient, I might add. Lester said that when he taught him how to waltz." Another tug of Ed's collar. "Apparently, Sallinger is making some alterations—what he told me when I asked what was to be discussed between him and Marshall."

"Alterations?" I echo. "What sort of alterations?"

"He said that you have to move tents, as he's put you in the women's sleeping quarters due to the rise in men coming in from America who need a place to stay. He's moving Marshall to another tent, too, among many others, and notifying him about the change...probably interrogating him about you being roommates and if he's done anything to offend you."

I blink up at him. "He hasn't."

"I don't suspect it."

As Marshall returns, he appears slightly bemused, rather queer compared the lively atmosphere of the party.

"Some unexpected news on your night out?" Ed plucks a glass of lemonade off of a waiter's serving platter.

"It was bound to happen," Marshall replies. "What I didn't expect, though, was Sallinger harassing me for the truth, asking, 'Did you do this?' and, 'Have you ever done that?' Obviously, he suspected me of doing something immoral."

"But you didn't." Ed's fingers thrum against the wooden table. "No need to worry. You can move in with me if you ever feel alone. I'm sure Lester and I can fit you in."

"Thanks, but I'm sure I'll get a new tent mate in no time, regrettably." Marshall grunts in dismay. "I'm so sorry, Frieda. Are you alright with the decision? Do you want me to talk to him for you?"

I let out a heavy sigh, my head pounding. "Thank you, but I'm okay with it. It's not like I won't ever be seeing you all again.."

"Pardon me, Corporal Joyce?" A voice behind me clears his throat. There stands a young man with long brunette hair and a glinting smile of straight white teeth on full display. He's in a soldier's uniform: gold epaulets, a matching lanyard tied to his shoulder. "Major Carl Fitzwilliam at your service. I've come to ask you to dance."

Out of the corner of my eye, I catch Marshall tense. Though he nods encouragingly, it's framed by a cold front directed towards the major.

"I'd be happy to accept." My voice sounds too airy, too dry.

Marshall clears his throat, stepping beside me, brushing his shoulder up against mine. He's bristling with apprehension. "Pardon me, Major, but may I have a word with Corporal Joyce first? It'll only take a second."

Fitzwilliam doesn't show it, but I can tell he's intimidated. "I don't see why not."

He takes me by the hand and leads me near the food platters. His glare settles back on Fitzroy, who strikes up some awkward small talk with Ed, who sips at his lemonade, unbothered.

A whisper in my ear, Marshall cautions, "Just a word of advice: Some men become animals when they dance. They get their hands all over you. I've seen it happen before." I can't evade his glare that chills the very marrow of my bones. "For your own good and for your own protection, I urge you: If you feel uncomfortable, dismiss yourself. Don't be afraid to inform me of what happened. I'll shoot him for you. No one deserves to lay their filthy hands on innocent people."

"I'm sure I'll be fine."

"Just in case, take it into consideration." His hand tenses on my shoulder. "You go and have fun. I'll be fine on my own."

13

NEW COMPANIONS

Fitzwilliam's grin is almost as blinding as his speech. He's obviously a wealthy man with a lilt made of a place I just can't locate. He possesses overbearing scents of spices that waft off of him. Most likely, he bathes in bathwater perfumed with them. It's far too unnatural, harsher than Marshall's rich aroma of coffee and cologne, which is much more pleasant to inhale in comparison to this stench. He's slathered it all over and has made himself into a stick of incense.

"I do hope Corporal Clark doesn't mind me dancing with you." His grin is artificial, there to filter his fear. I feel it too. There's his hazel eyes, pinned on us from the shadows, watching our every move over the rim of a wine glass.

"I wouldn't think so," I lie. "He pulled me aside to ask what refreshment I'd like after this dance is over."

"A gentleman," Fitzwilliam remarks as he places his hands on me. His grip is tighter than Marshall's; rigid, something I'm not used to.

Fitzwilliam is a gracious dancer, just like Marshall. But, compared to him, Marshall wins by a landslide. I can't blame him, when he's been a competitive dancer for years on end.

"Are you enjoying the party?" Fitzwilliam's voice is low, his head tilting to the side in question.

I choose to give him the standard answer. With a tight pivot, my heart squeezes in on itself as my stomach knots. "Quite so."

"I enjoy these gatherings, as there are so many people with so many stories. Interesting, don't you think?"

A little taken aback by the sudden conversation starter, I choose to play along. "I find that people come from all around, and that they all possess different qualities. Upon meeting them, it's quite peculiar to find out their personalities."

In the corner of my eye, Marshall has wormed himself in to dance with a dark-haired girl who obnoxiously flirts with him, calling him 'handsome,' 'sweetheart,' and many other names that he ignores with an averted gaze. Each time she attempts to make a move upon him, his face grows paler and paler. His lips move occasionally, but not for long.

"People are peculiar creatures." Fitzwilliam pulls my attention away from him with another conversation. "Different people leave behind different stories. I'm yet to uncover them, yet to uncover yours, Corporal."

"Interesting," I mutter.

As we pass each other, Marshall issues me an observational side glance before the girl grabs hold of him again with another bout of a conversation. He reluctantly turns back to her, ear still tilted my way.

"So, tell me, Ms Joyce," Fitzwilliams swivels me away, taking notice of our interaction, "your father was part of the army, was he not?"

A shiver scampers down my spine. "Indeed."

"I met him once on the Front. He was a runner; the soldiers were assigned to act like carrier pigeons and deliver messages from one point to another. Quite a risky job, really. He was a strong gentleman and had a brilliant hand at firearms, almost never missing a target. I aspire to be like him."

"He possessed a great talent, and had an eye for anything that moved." I fight the urge to smile at the praise after realizing it's been put in place to derail me, to make me spill something personal.

"You must have very fond memories of him." He bows as the music stops. "It was a pleasure meeting you, Corporal Joyce. I enjoyed our small chat. I hope it stretches further. Shall we meet again?"

"In time."

When he leaves, I wipe my hands on my skirt bitterly. With a sigh of relief, my eyes land on Marshall, shaking his head at the girl he danced with, waving his hands dismissively in front of her. "Please, Ms Amelie, I kindly reject your offer. I'm already occupied with business affairs and I just don't have the time. Perhaps I should introduce you to my companion, Lester?"

"Lester?"

"Yes. He's a respectful gentleman like me and is a dreadful bachelor and shall be until he finds his ideal lady. Perhaps he'd be the more favorable type for you? He has a lovely house in Dayton and is extravagant when it comes to meals. His steaks are simply sublime."

It's scary how Marshall can lie like that on the spot, creating an alibi in seconds. A terrifying ability, but useful if the enemy tries juicing information out of him, or when a threat appears. It both jars me and entices me into wanting to know what sort of lies he can structure, to what extent he can keep his opposition deceived. It also begs the question of whether or not he'd make a good detective.

Would he? I'm yet to find out.

Not waiting a moment longer, he takes her by the arm, directing her to Lester, who sits near the food table with a plate of roast beef in his possession.

"Ms Amelie, I'd like you to meet my friend, Lester." He lets her go, standing to the side with a polite grin. I lean to whisper in his ear, "What in the name of God are you doing?"

"Trying to introduce Lester to a girl. She originally wanted my tent number, my address back home and a time tomorrow for a tryst, but I denied all three requests and took the upperhand in setting her up with Lester."

Perhaps a matchmaker, then.

Lester gives Marshall a quizzical glance as Amelie approaches him. I hide behind his shoulder, watching intently to see how this interaction plays out. As Lester introduces himself, Marshall takes my hand. "We should leave them to talk. We'll hear the results later."

With my hands by my side as Marshall grabs two plates, he asks, "So, what's the deal with that man? He was eager to talk to you. Do I need to shoot him?"

I scoff as he hands me a plate. "He wasn't half bad...just weird. He asked me about my father and how people are so different, how they all have different lives. Something like that."

Marshall *hmphs* in response, takes a carving fork, and stabs it through his beef. "I haven't had real meat in ages."

"Marshall, are you listening?"

"Sorry, yes." He sheepishly smiles, his grip tightening. "He seemed peculiar. I'm still quite skeptical."

"Well, yes. And odd," I say as he takes a small bite of his beef, chewing. "I guess it's because everyone knows I'm the kin of someone important. They want to insult and tear me down."

"People praise you for what you're doing." Marshall stabs his fork through another slice of beef as I load my plate. "Ed does. So does Lester, George, and of course, I do, among many others."

"But that's just you four."

"I'm naming the people I know, but I believe there are more out there."

"You were quite unsure about me at first."

"Honestly, I was in shock."

"I get it." I sigh, taking a small bite out of the medium rare beef.

Marshall swallows. "Not only was I in shock, I felt I should respect you. I still do."

I turn my head away, divorcing my gaze. "You don't have to treat me like a special someone just because I broke some outdated rules, or because I'm different."

Marshall shrugs. "But you're *my* special someone. You won't be able to stop me from treating you as an equal. It's because I simply adore you. Who cares if you broke some rules? You're bold. I say that with all the admiration and praise I can give you. You're an inspiration to those like you who want to do the same thing."

Lester rushes towards us, grabbing hold of Marshall's shoulders. "Marshall Clark!"

"Lester! My beef! You're going to choke me!"

"Beef and choking be damned!" Lester shakes his shoulders. "You're a genius!"

"Me? A genius?" Marshall's bewildered, stabbing at his beef, popping it into his mouth.

"You were trying to set me up all along!"

"Huh? Oh! I thought she was your type and—"

"You genius!"

Marshall's brows have retreated to his hairline. He realizes what's going on, that victorious smirk making its grand return. "How did it go?"

"Surprisingly," Lester runs a hand through his hair, pushing it back, "really well. Ed and George were guffawing at the back of the room as they watched her talk to me. I've got her address. We're going to be writing to each other."

Marshall pats him on the back. "I knew it was right to get you two to talk! As soon as I saw her, I swore she was your type."

Lester puts his hands up in defense. "Come on, it's not like she'll be interested in me."

Marshall sets his now-empty plate down. "Lester! Don't make assumptions like that! There's always a fifty percent chance she's interested!"

"I agree," I mutter and I eat my beef.

Lester groans. "What do I do?"

Marshall lectures him. "Be yourself, first and foremost. Tell her all your favorite things."

"That's not enough! I'll just...I'll figure it out on my own for once."

"Good luck to you, my boy. Go find her again."

As Lester walks off, Marshall smiles. "I'm glad he found someone."

"You found her for him."

"I did. I'll say that I'm glad he's interested. I hope you don't mind, but would you like to dance with me again?"

"I'd love to. Let me finish this first."

"Of course. Lester's going back to her. You can see the two lovebirds clear as day."

Under the lights, I do in fact see Lester and Amelie conversing. I think it's the first time I've seen Lester grinning so freely with his smile actually creasing his eyes.

When I set my plate aside, Marshall takes my hand and escorts me yet again to the dance floor. He bows before placing his hands back upon me, leaning in so close that I can make out every little blemish across his cheeks. He's so close that I worry he'll kiss me right here and now in front of everyone, decency and society be damned.

"I've said it before, but I'll say it again." Marshall lowers his voice so it's only me that can hear it. His breath heats my cheeks along with his sensual leer. "You look divine."

A warm wave washes over me. "Thank you. You look stunning yourself."

He straightens at the compliment "Thanks, but your dress is gorgeous. It fits you beautifully."

Another hot flash. Another compliment that lulls me under his trance. It's addicting. My heart is practically begging for more. It's ever so fatal how he's got me wrapped around his finger like that. If he were to say something against me, I would snap.

"You should wear your hair like that more often." I coax him to say more. "I quite like it in that style."

"I don't think it would agree." He simpers as another sweeping waltz floats to my ears. I spot Ed sipping champagne with George, leaning back, relaxed in their chairs.

Like the first time, I don't fight the urge to lose myself in his closeness, his fond tenderness that reminds me that with this boy, I'm walking the line of the bonds that keep us together. The ropes are taut, our hands burned and scarred from holding on so tight. It would be as equal as death to cut the ropes from him, to have them lie frayed upon the floor with his wide eyes staring at me, wider than a deer caught in the headlights with the rope still clutched unyieldingly in his hands.

The lights spin overhead with each pivot, each whisper. I fear I'm getting far too lost in it all as I close my eyes, letting him take the wheel. I keep time with his movements, mirroring him the best I can. He keeps his silence, holding me close.

When I open my eyes, he's gazing down at me, the corner of his mouth quirked into a knowing grin.

"Look at you enjoying yourself." He pivots. "I knew you would."

The music echoes, the last note vibrating through the air until it fades.

I'm summoned back to real life, where I'm in his arms, holding him before he lets go..

When we return to the group, Lester is being harassed by Ed and George, who whistle teasingly as he lays out what happened between him and Amelie. His face is ruby red.

Enjoying the sight of it all, I hang back as the boys clamber over each other. I drag one of the chairs over and lean a hand against my elbow. My feet are hurting, toes wedged in my heels from all the dancing, the excitement. It's the type of pain that feels good, that's earned from having a good time. I do confess, I had more fun than I anticipated, more joy at a gathering than I've ever had in years.

I let my eyelids drop tiredly, feet creeping towards me as another waltz takes place.

"If you're going to ask me to dance again, you have some stamina," I say.

"No," Marshall says, "I just saw how tired you were and was about to say that I think it's time for you to retire."

"If only the fun could last forever." I stand and yawn, rubbing my eyes, thankful that there's no kohl on my lids. "I think I will. Tell the boys I said goodnight."

"I will." He takes one last look at me, scanning me head to toe. It may be the last time he sees me in this dress, and he takes it in before he flashes me a tired smile.

"Are you going to retire soon?"

"After I score another plate of that amazing beef, yes," he jests. "You go along to bed. Goodnight, Frieda."

"Goodnight, Marshall."

"Don't oversleep," he advises me, kissing my knuckles. "We leave at dawn."

* * *

The women's sleeping area isn't much different to the men's.

I feel a twinge uncomfortable as I walk through the many rows of tents, back in my uniform, with my satchel full of all my possessions. Many eyes stare at me as I walk to my assigned tent. With a grimace, I shuffle my way through groups of girls who're hanging up their linens, pinning their hair back for bed, or lacing up their boots to set off to their shifts as nurses or volunteers.

Whispers are heard at every corner as I pass, keeping my head level, following Marshall's advice of keeping my eyes up, abandoning the thought of showing any sign of weakness. The sound of giggling behind tent curtains and the sight of pointing fingers irks and claws at my nerves. I'm prickly all over just hearing what they're whispering.

"Look at her, all high and mighty. Thinks it's cute to stain her family name."

"Was all that embroidery too boring for her?"

"Perhaps this is her way of finding a suitor?"

"Who does she think she is?"

I have to halt and cool my blood as it pulses red-hot through my veins, my instincts telling me to turn, to yell at them.

That's when I hear the screaming.

Upon impulse, my grip tightens upon my bag as my legs take me just the smallest bit faster under the weight of my belongings.

The scream is shrill against the night air. Its closeness chills me.

Someone couldn't possibly be attacked in a campsite, could they?

The scene I shortly come across sends a shudder down my spine.

Clothes, garments, and bags are strewn across the ground, trampled upon, ripped to shreds. My foot comes into contact with jagged fabric from the hem of a chemise: white, stained with brown dirt in patterns only the sole of a shoe can hold.

The scream rings through the air again. My eyes train themselves on a group of girls yelling and squawking as they hold another down. A foot meets her back, a dull thud, as words of profanity are tossed around. The girl is crying, pleading for them to stop.

I can't turn away. I can't become another bystander to her pain.

"Just what do you think you're doing?" I square my shoulders, dropping my satchel lightly on the floor beside me. My voice carries, echoing across the campsite.

At least four pairs of eyes turn on me. A prickle rises under my skin.

One girl's crimson lips part. "Move along, Joyce. This doesn't involve you."

"Get away from her." I don't take any chances to stall. I need to put an end to this quickly.

Another girl's laugh cracks through the tension. "And what're you going to do? Report us to Sallinger? Tell him we've been disobedient?"

"Easily." I take a daring step forward, challenging the leader's glare. I keep my chin up. "He doesn't condone men engaging in fights. Would this be any different?"

"Quit it with the witty challenges of yours," a third voice chimes in. "You think you're so tough?"

"No witty remarks, all the truth. If you don't want to suffer his wrath, let her go at this instant."

The fourth girl steps forward and challenges me. She's taller by just a few inches, her heels giving her some added height. Her arms are long, hard muscles rippling under her sleeves. "You better get moving, unless you want to be next."

"I'm not moving until the girl is safe from the clutches of your lot." I crack my knuckles threateningly. Her eyes darted to my hands, my feet that stand shoulder-width apart. "Now, I'm not keen on getting my hands dirty, but maybe just this once, I'll let it slide. How would you feel about being my first punching bag?"

The girl's jaw hardens. A smile that doesn't touch her eyes reaches her mouth. "You don't scare me, you squirt."

Pain in my knees sends me buckling to the floor.

The hostage screams for her captors to stop, to refrain from hurting me any more.

Challengingly, I hold a sturdy glare through the pain, clamping my jaw shut to hold in a scream.

"Always getting yourself into trouble, aren't you?" Before I know it, a fist grabs my hair by the roots. I don't submit, internalizing a whimper. "You're a complete and utter waste of our time."

When she gains no reaction, she bends down, hand resting on her knee as she pouts her bottom lip.

Her fist tightens in my hair. She tosses me to the ground, letting go with my scalp burning.

It takes everything in me not to rise and punch the living daylights out of her or tear her insides out. With those arms and her height, I wouldn't stand a chance. To her, I'm a mere pipsqueak.

"Come on, ladies. Leave the runts," she calls.

Just as I asked. Just as I ordered before I got my kneecaps taken out and my hair pulled, the girl is let go of.

As they disperse, they make sure to step on me. Heels dig into my stomach, my back, my arms. I only offer so much as a grunt, lying there as the pain subsides.

Struggling to my feet, the girl hasn't moved off the floor, cowering in the fetal position with bright blonde shocks of hair covering her face. When I stand over her, she whimpers.

"I won't touch you." I crouch beside her. "They're gone now."

Separating her fingers to look at me with wild gray eyes, her body relaxes. "They're gone?"

"Gone." I reach over to start tidying her belongings. My knees ache. My head throbs as I feel her eyes burning into my back as I clean, when I hand back her case.

"Thank you." She sits up, her cheeks stained with tears and grit. "This is the first time someone's ever done this for me."

"Don't thank me. I couldn't stand by and watch you get beaten like that."

A bruise is forming on her jaw as she tucks her hair behind her ear. She still eyes me carefully. I give her a hand and help her to her feet. Her eyes continue to look at the floor with some sort of fear. Shyness, perhaps?

"I hope it's not too forward of me to ask if those girls have been doing that to you for a long time?"

"Yes."

"I'm sorry. I really am." I reach to pat her shoulder, but I don't want to take any chances in scaring her away when I've just gained her trust, so I pull my hand away. "I'll put in a report about them soon. They won't bother you for a long time. What's your name?"

"Colby. I know who you are, Corporal Frieda Joyce. You're a war legend, coming here under a false name."

"I figured you would. That's a nice name, Colby. Do you have any friends I can take you to?"

The girl, Colby, nods and directs her eyes to the rubble pathway leading up ahead. "Yes. Up the hill."

"Do you want me to walk with you? It's okay if you say no. I just want to make sure you're safe."

Colby gives me a childish shrug. "I don't mind."

I gather my bag, handing her hers. "Lead the way."

We walk in silence. Colby holds both of her pale hands tight around the handle of her traveling case in front of her as she walks. Each noise that sounds in the night air sends her flinching. I can't imagine how much of a struggle it would be to harness that much fear, so much fright that something is always out to get you: the evidence that trauma is existent in her mind. I don't pry any further into the idea.

We enter a clearing with tents standing compact, close together, with numbers ranging from fifty and onwards. I highly suspect my tent is around these parts. I scan the area for tent fifty-four.

Before I can get a proper look, another blonde girl rushes forward. She has the same gray eyes, wild and searching her.

"Colby! What happened to you?" Her eyes dart to me, a ferocious flare, not from the firelight, brightening them. "What have you done to my sister, Corporal?"

I take a step back, uneasy.

Colby reaches for her, tight, pale hands gripping her at the elbows. "Cathy, you have the wrong idea! Corporal Joyce helped me! They saved me from those girls."

Catherine stares me down. "I apologize for the aggression, Corporal. My sister tends to get into a lot of skirmishes that I wish she didn't. I'm Catherine Jansen, Colby's identical twin sister."

"Frieda," I incline my head sharply, "but I'm sure you know who I am."

"Of course we do. The news of your identity spread like wildfire." Unlike her sister, Catherine wears her hair in a loose braid. Colby wears hers in low pigtails that reach to her waist. Catherine embraces her when she whimpers of pain. "Colby, you're shivering! Let me take you inside. I mean to repay you one day, Frieda."

157

"No payment needed. Except, do you know where tent fifty-four is?"

"Tent fifty-four?"

"My new tent. I've been moved."

"Splendid! A new neighbor!" Catherine claps her hands together. "How exciting, Colby! A new friend! Just your luck, Fey's in that tent as well. Ah, here she is."

Another girl comes over to us. She has beautiful, delicate features, her lavish locks the color of a blackish brown against her pale skin.

Her eyes are a deep and tawny brown. Her lips thin at the scene before her. "Did someone call my name?"

"Indeed we did, Fey." Catherine gestures at me. "This is Corporal Joyce; your new roommate."

"Corporal Joyce, huh?" She sticks out a hand, offering me to shake it. "I never thought there'd be a day where I'd actually meet you in the flesh. A pleasure to make your acquaintance. I'm Fey Huáng."

"As to you." When she shakes my hand, her grip is firm, as if she truly means it. "Call me Frieda. I'm not fussy about formalities."

That sounded way too much like what Marshall would say. His habits are growing on me.

"Okay then, Frieda." Fey ushers me to her tent. "Shall I help you unpack?"

"I'll be fine on my own, thank you. It's late. I don't want to stress you too much."

"Please, not at all."

She begins unbuttoning her nurse's uniform. I look away as I set up my sleeping arrangements. I reach deep into my bag for a comb and run its teeth through my curls, whimpering when a knot pulls at my locks.

Fey's sitting on her own stool, undoing a girdle. Her hair drapes over one shoulder in a loose ponytail. "Did you go to the party tonight?"

"I did, actually." I accept her offer of small talk, her lips curving into a smile. "Did you?"

"I did, but I grew restless only an hour in. All the men were trying to amuse me with compliments and pick up lines. It was tiring."

"Men these days," I scoff and fold my tunic to the side. "They think that with a compliment, a wink, plus a smirk or two, it'll whoo us and send us head over heels."

"Exactly!" Fey exclaims. "It was ghastly, being in the center of it all."

"Don't let them get you down. One day, you'll find someone who has morals and is of the perfect kind of people, it depends."

"Does he treat you right?"

"*He?*"

"You know...Corporal Clark?"

It takes me a moment to answer. To grip at the right words. *Yes* is too much of a bland answer. Far too generic.

"He treats me as an equal. No side on the scale is ever more weighed down than the other. I wouldn't have it any other way."

"Then that gives me hope that there are some men who know some common decencies." She's fastening her robe's belt tight around her waist; white and cotton. "If you don't mind, I'm going to retire."

"I was going to do the same. It's been a big night."

"Sure has been, and an even bigger day tomorrow." Fey makes herself comfortable, turning her back to me as I settle down. "Goodnight, Corporal."

"Goodnight, Fey."

* * *

I remain restless as the temperature dips below zero.

Fey is fast asleep, tucked deeply in her blankets as I stare at the wall with my teeth chattering. I've put my overcoat, my arm warmers, and an extra pair of socks on. I achieve no luck in guarding away the cold.

Visions swim in my mind's eye. Visions of today, visions of tonight. Well, more from yesterday, as I check Fey's watch that sits on the top of her traveling case with a fading picture framing a couple. I know they're her parents: the same deep-set eyes, same straight, dark hair. Their arms are linked while they stare stoically out of the frame.

The visions don't disappear as sensations come on the rise. My shoulders and my hands still remember his touch and the swaying pivots of the waltz. My eyes still remember him with his hair slicked back, eyes full of hope and laughter.

My chest tightens at the thought of him. I miss his warmth, his comforting silence, and whisperings before we went to bed, even the cursed bedhead that plagues him every morning and the snores that kept my fears at bay. I imagine he feels equally as alone, staring at the old space where I used to sleep with tired eyes. Unless he's changed his mind in sleeping with Ed and Lester until his new roommate is decided.

The wind howls outside; wolves out on a prowl, singing to the moon. The fine hairs on the back of my neck and gooseflesh rise with the fear that comes from being awake and alone in the night. I try to calm myself by counting my heartbeats, taking deep breaths, even resorting to trying to remember passages of books word for word.

If there were no walls separating us, I'd run straight to him. I'd take the familiar path back through the tents, prodding and poking him awake as he'd grunt and yawn, eyes sliding into realization when he sees it's me, that I'm back for just one night. I'd pray for him to take me in his arms and keep the cold and the fears away.

I've never been more scared, more terrified of being possibly the only one awake at this hour. The fright itches under my skin, an itch that I just can't scratch.

I shut my eyes, trying to remember the party, the lights, the sounds, piecing together the music that was playing, the food that was served.

My nails dig into my arms, and I squint my eyes shut.

14

TRAVELS

I swat away a hand that shakes my shoulders to awaken me. Through scratchy and quite possibly bloodshot eyes, I find Fey leaning over me in her robe and nightgown.

"Good morning, Corporal." She gives me a minute wave. "Time to wake up. It's almost breakfast time."

Reluctantly, I sit up and hurriedly dress myself. I take the liberty in pinning my bangs back from my face for today. "Are Catherine or Colby awake?"

"They're usually on the morning shift. They volunteer a lot to help with rations and other affairs."

Pinning my puttees and smoothing the wrinkles in my breeches, I'm off after I've cleaned my teeth. The sun is abnormally bright today; a rosy pink, a gentle orange against the clouds in contrast to the pale snow under my feet.

For meals, we've situated ourselves across a clearing. Nurses hand out rations as we line up and wait. I suspected we'd be offered a nicer meal now that we're in a richer part of France, but it's always the same. It makes me look forward to the meals on the train we may have over our days of travel back to the Front.

Most soldiers have brought their blankets and extra layers out to keep warm. I don't blame them, as the risk of contracting hypothermia is far too common when you're out in the cold for too long. We need to stay as healthy as possible if we're to survive through this war, through the colder seasons.

I scout the crowds for Marshall, Ed, Lester, anyone I know, with my tired eyes which I know for certain are bloodshot after I looked into a compact mirror. When I see a shot of black hair sticking up at the crown, I know that's him. Even from miles away, I'd know it was him.

He's decked himself in his thick trench coat, pulling his cap over his brow to keep his ears warm. His hands are clad with his leather gloves as his cheeks and nose redden with heat rushing to them as he sniffles. He's folded his arms over his chest as he clutches his sister's blanket tight, worrying at his bottom lip, chapped from the cold.

Trudging through the ankle-deep snow, I pop my collar against the winds still howling in the early morning. My feet crunch into the icy layers, leaving footprints in my wake as I stumble over.

When he hears me coming, he turns his head with a warm exhale escaping his lips. "Good morning, you. I knew it was you coming to greet me. It took a while to find me, so I apologize."

My greeting comes out far too blunt to be considered cheerful. "I just got here. Overslept."

"Did you not sleep well last night?" He stuffs his gloves into his pockets. "Too excited after the party?"

"Do I have to be honest?"

We've moved farther up the line when he replies cautiously with, "Only if you want to be."

"I missed you, you fool. You kept me up all night with thoughts of dancing, the party, everything."

There's a pause before he breaks into shameless, boyish laughter. "Aw, Frieda! I'm flattered that you're thinking of me! I don't think you want to admit it, but I truly did make your night memorable."

"Fine. You did. You really did, and I thank you for that. I panicked a little from the change of environment, I guess."

I expect him to become judgemental, to throw in a joke, but he doesn't. He reaches for my hand and squeezes it tenderly, with care. Understanding. "That can happen. You're so used to one circumstance and then you don't consider another. I was a bit like that, too. Last night, I didn't fall asleep as easily as I'd wanted to. I slept alone, and the silence was about to make me desperate for a distraction. You have no idea how much I miss your company. Perhaps you'll sneak in one time?"

"If you want to suffer the wrath of Sallinger and even more rumors—"

"I merely jest." He cuts me off. "But, to be honest…" He lowers his lips to my ear, warm against the cold. "I wouldn't mind if you did every once in a while."

"It's not even past five and you're already making these unholy remarks!" I shrink back, flabbergasted. "Shame on you!"

"You have to admit that it riles you up. A shot of adrenaline to help start the day." He snorts. "In all seriousness, I truly missed you."

I elbow him in the ribs. "I missed you too, you oaf."

He reaches to pull me close, but I take a step back as Lester approaches. He's stretching, yawning with a thin blanket across his shoulders.

"Lester!" Marshall greets him as he pulls back his arms. "Today is the day."

"Indeed it is," Lester replies. "I don't want to go back."

"Well, you have a woman now to keep you company. At least that'll be something to look forward to."

"I don't even know if she's serious about this...this 'penmates' thing...whatever you want to call it."

"Time will tell," is Marshall's sole advice, "time will tell."

Ed is next to turn up, wrapping his coat tighter. He's glancing around nervously as he approaches, tipping his cap against the cold. "I haven't gotten a letter from Alice yet. I'm terrified something happened to her. Has the postman been around yet? Is—is he coming?"

"Maybe she forgot to write to you, or there's a delay in the post?" Lester pats him on the back sympathetically as Ed nervously fiddles with his ring. "I don't think the mail will reach us here."

Ed lets out a whimper, and as he starts pacing, he limps.

I take the opportunity to ask, "You're limping, Ed. Did you hurt yourself?"

Lester has an arm around Ed's shoulders to stop his pacing. "There was another skirmish last night. A few drunkards decided to tear through the tents. They went to Marshall's first and ripped apart the letter he was writing to his father and punched him in the stomach when he tried to retaliate. Then they went to Ed's tent and as poor Eddie was packing away his things, they decided to ambush him...He fell and sprained his hip."

"Oh, I'm so sorry to hear that."

"They nearly took Edith's blanket I was wearing to keep warm, too," Marshall adds bitterly. "I'd never forgive myself if I lost it."

I reach for his hand. "Are you okay? Is your stomach okay?"

"I'm fine. It hurt a little earlier this morning. I should be fine now." He squeezes my hand for further emphasis that he's telling the truth. "Where's George, by the way? I haven't seen him since he disappeared last night."

"He's sleeping in. I went to check on him." Lester steps forward with us in the line. "I'll pick up some extra rations for him when he wakes up."

"But we're leaving soon." Marshall checks his pocket watch. "We have to wake him now. Like, right, *right* now."

"We will. Just after we eat," Lester says.

As Ed makes his way slowly to George's tent, he calls, "Make sure to get some rations for me!"

Marshall nods as he leaves, eyeing me as I play with my sleeves.

"I must tell you," I say, "I got myself into some action last night by standing up for a girl who was getting harassed."

Marshall exhales uneasily. "Did they do anything else?"

"They only kicked me in the knees and threw me to the floor. Nothing else."

He wraps his coat tighter around himself, rubbing his hands together to get rid of the cold with the folded blanket still pressed against his chest. "I'm just glad you aren't seriously harmed. Is the girl okay? Are you okay?"

"She's fine. I'm also fine. I took her to her sister and her friend. Fun fact: They're all so nice. One of them is my new roommate."

"Admit it, though. You miss me, don't you?" he teases.

"I do, I do." I give him a chafing glare, winning a half-suppressed snicker.

As we grab our rations, Marshall grimaces. "They burnt my toast."

"Be grateful." Ed limps over to us, cursing at his hip with George following close behind. "Be grateful that you got food. I found him ambling over with his nose sniffing the air like a rat in a pantry."

"I'm glad I found you guys," George says through his yawn. "Good morning, all."

"Of course, and good morning." Marshall takes a bite of the parts that aren't burnt. I merely nibble at my slice, grimacing at how burnt it is.

My eyes droop the smallest amount. I don't stop myself from leaning on Marshall's shoulder as another cold blast of wind whistles by. His arm loops around me, engulfing me in the fading smell of his cologne from last night and the scent of soap. The earthy smell has been rid from his odor, and I hate to admit that I miss it with the sense of safety it gave me each time he wrapped me close. He unfolds the blanket and pulls it around the both of us, pinching it tight around my shoulders.

"So Lester, about this Amelie woman I've been hearing about, are you actually thinking about getting with her?" George asks over his breakfast.

"Well, I think it's worth a shot." Lester shrugs. "Why not?"

Ed takes another bite of his toast, the crunch making him grimace as he talks with his mouth semi-full of bread. "How did you meet her?"

"Marshall actually introduced me to her last night. Surprisingly, we hit it off and are getting to know each other."

"I knew she was your type." Marshall shifts beside me, cross-legged. I take it he's finished with his toast, because he dumps it in his empty meat can. I make a somewhat risky attempt at shuffling closer and pull at the blanket's hem as he takes a sip of hot chocolate that leaves a brown mustache on his top lip.

As he wipes it away, he cranes his neck and suppresses a titter. "Hello."

"Don't look at me like that," I grumble. "I'm cold."

"Hi, cold," Marshall snickers, "I'm—"

"Whatever you do, don't plant that bomb." With an elbow to the ribs, he nearly spills his drink.

"Easy, easy." He places a hand where I've jostled him. "I'm still fragile from last night's sneak attack."

"I'm so sorry. Did I hurt you?"

"Don't fret, my sweet. Not at all." He waves away my worried questionings that spout out of my mouth. "Come here."

It's all an exhilarating rush to me, really. It's the feeling of his side against mine, our bodies pressing together under layers of wool. His arm caresses my shoulders with such gentlemanlike care. It all feels wrong, so improper in society's eyes.

But we're not in front of society.

We're in a field full of snow, protecting each other from the cold, offering as much relief as we can in the form of heat. If a man such as Marshall, who has such a strong sense of morality, isn't feeling one pint of shame for his present doings, why should I?

With my hand draped across my stomach, I catch him offering me some hot chocolate. When I shake my head, he draws his cup away. "Not one sip?"

"I don't like hot chocolate."

His distraught face is enough to see that I've shattered a fragment of his heart.

"Why ever not? What has it ever done to you?" he pouts.

"It's too sweet for me." His face only twists even more. "But I'm happy you like it."

Gaining some of his composure back, he takes another sip. "For once, they make something that tastes good. It tastes like childhood all over again."

"A nice way to put it." I pull him closer, his cheek nuzzling against me momentarily.

"Mm, but the nostalgia is more bitter than sweet. The more you miss it, the more sweet it is. It's the longing, the wish to be back in easier times that makes it so bittersweet."

"You say that by just making a metaphor over hot chocolate?" I arch a brow.

"Look, I miss being a child. Those times were easier."

"I couldn't have said it better myself," Ed adds. "What I'd sacrifice to have that sort of freedom again."

"Amen," George raises his cup, "but don't complain too much until you get as old as your old man here, when your skin starts to sag."

"It feels a lot like that already these days." Lester drinks out of his canteen. He too has skipped getting hot chocolate. "Time just moves faster."

"Times are hard, but they're another rolling stone obscuring your journey to whatever your achievements may be. If you let the stones crash into you, your skin will become a body of armor to protect yourself." Marshall takes another sip of chocolate. "Basically, you must endure hard times to get to where you want to be."

"Someone fix him," Lester teases. "He's broken and speaking philosophically again. God forbid he makes another one of those awful analogies."

* * *

Another night aboard the train falls with the hills rolling outside the window. The wheels *chug-chug-chug* past. The stars wink down at us from the sky as the lights sway up above in my lodgings. My bunkmate is Colby this time. She's fast asleep upon her mattress as I read by candlelight. Marshall let me loan out *Anna Karenina* for the journey, an admittedly gracious gesture to humor myself with his scrawled annotations on the sides and margins of the pages.

Of course, Marshall and I were separated. We're only able to meet from breakfast all the way to dinner. After that, the lights are turned off on our time together for the day, providing some much-needed space away from each other to relax before going to bed. There's no dramatic sneaking into each other's rooms, no secret trysts, no venturing out into the dark hallways of swaying compartments.

Although, I often sneak glances of him in the hallway through the peephole of my door. He often speaks to Sallinger, dips his head in response to his words. Their conversations are muffled, but I sometimes hear him repeat certain words or recognize them as he shapes his lips.

It's all so peculiar. He rarely smiles during these conversations. It's obvious he dreads them.

During breakfast, he stumbles uneasily into the dining car.

His eyes have darker shadows forming beneath his drooping lids, his face blanched, cheeks even more hollowed out than before. His jaws are glued together, unmoving, as he trods unusually solemnly through the rows of dining tables with his hands in fists, knuckles white with the tension. Against his ashen complexion, his eyes are also weepy, as he mumbles a good morning and takes his place across from me, next to Ed.

He looks horrible.

The horribleness doesn't go away. His hand shakes as he picks up his mug. The angle he holds it threatens to spill the bitter tea absentmindedly all over the table. He's barely touching his sandwiches and holds a hostile staring contest with the floor. His free hand is tapping against his knee as the wheels of his mind turn. He's thinking, deep in thought as his teeth absentmindedly gnaw at his chapped lip.

My stomach churns, performing an entire trapeze act when I look at him. He's steadying himself against something. When I catch his eye, his fleeting gaze only holds for a few short seconds before it returns to the carpet.

Something is definitely wrong. I can feel it when I look into his eyes. Hear it when he speaks with short, sparse words.

"Marshall," Ed's voice makes him flinch, "you're not hungry?"

Marshall doesn't look up and replies dully, "I'm taking my time."

"You've barely touched your food."

"My stomach has been upset since yesterday."

It's obvious he's lying. Far too obvious. He's let his façade slide.

"Excuse me," he stands hurriedly, fast enough to send his cup rattling on its saucer as his knee knocks against the underside of the table, "I'm full. I have some work I need to get done for Sallinger."

As he exits the dining car, I excuse myself and follow close behind. Ed doesn't question it.

He rounds the corner and stalks through the narrow walkways, shoulders tense. I reach to grab him by the arm with such a force that stuns him to become as still as a statue. His eyes are full of pain that I'm yet to understand.

Without a word, he tries to pull his arm away, but I refuse to let him go. "Frieda, what's—"

"I want to talk to you." I force the words out, not knowing what's to come. I sound out the next words with a stronger weight, more urgency. "I need to talk to you."

"Can it wait?" He's not bothering to put up a fight. "I have work I need to attend to."

"Stop lying to me." I resort to giving him a pleading stare. "There's obviously something wrong. I can see it getting to you. Please, Marshall, if it's me, I apologize."

Marshall stutters. "Frieda—no, why would it be you? It's not you at all."

"Then what is it?"

Marshall doesn't answer. Instead, it's his turn to pull me along as he marches through the carriage, opening a door to a vacant, tidy room. There's one bed out of the two in here that's unmade with Marshall's belongings lying in a pile across the blankets. He pushes his things aside and sits, head in hands.

"Fine, I'll talk." With an unsteady breath in, he begins. "So much is going on and I just can't cope. You won't believe how much is going on."

"I can imagine."

"No, you can't." His voice hardens at my offer of sympathy. "You can't, alright?"

"Then tell me what's going on." I dare to sit next to him, minding his belongings, his tense limbs, his gnashing teeth. "I'll try my best to understand."

"My sister," Marshall hesitates, "was requested to be sent to the Front in a few months' time. My uncle passed away and I can't attend the funeral. My brother's baby is about to be born and I don't know how long it'll be until I see them, or if I'll see them at all."

"What about your conversations with Sallinger?"

He's bewildered, eyes wide in alarm. "How do you know about those?"

"Outside my room, you two talk. I can hear you both through the wall."

Marshall's throat bobs, face paling, taking another breath in. "Sallinger is wishing to put a few corporals forward to be promoted to sergeant. He wants to make me one in a few days. I don't know if I can uphold the position."

"You should be honored to receive such a promotion so quickly."

"That's what *he's* telling me." He rakes a hand through his hair, shuddering. "Not only that, but the General is coming to assign me my position."

"What about your sister?"

"I don't want her to be scarred from the war. She's just a small, fragile girl who doesn't need to live every day in terror, seeing blood, bone, viscera, and death everywhere. I don't want her shouldering the guilt of people dying by her hand when she can't save them. I want—I *need* her to stay home." He digs the heels of his hands into his sockets, breaking right in front of me. I rub small circles across his back as he issues a moan of struggle, pain, despair. "I just want her to be safe. I don't want her to feel guilty for the rest of her life. I don't want her to die."

"Have you tried talking to her?"

"I've sent letters, but she won't listen. She's always been so stubborn."

"About your uncle, I'm so sorry. About your cousin, congratulations. Can you ask for a service leave?"

"They're not *letting* me!" he half-shouts through gritted teeth, looking at me right in the face, balling his hands into fists. Eyes alight, his teeth gnash together, a muscle in his jaw jumping. "I'm trapped here, Frieda! I don't want to be here anymore!"

I take a handkerchief and wipe his eyes while he stays deathly still under my cautious movements. His arms open, beckoning me. When I pull him in, he grabs on for dear life.

The poor man is terrified.

"I just want to go home. I'm sick of being scared of death every day, feeling hungry, ill. Sick of the stench and the tiny spaces they call trenches. I'm tired of not getting enough sleep at night, waking up to gunshots almost every morning."

"We all are, Marshall. You have a lot going for you, I understand."

Marshall's hands reach for my cheeks, cupping them in his warm palms. "Thank you for being here. I'm sorry for being so cold."

"You don't need to thank me."

"I do."

"You don't. I'm sorry about what's going on with your life right now...I really am. I wish I could do something about it."

"Just stay by me," Marshall pleads. "You'll do that, won't you? I hate doing this alone."

"I know. I do too."

Marshall's eyes stray across my face, sandwiched in between his hands. From my eyes to my lips, through his flickering gaze, he's considering what he should do in the silence. His face stiffens as he crash-lands back into the present. "Sorry, I got lost in thought."

"I figured. Did you sleep last night?"

"Not very much."

"How much have you eaten?"

He scratches behind his ear—a nervous tic—before his hands sit back in his lap. "Not much."

"What I want you to do, when dinner is served, I want you to eat as much as you possibly can. Obviously the lack of food you've been eating is doing you no good at all. I want you to stay healthy."

"If I have no appetite, how am I supposed to eat?" Marshall's question is twanged with a tremor of pain, reluctance.

"Force it down." I sound like my mother: stern, strict, and ordering people around. "Force the food down. Once you start eating, you get hungry. As you said to me: Eat your fill, stay hydrated, and get enough sleep."

Marshall releases a false, airy laugh. "It's funny, really. I give others advice when I can't listen to my own."

"Try. If you want to make it out of this war alive, all you have to do is try."

Marshall nods while he takes my words into consideration. "For you, I will. When I see Edith...if she comes here...I won't let a single bullet graze her."

"That's being a good big brother."

Marshall's eyes darken as he descends back into his thoughts. "Maybe I can just wound myself and get sent home, see my cousin and pay my respects to my uncle. You should follow me a few months later, get admitted to a hospital back home. I'll visit you as soon as I can."

"If only we lived in a fantasy world." I give him a perfectly logical answer. "I'm not risking my health for something only a person could dream of. You're not planning it, are you?"

"Despite my tolerance to the mental pain I've suffered all this time, I dislike physical pain greatly."

"That's comforting. But really, would you be willing to risk mortally wounding yourself in order to get what you want?"

Marshall rubs the fabric of the wrinkled sheets between his fingers. "I haven't really thought about that yet. When I got shot in the shoulder, the pain wasn't that bad."

"You were screaming in agony. Don't deny it now."

"What I mean is it's not as bad as getting shot in the chest or the stomach, is it? I can't imagine the feeling of the blood pooling out of you right before your eyes and soaking through your tunic. The feeling of losing consciousness so quickly and seeing stars before you black out must be terrifying. You try to move, but your body won't obey due to the shock. It's not as bad as that, is it?"

"You don't know that for sure."

"You're right. I don't. I was leaning toward the idea of gaining a head injury or attempting to break multiple bones from a fall."

"You're risking too much." I wince at the thought. "Marshall, I love you. If anything fatal were to happen to you, I wouldn't forgive myself. The plan to escape this war is suicidal...what you're thinking is suicidal. It could end up with you dead or scarred for life. Your family would be wounded by the mess you'd get yourself in."

His scarred hand reaches to wipe his eyes as his lips tremble. "I just want out of all of this, Frieda. Conscription didn't give me a choice of what I wanted to do with my life. They just sentenced me to death like it was nobody's business. After seeing so many men wounded and hearing that they went to hospitals away from the Front, I couldn't help but think if that was my way out. But wounding myself would be seen as selfish, wouldn't it? If I could tell my past self something, it would be to put those damn conscription papers the *fuck* down."

He's shattering in on himself, hissing with the pain of it. I've never heard him swear. He barely uses foul language like that, save for an occasional 'dammit' or 'hell.' It's not usually as grandiose. If he's taking his use of profanity up a notch, he's truly conflicted.

"I'm sorry, I scared you. I shouldn't be talking."

"No, no. Get it out."

"But I scared you. You're sure?"

"Don't think I'd be scared of helping someone in need. Your swearing isn't enough to fend me off. Don't even try, because my stubbornness is blinding."

"I'm just tired." He hangs his head in shame. "Tired of working, tired of fighting. I'm tired of waking up and praying that I don't die that day all for the sake of my family. Tired of being afraid that something will happen to me while I'm sleeping. My gears are rusty, tired. So damn *tired.*"

"I understand. I am, too. We're all tired. I see it every day in everyone, how exhausted they are, working nonstop."

I reach to brush the hair out of his eyes. "But everyone, despite being part of an army, is fighting something inside themselves. You're fighting for your family, a selfless act. You're fighting yourself, and I can't believe you've been fighting for so long. You stumble, you fall, but every step you take is a step to victory."

His mouth twitches apprehensively. "Can I just...can you just...I need some time to myself."

"Of course. You'll be okay? You'll come to the dining car for dinner?"

"Yes." Marshall slouches, hands clasped together in the space between his knees. "I need time to gather my thoughts." I stand and ruffle his hair. He doesn't grimace, but takes my hand, giving me a weak smile. "Thank you."

I bend down to kiss his forehead, but he snags a shameless kiss on the lips, which takes me by surprise. He stiffens when he's realized what he's done.

"I'm sorry!" he gasps. "I wasn't thinking—"

"It's fine, it's fine! Look, I'll leave you alone now. You'll be okay?"

"I'll be fine."

The words ring in my head as the memory of his mere touch haunts me when I close the door. I hurry down the hallway, careful so that no men see me as I run past.

The words chant in my mind once I reach my chambers, closing the door tight behind me as I flop onto the bed.

He kissed me.

The words sound too surreal for them to actually be true. It'd been the ghost of a kiss. His lips skimmed against mine. Did that count as a kiss? A snog, even? What's even considered a snog? What's the difference? My lack of knowledge on true romance, despite reading so many romance novels, comes up with nothing. I cover my face with my hands in shame, trying to extinguish the wants, the needs my body tells me.

He kissed me still sounds unreal, horrendously untrue, even after I assure myself he did in fact kiss me, even if it was for half a second, or a mere peck on the lips.

He kissed me still feels too offputting to think, too shocking to realize as my feelings cave in, his face burning behind my eyelids as my heart skips a beat.

15

White Wine, *Crème Brûlée*

The dining car is full of life and sound when I slide open the squeaky door. The tables are clad with dark tablecloth over their light, varnished tops, candles with little flickering yellow flames heating their ombres.

Marshall sits in the far corner, a book in his hands, by the candlelight. He's tidied himself up as he leans his cheek on a fisted hand, reading. A habit of his is to squint at the words sometimes, trying to make them out. He complains it's because he didn't bring his spectacles with him.

When he turns the page with his index, he's still rigid, leg jogging under the table as he immerses himself with his novel. It's a rather thin one—probably about a hundred pages or over from where I can stand and observe it.

I amble over. Soldiers around me are fixated on their meals, grinning at a joke their friends tell or talking with a waiter. None of them pay any mind to my presence. I'm ever so thankful for their concentration lying elsewhere.

He doesn't look up as I draw near, just able to make out the title of his book before I reach for the head of my chair to scrape it back.

"*Pygmalion*, huh?" I sit, folding my legs over one another. "I didn't know you read playwright."

His face softens as he bookmarks the page he's on with a photograph. Two men are in the frame, both possessing a swirl of dark hair, embracing each other in an affectionate hug. Ed and Marshall, I presume. What a lovely photograph to keep as a keepsake of such a wondrous connection.

"I do from time to time. It's different from what I normally indulge in."

He sets the book down, giving it a light pat on its cover. His fingers thrum against it, and I take note that he's been picking at his cuticles, which have black splotches of ink drying on them on his hands as his fingers keep up the speedy and idle rhythm of *tap-tap-tap-tap-tap* against the leather of the book's front.

"You've been writing, haven't you?"

"Pardon?"

"Your hand," I point, "it has ink on it."

Marshall looks at his hand, emitting an amused groan. "As hard as I try to wash my hands so thoroughly, there's always that one stain that stays."

"Well, ink isn't easy to wash away."

"No." Marshall sets his hand back down, observing it for a few more seconds before looking up.

"Are you feeling any better?"

"A bit more relaxed," he replies. "It's been a little bit easier."

"It's because you were bottling it all in, internalizing it." I lean forward on my chair as a cloud of steam from the train floats past the window. "It may not seem like it, but it was weighing you down."

He pauses before speaking, unsure of what to say. "That's a habit I need to control. Sometimes I do it and don't even know I am. It's ridiculous, really."

An uncomfortable pang goes through my chest, so I decide to change the subject. "How long did I keep you waiting?"

"Not long." Marshall looks over my shoulder at a nearby clock. "I only got here ten minutes ago."

"Ten minutes?" I gasp, guilty. "Look, I'm so sorry—"

"It's fine." Marshall interrupts my many nervous sparks and apologies. "It wasn't that long. I had Mr Shaw keeping me company while I waited. How do you feel about a glass of wine?"

"I don't think I'm old enough."

Marshall snorts. "We're not in America, Freddy. The drinking age here is eighteen."

My chest tightens with my hurried, anxious decision making as he awaits an answer. He means no harm, but his patient gaze makes me shudder. "It's just that I've never had alcohol."

"How about this?" Marshall's tone is soothing, negotiating. "I'll order the wine anyway; two glasses to set on the table. If you feel comfortable, the wine will be there for you to drink. If you don't, leave it. How does that sound?"

"That would be preferred, but I don't want you wasting money."

"Nonsense. It's complementary." Marshall shakes a dismissive, inkstained hand. "I don't see anyone else paying for anything."

"Seems fair," I reply. "Anyways, where are the rest of the boys?"

"Everywhere," Marshall responds, "and nowhere. Ed wasn't hungry when I asked him to accompany me and is in his room, writing. I suspect it's how tense he is about Alice. George and Lester are busy with Sallinger. Maybe they're being assigned a job I don't know about? Sallinger upgrading me to a sergeant is nonsense when he doesn't even give me a task."

"And do you want to do it?"

"I'll do anything that doesn't risk my life, yes. I'm here to fight, but that doesn't mean I want to." He calls over a waiter with a wave and a smile that would set anyone's heart aflutter if he were to give her it from across the room. "Two glasses of white wine, please."

"I am sorry, *monsieur*," the waiter says, his accent of heavy French. "I do not understand the...the English."

Marshall is lost for words, fiddling with his mouth to try to find them before I speak up. *"Je suis désolé, nous sommes américains. Il ne comprend pas le français. Deux verres de vin blanc, s'il vous plaît."*

The waiter writes my order down as I thank him, wiping his forehead with a sigh of relief.

Marshall tuts. "I've forgotten that they don't speak much English here. I should take up French."

I fiddle with my sleeves. "It would be useful, and you could talk to me in French."

"You'd probably laugh at my accent."

"No," I deny his predictions, "not necessarily *laugh* at it, but teach you how to improve."

Marshall thanks the waiter in French as he brings out the wine, pouring each of us a glass. As the waiter leaves, I break into laughter. Marshall gasps. "I knew you'd laugh at me!"

"No! I'm laughing because you pronounced it so well!"

Marshall hides his face in his hands, letting out a sob of embarrassment. Once he recovers, he clears his throat and angles his eyes at my wine glass, which sparkles and fizzes with the freshly poured liquid.

"Remember what I said."

I take the glass by the stem as the smell of alcohol and grapes overwhelm me. Marshall watches, waiting for me to take a sip. He gazes intently at me, nodding his head slowly, as if to tell me to drink once the glass meets my lips. I take a small sip, the taste thick with age and sparked with alcohol. It's not heavy, but rather light.

"I had my doubts, but it tastes quite nice."

Marshall takes this as a confirmation that he should drink with me, taking a slow and easy sip, setting it back gently upon the clothed table. "I'm glad you like it. I wasn't too sure in the beginning whether I'd like it or not, but it grew on me."

After taking another sip, I change the subject again. "Did you rest?"

His fingers continue to thrum over the leather cover of *Pygmalion*. "I did, actually."

"You look better rested."

He takes the compliment with a mere shrug. "The wonders of sleep and relaxation."

As Marshall points to the menu and is able to communicate in simple English with the waiter, a grin spreads across his face. "I'm glad he understood."

"Just hope he *fully* understood that you wanted a 'rib eye steak with extra gravy' and that it had to be 'well done.'"

"I have to tell them what I like to eat, don't I? What did you get again?"

"A filet mignon. I'm not too hungry tonight."

My worried gaze reflects in his own dark irises. "Is it your nerves?"

"I guess. It feels unnatural, too, eating all this...premium food...while there's men back in the trenches starving and eating canned products all the time or nothing at all."

"I feel a bit selfish, too," he replies. "At least we're not the men back home who are too cowardly to even step one inch into the mud."

"Some are medically afflicted. Be mindful of that."

"I know that. They can eat all they want." Marshall takes another measured sip of wine. "It's the cowards who don't commit who should feel selfish. Eat what you can. Don't feel guilty. This may as well be the last good quality meal we'll have in months."

"It's also that in a few days, I'll be in Death's clutches again." A chill rushes through me, biting into my skin. "I've always been scared by the sound of gunfire, the sound of destruction all around me, resonating in my belly. I'm just...scared."

"Everyone on this train is." His *tap-tap-tapping* grows faster. "I am too."

"But you've been here since God knows how long." My muscles stiffen as the words fall out. "You have such a precise aim, and you—"

"*Shh!*" He puts a finger to my lips, silencing and interrupting me. "You were raising your voice just a smidge."

"I'm sorry, did I—"

"*Shh!*" He shushes me before I can continue. "Don't worry about it."

"Did anyone—"

"*Shhhhhhhhhhhh!*" he hisses. "Don't worry, no one heard you."

I sit back against my chair after he removes his finger slowly, his eyes locking with mine. "Yes, Frieda, I'm scared, even if I have the potential to be an elite marksman. I'm also worried about losing everyone to the war. I'd trade my life for theirs."

"That's very selfless."

"Yes, and I'm worried about *you*." His fingers brush against his steak knife's handle. "I'm worried about all of my friends, my family, amorous connections." Before I can say anything, he adds, "Don't leave me just because you think it'll make the load a little bit lighter. It would make it heavier, for I love you dearly and would snap every bone in my body in half to protect you."

"I'd do the same, honestly." I dig my nails into my palms. "It would be too much to bear, to lose someone like you."

Marshall's face morphs into the ghost of a smile. "Well, thank you. Let me tell you a story to lighten the mood."

I anxiously take another sip of wine as he clears his throat, leans in and clasps his hands together, ready to start his tale.

"The reality of how my aim is so spectacular is that when I was a little boy, around eight or nine, my father used to take me duck hunting. I despised it. I still do. Every outing, every bullet I fired, I hated it. I remember the first gun I held, when I was sixteen—some sort of shotgun—and as soon as it fell into my hands, I, being a lanky twig of a teenager, tripped over myself from the weight of it. My father saw that the shotgun was weighing me down. So, instead, he gave me one of his pistols to inspect."

"Isn't it dangerous to give children guns?"

"My father had the safety on and watched over my shoulder like a hawk, his grip still strong on it. Anyway, it's some sort of Clark family tradition where the men go out and shoot a few poor ducks out of the sky. It's an outing I'm not going to take part in, nor will my children. It's cruel to let a child see a harmless animal die right in front of them at such a young age. I ever so happened to be forced to go with my father, my uncles, cousins, and my grandfather across the river to hunt with them. There, they taught me how to shoot, and I detested the activity straight away. Just seeing the poor feathery things go limp before your eyes is a sight you don't want to see ever again."

"I can imagine."

"Yes, and when I was seventeen, Father kept taking me to shooting ranges to practice. At eighteen was when I had to put the guns down and my pen up, as I was busy getting ready to undertake a degree in nursing. That was until the war broke out and conscription was happening all around. Scared that I would get drafted sooner than I thought I would, I had to keep practicing. A sad story, but it's true. A full circle, but that's how life is sometimes, isn't it?"

"Your father is a lot different to mine." He listens to me with a keen shine in his eye. "I only got taught how to shoot when it would be absolutely necessary to protect myself. No hunting trips, no family traditions, but it stopped once I was seventeen. My mother would scream at him that he was sullying the family name by teaching me to shoot. That was her only problem with him. He only tipped his head back and laughed, as he said he was teaching me under means of self defense. We had to do the lessons in secret. My father and mother still loved each other, but that was the one thing they couldn't agree on. In front of my mother, my father would teach me how to be a wordsmith and read heaps of French poetry out loud. My grandmother read them to him when he was a child. When he came home from work, he'd always be humming a certain song that was recently released or an old French tune I never heard of."

As the food comes, we tuck in. Marshall is still listening as he pours the gravy over his steak after he's cut off a piece to see if it's been cooked to his standards.

"My mother gave my father hell for placing a gun in my hands, too." Marshall grins, at the memory. "It's a normal reaction. Most people wouldn't give their child a weapon."

"Indeed."

"But what a contrast! I'm honestly surprised they were able to become friends with such different personalities."

"You do realize that if they didn't become friends, neither of us would be sitting here together now, right?"

"We might, but we would have a very different relationship. I'm thankful that they found each other."

"You make it sound so romantic when it really isn't." I take the salt and pepper shakers and lightly season my filet mignon.

"It is, in a way." He uses his fork to separate his salad from his mashed potatoes and meat. He's pushed them into three corners of his plate. I don't say anything about his quirk. If that's his way of life, why should I disturb it? "But it is romantic. We got to meet each other the way we did." He digs into his salad first. "And here we are, sitting in a train compartment on a random date. Love in the time of war."

I incline my head as I slice into my filet mignon. "Marshall, I shall break it to you right here and now. You're certainly a lovesick young man."

"I'm flattered." He takes a bite of steak after he pours gravy on his mashed potatoes. "It's not very often I get to be around someone like you, dear."

"Now you're just flirting."

"No, I'm simply expressing how I feel."

"And you're free to do so."

His eyes shine and meet mine over his plate. I wasn't wrong to say he's lovesick, and he knows it himself. His feelings are true. His body language doesn't prove otherwise.

"So, your father seemed like a lyrical man." He gazes at the small town that's visible over the horizon out the window, the sunset shining rays of orange and pink across the sky. "When I met him, he was extremely verbal. I liked him. I was just busy, and I feel as if I gave him the wrong impression of who I was."

"If I could tell him now about you, I would."

When he chokes, I panic.

He pushes away my fearful proddings and tirades of *are you okay* with a wave of his hand, breaking into laughter. "Silly me! My food went down the wrong way."

"I thought you were dying on me or something." My voice trembles, my speech quickens, and my heart races. "I'm sorry, I got scared—"

"Hey, slow down," Marshall splutters through a cough. "I'm still here. Just a little mishap with swallowing. No need to feel anxious, but I do admit it was very jarring and unexpected."

"I'm sorry, again. I get worried over everything."

"It's fine. Honestly, it really is." I settle back down in my chair and continue eating.

I jump at the weight of his hand on my knee under the table. His fingers are delicate against the fabric of my breeches. He mutters, close enough for me to hear, "I'm not going to tell you to stop worrying, but just know you don't have to worry about me."

"But I—"

"*For now,* you don't have to worry about me. Enjoy these last few hours of peace. I asked the conductor earlier. He said we'll be back in around a day or two. We passed Paris hours ago. The city was in the distance, but you could still see the lights. I was going to wake you up, but then I remembered that I, a man, couldn't just simply walk into your room while you're sleeping."

"You could've knocked on the door."

"It would look suspicious if anyone saw me in the feminine quarters. I'm not so brilliant at disguising myself."

"But about the lights," my hands give way to minor trembles, "were they pretty?"

"You would've been mesmerized." He's swimming in the memory of the Paris lights. "The hills were silent and the trees were dark, but you'd see the Eiffel Tower and the lights of the Arc de Triomphe while the church bells of Notre Dame were chiming. I wish we had the time to go see the city in person while we were back in Le Havre."

"There will be a time. With or without me, you'll go."

"That sounds sad." Marshall's hand shoots back. "Like, very depressing."

My breath catches in my chest, me wanting so desperately to take back what I said. "I know."

His eyes have never felt so intense. "Frieda, darling, you're turning pale. Do you need to retire?"

"It's the thought of something happening...to us, to the world. Change."

"I'm here." Marshall's gaze remains on my face, steady and patient. I guess he let my remark slide. "Nothing will happen while I'm here."

I ask, my voice still trembling, "How can you be so sure?"

His reply is uncertain. He chokes on the words. "I'm not."

I can't stop my throat from closing up, my chest tightening, far more constricted than the inside of a laced corset. I let go of my silverware as my vision swims. It pools, the world blurring before my eyes. Warm liquid I can only register as tears threaten to spill down my cheeks in a rush of miniature waterfalls.

"I'm scared, Marshall."

The words slip out in a whimper. He doesn't laugh, doesn't tease me. He merely holds his eyes upon my face and takes in my unforeseen panic.

"I know." He drops his voice to a comforting grate, sympathetic at most. "Frieda, please tell me where your mind is straying right now."

"Over dinner?"

"Dinner be damned. I want to take care of you. My stomach can wait. Take your time, dearest. I'm right here, where you need me." He hesitantly reaches for my hand over the table. When his fingers brush mine, I let him and his contagious warmth in. He's enveloped me into a bubble of trust; a safe space for just the two of us, stability.

"My chest..." I wheeze as my throat dries. My eyes stray all over the room, looking for an escape. "My chest is on fire."

He replies, "I know. Try to look at me. Only me."

"My throat's going to close up...It's tightening up on itself."

"I know." He draws slow, lazy circles over my palm with his index. "Frieda, honey, I need you to breathe with me. Here, let me wipe your eyes."

I freeze as he digs through his pockets for a kerchief, dabbing delicately at my eyes when I blink up at him. My eyes probably appear innocent and full of fear to him, but he says nothing as he folds the kerchief. The tickling circles return. His eyes lock with mine.

"I'm scared." I struggle to keep my voice from wavering. "I don't want to go back. I don't want to die. This all feels wrong. So very *wrong*."

"I know." This is the fourth time he's said those two words. "You're not alone with that feeling, my dear. I have it too. I understand how you feel. Fear strikes a plentiful of chords in us. Some feel their fear greater than others, but don't let that provide the answer of how strong you are."

My throat burns as I gulp. The compartment rocks across the tracks, steady, chugging ahead.

"Can you breathe with me, Frieda? Do you think you can do that?"

Hesitantly, with my thoughts screaming inside my head, I give him a dip of the head.

Following a steady count of *four-seven-eight* we inhale, counting to four. We hold our breath, counting to seven. We exhale, counting to eight. We do it five times. He says it's an overused but helpful strategy as my chest loosens bit by bit, my throat extinguishing its flames. My hands still quiver and my stomach flips. It growls.

When he hears the grumble, he snickers. "Someone's hungry."

"Not yet." I stare at the tablecloth. "You start without me."

"I'm not eating until I've made sure you're okay."

"It's starting to die down."

"Will you try eating a little bit? One little piece at a time. We'll take it in baby steps." When I don't answer, he racks his brain for ideas. "How about I read to you?"

"You wouldn't. Not over food."

"Worth a try." He sighs. "Say, what's your favorite dessert?"

"You're really trying to coax my worries away by buying me dessert?"

"It wouldn't hurt. Maybe we can share something after dinner: comfort food," he suggests, delicately, with a spark in his eye. "You're getting some color back, which is good."

"Am I?"

"You are. Did the breathing help?"

"I have to admit, it kind of did. I'll have to hold onto that."

"I'm glad. I really am. I hate seeing you so distressed."

"It's my fault."

"Hey," he grips my hands, "no one's to blame for your anxieties. Don't try to apologize for it, because you have nothing to be sorry for. You needn't be sorry for whatever you're feeling."

"I guess, but I feel so guilty when people worry about me." The last of the tension leaves, and I move on. "By the way, it's *crème brûlée.*"

"There's no need to feel any sort of guilt." His face contorts into a question at the name. "What's that? A *crème*...brew-what?"

"*Crème brûlée.* My favorite dessert. You asked earlier. What about yours?"

"Red velvet anything." He picks up his fork when he sees me do so. Thank God for the food still being warm. "You'll have to explain to me what that is. I've never had it, nor have I heard of it. Maybe we can try it after dinner?"

So I explain it all to him.

After dinner, he loves it as soon as it hits his taste buds.

* * *

Marshall's rambling on and on about Sallinger organizing his promotion, which he announced to him in the final hours of the train ride that the decision was definite. He's grumbling about how he won't be able to sew his chevrons on once he gets a hold of them and that he'll have to suffer through the nurses trying to flirt with him as he goes to the medical tent to get them sewn on.

He can barely hold a needle with his clubbed thumbs, sticking out like knobs as he digs his hands into his pockets in indignation. They're a full three quarters smaller than a normal thumb. He's gabbling about how they're his biggest insecurity, how they've brought him so much trouble and that he worries that if he becomes a nurse, he won't be able to administer stitches.

When he gets off topic, Ed rolls his eyes and tells him that his hands are completely fine, that it's only a minor difference, that he'll sew his chevrons on for him, that he'll be taught in his course to become a nurse how to sew and that the size of his thumbs won't matter.

Lester picks on him for having 'baby hands,' and Marshall nearly loses it, giving him the death stare as he fires back with a hot-headed comeback of Lester's romance-lacking way of life. The two of them throw words against each other before George pulls them apart and makes them issue an apology to each other like school children. Lester says sorry apathetically. Marshall can't even look at him, his face darkened from his insults.

"Blasted git," he mutters under his breath as he fastens his pace. His boots crunch through mud, dirt and gravel as he tips his cap over his eyes, spitting out another curse.

I fall into step beside him, his jaw tensing as he glares at the ground.

"Are you alright?" I reach for his arm, but he doesn't budge.

"Just frazzled," he assures me, stiff. "Don't worry. This'll all be soon forgotten. Men don't hold grudges."

"I sure hope not."

"Trust me. Give it a week and it'll all blow over. We'll sleep on it." His posture says otherwise. He's straight as a pin, shoulders squared.

While we venture farther into the Front, Lester and Marshall keep a safe distance to stop themselves from reaching for each other with George in between them, acting as a wall.

Like a whip, someone calling our names cracks through the air.

The boys stop, heads swiveling like watchful owls as they attempt to locate the call.

When they do, they sprint head-on towards it and clump themselves into a group hug, screaming at each other when someone steps on or pulls a limb. George towers over them all. Ed is caught in the middle. Lester rushes to get away when it gets too out of control. Marshall, being the shortest, gets stuck under arms that squeeze and restrain him.

For the life of me, I can't hold in my laughter as one of their voices crack as they screech out a singular name.

"Sam!"

It takes me a moment to register that there's not four, but *five* men in their disorderly clump. They're all cheering and patting each other on the back. A man with sandy blond hair makes an attempt to pull away from their grip.

"God Almighty, let go of me!" He pushes away their arms that reach to grab him, shoving Marshall back a little too forcefully as he reaches to tickle him around the waist, sending him flailing into the snow, his face softened by laughter as he clambers back up to his feet.

Once it all calms down, George asks, "Where were you since September, Skipper? We haven't heard from you since!"

The man reaches to dust Marshall's back free of snow. "Me? I was on the Southern Front. I felt horrible—I didn't get to say goodbye! It was on such short notice, and the mail slowed down in the mountains, too. I was freezing my ass off before I came back."

"In Italy? Damn," Ed marvels, "must've been a fine ride up those Alps."

I step shyly into the group, the man's eyes looking over me with interest. He points, asking, "Did you make another friend, Marshall? Who's this little guy?"

"This little fighter, Samuel Westbrook," Marshall's hands land softly on my shoulders, "is Corporal Frieda Joyce. She has a lot of might for such a small package."

I almost groan at the remark.

"The news may be slow on the Eastern Front, but I've heard of you...I've heard lots about you..." Samuel says. "Esteemed Corporal Joyce. You're practically a war tale."

"Please, I'm nothing special. I'm just another soldier. Another specimen."

"If you say so, humble one," Samuel teases. "Oh! I also heard that Marshall and you are—"

"Yes." Marshall cuts his gossip short. His hands have stiffened over me. An ache in my stomach forms. "We are."

Our relationship is new, still so very new. I get it would sound odd saying it after just getting together not even a full month ago. It takes time for things to knit together and work out.

He opened himself up emotionally to me, told me his feelings, and even admitted on the train that he was lovesick, absolutely smitten. Yet he can't bring himself to say formally that we're—

"We're together." He's read my thoughts, somehow. A shiver sets in as he offers a snort. "Ah, I've finally said it. It feels good."

Sam only smiles. "Well, you two, as long as you're happy, that's what counts. Don't get frisky just yet."

"Just you wait until I get a hold of you!" Marshall barges forward and grabs Sam by the waist, pulling him down into the snow, into a playful skirmish, which results in chests heaving with laughter, snow dampening hair, and the brightest smiles.

16

Blending Blood

With my tent sorted and bag unpacked, the news of an assault for this afternoon gets handed down the line to me along with my placement.

The front line.

The words themselves are enough to make my hair stand on end.

As I make my way through the campsite with my webbings on, gun loaded, I don't speak a word as I slink through the crowds. Fey, Colby, nor Catherine have returned to their tents yet, leaving me to venture out and wait for the boys, decked with their guns and webbings, metal caps fastened tight with the straps digging into their chins.

I stop in my tracks as Marshall's voice comes in a mumble as he converses with Sallinger. He's anxiously playing with his identity tags in one hand as Sallinger takes a long pull from a cigarette. He turns his head to blow away from Marshall, the smoke pluming from his lips as he instructs him. "Corporal Clark, you shall help with the digging during the assault this afternoon. Please notify Private Westbrook and Private Abernathy, as we need their help, too. Abernathy has been slacking off. Westbrook needs some hours added to his time card."

"Right away, sir," Marshall complies. "I'll do my best."

I start to turn on my heel, but it isn't long before his eyes land on my back.

"Corporal Joyce," Sallinger takes another pull at my nerves along with the nicotine, "are you ready to go over the front lines this afternoon?"

Marshall's rigid. I don't look at him. I can't.

I dully murmur, "Yes, sir."

Sallinger *hmph*s, satisfied, throwing his cigarette into the snow, stamping it out with his foot. "I'll see you two in your assigned places. May God be with you both."

As he dismisses himself and is out of earshot, Marshall's hands clamp on my shoulders, his eyes wide, helpless. "You can't go over the line."

"It's what I need to do." His hands tighten, digging into me as if he's trying to wake me from a trance. "Sallinger wants what he wants, and I'll give it to him."

"Wake up," he begs. "You have to argue with him. We don't want to lose you. *I* can't lose you."

"Marshall," I lay my hands atop his, "I'll be fine. I've thought of something."

"What is it?"

"I'll go over the top, probably snag my hand on some barbed wire and fall, pretending to be shot. It's as simple as a dog playing dead."

"But the risk of actually getting shot is far too great." He leans forward, his hands growing tight on my shoulders. "You're being hypocritical. I said the exact same thing on the train, which you rejected."

"I know. It's ridiculous, and I'm sorry." I dare look up at him, his eyes blazing. "If I do get shot, know I—"

"Don't say that!" he shouts, his nails digging into my epaulets. "Don't you dare start grieving when it's still uncertain what your fate may be!"

I try hard to shove my shame down. "Please listen to me."

Marshall quietens almost in an instant. His eyes watch me like a hawk as he blinks back tears that don't fall.

I lower my voice to a comforting whisper. "Whatever happens, Marshall, if I survive, this monologue won't be for any other times we're sentenced to the front line. You'll only be hearing this once. I don't have the heart to say goodbye a second time."

He inhales a long breath, waiting to hear what's next.

"If anything is to happen, before it's too late, I want to tell you that everything will be okay. I know you'll be heartbroken, angry, saddened, for a very long time, but it'll pass when you feel ready. Grief is normal. Missing someone is normal, but it'll pass. Good luck with being a sergeant, as it's a brilliant achievement only so many men can get."

"What happens if you get wounded?" He sounds like a lost child. "What happens if you get wounded and survive?"

"Don't worry about me." It doesn't take long for a choking sensation in my throat to barge in. "Being selfless is a gift, but you need to start putting yourself first."

"No. God, it sounds so childish, but I keep having nightmares of people I love dying. They've made me scared. I don't want you to die. If you die, I'll die with you. It's the fear of someone I love running off and never coming back. I can't lose another. I can't stop fretting."

"I know, and I'm sorry. You're going through something so hurtful that no one should have to. It's my fault for being here."

"No, it's not. You came here knowing what your outcomes could be. You looked Death in the eye and said, 'you don't scare me,' while I'm here, cowering like the chicken I am, screaming at it to not leer any closer."

He peers down at his watch, letting go of me, closing the lid with care. "Time's almost up. We better get going." The hurt in his eyes is enough to send me reeling "Stay alive for me. I'll never forgive you if you don't. Give them hell."

He gives my hand one last squeeze, his eyes looking forward, hollow, as he pats me on the shoulder, pushing past.

I reach for his hand, pulling him back. He can't bring himself to look at me, but he's listening. "I'll try. I'd never forgive myself either."

I get one last look at him before he vanishes from sight.

My eyes remain dry as I make my way through the snow to the front line with other shivering soldiers leaning on the walls like they're waiting on death row. Some turn to scowl at me, throwing insults into the open air. I keep my gaze low as I squeeze on through.

"How many damned minutes are there till we die, Keegan?"

"About twenty, Marcus."

"I was lucky to have written a letter to my dear Marge this morning. By the time it gets to her, I'll probably be gone."

As I brace my gun against the wall and sit, leaning my head back, I close my eyes, trying to blank out my mind, hollow myself out, and stop my nerves from sparking. It's hard to imagine that a few hours ago, I was in a dining car with Marshall Clark: his black hair bent by sleep, hazel eyes melting into mine. His smile was crooked, but so wide. Now all I see in him are tears running down his cheeks, eyes wide as he snarls and yells for me not to surrender to death.

The minutes that pass by are agonizingly slow. One of the soldiers invites me to play a game of Blackjack to pass the time. The anticipation doesn't help the roaring in my ears die down.

The captain comes ten minutes prior to the assault to assign the waves of soldiers that are to go over the top. My heart starts beating out of my chest as he points to me and assigns me to the third. Luckily, it gives me time to think up a plan to survive this assignment.

If I'm to fake getting shot when the machine guns fire, I need blood. My hand will suffice against some barbed wire, and I can smother it over my uniform. But then, if the wound is too deep, how will I seal it back up again?

The plan is suicidal. Plus, it's risking the possibility that I could be punished by Sallinger. My head hurts from thinking too much and possible dehydration.

Marshall was right when he said I was being hypocritical. I saw how flawed his plans were, only to adopt them into my own head on impulse, to attempt to cheat Death.

"Three minutes, Marcus," the man, Keegan, mutters. He shuts his pocket watch and turns to me. "All the best, Corporal."

"As to you, Private."

I start to pray, my heart beating faster and faster as the captain passes through. His metal cap is dipped over his eyes, a silver whistle clutched in his fingers. That little thing will cause Hell to break loose, blood dyeing the white snow a deep red. Gas will spread and suffocate us all. I've seen what it did to Marshall's body. It left behind scars and boils that may never go away. I'm afraid of what it'll do to the others once they climb over.

"Less than a minute now," Keegan sighs. His hand trembles as he kisses his ring finger, a simple bronze band wrapped around it.

I shake obnoxiously hard as the first wave assembles themselves on the ladders, one foot raised and ready to climb as the first few explosions splinter the ground. Shrapnel sprays into the snow in pellets. I have to cover my face to keep myself from being peppered with them as some *plink* against my helmet.

"Ready, men? On my whistle!" The captain's voice is frightening against the crashes and bangs of war. As the whistle blows, a man in the second wave crumbles to his knees and cups his hands over his ears, screaming, pleading not to send him over.

The captain raises his boot and kicks him straight in the nose, yelling insults at him.

If my plan follows through, I may not even make it to Sallinger. I'll suffer at the captain's hands instead.

Gunshots spit through the air and whiz by. Over the top, man after man falls and disappears from sight. One is starting up the rungs of the ladder, but his body falls back into the trench. On his forehead is a depression made only by a bullet hole, his eyes wide, glassy, as his blood splatters across my face. Distress slams me into the wall with a scream howling from my mouth. I can't tear my eyes away, no matter how hard I try.

I'm sick, watching the blood ooze out of his head. The sight overwhelms me. My stomach mirrors my disgust as I turn away and heave the remnants of my breakfast into a nearby waste bucket while the second wave prepares to go over. I can't help the tears that fall from my eyes and the wails that escape my mouth with acid bathing my tongue.

The captain eyes me with disgust, tutting as I recoil into a corner. "Corporal Joyce, get yourself together." He summons a slice of cruelty as he kicks the fresh corpse to the side.

It sends me reeling, words pouring out of my mouth like an open faucet; unfiltered and free. "Please sir, please don't send me over. I'm so sorry. I didn't mean to—"

Smack.

The back of his hand meets my cheek with a force that I'm unable to comprehend.

"I said to get yourself together! You're going over, whether you like it or not!" Another smack to the face. "Sallinger is paying me to send you over. If I don't, I lose profit. I'm not going to let that happen. Once the second wave is over, I'll watch you get torn apart myself, got it?"

I don't reply, my cheeks stinging as he storms off. My tears run dry as the whistle blows once more. Just the sound of it is a kick to the stomach from the captain with his taunts.

My thoughts race at a million miles per hour as he orders us to line up. I clutch my gun tight in my hand, my other on the rungs of the ladder.

My throat stings and stinks of bile. There's pain in my temples as the rest of my body aches. A thousand possible outcomes rage on inside my brain. My last words to him play like horrid record tapes. My shoulders still throb from his fingers acting as talons as he pierced me with his sorrow.

It all fades to black, and I murmur a small goodbye.

I open my eyes.

"Ready, men?"

Everything comes back to life as I make my way over the top, the whistle screaming in my ears. I forget all about my plan and run like my life depends on it. I make sure to let loose a few bullets before the machine guns fire. I dive to the ground to avoid their unforgiving aim, rising once the shots stop, heaving myself to my feet—

Warmth spreads across my side. Searing pain bites its teeth into my body.

When I glance down, my face pales.

Barbed wire has impaled my left side, making every move feel like my body is on fire. If I try to free myself, the wire snags deeper and speeds up the process of blood loss.

I have to wiggle free.

As I work to free myself, my vision spots. I try to still my panicked breathing. My hands come away red with my own blood as I fall into a heap on the ground. The blood's uncomfortably warm and sticky as it soaks through my uniform. I don't move, but dig through my webbings to grab a roll of gauze and press it to my side to staunch the flow.

The blood seeps through in no time, and I start to give up.

"Marshall..." I can't stop myself from rambling, his name stuck on my tongue. If he couldn't look at me when he left, he wouldn't be able to look at me now: ruined and disastrous, a corpse, when he says goodbye for the very last time. Normally, I'd be rushed to hospital for stitches and probably be fine, depending on how deep the wound is.

If it's severed any veins or arteries, I'm done for. Infection here is common and will catch up to me sooner or later if the medics don't arrive quickly.

Despite having the most up-to-date methods and procedures to protect us from disease and harm, we're merely humans. Anything can hurt us. We die so quickly and we don't even know it.

The gauze becomes damp in my hands. The world fades away. My grip loosens on the roll.

I'm slipping away.

I don't cry. I feel eerily at peace as I concentrate on the clouds rolling up ahead, the disgusting warmth spreading and spreading in a puddle of crimson beneath me.

"Marshall..." My hand tightens around the gauze at the thought of him. "I'm so sorry."

I close my eyes against the waves of nausea, my heart pounding against my rib cage.

A wiry, metallic buzz fills my head from all sides.

So, this is it, I think. *It's been a good run.*

With a final, morbid laugh, I'm swept into the dark.

* * *

The quiet is violent, though not entirely silent. There's an occasional squeak of metal against metal, little tingling pains here and there across my body. Something warm is pushed through me. My veins and arteries tingle as they let it flow through their walls and pump through my system.

My heart jolts back to life as my pulse quickens. My eyes are blinded by the lamplight.

There's someone crying, sniffling. When I groan and alert those around me that I'm awake, Ed's the first one to my bedside.

"Thank the Lord," he breathes. "We thought we'd lost you."

"Ed..." I reach for his hand; cold, yet solid. "What happened? Marshall...Is he here?"

"You got pricked by barbed wire." He brushes the hair out of my face. "You lost some blood...needed to do a transfusion. The medics received you as quickly as they could. Marshall is here. Right here."

"Where'd you...where'd you get the blood?"

It takes a moment. Then it all adds up.

The pricks I felt in my veins, the sudden warmth, Marshall with his face in his hand as a medic extracts a needle from his arm and hands him a cup of water. He's horridly pale as he reaches for it, taking small sips as he slumps in his chair. He's getting a tourniquet removed, his track marks wiped with antiseptic wipes and bandaged up.

"I know, it's overwhelming to see. You were losing a lot of blood. As soon as he saw you, he ran. He sprinted as fast as he could as they were looking for a donor for the transfusion. He said his blood type was...A+, I think...So we took your sample to see if he could donate. He was a match."

"He did all this...for me..."

"He did, and he'd do it a thousand times over."

"He didn't have to."

"We didn't have time. If we waited any longer to take another sample, you would've died." He clasps my clammy hands, turning to Marshall, who's held by the nurse to support him as he makes his way to my bedside. His face is ghastly pale, eyes and nose red from crying, voice hoarse.

He peers over and puts an unsure hand close to my face. "Oh God..." Marshall touches my cheek, breathing a sigh of relief. "I thought I lost you. Thank the Lord."

"You...you gave me..."

"I did." He notices the concern in my tired eyes and rushes to add, "I'm fine. I really am. Just a little woozy. I'm more concerned about you."

"I cried so hard...the...captain..." It all comes back far too fast for my groggy brain to perceive the words choking out, the tang of blood still on my tongue while my memories fog. "He slapped me...again and again..."

Marshall doesn't speak aloud his conscience, looking down at me with a face made of stone, but he still bristles. He patiently waits for me to find the words.

"I ran...I ran...I just..." I close my eyes, squinting as an ache almost diverts my train of thought. "I ran...and I...started bleeding...before I...before I blacked out..." I focus on his face, the tears finally falling. "I was...going to..."

"You weren't," Marshall denies. "They got to you as soon as they sent the fourth wave over. I saw everything, heard everything. The men on horses were hauling you back to the medics. You were...you were a sight I never want to see again. I felt helpless watching." He chokes on his words. "You're shaking, my darling. May we please have a blanket, Miss?"

The medic sets off to grab an extra blanket. Marshall scoots his chair closer. Ed leaves.

"How much blood did they...did they take?"

"Not a lot. It wasn't all mine. They had some blood bags on call, luckily."

Once he's handed a blanket, the nurse packs up the transfusion kit and makes her way out to leave us alone. The fabric is scratchy against my chin as Marshall tucks me in nice and tight with all the gentle care in the world.

"My body..." I manage through the agony in my side. "It's on fire..."

"It'll be like that for some time." Marshall brushes out my hair with his hands. "They've already given you some painkillers. I don't think they'll give you any more."

I reach to take his hand as another wave of pain crashes through me. "Why is it so dark? Marshall...Why is it...so dark...I can't see clearly..."

"Don't fret." Marshall reaches to turn the dial of the oil lamp on the bedside table. "It's just after five. I turned the lamp up brighter. Is that better?"

"How long have I..."

"Not long. The assault ended about three hours ago," Marshall hushes me. "Try to rest. You get better faster if you sleep."

"No." I shake my head like a defiant child. "I can't...I need to see you..."

"I'll be right here." Marshall rests his chin on his arms. "I'll stay right here."

"You'll...leave in the middle of the night..."

"No, I'll be right here until they wake me up for roll call."

"Promise?"

"I promise." He fixes the blanket that somehow manages to slip away from my chin as I shift beneath it. "Try to close your eyes."

"No. I want to see you..."

"And you are." Marshall settles beside me. "I'll tell you some good news. The General is coming to award me my position in a few weeks time."

"Sergeant Clark," I mumble. He sets two fingers over each of my eyes, closing them for me when they get heavy. "Has a nice ring to it."

He dials down the lamp's brightness. With my eyes closed, I say, "You...saved me."

"And I would do it again." He shifts in his chair. "We should rest. You're wounded, I'm sleepy from donating blood."

"You say it like it's an everyday occurance."

"*Pft*, as if. I don't think I'd survive...quite literally."

"Thank you...I mean it." I open my eyes and find him gazing back at me. "You saved me...Thank you."

"Don't thank me. I did what was right." His eyes close once he's comfortable.

"Goodnight, Frieda. Rest well."

"Rest well..." I trail off before I can say his name, reaching for his hand, clasping it tight as I go off to sleep.

* * *

The first thing I notice when I wake is the weight on my stomach and the pain in my side.

I don't open my eyes straight away. I know who carries that certain weight, who put in a pledge that they'd stay all night despite the discomfort that's sure to follow. We slept all the way through, plagued by exhaustion from donations and receptions of blood and shock.

When I open my eyes, Marshall has a blanket over his shoulders. His head rests on my stomach, pillowed by one of his arms. The other stretches out with his fingers intertwined, lax in mine, his face buried in the blanket. My limbs ache as I shift to get comfortable, emitting a small groan. I note that almost every move equals another stab of pain.

My moving isn't enough to get him to stir awake, as he stays put. I honestly feel bad for him. He hasn't gotten a proper place to rest for a matter of hours, and this cot only fits one person. He'll be in horrid pain with muscle cramps.

His eyes open as he sits up, stretching and cracking his limbs one by one, touching his temples with his fingertips, face screwing up like a raisin.

"That's one way to wake up and draw attention to yourself so early in the morning."

Marshall's only response is to settle back down with a grimace. "My body just went on shutdown mode as soon as I stood up."

193

"You poor thing."

He checks his watch, nodding at the time. I whimper as I turn on my side to look at him as he settles back into his perch upon the chair. "It's early." He pulls at the blanket, setting it back under my chin. "Go back to sleep."

"I'm not tired."

"You will be soon." He places his watch back in his pocket and uncovers an envelope that's been crushed at the corners. "I have a letter from my father. I haven't opened it yet, but I may as well read it while I still can."

I move closer, resting my head on the lumpy pillow as he picks the envelope open.

"When did it arrive?"

"A few days ago. I haven't had the time to read it with everything going on lately." He unfolds the parchment. "I'm always worried when I read his letters. What happens if something occurs over there?"

"Your father isn't fighting?" I ask...and scold myself harshly. Another insensible question.

He doesn't seem to mind. "He was traumatized after, I'm afraid to say it, your father died. He injured himself in order to get out of the war." He notices my sour, regretful expression. Marshall took after his father with his impulsive, dire plans. Like father, like son. Now, there's not just one, but two hypocrites among us. "Just don't feel bad about it. Your father saved mine's life. He and I are forever grateful."

He then looks down at the parchment and reads to himself. It's silent as he does, folding one leg over the other as his eyes scan the page.

"Good god. Listen to this." He points a finger to the words on the page. "*Yvette*—my brother's wife— *has given birth to your new niece, Kara Evelyn Clark. She's of a healthy weight, is a beautiful little girl, and already has her father's hair.*"

I let out a bout of laughter.

Marshall snaps, "What?"

"Uncle Marshall."

"Shut up." He blushes. "I've never heard of the name 'Kara.' It sounds quite nice."

"It sounds wonderful." I try to sit up, but Marshall braces a hand against my shoulder. "Where's my tunic? I'm cold."

"Well," he rests the letter atop his knee, "you see, after you bled out, it was covered in blood, so I sent it to the laundrymen. It should be back in your hands soon."

I look down at myself, wearing thermals and arm warmers to keep warm. They aren't doing much for me at the moment. "But I'm cold."

He situates the other blanket over me and scoots his chair closer to the bed. "I'm cold myself. I'm sorry, I can't do much."

I close my eyes as he continues to read. With a grin, he reads to me as I bury myself in the blankets. *"Please do tell Ms Joyce she's welcome in our household at any time, as her father was a close friend of mine. What you're saying about her, reminds me deeply of who exactly her father was: bold, brave, and independent."*

As he folds the letter into his pocket, the nurse walks in. "I need to check up on Corporal Joyce, if you'll excuse me."

"Of course." Marshall stands, leaving my side with a drained smile.

As she examines me, I can't help but examine the wound myself.

It's a wide set of stitches that start just under my ribs and end before my hip. It's painful, and has dry blood crusting around it. As the stitches are cleaned, I listen in on Marshall talking to someone behind the curtain, most likely another wounded soldier. It's a friendly conversation, though I can't hear much to be certain. Their volume is kept at a whisper to keep from disturbing those still sleeping.

The bandages are set in place. I'm fully dressed again. The nurse writes down her findings and explains that there's some tissue damage done by the barbed wire and that it'll take weeks to heal. I groan in discomfort, glaring as the curtain opens with a bright stream of light.

Distant footsteps sound as the flaps of the tent close. It must be time for roll call already.

Only in a matter of moments, I find myself immensely bored and retreat to closing my eyes to go back to sleep and pass some time.

The tent flaps open again.

Lester enters. He's disheveled, wrecked and exhausted, shoulders slumped. Dark circles have formed under his eyes. His face is too pale.

"Lester?"

"Good morning, Frieda. How're you holding up?" He grins tiredly, gathering a box that sits on a table and sets it under his arm.

"I'm managing. What're you doing here?"

"I'm helping Sergeant Collins deliver medical equipment to the front line. They're running short of it."

"In your condition?"

"I'm fine, Frieda." He attempts to reassure me. Gunshots and explosions shake the ground, Lester breathing out a reluctant sigh. "There's an assault this morning."

"Another one? We lost too many men yesterday."

Lester slings a heavy-looking bag over his shoulder, refusing to look at me. His face hardens. "Good day, Frieda. I have to send this over or else we'll lose many more."

"Lester, tell me who's down there." A sharp pang hits my gut with worry. "Is there anyone we know?"

"Ed is in the trenches up north," Lester answers. "Marshall is stationed down south."

A light sheen of sweat dampens my brow. "What about George? The man named Sam that I met yesterday?"

"They're both in the east."

"Damn," I hiss, my wound throbbing as my head spins with worried thoughts. "They're all going to get killed! Marshall donated blood only yesterday! He's practically anemic!"

"No one's going over today. They've lost too many men, as you've said." He opens the tent flaps. "Still, pray they come back unharmed."

The tent is silent. Each bang or crash from outside makes me jump. A small, irritable twinge eats at my insides with distress wiring its way through my gut.

None of them told me they would be taking part in this assault. None of them said anything about going to the front lines.

I ball my hands into fists, slamming one against the bedside, wincing at the shot of pain that buzzes through my arm.

"Blood boys!"

17

MARSHALL'S INTERROGATION

The racket stops at about midday with the sun high in the sky.

I've been forced to stay in bed all this time, having thoughts run laps around my head as each painful minute of the clock goes by. I've been picking at the scabs on my arms nervously, trying to distract myself, but each explosion is a whiplash that no distraction can keep me from feeling.

There's a rustle as a group of men haul themselves inside. They're all yelling at each other to help carry their wounded friend as they grip his arms and legs. I turn my back against them, cursing.

"Get him on this chair!" Ed shouts as he pulls back a chair, the legs scraping and screeching against the ground. "For Christ's sake, Marshall! Don't treat him like a doll! You'll drop him!"

Marshall grunts. "It's not my fault Sam's practically a bag of bricks!"

"I'd watch yourself if I were you!" Sam grits out.

Once he's seated, footsteps creep to my bedside. A hand brushes my back, and I bolt upright, swallowing and forcing down the pain that wrecks my nerves. The surge of blood to my cheeks roars through my ears. My insides turn themselves inside-out.

Marshall jolts back, his face slightly brown with smudged mud across his cheeks, his nose. "It's just me, calm down—"

"Calm down, Marshall? Calm down? You want me to *calm down* when the lot of you vanished upon me for nearly a whole day without saying a word?"

He bristles against my rising voice. He doesn't yell back, croaking out, "Frieda, I can—"

"What? Can you explain?" I snarl. "You're anemic from giving blood yesterday, for crying out loud! You could've easily fallen ill! Shame on you, Ed, Lester, George, and Sam for letting him out!"

"Frieda!" Ed gasps. "Let us explain—"

"I will *not*! Do you know how worried I was that all of you had gotten hurt somehow after *Lester* told me where you all were?"

The boys' eyes land on Lester, who shouts back, "Christ! You asked where we all were to begin with!"

"I was terrified for you all!" I shout louder.

"We're obviously all safe and sound. There's no need to be worried anymore." George gets handed a medical kit by Ed.

His words only rile me up even more. "That doesn't stop me from being angry at you all for being incompetent and not coming to tell me where the hell you all were before you went to your stations!"

The tent snaps to life. Lester is snarling away. George is trying to reason with us. Ed shouts at Lester to watch his tongue. Marshall is covering his ears against the ruckus, his mouth fumbling with incoherent words before he squints his eyes shut and yells out. His voice strains with the words as their volume towers over everyone else. "Shut up, everyone! Shut up!"

Once silence sets over us, all heads turn to him as he uncups his ears and opens his eyes. His shoulders square up and a glare takes over his gaze. Like a judge silencing a courtroom with a gavel, he slams his fist against the bedside with a deafening bang that sets everyone on edge. The look of him is bone chilling.

"Are we not adults? Can we solve this without acting like a wild pack of baboons? The noise of this room infuriates me!"

"She—" Lester starts.

"Did I ask you to speak, McDouglas?" His head whips to Lester, who freezes. "Did I ask for your opinion yet?"

Lester bristles.

Marshall presses onward. "Screaming and blaming each other will get us nowhere. Absolutely nowhere." He paces the space of the tent, eyeing everyone. His cold glare has my heart growing horribly faint when his eyes land on me. "If I may request that we sit *down* and talk it out like proper problem solvers and move on from there? Is my request for a discussion to be answered?"

With a myriad of nodding and affirmative mumbles, Marshall surveys the room, carrying on. He's pacing with his hands behind his back. The cold stare he issues everyone makes him just a little more intimidating. It's a sight I never want to see again.

"Now, shall we start from the beginning?" His face softens, sitting himself next to me, decidedly playing the role of a moderator. He rests his forearms against the head of his chair. His eyes take another sweep of our faces.

"Frieda?" My name curling off his tongue has me stiffening at the sound. It's the same type of fear that arises when my mother calls my name; a fear I never want to feel in any situation. "You said Lester told you where we all were?"

It feels all too much like a lawyer questioning a witness during a trial.

"Yes," I answer, my eyes digging into the floor. "He said you were all out during today's assault. I got so worried because so many men died yesterday and that it was possible you were going to go over the top."

"I said that no one was going over," Lester adds. For once, he's civil. Marshall eyes him carefully. "I didn't want to worry you, and I'm sorry that I did."

"I know. My nerves got the best of me. I accept your apology. I should really be the one apologizing for all of this."

"Understandable." Marshall's eyes are soft as they lay themselves over my shaking frame. "You could say you got a bit spooked?"

"I did. I was even more worried, knowing that you gave me blood yesterday and had to go out and fight."

"They took about half a liter, nothing too much. I feel fine, I really do. My red blood cells are hard at work making more."

"That's not all," Ed jumps in. "We were only notified this morning that any of us would be taking part. Right after roll call, they called us up and marched us to the front lines without giving us any choice to object. We didn't have the time to tell you at all, and I—we apologize. We understand you were worried."

"Please don't apologize." My voice turns husky. I dare to look up. They're all staring at me, eyes digging into my skin. "I'm so sorry I caused all that arguing over one simple mishap."

"No, no," George disagrees. "It's our fault for not sending a telegram or something."

"You wouldn't have had time to write one," Ed says.

"Can we just say it was all my fault because I was the one who—" Lester starts.

"*No*," Marshall objects, "we will not. We all did something wrong, and accidents will happen. People make mistakes, but they're there to teach us where we can improve. This is a misunderstanding, a spook of the nerves, which are both equally understandable. We can move on from this."

"We can indeed." Ed nods. "Yelling got us nowhere."

"It did, kind of." Lester shrugs. "It got Marshall to scream like a banshee and have us all sit down and explain ourselves."

"I'm not one for arguing." Marshall winces. "I merely want to keep the peace."

"Oh, God, I messed up." I hide my face in my hands. "I messed up big time."

"Aw, honey, no." Marshall reaches to pat my shoulder.

"No, I did. You're mad at me. You want to leave. You all hate me now."

"Simply untrue," Ed replies.

"Nope, not true." Sam finally puts in his two cents through the pain of his injury.

"Not even a shred of hatred for you is within me as of now." George leans forward on his chair and starts unpacking the medical kit. "I'd say we all appreciate you worrying about us."

All the boys nod in unison, some offering kind smiles and pats on the back, tending to Sam's injuries as the tension recedes and the order of the group is back to normal.

"You're lying," I murmur and hide deeper behind my hands. The scrape of chair legs come closer. The weight of someone leaning forward on the mattress makes me wedge myself even deeper. "You're all lying."

"Hi," Marshall mutters. The sound of his voice compels me to remove my hands. He's leaning with his chin in his hand. "Let me just say we're not lying about being thankful for your distress."

"But you're obviously mad—"

"Hush," he shushes me, "hush, my love. Remember what I said earlier about men not holding grudges?"

"Yes?"

"The reason why is because they simply can't." He giggles and leans closer. "I mean, some are able, but they resolve usually in about a week or a few days, unless you have a vendetta or really hate the person."

"You probably hate me now, then."

"Your mind is tricking you, my dear," he counters. "It's telling you things that are simply not true. We love you too much to hate you. I, for one, could never hate you."

"You must have some tolerance."

"I'm quite agreeable to a lot of things." He presses his lips against my ear to whisper, "But I think you're the most agreeable thing of all."

He lays a kiss on my temple. I reach for his hand once my throat starts to close up again. He hears me hyperventilating, as the panic and the thoughts set in, graceful and patient, and lets me grip his hand tight.

"Remember the breathing technique I walked you through on the train?" When I nod, he eyes me carefully. "Do you want to do that or something else?"

"Fine. I really don't care. Whatever." I wheeze as he reaches to stroke my hair while I let out a whimper from the commotion behind him.

"Concentrate on me. Nevermind them." He pulls the blankets over me, gripping my hand, placing it over his heart. "Whenever you're ready, keep concentrating on me and start counting."

With his words, my own heartbeat is loud in my ears as I inhale. "One...two...three...four..."

"Hold...two...three...four...five...six...seven..." he counts in a low murmur.

"Out...two...three...four...five...six...seven...eight."

"Good, you remember!" He offers a comforting smile. "Shall we go for another round?"

Upon our third 4-7-8 count, George taps Marshall on the shoulder. "We need your help. You're a nursing student and the nurses are all busy."

"I'll see what I can do. I'm no doctor." His gaze returns to me as he gives my hand a quick squeeze. "I'm sorry I have to leave you so soon. You'll continue the pattern, won't you?"

I start to feel heavy, my eyes threatening to close. "I'll try."

"That's my Freddy." He gives me a wider smile, turning tending to Sam's wounds.

"Oh, for God's sake, get me a bandage!" Sam yells. "I can't wait here for all of eternity!"

Marshall starts going through his webbings and takes out a roll of gauze that's waiting at the ready. "You might've broken your ankle—"

"It's for my hand. Dammit, Marshall," Sam spits, taking off his shoe, cursing as he elevates it on a stool that sits nearby. He peers at his bleeding hand. "Barbed wire got me like it did to her. Won't be able to shoot properly for a few weeks, judging by this wound."

"Which hand is it? Is it your shooting hand?" Marshall inquires and bends to inspect it.

"No, but I won't be able to hold a pistol or a rifle properly otherwise. It's my left hand, see here?"

"Mm. Be thankful your trigger fingers haven't been affected." He accepts some antiseptic from Ed and starts cleaning the wound. "You wouldn't be able to shoot at all."

"Shut up, smartass," Sam grunts.

Marshall ignores his insult as he surveys his hand. "It appears to be just a soft tissue injury to me. I'll bandage this up and try to find a medic to look at your ankle. Keep it elevated for now."

"Whatever you say, Doctor."

Marshall unrolls the gauze, wrapping it a few times around his hand after he cleans the dried blood off of his skin. He lets out a sad sigh. "My best rifle got clogged with snow that melted overnight after I polished it. A shame, really. It was truly my best rifle."

"You have another one, don't you?" Lester leans against a wooden post and observes Marshall's bandaging skills.

"I managed to get a flare gun in my possession not long ago." Marshall shrugs, almost too cheerfully. "I sometimes order replacements, or I find guns on the front line and take them. Better than leaving them to gather dust and mud."

"You probably raid corpses from time to time," Ed jokes, elbowing him in the ribs once he stands.

"Please don't. I tripped from a shockwave." Marshall sits, his arm cradling his ribs. His eyes follow a familiar figure walking into the tent, hauling a stretcher, another nurse following behind.

Colby's hands and sleeves are covered in blood, her platinum hair tied back in a tight bun, stray hairs flowing in the breeze that makes its way through. As the soldier in the stretcher releases a groan of pain, she bends down to speak. "Sir, please keep the gauze pressed on the wound. It'll stop the bleeding."

"Don't tell me what to do, woman!" he howls, and she flinches.

Marshall leans his cheek on a fisted hand, still cradling his ribs. "Men these days."

Colby's speaking with a male medic. Marshall inclines his ears to listen in. "We won't be able to get them all here in time. Do you understand that? Most of them will die from blood loss—"

"Do as I say, or else there will be punishments. You're wasting time by chattering your little mouth off."

Marshall stands with a grunt of pain. He taps the medic on the shoulder. "Mr Medic?" Marshall is shorter than this man, but he presents himself as superior nonetheless. "I would like to ask if I'm required for some assistance, as I can see you're struggling. Also, if that's your way of treating women, I'll have to file a report to Sallinger about your misconduct. What a naughty boy for treating women so horridly."

The medic's eyelid twitches as Marshall stands his ground. Colby stares, wide-eyed, as Marshall tilts his head to the side, waiting for an answer, drilling a hole into the medic's face with his eyes. He never blinks, holding firm.

If looks could kill, Marshall would've slaughtered many with those eyes.

The medic *tsks*. "Fine. Help the nurses lift the men on the beds, Corporal."

"Brilliant." Marshall's gaze is still endangering as he passes the medic, purposely bumping him on the shoulder.

"I never thought Marshall would do other people's jobs just like that." Lester watches as he disappears from sight, rubbing his hands together as he sets off to work.

"Do you see his motive, Lester? It's quite clear," Sam remarks. "He's protecting her."

The two of them chatter away as he reappears, lifting a stretcher and listening to the nurses' orders. Colby watches with admiration as he gets down to business in carrying out a thorough first aid operation on a man's leg to staunch the bleeding, his hands coming back crimson, but he can't care less. He says something to the soldier, who nods dully before Marshall runs back to retrieve another stretcher.

It isn't long before he grows tired and the nurses tell him that he's done enough after he makes an attempt to assist with more stretchers. He washes his hands in a nearby basin and sits back down on the chair by my bed, clearly pleased with himself.

"Good going, chap," Ed grumbles.

"T'was nothing," Marshall replies. "I merely aided them. How're you feeling, Frieda? Any better?"

I wrap my arms tighter around my chest, whimpering. "The panic's nearly gone, but the pain, oh, the pain. It's like it's eating my insides."

"You poor thing." Marshall winces at my whimpering, reaching to squeeze my knee affectionately. "It'll get better in time."

As a nurse comes to check Sam's ankle, claiming it's just a sprain and will heal with a bit of rest, the three of them leave. Marshall volunteers to stay behind.

"You're not sleeping here again, are you?" I ask.

Marshall shakes his head. "I wanted to bask in your company for a little while longer and see if you're alright."

I point to the bridge of his nose. "You have a cut there."

"It's a scab. Nothing special." He stands, moving to lie on the bed as I cross my legs under the blankets, giving me a playful look as he rests his head near my knees. "How do people sleep on these things? It's literally a rock. I don't see sleeping on rocks as a great way to rejuvenate."

I puff out an uncontrollable chuckle that hurts my sides.

"Do you like sleeping on rocks?" He blinks up at me, eyes shining. "It doesn't sound too appealing to me."

It's clear he's trying to make me laugh, and it's working. "Shut up."

"I like looking at rocks, but sleeping on them will definitely break my back."

"You goon." I can't control my laughter. "Stop making me laugh."

Marshall clears his throat as our laughter dies down. "I have news from Sallinger. I'll be promoted in a week."

"The General is coming in a week?"

"Yes." Marshall rubs his eyes, exhausted. "He's coming to promote me and a few others."

"I'm proud of you." My eyes start to close on their own as I recline into the pillows, shifting under the blankets. "Very proud."

"I'm honestly terrified," he says. "The General is an extremely intimidating man."

Cheekily, I respond, "Intimidate him back."

"That's not how it works." Marshall stands and grabs a washcloth to wipe his face of mud. "No one intimidates the General. If I were to try, he wouldn't splinter under my glare. He'd just swat me across the head."

"Back there with the medic, you were great at intimidating him."

"He's a coward."

"If you become a sergeant, you'll become more intimidating."

"I don't think there's much to be proud of in becoming a sergeant, really. It's just a fancy new name for me."

"You gain more power." I brush the stray hairs from his face; soft under my touch. He closes his eyes against my touch. "Sergeant Clark does have a nice ring to it."

"Also, Alistair's been promoted to sergeant major. I can't imagine him in that position." His eyelids flutter. "I'm exhausted. Another day of suffering is ahead of me."

"Think of it as another battle won; the battle of staying alive."

After blinking rapidly to keep himself awake, he finally caves in, letting his eyes close.

I hand him my canteen, noticing his lips are the slightest bit chapped. "Drink."

He takes slow and sure sips out of it, handing it back and lying back down on his side. His brows knit together in disturbance. "My back is in pain…"

"Rest here," I offer.

"What about you?"

"I might. I'm not too sure."

"Just don't watch me while I sleep. That's creepy." His eyes close again as he shifts to get comfortable. He makes sure to give me some room. "If you need anything..." he's trailing off, "I'll be right here..."

"You're sure you're fine sleeping at the foot of the cot like a dog?"

"I'm merely here to keep watch. I've slept in spots worse than this."

* * *

The blizzard has died down to a soft snowfall. Outside, the world is completely white, the snow thick and heavy on the ground as more comes in soft flakes.

Marshall's found a way of making himself comfortable. His head moves from being flat on the mattress to near my feet; a close and nearby weight. He often stirs, perhaps from a bad dream or sore muscles. Ed came in earlier to give us both rations he had stolen. They sit on the rickety bedside, remaining untouched. I didn't feel too hungry. Marshall left his rations half-finished.

Once again, he stirs, brows furrowing as he emits a moan of discomfort, possibly having another one of his countless nightmares. His lips mumble jumbled words as he twitches his limbs. His fingers curl in on themselves. So do his toes. His eyes move beneath his lids.

"Bombs…" His words are now audible, understandable. "Hide…"

I reach to run my hands through his hair, his body tense. I observe his sleeping face, noting the fading scar on his temple and the light freckles that spot his cheeks like stars.

As he takes in a large inhale, he shuffles towards me, most likely sensing my body heat. "Frieda…?"

I immediately snap to attention. "Marshall?"

"Frieda...are you there…? I can't see…"

"I'm here." I continue stroking his hair as his fear grows.

"Frieda...I can't see...I can't...I can't breathe."

"You're breathing just fine," I whisper, knowing he won't be able to hear me, but I do so anyway.

"Frieda...where are you? My eyes...I can't see...Frieda…"

He mumbles my name a few more times before his eyes snap open, his body jolting as his chest heaves.

"Bad dream?" I ask once his panting subsides.

He's speechless for a few moments before he blabbers, "I was blind...there was gas…"

"It's over now. It's just a dream."

He looks away, hurt shadowing his dark eyes.

"I hope I'm not interrupting anything," a voice calls. We both look up to see Lester with his arms folded, watching us in the dark. "They need you down on the third line."

"More digging?" Marshall sighs, sitting up and stretching. "I did that yesterday."

"And they want you back on the third line to do it again."

"Alright, alright, calm yourself." He slides off the bed, giving my hand a quick squeeze before he walks away with Lester.

One minute, he's vulnerable, mumbling my name in his sleep, shocking himself awake. The next, he hardens back into a soldier; a ripped paper man with a heart of glass that may one day shatter. And the next, he's gone, evaded from my line of sight. His warmth fades with his company.

18

During The Night and Letters

With a bit of luck, Marshall comes back from the third line just after dinner is rationed out.

It's freezing cold tonight. The snow gets thicker each minute as the storm yowls outside. The wind becomes a pack of wolves howling in the light of the ethereal moon, singing their haunting tale of woe for all to hear.

As he stumbles back into the tent, he's covered from head to toe in snow. The wind pushes him back as he struggles to close the entrance shut to keep the heat in, shivering from the cold. His hair and eyebrows are almost white from the amount of snow caught within their locks. He's practically a walking dandelion. He bats his eyelashes, wet with snow.

"Oh God." I stifle a laugh. "What happened to you?"

"They made us dig through ice, snow, and dirt. Triple combo." He gives me a sarcastic thumbs up and shakes himself like a dog shaking off water, spraying snow across the floor. "I didn't think winter could get this bad at the beginning of the year."

"Time flies, huh?" I remark as he dusts off the snow still clinging to him. "Can you believe it's already January?"

"No, and I still believe winter isn't capable of being this bad."

"Well, it can, and it'll get worse. Don't ever underestimate the cold heart of Winter."

He sits at the foot of the bed, his hair a mess, collar askew. The circles under his eyes have gotten darker. His shoulders slouch farther than the day before. He's worn out, eyes half closed as he flops onto his back.

"You should've seen Ed. He's going to have a hard time getting the snow out of his hair. It's both long and thick."

"So, the both of you look like human dandelions?"

"Mostly, yes." He unbuttons his damp coat, leaving it to dry on a chair, and reveals his tunic. He's lost a dreadful amount of weight. "I'm shocked that they make us work in below-freezing weather. I mean, look outside. We may as well be snowed in by the next hour or so."

"You'll be trapped in here if you don't move quickly."

"You think I want to go back out there?" he retorts, his tunic undone at the first two buttons. My sensibility tells me to look away as he unbuttons it farther. "I'd rather stay here until the storm dies down."

"If you're going to stay, don't pester any of the nurses for a bed. A wounded man may need to lay there if there's an assault during the night."

"I'll sleep on the floor if I have to."

"If you do, make sure not to get in the way of moving stretchers."

"Sure, but it's unlikely that they'll send men out in this weather. They'll wear out in a matter of seconds."

"Please, Marshall, sit down. You're swaying and look as if you're about to pass out."

As he sits on his chair, my heart wants him to come closer, to slide under the blankets with me—to sleep, of course. I curse myself at my borderline wanton wants.

"I've eaten, I've drank, but why do I feel so dizzy?"

"You're tired," I answer, even if he isn't seeking one. "Sleep."

"I can't. There's a storm outside."

"There's nothing stopping you from making yourself comfortable here."

Marshall's cheeks darken into a deep shade of red. "You're suggesting I sleep with you?"

*Shame, shame, shame.*My mother shouts inside my head as I nod. *Shame on you! Shame on your name! You're letting a man in your bed before marriage! Shame on your purity!*

"Really? Are you sure?" he asks.

"It's for only one night. It's nothing special, nothing other than just a place to rest."

"Like I'm going to wedge myself in with you and cause you even more pain."

"I'll manage. I'm getting better every day. I'm sure I can handle you. I did last night, didn't I?"

"Fair call." He still sounds unsure. "I don't want to offend—"

"Come on, it's not like we're going to be doing anything immoral."

His teeth skim over his bottom lip at the idea while more blood rushes to his cheeks. "Frieda," Marshall draws on cautiously, "We don't match in a bed if we're unmarried—"

"Are you really letting your morals have you catch hypothermia?"

"What I'm saying is something might happen that'll make us regret this—"

"You're analyzing this situation far too much. I'm not offering to bed me. Jesus, Marshall! Is that what your thoughts are diverting to? Bedding me? Truly blasphemous, your head is."

"You amuse me, truly," he straightens in his chair, "but no. I have brilliant control over my desires."

"Then I'm sure you'll have that *brilliant control* over your impulses."

"I'm just not too sure—"

"Just stay here! It's completely fine! It's just like how we slept in the tent!"

"Are you sure?"

"I'm sure."

"Completely sure?"

"Yes."

"Absolutely sure?"

"For God's sake, Marshall! When will my affirmations be enough to reassure your conscience?"

"I'm making sure that I don't make you anxious or harm you in any way, because I would never forgive myself if I did!"

"I'm sure you won't do anything that will potentially hurt me, as you're already cautious enough that it would be impossible to do so!"

His silence lets me know that I've won. In the lamplight, his eyes shine as he stands, slides off his gloves and leaves them on the chair with his coat. His brows furrow, teeth chewing at his bottom lip.

"Is something wrong?" I ask, shuffling carefully to the side to make room.

"Big day," he gruffly replies as he reaches for the collar of his tunic. "I'm going to turn the lamp off."

He leaves his tunic on with the first two buttons undone, arranging his webbings, laying a pistol on the chair with a small *clunk*. I guess it's a habit for Marshall to sleep with some sort of gun by his side at night. The lights dim, and his feet pad across the cold floor as he slides off his shoes after he unwraps his puttees, leaving his three layers of socks on his feet. His hand meets the blanket as he makes his way to his side of the bed, about to draw it back.

He looks at me with a still-unsure glaze in his eye. "Are you sure?"

"Positive."

As he hesitantly makes himself comfortable, my mother screams louder inside my head, disapproving of my actions. It's not like anything will happen. I trust his word.

It's a tight fit. Our bodies press up against each other even if we move to the edges of the cot. I take it that being one of the shortest members of our group has its perks, as he's still able to squeeze in beside me and make himself at home.

He doesn't take up too much space and reclines onto one of the pillows I hand him. "Actually, yes, I think I needed this."

"I told you. And look, there's space for the both of us. Nothing of what you're thinking is going to happen."

He doesn't break into his usual soft smile. His face is like stone, unchanging. "It's just a bit weird, you know? Far too weird."

"No explanation needed." He struggles to keep his eyes open, his eyelids fluttering frantically to keep himself awake. "Go to sleep."

"I need to keep watch."

"For what, exactly?"

"In case you're in pain in the middle of the night."

"No need. I'll be fine." I meet his eyes as they stare back at me, and shuffle closer.

"Are you sure?" he asks once more, barely a whisper.

"How many times have you asked that and I've said yes?"

He considers it and closes his eyes. He's falling asleep mid sentence. "You know, if you need me, I'll be right here."

I mumble a goodnight, finding him already asleep beside me. The storm billows outside.

* * *

Early nighttime turns into early morning. The temperature yet again threatens to chill every inch of my insides. The blizzard and the wind howl through the campsite as the last of the heat from the furnace dies out.

Marshall's warmth isn't enough to keep the chills away as he remains deep in sleep beside me. He's stayed as still as a rock all night, the only movement being the steady rise and fall of his chest with the occasional groan or sniffle.

I peer over at him, sleeping with his cheek pillowed by his arm, mouth wide open with audible, quiet snores. His other arm is folded over his stomach, hair becoming even more untidy; the pillow muses and ruffles it.

He didn't have to stay, but he did. He was so quick to give in, and I still feel so guilty, thinking I've forced him into something he didn't want to do. I admit, he's selfless to take my own personal comfort into consideration. But his safety was what mattered most. Morals and society be damned. The last thing I ever want to see is Marshall's frozen corpse: black and blue from frostbite with a toe tag, like the men in the trenches from the last assault. I don't want him getting lost in the snowstorm either, to be out in the cold so late at night.

It's far too cold for me to give in to the drowsiness creeping at the corners of my eyes. I move closer to his sleeping figure. A stab of pain pierces my side, slicing through my nerves. I release a howl, whimpering as it ebbs through me.

Marshall's eyes snap open at the sound, bolting upright, grabbing me by the shoulders to steady me. His eyes are wild, searching me frantically. "Are you in pain? Did something happen? Do I need to call a medic?"

The pain is almost blinding, his hands patting me down. He pulls me close, asking, over and over again, several other questions, but the nagging agony of my wounds bolts my jaw shut and prevents me from answering.

"It hurts," I manage to cry out. "My side...it hurts."

His gaze lowers to my wounded side and darkens. "I was right. I shouldn't have stayed. I've caused you more pain than you can afford."

His paling, guilt-slammed face is a kick to my stomach. "Trust me, you did nothing wrong."

"Are you sure?"

"That's nearly the thousandth time you've asked that. Yes, I'm sure. You were as still as a stone all night. It was freezing, and I was cold. I tried moving closer to you to keep—"

He doesn't want to listen, shaking his head at my reasoning. Springing up and out of bed, he stalks quietly to his chair, picking up his coat by the collar.

"Please!" My voice is caught between a whisper and a hiss. "Will you just listen to me?"

"I am," he snaps, daring to avoid my eyes, "but I can't not feel guilty for taking up space that could be used to make you heal faster with more comfort."

"Honestly," I press my fingertips to my temples, rubbing back and forth, "I appreciate your concern, but trust me, it's completely fine."

"Completely fine, is it?" he replies snarkily. "Completely fine when I woke up to you screaming in pain with me beside you? It was bound to happen one way or another."

"Do you hear yourself?" I clasp my side, throbbing with another fresh pang. "Did you hear me when I said you didn't move all night? Let me repeat myself: *All night.* How were you supposed to even do anything when it was my fault for moving closer to you to keep warm because it's deathly freezing right now?"

"Because—"

"I know what you're going to say: You took up space that I could've had to be more comfortable while recovering. You've said it before, I don't need to hear it again. I'm more than thankful that you decided to stay rather than freezing your ass off outside. I appreciate your selflessness, I really do, but please trust me when I say you did absolutely *nothing* wrong."

"Look, I'm sorry, alright? It's all my fault for being so careful. If I didn't stay, we wouldn't be fighting right now. You'd be in less pain than you already are."

"We aren't fighting," I argue. "We're working through a misunderstanding. We'd be fighting if I were angry at you, which I'm not. Not in the slightest. Unless you're angry at me for something?"

"How could I be angry at you?" he replies. "You've done nothing wrong."

"And you haven't either," I reply. "Trust me, please."

He's growing agitated, gritting his teeth to stop himself from screaming. He looks at me incredulously. "I don't know."

"What don't you know? Tell me." I try to measure my voice, listening.

"I don't know. Look, I just don't know, okay?" He starts pacing, running his hands through his hair and squinting his eyes shut, gnashing his teeth. "Why am I so selfless? Why am I so damn guilty—"

"Marshall." I beckon for him to come close, looking him in the eye. His are alight with panic, uncertainty. A sick feeling in my stomach comes to life. "Come here, please."

First, he hesitates. Then, he creeps over and sits beside me, coat in hand. His head is hung, eyes boring a hole into the floor.

"Can you look at me?"

"I don't want to," he mumbles back.

"Alright.' I lean forward, swallowing. "Can I touch you?"

"Please don't," he chokes. "Keep your hands where I can see them. When I can't, I get uneasy."

"My hands are right here." His eyes flit to my hands that move to fold in my lap. "All I ask of you is to listen to me. Can you do that?"

"Of course." He's picking at his cuticles, leg jogging at a million miles per hour.

"Thank you. Can you first tell me why you feel so guilty?"

"Seeing you in pain, seeing you suffer. I feel like a disturbance, making this cot a tighter fit with the both of us in it. I feel like I'm bringing you only discomfort, no relief whatsoever."

"Is that all?"

"I guess so."

"Okay." I nod. "Let me just say that the cot is a bit tighter, but that's not a bad thing. I honestly couldn't care. I know seeing...this...is a lot to take in. I also know you don't like seeing those you love suffer, and I'm so sorry you feel so convicted. Rest assured, you're not a disturbance nor a discomfort. Not at all. You're the complete opposite. I appreciate that you're here beside me, keeping me safe. I really do. I'm also sorry that you're feeling this way. Whatever I can do for you, I hope it makes you feel a little bit better."

"I'm sorry." He dips his head even lower. "I shouldn't have done that."

"Shush, it's all in the past." I reach to ruffle his hair, but stop, remembering his request not to be touched. "It's getting late. You have to go back to the lines in the morning. Are you going back to sleep?"

"I'll sleep on the floor."

"No, sleep here, with me." I make room for him, patting the empty space confidently. "The floor's too cold, and you'll be risking a sore back—unless you want to, wherever you feel comfortable."

"Then again," he considers his options, "the floor is so cold that I can feel it even through my socks. Are you sure?"

"Positive," I reply. "I'm completely sure."

With a hint of caution in his movements, he pulls back the blankets and shifts carefully back beside me. Slowly, he opens his arms. "You wanted my warmth? Well, here you are."

"You're certain? You told me not to touch you."

"I'm a bit better now, thank you."

I make myself comfortable on his chest in the crook of his arm.

"Thank you for not yelling at me," he mumbles.

"Why would I yell at you?"

"Often, I get people yelling for me to shut up with repeats of 'it's not your fault' with no explanation, something like that. I get the 'stop asking and apologizing over and over again' phrase quite a lot. I can't make sense of things being said when there's no straightforward answer. It's all too confusing to even explain."

"I see nothing wrong with that."

"Other people do. They say it's too annoying for them."

"Don't fret." My eyes flutter shut. "It doesn't annoy me at all. I'm actually quite grateful that you're so sure. It's good to have someone who wants one hundred percent certainty. It really does provide a sense of clarity."

212

"You think so?"

"I do." I reach for his hand, squeezing it. "You're a good man, Marshall. You're brilliant. So perceptive, selfless, and caring. No matter who tries to shut that part of you down, don't let it die, for I, plus all the others who know and love you, wouldn't have you any other way."

"That means a lot. You have no idea."

"I have some idea of the weight my words carry. I hope they make you feel the slightest bit better." I start to doze off as sleep takes over, the last of the pain settling down. "I think we should get back to sleep. I don't want you to be too tired for tomorrow."

"Of course." He lays his coat over us like a blanket, tucking it in close. Then, he tenses beside me. "But are you certain?"

"I'm completely certain, Marshall. Completely certain that I want you beside me as of now and in the future."

* * *

When my eyes open, it's dawn, judging by how the sky is turning pink with the sunrise outside.

My shivers, brought by the howling winds, are kept away by Marshall, whose arms are hugging me close under the two layers of scratchy blankets plus a trench coat that traps our heat within them. He sleeps soundlessly next to me with his lips exhaling warm air. The smell of coffee and possibly a whiff of sprayed-on cologne wafts past my nose. Being this close to him feels far too unnatural, but it's a feeling I'm willing to get used to.

Him and I fit together, strangely enough. His presence is most certainly calming, keeping me safe during the night. His breathing is what steadies me, his heartbeat hammering contently in my ear as I lay my head on his chest.

In his sleep, he clears his throat and makes the move to shift closer with his hands wrapping me towards him, fingers splayed across the small of my back.

When I shift, a dull ache arises in my side. The pain returns, and I whimper louder than I want myself to.

At the sudden noise, he peers at me through squinting eyes. "It hurts again?"

"I can handle it."

"I can call for a nurse." He's drifting off again. "I can get some more painkillers."

"No need." I refuse his offer. "It comes and goes."

"I want you to sleep comfortably," he mumbles. "I feel bad, knowing I'm the one getting all the sleep and you're not."

He yawns, reaching to stroke my hair, still clutching me close. His fingers brush against my neck and hands, his words becoming warm exhales along my cheeks. "Your hands are cold."

"They're not bothering me."

"Let me warm them up. Cold hands aren't pleasant."

He takes my hands and sandwiches them in between his, rubbing his palms along them carefully.

"Your hands are like a fireplace."

Marshall snorts, taking my other hand. I become attentive to his palms, their texture. They're rough; the aftermath of all the tiresome work he's done on the Front. "I'm glad. It's the gloves, I'd wager."

My eyes close against the wind howling outside. It acts as a filler for the silence between us.

His rest on me, and his sleepy chuckle returns. "You're going to fall back asleep again, aren't you? I'm not complaining."

"Says the one who rejected my offer in the first place and took a mighty lot of convincing to get back here."

"*Hmph.*" He lets go of my hands, pillowing the side of his head with a bent arm.

The next few words slip from my mouth faster than I can stop my lips from shaping them. I'm caught off guard, waiting for the destruction to soon follow. "You do realize that tonight, it won't be like this, right? You'll be going back to your tent."

His heart frantically speeds up inside his chest. I can envision his dreadful expression even from behind my eyelids. "I know. I know it all too well."

It hurts to hear him say it, but there's no escaping the truth and the reality of the war. He knows as well as I do that he can't disobey his orders, can't deviate from his missions, his work, his assignments, that if Sallinger orders him to charge into the enemy trenches, as much as he despises it, he'd do it anyway.

He's well aware that men aren't supposed to share a bed before marriage, as it's seen as immoral. But here he is, staying by my side as society reprimands him and makes up stories that say he's doing anything other than guiding me through one of my most painful nights, being there to support me.

Rumors that he did in fact bed me will fly. We may not hear them, but that doesn't mean they'll be non-existent. The idea of them doesn't stop him from staying, from keeping by my side all through the night. He's willingly stepping into the flames of society, not caring if they burn with his reputation lying in ashes on the floor. He can overcome their heat; people's words licking at his feet. He can muster the courage to keep walking, to feel his body burn away into embers with each insult. He can keep pushing forward as lies and trickery bite his ankles at every corner.

When he sees fire, Marshall doesn't run, doesn't retreat. He steps right on through, regardless of how bad it burns.

He moves even closer, as close as he can get without causing any pain. He shields me from the cold, enveloping me tight against him.

If only moments like these could last.

* * *

I wake once more to the wind blowing into the tent, screwing my eyes shut against its noise in disturbance, reaching for Marshall's side to find it empty and cold. I spiral into a panic until my hand lands on a folded piece of parchment. It's from his journal that he carries all over the place, one of its edges ripped from tearing it from the binding of a book.

I reach to unfold it, rubbing my eyes for them to focus on the scrawling script before me.

My little, most fantastic love,

I'm so sorry I had to leave you so abruptly yet again, but I made sure to tell you where I am to stop you from stressing. I'd hate to make you even more anxious after what happened a couple days ago. I had to leave for roll call, and I felt so bad because I had you all cuddled up and comfortable and had to let go of you to leave. It felt so horrid getting out of bed to depart.

In all honesty, resting with you was quite nice, and I'm ardent when I say that it was a warmth I haven't had for a long time, and I already miss it dreadfully as I write this letter by your bedside. I may or may not have given you a little, light, departing kiss on your cheek. Just a little peck of my affections that'll be sure to leave an imprint on you for long enough.

I've thought about what you'd said to me last night many times over. I'm aware my cautiousness can be a bit overbearing sometimes, and can be a bit frustrating for you and I both. I just wanted to thank you for being so patient with me. It truly means a lot. You honestly don't have any idea what your words mean to me. I'll strive to be the best man I can be, cautious or insensitive, however you'll have me. I'm glad you can actually tolerate my constant queries. Really, I am.

I know how stubborn you are, and I'll only say this once. If you're in an agonizing amount of pain, please don't refrain from ordering more painkillers. They'll help you greatly.

I have to leave now, and I'll see you later today. Rest easy, mi amor.

Sincerely,

Marshall

I can't help but smile. So much affection in one letter from one man.

As Colby comes to conduct a checkup on my wound, we strike up a friendly chatter. She even has the nerve to inquire about my bedmate.

"Was that Corporal Clark in bed with you last night?"

"Why do you ask?"

"I was on duty from four," she gossips, brushing out my hair. "I was tending to a man who unluckily bruised half of his ribcage the day before. I don't understand how you two slept through his howling and baying. At six, I caught your good sir in the act of bending over a nightstand and writing furiously fast into his journal. I was worried he'd rip the page with the amount of pressure he was applying to his nib."

"Seriously?"

"Seriously! And then I said, 'what are you doing here so early in the morning, Corporal?' He got such a fright that he nearly tripped over his own two feet. He said he didn't see me and something along the lines of 'my poor love is suffering greatly. I'm here to comfort her' and asked me which painkillers would work best for your discomfort."

"Typical Marshall," I groan. "It wouldn't be normal of him not to ask. He wants the best for everyone."

"Consider yourself lucky for having a man such as him so enamored by you." She giggles girlishly as she gives me some painkillers, which I swallow hastily. "Men like him are almost a one-hit wonder nowadays."

With that, she's off.

* * *

Fey and Catherine come in later that day to assist Colby with her duties. There's been another assault today, and I haven't heard any word from my friends.

I busy myself by reading the letters that've been sent from my family up in Seattle. My grandfather, too old to fight. My uncle, losing a leg in a bombing. My aunt, who's busy with five children who are my cousins.

My grandfather, Alexander Joyce, is who I read from first.

My darling grandchild,

It brings me great joy to know you're still with us at the time that I write this. I expect this letter to be held up in the post regarding how many letters a day are being sent all over the globe. Also, Happy Holidays and a Happy New Year! 1918!

Things back in Seattle have been slow, and I miss you visiting me almost every weekend—if you can come home next Christmas, I do hope we can go out together. Maybe to the cafe down the road, or the bar for dinner, as you're now a young adult? Your grandmother would love to see you, too. We both miss you, my dear. We'd love to see you very soon. We still have your favorite Earl Grey piled high for when you come back from your travels. We do hope all is well in Europe. Study hard, study well.

Je t'aime vers la lune et retour.

Alexander Joyce, Pépé and Adèle Joyce, Grand-maman

I tuck it away with a sigh. My mother must've told him I'm studying abroad or something. My grandparents are behind the times, as they don't read the papers often. But, I'm sure they'd be well aware of the war. She probably said I was in a neutral country, like Norway, for example.

I pick up the next letter; one from my uncle who lives up in Renton, the one who lost a leg.

My special niece,

Words can't explain how shocked I am to know that you've been in Europe this entire time, fighting alongside the boys in the trenches. My God, Frieda! Was your head attached when you made such a bold decision? Look what the war did to your poor uncle over here and, I hate to say it, your father. It's suicide, my dear, signing up. I'm more fearful than I am angered, my child.

I will make the common joke that you have a higher chance of finding a suitor over there, as there's men crawling all over the place. Then again, please be careful. I know you're stubborn, so I won't try to change your mind. Be very, very careful, as you know what men want these days.

Get back to me as soon as you can. Stay safe. Merry Christmas and a Happy New Year.

Yours sincerely,

Isaac Joyce

A shiver runs down my spine. My uncle always jokes about finding a suitor as I grow older, moving further from childhood to adulthood. Though he means well, his letters leave a minute chill.

As I unpack the next letter, I draw the blankets closer to protect myself against the cold.

My darling,

It hurts us to know that you're away in France and won't be coming back home for a very long time. You know that Theodore will miss your French lessons dearly. Madeline will miss seeing you at ballet practice. Lydia and Virginia will miss you coming over every so often. My youngest, Benett, will miss you helping with his math homework. We respect your choice in choosing to travel to Belgium, and if there's anything you need, we'd be happy to host you for a while before things die down at home. Uncle Otis is cleaning out the attic, so we might be able to place you in there if you ever decide to come back any time soon. I understand you're going through a lot at the moment, my dear niece, my most favorite niece of all.

Your mother has been worried sick about you at home. Her new husband and step-daughter came last week to meet us. Fitzroy South is a peculiar man, and his daughter seems rather entitled, nothing compared to the brilliant little songbird I know.

Rest assured, we're fine here in our home, safe from the war and the commotion of the world. Please be back soon, and stay safe.

All our love to give,

Auntie Ruth, Uncle Otis, Theodore, Lydia, Madeline, Virginia and Benett Wilhelm

My hands then curl into fists atop the blankets as an ache hollows out my stomach. I feel ashamed after reading these letters; ashamed of my choice to travel here when so many others didn't even get a say in their decisions. It gets harder to breathe as guilt, blind anger, and resentment against myself fill me from top to bottom. It's a suffocating feeling, one that makes me want to scream and cry as it wrecks my insides.

* * *

I lie in bed for the rest of the day, shaking from both the cold and all the negative emotions I'm bottling up forming one huge storm cloud over my head. I don't bother to turn and see who enters the tent.

Chair legs scrape across the floor as the person pulls it up close, sitting upon it while their titter rumbles near my ear, dripping with affection.

"I'm back." Marshall's voice sends me jolting. It's grating and deep, somehow enticing. I hate when he or anyone sees me like this; vulnerable, about to fall apart. I never want him to see me like this ever again, but here we are. "Were you trying to sleep?"

I look over my shoulder to see him leaning forward with his elbows on the mattress. He sees the tear stains, my reddened eyes.

"Were you crying?" Marshall's smile fades. "Frieda, please, what's wrong? Are you in pain again? Whatever it is, I can—"

"I got some letters today." I don't look at him. I know he's coming closer. His breath plumes against my neck as he listens, his hand firm on my forearm. "They all felt like they were telling me off."

"About what?"

"Me coming here to fight when I wasn't supposed to." I feel like screaming. "They're all begging me to come home for them to punish and scowl at me for everything I've done."

"Your family?" Marshall asks.

"Yes. Now I feel bad because I did something I wasn't supposed to and I'm still doing it, fighting when I'm supposed to be a nurse or a maid or married off to a suitor by now. Marshall, I'm in so much pain and I don't know if I can stand it anymore."

Marshall's eyes are like magnets, dragging my gaze toward him like a piece of metal to a magnetic pull. He hesitates. "Frieda...I'm so sorry...I..."

A fresh set of tears falls. Marshall is so close that I can see all the tiny details of the engravings on his service medal, pinned to his chest and dangling from his breast pocket, as he leans in.

"Let me say this: Even if you don't feel it within you," he takes my hands, new bandages on his fingers, "you might see a person who's a disgrace, an imperfection of what they should be. You might see someone who's let everyone they know down, a person who's fragile and breaks every single day of their life. To me, I see a person with potential, with bravery coursing through their every step. I see them as perfect."

"That's only you," I argue.

"Well, ask my friends. Ask your friends."

I wipe my eyes as he moves closer, squeezing my hands in his. His face is so close to mine, and I can just make out the dark flecks of his irises. His frown is set in stone.

"I'm tired of existing at this point." The pain in my side takes another bite out of me. "Will the pain ever stop?"

His hand moves to my face. I succumb under its heat. "Exist with me right here, right now."

I'm lost for words. He looms over me, the pain in my side throbbing in time with my speeding heart. His eyes are the embers of a dying fire, glinting in the low light of the tent.

I open my mouth to speak. Instead of words forming, nothing comes besides a strangled sound of struggle.

"I know you're hurt." He breaks the silence, his other hand holding mine. "I understand that, and I'm sorry you feel this way. If I can be of any comfort, tell me."

The pit in my stomach only grows. I don't want to pull him deeper than he already is into my mess, even if he feels like he's stable enough to help.

His expression is desperate, and I melt just looking at it. My lips part to speak yet again, but I'm unsure of what to say. The heat of his hands against my skin and the sensation of his bandaged fingers locked with mine are already a lot to take in.

"I'll try," is all I can muster.

"Just remember, Frieda." His eyes that stare at my lips aren't hard to miss. "You're everything to me. I'd do everything in my power to make you happy."

With his collar astray, he gets closer, never leaving. I argue, "I'm no one, not your everything. Total happiness is impossible."

Marshall's laugh sets me on fire. His voice returns to that low, somehow-sensual rasp. "You're *my* someone. *My* everything. We can only dream of happiness, can't we? Dreams only come true if you truly believe in them. I believe and hope I can make part of that dream a reality."

The world slows as he leers closer, and I don't hesitate to pull him in.

His touch burns like whiskey. He brings a heat that doesn't just warm my mouth, but my entire body. His hand keeps its grip on mine as he moves closer to deepen the kiss.

My thoughts are no longer along the lines of *he kissed me*.

He is kissing me. Marshall Clark is kissing me.

I can't spare a care in the world for whoever sees, the sudden euphoria of the moment kicking me with a boost of energy. He cups my cheek. My name plumes from his lips on an in-breath as he goes in for more.

Delicately, he's the first to pull away and barely looks stunned, as if he's been preparing himself for this moment. "Is this how I can be of comfort to you?"

"In a way." I'm out of breath. His laugh rumbles in his throat. "But besides the kissing...I don't know. Just do what you're doing: being there for me when I need someone."

"Of course." He offers a smile. "You have to admit, the tension of that kiss was quite saucy, don't you think?"

"You better shut up. Once I'm back on my feet, you'll regret ever saying that."

"When you're in good health, enlighten me," he flirts. "I'll wait. I'm sure what's yet to come between us will be most divine."

19

JANUARY

Weeks fly by: nights in the tent with a thorn in my side, my stitches healing, the pain fading. I'm able to walk laps around the small tent, getting used to being back on my feet with barely any pain breaking my stride. My legs cramp from days spent in bed, and when I make an attempt to revisit an old stretching routine from ballet class, my side aches, so I leave it be.

Tonight, Marshall's fingers are busy in my hair, brushing out the knots with his hand. He's attempting to braid the short locks when he cracks a question. "I've been keeping an eye on the date," he interlaces my hair tighter, "it's someone's birthday tomorrow, isn't it?"

"I'm surprised you remember. I'd let the date slide if no one were to remind me."

"For your information, I have a calendar, plus that excellent memory of mine." He chortles, and gives up with his braids. "We'll have to celebrate tomorrow."

"If it's too much—"

"Not at all. No one deserves to have their birthday ignored!" He pouts and presses his face into my hair. "And I want the special lover of mine's day to feel special. One full day of freedom and fun to cheer on making it to another year. What more could you ask for?"

"Sounds delightful." His warm exhale plumes across my nape. "Perhaps you'll score another kiss of gratitude."

"I'd like that." He pulls me against him with a chuckle. "I'd like that very much."

"You git! You're desperate!" I turn my head to find him looking at me with a devilish smirk. He's obviously thinking about it, failing to hide the fact when his smirk turns into a coy smile.

"I'm merely suggesting the idea, and I feel bad that I can't get you a gift, so I may as well give you the kiss of a lifetime instead." He speaks slowly, exaggerating his words. His eyes flit to his pocket watch. "We'll save the discussion for a later time. It's late. We have to get our beauty sleep for your big day."

"Come on, I'm only turning nineteen." I settle into bed. He stands up, out of the cot, onto his feet. He shakes out both blankets and sets them over me, dousing the lamp.

With his hand upon the switch, he bends to meet my gaze. "Another year, another step into the big, wide world. Being nineteen seems like years ago to me."

"You're *so* old," I tease as he slips his gloves on.

"*Shh.* If you don't stop talking and go to sleep, I'll become even older before you know it."

"You're horrible." I groan as his silhouette ventures back to my bedside. "Absolutely horrible."

In the dark, his voice rises and falls in amusement. "But you seem to like that type of thing."

"You got me. Of course I do."

"I'll make sure to see you as soon as I can tomorrow morning. I want to be the first to wish you a happy birthday."

"Committed," I remark as he exits. "Goodnight, Marshall."

In the dark, his smile is made of angles, yet soft with care. "Goodnight, Frieda. Happy early birthday."

* * *

The sound of guns grab my attention. I grip my rifle. The ground shakes beneath my feet, and my teeth chatter when the dense, colorless fog sets in over the trenches.

Someone screams. It's a dreadful, high, and strained scream. Too close to a wounded animal.

My feet trot across the creaking wood beneath my heels. No matter how hard I try, I can't stop running, can't stop venturing farther into the fog that grows thicker at every turn. The scream sounds again, and my ears follow it.

I skid to a halt when I reach a fork in the road—more rather in the trenches—with Marshall on his knees. A knife has been wedged into him, blood pooling from the entry wound as he pulls his hands away. They're red with the horrid fluid as he screams for mercy.

Before I can run forward to help him, a hand appears out of the darkness with a pistol cocked at the ready.

Marshall's like a deer in the headlights, screaming at his attacker to not come any closer. I'm frozen to the spot. Stiff, unable to move. I can't move my jaw, can't open my lips to scream at him.

A finger squeezes upon a trigger.

Marshall's screams cease. His body grows stiff. His head throws itself back. He crumples to the floor, dipping fully into his own blood oozing through the floorboards.

Footsteps clunk against the wood, the sound of metal smacking against one's palm as they *tsk* and kick Marshall's corpse out of their path. I want to run. I want to scream. I want to alert someone nearby that Marshall's been shot and stabbed.

Bile threatens to rise in my throat as Andrej steps out of the shadows.

"For a man such as him," his Austrian accent pools around me, carried by the wind, "I didn't think he'd have that much blood. How much would you guess? Six liters? Five? He's not the tallest, so I'm leaning more towards five."

He continues the sick *tap-tap-tap* rhythm of the pistol smacking across his palm. I don't utter a word.

"Why so silent, my dear? Your boy just got shot. Wouldn't you like to scream in anguish at me? Threaten to shoot me with that rifle of yours? I feel terrible, seeing you stand in shock like that."

He takes another step closer, giving Marshall's slumped body another kick. His jaw juts back, eyes staring at me, glassy, mouth open, bottom jaw lolling about. I crack open my lips to scream, but it dies on my tongue as Andrej lines his pistol with my chest, my heart that beats horridly fast.

If the dead can haunt the living in their dreams, his specter has come back to execute his unfinished business.

"I was only jesting," he sneers. "Wouldn't you like to join your mister in the afterlife?"

My mouth finally opens to expel a curse, my arms fixing themselves tighter upon my rifle.

He beats me to it, his fingers squeezing the trigger. "Thought so."

The light has never been so blinding.

* * *

"Good morning, sunshine," a familiar voice whispers in my ear.

I groan and push him away, his cold cheeks squished under my fingers. "No, no good morning."

A noise of discomfort comes from him. His hand closes around my wrist, pulling it away from his face.

"Yes, it's time to rise and face the day."

"No, no time...I don't want to."

Marshall pokes my cheek. He doesn't give up. "C'mon, today's a special day!"

I let out a moan, swatting him away, refusing to open my eyes. "No."

"My dearest, please, just for me?"

I finally agree to open my eyes to see Marshall with his hair drizzled with soft flakes of snow. His eyes meet mine as his smile crinkles at their corners. His mouth then opens to start singing 'Happy Birthday' with clicks of his fingers in time with the beat. I hide back under the covers when he finishes, groaning as his hands peel the warmth away. His laugh is dreadfully loud, and I have to give him the stink eye.

"You knew quite well that I would be here as soon as possible to wish you a happy birthday, no?"

"I didn't expect you to be this early," I grumble. "Your singing isn't that bad, either."

He stifles another laugh. There's something new about him. Something's been replaced, newly installed. "I'm glad. You don't have to be in pain today. The nurses are discharging you. You've finally healed, so there's more we can do on your special day."

I sit up, the pain in my side that used to burn like a hellfire has now dulled and is simply a light ache. If he's just made another innuendo, I don't pick it up or say anything in return.

"Now then, out of bed!" He pulls the blankets back and makes me squeal from the chills immediately hitting my body. As I pull my tunic back over my shoulders and button it tight, he stands with his back facing me to give me some privacy. He rolls his shoulders and whistles a low note.

Yes, something's definitely different about him.

"You're a sergeant now?" I gasp.

"Mmhm." He nods, without turning to look at me. "I'm glad you noticed. The General came earlier this morning to promote me. I had to keep irking Ed to sew the patches on. I wanted to surprise you."

"Haven't you done that enough already?" Once fully dressed, I get a better view of his chevrons and the two stripes that blaze in gold against the earth brown of the patch.

With shaking legs, I creep to take my old place by his side. He flexes his new epaulets with another slow roll of his shoulders. I can't help but snort.

We exit the tent and get slapped in the face by another deathly cold drought. I've never realized how warm the tent was compared to the outside world, and now I feel terribly guilty for the soldiers, having to work through the January snow. It's been awfully quiet for the last few days while a blizzard settled over the battlefield.

My feet freeze with every step of the way to the mess hall. Though it's probably been hours since the last snowfall, the wind blasts across my cheeks and bites at my bare fingers.

There's the repetitive clang of shovels as men dig deeper through the ice. It crackles with each *plink* of their shovel's tip.

Ed catches up, panting as he skids to a stop in front of us.

"I came as fast as I could"—he puffs, bending over, drawing wheezing breaths—"to wish you a happy birthday. I ran to the tent straight after roll call, ran to his tent, and came here to find you."

"I hope we didn't make you run too far." I pat his back as he coughs, covering his mouth. "Are you catching a cold?"

"No, not at all. It was worth the exercise. I'm still in perfectly good health." He cracks a wicked grin. "So, nineteen, huh? Another step into adulthood."

"I guess you can say that."

Ed's smile falters as he turns to Marshall once he recollects himself. "I overheard the General speaking about your brother."

Marshall sighs. "Has he gotten himself into trouble?"

"No, no." Ed shakes his head. "He's being moved to the regiment. Permanently."

Marshall stomps at the floor in disapproval. Even I develop a foul taste on my tongue at the news. My memory of Alistair in the trenches is fuzzy, yet I can still remember his scolding words. They've etched themselves deep into my skin.

"That rat will do anything to undermine me." Marshall glowers.

"Is there ever any resolve between you two?" Ed asks. "The last time you forgave and forgot was when you spilled wine over a white tablecloth."

"That was Alistair, thank you very much."

Ed *hmphs*, placing a hand on his shoulder. "He arrived this morning with the General."

"That vermin. Where is he?"

"The last time I saw him, the *vermin* was setting up his tent a few miles away. You can try to find him at breakfast."

"Like hell I will," Marshall snaps. His eyes stalk the crowd and shift to focus on an emerging figure. "I'll smash his head in!"

"Smash whose head in?" A voice sounds behind us. Marshall freezes. "And here you are, giving me the bad rap when you yourself are the main instigator."

Compared to Marshall, Alistair is way taller; around Ed's height—maybe even taller. His eyes are still capable of piercing through me as he peers at the three of us, clasping Marshall by the shoulder, who snarls up at him.

"Marshall! God, how great it is to see you still here." He looks him in the eye, Marshall glaring. "Congrats on your promotion, by the way."

Marshall's reply is cold. "Thank you."

Alistair searches for another conversation starter, scrambling for words. "Did you get any correspondence from home? Father? Yvette?"

Marshall scoffs. "I thought you'd be getting all the letters, not me, Alistair. Congratulations, by the way. You're finally a father."

"Hah, thanks. You, Brother, are now an uncle."

Marshall's glare ceases, face softening. "Kara, huh? How'd you choose it?"

"What?"

"The name of your daughter. Did you forget, Alistair?"

Alistair dares to smile. Marshall sniffs at the sight of it. "Yvette mailed me. We decided together that if we had a boy, we'd call him Jacob, and if we had a girl, we'd call her Kara."

"And now you have a daughter. I do like the name Kara..." he struggles to deliver the complement, "very much. You chose well."

Alistair edges closer to his brother as Ed whispers to me, "I was expecting them to be at each other's throats by now. I guess not. Perhaps something's changed between them? We'll know soon enough if they plan on tearing each other apart."

Marshall takes a cautious step closer, returning his gaze. They seem to be reconciling, as Alistair pats him on the back and mutters something to him, which his brother nods to in return. As Alistair takes his leave, Marshall slumps his shoulders and watches.

I tap him on the shoulder, making an attempt to link arms. "Are you alright?"

He's gazing down at me with glassy eyes. "Oh, I feel bad about what I said earlier."

"But you've resolved your problem." He wipes his eyes. I squeeze his shoulder. "Didn't you two apologize to each other just now?"

"Yes, and he also told me that we're in an assault together later tonight."

"Is there anyone else?"

"Sam, that's all. We're on the second line for today. Lucky Edward Surry's going to be busy digging even more trenches."

Ed tips his cap back in acknowledgement. "Yes, quite. I'll be placing more barbed wire, too."

"As I've said, lucky." Marshall *tsks* at Ed. "I've been on the third line for three days straight and all he's been doing is help wash clothes and wounds without the worry of getting hurt."

"Watch yourself," Ed warns. "You're not the only one suffering here. I'll be in charge of deploying gas bombs in the trenches."

A spark of shock flares in Marshall's eyes. "That's equal to suicide!"

"Not if you know how to handle them." Ed takes his rations as we're given ours.

"And you're perfectly fine with risking your life just for this?" Marshall gasps. "Eddie...my Eddie...please, I can't let you do that."

"I can't disobey my orders, Marshall."

"*Edward.*" Marshall grabs a hold of him, growing more and more frantic by the second, shaking him as his hands curl into Ed's collar. "You can't do this. Listen to me before you go ahead and kill yourself!"

"Marshall, listen to *me*! All we're doing is planting them, not setting them off. We'll be wearing masks, too. Calm down."

I feel helpless watching them fight. Unsure of what to do, I raise my voice. "Marshall, let's do that breathing exercise you and I have been doing together, yes?"

"I'll be back before you know it, Marshall. Yes, let's take a breather. Good idea, Frieda."

Marshall is shaking his head rapidly from side to side, rejecting each of our offers. His grip grows tighter on Ed, shaking him harshly. "Listen to me! Please don't do it!"

Ed brings Marshall into a close embrace, his friend breaking down in his arms. I have to look away as Ed mutters, "All I'm doing, Marshall, is planting the bombs where they're required. They're sending another group of men to set them off, men more experienced than I am. I'm not going anywhere you can't reach me. I'll be back before you know it."

Marshall flinches, but holds his gaze, his eyes full of fear for what's yet to come.

"Promise me," he begs. "Promise me you'll come back."

"I promise." Ed pinches his cheek lightly. "I promise."

* * *

I glance at my surroundings—clouds up ahead, smoke rising in tendrils—as I screw my eyes up against the wind.

As always, the trenches stretch for miles on end in diagonal lines that branch out like the roots of a tree: all sharp angles, still in the works, yet still so far from being complete.

Beside me, Marshall is shaking all over, staring at the ground. When I pull an arm over his shoulder and bring him close, he doesn't look up as his grip on his gun tightens. He's lost in thought, the light in his eyes distant. He's worrying about Ed, whether he wants to admit it or not.

Once the whistle blows, he doesn't crash back into reality like he always does.

"Marshall, speak to me." I move my hand from his shoulder to his back, rubbing small, assuring circles into him.

"I'm scared." His voice cracks as he answers. "I'm scared for Ed."

I flinch from the explosions. "I know."

At the sound of something hurtling through the air, he snaps back to life and pushes himself forward to grab and knock me to the floor. With his hand braced behind my head, I'm wide-eyed, frozen in shock as he gets up to check if I'm uninjured. Now his eyes are full of emotion, a tidal wave of feelings that I can't decipher.

"Bombs." He helps me up, trembling, as he fixes his metal cap. "Shrapnel."

His hands retreat to his gun, holding it tight to his chest as he shakes with each quake of the earth, each flash and bang.

As I get up, I take my own gun and crouch beside him, nudging him lightly. "I don't think we'll be going anywhere tonight."

Marshall forces out a cold laugh. "What a way to spend your birthday, huh? Next to a broken man in a trench."

"Honestly, I couldn't care less. I don't feel any different."

When another explosion hits, I jump into his arms, letting him steady me. His hand goes to the small of my back as I bury my head into his chest, under his coat lapels, against the cursed shriek of the whistle, sending another wave over the lines.

"I don't want to go over. I don't want to die." I hold him tighter, his scent of coffee long gone, overtaken by dirt and mud.

Tears pick at the back of my eyes, stinging at their corners as he straightens the straps of my helmet, pushing back strands of escaping hair. He lets go of me to reload his rifle, turning the safety off. His grip upon it is tight, yet handling the gun with care. "They haven't given us any instructions, so I doubt we'll be going over."

Shrapnel spits over the lips of the trench. Everyone around us ducks to take cover. My head throbs from the noise reverberating off the walls like the drumming of a chaotic marching band. It's enough for me to groan in irritation and raise my fingertips to my temple.

"Why did they even put us here in the first place?" I yell over the gunfire and screams.

"In case one of the men on the front line is gravely injured. They send one of us to take over, like a substitute." He pats his shirtfront down, free of dirt. "We're mostly a support line."

I shiver. It's not just the front line waiting to die, but us, too.

Marshall yelps as something strikes him. His right hand is oozing blood slowly out of a fresh wound. He's quick to curse and dig through his webbings for his first aid kit, grabbing strips of gauze to staunch the bleeding, wrapping the bandaging around his hand before he returns his grip upon his rifle.

"Shrapnel." His voice is accentuated with pain. "We should find one of those burrows that the other soldiers dug out and hide in there for a while."

With another whistle of bombs blasting into the dirt and the droning of the occurring air combat in the overcast sky, I snatch his hand as we push our way through the trench. He uses mainly his shoulders to carve a path, barking at other brown tunics and metal helmets to clear away for us. Sometimes the butt of his rifle stabs a few men in the back.

He catches me off guard when he abruptly halts in the middle of the path. He points silently, shoving his rifle inside, climbing in himself. He's a mess of limbs before he works his body into a corner, crouching with his knees drawn to his chest. I myself can squeeze in with less difficulty, pressing more fingertips against my pulsing temple. The pain has gotten worse as the battle rages on ahead.

His eyes train themselves on me and my pained expression, chewing at his bottom lip. "What's wrong?"

"Headache." I struggle to become louder than the bombs and bullets as the pain increases.

I try to steady my breathing that's picked up the pace in my lungs, but I cough instead. My throat becomes scratchy as I start choking, choking on my own air and spit. My breathing is shortened as my vision starts to blur at the corners. I keep trying to breathe, but it gets harder and harder with each inhale.

Forceful hands go over my face, making me scream until I find his eyes behind a gas mask looking straight at me as I gain my breath back.

That's when I see it.

A cloud of colorless gas that bears a close resemblance to smoke clouds around us. Little pinpricks of unstoppable pain poke at my skin like millions of tiny needles. Marshall grows stiff beside me, frozen in place. I start to think he's passed out until I hear him cry out, "Edward! They set off the gas bombs! He lied to me!"

"You can't see him now!"

"I have to!" he shouts and stands, sprinting through the trenches, only to face the swarming gas and the men dying in its wake, those unlucky enough not to have a mask on their person, to suffer. He halts, stranded, looking for a way out.

I stop not too far behind him and grip his wrist. "Didn't they say they were setting them off at midnight? Look, the moon hasn't even reached its peak!"

"You're saying that this wasn't us?"

"I'm not sure." I squeeze his wrist. "We'll find him. He'll turn up sooner or later."

A scream rings through the trenches.

Marshall's quick to dart towards the sound, leaping over corpses of the fallen, risking his life to bolt through a passing gas cloud like a madman; a bull hurtling at full speed ahead to a red flag.

I follow close behind with more awareness of my surroundings. I find Sam: the owner of the scream.

A familiar figure lies cold on the ground.

Marshall's mouth opens to form a loud, shrill scream to match Sam's.

It doesn't take me long to recognize the long black hair, the wedding ring on his finger.

Edward Surry has been knocked out cold, his face covered in blood, features barely recognizable.

"We have to get him to the nearest tent as soon as possible." Sam beckons Marshall forward. "Grab his legs. I'll take his arms."

With little to no hesitation, Marshall and Sam heave Ed up and off the ground, leaving me to helplessly follow behind as they make sure not to drop their comrade. My breath keeps catching in my throat. Either from the sight of Ed, or the gas that's been released.

It's a slow and enduring process to get Ed into one of the hospital beds, Marshall whipping his mask off and checking Ed's pulse while the nurses race into action and tug him away. He's relieved when he finds it, but is only let down by a slow and soft drumbeat. He's trying not to cry, trying not to let his emotions get the best of him, but fails miserably as the first of his tears choke him and leak out.

Ed's face is now horribly discolored. His nose is far too puffy and unnatural. His left eye is swollen and clouded; blind, by the look of it. A wide gash on the side of his head shapes a crudely arched scar. It's hard to remember the handsome man who smiled behind those eyes: one blue, one brown. Innocent and caring.

Marshall's lips move uncontrollably fast, his words whispered as he takes one of Ed's limp hands in his while the nurses inspect his wounds, bandaging up his face and leaving him to rest. Marshall stays by his side, fingers interlocked with Ed's.

I want to reach out for him, but I decide to leave him as he rests his head on Ed's heart, listening to it, muttering inaudible words under his breath as he stares into space, his eyes distant as they stare past me, unblinking and dazed. He's counting heartbeats. Each rise and fall of his chest.

"I can't imagine what he's feeling right now," George whispers in my ear. "He's known him for so long that they're practically brothers."

Ed stirs, his voice hoarse. "My face...It's on fire..." His speech is slightly impaired, as his bottom lip has many wounds across it, inflamed, burdening him with a lisp.

Marshall shoots upright, daring to look him right in the eye to take him in: still alive, still in this world. "Edward Alfred Surry, tell me what the hell happened with you and the gas. They weren't supposed to set them off until midnight!"

Ed hisses, his voice gratingly low, "They weren't our gas bombs! The Germans threw them over their trenches into ours!"

Marshall winces as Ed spits, coughing his lungs out. "How're you feeling?"

"Can't you see what happened to me?" Ed squawks.

"Indeed." Marshall digs a hole in the floor with his eyes, breathing out an uneven sigh. "I'm just glad you're alive."

"I'd rather die than be like this. My face is on fire. Is there any morphine around here?"

"I don't think so. I'm sorry."

Ed howls. Marshall creeps away as he does so. His legs thrash under the sheets in retaliation to the agony of his wounds. I retreat into a corner at the sudden noise.

Marshall's hand goes to Ed's hair, stroking the black locks, running his fingers through them, shushing him. "Easy, Ed, easy." His voice is a soothing murmur. "If you move so much, it'll make it worse. Sleep."

Ed protests, "Sure, while my face burns off!"

"You'll recover faster if you sleep, Eddie," Marshall reassures him. "It'll give you the slightest bit of liberation from the pain for a little while, too."

"What I need is some damn morphine," Ed grunts. "Then I can sleep and forget that I'm slowly dying at this very moment."

20

DEPARTURE

Outside the tent, I wait for the bickering to die down as I dig into the snow with the toe of my boot absentmindedly. They've been in there for God knows how long. There's occasional thumps and bangs of Ed's struggles, scuffles, and screams, his chants of 'please stop' and 'you're hurting me.' It's all so terrifying to listen to. I have to cover my ears to suppress the sound.

Marshall ventures out quietly, hands covered in blood. He washes them in a nearby trough, staining the water red. "They've knocked him out with a sedative. He started screaming at the nurses to give him morphine. He'll be out for quite some time."

"So I heard. The walls are thin here."

He folds his arms as he stands, stiff beside me, defending himself from the cold. He's shaken, pale, exhausted. The circles under his eyes are darker now compared to just hours before: deep, dark craters against his ghastly complexion. I move his hair out of his eyes, his lashes fluttering in response.

"You should rest," I say. "You're a sergeant now. You can't function while running on little to no steam."

He releases a vaguely amused giggle. "You don't think I'm already lacking steam?"

"I'm serious." I hold my gaze on his face, him looking away as it digs past his mask of bravery.

"I have to look after Ed."

"No, the nurses will. He's in the best of hands now."

"He's been my closest friend for nearly all my life. Please," he sharply blinks back tears, "I need to be beside him." His eyes flicker with hope when I don't say anything in return. "Please, my darling, just until he falls asleep?"

"And you're not?" I argue.

"I will. I swear it to you."

"How do I know you're not lying to me?"

"I promise you, I'm not."

As we step inside the tent together after a long while of protests and reasons, Ed is grumbling away at Sam as he lies in bed.

Marshall takes a bottle and a spoon from his bedside. "Ed, the nurse told me to give you your medicine now."

Ed only glares when I sit down. He truly does look like he's suffering.

"Feeling any better?" I ask him.

He scowls. "Not really. Everything hurts to no end. I doubt the medicine Marsh has there will do any good."

"This will help. I'm sure of it." Marshall pours the clear liquid into a spoon, his hands careful not to spill any. "It may not be morphine, but it's a painkiller."

"That looks revolting. Don't you give that to me," Ed snaps.

"I know you hate taking medicine, but this is the only way you'll feel better."

He gestures wildly at Marshall's spoon. "I'm not taking that crap!"

He simply sighs. "Sam, please hold him down."

Ed snarls as Sam hurriedly holds down his limbs and pushes his head back. "Gah! Get off of me, won't you?"

Marshall puts the spoon in Ed's mouth, forcing his jaw shut, delicately urging him to swallow as he coughs and gags. Their eyes lock, and Ed's throat bobs with a swallow before Marshall releases him and hurriedly hands him his canteen.

Chugging its contents, Ed spits, "Thanks, the both of you. That was probably one of the most disgusting things I've ever tasted in my life!"

"It'll kick in soon," Marshall says, and sits next to me, rubbing his eyes. Sam sits on the other wooden chair—the creaky one—closest to Ed, who's yapping away at how disgusting the medicine tasted.

Marshall lays his head back and sighs while he closes his eyes. He's tired, nodding off to sleep.

The radio blasts with a news jingle. Sam turns the volume up, paying attention to the reporter's voice.

"Previously at the Western Front—"

Marshall's eyes snap open.

We both listen closely.

"The Central Powers have a new casualty rate: a new tally of 3,003,300." Marshall clears his throat, acknowledging the news. I lean forward in my chair. "The United Armies are steaming to triumph out there. A casualty rate of 4,000,050 rises along with the boys in the trenches. Brave heroes donating their lives for the greater good."

Against the radio, Marshall is resting his chin in his hand, eyes closed. I brush the hair out of his eyes as the outro of the newsflash plays. He remains half asleep, shoulders slumping.

"Yeah, right. *Donating*," he comments. "We were forced here, you goon."

"Marshall's conked out," Sam observes. "Look at him. Poor man's tired out of his mind."

"No I'm not," Marshall objects.

"I told you to rest," I whisper.

He opens one tired eye and whispers back, "Not until Ed falls asleep."

"*Please.*"

"I said I would, not until Ed falls asleep. I need to make sure he's okay."

Ed sits up in bed. "I'm right here, and I'm perfectly fine. I'd be better if everything didn't hurt at this moment."

"The medicine will kick in, Ed…" Marshall yawns, fighting sleep. "You'll feel better soon."

"No matter how many times you say that, I just won't believe you," Ed retorts.

Marshall clearly isn't in the mood, or doesn't have enough energy to argue back. He groans, his face in his hands.

"I told you to rest, Marshall," I nag.

"Again: Not until Ed falls asleep."

"Marshall, look at him. He will, soon. He's about to nod off," Sam says.

When I look up, Ed's eyes flutter shut as he turns away, his back facing us.

Marshall heaves himself up and out of his chair. I follow, him tripping on his own two feet when he stands. When he turns back to look at me, he asks quietly, "What're you doing?"

"You were about to fall and hit your head. Please, Marshall, go to sleep."

He leans down to whisper in my ear, his voice low and secretive, "I need to talk to you. Meet me outside in five minutes."

"What're you whispering about?" Sam asks.

"I was just saying goodnight. You know how people do it, how do couples act like they're married? Giving their partner a kiss on the cheek?"

Sam's brows furrow. "But you aren't…married?"

Marshall winks. "Yet."

My heart thuds in my chest. My brain goes haywire as my thoughts flood my head.

Something's happening. I don't know what it is, but it's happening.

As Marshall exits, I wait five minutes before dismissing myself, my heart thudding louder and louder.

I find him sitting on an abandoned fencepost, looking out at the night sky.

"Beautiful out tonight, isn't it?" Marshall rests his hands on his knees, swooning up at the stars. "If I were at home, I'd be reading by candlelight."

I skip the pleasantries and interrogate bluntly, "What're you getting at, Clark?"

Marshall's face is shadowed, only some of the lamplight gliding over his cheekbones. "I said I needed to talk to you."

"But you also wanted to look after Ed."

"He's asleep." Marshall shields his eyes from the piercing wind that blows our way. "I'm about to sleep too, but I need to talk to you. Urgently."

"About what, exactly? You're being so vague."

Something changes in him. His fingers tap against his thigh relentlessly.

"Frieda, please sit down."

My heart rate only increases. I start catastrophizing. The tinny and painful voice inside my head chirps happily.

He's going to leave you.

He doesn't love you anymore.

What if he didn't love you in the first place?

Not moving to sit, I can't stop myself from blurting, "You're leaving me, aren't you? You don't want anything to do with me anymore."

"Frieda, no." He steps in front of me, off the fencepost, and so close that the faded freckles of many summers ago are clear on his cheeks. They make me self conscious of mine, which are still so very bold. "I don't know how to break this to you, but listen. This may be the last time we'll see each other."

"What do you mean?" My legs shake. My hand reaches to grab hold of him, but it flops back to my side before my fingertips can even brush him. "You're leaving me, Marshall, just say it. You're—"

"This wasn't my choice." He's the one to grab me. "I've been appointed to a position in Italy on the Southern Front for a little while, until May. What I'm saying is this might be the last time we see each other, if anything happens."

I'm growing lightheaded. "Till May?"

"Yes, till May."

"But...why?"

"They need help with the new regiment...for a while, to get it onto its feet."

"When do you leave?" My eyes search him. He's doing the same.

"In two days," he answers. "Two days."

"You could've said no." I look into his eyes, but he's beaten me to it. "You could've rejected the offer."

"It wasn't an offer." The wind whips at his hair. "It was a direct order from Sallinger."

He takes a step forward, his hands around my wrists. "Frieda, please, deep breaths. I'll try to be back before my birthday, okay? I'll try."

I had completely forgotten his birthday was on May twenty-first. Not that it matters now.

He takes another step forward, his fingers growing tighter. Tears don't fall...yet.

I can't bring myself to look at him anymore.

"Frieda, I'm so sorry—"

"Don't apologize to me when it isn't even your fault!" I bare my teeth. Marshall flinches. "There's no point."

"I was going to apologize for making you so distressed!" His hands go from my wrists to my cheeks, his bandages scratching against my skin. His eyes are blazing like a forest fire in the dark, glistening and watery with his own tears that threaten to fall when they're needed. I'm left speechless. "I'm so sorry. If I didn't tell you, you'd find out another way and be more distressed than you should be."

"You're going to leave me. Just like my mother. Just like my father."

"I never said I'd be leaving you. I can still write to you. How does that sound?"

"But you are. You're leaving." I dismiss his attempts at calming me down. "It doesn't matter if you're going to write to me or not. You're leaving Belgium. Leaving *me.*"

"I'll be back. Again, I can write to you."

"Not if anything there kills you," I snarl.

"I'll be careful. I don't think they'll send me over. I'll probably be one of the personnel blowing the whistle."

"*Be careful,*" I mimic, in a high-pitched whine. "They can still send you over."

"If they do, I'll injure myself and go home. You'll see me there."

"No. There's still a high chance you'll die!"

Marshall doesn't look the slightest bit fazed. He closes his eyes, bringing his forehead to mine. Warm air spreads across my face against the cold. He's so close, but so far all at the same time. "I'll be careful. I'll try to stay strong. Frieda, come to my tent for the night. Just for tonight."

I take a step away from his clutches and observe his face: the beautiful man that I can call my own every single day.

His eyes are burning into mine, the ones that trap me with their stare every time.

Lips, quaking with fear, the same ones that could plant as many kisses as he can supply.

Arms that shake against his frame, that could hold me from dawn till dusk.

Shoulders, squared and waiting to carry more of our troubles.

His throat bobs, awaiting an answer. "*Frieda.*"

I can't, for the life of me, find any way to hate him. He's caught himself in the eye of the hurricane.

Hurricanes, like wars, are unforgiving. They take away the things we love. They divide us over their sirens. Their havoc wrecks our small wooden houses of emotions.

I take him all in, and when he leans in, I don't comply. He's already done enough damage. I don't need my heart broken more than it already is.

"I'm sorry, Marshall. I can't come with you."

He blinks once, then pecks a quick kiss on my lips. "That's fine. I understand."

"You'll be okay?"

"I'll try to be." He bows his head, ashamed. "I'll miss you."

"I'll miss you too." I want to throw my arms around him so bad, envelope him into a familiar embrace, but I don't. I can't. "I have to sleep. I'm on watch first thing tomorrow."

His eyes are still blazing, hands trembling as they curl in on themselves. He forces the words out, dismayed. "I see. Goodnight, Frieda."

"Goodnight, Marshall." I get one last look at him, letting myself, for one second, reach for his face before setting my hand down. He yields under my touch.

"I love you," I breathe.

His mouth twitches momentarily, letting the words sink in and smooth his features. His smile is bittersweet as he takes a step back, his parting words ringing loud and clear.

"I love you too."

* * *

The next day is just as dull as the last.

At the first hour of dawn, I slump against a fallen tree, drenched in my own tears that soaked my eyes all through the night. It was too much to bottle up the feelings, the anxieties that lurked behind my eyelids once they closed.

Upon turning away from him, I immediately regretted my choice, but didn't have the strength to turn back and see his face light up just hours before his departure. Not after all that had happened just moments before that sent us crashing down.

Marshall probably hasn't woken up yet, as it's still too early for roll call. Though he wakes an hour earlier, I don't think it's his time just yet. After last night, I guess he'd be sleeping in, escaping his fate.

My mind, as much as it hurts, keeps running back to him. Would he have cried, too? How long did he keep himself awake with his thoughts? Did he attempt anything dangerous during the night?

I'd never forgive myself if anything happened to him. Despite his strong mind, he's weak at heart; a sensitive boy. Sometimes the heart takes the controls and makes us make foolish choices, makes us do horrible things that tell us they'll take the pain away.

It's your fault you didn't go back with him. It'll be your fault if he attempts anything.

The thoughts sting. I flinch as if it's a physical wound.

With a sigh, I brace my rifle against my legs, staring at the sky, trying not to doze off. The morning bugle blows, signaling for everyone to rise and start the day. It's agonizingly loud and leaves a nasty ringing in my ears. I stand, knowing I won't be able to see anything from here. He won't see me until later, where I have to work on the third line to help build the trenches. They've been going at it for months and still haven't covered much ground.

There's the distant yelping of commands as the names are called. The roll call station isn't that far from where I'm positioned.

"Sergeant Clark, 21786!"

"Sir!" His voice snaps a wire inside me, makes me jump, as he replies. He still sounds tired, voice cracking, not fully warmed up in the early morning.

"Corporal Surry, 21787!"

"Injured, sir!" he yelps once more, an eerie silence following the echo. I don't expect him to want to get a reaction.

As they're dismissed, my body starts to ache. My eyelids droop. I got two hours last night, wishing that I could gather more if I hadn't kept tossing and turning, trying not to wake the whole regiment by pacing around the fire and kicking rocks, snapping any twig I could find to let out my anger.

I'm not angry at him, but at Sallinger. He knows perfectly well that Marshall's only recently been promoted, yet he sends him to a place far away from the land he knows and expects him to obey.

It hurts, not being able to rush over to him. As much as I'd like to, I can't. I suppress the thoughts to just run out of this trench and into his arms, but that would be risking a bullet or blow that I don't want to endure.

The hours go relentlessly fast, and the major lets us go.

My quest to find him begins.

Alistair is busy digging on the third line this morning. The group of men they sent out to work have been here since six, working nonstop, digging until their arms detach. When I walk past, he waves, his face dusted with soot and grit, remnants of the ground below flying up when he digs.

As I make my way to the medic tent, Ed's struck up yet another argument.

"Shut up! It's not like it's the end of the world, Marshall. It's just facial hair!"

"I hate it!" he complains as he observes himself and his stubble in the mirror. "I like my face clean!"

"I understand that," Sam says, "but it won't hurt you."

"But it scratches like—"

"Marshall, look. If it's there, it's there. You can't help it," Ed snaps. "You don't desperately need to shave at this moment. Maybe you can grow a beard. How do mutton chops sound?"

"Hell no. How could you suggest such an outlandish idea?"

"It's the time for a change, so why not go for it? It would look wicked with your cheekbones."

"Absolutely not!" Marshall takes none of Ed's teases and points to his dark stubble. Not even much has grown. "You see this? I want it gone as soon as I can get it off."

"Take the mutton chops into consideration!" Ed teases.

"Heavens no!" Marshall groans. "I'd look simply appalling!"

When I round the corner, the yelling dies. I catch him sitting back in the chair near Ed's bed with a hand over his chin, analyzing his stubble and muttering strings of curse words under his breath as Ed is given his medicine, coughing at the taste.

"Good morning," I mumble, his head turning at the sound of my voice. There's shadows of many missed meals hollowing out his cheeks. On all of them, their uniforms hang like a jacket on a clothing hanger: limp and lifeless. I start to feel thinner myself every day, my limbs aching with every move. We become more and more skeletal from day to day.

"G'morning," he replies, not standing to embrace me. I don't blame him. He looks like he's going to fall as soon as he stands, but he manages to crack a small smile. His words sting like a papercut. "You slept well?"

Unable to think of a lie, I shrug, sitting next to him in silence.

I can feel his stare as he watches me. He gets the cue that I don't feel like talking all that much, but he still briefly rests his hand on my knee.

I'm still here. He communicates with his fingers that lightly squeeze my knee.

When they leave, when no one's looking, I grip his hand tight, him jumping at my touch. He's staring straight ahead, squeezing my hand. It's a silent affair, none of us talking as Sam feeds Ed a second dose of his medicine. His gags are loud, but neither of us flinch.

"Marshall, have you packed everything you need?" Sam asks.

His head dips, his eyes downcast, distant. "Yes."

Even in his voice, it's clear he doesn't want to leave. He may put up a brave act for Sallinger, but just looking at him, he's more than just reluctant to go.

"What time are you leaving tomorrow?"

"Dawn." His reply is stale, his hand falling away from mine.

When the tent flaps open, Alistair appears.

"Good God. Soon enough, the whole Clark family will be in here," Ed grunts.

Marshall stands at the sight of his brother. The coldness previously shared between them is forgotten, but some tension still remains. His shoulders shake as Alistair's eyes lock with his; blue into hazel. "I heard you were leaving."

"Just now?" Marshall's voice lacks any sort of animation.

"I was on the front line for a week, Marshall. Do you expect me to hear anything there?"

Marshall lets out a tired sigh. "No."

Alistair takes a step forward to embrace his brother. Marshall shrinks in his arms. "When will you be back?"

"Around May," he mumbles.

"Your birthday, hm?"

"It doesn't feel like that anymore. I'm just going to be twenty-one and that's the end of it. I'll see the same trenches and the same people for years on end."

"We'll be here together," Alistair says. Marshall buries himself deeper into his chest. In the trenches, he's a brave and strong young man. In his brother's arms, he's just a fragile little boy. "When I see you in May, I'll try to spend as much time as I can with you. Edith is coming to the Front soon. We'll all be together again."

"I don't *want* that." Marshall shudders. "I want to go home."

"Many people do." Alistair buries his face in his brother's hair. "I want to see Kara, Yvette, and the rest of the family. I want to see Father again, I want to see you graduate from college and get a job, settle down and have a family like me with whoever you choose. I want to see Edith do the same when she grows older. I want to be an uncle."

"That won't happen."

"I predict it will. You're always too pessimistic." Alistair grins. "Just like Mother."

Something snaps in Marshall as his shoulders stiffen. Alistair senses it immediately, rubbing his back in small circles. "I shouldn't have said that."

"I'd rather be with her than down here in this filth."

"No, you wouldn't. Think about how all of us would feel if you were gone."

"You wouldn't care. You never did when we were back home."

"Didn't I? You don't remember when I carried you up to bed after you fell asleep on the couch in the library, exhausted from studying? You don't remember when I gave you food in your room when you couldn't get out of bed all day because of how hard you cried, and for how long you stayed up to the point where you'd pass out from just standing up? I heard you sobbing through the walls. I felt heartbroken not knowing what to do."

My chair scrapes across the floor as I stand. "Alistair—"

"Don't, Frieda," Marshall cuts me off sharply.

"Do you need time?" I ask.

"I think so. Thank you, Frieda," Alistair says.

I jump at the sound of a sudden scream. Marshall's wailing into Alistair's chest. His hands go to his hair, hushing him. Part of me wants to run over and envelope him in my arms, anything to stop the pained whimpers and moans escaping his lips. Alistair doesn't budge, holding him against his chest, staring at the floor with a face as blank as unused parchment. He's unsure of what to do, frozen as Marshall lets his terror run free.

When he quietens, he grabs hold of Alistair's collar, his knuckles digging into it as he hyperventilates. "I don't want to go, Ali."

"I know you don't, but you have to."

He removes his hand from Alistair's collar, shaking and stepping away, wiping his eyes with the heels of his palms. I put a hand on his shoulder as he hides his face from me, which I know is tearstained and puffy. "Marshall, please, sit down."

"Frieda—"

"You're swaying. Sit down."

Hesitantly, he sits, burying his face in his hands as Sallinger steps into the tent.

"Good morning, everyone." He waves as everyone stays silent. The tension around us is so thick that you'd have to cut through it with a knife to be rid of it. "I'm after Sergeant Clark. The Major has made a request that you leave this instant for Italy."

"R-right now?" Marshall looks up, eyes wide, face contorted horribly. "He said that I didn't have to leave until tomorrow!"

"Yes, but he had gotten contact from the navy via telegraph that there'd be a storm tomorrow at dawn. It wouldn't be advised to travel during that time."

Marshall's eyes shadow over, his hands turning into tight fists as he snarls. This is the first time I ever hear him talk back to a higher up, breaking his bond of obedience. "I'd rather drown."

Sallinger doesn't budge, doesn't show any sign of offense. "Come with me, Sergeant. Take your things. Your boat is waiting."

Defeated and deflated, he stands. When he takes his first few steps forward, I step in front of him.

"Lieutenant Colonel," I hold my gaze, Sallinger's brow twitching with a hint of faint annoyance, "could I possibly talk to Sergeant Clark before he departs?"

"Make it quick. The boats won't wait long."

I take Marshall by the hand behind the tent. My name is all he can say before I interrupt him. "I need to talk to you before you leave. I was going to say it later tonight, but I need to say it now."

"Whatever you need to say, let it out." His eyes remain red and puffy around the edges. He dares not to look at me.

I take both of his hands. "I'm going to miss you so much."

"I'm not doing much. Just conducting drills and blowing whistles."

"Yes, but I'm going to miss you."

He hesitantly lets go of one of my hands and lays a cold palm against my cheek, stroking it with his thumb. "I'll miss you too. Really, I will. You're the thing that's keeping me going through all of this."

"I hope that isn't bad."

"It's the best thing that's ever happened to me."

"Please Marshall," I sob, "don't forget me."

Marshall only huffs. A sad smile spreads across his lips. "How could I ever forget my pride and joy?"

I wipe my glassy eyes, his thumb hovering over my lips, taking all of me in. The hurt in his eyes is starting to reflect in mine as I place a hand on his wrist, his pulse thumping in his veins.

He's still here with me, but not for long.

The words choke themselves out. "Stay alive for me."

His lips part, struggling for something to say in return. He turns over the words, cogs whirring inside his brain. But he comes up with nothing.

"I'll try," are the only words he can muster. "I'll try."

His hand slides down to cup my chin, tilting it back tenderly so that our eyes meet. He's leaning in, eyes weeping and ferocious. He's getting closer, so close that if I were to look up, I'd knock him in the nose.

He holds me like that for only a few seconds before asking quietly, "Can I kiss you?"

I'm hesitant to answer, his teeth biting the inside of his cheek nervously.

I consider my choices. If I don't kiss him now, I may never get the chance again, but it would be an easier goodbye. If I do, I might just never let go.

Instead, I wrap my arms around his waist and pull him close. The words come in a weak whimper. "Hold me."

He pauses before reaching to wrap me closer, his chin resting atop my head. "Alright. This is better for us, anyways."

"What do you mean?"

"If I were to kiss you, I might just have to take you with me."

"I'd like that."

"Oh, you wouldn't. You would regret it."

"If I ever got the chance to walk hand in hand to Hell with you, I wouldn't regret one bit of it."

We start swaying, holding each other a little longer before his grip loosens. He swallows audibly. "I'm sorry. I have to go."

"Of course." I let go of him as he steps back. "Safe travels, I guess. I'll see you in May?"

"Yes," he reaches to latch a quick kiss to my forehead, "in May."

"And now you're leaving."

He squeezes my hand one last time, offering me his bravest smile. "Why would you say I'm leaving when I'm never truly gone?" I close my eyes as his hand leaves mine, a final whisper reaching my ears. "Please stay safe. Be brave for me. We'll meet again soon."

I nod, a little too sure, against the sound of his boots crunching in the snow. His steps grow quieter, farther away, as he widens the distance between us.

I don't open my eyes. I don't want to see him leave. Don't want the horrid scene of my protector departing from my side engraved into my mind.

His footsteps become quieter and quieter. His confident trample has turned into a reluctant mope. His smile has faded, turning into an awful scowl that worries at the corners of his mouth.

He's no longer my Marshall Clark, but a stranger, a horrible, dark side of himself that eats and feasts on his lively shell.

He's no longer my sweet boy with a cherished, luscious, and heartbreaking smile, now a decomposed corpse of who he used to be, somebody I used to know.

I mumble one last 'I love you' into the wind, hoping that the last of his light is still there to answer back.

There's no reply. Only silence and the echoing crack of two broken hearts.

He's already gone.

21

GONE

I stumble back to my tent. I don't want to see him leave, leave Belgium, leave me. It would hurt far too much, giving me more grief than I can handle.

I brush away some stray strands of hair and take in a deep gulp of air to steady myself. It's strange how your life can turn upside down as soon as something that gravitates you spins out of orbit.

As I lie down, I grow faint, clutching my lapels, tearing at my clothes to get the pain that stabs me repeatedly in the chest to go away. It gets harder to breathe as the tent grows out of focus, as I blink back tears. I want to tear my hair out. I slam my canteen against the ground, the metal thumping against the earth as I let out a scream I didn't know was inside of me.

Someone comes crashing in. Fey booms over my screaming, "Frieda—Corporal Joyce—what's—are you alright?"

"Fey, we need your help with the stretchers. The men that keep coming in won't stop coughing and falling over their own feet," an unfamiliar voice says. One that I don't care about at this very moment. "Please don't tell me Corporal Joyce has fallen ill as well."

"I don't know! I just heard her scream!" she shouts back.

"He's gone." I grab Fey by the shoulders, looking her in the eyes. "Fey, he's gone—"

It's not hard to miss her perplexion. It's written all over her face, the quizzical arch of her brow. "Who's gone?"

"Marshall!" I shout. "He's gone to Italy—"

"Hold on," the voice says again, "Marshall who?"

"Marshall. Sergeant—"

"Slow down." Fey splays a hand across my back as I sob. "Who's gone?"

"Sergeant Marshall Clark. He left for Italy and won't be back until May…"

"Damn, Marshall," the voice speaks again. And from what I can see, this nurse has black hair and blue eyes. "He promised me he'd be here. Turns out, he isn't. Do you know of Alistair Clark?"

"Y-yes! That's his—"

"Brother, yes. Our brother."

This stops me dead in my tracks. My hands dig into the grass and pull it up by its roots. The nurse has folded her arms as she frowns at me.

"E-Edith?" I stammer.

"How do you know of my brothers, Joyce?" She glares, placing her hands haughtily on her wide hips. "How do you know my name?"

"Marshall...He's—he's my"—I gulp, swallowing—"my partner. He wrote about you in the letters! He kept telling me all about you and how nervous he was to see you!"

She's rendered into silence, bringing a hand to her lips as the hostility on her face vanishes. A sheen gleams in her already-bright eyes. "He never told me he's been dating a Corporal. Where did he go?"

"Italy. The Italian Front. He mentioned you from time to time. You were a nurse in training."

"No, just a volunteer worker." She bends down to get to my level. "You really are Frank Joyce's youngster. You look just like him."

"Please go. Get back to work," I grit out as she reaches to cup my face delicately, wiping my eyes with a kerchief.

To my dismay, Edith sends Fey away. As she leaves, Edith Clark now sits beside me on the ground. Awkward silence hangs in the air as she leans farther forward to observe me.

"So, you're here, huh? Frieda, was it? How come you aren't back home or a nurse?"

"I don't want to talk about it," I mumble.

"Fine, but your name was Frieda?"

"Yes."

"I remember you vaguely. Very vaguely. You and your father used to come from Seattle to see us. I'm honestly surprised you found love in my brother." She chuckles, as if her own remark amuses her. "He's usually a very closed-off person."

"You'd be surprised."

She plays with her hair between her fingers, grinning. "Tell me, what's he like?"

"You should know. You're his sister, aren't you?"

"I really didn't see him settling down with anyone. I half-expected him to live a life of loneliness and singularity." I'm silent as she presses forward. "I'm sorry, was I too bold?"

"No." She smooths my hair out of my face while I take note of the peculiar thumbs that she shares with Marshall; clubbed, short little knobs. "He—your brother...he's kind, very kind. He's quite satirical when it comes to humor. Not to mention, he's plain handsome."

Edith snorts. "That's what everyone says about my brother. He's a handsome devil. His looks bewitch everyone. So, why did he go to Italy?"

"He's helping out with ordering the new platoon that's coming in, plus blowing whistles on the front lines."

"With the flu flying around? He'll flip when he hears about it. He hates getting sick."

"The flu?"

"They believe a strain of the flu is going around. It's reached the trenches here and in Italy. It's a widespread pandemic as of now. It's most likely that everyone here will catch it one way or another due to all the close contact we have in the trenches and their vile conditions."

"Darn, it can't be that bad."

"It is, I'm afraid." She plucks a long blade of grass and starts tying knots in it. "People are dying from it."

Right. Marshall will definitely freak out.

"We'll probably never live to see the end," she says, being far too pessimistic for my liking. Another trait she shares with her brother is that over dramatic flare that caused me to cackle far too many times.

"We will. We will survive this," I say as she shifts and smooths her skirt.

She's sitting close beside me with her hands folded neatly in her lap before she starts to fidget. "I just want to go home to Philadelphia where it's safe."

"I would say that I would like to go back to Seattle, but no. I don't."

"Why not?" she asks.

I hesitate before answering, "My mother hates me. She despises my guts and I can't understand why. Because I'm her late husband's kid, she says sometimes. I still haven't got a clue. After my father died, she remarried while I was away at the training camps."

"Can't you live with your aunt? Your uncle?"

"I've gotten a few letters in the mail from my relatives saying I could hunker down with them for a little while, but I don't want to burden them. Especially with what's happening as of late, I don't want to put more weight on their shoulders."

Edith has a small grin lining her face. "The Clarks are a pretty open family. If I remember correctly, we have a spare guest room. You won't burden us, I'm sure." My hopes rise when Edith adds, "I'd love another person in the house. Marshall would also love to have you with us. It'll be good for him to have a companion that isn't one of his siblings, as much as I hate to admit it."

My only reaction is to shrug meekly. It's too much for my brain to handle at the moment with him leaving, only to be invited to move in with one of his other family members. As if I could ever run from him. When a Clark family member leaves, another is quick to take their place.

After I clean myself up and make it less obvious that I suffered a meltdown over one of my closest people leaving me, I follow her out of the tent and into the open.

Outside, soldiers are loading corpses onto wagons, grimly talking amongst themselves as they work. The sight is chaotic.

The corpses lie with their cheeks and lips dipped in a deep blue among pale, stark, and lifeless faces. The smell is horrendous, bittersweet. I gag as I stumble on by.

Someone coughs amongst them, his hand splayed across his chest as he bends forward, lips turning blue. His wheezes are heard from miles away. He's slumped against the cart, clawing at the front of his uniform and puffing for someone to assist him. No one dares move closer to the sickly man, fleeing away with the fear that they themselves will get a taste of the lethal plague.

In almost a millisecond, nurses decked in a clad of protective gear stream forward with a stretcher. The only parts of their sweating and exhausted faces visible are the eyes that watch over the healthy men like hawks, their brows knitted together profusely with a headache that I can only imagine is turning into a disastrous migraine. They look as though they haven't slept in days, haven't sat on a chair or stool to rest, haven't been offered a sufficient meal or a sip of water.

Marshall will definitely go feral if he hasn't heard the news already.

The yelling grows louder, hurting my ears as I pass. I lose sight of Edith as she disappears into the crowd. It's a miracle to my throbbing temples when the yelling of the sickly man and the nurses die as they haul him away, but the commotion prevails as a mob of tall, burly men behind a horse-drawn ambulance and a supply truck whoop and cheer as a fight breaks loose.

I slink through the men and their muscular arms that pump their fists in the air when another punch or jab is thrown. The crack of a sharp smack to my flank has me turning violently around to meet my offender.

It's not hard to find him, standing tall, proud of his wrongdoings with dark hair and large, round, and gray eyes with a wrung-up towel bunched in his hands, guffawing along with his friends. He'd be a handsome man if he didn't have such repulsive antics. My fists curl at my sides as he makes tutting, smooching noises with his lips.

"Hey beautiful!" His catcalls send bile rising up my throat. "C'mon, give us a smile! You look rather tired today, Joyce. Perhaps you should stop being such a tease and use my lap as a resting spot?"

When his friends hoot and whistle, my frown only grows.

"I would consider it, but when there's a chair around offered by a man who doesn't use the instincts of his manhood as a moral compass."

I turn swiftly away and carry on with my business.

In the center of the ring stand two privates, bashed and bloody. This isn't the first time a brawl had to be separated amongst the lower ranks. In my first few weeks of knowing Marshall, he punched a man straight in the nose after he threatened to do sinful things to me behind closed doors in such a profound way. His ideas crawled like bugs under my skin.

I never saw Marshall so angry before. He called him a coward, insulting him about his presumptuously small load and threatened to shoot him if he ever laid hands on me. This resulted in Marshall taking a slap to the face and insults to his family name before a major came to break the two men up.

Compared to that mini outrage, this is far more grandiose.

Another punch is thrown to the smaller man's stomach, a chant of *fight, fight, fight* breaking out before I shout over the din, "Private Matiér, Private Cans, stop this at once!"

A Southern accent unfolds from his lips as he snarls a foul name at me, still holding Private Cans by the collar. "Out of the way.."

"*Matiér*. Hands off of him, or else I'll have to file a report of misconduct."

This threat usually gets the men reeling, sends them panicking and back to obeying their higher ups. With Matiér, he cackles. "Are you kidding me? You *are* Sallinger's pet after all!"

I stay put, taking a daring step into the ring, shoulders squared, arms at the ready to defend myself in case this goes off the rails.

Marshall would faint if he saw me in such a situation. Unfortunately, for him, he can't be here to clean up my mess and act as my bodyguard.

I can sharpen my knives in the shadows as easily as I can sip tea at a luncheon. There's no inbetween of what I'm capable of.

"Sallinger's chihuahua wants to play! She wants to nip at my toes!" His grin is lopsided as he comes closer, breath stank, reeking of alcohol. He has to be four or five inches taller than me, at least. The thought of suffering under his weight is enough to cause me internal panic.

"Tell me what happened," I make a weak attempt at keeping my voice level, "and we'll sort this out the easy way. We can all go home unharmed at the end of this. Unless your bravado prevents you from doing so—"

A punch to the chest.

Fingers knot in my hair as Matiér holds me hostage. My breath rattles in my lungs.

I went off guard too soon.

"My bravado? Please, Corporal, you're kidding me! Private Cans knocked my rum outta my hands and called me a scumbag. *You* must have some dumb nerve coming here acting all high and mighty, sweetheart. Go sit on the sidelines and enjoy the show like you're supposed to. Like the rest of your lady friends."

I don't flinch at his words, as I've heard them formulated in many variations thousands of times over. His hands grow tighter, and this time, I whimper as they pull at my roots. "I've been wanting to mess up that pretty face of yours for such a long time, but your boy toy would beat the crap out of me for doing so. He isn't here right now, is he? Poor doll."

I'm thrown to the floor and get a kick to the stomach as another wave of laughter flows easily through the crowd. My whole head throbs as I scoot away, hissing in pain as he leers closer.

The laughter and the chants that rise up swallow me whole.

* * *

"I won't let you cut off my arm! I won't!"

A young soldier has been putting up a fight with the nurses for two days straight as his arm dies right in front of him, reaching the point where his fingers have gone blue as his lost limb hangs lifelessly from its socket. He got shot in battle, Edith says. The bullet, lodged deep into his arm, has left it beyond repair. With his fear of pain, which he's claimed many times already (eighteen and counting), many approaches at getting him to agree to amputate have failed.

The spread of the flu has gotten dreadfully worse. It's only a matter of time before all of us catch it and die, turning blue like the rest of the corpses I've seen the past couple of days.

Edith reasons with him for what would be the thousandth time. "Sir, your arm is dead. Do you hear me? *Dead.* We can't heal it, it's way beyond repair. We have to—"

"I'm not letting you cut my arm off, woman!" he snarls, barking at her in fear.

"Frieda, get the gigli saw please," Edith sighs, drawing gloves over her hands before she tightens her apron. "Things will get messy. Please look away if you're squeamish."

I carefully hand her a coiled wire with silver handles from a nearby surgical kit as the soldier yells, "Get that thing away from me!"

Edith straightens her apron and flexes her gloved hands, taking the saw from me with an ease that's far too uncanny for this moment. "Sir, you'll die of an infection if we don't do this now. A prosthesis will be fitted as soon as possible."

"She's right, you know," Sam adds while he sits with Ed and helps him change his bandages that cover the left side of his face. They've been watching the whole scene play out, flinching with every new scream and struggle. "You're more likely to die in pain if you don't get that arm chopped off. The procedure can't wait. You've already waited so long that your arm is about to just drop off."

Alistair enters the tent, holding envelopes, matching black leather gloves to his brother on his hands. "Did I walk in at the wrong time, Edith?"

"Not at all." Edith's calmness is far too bone-chilling. Her smile is even worse. "I needed a big strong man to help me, and here you are. Right on time."

"What do you need help with?" He sets the envelopes on a nearby table and takes his place next to her, face contorted in pure disgust as he observes the scene before him.

"I need a few people with strong arms to hold this fellow down. We need to amputate his arm. You see how ghastly it looks? Sam? George? Maybe you two can help, if that's fine with you both. Frieda, too, if you don't mind."

"I'd rather stand back. I don't like looking at people's insides all that much." I wave off her request. "Bad stomach."

"I'll be fine," Sam stands to help. So does George, Lester staying to finish helping Ed with his bandages as he eats, his jaw rigid.

I obstruct the horrors of the operation from my sight and sit next to Ed at the foot of his bed, trying my hardest to ignore the closing of the curtain, the screams that follow, the saw meeting flesh, cutting into bone a few short moments afterwards. Ed's distracting himself by spooning the remnants of his lunch into his mouth. How can he eat while an amputation is taking place just inches away?

"Hey," I approach him on the side that isn't plastered with bandages, "did you take your painkillers?"

Ed curtly nods, his mouth full of beef. "Nurse gave me an extra dose of morphine. Not good. Needle bruised my arm."

"He had a shot of morphine to help him, as he complained that his head was in so much pain that it would explode. Don't get addicted to that stuff, okay mate?" Sam says as he pulls bloody rubber gloves off his hands. Again, his smile is too oddly placed for me to handle.

"When's Marsh back?" Ed sets his can down, taking steady sips from his canteen, careful to not let the water dribble too much down his chin as he takes it in at an awkward angle.

"We've got to get you a straw." Sam swoops in with a napkin and wipes hurriedly at Ed's chin, which makes him groan from embarrassment.

"Not for a long time, Ed," I reply. "I take it he's busy."

"He'll write, right?"

It feels like I'm consoling an anxious child when I reach for his cold hand. "I'm sure he will."

"It appears this has appeared right on cue," Alistair taps me on the shoulder, handing me an envelope, "from Sergeant Clark himself."

Taking the envelope, I turn back to Ed with a good-natured smile. "See? He may not be back now, but he's here in his words."

Wasting no time at all, I flip the envelope open and read its contents.

My darling Freddy,

I'm sending this letter along with the confirmation that I've arrived in Italy safely and am well rested from the trip. My fear of boats is slowly going away. I must say, the Italian Front is nothing like the Western Front, where everything is flat. Everything here is so hilly, as we're a few miles away from the Alps. They've stationed snipers on either side near the mountaintops. Everything here feels so new, even if it's the same system used over in France.

My love, although Italy is a beautiful sight despite the war blazing on, I can't ignore the current flu pandemic occurring at this very moment. I can't stress enough how very worried I am for your safety, the others', too. It's just as alive in Italy as it is in France and will probably stay like that for a long time. Try to bathe as often as you can, don't touch contaminated objects, and do not stick around those who excessively cough and sneeze or are unwell. If I am to catch it (I pray that I don't), please, stay away from me, as I don't want to get you infected either, though there's a very likely chance we'll both fall ill no matter what we do.

Upon arriving in Italy, the pocket watch you gave me started to buffer, as I had thrown my coat on one of the ship's beds. It fell onto the floor! I'm utterly ashamed to confess such neglectful treatment of such a precious object. It's in perfect working condition as of now, ticking away, but it died on me for a half hour. It reminds me that you're still here with me. Each tick reminds me of how long I have until I can see you again. This isn't the most logical thing to say, as I don't know when I'm returning with the pandemic going on and my role in helping around here. I just hope I'm able to leave sometime soon before conditions worsen.

Is Ed okay? The last time I saw him, he was in great pain. Sam, Lester, and George, too. I know Alistair is fine, as always. There never seems to be anything wrong with him. Also, I received a telegram from Edith earlier this morning about how she's going to be at the Western Front at such a bad time with this sickness going around. Maybe you can find her and write back about how she's doing. I pray that none of you fall ill and work the best you can in these hard times. It hurts me to see so many individuals dropping like flies nowadays. The war has just gotten deadlier.

I apologize that this isn't much on my behalf, and I hope you get back to me soon.

Kind Regards,

Sgt. Marshall Clark

I hold the letter tight in my hands, his handwriting creasing under my fingers as they start to shake. The weight on my shoulders returns as thoughts of him crash like a tidal wave. It finally hits me how much I really miss him, his presence fading every passing minute.

I close my eyes to stop the tears from pouring. I've cried enough already these last couple of days.

Ed's peering over my shoulder and seems to be reading along with me. He sighs when I fold the letter back into its envelope. "He hasn't written much. I knew he'd start to freak out."

"He would before he even got on the boat. They'd check him for symptoms and pull him out of line if he were ill. He'd be back here or in another hospital in isolation. That would drive him up a wall."

"The people who're most likely to fall ill are Edith and Ed because of their proximity with others," Alistair says, washing his hands in a basin. "Edith, dear Sister, Ed, please take every known precaution and protect yourselves."

"I barely go to the infected tent, Alistair." Edith sits on a rickety chair, unfazed by the amputation she's just performed. How she does it, I still don't know. "They say I'm not ready. I've only been sent here a few days ago."

"And I'm grateful for that." His hand goes over her shoulder, patting it after he's dried his hands. "Ed, please protect yourself, too."

"I can do that." Ed lies back, groaning in pain. "I'd do anything to see Alice again."

"You will," Alistair reassures him. His gaze lingers on Ed. Their eyes lock.

"You sound a bloody lot like your brother. I thought you were that amazing git for a second."

Alistair's hands fall to his lap as he reclines on a folding chair. "Sometimes I look at him and think I'm looking at a mirror image of myself, and it's terrifying."

Ed chuckles lightly. "You're lucky you're both still so handsome. Look at me. I look like an old hag with these bandages on my demented face."

"I still think you're handsome, Ed." Lester smiles as he takes a swig from his canteen. "Inside and out."

Ed closes his eyes, leaning his head back against his pillows. "If only, Lester. If only."

Deep in thought, I come to terms with the possibility that Marshall may be gone for even a bit longer than 'until May.' I may not even see him for the next few years. He might fall out of love because he'll grow sick of waiting to see me again. He'll get tired, become infatuated with someone else who stumbles across his path. I can't blame him. I'd get tired of myself too.

But then again, if a person wants something desperately, they persevere. I've been in that spot many times before. I don't even know if I'll love him the same by the time he comes back, nor what I'll do when I see him again. I'm fearful of the man he'll become as he grows rougher with the changing tides of war. He may be completely shaken out of his skin, hard as a rock, as that wondrous heart of his turns to stone, screaming himself awake as nightmares plague him.

Would he still be my Marshall either way?

Yes, a thousand times yes.

If he had to take up a life in a wheelchair or hobble down the halls with a cane, I'd be by his side no matter what. No wound or battle scar will impair the love nor the admiration I'm willing to share with one man. If we have to go through something, we'll go through it together. I won't settle for anything less.

I exit the medic tent and set out to the grass outside, taking in gulps of air. It stinks of smoke as I breathe it in, capturing it in my lungs, polluting my airways. My limbs shake as I hold the letter with a tougher force, my fingertips running over the etchings and engravings from his pen as he wrote this letter just for me. The thought is selfish, so I shove it away.

His voice floods my head. His smile, his laugh, and everything about him overflows within my mind. It makes me stagger. My head develops a splitting pain when all my thoughts of him spill like water out of a broken glass as I start to shake. I know all too well that it's not just from the cold.

My knees wobble like jelly as my body fails to fight the overwhelming feeling of having someone you love miles away, and when you outstretch your hand, you can't reach them or even see their face.

That's the very thing that reminds you they're gone.

22

German Offenses

Back in my tent, the sleeping bag is cold. Everything is cold while Fey's side remains empty. She's working hard on a night shift to assist with the treatment of all the sickly admitted constantly. Day by day, the numbers have multiplied and reached a deadly tally. I've never washed my hands more times in a day than I have in the past few hours.

My head keeps spinning with thoughts of him. It's just him; everything about him that my brain refuses to let go of. When I close my eyes, his silhouette stands clear against the lamplight, a picture beckoning me to enter it, only with an inevitable glass wall in the way that can't be smashed apart no matter what weight you throw at it.

If only I could feel his hands shake me awake with a voice that sounds like gospel against my ears as it calls my name. I'd let the tears pour, melt in his arms and stay put until I fall back asleep.

As I curl myself into a ball, I still have the letter scrunched in my fist: a painful reminder that he won't be back until God knows when. I'll have to grow up and take care of myself like I've been since my father left for this war and never came back. I'm not weak or someone who relies on a man to take care of her and kiss her wounds each time she falls, each time she falters. I've reached greater heights.

I don't feel like moving, so I let my body calm itself down and close my eyes in the process. The wind rustles outside against the tent, the sound of footfalls coming closer.

"Corporal Joyce!"

I don't open my eyes to the sound of the voice at the tent's entrance. I must be dreaming already.

"She's fallen asleep, Corporal," an unfamiliar voice chuckles. A masculine voice.

My eyes snap open, and I scamper as far as I can from the two soldiers who've barged into my tent.

"By God, did anyone tell you it's rude to barge in on someone while they're sleeping?"

"Our sincerest apologies, Corporal," the one on the left says. "We didn't mean to frighten you."

The one on the right dips his head. "Sallinger needs you on the east side to help with the stretchers. Remember to wash your hands thoroughly and cover your nose and mouth. Wear the gloves they supply you when handling the ill."

I sit up, sleep threatening to pull me back down. "Right away, sirs."

"I have to warn you, Ms Joyce, this is no pretty sight for you," the one on the left says grimly.

I don't suppress the heartless guffaw that rises in my throat. "You amuse me, sir. You'd be surprised by what I've seen. Please, say that to all the pretty nurses here."

I stroll out, grumbling out any curse word I know in both English and French. The cold bites at my frame as I find the nurses.

"Corporal Joyce." One of them looks up, her eyes tired and devoid of energy. "You're not ill, are you?"

"Last time I checked, I didn't have any symptoms." I step inside. "Sallinger appointed me to assist you with the stretchers."

She breathes a relieved sigh. "Thank God for that. We have barely enough nurses on staff as of late. There's men dying right now as we speak. Please go get some gloves and a mask."

Once fully equipped, I follow the young nurse out into the field where men lie on stretchers, coughing or gasping for air, their lips and cheeks blue as their lungs struggle to inflate.

I bend down to grab the handles of one of the stretchers, hissing as my muscles ache as I hoist him up. His breaths rattle. Much like an asthmatic when they have an attack. He coughs, and I try to lean back when he does so.

"Mariam," he wheezes. "Mariam…"

After we lay him down, I race out to grab another, then another, and another after that. One dies on his stretcher and joins the many others lying on a wagon. I have to look away. Some vomit might just get the chance to escape as the stench of the cadavers perfumes the air.

Someone shouts my name, skidding down the hill and spraying snow across my breeches. "Frieda! Come with me!"

"Alistair, I'm working."

Alistair is as pale as death, teeth chattering, uniform unkempt. "This is urgent!"

"Alistair! I said I'm busy!" I yelp back at him.

"Shut up! Listen!" Alistair screams, shaking my shoulders. "It's Marshall."

I'm tense, a needle injecting a dosage of shock into my veins. "What about him?"

"He's…" Alistair hesitates. My panic rises when his hesitation prohibits him from speaking.

"Alistair, what happened to him? Tell me!" I beg him, taking his hands in mine. Like his brother, he can't hold eye contact while facing conflict.

He chokes out, eyes squinting, "He's been shot! My brother's been shot!"

The floor caves under my feet at the news, quaking as Alistair swallows back tears.

The words are another jab to the side, tearing open another hole in my heart.

Shot.

Marshall's been shot.

"He told me he wouldn't be fighting!"

"I received a telegraph from my friend over in Italy who works at the hospital. He wasn't fighting, just doing his job as a whistle blower."

"Then how did he—"

"The nurse told me he was perched on the ladder, blowing whistles. A sniper got him in the abdomen."

I'm frozen, paralyzed. "Is he…"

"He's in the medic tent, stable for now. He hit his head on the way down. His thoughts are fuzzy and his speech is slurred, but he's stable. I also received this." He hands me an envelope from his pocket, hands shaking. "All of us got a letter from him."

I clutch the letter so hard that it crinkles.

When I open it, Alistair squeezes my shoulder. "I'll give you some time."

I stare down at the small brown envelope, unfolding the parchment inside. I start to grow short of breath when I catch sight of the ink blotches staining the parchment; writing with a clumsy hand. I hurry to decipher his font nonetheless, rushing to read his words.

So dark. Can't see. Everything hurts. Removed bullet. Stitches. Head hurts. Mind foggy. Can't think. Don't want to leave. Don't want to say goodbye. I'm so tired. I love you.

I race back to the medic tent and steal a pen plus some parchment and scribble hurriedly back to him, following the return address on the envelope. A nurse catches me in the act, but I don't look up, fastening my writing speed with her coming close to inspect what I'm doing.

" Joyce! You aren't done here!"

"I have to run an urgent errand! I'll be back soon!" I call. She scowls.

I send the letter and march back to the medical tents, wrapped in both of my coats (one being my father's heavy overcoat, the other the standard trench coat) with my cap atop my head. It's surprisingly cold for the end of February. Spring's going to be here in less than a few days, but winter remains relentless and refuses to thaw.

My coats aren't enough to keep me warm, the cold still biting at my edges. My hands are turning painfully stiff under my rubber gloves I haven't taken off just yet as the chill starts to set in. I'm itching to ask Alistair where he and his brother bought their leather gloves that have inner linings of wool and to put on some extra thermals to trap in my body heat. I could always order a pair of extra stockings, but they're quite expensive in the market nowadays. Especially when they're made of good quality wool that, as of now, can only be rationed out to only so many.

My hands fasten around a stretcher once more, my arms groaning at the weight of the men I have to haul. One coughs, and I almost jump back. Despite having the extra protection from contamination, both gloves and a mask, the sound is terrifying all the same. At any other time, it would be a simple cough, a filler for silence. Now, it's the equivalent to the call of Death fast approaching on his mighty steed, ready to harvest the freshly deceased with his grand scythe.

Once I'm dismissed in a matter of working hours later, I dispose of my mask and gloves, wash my hands, then head back to the medic tents, Lester leaning over Ed's bed in deep conversation.

"You'll be fine, Eddie. It'll take some time to heal."

"What if it doesn't? I can't live a life where whenever I talk, it feels like my face is on fire."

"I know, but we'll all have to get through it together. You, me, George, Sam, Frieda, even Marshall. He's not here right now, but he'd be saying the same thing if he were."

"Make up your mind," he teases, his face void of any jesting grins or smiles. "Do you hate the man or do you follow his advice?"

"A bit of both, really," Lester sighs. "He's arrogant...cocky, sometimes, but he's worth staying by."

"You have no idea how sick I felt when I heard he was shot," Ed whimpers. "He's like a brother to me."

"I know, Ed. I know." Lester takes his hand, avoiding his gaze.

Ed pulls his hand away, staring at his bedsheets. "Please leave me alone for a little while."

"Do you need anything?"

Ed deadpans, "Yes. Time to myself."

Lester hesitates. He dismisses himself with dismay etched into his face. He stops when he sees me waiting and mutters in my ear, "He hasn't eaten anything since yesterday.."

"It could be the news that's making him have less of an appetite, or his wounds. I think you should leave him alone for a little bit."

"Were you eavesdropping?" Lester fixes his cap so it sits straight and tipped atop his brow. "If you were—"

"I was going to go in, but I saw you two and decided to leave you alone."

Lester shrugs, taking in a long inhale to steady himself. "Any news from Marshall at all? Sucker got hurt pretty badly, didn't he?"

"Shot in the abdomen. He's scared out of his mind." I run the contents of his sparsely-written letter over inside my head. "He's in heaps of pain, can't think straight, and is worried he'll die somehow. He's panicking inside and out."

Lester pulls on a pair of woolen gray gloves. "He hates when he's wounded or sick. Every little thing that's wrong with him, he stresses over. I wouldn't be surprised if he's stressing about death right now. Along with the pandemic? The man's going to have a lot on his mind...Hypochondria at its finest."

"I can't blame him. He nearly died of scarlet fever when he was a little boy. It could be the trauma or survivor's guilt. I'm not too sure."

"I'll let you in on something. Ever since I met him at the training camp, I thought he was a nutcase who only knew how to shoot guns and get up to no good by chattering away like the chatterbox he is. Once, he got really badly screwed up and ended up breaking a rib after a self defense drill. He was yelling at the nurses that he was bleeding out when he wasn't. Ed had run in to hold and calm him down. He had a meltdown, and I'd never seen him so distraught. We were sitting in our lectures for first aid a few months later when the lad taught me how to tie a tourniquet when I kept failing. He's always been scared out of his mind when it comes to health. I never knew why he was so frightened. He never told me."

I'm unsure of what to say. My mouth isn't able to shape the right words, nor can my brain think of any. But I spot Alistair not too far away, carrying a heavy trolley of what looks like bombs, but appear to be something much bigger.

"Tell me, what're those Alistair's carrying?" I point at Alistair as he emits a strangled noise of struggle. He loads more of the heavy things into the trolley with care.

"Those, my friend, are canisters of mustard gas. Dynamite is in the mix, too. They've been stocking up."

"Mustard gas?"

"Mm. Much stronger than carbon monoxide or tear gas. They've been stacking up for the upcoming assault after hearing via correspondence that the Germans are going to be attacking later this month."

"So they're using the gas and the dynamite to—Mother of God!" I'm weak in the knees at the idea.

"It'll be time to get back to the front lines soon. It's best to make do with the peace you have until then. I wouldn't tell anyone, though, as it would stress everyone out once the gossip takes flight."

I try to steady myself, my knees still shaking. Lester side-steps away from me.

"Where are you off to?"

"Work. They need me to fix some barbed wire on the front line. Since it's all peaceful now, I hope I don't get shot. I'll see you later."

He marches off and leaves me alone with my thoughts swirling inside my head.

I was never notified about a German offensive.

It's all coming to me so quickly. That's why the Germans are limiting their attacks nowadays. Why it's been so quiet on the Western Front.

Lester's blond hair disappears as I take in the news. Ed's talking to himself inside the tent. I shouldn't bother him, but I need someone to talk to. He's always been there for me. My head is hurting from thinking too much, and I need something to nullify the pain.

I feel incredibly guilty as I make my way into the tent.

"Corporal Joyce," a voice speaks behind me, stopping me from moving any farther. "Please report to the front line."

I turn to find myself eye to eye with another corporal, judging by his chevrons.

I echo, "The front line?"

"You've been ordered to report to the front line by Lieutenant Colonel Sallinger. You must take your webbings and rifle immediately."

Ah, I see. They're taking me to the front line to fight when the time comes. Another pawn in their games.

I exhale a terribly long sigh and go back to my tent to collect my belongings that are deemed necessary. I don't get a chance to say goodbye. I'm shoved in line like a prisoner on death row.

Soldiers all around me are conversing, leaving me alone in this cramped space, and I start to shake with fear. I spot Sallinger over the swarm of dirt-colored caps. My stomach threatens to empty itself, and I have the need to run away, even if I get a bullet to the back as punishment for my insubordination.

I already know what Sallinger is going to say. I already have a prediction of the dire circumstances he'll put us in. The mask he wears doesn't hide the fear and anger he feels like so many of us here. It's the fuel for our battles, the fuel for the war. One man's fear is another man's anger. One man's anger is another man's fear. The doors revolve far too often from person to person. The war's patrons devour it for breakfast.

"Gentlemen, attention!" His eyes don't bother to sweep over us to check that we're all listening, but the shudder that flies through is enough to establish that everyone is. "I need you all to pay close attention to what I'm about to say. There's been word going around that the Germans are going to successfully perform an offense here on the Front, and we need all the support we can get to stop them. We've summoned you all here to assemble yourselves along the line to defend it. Snipers, machine guns, patrols; you'll be grouped into these small subsections."

I cast my gaze to the floor, listening through and through.

They know about the gas Lester and I saw Alistair carrying earlier, but they don't mention it through the entire lecture of the battle plans.

There'll be more reserves. Some soldiers are put in an 'outpost zone,' a 'battle zone,' and a 'rear zone.' I quiver in fear at the newly announced battle tactics, even more when I'm placed at the 'outpost zone.'

My chest aches at the idea of the amount of smoke I'll breathe in, the gas that'll burn me with every chance it gets, the risk of dying. The men around me narrow their eyes against the never-forgiving wind that comes our way, most of them towering over me in height. Sallinger's eyes meet mine; dark and stern, much like my father in almost every single way. He barely blinks, holding the glare as his lips move, his hands venturing over the rifle in his clutches.

I lower my gaze, just like I did whenever my father gave me that same type of glare Sallinger's wearing.

The world slows as he approaches me. "Corporal Joyce, a word, if I may?"

I bow my head out of compliance. "Of course, sir."

He leans against the dirt walls of the trench, folding his arms against his broad chest.

Very unofficial, I comment internally.

"I got a telegraph from Lieutenant Colonel Alberts on the Italian Front regarding the condition of Sergeant Clark. His wounds were worse than the nurses anticipated. He's stable. Besides the shot in his abdomen, his appendix was ruptured by shrapnel and had to be removed. He's in recovery."

I take it the bullet hit deeper than previously thought. An organ ruptured, but not vital.

"May I ask why you're telling me this, sir?"

As if I'm not taking on enough bad news already, Sallinger continues unpacking the situation. "He's also sustained minor damage to the head—a concussion, apparently. Due to the pandemic, I don't think he'll be returning any time soon, even when he's at full health. I'm not risking an outbreak here when we already have so many soldiers already ill."

"The flu's already here, sir," I argue.

"Then I won't increase the probability of spreading it. Not when this war is all the rage," he almost snarls at me.

265

I bite the inside of my cheek. I've narrowly missed my head being bitten off yet again, plus a notice of demotion being slid across the table.

"Of course, sir," I reply, monotone, a machine, the very thing Sallinger wants me to be, what he wants everyone to be so this operation can go along smoothly. The other men are gossiping around me as I watch him leave.

I catch a glimpse of No Man's Land over the horizon; the sliver of land that both us, our allies, and our enemies are trying to take over. I'll be fighting for my life yet again whenever the Germans decide to attack. It's the most painful time to wait for. My life is already ticking away on the clock, except that clock is speeding through time with no way of stopping. It's flooring the accelerator to no avail.

"Is that Joyce over there?" I overhear the men that are deep in conversation, sitting upon a wooden bench, uneven from many blasts and shots chipping it away. Bite marks from the war's hungry jaws.

"Great Scott, it is! She hasn't changed a bit. The last time I saw her, she was sharing a bed with Sergeant Clark in the medic tent."

I scowl, now knowing that they had been spying on me.

The captain who almost grinded me to a pulp stops to talk with them. I'm one inch closer to wanting to blast someone's brains out. I crack my knuckles irritably at the sight of him.

I want to demolish something, tear it apart. But the Front remains quiet for now, getting ready for the havoc that's yet to come.

All we have to do is wait.

PART II

THE ITALIAN FRONT

MARCH, 1918

MARSHALL

The First Interlude

The guns are the first thing I hear as my eyes open to the dawn of a new day. The ground rattles above me, men screaming at their stations, the whistle blowing to send a new wave over. The men in the dug-out sleeping quarters are stirring, one of them calmly reading a newspaper in the far corner.

"G'morning, Mr Clark." He lights a cigarette, tipping his cap backward to reveal a scar running diagonally down his face.

I've been assigned as tent mates with the scum of the earth—from Arkansas, he says—and Italy has been anything less than comfortable. The men here become one with the shadows: lighting cigarettes, chugging alcohol like there's no tomorrow. My liver and lungs hurt just looking at them, my mouth running dry each time they offer me a swig out of a grimy flask.

I haven't bathed in the past few days. My hair's gone all greasy, and I haven't gotten the chance to wash my uniform. I know I shouldn't be complaining when the rest of the men here have been on these lines for days on end. They often remind me of it, asking about how *they're* doing, how *they're* faring.

No one cares about Marshall Clark here in Italy. He's non-existent, nothing but a war tale. They always want to know what his partner is up to these days, jarring and poking me with questions, asking if we tossed around or got anywhere near. My eyes are strained just from the amount of times I've rolled them at such audacious questions.

"Oi, you! Are ya deaf? I'm talking to ya!" he spits. "Perhaps your ears are clogged so much with cotton that your eardrums are ruptured?"

My mother always told me that you should be polite to everyone. Even to those who turn against you and make your life a living hell. Her teachings have stuck with me all my life, but I've gotten to the point where I've somewhat doubted them. It's not acts of kindness she wants me to fulfill, but common decency. Kindness and common decency get us to higher stakes. Being unkind and unfair only digs a bigger hole, makes us stoop lower and lower.

"Sir," I rise up and off the wall, wincing at how sore my back is, "I apologize. I was still half asleep. New assault today?"

"Death's business is booming." He takes a drag, puffing out a cloud of smoke that has me choking. "I gotta say, I hate the way you talk. All that rich boy jargon is making my ears bleed."

Before I can retort, there's a shadow cast along the wall in the candlelight.

"Sergeant, good morning." The shadow tips his cap in stubborn urgency. "You're needed in the field for whistle blowing again."

"Again? You don't say." I feign excitement, rising to my feet and dusting my front. I dip quickly back down to grab my rifle and fasten my webbings, preparing myself for yet another fight.

It's uncanny, being the one to sentence someone to death rather than being the one to run to it.

Brushing my ragged hair back, the cigarette smoke tickles my nostrils as it perfumes the air with its sickly sweet scent. The man offers me some, but I reject it with a noble turn of my head. Smoking is for men who want to dig early graves.

The guns and shells rattle on overhead as I poke my head outside, strapping on my metal cap with my rifle in hand. I've forgotten my trench coat, feeling exposed, naked, without it. It's like a second skin, a safety net with its comforting weight on my shoulders. Sometimes, I like to run my hands through the material; the rough wool that fits snug against my frame.

My hands toy with the silver whistle I was given at my first meeting with the drill sergeant. Hands shaking, I clench it with whitened fingers against the cold. I've forgotten my gloves. I'm getting more and more forgetful these days. Perhaps I'm growing prematurely senile.

"Sergeant Clark! A late riser, as always." My name echoes across the trenches, in the wind, in my ears as I train them to follow the sound. It's raining heavily this morning, the raindrops tinkling against my helmet, a racket similar to that of a storm belting against a tin roof.

Each step I take is a step towards my doom, my downfall. One that's confidential to the singular man known as God, who has all the power in the world to push me to my limit regardless of how I stand, how I fare.

"Restless night, sir." I have to raise my voice over the din, sticking my hands in my pockets with my rifle slung over my shoulder. My eyes take in the waves I'll be ordering over the top, the few unlucky men meeting their demise. They refuse to look me in the eye. Some are praying. Some are crossing themselves and kissing their ring fingers, murmuring words of indefinite goodbyes. I see it everywhere when fighting along the lines: the praying, the devotion to someone back home. There's no escape from the dread that lingers over us in a dark stormcloud.

"As always," he pats me on the shoulder as the gunfire dies down, "best of luck, sergeant."

My jaw clenches. The men prepare themselves. The first wave clings to the rungs of many ladders. The second are taking their last shots of whiskey, going in for another round of praying as I raise my whistle, ready to deliver the signal.

Bang.

The pain is searing hot. The impact sends me doubling over as a strangled noise erupts from my lips. My rifle clambers to the floor. Blood stains my uniform. It starts to burn, starts to eat at my insides.

My hands come away red.

I know this pain from anywhere. It's engraved itself forever in my mind.

The world slows. My head starts to spin. Immediately, my hands reach for the gunshot wound to staunch the bleeding. The drill sergeant is wide-eyed, staring, as I stagger, losing my balance. I have just enough time to grip the ladder, gasping for air as I hurriedly search through my webbings for bandages.

"Sir, I have to get you to the nurses—"

The rest of his hurried words die under the ringing that shouts in my ears. He's far too late to take action, to catch me when I start to fall.

There's a dull crack as my helmeted head meets the floorboards. My blood forms a dark, murky pool beneath me. The warm, sticky feeling of it is all I feel before the world goes dark.

To calm the persistent bleats of panic inside my head as men with stretches clamber over, I go over the last letter I'd written to Frieda just hours before, left unfinished.

My Angel,

Most would see the opening line as presumptuous and outrightly bold for a young man in love to write.

It brings me great joy to say that I'm safe. For now, at least. The fun hasn't started yet. I have just the right amount of time before the big guns come to try and defeat us. Before it slips my mind, I decided to write this down.

Before I start my new assignment as a whistleblower, I just want to say that I miss you ever so much. My feelings remain unchanged. I hope to see you again...Hopefully in a better world, where war is a thing of the past, where I can sweep you up and away in an instant to take you to paradise. Of course, this paradise will be of our own creation. What do you say? Sounds like fun, doesn't it? It may as well be our little slice of Heaven on Earth.

There's a sour grunt from one of the medics as they carry me out of the trenches, my eyes fluttering shut with fatigue, the drainage of my strength.

I, for one, would like a humongous bookshelf to house our new editions of our ongoing collection. How marvelous would that be? A great big library for both you and I to surf the waves of our imagination? I couldn't ask for more.

The needles are ice against my skin, dragging me under, as the doctors drown me with anesthetic. The medics are shouting.

How about you, my darling? What fine additions would satisfy the most revolutionary soldier? I'm open and willing to let pieces of you in, as I'll never grow full. With these pieces, I'll sprinkle them like stardust across the night sky as we, together, just you and I, dance along the fine ballroom decorated with the desires of two great minds.

Two great minds. Two great imaginations. Who could ask for more?

Her eyes. Her laugh. Her freckles upon pale, blushing cheeks. I wish to take them in all over again like the first time every single day, breathe in her smell anew so that it never dies off.

"Frieda."

Her name is a song across my lips just waiting to be sung before the nurses put me under.

The world is silent. All joy and music is forever lost in the quiet.

23

THE HOSPITAL

The walls are white and sterile with cracks running up and down their faces. The windows only give way to a little light from the barren world outside. It's like a cage in here. The bed is my cell. My stitches are my chains. It's been like this for weeks: weeks of pain, weeks of challenges.

My head throbs as I attempt to sit up, only to be met with a stabbing pain on the left side of my brain that's burdened me ever since the incident happened on the front line. I can still remember it clearly. I didn't feel the bullet when it entered my abdomen, but the shrapnel when it dug in and splintered my skin. It hurt like hell; something I never want to experience again.

My vision is still murky, blurred, still waking from a deep sleep. I force my eyes to strain their focus on the entrance of the hospital ward: the same dark doors, the same row of beds, the same patients. The same *everything*. The drought creeping in under the doors makes me shiver through my thermals I'm wearing to keep myself from catching a chill. I start to think sometimes that they don't pay attention to their heating system here, as I've gone to sleep almost every night with shivers deep in my bones.

The doors open. I'm greeted by the nurse who had initially carried me in on a stretcher a few days ago. All blood and gore, I was one of the many unlucky people who became a number on the wounded tally. She told me I was lucky. *Lucky* that I'd survived such a traumatic shot and came out of the appendectomy just fine, plus a hit to the head. I had told her of the time I was shot in the shoulder merely months before. She called me a miracle when all I felt like was a burden.

Sure. I'm a miracle, for surviving a disease that took my mother away from me, that gave me survivor's guilt and depression in turn.

A miracle, for becoming a shooting target for the Axis Powers.

A *miracle,* for simply leading this type of life I'm living; the life of a man whose head is an animal which will remain untamed for as long as he lives.

Sharee, I learned her name was, walks uncomfortably straight as she approaches my cot. "Mr Clark, a letter from the Western Front."

I open my eyes against the inevitable pain that sprouts across my body. "Who wrote to me?" I ask, picking at the scabs on my knuckles from another unlucky event with German gas.

She squints at the name. "Their handwriting is a bit sloppy, but it's Corporal Joyce."

My heart skips a beat. "Is she alright?"

"I wouldn't know. You'll have to read the letter and find out."

The wrinkled envelope is left on my bed for me to open. I don't stop my fingers from accepting it.

Frieda's correspondence is like a drug kicking into my system, a pleasant, light sensation that tickles the inside of my stomach whenever I get my hands on one of her letters. I get the familiar ache of not being able to see her, the chills down my spine, the fear of what the contents inside this new letter may be.

My Marshall sticks in my brain, but not as hard as *mon petit garçon* or *mon bel amour*, which I made a horrible attempt at asking one of the French intern nurses to translate for me. I never blushed so hard before. One time, when she was sent home, she proceeded to call me *mon ange doux et gracieux*...whatever that meant in French.

Words cannot describe how shocked I am at the moment about what has happened to you, being shot a second time around. Alistair came bounding towards me to give this horrendous news. I apologize for how much pain you're in, and I hope you start to feel better some time soon.

Please rest as much as you can. Eat anything you can. Take any step of recovery you can possibly get. You won't leave. You won't have to say goodbye, trust me. You made it out the first time. You can do it again.

Please stay safe. Stay vigilant. I love you.

Sincerely,

Cpl. Frieda Joyce

I lie back against the pillows, the words swimming inside my head. I close my eyes against the oil lamps illuminating the room, setting the letter delicately atop my bedside. The doors creak open as another figure slips inside the ward.

"I knew you'd be here, Skipper."

I open my eyes, the familiar nickname ringing a bell. A close friend calls me that all the time, even when insulting or lecturing me. The shadow standing over my bed is too recognizable, shoulders stiff from the cold.

"G-George?" I gasp. He's shortened his hair to a buzzcut. The golden-brown locks that fell into a fringe on his forehead are gone. "What're you doing here?"

"I arrived today." He sighs unsteadily, adding, "You look well."

"As if. I've been mutilated," I reply, lacking any form of my usual jesting in my voice.

"I can see that." George sits on the chair beside my bed, leaning forward. "No infections?"

"Not yet." His eyes align themselves with my abdomen. This time, I joke with him. "Look, you could just ask to see it. They're going to clean it soon."

Lifting the hem of my shirt, I show him the myriad of ghastly bandages and stitches wrapped around my lower torso. He winces at the sight of them.

"I don't think you're going back on the battlefield anytime soon, man," George says gravely. "Not with those in you. Are you stocking up on painkillers?"

"You bet. They don't work as well." I lie back down, the distant coughing of the flu ward echoing from a few doors down. I rarely get any sleep without hearing them scream to take someone in almost every single night. It spreads like wildfire, this new disease. "I got a letter from Frieda just now. She seems to be doing alright. Mostly concerned about me."

"Ah, I saw her a few days before I left. Private Matiér had hurt her, I heard. She was trying to stop a brawl, only to land in the dirt with a punch to the stomach and one to the chest."

Bile rises in my throat. "Who does he think he is? Damned weasel...messing with my poor Frieda. Is she okay? Why didn't you stop him?"

"I had no clue it was happening. The news flew quickly." George shifts uncomfortably in his chair. "I was working."

I feel the need to suddenly punch something, which is physically and regrettably unavailable to me at the moment, which only strains and pulls at my patience. "Matiér, was it?"

"Yes."

"I'll file him in for a scolding from Sallinger—no, something worse than a scolding...a demotion. I'll kill him once I get my best rifle back."

"I wouldn't risk getting in jail."

"Anything for the ones I love."

"You'd kill a man for—"

"I would. I would. I'd kill a man for hurting someone I care about."

George occupies himself by watching the nurses fly by, barking orders at one another. "Another case, I suspect. They've had a lot of those here recently?"

"Yep." The commotion grows louder as the new patient bellows out a chesty cough. "They don't ever stop for a single second here."

George winces as a nurse shouts at the top of her lungs. "Jesus, Marshall, how're you supposed to sleep here?"

"The thing is, I can't," I grumble. "I'm up all night because of them. Plus, there's another fellow here who has terrible night terrors. He screams almost every night. It keeps the whole ward awake."

"Now I see the dark circles." George observes my face, taking all of me in. "It feels like I haven't seen you in years."

"Do I look older to you? Is that the case?" I tease.

"Well, it *is* your birthday in less than two months. Maybe, your body is maturing faster to give you that twenty-one year old glow."

I roll my eyes, itching them as they tell their tales and woes of sleep deprivation. "You're joking."

George smirks, elbowing me just a little bit too hard. I grunt at the pain. "Oh, I'm sorry! I didn't mean to hurt you."

"I'm like an old man, George." I rub my wounded abdomen. My brow twitches in irritation. "Go easy on me."

The screaming gets louder. A stretcher with a body bag atop it pushes past the door as the same song from half an hour ago plays on the nearby radio, spilling across the room with its soft and mellow soundwaves.

"*In The Shade of The Old Apple Tree.* Henry Burr." George nods along to the crooning voice crackling out of the speakers. "I'm surprised they're playing English music here."

"It *is* an English-speaking hospital, George. You have quite an ear for music, don't you?"

"I wouldn't say that. I was expecting them to be playing Italian music. I guess not."

"They were playing French music not long ago. Not that I could understand any of it. I'm surprised Frieda can."

"She would feel the same way with your Spanish music."

"Hey, I don't listen to Spanish music."

"You should try."

"It's not my style."

The doors open once more as the man with the bad night terrors clambers in on a cane.

"Ey, Marcus!" he calls.

"It's *Marshall,* Abe. Not Marcus," I reply bitterly.

"Didja hear the screamin'? Ten more people died. One in the testing room down yonder just now."

George's teasing grin is fleeting. His jaw gapes at the news. "Is it truly getting that bad?"

"Yeah. There's a high chance we'll all be infected by the end of the year."

A muscle in my jaw jumps at the word.

Infected.

Infection.

The same word many doctors said to me many times over.

It's best to keep the bandages on, Mr Clark, to prevent any infections.

Please let us give you these antibiotics. They'll help fight the infection.

You'll have to understand, Mrs Clark, that you and your son are contaminated and need to stay in bed

and away from the rest of your family to stop the spread of the infection.

George's conversation with Abe flickers on and off as memories of younger days come back from one

simple word.

I remember the blooming red rashes that spread across our bodies, the pool of sweat I'd wake up to in the

middle of the night from my fever, my furnace-warm hands clasped around my throat when it was too

painful to swallow with the waves of nausea that followed, the vomit spilling from my guts.

My fingers spread across the notch of my neck at the thought, my jugular veins pumping blood in

panicked pulsations as the flashbacks become clearer, urging me to look at them, crashing into my train of

thought and sending it off the rails.

"Marshall?" George's voice calling my name brings me back to the present. "Are you doing okay? You're

not coming down with anything?"

"No," I let my hand drop to my lap, "just caught up in the past."

"The past of what?"

"It doesn't matter." I'm growing weak, shaky, uptight, so I shift to lie back against the pillows piled

against the headboard.

Images of my boyhood bleed into snapshots—movies behind my eyes—of the infection that wrecked my

mother and I; parts of a boy's world crumbling apart in his hands like sand.

Her death ripped the family in two, my father grieving for days on end, gaining almost no sleep at all. From my room, I'd hear him screaming out 'Alexandria' nearly every night. I told him I was to blame for her death, as I was the only one who could be near at the time to aid her. He yelled at me for thinking such a blasphemous thing, screamed even louder that I wasn't guilty, as I was merely a boy. I can't evade the paranoia I still carry, some fraction of the guilt that I'm yet to be condemned for.

"You're turning pale—"

"I'm fine," I snap. "In pain."

Yes, I'm in pain. In such traumatic, gut wrenching pain.

I should probably talk to Frieda, tell her all my woes and worries, let her bandage my wounds ten times over again, spoon feed and coddle me with her affection.

It hurts to be this vulnerable. My grandmother, who always saw me as such a strong little boy, would be furious.

"I want to see Frieda," I say a little too loud.

George's mouth opens to speak. His words almost vanish off his tongue. "You can't."

"I know. But God, I want to see her."

"Marshall, look, you don't understand." George takes a breath before he adds, "You see, there's supposedly a huge, *huge* offense that's going to happen on the Western Front. I saw it before I left. Frieda's been appointed to the front line."

My soul almost leaves my body. It scurries to take cover from the shock. "The front line?"

"Yes, the front line." George shifts uneasily in his chair. "They need anyone they can get out there."

My jaw clenches. "When's this offense?"

"They don't know, but it's presumed to be later this month. You might hear of it in the news."

"What about the others?"

"I'm not entirely sure. Ed's still in recovery. Sam is definitely on the second line. Lester, hm, Lester...I think he's on the third."

"But why Frieda? You realize it, right? They always put her in the direst circumstances. She's always one of their first choices. They might be trying to exterminate her."

"I don't think so," George disagrees bluntly. "Have you seen her strategy? She's fast, she's nimble, she's adaptive."

"Yes, but another soldier could be of the same level of ability. I just think they're putting her up as a target to mock her."

278

"Not to be rude, but these are just my observations: Maybe you think that because she's your partner? Because she's close to you?"

Usually, this would make me rage, but I lack the energy to strike up an argument as of late.

"No. Even if I love her to death, it's not because of that. It's just an opinion. I truly do think we're chugging down an unhealthy amount of sexist injustices nowadays."

"Understandable." George doesn't fight back. I don't want to argue with him or anyone else in times like these. I want to scream instead; scream at Sallinger for putting her on the front line without any second thought. It's no use, though. He won't be able to hear me no matter how loud I yell. Talking back to an officer is as good as death.

Another song plays on the radio. Another one I don't know the tune or lyrics to. It has a beautiful, swaying tempo, something I'd use in a competition with my old partner, Josephine. She was a butterfly with knives for wings.

George is tapping his fingers on his knees, also deep in thought. "About your wounds, what exactly happened?"

"I've told you before."

"Yes, but I must've forgotten."

"I'll tell you again, then." I heave a sigh and glance down at the bandages. "There was an assault. We thought the enemy had stopped firing, so they sent me to blow the whistle for the third wave to go over. As I stood to blow, a sniper shot me. Shrapnel also lodged into my skin upon impact. I fell and hit my head, so here I am."

"Good grief. That sounds like something out of a nightmare...Getting shot and enduring blunt force trauma."

"I know," I huff. "I was eligible to get my promotion for sergeant major, and then that happened. If I had paid more attention to my surroundings..."

"You still wouldn't have seen the sniper. They're quite well-hidden."

A twinge of pain prickles through me, my lungs cutting my airflow short from the sudden burst. George hurries to ask if I'm alright.

"I'm fine. Just in a lot of pain at the moment. Damn, that sniper got me good."

"He could've killed you if he had the chance." George helps me lie down in my lumpy cot, thinking it might be just a little more comfortable than sitting up.

"Can I ask you something, George?"

"Yes?"

"About Eddie, how was he?" His face clouds over with hurt, sympathy. "Is he taking his medicine? Is he resting? Has he recovered? Did he catch the flu?"

"It's nothing grave, but it's bad either way." George rests his hands on his knees. "He wants to be left alone for the majority of the day, becoming quickly shaken up and tired. It's the trauma of what happened that's affecting him. He's begrudgingly taking his medicine, though, and is resting. He hasn't caught the flu, either."

"My poor, darling Eddie?" The pit of sorrow and longing grows ten miles wider. "But his—is he alright?"

"He's recovering, just in a lot of pain at the moment, like you. Maybe you could write to him to cheer him up?"

"He could be missing Alice, too." I start searching for my journal. "He loves that woman to death and beyond."

"I'm sorry, but who's Alice?"

"Ed's wife." I reach to grab it, hissing from the pain, so George retrieves it for me. I tear out a page and dip my pen in the inkwell by my bed and start writing.

My Dearest Friend Edward,

I wanted to write to you and check up on how you're feeling. I know I left far too abruptly and that you're going through a difficult time both emotionally and physically.

Eddie, I understand that how you feel is troubling. I've been in that boat before. If you need anything, please don't hesitate to write to me. Even if your letter or mine is retrieved later, I'll always attempt to answer. You can also phone the medic tent here, too. I'll put the number in this letter down below. Just put in a request for 'Sergeant Clark' or say my name and the nurses will be sure to send me over to speak to you. If they can't, you can most certainly still write.

If I'm not available, there's always Lester, Sam, Frieda, or even Alistair, or Edith, who might

be able to talk to you (if you feel like it, of course). There's George, too, who you may write to

as well, as he's with me.

I don't have much space to write, but please feel better soon. Get lots of rest. Eat, drink, take

your medicine, and don't be afraid to speak about what your heart is bleeding for when you feel

the need. I love you, Eddie. You're the greatest friend in the world. I want what's best for you.

Feel better soon, Teddy!

Sgt. Marshall A. Clark

My writing is rushed and scrawled, pressed and etched with urgent markings upon the page. I fold it and

hand it to George, who sends it off to a nurse who now has the role of giving it to the mail carriers for it to

be posted. I watch closely as the nurse carries the letter away.

George stands and pats my shoulder. "You'll be okay, Skipper?"

'Skipper' is a nickname from long ago that George calls us boys from time to time. I asked him once what

he meant by it. He just turned to me with a good-natured smile on his face and said it was just a fun name

to call us. He also said it was a tic his family had adopted down the line. His father, his father before that,

and his father before him all share the same tic. He even complained of how confusing it gets at a family

gathering when one of your relatives is actually called Skipper. I could only imagine the chaos that would

unfold.

"I'm fine. I think."

"You think?"

"I think."

A sigh.

"I have to go get ready for dinner. I heard that Lambert riots whenever someone's late. He believes it to be 'unpresentable.'"

"He does. I've seen it happen." I bow my head in shame. On the first day here, I was late for dinner. Field Marshal Lambert had reprimanded me and droned on and on about how, as a sergeant, it was *unpresentable* to be late. He didn't take that it was my first day here as an excuse. "You better go before he catches you."

"Feel better soon, Marshall. Take it lightly."

"Thanks, George. Adieu."

Once he's gone, I cover my ears against the screaming bursting from the infected ward once more. As I emit a dreadful moan, there's the distant coughing and wheezing that can be heard through my pillow that's doing a poor job at muffling all the noises.

Ever since I was a little boy, I was terrified of those sounds and the way diseases spread like wildfire. I've been absolutely mortified all my life of contracting something that'll be the death of me: slow and enduring, the long way down.

"They never stop, do they, eh?" Abe remarks. My head throbs as the screams grow louder. The screams, the wheezing, the coughing—everything heard from that ward is a nightmare playing on repeat. "They keep gettin' louder and louder! These people keep dyin' every day and we might as well follow 'em."

"Please, Abe, stop." My plea comes out hoarse, my throat dry.

"We'll come out like the rest of 'em: dead, dolls of who we used to be, eh?"

"Stop!" I scream, a yelp that hurts my chest far too much as I push it out. Though I can't, I feel like running away. Anything to get away from all of this.

Like I told Frieda to do countless times, I count my breaths, try to slow them down each time. I start to grow dizzy and stare at the wall, my hands still over my ears. I toss the pillow aside.

If I just stay healthy, if I just stay away from those who might be ill, if I mind who I talk to, then I'll be sure to not fall ill. I won't become another statistic in their catalogs.

"Mr Clark?" Over my ragged breaths, a female voice chirps. "Rise and shine. Dinner's here."

"B-brilliant. Thank you." I sit up as a nurse sets the tray down. Good, she's wearing gloves.

Before I eat, I tear another page out of my notebook, letting my mind wander as my words scrawl slowly but surely across the page. Once finished, I fold the letter and take a peek at the tray that's been put on my bedside table. It's a small but generous portion of still-warm mashed potatoes and brisket which are touching each other, making me grimace before I pull them apart with my fork.

I know I should feel grateful for such a meal, but I can't help but feel guilty for accepting it, which makes the hole in my stomach grow wider, ruining my appetite. I stab my fork into the brisket nonetheless, all the while attempting to ignore the loud chewing that Abe provides. There's no escape from his noises. He seems to always know how to make the most amount of sound and annoy me further.

I have to force down the mashed potatoes, as swallowing them makes me feel the slightest bit ill. Putting my knife and fork neatly on the tray, I ask the same nurse from before to post Frieda's letter. She takes it with a curt smile and a quick bow, taking our trays away.

My hands shake, itching to do something other than just lying about. I take my journal once more and write, write about today and what I did like I've been doing since I joined the army. Hours upon hours of daily routines and events have been compiled into one weak little notebook that holds all the insights and secrets of my time at war.

I flick back to the day I met Frieda, not knowing it was truly her—October of 1917. It strikes me so boldly, how much we've bonded, how occasionally seeing each other when our fathers visited another, bringing us along, turned into loving each other to death.

I close my journal once I'm finished and set it back on the nightstand, reclining and closing my eyes against the flickering of the oil lamps they've lit. They flicker behind my eyelids and glow a dull yellow, lulling me away with each changing shadow, each note sung by the lullabies of the radio in the far corner.

I rest easy now. The pain in my side, once cumbersome, ebbs away as sleep takes its toll.

24

FRIEDA'S FLIGHT

"Good morning, Mr Clark." A voice wavers through my dreams of smiles and laughter, her face fading away. My time in this pleasant world is done. "It's time for your checkup."

All of me wants to toss the covers over my head and sleep for years. But I battle against it, rising and rubbing the sleep out of my eyes. It's presumably still dark outside—early morning—still too dark for my eyes to make out the shape of the hands of the clock.

"May I ask what the time is?"

"Just after five, sir." The nurse props me up with pillows. "Now, may I please see your wound? I need to check for signs of infection and scarring."

"Of course."

"Could you just please unbutton your thermal, sir?"

Unbuttoning my flannel, the nurse unties the bandages. With gloved hands, she inspects the wound and its trauma. I watch her hands with a steady gaze, the coughs from the ward breaking the silence of the halls as their owners awaken. I feel the utmost sincerity for the nurses not able to catch a break. If I'm to become a nurse, then I may as well meet the same fate.

What I find ironic about the whole thing is that I'm wanting to fight against the very thing I've been afraid of my entire life: pathogens, germs, bacteria, growths. Father almost fainted when I told him I had applied for a nursing course in college and turned white as a sheet when I was accepted.

"It looks good. There's no signs of pus, no signs of inflammation. No pain around the wound when I press on it?"

"Besides the pain of getting shot, no." I grit my teeth at the pain of the wound itself; the unpreventable dull ache it provides.

"Good, good. The stitches seem to be keeping it together nicely. I'm going to put a patch on it and give you some painkillers, okay?"

I already know where this is going to go, and I highly dislike it. Yet, I grin through it. "Okay."

She offers me a stiff smile with a wink. "Good man. Good man."

The nurse throws out my old, itchy bandages and fetches a needle, which makes me turn rigid as she fills it with clear liquid—most likely morphine or something of the like, but it makes no difference to my instincts telling me to run for my life. I clench my jaw and grow rigid as she injects the needle into my abdomen, the pinch like nails against my skin. She then swabs the wound clean, disposing of the needle and putting on a gauze patch, bowing and leaving.

"Breakfast will be served at 06:00, as per usual. Thank you, Mr Clark. Feel better soon."

"Thank you." I wince at the pain as I lie back down, growling at it burying itself deep into my abdomen.

Abe is groaning from his pillow and making the most obscene sounds I've ever heard, my face screwing up in disgust in collaboration with the pain. When he opens his eyes, I hurry to look away and pretend I'm reading my journal.

"Mornin', Marcus," Abe yawns.

"It's *Marshall,* for the last time." I've learned to despise the name Marcus after being called by it constantly and correcting him.

"Apologies, my memory ain't that good." He rubs his eyes and stretches, cracking a few bones here and there. "Didja sleep well?"

"Average."

More injured men start to wake up. The one in the cot to my right lost the ability to speak due to a terrible incident with a bomb, so they gave him a blackboard and chalk, and everytime he writes, my teeth gnash at the noise. The one to my left has an amputated leg and is waiting for a prosthesis. He mutters cold and cunning things in his sleep that make me shudder, and the other next to Abe got impaled by barbed wire. He came in not long after me. His wounds remind me of Frieda's when she had done the same thing, unable to speak clearly for a full matter of hours from the shock. It was far too painful to watch her stammer and stutter. I've seen the corpses of men who bled out onto that barbed wire, and God am I thankful that they saved Frieda just in time.

Another heaving cough echoes from down the hall.

"The flu ward seems to be calmin' down a lil'. Didn't make a peep all night."

I nod, still paranoid of the flu getting to us, to this ward, to me. I've heard sickening stories of what it does to people. It makes their lips and cheeks go blue as they struggle to breathe. They cough like there's no tomorrow and die from asphyxiation. I've observed, from overhearing nurses as they stream past, that most also expire from the pneumonia it induces as the illness worsens. I've eavesdropped on conversations about the deaths that follow. Most have been tallied as young adults—my age bracket—above all others. There's been no recoveries that I know of. I've never been so petrified.

"Did they not?" I stretch my arms. "They must be well-rested."

"Yeah and nah. A person died durin' the night. Saw the bag as they carried it down the hall."

There's a knock on the door. A nurse bows and clears her throat. "Mr Clark? Private Wellins has requested to see you."

"Let him in if you may." I grin at her.

George steps into the ward in a slow and cautious walk. While his eyes are open and alert, they're rather bloodshot. His hands are stuffed in his pockets while he surveys the room.

"Look at you, awake so early in the morning. I expected you to be sleeping in."

"I would sleep through the entire day if I could. I had a checkup. The bandages are gone...gauze patches now. What's the matter? You don't look quite yourself today."

Under the bright lights, his face is pale. "I...have some good news and some bad news."

"Lay it on me."

"Fine, but brace yourself. I got a letter from Lester, which is the good news. The bad news is that he scrawled a hard and bold *URGENT* on the front."

My throat runs dry. "What were the contents of this letter?"

"Ed is in recovery, but is starting to show symptoms of the flu. They've put him in isolation with many others. Sam sprained his ankle again. Lester himself is fine, but…"

"But what, George?" I make a weak attempt to sit farther upright, leaning in to hear him better over the screaming that arises. "Tell me. Ed is in the best of hands, but what?"

George stammers, grappling helplessly for the right words. "Frieda disappeared since they sent her over the lines."

A muscle in my jaw jumps. My head starts to spin. "A-are you sure that's what Lester meant?"

He pulls out the letter, unfurls it, and reads, "*It's to my great dismay to mention that Frieda hasn't returned from battle.*"

Immediately, my hand, fisted, clamps over my mouth as I bite down upon it to stop myself from howling. The sudden sensation of vomit rising emerges in my throat. There's yelling in my ears, George's hands on my trembling shoulders and the sharp and shrill exclamation of my lips shaping her name.

"Marshall, I need you to—"

"They have to find her, George! They have to! They have to find her!"

"Lester told me they're finding people quite quickly—"

"You're lying!" I scream as I start to pull at my hair. "You're lying!"

"I'm being completely truthful."

"You're lying!" I spit.

"Marshall," George hushes me, "quieten down. I understand it's distressing—"

"You *don't* understand." I bare my teeth, shattering myself to pieces as all the anger, all the resentment oozes and aches through my muscles, leaking into my bones. "You will never understand. Get me something to drink...Something strong—"

"I'm afraid I can't do that." His voice is stern, almost like a lecturer. "I can't have you intoxicated, not while you're injured. They will find her."

"When? In five years?" My stomach threatens to heave its contents at the thought. "She'll be dead by then!"

"You're thinking too much." George tenses under my icy glare. "Please collect yourself."

"That means she won't get my letter." I start to struggle for air. "She's going to leave—"

"She'll be fine. We have to hope for the best."

"I can't do this anymore!" I slam my fist on the wood of my bedside table, the bang resonating through my hand as it aches. "I can't be here anymore! I want out! Lock me up in a madhouse or in a prison! Anywhere but here!"

"*Marshall*—"

This is getting far too unbearable. I can't stop the paranoia that irks a chained, violent, thrashing and murderous side of me that I want to hold deep down for as long as I can.

"George," I rasp, grasping his sleeve, my knuckles turning white. "George, please take me away. Please, fire that gun in your holster...Fire it at me without any second thought. You'd do that for me, won't you?" The silence that wavers in the air is suffocating. I scream out to protest against it. "Come on, George! Say you'll do it!"

"*No.*" George pulls up a chair, my lips emitting a moan of misery. "Look at you! Where your head is right now isn't healthy. You're shaking, wounded, and paranoid. Please try to calm down with me."

My hands return to my hair, digging deep and pulling at the roots. "It's been in that same place for years. *Years.*"

George grips my hands tight, holding them down in my lap when I try to pull them back. "I'm sorry. I really am. All I will say is to breathe. You're turning far too pale."

I suck in a breath, the cold air painful in my lungs.

"You know what?" George watches closely as I bristle. "You seemed a lot happier with her than ever before."

287

I don't reply. Instead, I hand him my silence.

"I can see why. You understand each other so well. I found it humorous to watch as your relationship developed. Can I say something?"

"What?" I finally croak.

"You two were made for each other. I don't know how it happened, but it did. You'd become a stone cold killer for her if you had to. She'd do the same. She'll be there when you need her, and you'll be there when she needs you. Right now, she needs you. I can already predict what she'd be saying right now. Tell me if I'm right."

"What?" I croak again.

He pitches his voice to sound like Frieda. "I need you to stay strong for me. I need you to take care of yourself for me. I need you to help yourself for me."

"You're right," I mumble. How does *he* know? Of all people? "You're right."

"So, please do what she would want you to do. Think: 'What would Frieda do?' She will come back, I promise you. How many times has she already defied death? We have to hope for the best. That's all we can do for now."

I resume my silence, unsure of, yet again, how to respond. Pushing the thought of her out of my head for a moment, I ask, "Ed's coming down with the flu, too?"

"Apparently so," George huffs. "Marshall?"

"Yes?"

"You know what happens to those with this new illness, right?"

"I've seen it." I lower my gaze. A new wave of dread washes over me. My eyes start to burn as tears prickle at their corners.

"And you know of the outcome, don't you?"

With a gulp, I nod. "I might lose a friend."

George's hands clasp mine. "I'm so sorry."

"But there's a high chance he'll survive, right? He's young, only twenty-one! His immune system should be able to handle it!"

George is silent against my babbling, his hands leaving mine slowly, careful not to startle me like I'm a wild animal.

"Why not?" I sit upright. The shaking of my limbs grows stronger. "Tell me why."

"You already know that most of the deaths occurring are ones of young adults. You're at the highest risk of infection."

I'm lost for words, desperately grasping for something to hold onto. "There...there must be something..."

"I'm afraid not."

The world is crumbling at my feet as I furiously search farther, finding nothing. My hands start to quiver as my surroundings dissolve with my thoughts.

"Please, if you could...I'd like some time."

George hesitates, standing, bowing. "Of course. Do you need anything?"

"Just...my books from my tent, please. I'll die of boredom." I manage to crack a joke as he turns his back to exit, leaving me to finally fall apart.

* * *

Breakfast is going cold on its tray: biscuits, overcooked scrambled eggs, and dry toast. I consider taking the biscuits, but my stomach says otherwise. It performs a nervous and saddened trapeze act.

My eyes haven't left the wall, boring a hole into it. The poem I wrote in my journal remains splayed open on the table with the pen resting inside its pages. Ink dries on my hands as the words flash through my mind, the black and blue smudges blurring together.

Eye of brown, eye of blue.

Little did you know, I loved you too.

An angel that fell too soon,

Blue in the lips, the cheeks,

Purple as the illness eats.

On the next page, there would be drops from my tears.

A ruler of her own castle.

Lying in the gardens with flowers in her hair

In my arms tonight as the owls hoot.

Her lips are rose petals; soft and pink.

I'm sure I'd miss them if I were to blink.

A smile, a laugh so divine,

I'm sure I'll see it all in my dreams tonight.

And further down the page…

A helpless boy, a runaway with his love.

Gun in hand, heart as his armor,

His ribs hollowed out, his lungs cracking.

By God, who will save him now?

A walking corpse, pale and wide-eyed,

Sick and tired of playing War's endless game.

The world crumbles, and so does his life.

Footsteps emerge at the side of my bed and halt. There's a gruff grunt as the thump of books lands against the table. Usually, the sight of them would bring me immense joy. Only today, they're replaced with a severe case of apathy.

"How do you even carry these? They're heavy as hell!"

I don't look up. "In a satchel."

"I know, but you must be a weightlifter to be able to do that."

It's obvious he's trying to make me feel better, and he's failing. I don't reply, remaining silent as I don't bother to hurriedly close my journal.

"You've been writing again?" He flicks through the pages. Through my mess of poetry. It's never been my strong point.

"As always," I murmur. "It's one of my only senses of gravity."

"I won't pry. You didn't eat your breakfast either?"

"I wasn't hungry."

George pushes the tray towards me sternly. "Do I have to force it down your throat?"

"No. As I said, I'm not hungry."

"This isn't the time to joke around, Marshall. You need to eat to stay alive."

"So what? It's just one meal."

"Marshall Clark," George's brow furrows with his frustration, "eat for me, please."

I grumble in return, "I still don't feel hungry."

George shakes his head. "That won't be an excuse. Sit up."

"I told you, I'm not hungry! Do I have to keep rephrasing it to get it into your head?"

I can't stop the burst of sudden anger that explodes inside me. I'm growing irritable, and he knows it while he hovers, unsure of what to say.

I'm sure I've finally shut him up, but then he sighs. "Please, just a little bit for me?"

I shake my head.

"Remember what Frieda said? Take care of yourself."

"You made that up," I spit. "You made it all up just to make me comply and be less of a burden."

"No. You agreed that that would be something she'd say."

Watching as my body does so, I slam the tray to the floor. George winces at the sound as it falls. I feel like screaming or shooting someone. Perhaps both.

"Get out," I hiss. "Get out."

"I—"

"Get out!" I let out an ear-piercing scream, the rasp in my voice hurting my throat. "Get out before I lose it!"

George hesitates, taking a minute step back. "Mar—"

My hands resume their pulling of my hair, digging deep at the roots as my jaw clenches. I scream through clenched teeth, "*Now!*"

George gulps over my weak sobs. "Before I leave, I will request for you to please eat for me. Take care of yourself. Get some rest. I'll be back in a little bit."

I stare hard at my blanket, rapping at my temples with a fisted hand to knock some sense into myself. My limbs shake their hardest as my teeth grind together to stop another scream of anguish. The sensation of being watched by other patients and nurses alike is nothing I can avoid, but none step forward to make an attempt at calming me down. I can already predict the rumors that are going to plague me. They may travel with me all the way to France for all I care.

When you have a demon inside your head fighting to get out, to cause mayhem, you're automatically labeled as mad. *Mad,* they call you, without bothering to step in to help tame it.

Each whisper sends me further off my rocker as I mutter words to myself under my breath to calm the raging sea inside my head.

"He's shell shocked."

"Shell shocked? Are you sure?"

The taste of newly-drawn blood on my lip is enough to jar me back into reality. It appears that I've bitten my lip at some stage during my fit, but it's the least of my concerns. My head continues to swim in the lapping waves of my darkest thoughts.

"I just think he's paranoid."

"Paranoid? Did you hear that Corporal Joyce went missing?"

"Did she? Serves her right. Her family must be miserable at the news."

"I think they're already miserable for their wayward child. She's already been lost. There's no chance that she'll be found again."

Images are flashing through my head of when I yelled the exact same words to Alistair all those years back. I remember the trays of food left beside my bed when I was too caught up inside my head to even move an inch.

Leave me alone before I lose it!

My father had been so concerned that he called a doctor, as I was turning pale and losing weight rapidly. I was the equivalent of skin and bone. The doctor had asked me if I felt any bouts of sadness, apathy, mental pain, or anything. Too scared to find out where I'd end up, I shook my head. It went on for a painful three months, this exact relapse feeling like a life sentence.

The heels of a nurse's boots stop before my bed. With a sigh, she sits before me on George's abandoned chair. "Mr Clark—"

"Don't," I mutter through clenched jaws, placing an open palm out before me. "Please don't."

A dark hand reaches for my knee, covered by the blankets. Craning my neck to find its owner, she stares back at me with great big innocent, chocolate eyes that remind me far too much of a young doe. Her lips are full, colored dark with lipstick as she looks over me with a sympathetic bite of her lower lip. Her gray-streaked, wavy hair is tied back into a tight bun with an aged hand folded neatly in her lap as her other reaches for me.

"I'm so sorry," she says. The quake of her voice is enough to bring me to tears. What she shows is not false sympathy, but somehow, empathy. It's not hard to read that she's lost someone to this war, too. I can see it in her eyes, the way she looks at me like I'm one of her own.

I can't find any words other than, "you don't have to be sorry for me."

"I know, but it's the best I can do, sweetheart."

With a slump of my shoulders, her hand squeezes my knee once more, momentarily frozen before she draws it back.

"This person that you loved," she draws out her words to be of an even rhythm as they fall out, like notes against a metronome, "I take it she was special to you."

A bitter laugh bubbles on my tongue. "You wouldn't believe it. No one could replace her. It sounds imprudent of me to say so."

"No, no, it doesn't." All eyes are on her as she tries to tame the wild beast sitting in this very bed, his eyes bloodshot, skin pale from malnourishment. He's a walking skeleton; miserable and impaired. "Love is a forever changing thing that so many ever get to experience truthfully. It's a sickness, a weakness of the heart, but it only occurs to make you feel at the best of health when it comes. When it goes, it takes every last ounce of strength out of you until you feel like there's nothing left."

Odd. She summarized it perfectly.

"You must've lost someone too." I'm scared to speak it louder. "I'm sorry we have to share the same pain."

A pursing of the lips. Another sigh. "Don't fret, buttercup. Loss is what makes us stronger."

* * *

I usually don't sleep during the day. Not if I'm in the same mood that held me captive in my bed for months. But here I am, dreaming again.

It starts off in the library of my home back in Philadelphia: the books lining the dusty mahogany shelves, the circular window overlooking the river and the trees, open and letting in a draught. I'm sitting on my favorite sofa by the window, reading pages upon pages with words that feel so familiar, but are blurted out like someone's drenched them with water.

Frieda, to my surprise, is here, writing away at the desk in the center of the room. Her hand is quick, writing fast, not seeming to mind my company. I don't open my mouth to question her on what she's writing, nor do I ask what she's doing here. Her presence is already enough. A reason is not needed for when she's around.

There's a knock, three—no, four—thuds at the door. A rapping only one person in my family would do before entering a room.

Much to my shock, my mother opens the door in a nightgown: black and blue, a matching robe, the same one she wore when she died. My blood runs cold as her brown-black hair shines in the weak sunlight, olive skin, the same hazel eyes that mirror mine stare back at me.

I stand hurriedly, the word escaping my mouth. The word that hasn't left in the last eight years. Just the sound of it is like a lost song, a distant melody.

Mother.

When I step closer, the fever that made our cheeks turn red and our pores weep is nowhere to be seen. The freckles from many days under the Puerto Rican sun lie prominent upon her skin.

Frieda raises her gaze from her papers, her hands stained in blue ink. "Mrs Clark?"

"I remind you, Frieda, please call me Alexandria."

Her name echoes around the room: the name my father called out so many times at the funeral and during the night as he drank his sorrows away, the very name that brings my father to tears each time it's said. It's turned into a blasphemous thing in this household, as it brings someone to tears each time its sound haunts the walls.

"Are you alright, dear? You're pale." Her hand reaches for my face, my forehead covered in a sheen of sweat. Her hands are warm, welcoming, making me close my eyes against them.

I want to speak, but my lips can't form the words as my vision sways, pain streaking its way across my arms. In retaliation, I take a wide step back and hurriedly roll up my sleeves, the result stealing my breath away.

Red marks of a rash line my arms, creeping up to my shoulders and all over my body as my throat catches on fire, making me scream as the fever spreads.

My mother rushes forward, Frieda standing hurriedly to accompany her. "Marshall—"

"Do not touch me," I whimper, struggling for air as the room grows smaller. My mother's hand lands on my arm. "*Do not touch me!*"

If I couldn't save her eight years ago, I can save her now. Even if it's just a dream—

It's too late.

The last thing I see is the rash blooming across her chest, her cheeks flushing a deep red.

* * *

The shock of the dream has me bolting upright as soon as my eyes open back to the real world.

I roll my sleeves back hurriedly to find no signs of the blooming red rash, but scars from my days of war and silent battles with myself replacing it. Tears spike at the corners of my eyes, burning me as my stomach flips over itself. I hug the thin blanket tighter, staring out the window as my body calms itself down.

"Bad dream?" Abe asks. He's reading a thick pamphlet that sits on his lap. "Gettin' a lot of those lately."

"H-how long have I been out?"

"Half an hour, I'd say." He turns the page. "That George fella came back in to check up on ya not long ago—said somethin' bout a letter for ya."

"Another one? Did he leave it?"

"I didn't see nuthin' about no letter in 'is hands, but 'e did say 'e'd come back tomorrow or later to give it to ya."

"Of course." I slouch against the sound of a nurse's heels clacking on the floor as she walks by.

"I see you're finally awake, sir." She seems on edge, probably after what happened this morning. "Are you calm?"

"You've come to check my bandages, haven't you?"

"Yes. How'd you know?"

"That's what you usually do. You're carrying disinfectant and a gauze patch with you."

"Sharp as always. I have some good news for you. You'll be up on your feet next week."

"Do I need therapy?"

"No, but perhaps a temporary crutch to help you until you can walk without support and are up and ready to serve on the battlefield again."

"Oh, *great*," I mumble as I unbutton my shirt. She also carries my tunic. The sleeves that were once threadbare are stitched back together. My coat gets draped across the neighboring chair, the sergeant chevrons and epaulets winking at me in the lamplight, telling me of my position and who I'm meant to be.

"You're a sergeant, sir? I should call you Sergeant Clark from now on."

"It's fine. I'm not one for formalities."

My gaze holds on the uniform that's grown with me through my months of service in this war. It's the uniform that's taken so many blows, so many rips and holes, so many bloodstains, so much dirt and mud along with so many washes and gas residues. I concentrate so hard on it that I don't even flinch away from the coldness of the disinfectant as it's rubbed in on a swab.

"Your wound is healing up nicely, but please make sure to restrict as much pressure as you can on it. Even when you start to walk again, sleep on the opposite side or on your back, not on your stomach, as it may give you discomfort."

"Understood."

She applies the gauze patch, letting me button my thermal back up to protect myself from the cold. "Also, you didn't eat your breakfast—threw it on the floor. I could send a request for a small meal for you if you'd like."

My stomach growls in response, and I bow to the will.

The nurse grins and sets off.

* * *

It's sunset. The sky glows a beautiful orange. There's warm soup in my hands for dinner as the nurse who helped earlier stumbles in.

"Mr Clark, sir, it's Mr Wellins."

"Let him in," I mumble.

George comes in, arms folded. "I see you're finally eating. What was the change of mind?"

I skip past the question, dodging another argument that may play out if I answer. "There was a letter for me?"

George hands me the battered envelope haughtily. The handwriting isn't recognizable, rushed, but I open it anyway.

To my big brother, Marshall,

We have some good news and bad news. Some rather outstanding news that's had the greatest effect on all of us! The German offense is still going. I'm on duty on the third line, watching the men run up and over the lip of the trench and get shot down while others are dying of the flu...It's not a pretty sight.

How are you? I understand that the injury of yours inhibits you from fighting on the field—probably for a very, very long time, which may be good for you, as you deserve to rest and the time to rejuvenate. On the current affair, though, you may have a shiver after hearing this news. It's just remarkable!

The good news is Mr Edward sick and tired Surry, though he has the flu—they're now calling it the 'Spanish Flu'—is likely to recover and is self-isolating the best he can, telling us to not come close to him at all, but has asked the other nurses to update us weekly on his condition. He's been able to take some of his bandages off and is now sporting quite the face deformity. He shall receive surgery for it once the war is over. He's deaf and blind on the left side of his body, the poor lad. He'll be due for a hearing aid and a facial restoration surgery soon.

The other news I'm going to share is both good and bad, however you may deem it. I shall tell you of this remarkable news. By God, you will cry of either happiness or dread:

At around four this morning, we heard someone wailing outside the tent, screaming, 'help me' and,' I'm going to die,' lines from the mouth of, from when we ran out to find it, a terrified figure crawling on her hands and knees, covered in mud, coughing her lungs up. It was obvious that she contracted the flu, and the nurses had taken her up to the isolation tents to wash her up and check her condition. As soon as the mud was off of her and staining the floor of the bathhouse a murky brown, the branches of decaying trees out of her hair, it was unbelievable who it was, someone you may know very well and fought for her life every step of the way.

If you haven't guessed already, or are too scared to even guess the identity of this mystery figure, it is indeed your Corporal Frieda Joyce, who was missing for three days and a half since the offense began. The letter you got must've been delayed, as we haven't received a reply just yet. You may be

297

celebrating the finding of the long lost corporal, but her story of how she returned was terrifying to hear. She's not in the best state of mind; rather impaired and scatterbrained. She's not entirely the same as who she used to be.

Frieda begun to tell me that after she had gone over, she ran for her life over the large stretch of No Man's Land and was hit with mustard gas on the way, falling into a ditch where rotting corpses lay (the poor doll will be traumatized for life) and said it took her a century to climb out. Over each day, she was continuously struck by bombs. The shockwaves made her weak. She grew ill with the spreading pathogen and the corpses, but continued to crawl back with all the courage it took her. She was about to pass out when we reached her, and found that she suffered trauma to her right eye and is now blind. We had to remove it through an enucleation procedure. It's most likely that it's from the gas. She's in recovery now with a great amount of dressings on her face and is continuing to be administered morphine and medication for both the pain and the flu. She's suffering through night terrors, reliving her experience behind her eyelids.

I'll update you soon, my dear brother. In the meantime, the rest of the men are in the best of health they can be in, keeping their distance, washing their hands when necessary, as we've advised. They're good about it, obedient and willing to help. They're good men, working as best as they can.

When we meet again,

Edith Clark

My hand goes over my mouth as I delicately set the letter on my lap.

George finishes reading. "Well, shit."

"Oh, God, no," I murmur. "Frieda...Edward…"

George catches the spoon that drops out of my grip. "It's somewhat good news, otherwise."

"She climbed back all the way, knowing that it was do or die. Unbelievable!" Electric bolts prickle beneath my skin. "Oh my God. Frieda, my pride and joy...I should've rejected Sallinger…"

"Do you need time?" George asks.

Thankfully, I nod.

He rises to leave, a final hand on my shoulder. "Are you going to be okay? It's a lot to take in."

"I need time. Thank you, George." I don't look up. He *hmphs* before he leaves me to my thoughts. "I'm sorry for lashing out, by the way. I didn't mean to."

"Don't sweat it," George replies, and exits.

In the new silence, I duck my head. "Frieda, my little love, you're so strong. Too strong." My hands shake and resume their hold of the letter. All of me wants to run to her and be by her side, but in times like these, it's just not possible. Especially when she's in such a vulnerable state.

My hands now itch to gain possession of a pen, my journal, anything to write with. So I let them, though they're shaking like mad. The ink spills across the page and eventually stains my hands in dark currents as I write paragraph after paragraph after paragraph.

25

THE OUTSIDE

My adventures with my new crutch begin the following week as the nurses wake me up bright and early, carrying in the heavy wooden thing. Just seeing it makes me shudder, but it's probably better than staying in bed all day with little to no physical activity to get rid of my nervous energy. I'm growing restless, being cooped up here.

"You're finally back on your feet, Skipper." George grins as I sit up, taking my boots from his outstretched hands. I make a noise close to a squeak as I bend to tie the puttees, which clearly isn't possible just yet, with the crippling pain making a home in my side.

George sighs and bends down to put my puttees on for me along with my boots. "This will be the last time I do this for you."

"But I'm wounded," I reason with him and fix my slipping suspenders.

The nurse only grins, stepping forward. I should really learn her name, as she's been a massive help in making me feel better, hurtling me towards a quick recovery. The previous nurse who took the liberty in comforting me through my darkest days is there by her side, hands perched upon round hips with her graying hair down in a braid. When she steps forward, an excited little jolt jumps through me.

This is it.This is the little slice of freedom being served to me.

"Now, Mr Clark, you can steady yourself against the footboard and try to stand. Use the side you feel most comfortable with first."

Stepping onto my left foot, My hand grabs hold of the footboard, wincing as the pain in my abdomen burns when I stand. It protests and demands to be put back to rest like a moody teenager. With freedom comes suffering.

"He's alive! He's alive!" George teases.

"George, kindly shut up." I hold my side, poking my tongue at him.

The nurse hands me the crutch. The other steps back with a smile. "Place it under your arm on your injured side—yes, exactly like that. Here's a warning: It might get a bit sore if you use it for too long, but I don't expect you'll be walking much for a few weeks."

"Understood." I swallow, putting the crutch before me, fearfully taking my first step in weeks. George applauds as I take another, then another.

"Stop treating me like a toddler, George! I'm a grown man!"

"I thought you needed some encouragement." George stops clapping as I take yet another step, my feet somewhat solid on the ground. I keep going.

The nurses attend to Abe as George comes forward to evaluate my steps.

"Would it be possible to take me outside? I haven't gotten a breath of fresh air in what feels like years. I'm about to go mad." I can just smell the wind, feel it on my cheeks.

"Well, of course, if the distance isn't too much for a *grown man* such as yourself."

"Sure. If you're up to it, *old man.*" I elbow him, giving him the stink eye.

"C'mon. You're like a colt in the middle of a spring field. I'm only *ten* years your senior."

I gesture at my crutch. "A colt who can't walk."

"But you're lucky they learn quickly." George winks.

I take another limping step forward, stuffing my free hand in my pocket. "Lord, it's cold outside, isn't it?"

"I mean, it's spring, but it doesn't feel like it." George huffs, stopping me. "Hang on, you're going outside like that?"

I'm fully dressed, tunic and all, lacking gloves or a coat. I bite back a whine from the cold.

"Wait for me." I hobble back to grab my coat and slide it back on. I button it tight and pop the collar. The familiar fabric welcomes me, saying, *Welcome back, Sergeant.* I then shuffle through the inside pockets to find my gloves—the same expensive, black leather ones I was gifted when I shot my first goose. They've served me well, but the reminder of how I obtained them doesn't ever slide.

"I'm surprised that you didn't fall over," George goads me to act.

I don't take his invitation. "Do shut up."

We're off.

The ward is a lot to take in, since I've barely seen it. The halls are stuffy and smell of cleaning supplies with doors that lead to rooms identical to mine, beds occupying nearly every corner, stretching across the room with little to no privacy. Nurses are leaning against the walls—actual nurses, not the medics in the trenches. There's one or two of them around. Pots of flowers sit by the windows here and there, messengers walking to and fro with a satchel full of packages and letters.

"I expected this place to be bigger," I speak louder over the commotion, "like the hospitals back in Philly."

"It's a makeshift hospital for soldiers." George matches his pace with mine. "It's temporary. I wouldn't expect them to be using an extreme amount of room. They needed to build these wards quickly, I heard."

"I see, but do you mind going just a bit slower? I'm not as fast as I used to be."

"Sorry, slow poke."

He directs me to another wing where the doors to the outside world have been left open, probably for the nurses to carry stretchers in with ease without the struggle of getting someone to hold the doors open for them in case of emergencies.

My first breath of the outside world in a long time is one full of the tang of smoke and the acrid stench of fumes. The scents of the battlefield that I and so many others have grown so accustomed to all come back. The cold sends shivers across my skin. Even with my coat on, gooseflesh forms as I take another step outside. The sky is a deep winter gray. The snow gathers on the steps below, only just starting to thaw.

"We could go for a stroll, if you'd like. Just keep your distance with others."

"I think not," I reply. "I'll grow tired. You'll have to carry me all the way back."

"Not even around the block?"

"This is enough." I train my eyes down below, where the battle rages with the echo of machine guns, sprays of dirt blasting with each explosion and bullet. My eyes start looking for where the sniper shot me, recalculating my location from that day.

I was in the southern trenches, facing forward on the front line, just peering over the lip with my metal helmet on and a whistle just inches from my lips. Then the impact of a bullet exploded inside of me, sending my body into a state of shock while my head collided with the wood as my helmet fell to the ground. The sniper could've shot me in the head while he had the chance. I was still in their range of fire, but they chose not to. They must've thought a single shot to the abdomen would be enough to send me to the grave.

Coward.

I chuckle to myself at the thought.

George hears this and inclines his head. "Are you good there, pal? What're you laughing at? That's the first time I saw you smile in weeks. Is the real Marshall Clark finally making his appearance?"

"Oh, nothing." My smile doesn't vanish. "I'm just thinking back to when I could've died."

"Quite literally. You were shot in the abdomen."

An abandoned plane in the east causes a plume of mud and dirt to rise as it dives in a cloud of smoke. The pilot will definitely be dead, and I'm here to watch. "The thing is I could've died without even knowing it. The sniper was a coward."

"He still shot you fair and square in the—"

"Are you not hearing me out?" I turn to look at him, who flinches under my gaze. "The sniper could've taken his chance and shot me in the head as I fell. He didn't. If he did, then that would be one less of a life for the Axis Powers to worry about."

"Maybe he thought you'd die just from the shot or from hemorrhaging? Perhaps from sepsis, tetanus, or shock? There were many ways you could've died then."

"He thought wrong." I shudder from a cold breeze that numbs my cheeks. "He miscalculated. Once I find him, he's going to have to run for his life."

"I don't think you will. You don't even know what he looks like."

I sit on the bench nearby with difficulty, wincing as I lay my crutch at my feet.

"Hm." My memory rewinds back to the day Andrew had shot and taunted me as he revealed he was a spy. The damn rat. I'm glad Frieda shot him. I laugh once more. "The man who shot my shoulder was even worse."

"The Austrian guy you kept rambling on about?"

"He talked me to death. You'll never guess what happened to him." I don't fight back the evil grin that escapes. "He's dead."

"You didn't—"

"No, I didn't. Frieda did. She shot him, not me." I pick at the lint that's caught on my knee as George bristles at the thought. "I guess it was a returned favor for me saving her from nearly dying from that explosion."

"When you did something so suicidal you nearly came out obliterated? Ran into the path of a bomb set to blow you apart? Yeah, I remember."

I shrug it off. "What is a man so terribly in love supposed to do, George? A man with a heart so fragile that he couldn't bear to watch those close to him die in front of his very eyes?"

I think I've gone too far, as George stiffens.

I've hit him hard. I shouldn't have said anything. George stayed behind that night when Chip passed away. He was his brother. It seems he's still grieving.

"George, I...Did I go too far?"

"Honestly, yes." He's fighting back the waves of guilt and grief.

"I'm so terribly sorry. I didn't mean—"

George steadies himself. "I know you didn't."

"Please, sit with me." I pat the space beside me, chewing my lip. "You're swaying."

Almost obediently, George keeps his distance. He sits on the other side of the bench. His golden-brown hair is pushed back by the wind—Chip's hair—that he had cut short. I want to reach my hand out to grip his shoulder to calm him and tell him it's okay to cry, but rules apply that we must keep our distance to stop the spread.

"You know what?" I prod him with my elbow. My hands remain in my lap. "War sucks."

"That's the best thing you can say, huh?"

"Well, it proves a point one way or another." I close my eyes against another biting wind. "You can't help but agree with me. If you disagree, call yourself a masochist and a sadist and get on the road."

George changes the subject. "What do you plan on doing after the war, Skipper? Get a job? Get married? Start procreating and producing money that makes the world go round?"

It's now his turn to catch me off guard, silence filling the barrier between us.

"Get a job, yes. I'd like to be a nurse"—I run my hand through my hair; a nervous habit—"to sustain myself and stay alive."

"A nurse, huh? How's that?"

"I want to conquer a phobia. Also, I'd like to save those who need saving. After my mother died, I couldn't bear the thought of leaving those in need out to suffer. Human health also interests me."

"You'll get some good earnings if you work hard." He flicks away a splinter of wood coming loose from the arm of the bench. "What about your family?"

"They're fine—"

"No, I mean when you start looking for a partner."

Another bullet in my side. More painful than the one that left actual stitches.

A partner.

I have one person on my mind. I'm willing to wait until she's ready.

"You know me. I have only one in mind." I intertwine my hands tight in my lap. "As she says, I'm lovesick. When you say to procreate, that makes me laugh. I'd have some rather good looking children."

"Of course, the Clarks' vainness never ceases." George slumps in his seat. "Like your hair, it's always there in the genetic pool as yet another personality trait."

"I don't mean to come across as vain. My partner would supply all the good looks. It doesn't matter how they look, though. I'd love them, no matter who they are."

"You *are* at the ripe young age for marriage," George observes. "I don't think a dashing bachelor like you will have any trouble winning her over."

I have to force myself to clamp my jaw shut to stop myself from screaming. "Did—did any letters come through?"

"From who?"

"From anyone we know?"

"No, but I suspect a rather large wad of parchment from a special someone is coming soon."

I manage to gasp before I'm interrupted. "Oh—"

"I picked this up for you. It seemed important. Just remembered it now."

I reach for the letter George retrieves from his pocket, opening it to find my father's handwriting. Once I finish reading moments later, I let out a low groan.

"Is something the matter?" George asks.

"You'll *never* guess what he writes to me about. He's talking about Frieda. He thinks we're courting."

"And what does that mean to you?"

"I never imagined it. *Courting*." I exhale, a cloud of warm air spilling from my lips. "We're close, but...I just don't know how to describe it."

George smirks. "It's more than just courting between you and Frieda. Don't deny it."

"I won't." My stomach flips again at the idea of courting; something I've feared all my life. "Oh God, what do I say?"

"To whom?"

"My father."

"Well, you've been doing it for quite some time."

"He knows I'm scared of courting. He's even written, *my little boy is finally overcoming his fear and is getting ready for a beautiful union.*"

At this, George doesn't hide his laughter, his shoulders shaking with glee as he doubles over. "Admit it, you want to marry her."

"We've only been together for five months, George. It's not time to discuss it yet," I lecture him. "I must respect her wishes as she respects mine."

"You'll be thirty and still be stuck to that opinion."

"And you'll be growing gray hairs! That makes two of us."

George looks at the letter that's still resting in my hands. "Wow, he seems really fixated on the idea of Frieda becoming a Clark."

"And if she says no?" I worry.

"Ah-hah! So you admit that you want to marry her?"

"I haven't entirely made up my mind. She isn't my first relationship. The last ended chaotically. I'm afraid the same thing will happen."

"Who was it?"

My mind once again retraces the night his hair was tied back in its black ponytail. He leaned against my desk, cradling a glass of bourbon from the liquor cabinet in the kitchen in his long, graceful fingers. Two eyes—one a dark brown, the other a brilliant blue—were illuminated by the candlelight.

"Not anyone you know." I let the lie fall, casting the letter aside.

"Are you quite certain? I know basically anyone and everyone."

Another lie. "You don't know *everyone,* and it's no one in Belgium or here."

George raises a brow, questioning me. "I'll ask again. Are you certain?"

"They're a person of my youth. No one I'm involved with anymore."

"Huh, another secret of yours that you'd rather keep to yourself and not share with your friend?"

"If I shared it, it wouldn't be a secret." I lean back against the bench, the wind blowing in my hair, tickling my forehead. "The truth is, in a life as tragic as mine, for all the twenty years that I've lived, for once, the world has stopped spinning."

"What do you mean?"

Another smile—a true one—threads its stitches into my lips. "I feel complete. It may seem melodramatic of me to say, but I think I've found an anchor."

"An anchor?"

"Yes. An anchor to plant in my angry sea."

"You're turning into a poet. Did you smoke something? Drink anything?"

I don't move, savoring the feeling of the wind chilling me through my clothes, finally being able to feel something true. "She may be quiet, reserved, and fearful, but she's cunning. She's an angel, *my* anchor, and I love her."

He's perplexed, face etched with it before the realization kicks in. "Is this your way of saying you want to marry her, but you're too scared to openly admit it?"

"I haven't made up my mind. I'm terrified of the idea."

"Marriage shouldn't be scary."

"It's the idea of being on display for all to see."

"I'm sure they wouldn't do that."

"I don't want to put her through that," I say. "She already hates being the center of attention. I don't want to put any more pressure on her."

"If you do become engaged, you will technically be the center of attention. I know that for a fact."

"Of course you do. Tell me, what's it like...you know...being married?"

"It matters on the one you choose," he tells me. "Of course, with Frieda, I'm sure it'll be brilliant, no doubt. With Myrtle, it's the primary thing I care about. You'd kill yourself to keep the marriage safe, especially once you have children—especially after we had Howard—or else you'll end up as a lonely, miserable man."

I mope. "Sounds like a chore."

"Not so much. Don't let me discourage you. It's basically your relationship with Frieda, except she becomes part of your family and you become part of hers. She takes your last name and moves in with you while you expand your family by having children."

"Children seem terrifying," I gulp. "I mean, I'd love to be a father, don't get me wrong, but it's intimidating to think about having little boys or girls running around your house calling you 'Father' or 'Papa,' if you get what I'm saying."

George nods with an affirmative *mhm*. "It's not intimidating once you get to see them when they first step into the world. It's magical."

"So it would seem," I mutter. "This bench is feeling rather cramped. Care to walk further?"

"Do you think it would be good for you, being on a crutch and all?"

"It'll clear my head."

"If you fall, it's not my fault. It's entirely yours, old man."

"You're such a hypocrite, don't you know that?"

George chuckles. "Nearly died, and you didn't lose your sharp tongue."

"Trust me," I dip my head back with a titter, "It'll keep getting sharper."

PART III

HEALING

APRIL-NOVEMBER, 1918

FRIEDA AND MARSHALL

THE SECOND INTERLUDE

The world around me is full of light and sound, crashes and booms as I crash into the dirt.

As if the impact wasn't enough, sticks and stones are splinters in my side. Smoke pours from a nearby flame. I've fallen yet again against the shockwaves, the violence dancing in a sweeping tirade above me. My hands are scraped, littered with mud and dirt, stained brown.

I'm breaking, brittle, running out of stamina.

Back in the dance studio, when I was younger, my dance instructor told me that every twist, every turn, and every jump is part of a soulless set of choreography that only you can give meaning. When you grow tired, so does your interpretation. So do your feet.

In this war, your life is a dance that you must give a meaning to. Each turn and each pivot decides how far you'll fly, how far you'll fall, how long you'll live, how brutally you'll die. They don't care if you start growing fatigued or how tired your feet get to the point where you can barely walk from the exhaustion. They continue to tap their cane against the floor with a sudden urgency that snaps like hungry jaws in the midst of battle. Like ballerinas hungry for a song, for freedom, they're hungry for some sort of power to clutch onto.

I guess I've taken the wrong amount of steps, the wrong turn, somewhere along the line. My head is spinning, chest tightening as I lie helplessly on the ground. I long so desperately to dig myself deeper, bury myself head to toe, anything to escape this long and hard battle.

"Get up!" Madame Abadie would slam her cane against the floor, snapping those words over and over again. "The beautiful swan you were destined to be can't fly with clipped wings."

I'm not a swan, but a duck in hunting season: shot down, unable to move, pinned and ready to be slaughtered by starving hounds. Each cut to my ankles or my feet from the pointe shoes was another insecurity unveiled, another mistake made. Whenever they'd reopen, the insecurity would bleed through yet again. Each rise upon the platform of the shoes felt like flying. Each stumble or fall felt like I was descending to my death.

With each step higher and higher into authority in this battle, your pedestal rises. So does your fame. One wrong command or one wrong march is enough to send you clawing at the edge of a crumbling cliff that was once your kingdom, your castle, where you felt it was safe to rule. Mine is falling apart with each crawl of my limbs, each shielding of my ears from the commotion. I'm so utterly lost, forgetting the choreography of survival like an innocent dancer forgetting her solo.

Another gulp of smokey air scrapes at the back of my throat as I make an attempt to rise, to stand when the gunfire stops, bodies lying just meters away. I have just enough energy to pull myself out of a ditch before the next shockwave strikes with a bang that almost mars my hearing.

My foot slips. So does my grip. I go tumbling back to where I first landed, where my back cracked so loud for the entire Front to hear upon an impact that had the air gushing out of my lungs.

The sour-sweet smell is distinguishable enough in my nose, and I curse at the oncoming threat. Yet, I can't get my limbs to move a single inch, my chest heaving, oxygen trying to supply my body to keep it alive. I fear it won't have to worry for too long, as the cloud rolls over.

Unable to protect myself, I have no choice but to surrender.

At first, the perfumed scent tickles my nostrils. Then, it burns through my skin, my lungs. I abandon all thoughts of forfeiting to such a painful death and force myself to climb, to escape, as my eye seals itself shut and blisters. It burns far too much, leaking tears of pain.

The next wave are running at full speed, howling and crying out to their comrades to run, to fight. My scream for help is unheard as they stream past. I make another attempt to stand, to rise, to continue dancing, to continue fighting.

My head swims with the gas. My ears may as well be practically leaking with it, lips blowing it out like cigarette smoke.

I finally give way to the weight, the weariness, and pain wrecking my body.

I fall ungracefully back to the floor, waiting for death to take me away, a dead ballerina with a dance left unfinished.

26

Drowning, Part I

Frieda

They say that when you drown, you get the choice to sink or swim, to live or die, call for help or suffer silently. It's all a matter of your decision at the moment. One wrong misstep could send you sinking to the bottom of the ocean instead of aboard a lifeboat.

Another day. Another moment alive. Another moment above the surface, awake, gasping for air. I'm treading choppy and unforgiving waters yet again. I've chosen to swim, to live, call for help and a lifeboat.

"Good morning, Frieda."

The voice is tired, strained from exhaustion as it comes closer. There's the sound of a box being plonked down on a nightstand along with the shifting of many sheets of paper.

Another voice that's low and cautious follows. "Don't wake her. She's ill and needs to rest."

"Do be quiet, Nathan. Her eyes just fluttered. She's awake."

I've grown accustomed to one side of the world being dark as I open my eyes, my body on fire, throat parched, head killing me. It's the cost of being alive, the suffering, the pain, the drowning and resurfacing—at least that's what I call it.

"Did you sleep well, dear?" Edith slides on a pair of rubber gloves, her eyes shadowed from long nights of no sleep. When I'm awake, she yells at her colleagues until her voice grows hoarse, and the sound of new men being piled in drowns her out. I may as well start preparing to say goodbye, as death is fast approaching.

"I could care less." I shield my eyes from the light, raspy breaths entering my lungs. "I'm going to die soon, anyway."

"You're better than you were last week. Can you sit up for me, please? I forgot to mention that your patch may be able to be taken off soon if everything is healing nicely for us. You get to wear a clear shell in your eye called a conformer to keep the shape of your socket. Think of it as a bigger contact lens."

As I do, I stare up at the man hovering over my bed: a red cross on his sleeve, copper hair, and matching shadows under his eyes, small crescents of dirt under his fingernails. Another medic, carrying a satchel of medical supplies, staring me down with gray, stormy eyes. His skin is pale, dotted with plenty of blemishes, probably more than what I have all together.

"I forgot to introduce you to this bloke behind me." Behind her mask, she's smiling as she sticks a thermometer under my tongue. "This is my new assistant, Nathan Nelson. He usually rides on horseback on the front and hauls those who are wounded back here. Poor doll's been up all night wheeling carriages full of the sick."

Nathan waves a shy hello, holding an envelope in his gloved hand. It's obvious he's trying not to stare at my eye that's been severely damaged by the Germans' gas attack. The red and angry burns around it are symbols of survival. As ugly as it is, people want to praise it.

"Any other news about my eye?" I ask.

"No, but we're thinking that once the war is over, or after we put in your comformer for two months, we could put you on the list for a prosthesis."

"How quaint," I answer. "How will that help me?"

"They've already removed your damaged eye through a procedure called enucleation. What they'll do is take measurements of your socket and record your eye color. It won't restore your sight, but it's better than an eyepatch. You can wear it for as long as you want. There's no time limit. Nathan, where's the envelope that came this morning?"

"Apologies. I must've put it in my pocket somewhere. I've only got one from a week ago."

"Dear Lord, Nathan! Give me your pockets."

Edith sighs as she digs deep in his pockets. He holds his arms out awkwardly to shuffle through the pockets of his apron as well. "Boys, always losing things—here it is! Don't tell me you've already lost the second one in your hand just a minute ago. That one is equally as important."

"Right here." He hands it to her with care, holding her gaze as she takes it from him.

"These two envelopes came for you this morning—he wrote one for me too—asking how you were."

"Who's *he*?"

"You know who *he* is." Edith sets the envelopes on the blanket, familiar handwriting on the front. The day he sent it is marked from a few weeks ago. The mail must've been delayed.

I stop before I say his name, being accustomed to not saying it for days on end. "He wrote to me?"

"Indeed he did. There's a shortage in mail carriers at the moment. You should read both of them."

"My eyes are too tired." I groan. "Please read them to me."

Edith complies and opens the first envelope, reading aloud: "*My dear Frieda, before I get into any nitty-gritty detail of my current affairs, I know you probably won't get this letter until much, much later, but I felt like responding to your letter as soon as I possibly could.*"

"Which letter was this?"

She pauses to answer, "I presume he means the last letter you sent before going over the top."

"Oh, I'm sorry."

"*Before I say anything about what's going on, I'm going to say it. I miss you, Frieda.*" The words hurt me on the inside, the longing returning. "*I don't feel like I'll ever be able to say it enough. I miss your smile, your face—especially all the little freckles that you don on it. Don't stop me when I say this, but I also miss your lips and the voice that pours from them. What I miss most is you by my side and the personality that makes me want to smile for the rest of my days.*"

"He's infatuated," Edith sighs.

"Keep reading."

"*I will ask, how are you? I understand you're in a troubling position, and I worry every hour for your safety. I'm sending all my love and prayers over to you and will pray to God that you come out unharmed and safe when you return. I trust you'll take care of yourself. I've noticed that you have quite good awareness of your surroundings and are incredibly agile. Your whole body seems to move with you on the battlefield. Could it be that being a ballerina has made you stronger in these aspects? I mean, you have to look where you are so that you don't jump on the person next to you, plus the spotting, the turns, and pirouettes you have to do, and how flexible you could be.*"

Marshall, fluent in the art of flirtation, never fails to make me cover my face.

"*On the topic of my health, I'm in recovery at this very moment near the ward where the flu patients are taken care of. My lord, am I terrified of falling into that ward! Just thinking about it makes me shudder! As for my current wounds, yes, the nurses were able to remove the bullet successfully under the knife. The pain isn't too much to bear—just a small jab. About the stutter, it's nearly gone. It was the forming of the words themselves, but it doesn't so much affect me as it originally did. I'm starting to feel better, but all the screaming, coughing, and transmissions are what's keeping me back as I lie here in this hospital bed.*"

The pit in my stomach grows. "He must be dying to get out of there."

"*George stopped by today to tell me the news of what's happening over on the Front. It's all very tragic at the moment. I don't know if you've heard, but Ed's wellbeing is declining fast and his behavior is quite...how do I put it...maladaptive? I worry for him. Perhaps you could talk to him for me, or Alistair, for that matter? Though my brother can be a complete pain in the ass, he also has a knack for talking to people. I wouldn't trouble Edith about it much, as she's already very sensitive. How are they doing, by the way? Are they well?*"

"Are you two doing okay?" I ask Edith, unsure.

"We're both right as rain. Calling me sensitive, what a tease."

"What about Ed? Is he—"

"He's stable."

I exhale in relief, my heart skipping a beat.

"I'm running out of space to write and dinner is going cold. Please write back as soon as you can, as I'm aching (quite literally) to hear more from you. I love you so, so, so very much...to the point where I'd break my back if I had to to save you. 'You must allow me to tell you how ardently I admire and love you.' You may remember this quote from a very famous Jane Austen novel, my dear, as it captures beautifully how I feel about you."

Edith registers this letter, setting it on my bedside. Before I can say anything, I'm fading away, drowning once more.

* * *

When I start to drown, the world goes black, then surges with color as my subconscious takes hold, twisting reality into my dreams that plague me each time I go under.

It's the same set of hallways that form around me. The same oil lamps that flicker as the wind threatens to blow out the flames. There's a piano downstairs, someone playing a slow and beautiful ballad—probably Chopin.

In the real world, it's unseen on one side, halving my senses, depriving me. In my dreams, I can see thousands of miles away, everything screaming with color and light as I walk by.

I descend the stairs. The familiar shape of Alistair is at the piano, hands elegantly poised upon the keys, body moving with the rhythm and each sound that echoes through the walls. Edith is at the dining table with her father, sipping tea in the same gray frock she always wears. Cooper Clark is the same as I remember him from years ago, laughing along with Edith. The last man should be in the library, poring over thick tomes of literature the last time I left him when I woke up; a doll in a dollhouse waiting to be played with again.

Opening the doors to the library, the room is empty, books from many shelves strewn across the desk. It's abandoned, along with the armchairs surrounding a coffee table where he usually sits and lounges, placing his feet on the ottoman as he reclines with a throw blanket as his eyes skim the page. In my dreams, the bandages and scars from his fingers are gone. The hollows of his body and the bones gliding under his skin are gone. He looks as if the war never existed.

Reentering the dining room with the forever-haunting keys of Alistair's piano, Cooper Clark looks up with a smile that never fades as Edith takes a sip of what I presume is rose tea in a pristine, white cup.

"Frieda, nice of you to bless us with your presence again," Cooper acknowledges me. "You vanished again. Marshall left the library by himself. Quite strange, your disappearing acts are. You're quite the illusionist." I don't say anything as he resumes sipping at his tea. "He's out in the yard, trimming the rose buds. They grow nicely around this time of year. Take some dark chocolate for him to munch on while he's trimming. It's his favorite."

Taking part of the chocolate, I creep through the open doors and down the deck's stairs to see him trimming, indeed, red rose bushes in the garden, dressed in a hickory brown waistcoat and dark gray slacks, sleeves rolled up against the heat of a fast approaching summer. His hair is combed neatly back, freshly styled in an undercut. The real Marshall would flip if he ever had to style his hair like that. He was absolutely repulsed when Ed suggested it.

As my heels hit the lawn, he raises his head and smiles, eyes illuminated by the sunlight. It's not the uptight smile he has in the trenches, but a true, relaxed smile I saw on him at the party as he waltzed. Whenever I wake up, I have a pain in my chest—a pain of longing—and want to see *him* again. But he's a thousand miles away. Simply untouchable.

"Hey," he waves, the trimmers in his gloved hand, "you disappeared again."

"I did?"

"But now you're back." He sets the trimmers down, gesturing at my hands. "And you've brought...what's this...chocolate?"

"Your father said to bring it to you, so I did."

Marshall—a dreamlike figure acting in his place—unbuttons the top button of his shirt, exposing the smallest amount of his collarbone. I bite my lip as he fans himself.

"God, it's hot for a spring day. Thanks for the chocolate. We should head inside before it melts." He offers his hand with a minute bow, taking off his gloves; a gesture that the true Marshall would do to jest and trick a smile onto my face when he thinks I'm troubled. "Shall we, my love?"

Without thinking, I take his hand and walk with him, his smile never fading as it all fades to black.

I resurface.

* * *

The first thing I feel when I wake up in the dark is the sudden weight on my chest and the suffocation that comes with it. I'm shaking all over, my fingers turning blue.

I sit up, coughing up a storm, clutching my throat which is engulfed in flames as nurses rush over to pat my back. I cough up the bloody fluid that they say is clogging my lungs, their gloved hands prying away mine that close tight around my neck.

"Remove her hands! She's going to choke herself!" one of the nurses orders over my coughing, tears stinging my eyes. Edith rushes forward, nearly tripping over her skirts to help settle this all down.

Caught in the fight-or-flight response, my eyes widen as hands clamp down on my shoulders. "G-get o-off of me!" I try to scream out, more coughs erupting from my throat.

"Breathe with me. You'll only make it worse by yelling. Ladies, please, I'll handle this."

The nurses dissolve from the scene as Nathan slips in, carrying a pitcher of water and a medicine bottle with a spoon. I slump forward, letting in raspy breaths, but Edith delicately pushes me back upright.

"I need you to sit up, darling. It'll clear your airways." She keeps her distance while speaking to Nathan. "Nathan, sweetheart, please bring her a blanket. She's shaking all over."

"Any blanket?"

"Yes. There should be some in the storage cabinet. Thank you." As he leaves, she sets the water and the medicine in front of her. "Would you like some water?"

I shake my head, attempting to focus on my breathing. Nathan returns, a small smile on his face as he sets the white blanket over my shoulders, sitting on the wooden chair by the bed. His brows are furrowed and act to mirror a concerned parent overlooking their child. It would make me laugh...if only I could. His long legs fold over one another. His hands sit, clasped, in his lap, back straight and poised.

"Do you feel a little better?" Edith asks, reading the medicine bottle's label. "Your coughing has died down."

"My throat..."

"What about it?" Nathan asks, leaning forward. Edith doesn't stop him.

"It burns," I sob.

"Maybe a small sip of water will help?" Nathan stands, pouring water into the cup for me to drink out of. It's a small metal cup with a matching metal pitcher that he holds out in his gloved hands. I peer up at him, his hair a dark auburn in the moonlight. He looks too ethereal with his cold, stormy eyes.

"I don't bite." Nathan tries to reassure me, continuing to offer the cup, tilting it. "It's just fresh drinking water. No poison, no arsenic. Nothing but water."

"You should work as a salesman instead of a medic," Edith jokes.

I reach for the water, making sure that our hands don't touch. Despite the fact that his are gloved, I'm still cautious.

"Thank you," I mutter.

"Frieda," Edith speaks as I take a small sip of water, cradling the cup in my shaking hands. "You conked out before we got to read the second envelope from Marshall. Did someone slip you a sedative or something?"

"I'm just exhausted. We could read it now."

Nathan fetches some matches, lighting an oil lamp hanging from the wall. He gestures to the envelope that sits unopened next to the one that was read before on the wooden table. The parchment is folded neatly, unraveling before me as I unfurl it.

My dearest love,

There's a song that George told me about when we heard it in the cafeteria this morning while having breakfast (not the most appetizing thing in the world). It caught my attention when it played on the radio. It was called Let Me Call You Sweetheart by Henry Burr and the Peerless Quartet. It was apparently a cover, but the swaying tunes and the slow tempo made me close my eyes and feel at peace for once, thinking of you, until George burst in and told me the song was seven years old. I had gone my whole life not hearing it. It came out in 1911.

Despite my current shock of not hearing a seven year old song until now, I will announce that my wounds are healing perfectly fine and that I'm using a crutch for support. But what I truly want to know is how you and the rest of the men are faring with the whole pandemic and the

German Offense. Have your flu symptoms died down? I'm starting to get a cold myself with a few sniffles here and there, so I'm isolating myself under the watch of the nurses, who are all being very supportive. For once, I'm not flipping tables about the idea that I may be developing the flu, which is a very high possibility. I could also just have the common cold, as I'm not having any difficulty breathing. But, for you, I've seen nurses let the flu patients bathe more than us healthy men. The steam works as a decongestant...Smart women! Maybe you can request to Edith this idea if you feel up to it. Don't move about so much, as bedrest is crucial.

Have you heard anything from Edward? The last I heard of him was that he did indeed have the Spanish Flu and is serving more time in the medical tents as his body heals. I'm worried, as his wounds may get infected and that it's taking a huge toll on his health. I'm quite sure about Alistair, as his immune system is like a machine. He never seems to get sick, never seems to hurt himself. Consider it a rare occurrence to find him coughing into his sleeve for reasons other than choking on a drink of water. Then, you can laugh at him for it. But not right now, as it could mean something severe. I've heard that this virus is highly contagious. About the boys, it was also mentioned that they're all keeping themselves safe. I should send some confections in the mail for you. The chocolates I've scored here are quite nice. I'm sure you'll enjoy them.

Stay healthy, stay safe. My best wishes are with you. Take care of yourself.

Kind Regards,

Your Marshall Clark

My eyes hover over his name, his handwriting, his everything. Each time I look at it, it hurts me even harder. His writing is slanted, which is probably from my wounded convergence. The pang in my stomach reappears as I think that, with this loss of an eye, I won't be able to see him clearly ever again. He doesn't know how badly scarred my face is, nor what I look like with an empty socket.

He still sees the person he once knew: the person who wasn't afraid to look at him with *both* of her green eyes, who he made smile without being ashamed, who he made feel at peace whenever he was around. I was the one who wanted to hug the living daylights out of him each time he came back from the front line, the one he danced with, all the while knowing that all eyes would be on us, enjoying himself either way.

"I'm not afraid." He spoke to me that night on the boat from Seattle when I awoke from a nightmare. He was quick to rush to my side, to gather me in his lap and brush the hair out of my face, the tears off my cheeks. He held me close, his tired eyes staring into mine, full of promise. "I'm not afraid to love those who are different. I'd never leave you. *Never.*"

I get lost in the memory, setting the envelope to the side, closing my eyes. An echo of his presence bleeds from the words on the page as it all floods back inside my head.

He had bent down to kiss me that night, and I declined. Without uttering a word, he'd gathered me in his arms for just a moment, making himself comfortable on the floor. He slept like that all night with his hand holding mine as it dangled off the bed to keep me at peace.

Marshall doesn't break promises. He fulfills and exceeds them.

"Frieda?" Edith's voice is far away as I settle back against the covers being situated at my waist, Nathan murmuring a goodnight against my ear.

"She's falling asleep, Edee. Your brother's words are like a lullaby."

"He's always been the very verbal type," Edith sighs, checking my breathing. "Ever since he met her, he's never stopped talking! I can imagine his smile. He hasn't smiled like that in years."

Nathan chuckles. "Just be glad he has someone else to bother."

"I think she's his first beacon of hope in a long time."

Nathan is saying something. Before I can catch wind of it, I fall back.

But this time, I'm not drowning.

I'm dreaming.

* * *

I'm not in a garden, holding hands with a manifestation of a boy who I'd let break down my walls, but in a grand ballroom, a golden candle-lit chandelier dangling from the ceiling. The dark, varnished wooden floor is worn down by dancing heels. Haunting music sways its lulling tune. I begin to feel lost amongst the crowds, unsure of where to go.

I remember this place from somewhere far, far away. The event was a party held by one of my father's friends from the richer end of Seattle. I forget the man's Christian name, but I fell for his son and engaged in a secret love affair. Compared to the vile scum of the earth who practically bathed in money-scented soap and told me of the many riches he'd gift me if I accepted his ongoing marriage proposal (pure bribery and manipulation, I must add), Marshall would run circles around him and continue running until he himself blew out of steam many miles away.

That's when I find him. His presence still haunts the deepest depths of my memory, no matter how far down I bury him.

In strides Henry Thompson in a dark, glamorous suit. His coffee brown hair is slicked back in its cloud of soft curls as he peers at me over his winged collar. His sneer is the deathly venomous mark of a wicked man, one that crept in the dark alleys and brothels with too many women to count, still possessing the audacity to claim that he loved me. He lied purely to my face.

I grimace at my rashness along with my fear of solitude for not letting him go sooner and my constant acceptance of his pleas for forgiveness.

He used and abused me. I won't let it happen a second time.

His face is set in stone: jaw clenched, chin angled with a despicable flare of arrogance. When he approaches, his lips stretch into a suggestive smile. My blood runs cold at the reminder of its existence.

"Frieda," he purrs, sober, but deliberately slowing his movements to give them a sensual, drunken air. "Is my little bluebird enjoying herself?"

My lips are glued shut as he perches himself right by my side. He tilts his head to me, his hand going between my shoulder blades. It's a small, unsettling wisp of air on my back.

"There's quite a lot of French being spoken at this party. Your father is pouring out words of it." He leans down to press his lips against my ear. "Perhaps you could teach me some tonight?"

My legs work on their own, backing away, as the door to the ballroom opens, men with black hair streaming in one by one, a lick of gray hair in the front, the other as tall as a tower. The third trails behind them with his gloved hands stuffed in his pockets. My heart throbs at the sight of him.

In this dream, he's as untouchable as ever. Marshall, his father, and Alistair have entered my mind once more. They're able to break in at their own will. I want to run over and throw my arms around him like the night in Le Havre. But this is a dream of the past. He wouldn't feel the same for me as I do for him here.

"Ah, you're watching the Clarks. Dreadful family, though they're of the upper-middle class. They don't earn as much as me in their tiny house in Philadelphia. Cooper's sons are like dogs following their owner."

My eyes don't remove themselves from Marshall as he forces his chin up over his winged collar, broad and padded shoulders squared. His tailcoat fits snugly against his frame, eyes the color of cold coffee as he streams past, quickly fixing his hair to the side as his father instructs him to fix his posture.

"What a dreadful excuse for a man," Henry sneers. "He scuffs the ground and walks like the homeless in the streets."

I want to hit him, smack him, for saying such things. I cool myself down with the thought that when I wake up, I won't have to see him ever again, that this isn't real. But it isn't enough.

"I...Excuse me."

I slip away, walking fast through the crowds, trying desperately to find my father, Cooper, Alistair, Marshall, anyone I know, to save me. As I wander farther, the weight on my chest grows as the dizziness comes hand in hand with the promise of fainting. I lean against the wall and clasp my hands around my throat, trying to escape the unease.

As I squint my eyes shut, footsteps come my way and halt. I don't dare open my eyes to identify their owner.

"Are you okay?" The voice is achingly concerned, low against the swaying tunes of the music, tapping me on the shoulder. His cologne stings my nostrils, his familiar warmth so painfully close. "Hey, I asked if you—damnation—can you hear me?"

Daring to take in another inhale, I open my eyes to find eyes—*his* eyes—blinking back at me. Familiar, but distant.

"Did you have too much to drink?"

"Mar..." I stop myself. "Mr Clark, I—"

His composure nor his patience are spoiled, growing more and more concerned. Typical Marshall: forever patient. He edges towards me and asks, "Are you drunk?"

"No. Is my father around?"

Perplexion crudely contorts his brow. "I don't know who your father is."

"Mr Frank Joyce? Is he nearby?"

The confusion ceases into familiarity. "Mr Joyce...He's your father?"

"If you could tell me where he is—"

"You look like you're about to pass out." He lowers his voice, linking his arm with mine. So much care in one singular gesture. "Let me take you to him."

This is too much. Being transported back in time is too much. His dreamlike presence is too much, far too much, though it makes me want to linger because of *him*.

I close my eyes as we walk.

"Mr Joyce, Ms Joyce." Marshall sounds vaguely reluctant to let me go. "I found her appearing as if she was going to fall over herself."

I don't dare open my eyes. I'm not ready to see him again. Not after the funeral, after the unveiling, after the many weeks of grief and silence. Some men need to stay dead.

Carved and refined by French descent, Frank Joyce tuts. "She must be still ill. She had a headache not long ago. Thank you for retrieving her, Marsh. It's a good thing she had you nearby."

"As always." He bows, arm slipping away. The familiar weight of my father's hands—something I should be yearning for—lands on my shoulders as he steps back to let him take hold of me.

"Mr Clark?" I reach out for him, grabbing his sleeve.

His eyes blink back his shock, waiting for me to speak. "Ms Joyce."

"Shall I see you again?" I sound too out of breath, too light, far too desperate.

A pause.

His lips move, unsure of what to say. Face softening, eyes creasing, the tiniest hint of a smile rises at one corner of his mouth. "In time, I'm sure. Goodnight."

As he turns on his heel, every instinct in my body is telling me to run to him, to grab his shoulders, run my fingers through his hair and slam his lips against mine until I lose my breath and have to pull away while his arms, unashamed, pull me closer with the all the urgency I need to tell me that he wants to do more than steal the night away on the dance floor. I have to stop myself before my longings get the best of me.

Here, in this dream, he doesn't think of me that way, doesn't see me as his 'pride and joy.' He perceives me as another naive little child who got lost at a party. An annoyance.

"Are you okay, *ma chérie*?" Wild chestnut hair. Tawny green eyes. Faint freckles on his cheeks. All these simple things mark me as his offspring. I almost choke.

Why did I have to open my eyes?

"Fine" is all I can muster.

Everything dissolves, and I rise to the surface once more. Though I wouldn't really call it 'rising to the surface' this time, as I still am very much underwater. The party becomes part of my distant past yet again.

My boots are drenched in mud, the air stale and full of smoke, all life erased as a barren landscape takes its place.

The Western Front is cold. The trenches are empty. Bodies of dead and gone men, horses, decaying wagons and fence posts remain strewn across the ground. There's a high-pitched, unrecognizable ringing in the air as footsteps come to a stop behind me.

"Admiring the view?"

My whole body is dunked in ice. He's back, here before me in the middle of the battlefield. The voice I haven't heard for months, the one I dread, belonging to someone that made my life a living hell sends my skin crawling with my fingers twitching at the sudden need to wrap my hands around his throat until his lips turn blue as he dies once more by my cause.

Andew—Andrej—Johannes stands with his hands in his pockets, his battered uniform hanging off his frame. His head is inclined teasingly as he stalks me; a predator observing its prey. His eyes are like Henry's: cold, menacing, and vicious.

"What's this? No 'hello, *Andrew,* how are you?' No 'how's the afterlife after I shot you in the chest, *Andrew?'* Even a round of applause would be nice."

"Why are you here?" I hiss. "Get out of my head!"

"Calm down. You never let me rest, do you? Not even when I'm dead! I come unarmed." He removes his hands, palms up, from his pockets, holding them up so I can see. "See? No knives, no sickles, no merciless guns hiding under my sleeves waiting to shoot your lover boy."

The hairs on the back of my neck rise at the memory. He presses on with a sickening, cold chuckle.

"Anyways, where is he? Not with you?"

"Why should I tell you?"

"I'm not here to harm you, even in your dreams, Joyce. My days of being an undercover spy are over—all my days are over. It's so dark here. It gets so lonely, despite how many parties you attend, how many gatherings, it just gets so *lonely.*"

I'm lost for words. He steps closer. "Let me tell you, it hurt when you murdered me. When that bullet flew right through me, it was all *red*, beautifully bright red! The last thing I saw was your face as you shot me with my blood all over you. I'm surprised you have such a good aim."

The words come out to their own accord; cold and merciless. "It was a spar of the moment. It's better with you gone."

"Has it?" Andrej sighs. "It's a real shame that I put you through so much, sending you home and thinking a target had been dealt with while moving on to the next. I want to—"

"You came into my dreams to apologize? You're sick. Truly sick."

"Here's the thing, Joyce," Andrej kicks the shoe of a corpse, his nose wrinkling in disgust, "I had no intention of killing you. *He* was my initial target. His marksmanship and ability on the field was a threat to my employer, the big boss. He had many other spies who came back after eliminating their targets who thoroughly reported on his skill before I was appointed. You weren't a target. You were merely an *obstacle.*" He spits the word out like it's a putrid dish he's just tasted.

"Great to know, but you failed. To me, who you said couldn't fight for herself many moons ago, who shot up your lungs with a single bullet."

He swallows back his defeat. "I thought getting you sent home would be enough. Turns out, you're a more valuable pet of Sallinger's than I had anticipated. I didn't get much time to stalk the man. He's quick, one place once, then another the next. It was hard to even get an ounce of information that may help my employer win this war. He didn't let me in so easily."

"You were stalking him while I was gone?" I'm not surprised. "I should've told you he was suspecting someone was after him all along."

That horrid, menacing laugh erupts. "No wonder he was so hard to snatch away. I was thinking of suffocating him with his pillow as he slept, but the clean up of the crime scene would've been too much of a task, though I could've said that he died in his sleep, but it would be too suspicious. Plus, the gun he had by his bed was easily within his reach. My employer would be slamming his hand into a mirror once he learned that I died without getting rid of him. He's a walking target, and I find it almost hilarious that he got shot once again a few months later by an enemy sniper. The man is made of steel, I must admit."

"But why not just kill me too? It's obvious that you wanted to."

"I did, I must admit. You were an annoyance, but not a target."

"What of Marshall? Is he still a target?"

"I wouldn't think so. They may think him dead, as he's in recovery. But, as soon as he shows his face on the battlefield, if he comes back...well," Andrew snickers, "who knows what they'll do to him."

There's rampaging footsteps, someone panting to my left, their boots squelching in the mud. Bending forward, planting his hands on his knees, is none other than Marshall Clark, puffing before me—nothing like what I saw moments before. Sweat drips from his forehead, fringe sticking to it as he pants.

"Marshall—"

"Frieda!" He breathes my name, hurriedly fiddling with his pockets, in search of something. "What're you doing here? Please come with me. We have to go. Come, run with me. They're coming." He wraps me close, patting me down. "Are you hurt? Please don't tell me you're hurt—"

"I'm fine! Who's—"

"How lovely of you to suddenly barge in on our little conversation, Clark? Enjoying the ambience? It's lovely, isn't it? Nice and calming," Andrej teases.

He freezes, hands stuck on my upper arms, gaze whipping from me to Andrej. His feet are quick to take hurried steps back.

I stammer, "I-it's not what it—"

"*You.*" He steps in front of me, barking, "What're you doing here? You should be dead!"

"The afterlife got boring. I was just having a conversation with your lovely lassie about what would happen to you if they were to catch you. Weren't we?"

His worried eyes flit from me to Andrej again. "Let's go. They're going to kill us."

"I don't think you're going anywhere. Up there? There's still remnants of mustard gas, so good luck not getting burnt."

"Do you have a gun?" I ask.

"Only one round left." He gestures to the pistol in his pocket. "I used the other two up."

"Use the round."

"I'll have to fire wisely unless you have any spare ones lying around."

"I'm unarmed."

"Is this one of those couple quarrels? Because I'm growing bored to death!" Andrej groans.

"Get back!" Marshall hisses, glancing over his shoulder feverishly. "Is there anywhere else we can go?"

Andrej grins. "Better start running, boy. The hounds are sniffing out your tail."

Marshall hauls me over his shoulder without warning, taking off. Andrej watches us go with that sinister smile plastered on his face. The commotion arises behind us.

"How many of them are there?" I gasp.

"Three! Shit, if Andrew is with them, that makes two against four!"

Andrej's voice echoes all around me.

You were merely an obstacle.

You were an annoyance, not a target.

He's a walking target.

A *walking* target? Andrej never said anything about a *hiding* target, one too difficult for the enemies to find. If there's one person I can save in this dream, it'll be Marshall.

"The trench!" I shout. "There should be some old tunnels in the trenches!"

"What the hell are we going to do with old tunnels? Find some bombs?"

"Hide!"

Marshall leaps into the ditch, fighting to stick his landing with my weight on his shoulder and the rubble skidding at his feet. He observes the area, setting me gently on the ground. "Over there. Once they give up on finding us, we'll try to find a village nearby. No, the docks. There should be a rowboat or some horses, maybe even people."

"But there's a war going on! The town is nothing but ash!"

Marshall pauses, staggering before he beckons me after him. "Follow me. We need to get under cover before they find us."

We hurry into the bunker, me first, Marshall following close behind, peering out.

A hand clamps over my mouth.

A pistol cocks just inches away from my temple; Marshall's pistol.

"You're with him, aren't you?" he spits, forcing me to the floor. "You're with *them*!"

I shake my head rapidly from side to side, my eyes wide. His teeth are bared, snarling like a rabid dog. Tears are forming as I whimper, kicking, but it's no use against his suffocating weight.

"Don't give me that." Marshall's pistol moves from my temple to my jaw, pressing where my jugular vein is pulsating frantically. "Don't act all innocent when, clearly, you're with them! There's not three, not four, but *five* of you!"

I let out a scream from behind his hand. His fingers are ready on the trigger. I don't stop sobbing and kicking underneath him.

"Just say it!" His hand clamps down harder against my mouth, my nose, as all strength leaves my body. Ugly, wretched cries form, gurgling in my throat.

"I knew it. I knew it! I should've never trusted you in the first place, never should've let you in. Because of you, all of our friends are dead. You're a plague that I'll gladly get rid of."

I close my eyes, the sobs and cries never stopping. The blast of gunpowder is loud against my ears.

White light sends me spiraling.

* * *

I wake up once more; drenched, shaking, sobbing, in a pool of my own sweat, screaming out his name until my throat is red raw.

My hands are gripping the bed sheets tight as Edith and Nathan rush over to settle me back down. Nathan is sitting by my bedside and clutching my hand. Edith wipes my eyes clean of tears. There's a rushed muttering of 'the poor thing' from Nathan with Edith shushing him as my eyes flutter shut.

They stay put for the rest of the night, watching over me in Marshall's abandoned steed.

27

Promises and Memories

Marshall

Isolation has never been fun. George can't see me, nor Abe, even if he's an annoyance. I grew too used to his company, even if I couldn't understand what he was saying most of the time in his thick, Southern accent.

The last time I was in isolation was when I was coming down with strep throat at the age of eleven. I was cooped up in my room and unable to see anyone while I was ill. We had guests from time to time, bringing chocolate when I was sick; mainly aunt Paula giving me hampers of cough syrup, painkillers, sweets, and books for me to entertain myself with. There was that, plus some tea tisanes that my mother brought up for me to drink: mostly ginger, peppermint or lemon. Sometimes, she put honey in it to help my throat be less of a nuisance.

Today, I sit by the window, re-reading, for almost the third time, *Pygmalion*, as the gunfire outside keeps me on edge. It's so surreal, knowing I'm not fighting for my life while so many others out there are. Instead, I'm fighting a battle of my own—a wounded abdomen and a cold that may or may not be the Spanish Flu—while I await a response from Belgium. My head pains me with the bangs and blasts along with my eyes trying desperately hard to focus on the words of each page. Each blast is another arrow slicing through my brain, the dull ache throbbing persistently, so annoyingly present that I throw my book on the table and cover my ears.

"Damnation!" I hiss as the book falls to the floor while I bend over the table, gripping my crutch tight. My lips are chapped from dehydration as I reach for my mug of water, the liquid cold as my head continues to pain me. There's a shake in the earth each time another crater is dug by the bombs. I feel it under my feet, spraying debris and soil over those who are near. The shockwaves then rip them to shreds.

I surrender on the bed that sits in the middle of the room, picking up my book and setting it neatly on the nightstand. I carefully sit myself down, placing my crutch against the side of the headboard. My vision sways with each movement I make, the dull ache still pulsing across the front of my cranium.

I should order some painkillers. Anything to get rid of this pain. Anything to bring me the smallest bit of relief, make me feel better, let me forget I'm ill along with the phobia that plagues me. It crawls under my skin like a bug I can't simply rid myself of, one that feeds off my terror—perhaps a parasite, in a way where it feeds off of its host.

Yes, that may as well be what my fear is; a parasite, feeding off of a host until they die or run out of nutrients. A host, which is me.

As of now, I'm a full course meal.

It's crawling through my body: behind my eyes, my set jaw, the shakes of my thin frame, even through the pulse in my veins. Shadowed memories of the tangled bedsheets, beads of a feverish sweat, my stomach flipping over itself each time I stood—a body of a boy fighting to survive. They all come back one by one.

The knock on the door is a summoning, telling me to deviate from the road of memories.

"Mr Clark? I've come to check on you."

It's the nurse again. God, I should really ask her for her name after all she's done for me.

The answer I give is a dull, tired 'come in.'

As the door opens, she's wheeling in a cart of medications and linens—things that are irrelevant to me and this small room. She wears a mask, a familiar white apron across her front, her dark hair pulled back in a complex braid.

"I've come in to check on your symptoms and your progress with that wounded abdomen of yours."

"Of course." I wince as another stab of pain comes. Another arrow to the head. "My head feels like the battlefield outside...painful, hard to endure. You don't have any painkillers, do you?"

She pauses before she goes to her cart and pops out two tablets, pouring a glass of water from the pitcher by the window. I take the tablets and the glass gratefully, swallowing both in a single gulp.

"So, how are we feeling?" She digs through the cart, going through a packet of gauze bandages. The sight of them has grown uninteresting to me. "Any signs of infection? No inflammation?"

"None."

"How's your walking? Feeling confident?"

"Give me a break. It's only been a week." The question is tiring. Each nurse that walks in here asks the same thing every time. I've learned to go on autopilot and say that it's going fine, just *fine*. But now, I don't, as this is a medical examination. "My core feels a bit stronger."

"That's good news. It should all come back to you soon. Your legs feel okay?"

"Yes, they feel just like before." Just like before, if I hadn't lost so much weight.

"Just like before?"

"Sturdy, stable."

She hands me a gauze patch while in her other hand is a thermometer. "I think you'll be able to put this on before you go to sleep. It's like a sticker. I need to take your temperature and check your nodes."

Once the thermometer goes in, I gaze at the floor, avoiding eye contact as she removes it. "Hm, just above normal temperature."

Even if the number is just a few units above the normal body temperature, it sends me flying, jumping at the news. "Wh-what's the number?"

"Thirty-seven point six," she says.

I start to shake. "What's that in Fahrenheit?"

"About ninety-nine point six eight. You're shaking. Fever chills?"

I swear, I'm just about to lose it. "No, just tense. I...I don't like getting sick."

A small smile teases at her lips. "No one does. I'll make sure to fix you back up. You may call me Heidi, by the way."

"Heidi," I mumble as she tilts my chin a little farther back. Her cold fingers press on the head of my mandible just under my ears. My jaw clenches. Even from a simple brush of fingers, illness can spread.

"It's alright." She grins calmly. "You're tense. Does it hurt?"

"A little," I croak through a clenched jaw.

"Hm." She moves her hands farther down my neck, still cold against my skin. "Does it hurt here?"

"A little."

"You poor thing, getting sick at a time like this," she sighs. I shudder as she pushes my hair back from my eyes. The gesture sends an uncomfortable shiver through my body: too sugary, too affectionate. "Just like your little friend."

"P-pardon?" I clear my throat, which is a terrible idea, as the pain spreads like wildfire.

"You're lonely, aren't you? Perhaps a lady friend would benefit you?"

"Miss Heidi," I glare, brows furrowing, hackles raised, "I—"

"It would benefit you, wouldn't it? We could have a night to—"

"I have a partner. They're sick with the flu."

"They don't have to know, does she?"

"I will repeat myself: I have a *partner*. Do you think I'd partake in such a foolish and unfaithful idea? No, and I won't." I edge farther away. "They're sick with the *flu* and there is never a day that goes by where I'm not worried about them. I love them with every part of me. I care whether I break their heart. I'm putting it nicely, and if you suggest this horrid idea again, I won't be as nice."

Heidi stands straighter, abruptly, taking steps back and away from my glare. "My apologies, sir. I...didn't know. We'll keep you on high alert for any more symptoms and will provide more wellness checks. Good day."

She sets an envelope on the bed, pushing out the cart, and closing the door behind her. Shocked, I open the envelope to find George's rushed handwriting. Reading on, I roll my eyes when he notes that a few nurses had heard us talking a week ago about courting, presumably gossiping about either Frieda and I's upcoming union, and a plan of taking me away for the night.

I take it that Heidi was one of them. The idea curdles my blood, twists my gut inside out. I almost retch.

I sit back on the bed and squint as my head still pangs me, the painkillers not setting in just yet. As I finish reading George's charged and angry letter, my head dips back against the pillows, a low groan escaping my lips as it continues to throb.

I feel like just closing my eyes and letting sleep swallow me. I can no longer take walks, no longer see anything that's beyond my window or the door when it's open, the memories of my past all flood back to days that felt like years as they took my youth away; days of sleeping on the couch made into a bed for my mother and I when we fell ill.

Countless books started piling up with dogeared pages or left open on a certain part, the plot boring me, not able to distract me from the pain of simply living. I remember screaming out the word 'mother' as she cradled me and told me it would all be okay. That she loved me to the moon and back, apologizing that she couldn't be in mine nor my family's lives any longer. That she had to say goodbye so soon.

Vive para mi, mi pequeño Marshall were her last words before she faded away right before my eyes. *Live for me, my little Marshall.*

When my mother died that morning with her arms around me, I couldn't stay in that room any longer. The memories of her body growing increasingly cold in my arms were too much, something I didn't want to remember each time I reclined on that couch. I'd screamed that it was all my fault as the body collectors came to take her in their car in a bag, unable to make contact with anyone from how ill I was. Even when I recovered, I felt guilty and closed myself off for four years: four years of falling asleep in the study with an excessive amount of assignments from middle school, later a large pile of AP English and Biology homework. Alistair carried me to bed most nights.

I met Ed upon the week of my fifteenth birthday; the week where I nearly kicked the bucket after struggling for so long with thoughts and urges of death stemming from my grief and survivor's guilt. He pulled me over in the hallway when he saw the marks—the scars—on my arms and asked for me to talk with him at lunch.

"Do you know why I pulled you over?" he asked, sounding far too much like a cop.

"To pick on me? I don't know, why?" I wasn't in the mood to play around. I barely slept that night and had just failed one of my assignments that I'd studied for weeks to pass.

"I saw your arms."

"They're just cat scratches."

My heart quickened at the lie. His eyes never looked away; two semi-colored irises staring into mine.

"Your cat must be a hostile one. I'm not buying it. I'm Edward Surry, and you're not alone." His hand had extended to shake mine.

I was quick to draw mine back. "Seriously, you don't have to help me. I'm fine."

"Clearly, you're not." His words wounded me. "I want to help you. Marshall, wasn't it? Quite an abnormal name."

It was my turn for my words to choke me. "My mother picked it."

Just like that, Ed had wormed his way into my life. The night I had planned everything out turned into a night of tossing and turning in bed, fighting the urges, the scars fading from an angry red to a light pink, a frown turning into a relieved smile as the clock struck twelve on my fifteenth birthday; another year lived.

I remember bolting straight to him that morning, hugging him so tight.

Eventually, it turned into a close friendship, but my feelings for him grew from day to day. I never told him, as I would have no idea what he'd answer with, and people like me are shunned by society, seen as unnatural, as a sin. But why is it that we are told to believe that love is such a cherished thing, but still caged by oppressive rules that dictate who we must and must not devote ourselves to? Why can't we ever be free?

It was until Ed was put into an arranged marriage with Alice at the age of eighteen. I knew that he and I were never going to work, but the shockwave that hit me made my heart shatter so badly that eighteen year old me broke a whole set of wine glasses by throwing them against the wall in the midst of heartbreak.

I hated Ed until we reconciled during after school hours when he had enough of me avoiding him. I told him all about how I felt; the loneliness, the isolation of my individuality, how closed off I felt from the rest of society because of who I was. He didn't shy away, but accepted me for what I was and what I would grow to be.

Still, he looks out for me, knowing that I grew weary about the time of my birthday. He must be still so scared that I'll do something at age twenty-one. He saved my life each birthday for a good six years and must be scatterbrained, dealing with the flu, a gas wound, and the idea that his best friend for almost seven years will finally off himself with God knows what. It's now my turn to be cautious of him, as he's also fighting the war and himself.

My eyes struggle to stay open as I blink back the memories, my headache starting to subside. I sit here on this bed, alone in the stale air of this sterile hospital room. Fears of falling victim to the pandemic crawl under my skin as the battlefield booms; a forever chaotic orchestra. For once, I wish that I was able to help and do something instead of just lying around, indisposed. I wish I had some company: George ranting in person about the nurses attempting to chase us down, another written letter from Belgium, updates on Frieda, updates on Ed—anything to entertain me just for a little while. I'm getting greedy for a distraction. It may as well be the end of me.

My thoughts lurch and spiral back to the day I had left her. Left *them*.

Sallinger bursted in on us and told me that I needed to depart that afternoon. The fear of it all had hit me in multiple places—gunshots—my airways constricting me as Frieda asked to talk to me before I left. I pondered that night on the boat if she was mad at me for leaving on such short notice. When I tried to pull her closer, she tensed, declining and pushing me away. It hurt, but I understood what she was trying to do: make the separation less difficult than it already was. Despite her efforts of reducing the pain in both of us, it grows every day on the inside as I yearn for her touch, the sound of her voice. I'm worried that one day, when I reach the lowest of the low, I'll snap, turn into a monster rather than a man. I'll sink my fangs too far into another loving heart, far too deep to staunch the bleeding, the damage my hunger may bring.

I could conclude that she was indeed mad. Not at me, but at Sallinger. She said the three words as I turned away, my tongue tied, not ready to capture the image of tears falling down her face, an image that would be stuck on replay in my mind if I had dared to look back. I felt like throwing up my entire breakfast as soon as my feet hit the docks. Not just from my absurd phobia of boats, but from the reality that I was actually *leaving* and setting off into the unknown.

She begged me to not forget her. I was worried too that I would, even begging my own brain to keep her memories prominent.

Although, the truth is, she's never left her little cozy space inside my head. I've never forgotten her as she visits me in my thoughts almost daily; usually in an array of paranoid questions in regards to how she's doing, if she's hurt, if she's pining just as I am.

After the commencement of the German Offensive was announced, the thoughts turned into prayers. I prayed every night that she'd come out alive if she were sent to the front line and that she'd still be there for me when I returned.

But now, I feel horrible knowing that I can't reach her as she fights for her life. If only I could grab her hand and hold her close, comforting her through the delirium that most of the victims suffer as their bodies cave in on them, singing her soft songs and reading to her. I'd do anything to provide her as much comfort as she needs while fighting a battle that could possibly be won by an extremely slim sliver of a chance.

The painkillers still aren't setting in. I'm about to bury my head in the pillow and scream as the pain knocks persistently on the door of my skull. It rattles around like a loose bolt in an engine. I clench my jaw, exhaling through my nose. Another strike of agony nearly blinds me. Closing my eyes against it, they grow heavy as my vision swirls.

I'm still not able to render what happened. The nurse who had been so nice to me—*Heidi*—who had gotten me through hell, asking me to start an affair with her without Frieda knowing?

God, how that would break her.

I've seen what happened when my uncle and my aunt Paula fought about an affair he was having with a barmaid at a pub he went to in the previous month. It resulted in a divorce right away. No second thoughts. Thus, I can't imagine what would happen between Frieda and I if I accepted Heidi's advances. It would be uncanny for her to scream at me, for how quiet and reserved she is, even more so for her to backhand me just like Aunt Paula did to her ex-husband. I can't ever imagine Frieda as violent towards me or myself screaming at her like my uncle did to Paula, calling her wicked and sinful things that one should never call anyone under any circumstance.

I don't let my head wander any further into the idea, the painkillers fighting away the pain. Yet, the pain of overthinking and concocting false situations only limited to my imagination remains unsolved.

28

DROWNING, PART II

FRIEDA

My eyes settle on the outline of a disheveled figure that stands over my bed the next morning.

"Marshall?"

"Nathan." His voice is soft like the sun rays that glow through the gaps in the tent's walls, illuminating only half of his face. It's enough to see the shadows forming under his eyes and the paling of his skin, even if his complexion is starkly pale already. This morning, he's as white as a sheet, his autumn-leaf hair left ruffled and messy, eyes the color of a raging storm, bloodshot under ginger lashes. "Morning. Slept well?"

"Somehow." He takes a step forward, grinning as he sets a medical kit down. "You don't look like you slept at all."

Nathan huffs, smoothing his rumpled hair. "I'm used to it. Lots of overnight shifts, really. I did. Only three dreadful hours, though. I'm quite jealous of you, sleeping like a rock through all the commotion."

I don't know if he's joking, but I laugh anyway as he gestures to the medical kit. "Mind if I sit and do a checkup?"

With a nod, I ask him as he sits down, "Do you know any women called Colby, Catherine, or Fey?"

"The twins? I know them. What of them?" He takes a mask, puts it on and pinches it over the bridge of his thin nose.

"I'm worried about them. I haven't seen any of them since I was last in one of these tents. Are they okay?"

"I haven't seen them myself, but I do know they're safe. Colby is up on the front line. Catherine, too. I'm not too sure about Fey's whereabouts, though. If you could let me see your eye, please?"

I let him take off the patch, blinking rapidly, even though it does nothing for me. The world stays dark. At least I have more comfort without the patch suffocating nearly the whole right side of my face. Nathan slips on a pair of rubber gloves and prods lightly around my socket.

"How does it look?" I ask. "Ghastly? Like your next Halloween costume?"

"A little bit of bruising after an enucleation is normal, I've heard. It's not necessarily horrible, but a bit off-putting. It should clear up soon." Digging into his pocket, he pulls out a small dark box with some sort of lens. "Now, this is the second step to healing before your prosthesis. You can clap and cheer now. You don't need your patch anymore, only if you want to wear it. This, my dear, is a conformer. It looks like a large contact lens, doesn't it?"

"A bit."

"This is going to go into your socket to help shape and prepare it for your artificial eye. It's temporary, and some discomfort may follow. Whenever you're ready, I'll slip it in."

"Did you wash it? I heard you need to wash them first."

"I did, yes. I'm also wearing gloves, so there's less chance of any eye infections or anything like that." He chuckles and dips his head, gazing momentarily at the conformer in the box. "Now, are you ready?"

"Just get it over with," I mumble.

"I should warn you, it might be a bit painful at first—a little bit of discomfort. If you could lean back for me, that would be great."

Moments later, the comformer is applied. I'm as still as a rock while he pushes it in, shifting, blinking furiously and rubbing my eyes, trying to evade the discomfort.

"Let me have a look, please." He sets the box to the side before he bends to look at me. "Oh, good. You look amazing. Would you like to take a look?"

"Is it horrible?"

"No, actually. I think I did a pretty good job." He hands me a small compact mirror. "Now, if it falls out at all, just call for one of us and we'll have to wash it with soap and water for you before putting it back in. It didn't hurt too much, did it?"

I don't reply, ultimately lost for words as I stare at my reflection.

In the mirror sits someone I don't know, someone so vaguely familiar, yet so distant. I struggle to swallow my shock as a whimper escapes me.

On my face are bruises of purple and an ugly tinge of yellow along my swollen lid. A myriad of angry red burn scars paint themselves in disgustingly vivid patterns on the side of my face, starting at my temple, stopping inches before my top lip. As if I thought it couldn't get any worse. But then comes the hard part: seeing my socket with the conformer. Behind the clear shell sits some pale pink skin that has me blanching at the sight of it.

"I know, it's a lot to take in." Nathan packs the box away, standing over me. "Not every day that you lose an eye, is it?"

"Is it usually this bad?"

"You're one of the lucky ones." He sets back to digging through his kit. "Some have their ears chopped off along with both of their eyes."

Another whimper escapes me as I hurriedly hand him back the mirror, not wanting to look at my face a moment longer. My throat runs dry as the shock finally sets in. Bile almost rises to my mouth, my gut threatening to make me even sicker. All I see in the person staring back at me is a ghost, a shell of who I used to be. I want to so desperately cry, to sob at my ugliness, the brokenness, the marks of my suffering I now must carry for the rest of my life.

My hands tremor as I screw my eyes shut to stop the tears. Just doing so creates a new wave of pain that takes my breath away. As if the world would take my pain away for a single day. Whoever is looking over me is on the floor, laughing themselves silly while watching the marvelous scene play out.

They say that eyes are the window to the soul. It's truly a repulsive shame, a tragedy, for a soul to have a small fraction of its essence smashed and broken beyond repair. Without it, I feel yet again incomplete, helpless, stripped clean of power, left weak and crying on the floor, lying in my soul's demolished, fragmented parts, desperately trying to glue them back together.

Rendered speechless, I let Nathan carry on with his examination. He checks my temperature, placing the thermometer beneath my tongue, concentrating on the mercury that rises with my body heat.

He squints as he pulls the device away. "Your fever's going down little by little."

"Is that good or bad?"

Though I can't see it, I know he's smiling from underneath his mask. "Good, obviously. A small ripple leads to a tidal wave."

"Does it mean I'm getting better?"

"I wouldn't be so certain. It could mean so many things at the same time. Anything can change without any given time. Any chills or sweats lately?"

"Not as much as before." While he grabs a stethoscope, I ask through one of my waves of drowsiness, "Any correspondence?"

"Not since yesterday." His voice is a rumble, careful not to wake the other sleeping men. His surprisingly warm hands are against my back, brushing against my neck delicately and keeping his distance. "Hm, your breathing sounds a bit better. Does it feel a bit easier to breathe?"

"A bit winded."

"But better than before?"

I shrug. "I haven't really been keeping check nowadays."

"Understandable." His voice is comforting, checking my lymph nodes, fingers still warm. "You've been fading in and out of consciousness for the past few days."

"I call it drowning." My voice vibrates against his hands on my neck. "When I'm awake, I fight to stay afloat like you'd fight a current. Drowning is when I go under."

Nathan's answer is grave. "Let's just hope you don't stay under."

He stashes the stethoscope away and gives me a courageous smile, which is obviously a tactic to either clear the tension in the room or to get a grin out of me to make himself feel at ease.

As the lamps flicker, there's footsteps outside and a shiver in my bones. The person who enters the tent sends my blood running cold as recognition kicks in.

Dusting his shoulders of snow and wiping his pale face, the curly brown hair and tawny green eyes of the Joyce family stay prominent in my first cousin Jay Joyce, the eldest son of my father's twin brother. He wears a mask over his nose and mouth while he carries a heavy-looking basket of jars and medical supplies, his arms shaking with the tension of his muscles clutching the handles.

My lips part to speak, surprise shocking my spine upright. "Jay?" I squeak a little too loud.

Jay is older than me by a year and the closest friend I've had since I was a newborn. He's like a brother to me and was one of the first to see me once my mother's protective layer had dissolved and she had allowed my family to gush over me. Even my father had to bend to her ways and fend off the eager family and friends who knocked on our door to see me.

He looks around once or twice before his eyes settle on me, shocked wide open. "Frieda? What the hell are you doing here?"

"I'd ask you the same question."

He takes a step forward, but Nathan stops him. "I wouldn't come close. She's sick."

Jay lets out a frustrated sigh. "After almost a year of not seeing you, you wind up here at the Western Front before my very eyes. You're not a medic, are you? What happened to your eye? How did they let you in?"

"It's a long story. When did you get here?"

"I've got all the time in the world to hear it." He picks at a loose thread on the cuff of his tunic. "I enlisted months ago and *finally* got here only a few days ago."

"Uncle Isaac allowed it? He didn't exempt you?"

"He said it was a noble deed, apparently," he scoffs. "More like public pressure. Now, how did you get here?"

Nathan vanishes into the darkness of the early morning with his medical kit and leaves us to talk with a curt bow, setting off to aid another patient.

"I ran away."

"From Aunt Rose?"

"I know. I've been told many times. I then went under a fake name and got accepted into a training camp and came here."

"Do they know now?"

"Indeed they do. One of the medics ratted me out right to Sallinger, but I'm guessing he didn't know what to do with me and let me stay. Funny, isn't it?"

My head hurts as Jay searches for words, letting out little, exasperated noises. "But what about your eye?"

"Gas accident," I bluntly reply, not bothering to get into detail about being lost for three days, almost dying in a ditch, crawling my way back to the trenches.

"God, Frieda, if any man laid his hands on you—"

I don't know where it comes from, but a laugh pains my chest. It provokes Jay's old habit of his bottom lid twitching when he's irritated to return.

"Bold of you to assume I'd let them, Jay." I cough when the laugh tickles my throat too much, making me inhale with a wheeze. "You don't need to protect me."

Jay still struggles for words as he stands there, turning pale. "As a matter of fact, I do. I'm your cousin."

"You can't protect me. You can't even come near me while I'm ill." Another chill shudders through my body from the fever. "Besides, I have someone looking out for me."

"Like a secretary? I don't see them, unless it was that ginger from just a moment ago."

"Oh, he's not a nurse—"

"Edith?" Nathan's voice booms through my ears, my head paining me just the slightest bit more as he rushes back inside the tent, looking around for her. "Edith?"

"Oi, Ginger!" Jay hisses, making him freeze. "There are people sleeping in here! If you're going to yell, you do that outside."

Nathan pauses, his eyes meeting Jay's. "Wasn't yelling. Did you come here looking for something?"

"I sent over a basket of medical supplies that almost killed me carrying them up that damned hill for you. Just talking to my cousin."

"Jay," I start. "No need to be so cold. That's Nathan. He—"

"Well, *Nathan*, your yelling is giving us all a headache," Jay complains, Nathan flinching, setting his basket aside.

"I wasn't yelling. Jay, was it? I apologize if I gave you a headache. I'm looking for Edith, unless Frieda has seen her?"

Jay spits at him, hissing, "You know her on a first name basis? What are you to her, huh? Did you get her in trouble with Sallinger? What are you, her lover?"

Nathan's rendered speechless for a few beats, but his shoulders relax. "I believe you're severely misunderstanding our situation. She's merely my patient. I've been caring for her as soon as she was admitted after being missing, contracting the Spanish Flu, blinded by mustard gas. I work under the guidance of Edith Clark, the sister of Frieda's partner. Do you dare question my position any more?"

Jay glares as the pain in my head increases, throbbing in time with my quickening pulse while Nathan stands his ground, never breaking eye contact.

"Jay, please stop it," I almost sob.

Nathan steps to the side, gathers his basket and opens a cabinet, sorting the many jars, syringes, and packets into their desired spaces. He squints to read their labels. "Mr Joyce?"

"What?"

Nathan brings up a gloved hand, beckoning him. "Please bring me that basket you brought up earlier. Frieda, you didn't see Edith? I was going to ask her to help me sort these jars."

Jay curses under his breath and hands the basket over to Nathan, who continues sorting through the myriad of medical supplies. I lean back against the pillows and close my eyes, the sound of gunfire awakening and unsteadying me. I hack out relentless coughs that scratch the back of my throat.

Nathan's up and alert, rushing to my side to get me to sit up, pushing Jay out the way to reach me.

"What—" I try to speak between coughs as Nathan pats my back. "Nathan, what—"

"Don't speak. Save your strength." He continues to pat my back. "Keep your chin up. Deep breaths."

"I'm—I'm"—I wheeze, the air in my lungs crackling, cutting off far too soon—"drowning."

Everything dissolves and dilutes. There's a ringing in my ears along with the sound of Jay's screams, Nathan hurriedly fending him away, muted by the violent waves, my ears cupped by suffocating tides and their chill, sinking further down to the sea floor in an endless, unforgiving black ocean.

I'm drowning once more. It's up to the sickness to say whether I resurface or not.

* * *

This time, I've reached the ocean floor, the water filling my ears, burning in my lungs as the air pressure has my bones crashing in on themselves in this sea's murky depths, waiting to bury me in a watery grave.

There are no dreams this time. No Wonderland down this rabbit hole. No one to guide me through the chaos.

No Marshall as the White Rabbit, making me chase his fuzzy tail as he's there one moment, gone in the next, his pocket watch *tick-tick-tick*ing away in his palm as he dashes away.

No Andrej as the Cheshire Cat, with his sinister smile, his disappearing acts, his torments and riddles, no jarring jokes, picking away at my sanity like a hungry vulture, attempting to convince me that we're all mad here in this war, battling turbulent tides, unforgiving currents.

Alice is dead down here in the dark; sinking, submerging—not through her imagination, but the grim Challenger Deep. The merciless Mariana Trench.

Her boat capsizes.

* * *

Seconds fly by. A lifeboat and its crew pull me up to the surface.

"Stand back, Jay!" are the words that are screamed out when my eyes flit open. A flash of red hair is in the corner of my vision. Nathan's gloved hand is pressed to my wrist. My pulse beats weakly, my head tilted back, lungs gasping for air. An unfriendly rasp appears in my throat as Nathan watches me come back to life.

"Thank God," he breathes. "Can you hear me?"

Slowly, I nod and take in a few more gulps of air.

There's the thudding of footsteps—heels—as they bolt into the tent. Edith skids inside, her skirts a whirl of fabric as she halts.

"Nathan! I came as soon as I heard!" Edith pushes past him to me, still coming back from drowning. Her thick black hair is matted in a braid that looks more like a lion's mane as each lock frays and frazzles from either stress or the lack of self care, or how busy she's been with all these new cases popping up. "Frieda! You blacked out again. Aw, my darling, you're as pale as a sheet! Let me fetch you some water."

"Settle down, Edith, love. Rest, I'll get it." Nathan stands and sets off for water as Edith furrows her brow, peering down at me as I lie on my back in a pool of my own sweat. She takes a kerchief and wipes my forehead, taking my temperature all in one fluid motion.

"Your fever has gone down since yesterday." She sounds reassuring. *Too* reassuring as she tucks the thermometer back in her pocket after wiping it. "I see Nathan's put in your conformer, too?"

I dodge her attempt at small talk. "I didn't know there was something going on between the two of you."

She freezes at the words coming out at my own accord, my mouth agape. At this, Edith gives me a fatigued grin. "I'd expect you to know something was going on, since you're in bed all day with nothing else to do but observe. Yes, you're correct."

"Tell me."

Edith rolls her eyes. "You'd fall asleep before I'd even get to midway."

"In trade, I'll tell you how I met your brother. I promise I won't fall asleep. If I do, that's entirely on me."

"I'm off for the next half hour or so. Nathan's covering, I believe. He'll be late if he doesn't come back right about now."

"I'm so sorry!" Nathan gasps, coming to a halt with a metal cup of water, setting it on the bedside and helping me sit up, the cotton of his gloves scratching against my hands as they fly past. "They ran out of water at one station, so I had to run five tents over."

"Stop rambling. It's fine. Now get back to work, it's your shift!"

"Damnation!" Nathan yelps, grabbing his kit and breaking into a panicked sprint. "Jesus, I gotta go!"

Once he leaves in a flurry of tent flaps, Edith and I laugh, my chest creaking with each inhale before Edith clears her throat.

"Okay, as you were promised: Nathan and I met at a training camp in France. He caught my eye with that godforsaken red hair of his at the back of the room. We were paired up and volunteered at the local hospital together in Paris while not knowing any French. That didn't stop us from becoming close. After one of our shifts, he came up to me, looking like a child kicked in the street, stumbling over his words and asking me out to dinner."

"Did you go?"

"Of course I did. Who do you think I am to reject a man's invitation for a dinner date? When he did take me out, we were so lucky the waiters spoke English and that Nathan had found enough money in his wallet to pay for dinner with a jazz band on stage. The poor boy was so shy about the whole thing and even combed his hair down to look especially nice and buttoned his collar all the way up to the top. It was raining that night and he had forgotten to bring an umbrella, so he gave me his coat and had to suffer through the downpour. He's truly a gentleman."

"The date went well?"

"It did." Edith tosses her mane behind her ear, pearl studs winking at me from her lobes. "I racked up the courage to admit to him that I had fallen for him months later after many other outings together. He dropped his whole medic kit at the news and was scolded, but we ended up just laughing it off."

I reach for my metal cup, taking small sips of water to calm the soreness of my throat. "Well, congratulations."

"And you? My brother is a nuisance, isn't he?"

"Which one?" I shrug. She regards me wryly. "Kidding, kidding! No, he isn't." I shift in my place on the cot, the mattress always lumpy no matter how I sit. "You already know how our families are close friends, so I'll just skip through all of that to spare us some time." A cough. "I originally came here and just got off the boat, bumping into him while he was reading and walking."

"Typical."

"Typical?"

"I remember, when he was younger, at family gatherings, he would always carry two or three books with him in a satchel along with his journal. Sorry, carry on."

Another cough traps the air inside my lungs before I tell her the rest about our first impression, asking with an exhausted sigh, "Oh, Edith, please, how is he so extroverted? You've seen how big his friendship groups are and how all the men regard him, haven't you? He adopts them like children off the streets."

Edith huffs a laugh. "My dear, his personality, good looks and manners are contagious. You either fall in love or get annoyed, as his humor and teasing make you descend further into madness."

"Anyhow, when I told him I was non-conforming—well, he was eavesdropping—even more so the child of his father's best friend, he was bewildered. Most likely, to hide his shock, he started remarking how wonderful it was to find out he'd been sharing a tent with me. He's quite cocky and bold when he wants to be, making innuendos shamelessly."

Edith gasps. "I'll have to scold him as soon as I see him."

"That's not all. He confessed his feelings while I was boarding a boat to Seattle and spent the following month writing letters back and forth, coming up with all these nicknames and pet names, flirting in almost every single letter."

"Damnation!"

"He still does it from time to time. Upon collecting me from Seattle, he took me on a date before the boat ride back and danced with me at a party just after Christmas."

"Dear me," she giggles. "I'd *love* to break it to you, but he isn't going to let go of you that easily. He's infatuated. Expect him to get down on one knee as soon as he sees you and ask you to be his spouse with hearts for eyes and Cupid's arrow in his flank."

"No, he wouldn't."

"I merely jest." Edith flashes a tired smile. "He's extremely patient, my brother. You'll have the time of your life with him. I must warn you, though…" Her smile fades, a prickle of fear stabbing me in the gut. "He's prone to breaking easily. He's as fragile as glass. I never tell anyone this about him, but I feel you should know. My brother, though he's never been diagnosed, nor does he look like it, is extremely hurt and has suffered for three years now of what I think is depression."

"He told me only a fraction of his feelings." Another prickle. "I…I didn't know how to help him, so I just complied with what he needed…alone time. He never told me anything else about it and acts like it never happened."

"He's not really one to talk about his afflictions." Another cough from me as she explains. "He's been struggling a lot recently. As I've said, he breaks easily. He's a highly sensitive boy. He wears his heart on his sleeve. Sometimes, it gets to be too much."

"I see."

"And when it does, he relapses and grows irritable. He begs to be left alone, cries almost every night, eats barely anything, and claims he's given up. He pins all the blame on himself and he disintegrates, he fractures. When it gets to be too much for him and he has a sensory overload, please be diligent with him. Please show him as much patience as he shows you. If he ever lashes out, know it's not your fault. It's very unlikely that he would. He hates hurting people."

"Is there anything I could do? Boost his spirit a little bit?" I take another sip of water, choking back another cough.

"As I've said: Be patient, be diligent. Talk to him, listen to what he has to say. If you do that already, I congratulate you. He does enjoy reading books. Maybe read them aloud to him? He enjoys walks, chocolate…find some dogs on your way and let him pat them. If you make him smile, that's a small victory."

"Edith! You're needed in tent five!" Nathan comes back, puffing as if he's run a marathon. "There are more cases."

"More? This pandemic will kill us all once it gets the chance." Edith stands and dusts her skirts, adjusting her apron and collar. She turns to me and fetches a piece of paper, a pen, and a miniature inkwell from her apron pocket, setting it on the nightstand, winking at me. "Loverboy is awaiting a response."

As she turns, I set the parchment on my knee, wheezing in a breath as I grab the pen and unscrew the inkwell, dipping the nib in its black ocean of ink. Now's the time for letting my emotions run loose upon the page with each breath I breathe, each cough my lungs force out.

I sign off as my eyes close, setting the pen and inkwell upon the parchment as the ink dries.

I lie back against the pillows, the riptide catching me in its merciless current as I drown once more under its waves.

29

CORRESPONDENCE

MARSHALL

The following weeks in isolation have been rather unsettling as the symptoms creep in. I've been keeping track, writing in my journal:

Week one: First came the fever, then came the episodes of waking up in pools of my own sweat. There's no escape from the heat, the chills.

Week two: The fatigue I'm experiencing is horrendous. I nearly fell asleep while eating breakfast and slept the whole day away.

Week three: I woke up too many nights in a row, coughing up phlegm with my chest rattling for air. My lungs are on fire.

Week four: It's been decided by the head nurses for me to be admitted to the ward after collapsing on the floor before inspection. I've become another sworn victim of this virus.

It's June now, and another year has passed for me. I'm twenty-one. My birthday gift is this virus killing me slowly while the snow melts outside to make way for the peaceful spring weather. I feel dreadful, like the illness is eating away my insides as I lie in this lumpy hospital cot. The other patients' coughing send my nerves firing spontaneously with the fear of coming close and even being in the same room as them.

It's only my first day here in the ward and I'm already having a miserable experience. The flu, partnered with a wounded abdomen that's taking its sweet old time to heal, is causing me more than enough pain. I've grown impatient with it, contemplating if I should have argued with Sallinger to not allow me to sail here to Italy, but that would risk me getting dismissed or forced into going with no change in answer. Sallinger is a stubborn and prideful man. I could write to him now and exclaim how angry I am, but it would only be turned against me. My military experience has made me paranoid; a permanent scar on my mind that'll last forever if I make it out alive.

It's like a recurring habit or a tic as my mind takes another swerve to Frieda, who's confined to her bed as if trapped inside a prison cell—just like me. I have nothing else to think about. I don't even want to think about death anymore, despite it coming fast.

She hasn't sent me any letters, as far as I'm sure, since the one I sent her a few weeks back that hurt my head to write as the infection inside my body only grew. I find myself constantly worrying about the state she could possibly be in: Has she gotten better, or has she gotten worse?

The nurses open the ward doors and wheel in another stretcher with a man lying across it. His deathly pallor and sickly blue lips send a shiver creeping along my spine. They load him into the cot in the far corner of the room, as gentle as a mother sending a baby to sleep.

A few of the sleeping men stir under the thick blankets, tucked just under their chins to keep them warm, though they suffer from chills brought by both the cold and a fever. I would sit up and prop a book against my knee, but the idea of getting up and reaching for one makes me want to dig deeper under these blankets. I've tried once before. My vision swirled so severely that I nearly vomited.

I've gotten tired of staring at the same white ceiling, the same small window, the sound of men coughing and sneezing around me. All I want to do is grab my crutch and make an attempt to break out of here, but I would fall into a heap as soon as my feet hit the floor.

I wonder how the rest of my friends and family are doing. My father has an exceptionally fantastic immune system. Alistair takes after him. Edith's most likely decked in protective gear. Lester and Sam are apparently distancing themselves. I've received no news from George for a while, so I presume he's doing just fine. I worry most for Ed and Frieda. Frieda's case appears more severe than Ed's from what I've heard, as she's healing from surgery plus a disease. It all must be taking a great toll on her body as Ed recovers from milder symptoms and burns.

That fluttering misstep of my heart comes back for the millionth time as I propose my thousandth prayer that they'll both be okay, that we'll all be okay, and that this war and this pandemic will end soon so we can get back to normal. What would I do after all this is done and over? School? I'll be damned. Without all of this, I'd be there already. Would I become a nurse like I always wanted? Would I marry? Have children? If so, how many? There are far too many questions swimming inside my head at the moment. I keep losing track of all of them before I find an answer.

There's the fast-paced clicking of heels across the floor as another nurse strides with a clipboard and pen, forms clipped in place as they gather around the man's stretcher, dressed in their medical uniforms of white aprons, white caps with the red cross across the front, and high-collared dresses of a deep navy blue underneath. They talk fast, swooping down to gather information, hurriedly jotting all of it down.

Once they finish, they stream out of the room, but one nurse stops by my bedside. "Mr Clark, is it?"

"Yes, ma'am." It comes out in a tired and sickly groan; the sound of a dying man.

"I've been instructed to hand you these." She presses three envelopes on my nightstand with her gloved hands. "You've got mail."

"Thank you."

I take the envelopes. My eyes squint to read the small handwriting on all three of them, trying to distinguish who sent what, in the dying daylight, making out that two of these letters address me by my middle name, 'Ace.' Quite the peculiar middle name, but not as bad as Alistair's—*Quincy*. It makes me gag. The other is simply 'Sgt. Marshall Clark,' and the way I'm addressed brings me some anxiety, as I rarely ever get addressed as a sergeant in letters.

I set them aside, planning to read them once my eyes don't feel like they're going to close on me mid sentence. I attempt to ignore the coughing of those around me and steady my breathing when fear sits its familiar weight on my chest.

My eyes snap open in time with a bang outside, the air knocked out of my lungs. With that, it's decided that I *will* read these letters and see what they have to say.

Sitting up, the world spins as I reach for the envelopes. When I regain my balance, I take a lucky dip and pick blindly, attempting to fight the wax seal on the tongue of the chosen envelope, carefully sliding the parchment out.

To Sergeant M. Clark,

I will begin this letter by saying that I don't think I've given you enough credit for your service to the army, keeping the United States free of enemy threats. Your commitments will be well-rewarded once the war is over.

I had originally addressed this letter to you, Sergeant, after hearing that you're currently indisposed for an indefinite amount of time. You were shot a second time, in the abdomen, and have contracted the Spanish Flu. The nurses have written to me about the matter. My best wishes are with you.

What I did want to disclose in this letter is, since the German Offense, our numbers have dwindled. Our fatality rate has gone up in regards to the current pandemic and the Ottoman Empire's malicious plans to invade us. There are no more troops heading to Italy as of now and no more higher-ups to support them on the lines. What I ask of you, Sergeant Clark, is that once you've recovered, is that you return here at whatever time is convenient for you. Your support in Italy is no longer needed. I feel as though I'm in need of a right hand man to keep my men in order, as my current major and both of my captains have fallen ill. Since you've struck up a reputation as the sheep shepherd of the Front, you're the best man for the job. You have been nothing but resilient. You have kept your composure ever since your enlistment in July of 1917 and have truly lived up to your name as a sergeant and have never failed me or your superiors.

I understand this letter has gotten to you under such short notice. Please respond as soon as you can once you've recovered.

Regards,

Lt. Col R. Sallinger

My throat is painfully dry as I put the letter to the side, paralyzed from the words I've just absorbed. My eyes are stuck on Sallinger's name, failing to register whether or not this is real or if I'm in such a sickly state that I'm hallucinating. I blink once or twice. The words don't change their form nor their structure. My hands begin to shake as a cough scratches the walls of my windpipe. It's all going too fast for me to make sense of it, my thoughts all spiraling at deadly speeds.

Sallinger requests for my return to the Western Front, wishes me a smooth recovery and praises my commitment to his regiment, with rules set in stone that I followed religiously for months on end, all in the same letter.

My pulse crashes inside my ears as I reread his letter once, twice, even three times more before I set it back down and let the words form more clarity with each read. Once they register, I bite at my cuticles as the rest of the letter sinks in and several more questions are spoken by the voice inside my head.

Will it be the same as when I left?

How many will be ill?

How many men do I have to take care of?

How will I tell George that I have to leave as soon as I get better?

What about my family? My siblings? Frieda?

It gets to be too much to think about, and I want to run away from it all. Except, my lungs would give out before I even make it outside into the smoky air that clogs my chest. Anything would be better than the smell of sanitizer and cleaning products that are all too stale in my nostrils and have my head spinning. With shaking hands, I reach for the second letter, hoping, praying for something to calm me down.

My dearest brother,

Happy birthday! How are things? Don't think Edith and I have forgotten about your birthday. It's really funny, as you've turned twenty-one. Gotta find it humorous that you've turned the same age as the number of the day you were born, huh? I hope you cackle at this one. It's a once in a lifetime occurrence, little brother! We wished to send over something for you, but when we tried to put our heads together to think of a perfect gift for our little Marshall that wasn't a book for the tenth year in a row, something special for his twenty-first, we just couldn't think of anything. Our creative juices were running flat.

Funny story, actually. I sent Edith into the tent (I can't go in, as I'm not a nurse nor a medic—I can't risk falling ill) to ask Frieda what you liked. She only told us 'books, dogs, horses, and poetry,' so we asked if it would be fun to buy you a new journal to write poems and sonnets or even a novel in. Your last one is getting scratched up and seemed to be falling apart the last time I saw it. Perhaps a cool, rich pen with real gold on the handle with premium ink and parchment to match? Or a medical textbook, since you were going to college before the war began, you'd like to return to studying with all the time you have.

Little brother, Edith's description of Frieda's reaction has got to be the highlight of my day. She actually grimaced! Apparently, the space in between her brows wrinkled to the point where it seemed to hurt her when we mentioned buying you just a pen and parchment, claiming a medical textbook would be easily purchasable and that you deserve something better, as it might be a dull read. I don't know about that, as I'm not you. So, please write what you'd like for your birthday, and we'll try our best to surprise you.

Cut to the chase, I received an update from Yvette about Kara. They're doing well. Father was such a sweetheart and helped build a cradle for our little angel. Apparently, he holds her in his arms and puts a disc on the record player and dances with her, swaying her back and forth with the slow piano pieces you used to compete with. I remember, last time, you used a lot of Chopin's ballads. Some Mozart, too. Dear Lord, apparently he cried when he saw her for the first time! Yvette told me she's another of the black haired flock; our genes remain dominant.

Yvette also told me how excited she is to see you when you get back so you can meet your niece while I, my daughter. Together, we'll fall to the

floor and sob to the high heavens. I wish to see her as soon as possible. You may have to catch me if I faint.

Another thing Sallinger updated me earlier that he sent you a letter. You should be getting that soon. It seems like years ago, the last time I

saw you, before you boarded the boat to Italy. I know you've contracted the flu, and I wish you the easiest road to recovery alongside that bullet

wound in your abdomen. Shouldn't that be fully healed by now? By the way, we're planning on surprising Frieda about your return, so please

don't write to her about it at all. It'll spoil the fun.

I shall sign off here, and I hope to see you soon.

Alistair A. Clark

Folding the letter carefully, I take in a deep, struggling breath, choking when I inhale too much air for my lungs' liking. I hate to admit it, but I forgot about Kara. The pressure of healing from trauma, wounds, and now, the flu, plus worrying about my significant other are all too much and have taken up too much space inside my mind for me to worry about anything else. It hurts to say it when I truly do care about Kara and want to be the best uncle I can.

I can't wait to meet her. She's safe and sound with her mother while her uncle, aunt, and father are all out fighting for their lives. Though this is the case, I'm glad to get updates and know she's doing well. Although, both Yvette and my father need to stay vigilant, as the young don't stand a chance against this new virus. I stress a lot about the risks for young Kara.

Opening the last letter, the corners of my mouth lift into a smile when I recognize her handwriting, muttering her name softly to myself.

Dearest Marshall,

I write to you with a shaky hand this morning, as the rest of my body is weak. I feel as though my eyes will close any minute as I write this.

You might receive this letter late, and I apologize in advance if you do, but please thank Edith for giving me this piece of parchment to use to write to you—I feel I should, as I haven't in weeks.

I haven't forgotten about your birthday, and by the time this letter gets to you, your special day may well and truly pass where you're another year older, all the while staying truly young at heart with your wild, raging personality. Happy twenty-first, dearest love. May you be gifted with the best of health and luck in the near future. Wherever you may be in life, I'll gladly support you through it—through thick and thin. You're truly the light of my life and have gotten me through so much I pay you back a lot for it. Even when you're not here at the moment, I miss you so much that my heart winds itself up and sings the same three words each time I think of you.

I just received the news that you had been diagnosed with the flu, and I pray that you recover quickly. My best advice is to get lots of bedrest, eat as much as you can, and stay hydrated, or else you'll be living through Hell. Blow your nose a couple of times to get rid of the congestion it may bring, as it can get nasty. If you can afford the luxury, tea—especially peppermint—will help soothe your throat and put you to sleep. If you find yourself falling asleep, do. Its your body repairing itself. If you feel abnormal, please yell immediately for a nurse. I've made the mistake of not calling for one when I was at my lowest too many times.

I'm sorry to taint this letter with my sorrows, but Marshall, you said not to hide anything from you; a part of our deal all those months ago. Please bear with me, as I am drowning with this illness. I fall unconscious too many times and end up dreaming. You read that right. Dreaming. These dreams are all too peaceful for someone who's just drowned from the illness hitting them with a new wave of nausea and fear.

The first: We were presumably at your home in Philadelphia. It was frankly quite uncanny, watching Alistair play the piano (tell me, is he truly a musician?). Edith and your father were sipping tea at the dining room table and gave me a bar of dark chocolate to give you while you were in the garden, trimming rosebuds. I can't imagine you doing gardening. You don't seem like you have green thumbs. When I found you, you claimed I'd 'disappeared again' and that you were happy to see me. As soon as you took my hand, the dream faded away.

The second: It was a ballroom from my youth, a party that was going on, something like that. My old friend, Henry, was there, and you walked in with your father and Alistair by your side. You came to save me when the room started to shrink as you led me to my father.

The third dream was really an add-on to the second. The ballroom dissolved into the Western Front. Only ~~Andrew~~ Andrej and I were there, discussing his mission, which wouldn't be entirely true, as he was only a figment of my imagination. He was terrible—teasing me about the afterlife and how I'd shot him, calling me a murderer. You came *running out of the bushes and claimed someone was trying to kill you. We ran and ran until we found a trench to hide in where you grabbed and pinned me to the floor with a gun to my neck. You shot me. Just seeing your eyes burn with such hatred has left me scarred with a vision that I never want to see again. It terrified me so much that I awoke screaming until my lungs gave out.*

I truly do feel as though I'm drowning and sinking deeper and deeper each time, only to resurface until I sink to the bottom where no one can save me. I'm absolutely terrified that I'll leave without saying goodbye. I'm aware of the consequences of falling ill and the risks it presents. I hear them every day when Edith and Nathan tell me that I'm lucky to still be alive here in this hell that I'd rather black out of. I know I'm not the only one. Each patient here is growing more and more restless by the hour. They cry for their mothers, their wives, their children, for God. I don't think I can take this insanity: the cycle of this disease spreading as turmoil never ends. It's all too terrifying, Marshall. What would you do? How are you handling this? I heard you were in isolation. Hopefully, you're well, staying healthy and clean. I know how you get with germs, so please stay safe. Be careful.

I might pass out, so this is all for now. Until we meet again, my pride and joy.

Sincerely,

Frieda S. Joyce

P.S. Do not hesitate to shower me with letters...I read them all.

The last few words send my heart aching like Frieda has her fist around it and is pulling it out of my chest.

My pride and joy.

Is she challenging me to remember the last words I spoke to her in person? Is she trying to hurt me? If so, it's a bittersweet hurt that makes me want to wrap my arms around her and steal her and dance the night away in the park with the soft hum of a street band on stage. A longing pain spikes in my chest.

I rewind to the night I told her I was leaving. I made her more nervous than she should've been. I saw the look in her eye, the one she gets when she's anxious or unsure. Her movements turn rigid with apprehension.

I phrased it wrong. I knew she had the potential to break down. When she reached for me, I inwardly cringed at the hurt I didn't mean to cause. It hurt even more to see her babble, unsure of how to grip herself.

I racked my brain for a way to reassure her. The look in her eye sent me reeling. It pained me to see her upset, even more so when she pulled away. I thought I'd truly damaged her beyond repair. It was the last thing I wanted to do.

Leaving her was even worse. I never wanted to let go. It's either that I have terrible separation anxiety or I'm deathly sick with love. I personally think it's a mixture of both, stirred together in some terrible concoction.

I hold the letter for a little while longer, as if to absorb every trace of her left on the page through my fingertips like water through the roots of a plant.

The door opens again. A masked nurse walks in wheeling a cart of multiple thermometers, bedsheets, and jars. I know what this is. They do it every morning, every afternoon, every evening.

Patient check ups.

I file the letter away as she starts going around the room and checking each man's temperature, collecting reports on their symptoms and giving them painkillers or a glass of water when necessary. One man is complaining loudly of a migraine and severe chest contractions, wheezing in each breath, lips blue, eyes rolling back, slumping on his mattress. The nurse screams for assistance, but by the time the doctors and the medics get here, the man is long gone. He turns into a husk of what he was just moments before. I see it before the nurses can. I feel it in my gut, in the stillness of the room.

My skin crawls from seeing him die in front of me, how his eyes glazed over and detached from reality as they rolled back into his sockets. I try to blink it out of my mind, but the vision keeps coming. I give a little whimper, covering my mouth with my hand. My body shakes when they pull a white sheet over him on a stretcher they've wheeled in. A new bed is soon prepared with fresh linens, the dead man out of sight, as if he were never there.

My gut turns itself inside out when I see who's on the new hospital bed.

Surrounded by nurses, a man lies still, his eyes closed as they poke needles into his arms, injecting fluid into his veins. He coughs like there's no tomorrow.

My throat burns as I call out his name. "George!"

He doesn't pick up. The nurses are all over him as they stick in one needle after another. I call again and again with more and more urgency, more nurses coming to detain me as I make a move to push my shuddering, feverish body out of bed. I snarl wildly at their gloved hands as they clamp down on me, shrieking like my hair's on fire. They're dodging my teeth that threaten to bite into their arms when my limbs can't flail, when my nails can't scratch. Their hands are on my shoulders, my elbows, my knees, my feet. The weight of it all is enough to get me to scream louder and push against the force.

A needle glints under the lights, filled with clear liquid held in place by a plunger. It's waiting, ready to be pricked into my skin. I don't take the time to guess what's inside it, my throat dries as the nurse approaches.

"No! Get that away! There's no need for a sedative! Don't knock me out! I'll be good, I promise! He's my friend! I need to see him!"

The nurse with the needle looms over me. "Calm yourself. This won't hurt a bit."

"Get that thing away from me! I swear to God almighty, I'll be good. Get it away from me!"

"Are you scared of needles?"

"I'm scared for my friend! Please let me see him! No need for a sedative!"

"I'm sorry, sir. Seeing him will only transmit more germs." His eyes travel from me to the nurses as I let out a weak cry, pleading. "Hold him down."

Their hands toughen upon me as he pulls up my sleeve to inject the needle into the crook of my elbow, the prick digging under my skin. I continue to thrash my limbs, screaming against the nurses and their steady grips, their rock-hard faces. My hands ball into fists. My entire body tenses and tries to battle the drugs as they ooze into my system.

The world starts to grow fuzzy, my senses failing. I fight to keep my eyes open as my screams fade to whines. Their hands don't let go. Their eyes don't leave my face.

"Please." It comes out in a disgustingly weak whimper. "You have to let me see him."

"I'm afraid we can't," replies the nurse with the needle, staring at my tiring body. "If you move about, it'll only make your case worse and spread more germs. We need you confined to your bed until you recover."

"He's...he's my friend." My brain fogs over. "My friend...I...I need to see my friend."

"I'm sorry."

"Piss off..." I grunt as my body goes numb. My limbs start to feel detached from my frame. "The lot of you, piss off. You're going to..." a pause, my lips tingling as my head lolls. "...take him away...from me..."

The drugs take their hold.

My eyes remain shut as the world falls away.

* * *

When I wake, I immediately bolt upright, despite the tired ache in my limbs.

It's dark outside. The lamps are lit. The nurses are back to their checkups with heavy aprons, masks, and gloves on. A nurse on duty's head whips toward me as I shake the tingles out of my limbs. Her eyes are wide, as she's midway through stacking jars. I've regrettably scared her.

"Sir, did I wake you?"

I waste no time on small talk. "I need to ask about my friend, George Wellins. He's here. I know he is. Did you check on him yet?"

"Sir, I—"

"Please, ma'am, did you check on him yet? I was so worried that they hit me with a sedative. It's a long story."

"George Wellins? Yes, he's stable, for now."

"Thank the heavens." I exhale hard. A cough erupts in my throat, my head hurting like hell. "Also, tell your colleagues it's rude to stick a sedative into their patients. It's not a tranquilizer in moose season."

Her laugh sends a spike through my chest as she steps into the light.

Heidi's face is covered with a gauze mask, but I can tell she's smiling.

"Fun drugs, aren't they, Mr Clark?" She folds her arms as she stands over me. "Put you right to sleep."

My eyes narrow at the sight of her. "Ms Heidi, if this was your idea—"

"I wouldn't do such a thing. I'm not that type of woman. If it were me, there would be arsenic in your food."

My mouth opens to project a noise of shock, but she beats me to it with more gleeful laughter. "I'm kidding, I'm kidding. You never lower your guard, do you, Mr Clark?"

"Why should I?" I ask bluntly.

Heidi sighs and bends to gather more jars and put them on their respective shelves. I avert my gaze and lead it to my crumpled bed sheets.

"Is something troubling you?"

"No." The lie comes out easier than expected.

Heidi huffs, unsatisfied. "Men: making themselves look tougher than what they are. You mentioned you had a partner—"

"If you have something against them—"

"No, I don't. It's nothing like that. I have a husband."

"What are you trying to say?" I press, my glare etched upon my face.

"I want to formally apologize for what I did. I wasn't thinking."

I don't soften. My muscles are still rigid with anger, shame. "That still doesn't excuse you for what you did. You tried to take advantage of me."

"I understand if you don't forgive me. You seem troubled, sir."

"I'm on unfamiliar land, my friend and I are bedridden in the middle of a war, plus a pandemic, my friends and loved ones are all miles away, and I've got no one. No shit I'm *troubled,* Ms Heidi. Is that enough to say why?"

Heidi doesn't shrink back. She's strong. I keep my hands clenched at my sides. "Yes, completely. Your partner is Frieda Joyce, isn't she?"

"Why? Are you planning on poisoning her meals with arsenic too?"

Heidi doesn't stifle her snort at my cruel remark. "She's a large inspiration."

"She bent the rules. She broke them in half."

Heidi nods solemnly. "Indeed. I received a telegraph from my colleague, Edith, that she's staying in hospital because, like you, she's ill—all updates about her."

"Updates?" I jump. I can put my anger aside just this once.

"Yes. Today, she sat up and ate all her food and was able to read with one eye. That and news of a new conformer were sent down the line. Her wounds are healing nicely. She's recovering swiftly. To trouble you less, she's getting better."

"The letter she sent me must've been delayed." My hands begin to shake, chest filling with an emotion I can't explain. "That's wonderful news."

Heidi takes her cart and wheels it away, stopping at the door. "I'm sorry, Mr Clark. I understand if you don't forgive me, but best of luck to you. Make her happy."

30

RESPONSES TO A RUMOUR

FRIEDA

"Nathan! Nathan!" Edith's voice booms. I clutch Marshall's copy of *Anna Karenina* tight, setting it on my lap at her sudden cry. The book thumps against my knee, causing it to throb with a dull ache. Reading has proven to be most difficult, but I've been getting back into the swing of it.

Nathan comes crashing in, clutching his first aid kit, skidding to a stop on his heels. "Edith!" He sets his kit aside and grabs hold of both her arms. "Are you hurt? Are you ill? What's the matter?"

Edith holds back her laughter as sweat forms on his forehead. "Calm down. Step back, you're going to get me sick."

Nathan gasps, peeling his hands from her and dousing them in soap and water, scrubbing and drying them furiously. Their ruckus interrupts my reading as he fusses over her, asking if she's ill, hurt, even *pregnant* (this gets me questioning a subject I do *not* want to think about. Edith is seventeen, he's only a few months older).

"I told you to calm down." She puts her hands up, shrugging him off when he tries to reach for her again. "I got a telegraph from my father."

"Did you?" Nathan's shoulders tense at the word; a universal nightmare when it comes up in a relationship. "Wh-what did he say?"

"He said…" Edith fumbles with her pockets, Nathan coiling in on himself even more than I thought he would be able to. When I start thinking that's as tight as he can go, he tightens even more as he lies in wait.

"Edith, my love, I'm seeing stars. I'm holding my breath. What did he say?"

"Calm down. Nothing necessarily bad—"

"*Necessarily bad*? Edith—"

"He said that he'd like to meet you once the war is over, if you come back to Philadelphia with me."

Nathan pauses, considering it with a notch in his brow. "I'd have to write to my mother. Pops will be fuming back in Lincoln."

"You can say it's for a business trip."

"You're literally *helping* me *run away* from my parents to *Pennsylvania.* You're asking me to lie to them when in reality, I'm running away with a girl!"

"I didn't say you had to lie to them, nor did I say you were running away. Do whatever's convenient for you. We could write letters like Frieda and Marshall, or we could—"

"Could we discuss this when the time arises? I've got a lot on my plate."

Nathan uncoils as Edith nods. "Sure. I'm sorry, I didn't want to give you any stress."

His tired eyes bore into hers. I can see in them how badly he wants to wrap her close. I understand the feeling of a painful yearning of something right in front of you that you can't quite have. "Thank you. I'm just overworked."

"For what, exactly?"

"For understanding." Nathan bends the slightest bit forward to bow as a bang breaks the silence outside. With a groan, he asks, "Another assault?"

"They sent the men over the front line this morning." Edith leans against the wall, a tired sigh escaping her as she rests her head against the wooden beam. "The cycle never ends. I haven't sat down or rested at all since yesterday afternoon."

"Take the next shift off." Nathan plays with the straps of his apron. "I'll cover for you."

"You don't need to do that."

"I will if I have to." He leans against the wall with her, folding his arms, his eyes on me. Hurriedly, I bring my book close to my face as if I'm reading intensely. He releases a small chuckle. "Eavesdropping are we? I wouldn't suspect you to hear anything interesting."

"Caught red handed," Edith remarks over her shoulder.

"Since you're awake, how are you feeling?" Nathan slinks off the wall and walks over to me as he fixes his mask. "Reading since yesterday, huh? What're we reading?"

"Better than yesterday, actually." I mark my page. "It's Marshall's copy of *Anna Karenina*."

"Quite a...quite a thick book you've got there...Should keep you busy for a while."

"Marshall had a thing for thick books. He said the thicker it was, the more plot it had and the more entertainment." Edith shrugs. "I'm not surprised that he gave that to you. He also has *War and Peace,* which, Nathan, is even thicker. He read the entire thing in almost two days—stayed up all night with it, couldn't unstick his eyes from the pages."

"Good God." Nathan's shoulders slump. "I don't see how you or him have the patience to read. I never was much of a reader myself."

"How come?"

"I mean, I can read. Quite well, actually. But the thing is I never had the patience nor the time to read for fun. It's just not in me."

"How about I give you some recommendations?"

"Honestly, thank you, but I don't think I'm much of a bibliophile."

Edith is busy sanitizing her hands and pulling on a pair of gloves as she reads over a clipboard. A messenger walks into the tent with a satchel filled to the brim with envelopes and parcels.

"Ms Joyce?" He bows before Edith, handing her some battered envelopes. "Letters for her."

"Who is it?" I ask from my bed.

"The South family, Corporal Surry, and Sergeant Clark, ma'am."

Edith is quick to take the envelopes and thank him as he leaves, handing them to me. My hands shake as I carefully take the three letters into my lap and open the first one. The one I look forward to most is Marshall's, unwrapping it like an eager child on Christmas. His letter is irregularly thin and consists of a small slip of paper with a paragraph's worth of writing.

Frieda,

Not doing well. Eyes hurt. Head hurts. Everything hurts. Can't breathe. Doctors gave me a sedative. Can't write much. Going to faint. Hands are shaking. I'm sorry for everything.

Marshall

With a nervous sweat breaking upon my brow, I open the next letter. The handwriting doesn't come up in my memory, but I realize who it is once I read the opening.

Dearest Step-Child,

I hope not to cause you alarm at such a troubling time—how are you, first of all? Are you doing well? God, I hope you are staying clear of the infected, keeping clean.

The thing is, we're also in an increasingly troublesome time in Seattle. With you being part of the family, I felt I had to alert you, no matter how many times Rose protested against me sending this letter (she tried countless times to burn it or put it in a bowl of water so that the ink would run out of the parchment). Promise me you'll stay strong while reading this. Don't think too much about it, but the disease has spread to Seattle and into this household.

First it was Irene who had caught it from a classmate who was asymptomatic. She's in the Intensive Care Unit— so is your mother. I might be next. I'm not sure. What I want you to do for me is stay strong. I mean it. We may not be on speaking terms for a while after this letter is sent, as I may be in isolation.

Kind Regards,

Fitzroy South

I take another gulp before I open the last letter: Ed, who I haven't heard from since February. I almost choke as I unpack his letter, which is dreadfully thick.

My Dearest Friend,

It cost me a lot to deliver this letter, and I apologize if my writing is askew. My sight has diminished since the gas attack. I feel dreadful with the flu.

Months ago, I had received multiple letters from Marshall when I wasn't feeling like the greatest person alive (yes, I say that with humor. I am alive and I apologize that I couldn't get to you until June): thirteen letters, to be exact. Some were telegraphs. Most of them were letters written in his own writing or on a typewriter, pestering me. How many times has he shat the bed thinking about me? Do you know?

The thing I wanted to alert you about was this: Ever since I heard you were in hospital with the flu like I and many others with your...scene in the nurse's tent, there've been rumors. I've heard them all. It's almost like the time when you first announced you were a person with a catastrophic amount of men harassing you. I wouldn't say it's one hundred percent like that, though, as this may as well be worse. Please read what is enclosed inside this letter _very carefully_.

Marshall managed to send me a letter that had arrived just last night, detailing his current problems with his illness and everything in between. My darling, he sounded dreadful. He kept crossing out an obscene amount of words. His font was the same as a doctor's chicken scrawl.

What he had told me—from what I can remember—is that he had been getting a flu checkup from one of the nurses. 'Ms Heidi,' he called her. He had exclaimed, in all hurried and broad capitalized strokes of a broken man, that she 'put forth a vulgar request of unfaithfulness.' Now, he didn't confess to infidelity; he declined her advances as a faithful man should. It spooked him and made him dive into a state of despair, calling himself 'unfaithful' and a 'sinner' because he had been victimized and declined an advance. I know how shocking this can be for the both of you. I've experienced it myself.

Now, he's in a state of peril. He's not eating, nor is he drinking, and refuses whenever the nurses put food or drinks before him, knocking him out with countless sedatives to supply nourishment to his body. What he doesn't understand in his state of delirium is that without it, he'll die. He's incredibly frail.

Then there's this mysterious Ms Heidi he told me about. I heard it all from her friends here at the Front, and I hate to tell you that Fey is one of the gossipers. She wasn't the one who started it, but she's in on the gossip as most women are, chatting about topics that do them no good to be involved in. Please take none of it personally when you know it's nothing but a rumor. Ms Heidi needs to take accountability for what she's done. If anyone says anything to you, dismiss it. Please write him a letter. I'm so sorry that you two have to experience this, and I wish you the best of luck.

Edward Surry

Tears spring from my eyes. My hand clasps over my mouth as Catherine steps into the tent with her medical kit.

"Good morning, Frieda." She halts, her smile vanishing, lashes batting at me innocently as she takes in my sudden shock. "My dear, are you crying?"

"Cathy," I mumble and sniffle, "is this true?"

"What's true?"

"This." I hand her the letter that she takes in a gloved hand, sighing.

"He said...he said that Fey was part of it."

Catherine hisses, "That *bitch*."

That's not the first time I've heard her curse. It shouldn't come as much as a surprise. "Catherine?"

"I did hear her speaking about something like this. She's in for it."

"So she did say something?"

"Heidi did this?"

"Apparently. Who is she?"

"Heidi is a nurse. During training camp, she was a menace, nothing like your ideal woman, picking on the vulnerable men and using them for her benefit. I don't see it as a surprise that she tried doing him in. Her apologies mean nothing. She never changes."

She places a gloved hand with spread fingers on my back, her eyes sympathetic while her fringe shields them. "You know he wouldn't do that, right?"

"Would he?"

"This is exactly what Heidi wants. To tear you two apart." Catherine sets her kit down on the bed and unpacks it, retrieving and digging out a thermometer with a few other medical objects that *he* may be able to recognize. I shouldn't feel angry at him. I don't even know who my anger is directed at. "Countless times have I heard his name come from the postmen. You send letters day-in, day-out. His friend wouldn't be lying to you. Mr Surry is an extremely truthful man."

"My family was struck with the flu. He's doing worse than last time. Everything is going to Hell." I bow my head with the weight of it all. "I shouldn't get better. Leave me untreated."

"Don't say that. Everyone here deserves treatment. Don't let these problems get to you."

"They deserve it more than I do."

"*Lies.*" Catherine pops the thermometer under my tongue, watching the mercury inside it rise with my body temperature. "Everyone here deserves to recover." She takes the thermometer and squints at it. "101 degrees. It's gone down since yesterday. Let me check your nodes, please."

I sit farther upright and dive deeper into my thoughts as she presses cold fingers under my neck, making me think against my will about Heidi and Marshall. Her hands on him make me want to wrap my very own around her neck until she turns blue. I can't imagine how angry he is right now.

I freeze under her touch.

"I know, my hands are cold," Catherine says soothingly before she grabs her stethoscope and taps on my back. "Any pain here?"

"A little," I mumble.

"Okay, okay. Let me check your breathing."

After a few deep inhales, I start to feel dizzy.

Catherine nods, satisfied. "You sound a lot better. A lot less constricted than yesterday."

"Where's Colby? Is she here?"

"She's up in the east, third line in the assault."

At the word *assault,* another explosion shakes the ground. A squeal escapes me. "I will never stop getting scared by those bombs."

"That's not all. There's an air raid that's going to come soon."

"A *what?*" I gasp.

"An air raid. Nowhere near here, though. They're going more down south."

"Do you know Lester? Sam? George?"

"Private Wellins departed for the Eastern Front two weeks after Sergeant Clark."

"You're kidding me. What about Alistair?"

"I haven't seen Lester since this morning, nor Sam. I didn't catch wind of where they were going, but—"
A scream shreds through the air.

Catherine's attention goes to the source of the scream. In come a squad of nurses with a man lying on a stretcher. Lungs heaving, the man screams all his pain and agony out as blood soaks his uniform.

"Quick! I can't get the bullet out!" A nurse wails.

"Where was he shot?" Catherine sprints head-on toward the stretcher.

"In the arm! His forearm has a bullet lodged in it and his hand is impaled by barbed wire—we're going to have to amputate it! No chance of saving it!"

The cots around me stir from the commotion as Catherine bends over the man. "Sir, can I get a source of identity?"

"Alist...air..." he croaks, crying out, growing fuzzy and slipping away. "Please, madam...my brother...my sister...my...my wife...my daughter..." A pause. "Alistair...Ali...Quincy Clark. Twenty-three...August sixteenth, 1895. Please, don't let me die here..."

"Alistair, can you feel anything in your arm? Your hand?"

"Bullet hurts like a bitch." His eyes become wild, like a caged animal. "My hand is completely numb."

"Alright, alright, Alistair. Please try to stay calm—"

"Stay calm, my ass! Stay calm when there's a bullet in my arm? My hand has been rendered useless! Sure, I'll stay calm!"

My hand clamps over my mouth as Nathan rushes forward, a needle full of clear liquid in his clutches with a few more male nurses on his heels, rushing to pull on their gear. His hair is a streak of red against the dark and murky light setting upon the commotion Alistair is stirring.

There's a screech and a slap before it dies down with nurses chanting 'hold him down, hold him down' and 'gather his legs, his arms, careful!'

Nathan scampers away with the needle, now empty, the plunger pushed all the way down, disposing of it.

"N...Nathan?" I stammer.

He wheels around, his brow shining with the sweat of the summer heat. He's shocked, gloves covered in blood—Alistair's blood: red and murky, dried and cracked. "Frieda, what's going on?"

"I'd like to ask you the same question." There it is. My chest starts to close up. "What happened to Alistair?"

"Alistair sustained a bullet to his forearm. His hand was mangled by barbed wire that he managed to tangle himself in. The medics on sight managed to catch him. Now we have to amputate his right hand."

The air in my lungs catches in my throat. "Will he be okay? Does Edith know? Marshall?"

"They're sending word out to him now, and I volunteered to break the news." Nathan slips off his gloves, his hands pale and veiny. He breathes out a reluctant sigh, attempting to stand up straight as if to show the strength he lacks. "I'm sure he'll be okay. He didn't lose too much blood. Won't be losing too much flesh, either."

I stare hard at the ground, a million thoughts and images darting about inside my head. It pains me, makes me want to forget, steal one of Nathan's needles and inject whatever he gave to Alistair into my veins, regardless of what it does to me.

"Did you give him a sedative?"

"I did, yes." He's washing his hands in a nearby basin, face set and grim. "I had to. He was struggling too much. I honestly feel bad. Having a wound like his is terrible."

His eyes sweep over me, registering my face and paralyzed limbs as the shock sets deeper, chilling the very marrow of my bones. I close my eyes against the waves that puncture me again and again in the chest; a sword of a knight stabbing the heart of a dragon. No matter how hard I try to shove down and swallow the visions, they keep coming back. Everyone I love's faces are imprinted forever inside my mind, their voices crashing like waves in the raging black ocean that swallows me whole days and nights at a time.

It hurts too much. I'd give anything to forget just for a little while.

"You can't give me some of that, can you?"

"What?" Nathan appears perplexed. "Do you mean the sedatives? Oh, no. I couldn't, no. I don't have that ability, nor can I administer them for recreational use. I'm sorry."

"Fine," I mumble. "I want to black out for a little while. You know what I mean?"

"Everyone does." There's the clunk of jars and containers being shuffled around. "Everyone wants to run away from what causes them trouble because they're worried that it'll hurt them in a way that's irreparable. It's all part of human instinct, I'm afraid. Even I, who seems to have next to no problems at all, wants to run away from it all."

"Would you?"

"Would I what, exactly?"

"Run away from your problems if you were given the chance?"

"Running away would equal defeat. Essentially, you can't run away from your problems no matter how much distance you travel. They'll always be waiting, chasing you. In the end, running is only equivalent to letting a weed grow. If you don't douse it with weed killer, it grows and ruins your garden. If you don't address the problem, it only grows worse and eats at your insides."

Silence washes over the both of us; uncomfortable, a pair of talkers who are unsure of what to say next.

I speak of nothing more as he turns on his heel and ventures outside, leaving me to my lonesome with Catherine treating another patient on the far side of the tent.

I peer at Marshall's copy of *Anna Karenina*, cracked open from years of use, showing his name blotched on the inside page in his neat cursive. Everything about this book reminds me of him, even when he gave it to me a second time on the night when I had wounded myself with barbed wire.

He argued so passionately that I needed something to pass the time as I rested, bringing, the next day, a satchel full of books. He smiled so wide when he assured me that I could borrow it, and he never took it back. I guess he's under the impression that I'm still reading it after all this time, reading the wonders of Leo Tolstoy's work once more when I already have a thousand times before.

"Catherine?" I call as she finishes spoon feeding a patient their medicine.

"Yes, Frieda?"

"Do you have a pen and paper?"

"I do."

"Can I borrow some?"

"Sure thing. Hang on." She gives me a scrap of parchment and a thin granite pencil from deep within her pocket. "Are you writing something?"

My hand quivers for a moment, a lump present in my throat as I soldier on with my messy scrawl.

I stop, my brain going back and forth with what to say. A thousand words go through my head at once, firing through and fighting to come out as the pencil scratches lines upon the paper. It's a chaotic tidal wave of feelings. A heap of words bubbling on my tongue. A grueling sensation washes over me as I swallow back the words I choose to leave unsaid.

I believe this will be a very short letter, as I don't have much room to write. I got a letter from Edward about your distress on the current issue. I know, being the magnificent man that you are, you're highly faithful. I know its not in your nature to break promises. Especially ones as large as ours. Edward told me you rejected the woman. Even Catherine knows her methods.

If you had been unfaithful, I would be angry. In this case, where you've been forced into an uncomfortable situation such as that, don't think I'm mad, unless there's something you're hiding from me, which I don't think would be possible, as you yourself tell the truth even when there's no pledge to do so in the first place.

I hope you're recovering. I myself am feeling heaps better. Once you come back, whenever that may be, we'll rejoice.

Kind Regards,

Frieda

Signing off, I hand it to Catherine to send to the post. Before she leaves, I ask her about how Ed's doing.

"Oh," she sighs, "he's...he's not doing so great. He has an infection that we have to keep draining from day to day."

The lump returns, choking me as she exits, carrying the thin envelope with her.

The tent flaps close, leaving me alone with my thoughts that eat me whole.

31

I'm Coming

Marshall

It's now September, 1918. The number of cases being reported are high. The screaming, gunfire, and even more havoc leads on in its tyrannous rule. The sounds never cease, never halt. They roll and run around inside my head, always changing, always shifting like the storm clouds prowling up ahead. The flames of war still lick at my feet, burning my soles with their savage tongues.

Not for a moment, not for one second, the world moves. Everything's stopped, stagnant, like a photograph. But, for one blessed instance, the world shifts. It composes itself anew, a song in the making. Through all the sickness, all the violence, the world is waiting to unleash the beast of change.

I won my battle with the Spanish Flu at the end of August. Feeling better, I started to work on walking again while my lungs caught up, and started taking better care of myself. When I was able to break into a run like a newborn foal weeks later, the sun on my face, the nurses erupted into a round of applause. Some even started crying.

George was watching all the way. He recovered, too. The only evidence that he was ever ill is his dramatic loss of weight—found in both of us. He's been pale over the past few months. It anguished me that I couldn't see him once I was booted out of the ward and felt so bitter about being free.

During the first few days of September, after I gained all my balance back, the bullet wound healed to become a scar once the stitches were removed as I worked on the front lines and sorted men into their waves, blowing the whistle (this time, I didn't stand on the ladder, just in case there were snipers ready for a second round) and closed my eyes against the shots that rang in my ears, my head panging with each shockwave that stilled my limbs as my heart jumped out of my chest.

Now, I adjust the straps of my mask across my nose and mouth, reading the letter Frieda wrote three weeks ago, exclaiming how she was indeed going to get a prosthesis once the war was over. She's staying in the medical tent since Sallinger told her she couldn't fight due to her visual impairment, but she was able to score a few moments on the third line and dug new passageways, laid down new boardwalks once her breathing patterns returned to normal and once she recovered. Of course, with the flu, the damage to your lungs can be either dangerous or not at all, both of us so very lucky to have ones still soldiering on and surviving, inhaling a breath of a new day

She's still absentminded to the fact that I'll be returning soon. Lester, Sam, and I have been planning the reunion for almost two months now, Alistair chiming in a few times, since he has nothing better to do as an amputee with a bullet wound in his arm.

George emerges inside the tent. He too is wearing a white cloth mask and gloves for extra protection, his hair growing just over his ears, obscuring his vision along with the mask.

"Ready to go?"

George is staying here to aid the Italian campaign. Sallinger needed so many men to come back and help him. He won't be coming with me on my journey back to France. Regrettably, I'll be traveling alone.

I heave in a breath to still the thrumming of my heart against my ribs. "Ready as I'll ever be."

George makes way for me to step out of the tent with my satchel slung over my shoulder, shuffling past with my head ducked low.

"George?"

"Yeah?"

"Do you think she forgives me?"

"Of course she does. If she didn't, she would stop writing to you, wouldn't she?"

"I guess so." I take one last sweep of the tent before I turn on my heel with George following close behind. "I'm just scared. It's going to be so different from last time. What'll everything be like?"

"I get that," George replies. "Aren't you excited? You get to see your future spouse again!"

"George, we've talked about this. She's not my future spouse. We're just...I don't know..."

"She is. Don't deny it." George grins, clapping me on the back. "C'mon, Skipper! You'll see her and be as happy as a pig in mud. Give me a smile."

"*Hah.*" I give him a sarcastic huff instead, elbowing him. "My sister will be there. How much did she grow? Alistair—is he doing okay? Edward —oh, Edward...Lester, Sam! Without us, where are they?"

"Look, take a deep breath for me." George stuffs his hands in his pockets as I give him a scrutinizing look. "Come on, Marshall! I'm trying to help you!"

When I do, he nods approvingly.

"Good man. Listen, you'll be absolutely fine. Even Sallinger said you'll be like the park ranger you used to be; showing men around like a shepherd bossing around sheep or cattle—and you're getting paid for it! Think: No front line assaults, no certain death. All the while, you're making more bang for your buck while you spend time with Frieda behind the scenes."

"Sounds nice. Oh boy, George! Lest we forget the air raids! Oh, heavens, the air raids!"

George shrugs. "You're going to get a few of those once in a while, give or take. You can't prevent those. Get deep undercover and pray you won't lose an extra limb."

Another shrewd look is pointed at him. He has the audacity to laugh. "I'm kidding, I'm kidding, but not about the part where you can't prevent them. I'm sure you'll be fine if you stay vigilant."

We reach the train station that's well in the city. The trees are stripped ghostly bare along the rails in front of us as I check my watch. I'm running ten minutes early. More and more men approach the platform. One is in a wheelchair, the other leans on a crutch.

The third stumbles and dips his hat over his dark hair. "Sergeant Clark, heading home?"

I decide to joke to lighten the mood. "I'm not sure if you're referring to Belgium or Philly, Dominic."

"Belgium. You look like a whole new man now that you're not sick in bed and with a crutch under your arm."

"You look fine yourself."

Dominic only shrugs. "Private Wellins, fancy seeing you here! Coming with us?"

"Me? No, unfortunately. Just seeing this young man off. I'm off duty for the next hour."

"Ah." Dominic grins, eyes crinkling with his smile. "Best of luck to you, Private."

"As to you, sir." George bows his head.

I step away, leaving them to their own conversation as I watch the sunrise from the bench beside the lamppost and the map on the wall, shivering against the chill of the cold breeze. Leaves skitter and scratch at my feet in the wind. I'm debating unpacking my blanket to drape over my legs as my hands bundle together in my lap. My leg keeps jogging in anticipation.

Dominic clears his throat, still recovering from a sore throat brought by the flu. "Marshall, I presume you're going back into battle?"

"Not exactly," I reply. "Sallinger wants me to be his sheepdog."

His pale slate eyes blink in confusion. "Sheepdog?"

"He wants me to"—I mimic Sallinger's accent, his voice, drawing on his facial expression—"keep his men in order."

"It's better than predicting your death every single day, not knowing which will be your last, don't you think?"

"I'll still do it. I don't think I'll be let off that easily." I fix my satchel's straps and pick out my rations from this morning, munching on the crackers and corned beef I've grown too used to, my hand brushing

370

against Frieda's letter. When I think no one is looking, I kiss the envelope and mumble to it, "I'm coming, Frieda. I'm coming."

George is still busying himself, talking to Domic. I fix my mask and stuff the envelope with care back into my breast pocket when the approaching train toots its whistle in the early morning mist that settles over the station, the train's shape a large shadow before my eyes.

I look over at George, who crosses from Dominic to me and holds out a gloved hand. The train screeches to a halt, the doors opening. The conductors get their handy holepunchers ready.

"Skipper, you'll write to me, won't you?"

"Of course I will." I give him a good shake of the hand with a wink. "No doubt about that, *Skipper*."

George softens. "Tell the boys I wish them well. Frieda too. Take good care of her. Until we meet again. May God be with you."

"May God be with you too, my friend."

As my hands slip from his, I give him one last glance and a clap on the shoulder before I depart, showing a conductor my ticket. While he punches a hole in the small rectangular slip of paper, a sense of giddiness overwhelms me with a drop of fear put into the mix. The thought of seeing her again leads to me wanting to faint right then and there on the step.

Domic is trailing behind me as I greet the engineers and other conductors. I step inside the train. A steward escorts me to my quarters, which are a small, compact room of brown and white with an even smaller bathroom; much like the one Frieda and I slept in on the boat when I picked her up from Seattle except with bigger windows. My grand expedition across Europe feels so long ago. Centuries ago.

I set my satchel on the hook by the door and unpack it, taking out the few books I have and my journal. Using the inkwell and pen sitting on the windowsill, I crack open the brown leather cover and sit at the desk, writing away as the train departs. The train's gears *chug-chug-chug* under my feet while my chest tightens as my stomach flips over itself.

With that, another adventure begins. Another page is turned.

* * *

Dinner with Dominic was enjoyable. Probably the most enjoyable thing I've done since learning to walk again and recovering from the disease.

My main course was an amazing risotto. Dessert was some cherry pie that was passed out across the dining car as a token of thanks as we passed over the Swiss border; another step of freedom. We're in the north west part of Switzerland right about now, supposed to cross into Luxembourg by early morning.

I've lit a candle with some matches I found in the bedside drawer and write by candlelight, documenting my train journey yet again as the clock strikes midnight in Switzerland. The Alps remain in the distance, dark, mountainous beings sleeping far behind the glass of the window.

I continue scratching away at the page in my nightclothes, yawning as I write the last sentence.

I'm coming back to you, Frieda. Just you wait.

Leaving my journal open for the ink to dry, I stand, stretch, and draw the curtains. Blowing out my candle, I settle into the bed on the far left of the desk and get comfortable, staring at the wall until my eyes can't stay open. When I close them, her face is burned into my memory, raising a great load of questions.

Has she changed?

How will she see me?

What should I say to her?

Of course, Frieda may look different, or the same as when I left, with an empty right eye and a scar on her face. She may call it ugly. She may hide her face in fear of being called a disgrace, but I'll still cherish her either way.

My stomach flips again at the idea. The smile of a lovesick boy stretches across my lips.

After all this time, all the letters we exchanged, all the feelings that we've shared, all the moments we didn't experience together while being a thousand miles away, I still feel the same. It's a brilliant feeling, a wondrous one shadowed by the letter I sent Edward about Heidi and Frieda's short reply. The problem was solved pretty fast. Frieda's too kind, too forgiving for her own good. At least she has some of that soft and magnificent side still inside of her.

The churning feeling I get in my stomach still comes from the idea that I hurt her without intending to do so. I still feel bad about it months after it happened. It feels like a confrontation rather than a reconvening. She expresses that she misses me dearly and that she wishes for me to come back soon, all the while oblivious to what we've been planning.

I shift deeper under the thin blankets, pulling them over my shoulders, trying to disassociate from my thoughts to get some shut eye.

Finally, I doze off as the wheels on the train tracks move beneath me against an imaginary metronome that keeps ticking away.

32

UNTIL WE MEET AGAIN

FRIEDA

There's an abnormal hurrying about in the tent today as Edith and Nathan chuckle with each other. I'm not allowed outside, stuck inside, putting jars in cabinets and shelves, working out dosage amounts and logging them all in a journal, getting used to the new cloth mask I've been given once I recovered and a black eye patch to hide the damage done while my socket heals with the conformer inside it. I've made up my mind about getting a prosthesis. I don't want to be stuck with a conformer that needs changing every so often all my life.

With my impairments, I had a long talk over bitter tea with Sallinger about the issue. My nerves prickled with the suspicion of something being hidden from me. When I asked, all he said to me was this:

"I'm expecting a package. It's a special one and needs to be handled with extra care. I like to call it the *Ace Project,* or *Ace* for short."

My suspicions only heightened from then on.

Alistair's been bedridden ever since his accident, a new amputee with a stump for a hand. He's been helping with my work while I teach him to write with his left hand, his handwriting a scrawl that's closest to a child's when they just learn to write. Edith's been giving him hell for it with daily doses of sibling banter.

"Any new letters, Alistair?" I ask as I sit beside him and flip through pages of tables including the names of many patients plus my calculations in the corners. "No new news?"

"No, besides Kara smiling like there's no tomorrow." He points out the passage in his wife's neat writing. "I wish I were there to see it."

There's a crash of kidney dishes clanging to the ground. Edith swats Nathan across the shoulder playfully. "Nathan Nelson!"

"Please have mercy, m'lady! I didn't mean to knock over the dishes!" He laughs. "They were empty!"

Alistair grins as Ed stumbles into the tent. Over the course of healing, his face is still wrapped in bandages. Some cuts have turned into scabs around his mouth, but his eyelid and the skin around his socket remain swollen.

"Sir Edward! How're we hanging?" Nathan plucks Edith's claws off of him and sets back to work.

"The infection is nearly gone," he replies, pulling up a chair. He too has recovered from the flu, but still remains troubled, not inhaling enough air through his bandages and mask. I can hear him wheeze in a breath behind it as he gestures to Alistair's stump. "How's the hand?"

"Not there," Alistair says. "They managed to remove the bullet from my arm, though. I received the news that Marshall has recovered from both his injuries and the flu as well."

"He did?" I gasp.

"Man of steel, I tell you." Ed shrugs. "Getting shot twice, overcoming an illness that stirred up a whole pandemic while surviving this long. He's strong."

"But he's not coming back anytime soon," I sigh, moping. "The Italian Front still needs him to help with the men. Now that he's back in good health, he'll be on the front line again."

There's a brief pause as Ed and Alistair stare at each other. Another drop of suspicion makes my stomach heavy with nerves.

Alistair stammers, "W-well...you d-don't know that for sure. He could just be blowing the same old whistle. This time, he'll be wearing a helmet and be below the top."

"What do I know anymore?" I whine.

"There's a lot of uncertainty at the moment." Ed shifts on his wooden chair, picking at his bandages that're wrapped around his index. "I think, in time, it'll all work out. We won't know when. Solutions often sneak up on us when we're not looking."

"What they all say," I quip, growing quiet.

"Hey, Nathan?" Edith calls.

"Yes, dear?" Nathan's leaning over a box of syringes, heaving it onto a nearby table, wiping his brow free of a cold sweat. "What is it?"

"We were supposed to get a package today, were we not?"

"Yup. I hope it hasn't come late." Nathan whimpers as he pulls on a new pair of rubber gloves.

"What package?" I ask.

"Just some extra bed sheets, jars, the lot," Edith replies. "Sallinger ordered them when he saw the spike in cases."

"That's good of him." Alistair continues practicing his child's scrawl on a scrap of paper. "Really helps us. They should make a machine that drains the lungs of fluid at the push of a button instead of having to do it manually. I heard the people who die from the flu don't actually die from the flu itself, but the pneumonia it brings with all the bacteria growing in the lungs."

"Yuck!" Ed gags as the tent flaps rustle.

"May we come in?" Sam and Lester's masked faces pop through, their eyes creased by their cheerful smiles. "We have that package you wanted. If we could just put it somewhere—not the bedsheets—the special one Sallinger was talking about."

Nathan beams. "Of course! Bring it in! Is it *Ace*?"

"*Correctomundo*." Lester's grin grows lopsided in a rare display of glee.

The flaps open as Sam and Lester step to the side, a scuffle between not two, but three voices snarling at each other outside, followed by a collection of nervous laughter as a man stumbles in, almost tripping over himself.

With his hands dug into his pockets, cap is tipped over his eyes as he fixes the black leather gloves he dons on his hands, a mask is over his mouth, and he yelps at Sam and Lester to hurry with the boxes.

It all happens so quickly.

His arms reach for the brim of his cap, slowly but surely pulling it off with nervous grace. The whole tent has gone silent, hands clamping over mouths, eyes wide with shock and surprise as a storm of black hair comes into view.

Clutching his cap against his chest, his hand runs through the unruly locks, teasing each one. Eyes—dark hazel eyes—rise to meet mine.

The air is knocked out of my lungs at the sight of him; a walking skeleton, gaunt, his uniform the slightest bit baggier on his frame. Yet, his broad shoulders remain unaffected by his starving, hollow exterior. The sparkle in his eyes reveals that his soul remains unchanged, undamaged, still the same ecstatic, quick-witted man that sends out electrifying sparks of light and joy to those around him, who he draws in with his magnetic pull. His bright delight of a presence could light up an entire room and leave the ground shaking with his magnitude. His pull is undefeatable. His mind can't be reckoned with.

He's here. Right in front of me. His announcement of his arrival is waiting to explode into the air, a flashbang aching to blind those with his brilliance.

Marshall Clark stands shamelessly with a cocky grin across his face and a red satin bow tied around his neck. He puts one of his hands up to wave while he sings out a singular word, a tune that could get me up to dance any time he wanted me to. "Delivery!"

I'm paralyzed, stuck to the spot, my pen falling to the floor. It's a massive effort to stand and move my limbs even an inch. The tears well up as I rush towards him, screaming his name, his arms wide, accepting me into a ferocious hug, squeezing him around the waist and breaking down.

"Hell no—It can't be!" I gasp, gripping his upper arms. "Marshall, is it really you?"

His chuckle is enough to cause my stomach to flip, threatening to send waves of nausea wrecking their way through my gut. "Who else would I be?"

"Sallinger said that you'd remain in Italy!" My hands roam his waist, his shoulders, his face. "You...you're the *Ace Project?*"

"When Sallinger calls, I come." He reaches to wipe my eyes with the hands that I ached to feel against my skin for months on end. "Of course, he wanted his special package to reach its owner before he could put it to great use. I'm here to stay, my love. I'm back."

I can't stop the tears that fight to fall down my cheeks, turning my premature sniffles into ugly sobs as he brushes the hair out of my face. He presses my cheek to his chest. "You're as beautiful as when I left. Even while crying and soaking my uniform, you're truly captivating."

"I'm dreaming. This has to be a dream." His arms wrapping around me is a heap of information to suddenly take in. My legs threaten to send me to the floor. "I have to be dreaming."

"No, Frieda. This isn't a dream, nor will you drown. You've completely resurfaced. I'm not going anywhere."

Ed stands, reaching for him. "You're actually here! How was the train ride?"

"Huh? It was alright, nothing special." He shakes Ed's hand, continuing to hold me close. "I'm honestly exhausted."

"Marshall, the packages!" Sam calls.

"Oh, darn," Marshall sighs. "That's right. Hang on for one second. I'll be right back."

"You said you weren't going anywhere." The joke comes out in a weak whimper. I grip him tighter, pulling him close when he draws back.

"Anywhere from here," he elaborates.

"You haven't lost your spark yet." Ed claps him on the back. "It's good to have you back."

"It's good to be here," he says as he exits the tent, carrying boxes. "Frieda?"

Our eyes meet as he sets the boxes down, leaning on his elbows atop their lids.

"I know what you're going to do."

"Bother you with a heap of questions?" The question is far too wholesome, far too childlike when it leaves my mouth. It only makes him chortle.

"Exactly." He sits on the nearby chair, patting his knee.

"Are you kidding me?"

He blinks innocently. "What?"

"We're in a pandemic, Marshall."

"And we're both in the best of health, are we not?"

Not taking any chances, I draw up a chair right next to him.

"Your call," he pouts. "Okay, I'm not used to seeing the love of my life right in front of me after all this time."

"It's all such a blur. I can't believe you're back! I'm so very lost. What're you going to do here that you didn't do in Italy?"

"Sallinger sent a letter back in June saying that whenever I was ready, I could come back and be his right hand man. It means I have to keep his men in order. I won't be surprised if he places me as drill sergeant."

"You're not going over the top, are you?"

"I don't think so." He shrugs, unsure, in another dreadful beat of silence. "Your eye; I heard about it."

"It's ugly, I know—"

"No, no, no!" he interrupts and steadies a gentle hand on my thigh. "I didn't mean it like that! I was concerned as hell when I heard what happened."

"I'm sorry to have placed that on you."

He leans forward, closer. His gaze is magnetic. Now I truly see how worn he is. His cheekbones protrude far too much under his skin. The shadows under his eyes have deepened. Little fragments of who he used to be still shine through. His twinkling eyes never lie. "You don't have to apologize about anything. Of course I'd be concerned if my partner went missing and came back from Hell on Earth. I was beyond relieved to hear that you'd been found. I feel so lucky to have you still here with me."

"I'm so glad to have you back. Edith wanted to introduce you to someone."

"Edith?" He shoots a glance at his sister. "Who is this mystery person?"

"Marshall, this is Nathan." She points at Nathan, who waves as he handles more and more jars. "My assistant and my partner."

"Nice to meet you, sir." Nathan inclines his head, stiff as a board when acknowledged.

He grins, warm. "The pleasure is mine. No need for formalities. Call me Marshall."

Once Edith starts teasing Nathan again, Marshall chortles and positions himself to stare me down again. "Also, I'm so relieved you recovered from the flu."

"And you're walking again." I gesture to his abdomen. "How's the wound?"

"Merely a scar." He unfastens the bow and sets it aside, straightening his collar which has turned askew. "I think I can take this off now. Sam suggested I wear it and become one with the packages for dramatic effect."

"You looked rather ravishing with it."

"Thank you, darling. I needed some positive feedback."

I've never been more excited to feel that familiar exciting shiver that comes with his flattery.

"Ah, Christ, the lovebirds are back at it again," Lester calls. "I completely forgot how enthralled you two are with each other."

"And you, Lester." Marshall snickers. "What about your lady friend, Amelie? How are you two going?"

"I forgot you'd mock me about that too, bastard." Lester glares. "She hasn't written in months."

"Oh? Perhaps her letters are lost in the mail? That can happen."

"I think she's genuinely not interested."

"That's unfortunate. It was worth a shot. Perhaps, when you're ready, you'll find someone?"

"I hope."

Marshall then looks over at Alistair, who meets his gaze. "Alistair."

"Marshall."

He situates himself on the edge of his brother's bed, patting his knee. "How's it hanging? Learning to write again?"

"Of course," he replies, groaning at the effort. "I feel like a child all over again."

"Better than last week's sample, don't you think? Maybe you'll become left handed or even ambidextrous when your prosthesis comes in."

Alistair shrugs and screws the lid back on his inkwell. "Would be a wondrous talent, eh?"

Marshall takes the parchment from his brother, nodding at his scrawl. "Your hand is a lot better. It's legible."

"Is that supposed to be a joke?" he asks sharply.

Marshall chuckles softly, handing him back the parchment. "I meant your handwriting. Your hand*writing* has gotten a lot better."

Alistair reaches to ruffle his hair as Edith emerges. The three of them get caught in a deep discussion. A hurried billow of words fire between them. Marshall leans farther forward as Alistair nods along. Both their shoulders develop some sort of rigidity from whatever they're talking about, and when they dismiss themselves from the conversation, they all appear distraught.

I carefully make my way toward Marshall, bending to meet his shadowed gaze that stares at the floor. "Is everything okay?"

I've startled him. He snaps up to look at me. "You could say that. I'm tired."

"From the train? Or is it something else that's bothering you?"

"Nothing. Just the train. I spent a day inside the same small room. Cabin fever."

I give him a condescending look, causing him to flinch and avert his gaze. "Come, perhaps we should talk outside?"

Hesitantly, he trails behind me out into the chill air, keeping at least a meter away, as stiff as a board.

"You know you can walk beside me, right?"

"I...take social distancing very seriously."

His response is enough for a snort to blow from my nose. "You must be afraid of catching my cooties, then."

Gaping jaw, rendered speechless, his face only satisfies my teasing even more.

Outside the tent, his hands return to his pockets. He whistles an anxious low note when I turn to face him. He remains tense, brows knitted together. I've grown to know him so well to know that he hates this type of confrontation.

"Was there something you wanted to talk to me about?" His foot kicks a stone out of his path as he situates himself on the wooden bench. "You know I'm open."

"You seem anxious about something. I'm open, too. C'mon, spill the beans."

Marshall hesitates, leaning to rest his hands on his knees while he stares intently at the floor. "It's just that you hadn't written to me for almost two months. I was under the impression you hated me after what happened with that woman."

That woman.

It's evident he doesn't want to remember her. Doesn't want to be reminded of her actions.

"Marshall dear, no." I shake my head. "What's splintering that fantastic mind of yours? I could never hate you. I didn't write to you for so long because it was Edith who was keeping me busy with work. Let's get it straight. It's not your fault, but Heidi's, for making such an advance, unless you—"

"I said no," he hisses, tense. His eyes squint shut as his hands clench into fists. His voice trembles. "I said no! I thought I mentioned that countless times—"

"Hey, hey, I get that. I'm assured well enough that you're telling the truth. Don't worry." I put my hands up in a surrender. "I don't hate you, nor do I believe you were unfaithful. Take a deep breath with me."

His inhale is shaky, exhaling a relieved sigh through his nose. "I can't forgive myself for letting it happen. I was so blind to her motives."

"I'm truly sorry. But you know what?"

"What?"

The ghost of a smile prints itself along my lips. "I'm proud of you for saying no. You know what that shows me?"

"What?"

"That you're brave. I believe you. It wasn't your fault."

"I mean, of course." Marshall leans back against the bench. "If I let her go further, I'd slam my head into a brick wall to punish myself."

"You wouldn't."

"I would." He taps his index against his temple, giving me a playful grin. "I have a thick skull, so I don't think it would do much besides give me a splitting headache."

"You've been away for six months, yet you know exactly how to make me laugh."

"Of course I do." He warms my heart as he pats the spot beside him. "You're not going to stand throughout this entire conversation, are you?"

Gratefully, I take the spot, his shoulder brushing against mine. A fleeting spark of longing zaps between us; more of his magnetic pull dragging me in.

"So," his eyes brighten in the fall sunlight, "what happened since I was gone? Fill me in."

"Besides what I sent you in the letters? Not much."

"As Sam said: News is slow on the Italian Front."

"The German Offense is obviously over and done with. Not many assaults have happened since then. It's been mighty quiet here."

"Significantly less, compared to Italy. There were assaults almost every day." He reclines even farther, relaxing and unwinding. "I'm glad to be back here before it gets worse over there. I honestly feel lucky. Extremely lucky."

"I feel lucky to have you back well and whole. Red bow and everything."

"As I've said, it wasn't my idea. It was Sam and Lester's to add a dramatic flair to my arrival. I was too tired to object. Besides, I thought it was adorable, anyways."

"It suited you. You should wear it again."

He stifles a laugh, resting an arm on the back rest of the bench. "Red doesn't suit me."

"Worth a try."

Shifting to face me, he looks me straight in the eye. The butterflies inside my stomach and chest flutter to life yet again.

"I've said this plenty of times, but I've missed you."

"I've missed you too."

"No joke. I missed you so much that each thought of you felt like it was creating a sinkhole inside me. I might've turned into Swiss cheese if I were away any longer."

"I'm sorry. I didn't mean to hurt you."

"No, no, no! Don't apologize!" He stops me with a finger pointed at my face. "It felt good either way to have someone to care about. Now that I'm back, I can stop pining and actually spend time with you."

"As I've said, you're drooling over me."

"I feel no shame." Always fast to retort, he is. "Regardless of how the boys tease me, I have no shame."

"I'm touched." I place a hand over my heart, swooning as its beats quicken with his flirtations. "Really, I'm touched."

"Quoting Sir Arthur Conan Doyle"—he leans so close that the musky scent of the cologne he must've sprayed on teases my nose—"*you are my heart, my life, my one and only thought.*"

"Please have mercy on my failing heart, kind sir." I elbow him weakly in the ribs. He emits a bubbling laugh. "First a Jane Austen quote, now this."

"They convey how I feel. What better use would they have other than helping me express it? You have to admit, it sets you on fire inside."

"You got me. You've shot down and quartered me with your flattery." I hoot with a horrendously loud charade of laughter as his cheeks burn scarlet. His feet shuffle on the ground.

He innocently digs at the dirt with his toes. "Would a kiss make it better?"

"Not right now! We're in a worldwide pandemic, lover boy!"

It's his turn to clutch his belly as he laughs his hardest. I've missed hearing him guffaw. Just the sound of his laugh is enough for me to get high. "I know! I know! But we're both clear of the flu, so—"

"Okay, here's a thought." I jab an antagonizing finger at his breast pocket. "Once the war and the pandemic are over, I'll give you a nice big kiss to cure your longing heart."

"For shame! I can't wait that long!" His voice is close to a squeal, which makes us both double over, chests heaving with shameless laughter. He wipes his tearful eyes and reclaims control of himself.

"Frieda?"

"Yes, Marshall?"

"I must say it again. I don't miss just you, but the way you make me feel." His grin doesn't fade, eyes glassy and alight with joy. "You make me feel like a free man. Every time I talk to you, the feeling only grows."

"Touché. Marshall?"

"Hm?"

The words pour off of my lips—the first time in a long time, filling me to the brim with a warm sensation that's almost the equivalent to what I'd imagine is like swallowing a full glass of brandy. "I love you."

The corners of his mouth twitch. His grin grows wider as the words sink in. "I love you too."

Under the afternoon sun, he folds one leg over the other as his gaze lands. It sticks. When it breaks away, it's when someone rounds the corner.

"There you lovebirds are," Ed teases. "Keeping distance while staying close, I hope?"

"*Edward*," Marshall warns.

"Sorry for interrupting. I've got a message from Sallinger. He'd like to speak with you in private. He's waiting in the tent for you."

"Of course, the time has come to ascend to greatness." He waves Ed away and stands, dusting himself off as Ed shouts names at him like 'tomcat' and 'lover boy' as he slinks away. He glares at the sky while he lets out a loud, disgruntled groan, slouching his shoulders and moaning out loud, "And so, the work begins. Just when I thought I'd be free from labor for one moment, the Devil is calling."

"Face it. At least you don't have to go over the top."

"I don't know about that yet. Laugh at me if I get shot a third time. Third time's a charm." He tips his cap over his brow, turning to me, a grin appearing once again. He produces a short bow. "My dear, if Sallinger doesn't drown me in errands, I'll see you soon."

Darting around the corner, he leaves me, once more, alone; evicting me of his charm and company that I've missed for so long.

* * *

Marshall doesn't return till later that afternoon.

I pore over log books yet again, converting units and noting dosages. When the tent flaps open, he stumbles in with his cap under his elbow and a tired sag in his bones. He saunters in, producing a loud yawn, as if to confirm his presence, which makes me chortle behind my hand over my work.

"Mr Clark, so glad you're back." Nathan emerges, scrubbing away at the tourniquet which has kept him busy for the past hour. "How was Sallinger?"

"Again, Nathan, please, it's Marshall." He rubs at the corners of his eyes. "Yes, I was right to predict that he'd drown me in mountains of work. I have to help the drill sergeant tomorrow with roll call and inspection, meet the new troops at the docks and allocate them to their correct sections. Expect me to be a grumpy sack of potatoes once I'm finished with them."

"Apologies. Yes, Sallinger really does put a lot of work on his subordinates."

"A subordinate? Me? No, I'm merely an intern. Oh, if you're to wash that tourniquet, soap and water will only wash out so much blood. Hydrogen peroxide will get rid of it completely."

Nathan pauses his ferocious scrubbing abruptly. "How do I know you're not a murderer?"

"I'm not. Trust me. It's common knowledge."

Nathan's brows raise, questioning him as he stumbles past. "Alright. Thanks for the tip."

"No need." Marshall lets out another yawn. He waves to Edith and moves tiredly towards me, dragging over a chair, slumping on the table. His eyes meet mine as his fingertips tap against the wood when he croons, dragging his words out with a smirk, "Hello, most cherished one."

I pull back from my work. "You look exhausted."

"I *know*!" he groans, resting his chin on his forearms. "Too much—far too much work already. Sallinger rambled on for so long it nearly killed me." He looks at the book on the table and asks, leaning even closer, "What's that?"

"A logbook containing patients and their treatments," I answer. "I had to sit here all day, calculating like there's no tomorrow."

"Ew, math." He grimaces. "I could never imagine doing it all day."

"If you're to become a nurse, you might have to."

Marshall grunts, closing his eyes against the table, murmuring something unintelligible.

"What's the matter?" I ask, brushing hair out of his face. He melts under my touch.

With a pained expression, he's closing his eyes, chin resting atop his arm. "Tired," he mumbles, playing with the lid of my inkwell in between his fingers, fixing his mask to fully cover his nose before it slips down any farther. "I did sleep on the train, but sleep deprivation is finally catching up to me after all these months."

The folds open again as Fey stumbles in. I glare at her, being rewarded with a miniature flinch when she finds my eyes. Catherine and I tracked her down once I recovered and gave her a lecture on her gossiping. Colby follows close behind, waving in a minute greeting.

"Colby!" I grin. "Look who's back!"

"Is that—" She gasps once the realization sets in. "Sergeant Clark?"

"Hey." He tiredly gives her a two-fingered salute, still leaning on the table, the inkwell lid in his other hand. "Colby, was it?"

"Oh dear, what happened to you? You were expected back in May, but you weren't there—what—"

"Shot," he replies gruffly. "Got sick."

Colby cowers at his blunt reply, but I wave away her worries. "Don't worry. He's exhausted from the trip."

"I am a sloth. I would like to sleep twenty hours a day. Uninterrupted."

This makes Colby and I both giggle. "Okay, Marshall. You do that."

"No, seriously!" His eyes flutter shut as I stroke his hair. "Did you know that sloths sleep for twenty hours a day?"

"I actually didn't," I answer. Colby fixes her apron and ties her hair back, the same brilliant blue eyes as her twin sister grinning at me from behind her mask. "I finished the first few pages, if that's what you're here for."

"I'm here to collect supplies, but I'll be sure to give them to Ms Audrey once you're finished. By the way, I suggest you get ready for supper. It's nearly time."

"Food," Marshall mumbles.

"Yes, you sloth, food. You heard correctly. Thanks, Colby. You can take the pages now if you'd like. Don't overwork yourself."

"As to you, Corporal."

Packing up my things, I make my way to the entrance of the tent, waiting for Marshall while he cracks his back and stretches. "Shall we get Ed? I'm guessing that it's the same as always. Sam and Lester still wait for us?"

"Actually, Ed has to stay in the tent," I correct him. "He has to stay in close proximity, as he isn't discharged yet."

"What a shame," he sighs. "Nonetheless, everyone who doesn't know already will gasp once they see me. We're quite famous, as you know."

The grumble I emit only amuses him more. "All because of me."

"You don't ever shed a light on my good looks, do you?" he chides playfully. "I'm just pulling your leg. Just tonight, I'll give you the extra credit."

33

TWO HALVES OF A WHOLE

MARSHALL

Outside, the night is young. The clouds roll over the deep black sky. It's a mesmerizing sight to behold, the stars banding like freckles across the infinite universe—quite like the freckles of the person beside me: walking as straight as a pin, casting occasional glances my way with a hint of a smile on her lips. She inhales the night air, at pure bliss with the world. Her feet press step after step into the earth.

I'm hypnotized by her presence, longing to reach out to intertwine her arm with mine as we make for the mess hall.

She's beautiful.

She's here beside me.

She's real.

Miniature sparks of excitement spontaneously run down my spine as she doesn't fade away, nor vanish. I make sure to walk on her left side so that she doesn't feel alone, nor will she think she's lost me in the crowd. I start thinking I've either shrunk or she's grown, as she appears taller than what she was a few months ago. Unless she purchased new boots with a higher heel. Her hair's been cropped into a bob and spins in curls to frame her small face; way different to the angrily chopped hair I first saw her with when she first arrived. Her black eye patch keeps its place over her eye, her jaw set as she struts beside me.

"So..." I start to feel the imprints of the many eyes that settle upon us as we stroll on by. I was right when I said we were famous, eyes goggling at us like we're stars of the silver screen. "They're still serving the same old thing?"

"You can say that," she answers. "They had more beer a few nights ago."

"Did they really? Again? You didn't try it again, did you?"

"I did. It tasted disgusting, as always." She grimaces, remembering the acrid and bitter taste of the vile beverage. "One man brought blackjack along, which Sam and Lester started playing as I sat in the corner. I'm not one for card games."

Though she's the same: of the same body, the same face, the same Seattleite lilt, something's different about her. She's hardened up over the past six months. The Frieda I knew, from what feels like years ago, wouldn't take up the offer of trying beer again after knowing she didn't like it without anxious questionnaires of 'are you sure' and 'I don't want to put it to waste' upon many other phrases.

She walks with her back straighter, taking wider steps, strutting and pressing forward rather than retreating behind my back. She moves with ease, with grace, without shame or disgrace. She keeps her head high rather than at the ground. She has the faintest crease of a smile at the corners of her eyes, trading a frown for a content and promising gaze.

She's an entirely different breed with the heart of a lion. It frightens and thrills me all the same. She possesses the methodic twists and turns of a mind that's always churning; forever magnificent, forever growing stronger. This version of Frieda Joyce brings me great delight. It kicks me in the stomach with both excitement and glee. She's terrifying, dignified, and mighty. Although, I still love her the same.

"Really? You? Missing out on a fun game of blackjack?" I tease. "I thought you'd enjoy some good competition."

"Card games bore me dreadfully," she whines. "I'd prefer a nice sprint race to keep the blood pumping."

"Maybe someone will challenge you to one sometime." I peer down at her as she bristles. "You can run pretty fast, can't you?"

"I don't have these legs for nothing," she replies playfully. Even when she's the hound at the head of a pack, she still has the playfulness of a puppy.

"My sincerest apologies," I retort quickly.

Her gaze digs into mine. I'm reminded of how much I've truly missed her after all this time. She offers me a smile, a hand that can be held through an emotional touch rather than a physical one. It makes me weak in the knees.

Frieda from six months ago almost never smiled; she always grimaced or frowned. It was rare to get one from her and felt like a reward when I did. I'm glad that a little light is finally breaking through and that I'm here to see it.

"So, in Italy," she winds the conversation up again, an extra skip in her step, "what did you do to pass all the time you had?"

"You really want to know?" I ask.

"Is it bad?"

"If you consider it boring." I halt as a military car drives by, the driver tilting his hat as we cross. I wave to thank him. "I didn't sleep much. I wrote a lot. Every day, I'd make sure I'd written something. It was almost like religion to me. I'd read, write letters, and speak to George if I could."

"He hasn't returned yet?"

"They need him. I wish he came back with me."

Frieda nods, taking this information in. Her gaze darkens. This time, the smile vanishes, and she hugs her arms tighter around herself. "I wish the war would end. It's been going on for what, four years now? I don't care who surrenders, I'm tired of being used as a pawn by the higher ups."

"I wish this war never existed."

"Then we would never meet and be an unhappy, nonexistent pair."

I huff at the statement. "You really think that if the road was any different, we would've never met? I could walk a thousand lives and my heart would still come back to you in every one."

Her hand falls over her heart. Once again, I've been able to make her swoon. "That's probably one of the most romantic things you've ever said."

"Are my continuous flirtations and banter, coming exclusively from my mouth, seemingly unromantic? Gosh, I should improve. Sorry for being such a buzzkill."

"I didn't mean—"

"I know you didn't." I pull her close momentarily. "I'm teasing."

"As you do."

"Although…" I lean down to whisper in her ear as we stop to let yet another military car through. "I could master the art of flirtation elsewhere. I could make it part of my expertise."

"You scoundrel!" she cries out, flustered, but laughing. "If you ever say that in front of my family, you're dead!"

"Well, I'd never." I titter playfully. "My practices are reserved for only you to assess. I expect a full report with full marks by next June."

"My mother would ban you from seeing me if you say such suggestive lines in her company. You'd have to sneak in through the window next time and hide in my closet." Frieda shrugs, an impish grin solidifying. "But who is she to stop us?"

"I haven't even been here for a full day and you're already challenging me." I roll my eyes. "I'm glad to see you aren't scared of her anymore. Do I stand correct?"

"I've come to realize that she has no hold over me. Besides her position as my mother, she can't really control me like she used to. I'm an adult now. I can decide what I want to do with my life. I got sick of her abusing me since my father left for war." All hints and teasing leave. "Now, she's sick in the hospital from the flu along with my step sister."

"I'm sorry about that," I reply, not knowing what else to say. I struggle with giving condolences sometimes. It's one of the occurrences where you have to tread so lightly or else your whole attempt shatters. I want to comfort her, I really do, but it's hard to find the words to express how sorry I feel. "The flu truly is a pain to deal with. Especially with the second wave that came last month, don't you think?"

She nods, getting a place in line for the both of us as I scan the crowds for Sam and Lester over the many capped heads of soldiers. In the corners of my eyes, dozens of others stare back and make me feel small, shrinking behind my tunic. There's whispers of our names, a few pointing fingers impaling me in the back like an archer's arrows.

I turn to Frieda, who flinches under the pressure of their glares. It's the first mark of vulnerability I've seen from her since I've returned.

"Oi, you two!" Lester calls as he and Sam rush through the crowds. "First dinner together in a long time!"

"True," Frieda mumbles, looking over her shoulder. She covers her patch with her hair. It's obvious people are making fun of her, making her push her vulnerable wound into hiding. "They're looking at me, aren't they?"

I suggest, "I could always go over and—"

She stops me with a forceful hand clamped around my forearm. "No! Don't, please!"

I stop dead in my tracks as she looks away, biting her lip, hands trembling. "So, they *are* looking at me?"

"Just ignore them. They want attention, a reaction." Sam's gaze goes from her to me. He jabs a finger in my face. "I know what you're thinking."

I dodge it as it almost pokes my forehead. "What?"

"Being pretentious, threatening them to turn away like you always do."

"You mock me." I slump my shoulders, defeated. "I'm too tired to set foot away from you."

"Don't, once you have the energy."

"Understood, sir." I bow, joking, cold. "I can stay a good boy: nice and tame."

Frieda curses under her breath. "Edith told me to let my eye breathe from time to time—every few hours. What's the time now?"

I get out my watch. The hours really do go by in a flash. "Just after five."

"Damn," she hisses. "About time."

"You can take off the patch once you get your rations, can't you?"

"I guess." She watches as the line moves, growing uneasy. "You two go on ahead, Sam, Lester."

"We'll find you at a table?" Lester asks.

"Yes." Frieda's dismissal is curt as she reaches for her patch, to the strings that hold it, cursing again as the knot she tied is too tight to come undone. Lester and Sam move up a few spots, leaving us behind.

"Here, let me." I reach down to fumble with the knot. When it comes loose, she holds the patch to her eye. "Aren't you going to take it off? You know, let the socket breathe?"

"I don't want you to see me." Her voice is quiet, barely audible. It's enough for my lips to twitch with sympathy as I grapple for words. A promise. A comfort.

"I won't judge, trust me." I lower my voice to match hers. "I promise you, it won't make me think of you any different. I won't even regard it as much, nor will I see it as a flaw. It marks who you are. It tells a story only you are able to convey."

"It's disgusting," she retorts. "I hate looking at it. I hate seeing it in my reflection. I want to run away from it. But I can't, because it's on my own ugly face. It's hideous. It hurts when you can't run from yourself."

"Hey, don't say that when you have a man who would jump off the Flatiron Building if your life depended on it. I think you're beautiful either way. I'm not entirely perfect either. You should see the wicked scars along my back. Look at my hands, Frieda, see all these scars?" I gesture to the scar tissue that peeks out from my sleeves. "They're from the gas and many other incidents I've had. You still see me as a handsome devil."

"I do. Maybe because your looks don't matter to me. I wouldn't care if you looked any different. I'd still like you either way."

"I see you in the same regard. I don't care what you look like. As they say: It's what's on the inside that counts." I manage to catch her lips twitching to hide a grin. "One mishap won't make me see you any different."

"Don't say I didn't warn you." She sighs and tugs the patch off, looking right at me.

Her normally green eye is gone, replaced by what I presume is the conformer over healing pink skin. The skin around her socket is a blotchy, injured red, fading to match the inside of her socket with scars making lines along her cheek.

"To tell you the truth, it doesn't look that bad." I give her an assuring smile, looking her right in the face. "I don't mind it. Not at all. It's quite a mighty fine battle scar, if I do say so myself." I push her hair back from her face. "It tells people not to mess with you, shows that ferocious, undying flame burning endlessly inside that heart of yours."

"It's a bit childish of me to ask...Marshall, I'm feeling awfully tense. This is the first time I've taken my patch off in public. Will you...will you please hold my hand?"

"You don't need to ask twice." I offer my arm. She grabs my sleeve. "You've got a tough grip." Her fingers pinch my arm accidentally. "Too tight!"

Frieda fills my ears with shy giggles as we move forward. She's leaning against me, her arms looped around mine, shuddering when we halt.

I crane my neck to brush my lips against her ear. "Are you doing okay?"

"I think so." She adjusts her mask with her other hand, stuffing her patch in her pocket. "I feel strange like this."

"Let's be strange together, then. How about I tell you of the time I had in Italy where one of the French corporals brought his dog into the medical tent while waiting for a nurse to see to his injuries, hm?"

"Do tell."

"Alright. So, as I was learning to walk with my crutch, this French guy came in with his dog—a gorgeous Spaniel of some sort—trotting along beside him. You know I love dogs, so, naturally, I asked him if I could pat it while he was getting checked out, and the dog had jumped all over my front and was the friendliest little thing towards me. His ears...oh, Frieda, his ears! They were so soft."

"Spaniels do tend to have soft ears."

"I started crying when he started licking my face. His tail wagged at a million miles per hour. He was one happy pup."

"Did you get his name?"

"Beau, I think it was. It means something in French."

"Handsome," Frieda translates. "It means 'handsome.'"

"Yes, I was expecting you to know what it meant." I collect our rations and lead Frieda toward Sam and Lester, who've situated themselves at one of the tables at the back of the mess hall. Helping Frieda to her spot before I sit, I start taking off my mask to eat as she leans on the table, slumping against the wood.

She's lazily picking at the bread roll before her, groaning at it. "I'm getting bored of these meals."

Lester glares over his own dinner. "Be grateful. Unless this war ends and we all go home and have a feast, you can stop whining and—"

I give Lester a death stare, stopping him from flapping his mouth more than he should. Frieda remains unaffected. If she is, she's hiding it rather than telling us. Her eyes stay set on the table, her hands tensing into fists as she pushes her tray away.

His toughness falters. "Frieda—"

"It's fine, Lester. I know I'm being unreasonable."

The table goes silent. No one dares speak a word as they eat. The low *clink* of silverware sounds all around us, accompanied by the scraping of their edges against the beef cans. I force down my corned beef and take small sips of water to wash its almost non-existent taste from my mouth. Frieda picks at her bread loaf, taking small bites. Lester has scared her into eating. I feel horrible at the thought that I've somehow become one of the causes of her anxieties.

Frieda's hands begin to shake. Her jaw clenches.

"Frieda," I lean forward, "is everything alright?"

Frieda takes in a staggered breath, biting her lip, as she searches for an answer. I already know the response before it escapes her mouth. "I'm fine."

"We could step outside—"

"No," she stops me. "I'm fine."

"So, Marshall," Sam interrupts. "How's that bullet wound of yours?"

There's a pause. I direct my eyes to him, who opens his can of beef. "My wound? It doesn't affect me much. Still a bit of pain here and there." I touch my fingers to my abdomen, Frieda's eyes following them. "The stitches have been removed. Everything came out just fine."

Sam nods, scraping at the bottom of the can, satisfied with my answer. His brows knot themselves into one line as he scavenges for more, coming back unsuccessful. Frieda remains silent. Her gaze keeps moving between me and Lester, who also sits quietly and picks at his bread roll, taking it in tiny chunks between his fingers.

A shoulder brushes mine, Frieda taking the risk of coming closer. Her voice is soft against my ear, eyes alight with mischief. "Lester's moody because he found a new girl."

"Did he?" I gasp, Lester stiffening at his name.

"What're you young romantics whispering about?" Lester snaps. "Always have something to gossip about, don't you?"

The shock dissolves from my face. I lean on my elbows. "Don't worry, Les. Frieda was just joking with me."

"Joking?"

"An inside joke," Frieda adds, following the plot with ease. "One we made up in our letters. He got shot, so he's a holy man."

That stung. I clench my jaw. *Frieda, you've wounded me.*

"Well, he's certainly not the most innocent. He's sinned quite a few times—"

"Lester!" My voice rises a few octaves. I break into an embarrassed sweat. "No, not like that! I'm supposedly a holy man because my body is filled with bullet holes, get it? Hah-hah, yes, your face may shrivel up with embarrassment at hearing such an absurdity now! *Hardyharhaar!*"

Frieda breaks into a horrendously loud hoot which would have her mother rolling in her grave. Her face grows red. A glorious grin forms, and she clutches her chest as she coughs. She waves me off as my hand fumbles to pat her on the back.

"Oh my dear lord!" She bangs her fist against the wood, wiping her eyes. "Lester, how did that even correlate with—oh, Lester, no!" I've never seen her laugh this hard before, holding her stomach as she wheezes, calming herself soon after. "No, that's entirely different to what we meant. Good job for making me chuckle. Now we know how truly wanton your thoughts are."

Awkwardly, my face ashen, I reach for my glass and chug my water down. "I'm going to need a good visit to the bar once the war is over."

Frieda leans on her fist, acting to the equivalent of a flirty drunk: utterly chaotic. "I could join you."

As the color returns to my face, I sneak her a smirk. "And share some whiskey?"

"You've got it."

I take another sip of water, teasing her even further. "You've never gotten drunk before, I'm guessing. I don't know how long you'll be able to hold your liquor for."

Frieda retorts, "Worth a try."

Sam *hmph*s and takes a bite of his biscuits, dipping them in water (they're inedible if we don't dip them), shaking his head in disapproval. "Tasteless, as always."

Once we finish, we tidy up our eating space. Frieda ties her patch back on, the rest of us with only our masks. Lester straightens his cap, covering his locks that reach his ears. We all need haircuts sooner or later, if Ed feels up to it. He once teased me over getting a buzzcut. I almost slapped him, claiming it would be a curse to see me without my curly, boyish locks I've grown far too used to.

Frieda keeps her composure as she walks beside me. The major difference is that her shoulders aren't stiff, but more relaxed. She doesn't look like she'll crumble again. As the four of us walk, a line of soldiers march past, trailing behind a transport car with a driver that's hesitant at the wheel. He's carrying heavy loads, boxes of ammunition, bullets stocked high in their wooden crates.

I grow rigid as the clan march past in a hurry. "I don't remember hearing of an assault coming any time soon."

"They're sending new men over the front lines since most of the older waves got sick. I believe they're the night watch." Sam stands beside me as the car stops, men hauling the crates, shouting at each other as the sun goes down behind them in the distance. Once it's safe to cross, the men march into Death's clutches, footsteps echoing in my ears.

A radio starts up. A group of men start cheering when they get a line to work. I try to tune in to what the reporter is saying, but the volume is too low for me to make out any of his words that buzz with the radio's changing frequencies.

Terror spikes down my back as the drone of engines roar up above. I train my eyes to make out the many silhouettes of planes—biplanes—in formation. Their winged shadows are birds in the early night sky. A thousand snippets of disaster flash through my head all at once. I'm stuck to the spot, remembering the crusade of bombs that boomed as the bullet struck me, the crash that rung in my ears before—

"Marshall," Frieda's voice travels through time to bring me back to the present, "you're—"

"We have to hide. Now. Did you see the planes?"

"They're ours." Lester stops my fretting. "We've had more and more planes flying over. It's more and more of a recurrence now that the Ottomans are catching us like mice. They're not going to bomb us. They'd be brainless if they were to bomb their own side."

"It's just...bad memories." I dismiss the topic, the engines' groans fading as they fly away.

Frieda gives me a concerned glance. "I wonder what it would be like; seeing the world from above, like, at eleven-thousand feet. Would be quite a sight, don't you think?"

"I've been in a hot air balloon before," Sam replies. "Not for long, just for a joyride—I got airsick. We flew over the countryside. All those stretches of land and their fences turn to boxes, bricks, of many shades of green."

"Sounds wonderful," I comment over Frieda's shoulder, scanning the sky, paranoid, if more planes happen to fly above us. "Except I have a fear of heights. Eleven—what—thousand? I'll pass."

"But can you imagine zipping past in one of those beauties?" That rebellious, tomboyish grin returns on Frieda's face. "The engines sound amazing...So powerful."

"You should join the air force," Lester suggests.

"Heavens no. I don't even know how to fly a plane!"

"Flight training?" I offer. "I mean, if you were to join, then of course they'd give you some sort of training."

"Waste of time," she grunts, kicking a piece of rubble out of her path. "Besides, their cadets would most likely be as backward as they are here, times ten. Also, you're forgetting that I'm half blind."

"That shouldn't stop you from trying," I argue.

"As much as I'd love to fly one of those things, I'd rather have my feet on solid ground while I work, thanks."

I snicker. "A non-conforming aviator. Imagine that. You'd be making history."

"I'll let another well-deserving person take that slot. I think she'd be ecstatic upon receiving her award."

"It sounds tempting though, don't lie." I pull my gloves over my hands. The air is growing colder. "You could be famous. Rich, even."

"I'd rather not. I already have enough of a paparazzi," she jokes, winking at me. My face darts to the floor as a grin upturns my lips.

Lester enters the medic tent, Ed sitting by Alistair's bedside, watching over him as he scrawls over the parchment in his lap. His hand continues to quiver whenever he holds the pen. I'm sure the tremors will fade once his grip grows stronger.

"Good," Ed encourages him in a low murmur, "really good, Alistair. You're getting better and better with each print."

"Yvette might finally be able to read my letters," Alistair replies.

Nathan's busy lighting candles. I emerge while his back is turned.

"Managed to find some hydrogen peroxide?" I start with a joke, Nathan turning to look at me, running a hand through his hair.

His eyelids are heavy from fatigue, yet he provides a smile. "Sure did. It took a while, though. How did you know? Don't say it's from 'basic knowledge.'"

I stop before I tell him of my experiences with blood on bedsheets in sad, existential, nihilistic hours of the night, telling him an alternate story. I'll uncork the stopper of that bottle of trauma another time.

"Well, chemistry class, for one. Second, medical textbooks. You can also use it to clean minor wounds and cuts."

"You really are a future nurse, aren't you?" Nathan waves a match, whipping it out so that the smoke dances in the air. "I don't stand a chance when there's people like you running around."

"I think you do." I lean against the wall of the tent. "What you've done to serve? Truly inspiring. It doesn't matter how much medical knowledge you have, but how you help others. I've done next to nothing compared to a man such as yourself."

"Well, thank you. That's reassuring." Nathan dusts himself off, yawning.

I ask, "So, where are you from, Nathan?"

"Lincoln."

"Nebraska, right?"

"Yep. Edith told me she was from Pennsylvania, but she didn't say exactly where. It could be that I've forgotten."

"The three of us hail from Philadelphia."

"Popular city, eh? I've wanted to go there. Not right now, obviously, but someday."

"Perhaps you'll come back with us when we go home?" I shift, giving him a welcoming grin. I sneak a quick glance at my pocket watch. "Look, it's getting late and I'm on duty tomorrow morning. You look exhausted. We better get some sleep while we still can. Hard working men like us need our rest."

"I'll try. Goodnight, Marshall."

"Goodnight—oh, one more thing?"

"Yes, sir?"

I remove myself from the wall, inclining my head, standing straight. "Thank you for taking care of my sister. Please promise me you'll continue to look out for her."

"Of course. No doubt about that."

"Good man." I turn on my heel after I show him a flicker of my approval through a smile. "Sleep well."

Yawning, I rub my eyes and find everyone crowding around Alistair as another medic comes in with a trolley.

"Good evening, Jay." Frieda grins. "Got everything you needed?"

Jay blinks. "Pretty much. I got a message from Dad. Uncle Isaac says he's still well."

"Thank the lord." Frieda stands and brushes herself off. "Please get some rest. Ah—there he is. I have someone I'd like you to meet."

"Oh?" Jay cocks his head.

Frieda beckons me to her and the man. I step forward, producing a minute wave.

"I mentioned Marshall before, remember? This is him. He got back this morning. Marshall, this is Jay, my cousin."

"Pleasure to meet you, Jay." I reach out a hand for him to shake.

He takes a small step back to decline it, holding my gaze with skeptical green eyes. "Yes, a pleasure. Look, I'm going back to my tent for some rest. You two sleep tight. It's getting cold tonight."

As he exits, I groan from exhaustion. "It's been a long, hard day."

Frieda's equally as exhausted. "I think I'm going to get ready for bed soon."

"I should too…" As she turns away, I reach to grab her wrist to pull her back. "Frieda?"

Her eyes find mine. "Hm?"

"It's weird now."

I've caught her off guard. "What is?"

"Actually saying goodnight to each other again. Seeing each other in person after all this time. I'm glad for it."

"And now you're leaving me."

I pull her close, pushing her hair behind her ear. "For a matter of hours. It won't be like before."

Before. A dangerous word to say.

Her eyes darken at the word. "I'll see you at breakfast?"

"Of course. Same as old times. Care to walk with me?"

Once we say goodnight to everyone, we set out into the night. It's quickly gotten dark. Troops are getting ready for bed, and blowing out their lanterns. A chilly breeze drifts through the campsite.

A shiver scampers over my skin. "I used to take a lot of night walks once I got better."

"You did?"

"They kept me busy." I tread over the gravel walkway, not jumping this time as another roar, belonging to a plane's engine, sounds up above. Another triangle of them fly peacefully onward. "It cleared my head from everything going on. It all felt okay for a little while."

"I couldn't move for a few months." Her voice shrinks. It quivers. "My body was so weak from almost everything. Even opening my eyes was a pain."

"There were days where I kept falling back asleep because I was so weak." I keep up my measured pace, walking alongside her. "Was that when you had your dreams?"

"I kept passing out. Every time, I thought to myself, 'this is it. I'm going to die without saying goodbye.' But I opened my eyes and everything was okay. Sometimes I wish I could die. It would make everyone feel so much better. They'd have one less person to care about."

"I've done my research, and I'm also wanting to be a nurse. Judging by all the doctors I've seen, what the nurses are doing now, every patient's life matters. Especially at this time. One loss is equal to losing an entire world."

Frieda's silent, staring at the sky.

"If you died, Freddy, let me ask you this: Would that make the people who love you so dearly feel better? How do you think I'd feel?"

"I don't know...Sad? Burdened?"

The words slip before I think to stop them. "I was in your position years ago. I know how you feel."

Frieda halts, turning, her eyes digging beneath my skin. They show no anger, no distrust, but shock, as she bats them, almost dumbfoundedly, at me. "You kept that from me for so long?"

I swallow, picking anxiously at my cuticles. "I was scared. I'm sorry, I won't say anything—"

"Remember our promise—"

"—to tell each other everything? Yes, I remember. I broke that promise, I'm sorry."

"Shush." Her gaze impales mine again, sending a twitch up my spine. "You're thinking about it too much. To tell each other everything would take years if we did it all at once. We only know each other truly now. We're no longer background characters in each other's lives, Marshall. You don't have to tell me if you don't want to."

"I guess now that I've told you, you should know. You're an important person in my life. You deserve to know every inch of me, every light and dark moment that made me who I am today."

I shuffle on the spot, kick at the rocks under my feet, and unbutton the cuffs of my tunic. My fingers go to the pale, fading scars that sit horizontally across my wrists, my forearms.

"We should sit down. There's a lot to say."

34

GRIEF AND MOVING ON

FRIEDA

I can't stop looking at the lines on his arms. He feels my eyes on them, stuffing his hands into his pockets with an uneasy gulp.

Once I'm seated on the bench, he doesn't sit with me, but remains standing. His cuffs are still folded back. He's rigid, his lips babbling, searching for words to say, where to start.

There he goes again: running his hands through his hair, pacing in circles and muttering to himself, slamming his fist against an open palm, shaking out one nervous kink after another.

"Take your time." I try to reassure him. "I understand it's a sensitive part of your life."

Once he summons enough courage, he blurts out, "You'll think of me as mad."

"I won't." I lean forward, watching him closely. "Take your time."

"Fine, fine." He inhales. "I'll shorten it for you. Ever since my mother died, I thought I'd killed her because I couldn't take care of her when she needed me most. She died on me, and after I recovered, I felt extremely guilty for not being able to save her and stayed in bed all day, lying that I still felt ill even when I felt physically better, but not mentally. My head was in a dark place. You can imagine what it would be like for an eleven year old to experience such dark thoughts...that he was the one who killed his own mother, the woman who birthed and cared for him every single day of his life."

"You didn't kill her." I want to reach for him, pull him close, but he takes another step back. "It wasn't your fault."

He paces, his brain ticking away. "On my twelfth birthday, everything went to shit for me. I thought I didn't deserve to be alive after all that had happened, that my mother should've lived instead of me. I skipped nearly the entirety of sixth grade, my life becoming darker and darker. When I was thirteen, after so many pledges to not take it out on myself, these appeared."

He points to his wrists, the scars that line them, the horrible things I can't avert my gaze from.

"It was too much of a burden for me, so I had to find a way to get it out. I'd abandoned all the nonsensical pledges. My demons grabbed the wheel. I wanted to feel something for once, an escape from the nullification of my senses." He lets the words sink in, drawing his wrists back, rebuttoning his cuffs.

"Things kept getting darker and darker. Every fall, more lines. Another failure, another scar. They kept multiplying, but at least I felt in control for once. I wasn't capable of doing anything other than sitting

absentmindedly on the living room sofa, watching people pass with a half-read book in my lap. I was too

tired to concentrate on the words on the page. I thought about how I could be a better person. I stayed up

almost every night, falling asleep in class. My father thought I was still weak from scarlet fever, taking me

to all these doctors who asked all the same questions when I knew the answer, but was too scared to say it. I

settled it. On my fifteenth birthday, I would end my life. I met Ed a few days before because he'd seen

these and wanted to help me feel better. He did. He kept me clean, kept checking up on me, and treated me

like an ordinary person. On the eve of my birthday, I…"

All I want to do is reach for him. "You don't have to—"

"*No.*" He thrusts an open palm out in front of him to stop me. "On the eve of my birthday, I had

everything ready: the note, how I'd go, everything. I'll admit, I was scared. I was shaking, leaning against

my desk, rocking back and forth to calm my nerves. I lied on the bedroom floor for three hours straight,

sobbing with my hand over my mouth to not wake anyone up, paced my room for another two, tried and

tried again to fight the urges. Ed's words kept repeating inside my mind, telling me I could get through it.

Everything he said to me echoed until the clock struck twelve. I threw everything away, burned the note,

and cried. I was a scared little kid who didn't know what the hell to do. God, am I so glad that I survived.

Without Ed, I wouldn't be here—I don't even know where I'd be."

I'm speechless, letting the silence sink in until I'm able to mumble, "I'm sorry."

"No, please, don't apologize. It's not worth throwing a pity party over." He bends on one knee in front of

me to look at me with soft eyes filled with sorrow. "Frieda, I didn't mean to—"

"No, it's not that." I reach to wipe my eyes when they start to water.

"Am I in trouble? If you want to end it here—"

"Hush, you fool!" I interrupt. "Do you know how strong you are?"

"Not very."

"You're a man of steel." I stare at him with a ferocious gleam of admiration in my eye. "You're a soldier,

a victorious veteran of the war inside your head. You beat Death himself four times in your life and still

came back for more. You don't give up, you keep fighting. I don't care about your past, I don't care for

what you did. I care about who you are now and that you're still here and pressing on."

He clears his throat as I take the risky move of hugging him, squeezing him tight and burying my head

into his shoulder as he adjusts himself to take me in. I whisper quietly into his ear.

His breath hitches at the sound of my voice. "What was that?"

"I said that I love you."

He takes the risk of bringing me closer, his heart beating madly inside his chest, flitting nervously. "I love you too. If I could, I would kiss you."

"What's stopping you?"

"Germs."

"I have cooties now?"

"No, the ones causing a worldwide rampage. I'd catch your cooties any day," he jokes and wipes his eyes. He slumps his shoulders and holds on a little longer. "I missed this."

"What?"

"Hugs. I forgot you give the best ones." When I think he'll pull back, he melts farther into my arms. "Thank you, Frieda—in all seriousness, thank you for listening to me, for accepting me. It's all word vomit at the moment. I'm working on and editing it twenty-four-seven."

"You don't need to thank me, and I think the word vomit's fine the way it is." I slump against him, yawning and closing my eyes. "Let's sleep out here like this tonight."

He lets out a weak and airy laugh. "You certainly are a daredevil, aren't you?"

"Maybe, whatever your definition of the word is."

"What am I ever going to do to you?" He squeezes my arm. "I think it's time for the both of us to go to bed."

"You're leaving me?" I pout.

"I'll be here in the morning. Don't you worry."

"Take me with you! We can have a sleepover! You can braid my hair and I can curl yours!"

"You can't just sneak into my tent like that! This isn't some college dormitory love affair! Plus, as much as I would *love* you to terrorize my curls, I have to get up an hour earlier than you to get ready for roll call. I'm helping the drill sergeant first thing tomorrow morning."

"That's bonkers." I yawn. "Sallinger is a meany."

"And you sound drunk. Plus, you're overtired."

"You're horrible!" I playfully smack him on the back. "First you tease me about not being sure of how long I can hold my alcohol, now this! You're horrible, *salaud*!"

"I don't know what you just called me, but it sounds like a threat." Marshall backs away, playing with me. "*Mierda,* Frieda, *you're* horrible."

"*Shuddup!*" I slur my speech, him letting out a relentless hoot in response.

"Come on, gremlin. You need sleep, I need sleep, we both need sleep."

"Are we back to this again? I'm only five inches shorter than you!"

"I wasn't insulting your height!"

"I still take offense to that!"

We break into more absurd laughter before I slump against his chest again, the rise and fall of his laughter beneath me, the steady thrum of his heart against my ear.

"You're right, you're right." I slip away, standing and brushing the dust that's collected itself on my uniform. "I'll go to bed. We need to sleep."

"Good idea." He stands with me, giving me a tired grin, eyes creased both with fatigue. "I have to rest from my trip. I'll see you tomorrow?"

"Of course."

With a mischievous glint in his eye, he blows me a kiss before departing.

I make my way to the women's camp, waving a goodnight, letting my shoulders slump as I walk, cowering from the whispers that follow everywhere I go, the eyes that glare, the lips that smile patronizingly at me. As always, my name is tossed up in the air by a group of nurses hanging their aprons up to dry, shivering in their thin nightgowns, one wearing her frock over it in a weak attempt to protect herself from the cold.

Once I step inside the tent, Fey looks up from her journal. "Frieda—"

"What?" My mood immediately changes, anger filling my chest. "What is it you want to say? You want to spread more rumors now that he's back?"

Fey swallows, tense. Her eyes darken with fear. "I—"

"You know what?" I let the heat in the tent rise, turning the dial up as far as it can go. "After you were so, so nice to me when I first moved here, it's hilarious that you turn on me and spread rumors about my private matters, don't you think?"

"I'm—"

"No, no, no. I'm not done." I glare at her, worming my intended intimidation into her. "Don't you think it's hilarious that someone I *trusted* turned out to be the person fanning the flames over a minor incident, one that could be easily resolved if we had talked about it? Absurd, right? Is there not any privacy here? Are you using my personal matters for your entertainment because your work is so *dreadfully* boring to you?"

"I thought…"

"You thought what, Fey? You thought what?" I spit.

"I thought…" She shrinks against my glare. "Nevermind, I'm sorry—"

"I see how this is." I crack my knuckles, her cringing at the threat. "You apologize because you feel bad only *now* while being confronted, after spreading that little rumor like wildfire with no care in the world for how I would feel once I found out. Highly amusing of you to presume I wouldn't confront you about it, nor be here tonight telling you this, or even alive, for that matter."

"Just hear what I have to say!"

She's pleading, eyes spiking with tears. If I were less angry than I am now, I'd feel a shard of sympathy. My silence is enough for her to know I'm interested in hearing what she has to say.

"Whoever told you it was me spreading those rumors, you have it all wrong." She pulls at a dark lock of hair, eyes blinking back tears. "It wasn't me, I swear it to you! I was trying to stop the rumors! Catherine must've heard me talking and assumed it was me. I'm so sorry this is all happening to you. I can't imagine how you must feel."

I consider my choices. She could be lying through her teeth to save herself. But there she is, crying and pleading for my forgiveness and rambling on about how sorry she is, that she couldn't prevent it from happening, that she's so desperately sorry, that I'm going through something so trivial, so horrible, so—

"*Fey*," I interrupt her pleas. Her eyes are wide, innocent, yet tainted with fear. Her hands are clasped, body bent forward, as if she were praying. "Please don't fret." I bend to meet her gaze. "If you keep rambling on and on like this, your tongue will fall out."

Fey doesn't say anything back, paralyzed.

"I'm sorry for lashing out at you like that…I should've listened." I reach for her and clasp her shoulder. "Thank you for…you know, trying to stop the rumors. I need to repay you."

She relaxes under my grip, eyes remaining wide. "Y-you're welcome?"

"I should've listened," I repeat. "I should've just let you talk. My anger got the best of me."

"No, no! I understand," Fey answers quickly. "I understand what it's like to have someone undermine you like that. My family and I…we're…immigrants. All our lives, we've been tormented for it, gossiped about by the ones we thought we could trust, had our culture and language made fun of and ridiculed. Nowhere is safe for us. I understand how you feel."

I dip my head. "I'm sorry you had to go through that. I wish people embraced different cultures and peoples rather than moving to extinguish and oppress them."

Fey nods, sighing. "I do too. We can move on from this, can't we?"

"I think we can." I offer a guilty smile. I'm still reeking of it. It doesn't sit well in my stomach. I stand and turn away to get ready for bed.

"Did you talk about it?" Fey asks.

"What?"

"About...you know...the argument...if he…"

"There was no argument to begin with. It was all a great misunderstanding." I sit on my bedding as she settles on hers. "I think we should sleep. Just know everything's fine between you and I, okay?"

Fey gives me a confident nod before she turns over in a flurry of dark hair. "Goodnight, Frieda."

"Goodnight, Fey. I'm sorry, again...for lashing out."

"Please don't apologize anymore. Maybe your tongue will fall out instead of mine."

I let out an airy sigh and close my eyes. The tent is silent, the last of the light in the oil lamp burning out with the only sound being mine and Fey's breathing as we desperately try to catch some sleep.

My brain keeps cycling back to Marshall with his arms outstretched, his scars lining them, his eyes full of a ferocious pain that only he can feel coursing through him. It hurt to listen to him. It always hurts to see him break down into tears, to see him so vulnerable. I didn't mean to hurt him. I didn't mean to bring up bad memories. I feel disgusted after asking him, bitter at myself for hearing him speak of it so reluctantly, disgusted at myself for accusing an innocent woman for another's wrongdoings.

One word repeats itself; the steady *drip, drip* of water from a faucet not quite turned off.

Selfish, my head screams. *Selfish. So damn selfish.*

* * *

I wake up in a daze the next morning, rising to hurriedly comb my hair and throw on my uniform once I check the time.

I slept in for almost half an hour. Roll call is in fifteen minutes.

The time sends me into a panic as I hurriedly tie my patch over my eye and I burst out of the tent once fully dressed. Running down the campsite to the drill grounds, rifle in hand, soldiers gather in the still-dark dawn of a new day.

I ask a man hurriedly for the time: five minutes before drill; five to five in the early morning. The rest of the country, settled over the hills and far away, would be sleeping or getting ready to earn their innings at work or take care of their families, trying desperately to stop the spread of the flu all the same. I envy their secluded lives, the order still installed inside their homes, not overthrown by the sounds of gunshots and blasts threatening their impending demise.

Over the heads of many masked men and brown uniforms, a steady breeze drifts by, chilling me deep in my bones.

A voice cracks through the air like a whip. "Squatchin! Attention!"

My clutch upon my rifle tightens. Marshall emerges beside the drill sergeant with his head held high, eyes shining with a steely glare, and epaulets—bars of gold—sitting proudly on his shoulders. He's combed back his hair, or more rather, it's been trimmed and styled into a pompadour under his cap. The drill sergeant stands with gold epaulets of his own plus a stern and graying mustache that stops at the corners of his lips. He mutters something to Marshall, who replies and stands respectfully by his side. As he holds his hands behind his back, he finds me within the flock of brown tunics.

By the nerve of him, he winks. He has the audacity to *wink* with a devilish smirk during an official drill under the sergeant's nose.

I stop myself from bursting into laughter with the absurdity of his actions. He flashes me a grin as he steps forward to mark the regiment's presence.

Sallinger moves to stand by the drill sergeant with his eyes trained on Marshall's back, watching for any mistakes to pin him to the wall with. Marshall pulls out a pen and a clipboard, keeping his shoulders straight and rigid as he reads the names on the slip of paper. He methodically works his way down the list, reading the last names first and nodding as each owner yells 'present,' other men yelling 'away' or 'ill.'

"Joyce, Frieda!"

"Present, sir!" I yelp, cringing as my voice squeaks compared to the rest of the men, who hide their laughter which would cost them their position if it were to be let out. Marshall himself releases a huff of amusement as he ticks my name off, his gaze lingering on me as he continues his roll call.

Sallinger's eyes remain on him before he briefs us about today's plans. An air raid is supposedly happening, so we're to take caution as we work. He's assigned groups of men to dig the trenches, to drive supply cars and tanks, and tells us who will be going over and who would be in the reserve trenches in the event of an assault.

I remind myself that I'll be resuming work with Edith today rather than suffering the risk of going over. The thought is of minor comfort, but it doesn't save my nerves from fraying. Marshall listens intently and stores his clipboard away, chattering with the drill sergeant as Sallinger keeps briefing us.

"I would also like to introduce you all to Sergeant Clark. If you don't know him already, he's taking my major and captain's place for the time being, as they've both fallen both regretfully ill. Please send your regards. Keep an eye out for Sergeant Clark, as he'll be stepping in to help me for as long as the two of them are out. Any regards and requests for me, you send through him."

Marshall nods in acknowledgement. It's terrifying, watching him conform, becoming perfectly poised with his superiors chewing on him with all their claws and teeth. Just looking at him, he seems unaffected, or he's that brilliant at keeping up a mask, or he's *enjoying* this treatment.

Once we're dismissed, I set off to find him, but stop in my tracks when the drill sergeant guides and drags him into a conversation. His eyes never leave his face. Marshall's gaze never drops. Confident, he is, I'll give him that.

The sergeant gives him a slim set of papers, turning sharply to follow behind Sallinger, leaving Marshall on his own to read what's printed on the papers.

"Busy bee, aren't you?" I tease once the coast is clear. I jostle him on the upper arm. "Look at you, acting as a secretary."

He rolls his eyes and tucks his papers under his arm, failing to hide his amusement. "Hey, the good news is maybe I'll get promoted to sergeant major."

"You have the whole rank ladder memorized by now, don't you?"

"Not exactly," he argues.

"I'm still waiting for my sergeant promotion. I'm starting to think Sallinger's forgotten about me."

"You need the recommendations, obviously."

"I haven't gotten them yet. I think I know why."

"Because you just haven't been recommended?"

"Because I'm *me,* dammit!" I snap, and bitterly add, "It wouldn't be a good look for him. I should ask Sallinger to become a medic or something. That'll really make him laugh."

"I can put forward a notice. You could become a combat medic."

"You'd probably be better at it than I would be. You're qualified in that area."

"I'm sure all you need to know are basic medical skills, like how to tie a tourniquet, which medications work with what, how to clot wounds—hell, you could ask me for some tips."

"Have mercy. I'd have to wear a skirt, too." I let out a dramatic moan of despair. "A *skirt!*"

"You could be an assistant. There are plenty of those. Maybe for Colby or Catherine, one of your friends? I don't think it'll be that bad. Look at Nathan, he's having the time of his life."

"Fine, please put it down. Do I need to go somewhere for training?"

"I wouldn't know. Most likely, if you're just an assistant, I'd say you'd have to undergo minimal training. Since you're already here, Edith or one of the twins can give you some pointers." He clicks his pen, scrawling a note. "Combat medic, was it? Or do you want to be a stretcher carrier?"

"Wherever Edith is."

"Combat medic it is." He finishes his note, folding it in his pocket, patting it. "C'mon, Frieda, at least you'll get more action. Do you realize you have to go on the front line from time to time?"

"At least I can't be shot," I say. "Come along, we'll be late for breakfast."

"Another thing: Me and the boys won't be seeing you at drill or inspections, nor will you be eating meals with us."

"You'll come visit me, won't you?"

"Of course I'd visit my lover in waiting." He bumps me with his hip, making me squeal.

"You...you *connard!* You casanova! Curse you!"

"I know what a casanova and what a—*canno*—damn, however you pronounce, it are. By the way, nice voice crack during drill this morning."

"I swear to God, Marshall Clark, you know just how to push my buttons to the very limit."

"C'mon, I'm just teasing. You love me."

"I do. I shall profess my love for my helpless inamorato."

"Now you're poking fun at me!"

"Ha!" I prod a finger at his chest, laughing in his face. "How does defeat taste, Sergeant?"

"Just you wait until I get my hands on you—"

With a childish squeal, I take off with him behind me chasing my tail with a loud and teasing hoot. I skid to a halt once I reach the line for rations, turning to find him blazing through the crowd, tripping on his heels and panting, bending over and bracing his hands on his knees.

"My god, you're fast."

"You still haven't gotten your hands on me."

"In time, I will," he sneers cheekily. "You can't keep running like you've been running through my mind all day."

"Don't start. It's only six in the morning. So what, you wake up and immediately go 'oh, shucks, thinking about her now?' Is that how it is?"

Marshall's still puffing. "Terrible usage of a pickup line, I know. Never again."

"There you two are!" Sam calls, pushing his way through the groups of men that block his way. "Why do you both look like you've run a marathon?"

Marshall pants, "She started it."

"Nonsense, you goon. You were the one to start teasing me." I fold my arms. "It's funny, when you get back from Italy, you start up again. You missed me that much, huh?"

Sam shakes his head in disbelief. "I'll never understand you both. Besides that, Lester's coming soon. I've got updates from George."

"How is he doing?" Marshall asks.

"Good, apparently. He went over again and survived a gas attack. Iron man, I'll say."

"Brilliant. It just occurred to me how long it's been since I last fired a gun," Marshall observes and scratches the back of his neck. "I should go to the range in my free time, blast some rounds."

I knock him lightly on the arm. "I'll join you. I need to polish up my aim."

Marshall turns to me and smirks. I plant a hand over his mouth. "No. *Do not* attempt another pickup line on me."

"You caught me, shot me right through the heart!" He dodges and grasps his chest, letting out a choked and authentic groan of pain, leaning forward. "Sam, man down, man down! I've been shot!"

"What in the hell is going on here?" Lester emerges behind Sam.

"Don't worry, he's being obnoxious." I stifle a laugh as he lets out another groan of pain, getting down on his knees and reaching out to Sam and Lester, who backpedal.

"Gentlemen! Assist me! I've been shot by a beautiful archer!"

"Obnoxious indeed. It's"—Lester checks his watch—"quarter past six in the morning and you're already acting like you drank a whole barrel of beer."

Marshall rises and dusts himself off. "I had two cups of coffee today."

"Ah yes, the creators of all things evil: Marshall and coffee."

"I plan on having a third cup—"

"No!" Sam interrupts. "You won't be having any more coffee today. You've had enough, unless you want to go into cardiac arrest. Do you seriously have a death wish?"

"I'm only jerking your knees," he snickers.

Lester scoffs at him as he takes off his cap, running a hand over his pompadour cut. It's not too bold; a small lift with gel.

"Did you get a trim?" Sam is astounded. "Who did it for you?"

"I may have bothered Ed about it...He screamed at me for letting my hair grow so long and unruly. It was just past my ears when I came back, so he cut it. I came back the next morning asking him to style it, so here we are."

"I'm not used to all that forehead. You had that this entire time?" Sam reaches a hand out to smooth Marshall's hair, which he swats away.

"You're too cruel, Sam, you truly are." Marshall tuts. "You truly thought I didn't have a forehead?"

"How much did he cut off?"

He stands proudly, grinning from ear to ear, as if he's achieved something grand. "He got rid of some split ends and cut my fringe. Not too much. I can see now!"

Sam rolls his eyes. "Welcome to the club. Just a tip, don't show your forehead ever again. It's unsettling."

Marshall stammers, hurt. "A-are you saying you don't like my hair?"

"What he's saying, Marshall," Lester explains, "is that he likes your hair, but the amount of forehead you're showing compared to your usual is unsettling. I must agree."

Marshall stomps his boot down as we move up in the cue, taking his rations, giving Sam and Lester a glare as he passes.

"I think you insulted him a bit too much," I say as I take my rations and wait for the others, Lester snickering.

"Payback for teasing me about my love life. Wouldn't you say so, Sam?"

Sam sighs. "I'm sure he means no harm, Les. After all, I do admit you're quite unfortunate with the likes of women."

"Damn!" Lester hisses. "I'm not *that* bad that you have to side with that goon, am I?"

Trailing behind them, I find Marshall sprawled out across the grass with his clipboard resting on his knee. His hands are stained with ink as he writes furiously, the pages underneath stained black with words on the parchment.

"Hard at work?" I question him.

"Please, not now." He presses his nib harder upon the page, his head coming closer to his writing hand with each sentence. I peer over his shoulder and find that he's writing out his assigned errands under Sallinger's name in scrawled and messy handwriting. "I need to finish these for Sallinger."

"It's not even the end of the first day and you're already overworking yourself. Please eat." I prod him with his can of bully beef. "One bite to keep you going?"

"No." He pushes the can away with the back of his hand which is also stained with black blobs of ink along his knuckles and in between his fingers.

"Just one?"

"Please, Frieda, *no*." He pushes his rations away a second time when I try to hand them to him again and continues writing, signing things off and making confirmations. "I'll be done in a minute."

Hesitantly, I begin eating as the scratching and scrawls of his pen scrape against my eardrums. His scribbling continues.

I've had enough, setting my can down. "It's only breakfast time and you're already working your butt off."

"In a minute, *please*."

I narrow my eyes at him. Satisfaction oozes through me as he shrinks back.

"Marshall Clark, you are in the middle of a war, a pandemic, and working under Sallinger. A gentleman with a duty such as yours won't perform at his full potential if he doesn't have at least something to keep him running. You'll fail to cope and fall ill under the pressure. Young man, I demand you to eat. Not in a few minutes, not even one, but *right now*."

The silence buzzes like static. Marshall freezes, his fingers clutching the pen tighter before he sets his papers down and reaches slowly for his rations with a reluctant sigh. His nose scrunches in disgust as he peels away the seal of the can of bully beef before he scoops some out, gagging at the taste. No one here likes the bully beef, but we force it down. It's the best thing we have.

I watch him closely as he finishes the disgusting beef in record time, looking up at me with shadows of no sleep and stress under his eyes. "Can I work now?"

"You may, thank you." I continue eating as he writes next to me, spluttering and taking a big swig from his canteen.

"The beef is disgusting. What did they do to it while I was gone? Salt it?"

"I never realized," I reply as Sam chats away with Lester, who gags on his rations and soaks his biscuits in water. Everyone has to, or else the biscuits will break your teeth from how hard they are. Not to mention, they're as tasteless as dog biscuits.

* * *

I've just returned from helping Edith carry in new stretchers and sheets for the cots as the number of sick soldiers increases daily. A day doesn't go by when a new report is made, when a new case is found.

Footsteps stomp behind me. I jump at the sudden boom of a deep voice. "Corporal Joyce, just the person I wanted to see."

I wheel around just as Robert Sallinger emerges around the corner with his hands in his pockets, guarded against the fall chill. His salt-and-pepper hair is tousled by the winds, his wrinkled forty-or-so face cracks into a dim grin. "I'm glad you're back up to speed, one eye and all."

I release an unamused, flat laugh. "Sir, you amuse me."

"Yes, yes. How are the medical tents treating you? I understand you're helping out quite fondly and putting in a great effort. Mr Nelson told me quite a story of it all."

He's getting under my skin, picking away at my usually-impenetrable armor. "I'm being a good helper. It wouldn't be me not to help in times of need."

"Isn't that lovely," Sallinger remarks, taking in an uneasy breath.

"Is there something wrong, Lieutenant Colonel?"

"Sergeant Clark put in a notice. You wanted to transfer to work as a combat medic?"

"Yes?"

"It's unfortunate of me to say, but I'm afraid you lack the necessary requirements: training, uniform, approval—"

"I get it, sir, I really do. I didn't mean to trouble you. Now, if there's anything else—"

"The thing is, yes, there's more, Corporal. I received word from Seattle almost a week ago, a telegram speaking of Mrs Joyce—"

"Mrs South, sir. She remarried. I hate to correct you." Just the sound of her name causes me to tense. What trouble has she stirred up now? What condition is she in?

"Mrs South, then." He shuffles uneasily, rolling his ankles, brows creased. "You would know that she's an unlucky case of the flu currently flying around. I hope so, or I'm deeply sorry if this is your first time hearing of her."

"I've heard it all from my step father." A nervous prick taints my heart. "Did something happen, sir?"

A pause. A breath. A nod.

Another drop of apprehension intrudes on my already-sick, already-churning gut.

"I'm sorry, but she didn't make it. She passed in her sleep on Tuesday morning. Doctors say she stopped breathing from the fluid in her lungs. She passed away peacefully, I heard."

The air stills in my lungs. "She...she's dead?"

"I'm sorry for your loss, Corporal Joyce. Just know that she's in a better place now."

"Did she leave anything? A will, perhaps?"

"They're sorting through it now. They'll mail you the details soon. I truly am sorry. I'll leave you now, Corporal. You wouldn't want me around as you grieve."

Turning away, his head sinks, his gaze to the floor, vanishing from sight the way he came.

The news hits like a shotgun using me as a practice dummy with impulses crashing under my skin like tidal waves: run, crumple to the floor, let out a horrendous sob. More are to seek comfort, hide, swallow it all down like bitter cough medicine, stay strong and apathetic. They close in, circling like vultures amongst a dark cloud over my head on a sunny day.

My feet take off before I tell them to, shooting through the campsite. I sprint past the mess hall, past the medic tents, searching desperately for him, for a sign of his presence.

I've checked all the places he might be roaming. There's no sign of him at all, not even one through the many brown tunics and white masks, caps over brows.

Nothing.

My hand claws at the front of my tunic. My eyes flit through the mobs of men getting on with their work for the day, growing dizzy and breathless. I can't find that familiar face among the crowds.

I let out a suffocated whine as he arrives from the pathway to the trenches in deep conversation with another sergeant, poring over the contents of his clipboard. Once he breaks free of the sergeant's hold, I race toward him, gripping him hard by the elbow, startling him.

"Ow! What the hell—Frieda?" He blinks back his shock, eyes wide like an owl. "Frieda, what the hell? Why did you have to grab me like that?"

"We need to talk. *Now.*"

He senses my urgency. Without putting up a fight, he follows me. Dragging him to the bench near the shooting range as I try to control my breathing, neither of us sit down. He stands there, helpless and unsure. I hammer my knuckles against the insides of my wrists, muttering to myself.

"Is everything okay?" His voice is too loud in the silence. Far too loud against the speed of my racing thoughts.

"Marshall, please—"

"You're white as a sheet, darling. Talk to me."

"Can you be quiet?" I snap, trying to string a sentence together, figuring out a way to break the news before I vomit out my insides.

"Look at me please." Despite my obvious tension, he remains calm. It shouldn't infuriate me as much as it does now. "Whatever you want to say—"

"My mother is dead!" I snarl too loud. Anyone could hear if they were close enough. "Dead. *Dead*! She died from the flu! Sallinger told me moments ago."

Marshall's silence, ironically, drowns out my thoughts. I concentrate my gaze on him, my harried inhales and exhales whistling through my teeth.

"I'm so sorry...If there's anything I can do—"

"What should I do now that she's dead? Should I cry for a woman who cursed my existence? Cursed and hit the very child she herself birthed? Or spit on her name and celebrate her passing? I'm all alone now. I'm not worthy of anything, not worthy of you, a middle class morale with a large family and *parents*—"

"Frieda, Freddy!" His gloved hands reach for mine. I weakly hold on as if they're a lifeline. "Look at me. Don't say that please."

"What am I to do?" It comes out in a whine, a desperate whimper.

He hesitates, letting out a struggling sound. "Look, I understand what it's like to lose a parent, as you know. Although, I can't imagine the sorrow you feel from losing both of them. I understand you're angered, hurt, disoriented by the news. It's a terrible, gut-wrenching feeling to have someone you love go, and I'm truly sorry for that."

My voice raises itself to become louder. "She didn't love me. She hit me, burned me, neglected me ever since Papa went to this bloody war! She used me—"

"Shh, let's not focus on that. Please lower it a bit, breathe with me here. I agree, she wasn't the greatest mother in the world, but I heard that when you lose a parent, you're supposed to grieve."

The emotion behind his irises is indecipherable. He reaches to wipe my eyes with a gloved thumb. "Let it out. The worst you can do is suppress it. It's like pleading with the clouds to stop the coming thunderstorm; something you can't control. Emotions, as ugly as they are, are things we need to learn to feel. I'm here for you."

"But why?" I ask, choking on my tears. "I'm useless now. I have no immediate family, probably no income. Nothing."

Marshall cups my face in his hands. "You're everything to me. As dramatic and cheesy as it sounds, you're my everything. You're my sun, my moon, my earth, my stars—damn, just take the whole universe while you're at it. Mine and your father were like brothers; they were inseparable. He wouldn't let his best friend's beloved child slip away so easily, especially when his son is so amorously connected with her. I'll make you a promise. After the war, you'll come back with me, Alistair, Edith, and Ed to Philadelphia. Ed will of course reside back in Society Hill, where he moved during middle school with his parents and lives now with his wife. Alistair will be back with Yvette nearby. Edith, you, and I—I'm not sure about Nathan—will come to our house in East Falls and stay there with us. You'll be safe with me and my father who will go above and beyond to support you, I'm sure of it."

"You don't have to do that. Why waste space on me?"

"Because I care about you. I live and breathe for you and would do everything in my power to protect you, because as you've said countless other times, I'm chaotically in love with you. No obstacle or wave that may set us off course will change that."

I cover my eyes. The tears start up again, following his advice to just let it all pour out as he digs through his pockets to retrieve a kerchief, wiping my eyes again and again with no complaints.

"There, there," he speaks soothingly to me, continuing to hold my other hand. "I'm so, so sorry."

I shake my head, sniffing and speaking the two words 'I'm sorry' over and over again, him shushing me, assuring me that it'll be all okay in the end. He doesn't leave, doesn't curse and tell me to stop crying, but stays with me for what feels like ages. I'm sick to my stomach, wanting to run away from my problems like I always do. Knowing him, he'd take off and follow me to the depths of Hell, if Hell is even a place on Earth.

Once I grow quiet, his gaze doesn't fall away, but sticks, holding me to him. He wipes my eyes with his kerchief, which has his initials embroidered into it at one corner in red.

"Is red your favorite color?" I ask awkwardly, attempting to change the subject to distract us both from my sadness.

"Pardon?"

"Your kerchief—it's got your name in red. Is it your favorite color?"

"Oh," he blinks, "yes, actually, good observation. Especially dark red. What about you?"

"Green," I mumble. "Forest and sage green."

"Just like your eyes." His laugh chimes in my ears as he folds his kerchief. He's obviously trying to make me feel better.

The sadness drags on. It pulls at my heart, turning into a disgustingly powerful magnet.

There's an awkward silence between the two of us before I pipe up again. "I'm sorry for grabbing you like that earlier. How's your arm?"

"You didn't hurt me. You shocked me because all of a sudden, there's someone grabbing my arm and I didn't know who it was until you spoke. Honestly, I'm bombproof."

I look away, staring at his badge; a red ribbon holding the gold of the medal upon his breast, over his heart that still beats after facing so many nightmares on the battlefield, falling into the pursuit of Death. I can't stop admiring him for it, for staying so strong when almost every single challenge of life has been thrown his way.

His voice grows distant in my ears. "Everything okay?"

Leather touches my cheek. Dark eyes bore into mine. His face is inches away, every freckle standing out against his pale skin; stardust across boyish cheeks. They've started to fade compared to the last time I've seen him. So have mine from staying inside for all of the summer months, enduring a fever and a heatwave.

Not having the energy to lie, I shrug. "I haven't got a clue. It feels so different to when my dad died. When he did...imagine a radio wire for me."

"Alright, got it."

"When he died, the wire snapped in two—completely in half with all its edges frayed and everything. Now that my mother is gone, her wire snapped, but not completely. It's frayed, but I'm still wrapped and tangled in it. It's choking me."

Marshall's eyes crease along with his brows in thought. "Do you ever think why that wire hasn't snapped in half like your father's, then?"

"What do you mean?"

"It's hard for me to explain, but I have an idea why." His thumb presses against my cheek, stroking the skin below my patch and the cotton mask thoughtfully. "Perhaps it's all that she did to you that's causing it to stay? Everything: the abuse, the harm. It sticks, weakens the tension, the connection and the love between you two. Your father's wire broke completely because you had more tension, more love than you and your mother had. You let him go with ease. With your mother, the trauma still lands as painful as it did when she was alive. Now that she's gone, it's time to let go. You're free."

I stay silent, letting it all sink in.

"I understand it's traumatic, losing both of your parents. With your mother, after all she's done to you, I hate to speak like this, but now that she's gone, you have to move on. You have to get out there. She made you who you are. All of these scars you have toughened you up and every time you fell, you got back up again. Take as long as you need, but it's time to move on."

"How?" It comes out with a pitiful crack. I may as well end in tears again. "How? Tell me. How can I move on when she took such a large chunk of my life away from me? When you...when your mother died, you suffered three or four years of grief—"

"Depression," he corrects.

"Depression, stemming from grief and guilt. Correct me if I'm wrong. I may as well be feeling something similar at the moment. My mother told me to get over my father when he died, and now you're telling me to take my time to grieve. I don't know which one to choose. Should I just get over her or—"

"Hey, hey, hey." Marshall stabilizes me, holding me close. "Sit down. That's it, that's it.." On the bench, he presses me to his chest and continues to lecture me. "Another part of moving on from trauma is looking at whether your ways of coping will do you any good. Right now, you're in a dilemma about how you should react to grief because you've been told how to handle it one way, and now someone you trust is telling you to deal with it another, a way you're not used to. It's the same with taking another shot of vodka when you're already too drunk to stand. Would you take another shot of vodka and let it do more harm than good, or call a cab to go home for the night? In a way, they correlate. Trying to 'get over' someone will get you into deeper shit than make you feel better. It's like trying to hold down the alcohol in the vodka, which is damn strong, I might add. It's better to put the vodka away, call a cab, let the calm set in and sober up, like grieving and letting out the sadness."

"Very profound," I remark.

"Yes, so look at it from that perspective. Is it better to build up tension inside yourself and bottle up how you feel, or let it out and be rid of it to get some weight off your shoulders?" His hand ventures to my waist, pulling me in. His face is dangerously close to mine, but comforting all the same. "Would you rather take another shot of vodka and have a hangover the next morning, or give yourself space to throw it all up before calling a cab? Think of the vomit as your grief."

"Grief vomit."

"Exactly."

"I'll take it."

"Good, it's better to get it out rather than letting it make you even sicker."

"You're suggesting that I get drunk and imagine the alcohol poisoning as my grief coming out, huh?"

"It's not like that. It's all metaphorical."

I slump my shoulders, wiping my eyes for the thousandth time. "It's strange."

"What is?"

"Not having to worry about the next lash across my skin, what insults she'll scream at me as I enter the house. But it's sad all the same. She loved me so much, and as soon as he left, it all went away."

Marshall takes in a large inhale. "Perhaps she was dealing with her own grief? But it gave her no excuse to ignore what she did to you."

"Marshall, do me a favor. Resign from nursing school, become a psychologist."

"A horrible decision, really," Marshall retorts. "To become a shrink would be my downfall. I'd be dealing with other people's struggles as well as my own. It's not good for me."

"Fair call." I sigh. "An ethics professor, perhaps?"

"You really see me as the teaching type, huh?"

"Your way with words is just..." I can't think of the word.

"I see you're feeling a little better. See? Talking it out is better than holding it all in. C'mon, it's a common metaphor, and ethics are boring."

"But you're a legitimate wordsmith, Marshall," I drag on the ending syllable of his name in a whine, making him groan. "And yes, I thank you."

"Take all the time in the world. There's no rush. Go at your own pace."

"There we go again."

"What?"

"Whatever comes out your mouth sounds like gospel."

"I'm not preaching the Lord each time I speak, Freddy."

"Does that matter? Don't deny your evident talents."

"I'm *not*. It's common sense."

"For you," I say. "You're too humble!"

"It's not my fault that I give good advice because I want the people I love to be happy."

I jab him in the chest. He lets out another, dismayed groan.

"I hate to say it, but you got me. Fine, I'm good with words, good at giving advice. I have evident talents, but I'm not becoming a shrink, nor an ethics professor or a preacher."

"Good enough."

"You're terrible." He clutches his chest. "You're making me feel disgustingly warm..."

"Are you getting sick again?" Worry etches its way along my nerves.

"Garn! Don't you dare propose that! No! It's from you praising me!"

"You're getting all red," I tease.

He bolts to his feet, checking his pocket watch that stays attached to a loop of his breeches. I observe that the watch has a few knicks in its frame around its face and on the cover. "Revenge will come swiftly. It's just after three. We should head back before they think we're up to things even the devil himself would frown upon."

"You're suggesting—"

"Yes, I'm in fact suggesting unholy actions I'm not ready for in any shape or form. My father would disown me—no, he'd be more likely to stab me and make my skin look like salami with all those disgusting holes and put my head on a stick."

"Yuck." I gag and follow him back into the clearing, wiping my eyes.

"Exactly. And salami is disgusting either way—just thinking about it makes me—*bleugh!*" He shivers, disgusted when the image sets in.

There's someone clearing his throat behind us. We brake and wheel around.

"Sir." Marshall addresses Sallinger as the sergeant he is: hardened and strong, not the boy dealing with my grief and troubles willingly, experiencing my horrific banter all the same. "All the work is finished in the tunnels on the front lines."

Sallinger's eyes sweep over us. He catches a glimpse of my still-red eyes and nose staring blankly back at him before he nods. "Brilliant. I presume you were heading to your next job, Sergeant?"

He bats his eyelashes, oblivious. "I fail to remember, sir. My next job?"

Sallinger mutters something incoherent before he asks, "How long has it been since you've fired a gun, Clark?"

"Too long, sir. Before my accident." He presses a hand to his abdomen, as if a phantom ache still haunts him.

Sallinger's eyes drift from Marshall's hands to his masked face. "Go ahead to the range and shoot a few rounds. I believe you'll be needing your marksman's ability back sooner or later."

"Of course." Marshall bends to bow as Sallinger exits. He hisses once Sallinger's out of earshot, "Working under him gives me the shits."

"How? It's like working for a god."

"He gets so many requests, telegrams and letters, so many damn calls...Answering the field phones is the fun part. Tonight, I have to go to the docks and retrieve the men coming to our regiment on a ship from New York. For now, let's go shoot some guns."

35

THE *EIRSERNE KREUZE*

MARSHALL

We part ways and meet back at the shooting range, where the men stare as I enter with my rifle in hand. The cold, varnished wood is familiar under my fingertips, shaking my hand like an old friend. This is my favorite rifle; the one I use most often. It has an easy weight that feels good in my grip and is the least flimsy to handle.

My eyes scan the range for Frieda, who stands and watches two men fire their pistols, barely flinching as the shots ring out. She herself is unarmed, standing with her arms folded and her sleeves cuffed at her elbows, showing thin arms with scars running along them—battle scars—that set in well with her patch, casting her as someone you wouldn't want to meet in a dark alley.

When she hears me draw near, she merely turns her head while the rest of her body doesn't move an inch. A birdlike movement; a falcon surveying its next kill as it rides the waves before it dips, diving into the water with its merciless talons.

Her lips stretch into a grin when she sees the rifle. Any other person would quiver in fright if an armed soldier came their way. She points to the gun. "I haven't seen that one before."

"It's a M1903 Springfield sniper rifle. A beauty, isn't she?"

Her eyes don't leave the rifle. "Is it heavy?"

"Matters on how much weight you can lift. For me, not so much."

"Because you're suddenly a bodybuilder?" she jokes.

"Not exactly. I'm used to their weight. Though, I appreciate that you think I've hit the gym a few times in my life." I give her a wink, flexing an arm teasingly as I lug my rifle over my shoulder.

"Woah, slow down, tough guy. I didn't know you were that desperate to impress me."

I jut my chin up with a laugh. "Nonsense. There are far better things I can do that'll impress you."

As more shots ring out, her head whips back to the men firing at the targets nearby who hoot as one scores a headshot on the wooden targets, splintered from the bullet blasting through.

"You know what?" I interrupt the blasts and booms.

Her head swivels back to me. "What?"

"I don't feel like a Clark son when I say this, but I don't find much joy in shooting."

"So?"

"For men, they're like toys. For me, all they do is cause death and destruction. They'll keep evolving, get deadlier and deadlier, cause greater violence and tear people apart. It's funny how we have to resort to weapons to keep the peace of the brutality we created, don't you think?"

Frieda shrugs, her stance remaining unchanged. Somehow, even when she means no harm, she makes the hairs on the back of my neck stand on end. "I never cared much for weapons. My father decided to show me how to shoot in case the enemy invaded us or broke into our house, or whatever. Well, do what you need to do."

"You're not going to get in a few rounds?"

She scrunches up her nose. "Nay, I won't be firing a gun for years. I'd probably shoot someone on accident."

I prepare my ammunition, putting the extra bullets in my pocket, setting myself up: turning off the safety, loading the magazine, and pulling on the bolt to let a bullet into the chamber; religious steps my father had me memorize each time we went hunting, horrid memories of moments I didn't enjoy. When I move out, I'll never let a gun inside my house. Ever.

When I squint against the sun's glare, the Italian battlefield comes back to life, the shots echoing in my ears alongside the sudden spurt of blood I didn't even feel oozing from my abdomen. My senses failed to keep up as I tripped over my own heels, slammed myself into darkness as my blood wet the wooden boards beneath me...

I blink back the memories, taking aim, squeezing the trigger, letting the recoil bounce off my chest as I release an *oomph* against the force. I should've emptied my lungs out before I fired.

The bullet splinters the target in the shoulder region, a darkly humorous mirror image of past wounds and betrayals.

Jerking back on the bolt again, the methodic click sounds. I cast a glance back at Frieda, who stands, motionless, as if she's getting a portrait painted. Her eyes are trained on my back, her index taps against her bare forearm. I freeze before taking aim again, cursing as hospital beds intercept my mind's eye, hands coming away, bloodstains upon pale palms.

For a moment, I take a breather, relaxing my grip upon my rifle. Taking another shot, the target chips away at the neck region. I've narrowly missed the shot.

I give up when the other three bullets land in the chest, the opposite shoulder, and somehow, the top part of where someone's face would be. I turn the safety back on and carry the rifle with care.

"You're only firing one round? I thought you'd be leaving the target in pieces like you always do."

"You miss that, do you?" I joke. She tuts disapprovingly. "I'm not too keen on blasting wood today."

"Understandable. Say, should I have a shot?"

"Do you not remember what you said moments before?"

"Worth a try." She snickers devilishly. "I don't think my aim will be that far off."

"Are you sure?"

Her wicked smile only grows. "Don't think I'm incapable just because I've lost one eye. I've still got the other for miles to come."

I hand her a round and the rifle with a worried sigh. "Be careful not to shoot anyone other than the target, please."

Frieda waves me off with a dismissive hand. "No need to lecture me. Don't worry, my father didn't teach me how to spot a man from afar and kill him in various ways for nothing."

"My god," I choke out, "your father is just—oh, my—please say you're joking! *Do not* shoot anyone, or else you'll land yourself in prison."

"I know how the law works," she replies, with a cocky chuckle. "Don't worry."

I watch her closely as she takes my spot before the target, her grin sliding off her face. She slides into deep concentration, turns the safety off, loads the magazine, and pulls back on the bolt with little to no hesitation—much less in comparison to what I exhibited moments before.

The muzzle rises, aimed straight at the target.

Her first bullet rings in the air. The men firing their pistols stop to watch. The cracking wood echoes like thunder.

She lowers the rifle slowly and observes her shot, nodding meticulously once her eyes align themselves with the splinter in the chest region. She goes back for more, shooting four more bullets: two in the chest, another in the shoulder, the last in the lower abdomen, all guided more toward the left side of the wood, my hand landing on my previously wounded stomach almost on command, as if I'm the target instead.

She turns the safety back on and reapproaches me with a grin, handing the rifle back with two hands. "I didn't kill anyone, did I?"

"No." I take the rifle, carefully resting it over my shoulder. She hands me another bullet from a hand hidden behind her back. "Did you steal this off of me?"

"Maybe."

I let out a guttural laugh. "You truly are a troublemaker, aren't you?"

"Flirt," she hisses.

"It's my job." I wink. "Please, do enlighten me on your killing methods."

"But why?"

"For the future, if my patients don't stay quiet under the anesthetic."

"That's screwed up," she comments, "but brilliant." Frieda stuffs her hands in her pockets. "Unfortunately, I wasn't taught how to kill someone with chemicals, nor am I any good at chemistry, but he did give me information on guns and knives, especially self defense."

"Now I know I can't backstab you or else you'll tie me to the railroad tracks in no time."

She halts, eyes sharp with a teasing glare. "You were planning to?"

"No," I pat her shoulder nervously, "I merely jest."

The men around watch us pass. The news of my internship must have spread fast, because most are staring at *me*: the sergeant with the rifle over his shoulder, the marksman, Sallinger's new henchman. I start to believe it's the only reason why I'm here; to bend and bow to Sallinger's orders while his subordinates are ill. I'll be put on the front lines as soon as they're back—here or Italy, it wouldn't matter, because Sallinger would be more than happy to have one more healthy man fighting for him at a time like this.

Frieda whistles a low note as she passes the men who stare after her and suffer the wrath of my glare. They're bold enough to continue goggling once we turn the corner.

Storm clouds are rolling in, the sky a dull gray. Soldiers work in their respective places. I catch Nathan jogging across one of the gravel pathways into the reserve trench. His hair is a mess, disheveled. I haven't seen him all morning. All day, at the most. He brakes and pulls himself to a stop in front of a lieutenant who pales as he explains hurriedly with words that I can't make out from this distance.

My ears prick up. My eyes follow the sound thundering from the sky.

The cough and roar of engines is enough to tell me that planes are headed our way before I see their wings; Ghosts haunting the sky. A flock of birds with killer potential.

Men around us see them too. Some raise their rifles and take aim.

I don't hesitate to reach for Frieda's arm and pull her close.

The *Eisernes Kreuz*—one of the only German phrases I know—is painted viciously in bold silver, slathered on their empennages, wings, and rudders, descending while our shared terror climbs the scale with a ferocious takeoff.

We scram; rats running from a cat, diving for cover as the first bombs drop.

Now I know what Nathan was screaming to the lieutenant. He saw the planes first, tried to warn us, save us all.

A little bit too late, Nathan, I think, cursing him, the Germans, the war—everything be damned. Throwing my rifle into a tunnel, I grab Frieda hard and jump in as the bombs shake the earth. I stumble and trip from the shockwave and land hard on my stomach, facedown against the earth. Letting out a groan of pain, I rise to my hands and knees and struggle to keep my balance as dust plumes through the trenches.

Gunshots boom. Obviously some goons are hopelessly trying to bring one of the planes down.

By God, one succeeds.

Time slows for a second that feels like an eternity as the plane sputters and coughs almost like the flu patients back in their wards. It shakes. The engine starts to smolder, engulfed in great black clouds as it transits from a steady descent to a nose dive.

There's a scream.

Whipping my eyes away from the scene, I find Frieda screaming with her hands over her ears; a shrill screech like an officer's whistle. A blast narrowly hits our trench, spraying more and more dust as it crumbles in on itself. As reckless as I am, I rush forward, grabbing Frieda by her collar as more blasts wreck the world around us.

I'm knocked against the hard dirt wall of the trench, enduring the pain that spreads in spider webs across my back. I don't care that I've lost my rifle, that I've potentially sprained a few ligaments. Only two objectives flash inside my head that're far more important.

Save her.

Save myself.

I'm dragging her along with me. I won't agree to have it any other way. If she dies, I'll die just the same.

The blasts keep coming. I yelp when one falls near us, gathering her in my arms and bolting as it hits. My ears ring as we fly forward, landing on my side as the ringing and the blasts die down along with the engines. They're replaced by crackling flames licking at a dead man's plane which sits with its front crushed and its tail in the air. Its trim tabs and part of its elevator are missing, probably broken off or littered somewhere on the battlefield, hitting an unlucky soldier.

Below me, my hands are in fists. I cough out dust, my throat dry and parched. Frieda's covered in just as much dust as I am. Her body lies frozen beneath me in shock, panic, fear. Blood dribbles from a cut on her lip. Either she's bitten it when falling or she somehow cut it on shrapnel or a stray twig or rock. Her eyes are wide, her patch hanging loosely by a string from her ear.

The illusion of someone who wasn't afraid to fire a gun is gone. The fragile child with no parents and many vulnerable fractures takes her place.

"Frieda." Her name comes from my lips in a shaky mumble. "Frieda, look at me."

Her eyes; wide, one green, one cloudy, stare up at me. Her teeth are bared and bloodstained. Gasps for air whistle in and out. "Who—who are you—"

"It's me, Freddy, it's me." I speak slowly, sounding out each word. "It's me. Breathe with me. The raid is over. Breathe with me."

As her terror dies, her hands latch onto my forearms, my upper arms, my shoulders, my face, all pulsing with life and heat against the cold. Her eyes are searching, scanning me.

"Are you hurt?" She frantically examines me over and over. "Marshall, are you hurt?"

"No, no. Just sore." I cough, dust entering my airways, covering my mouth. I've lost my mask somewhere in the upheaval while running.

She attempts to rise, alert, before she weakly falls back down against the floor.

"No, Frieda, stay down. You're weak, and it won't do you any good standing."

Thankfully, she doesn't put up a fight and obeys. I crawl off of her and lean against the dirt wall, gaining my breath back.

"Marshall?" she calls from the floor, turning on her side to face me, clutching her stomach.

"Yes?" I puff.

"I should give you some extra credit for saving me."

"No need." I sputter, coughing up more dust. "I did what I had to do."

She starts coughing as well. "Protecting a comrade?"

"You're more than a comrade to me and you know it." I grab my kerchief and dab at her lip, ridding it of dried blood and grit, speaking to her as I do so. "You're so much more."

Something dives into the trench: a rescue dog—some sort of Shepherd—with a medical cross on his vest paired with Nathan, caked in dirt and mud, brown staining his red hair.

"Thank the Lord you two are okay! Edith and I were worried sick!" Nathan exclaims.

"Nathan, are the others"—I cough—"alright?"

Nathan nods solemnly. "Everyone else is okay. They didn't hit the medic tents. Sam and Lester came by after the raid to check in. Everyone is fine. By George, is Frieda okay?"

"In a state of shock." Another cough comes on the rise. "We're both okay, I think."

"Are you ill? You're coughing non stop."

"Dust and smoke, my friend." I give him a minute smile. "Dust and smoke."

"Sallinger was right about the air raid," Frieda says, sitting up once she gains her breath and strength back. "He could be the weatherman of death for all I care."

Rising to one knee, she coughs and spits blood mixed with saliva on the wood and dirt below us. She grapples for her patch and ties it back in place, wiping her lip as Nathan helps her up before me. We assist each other out of the trench with some lucky pats of the rescue dog's coat to make this catastrophe just a little bit better.

Nathan sets off with the dog to find more men. Frieda swears under her breath and curses at the sky in both English and French at the Germans—the *allemands,* in her case. Once she's done, she spits again into the dirt. We set off to the medic tents with the sun setting behind us.

All around us is death and destruction.

Bodies are wheeled in on carts. Wounded men stagger to their feet, falling, crying to God or their mothers, screaming in either agony or at the nurses as the line for the bath house grows for all the survivors who came back in one piece. The line for the medic tent is even bigger, and in the middle of waiting, Frieda leans on me.

"Is something wrong?" I grapple for her, which only gives her more space to wriggle deeper. "Are you in pain?"

"Cold," she mumbles. "Pain is an understatement. I'm in agony."

I keep my arm wrapped around her shoulders, letting her stay put against my chest. I fear she'll fall asleep standing up, as she starts to slump against me.

"And I thought today would be a good day," she continues to rant. I can tell she's clearly angry, disoriented. Plenty of people are like that after air raids or assaults. They get tired, hungry, dehydrated, and complain of sore but restless bones.

"Frieda," ahead, the line is slowly growing smaller, "don't let one air raid unsettle you. You survived another day. Hey, think of the awesome stories you'll get to tell your kids one day."

"If I want kids." She grows dazed and tired. "I don't know about you, but I don't think I'd want to suffer through childbirth."

"We'll have to wait and see," I ruffle her hair, "won't we?"

"Yeah, I guess so." She hiccups, closing her eyes. "But it doesn't sound too fun to sit there with a stomach like a balloon with your insides on fire. All for a gremlin to crawl out of you."

"That's your definition of the beginning of life?"

427

"Babies look like gremlins, don't they?" Frieda argues. "I don't know...maybe I want one, maybe I don't. There's a lot I don't know."

"You'll find out in time. You'll be the cool parent who has awesome bedtime stories to tell their children." I add quickly, "If you have them."

"I do know something, though."

"What's that?"

She pokes a tired and scarred finger against my nose. "I may or may not want kids, but either way, I want you on my team. We'd make a good one."

"Oh?" My cheeks heat up.

"Not good, but great." A new warmth creeps inside my chest. My heart quickens. "We'd go down in history as the best team ever made."

I hold her close, leaning down to give her a kiss on the forehead. "I'd like to be part of that team, then."

"You already are." She pokes me on the cheek, chuckling like a child. "You always have been and always will be."

"If we weren't in the middle of a pandemic, in a crowd of thousands after an air raid, I would be kissing you until we both end up seeing stars."

"I would like that...I really would." She grins devilishly. "Hey, Marshall?"

"Yes, Frieda?"

"Thank you."

"For what?" I meet her gaze again, which is abnormally bright after such a catastrophe.

"For staying by my side. For suffering my wrath."

"I wouldn't suffer anyone else's wrath other than yours, my love."

I make the move to grab her hand, squeezing it affectionately and keeping her close as we step inside the medic tent, continuing to let her lean on me.

Edith sprints towards us, wrapping us in a tight, heart-throbbing bearhug.

"Thank goodness you two are okay!" She sobs into the front of my tunic, kissing us both repeatedly on the cheeks. "If anything happened to any of you, I wouldn't know what to do with myself! Nathan told me he found you in a trench—I started having a meltdown then and there when I didn't know whether or not my big brother or best friend were okay!"

"We're right here where you want us." Frieda rubs her back, leaving me out in the open, feeling a touch awkward. "We're okay, my dear. Just really dirty, itchy, tired, in pain. Not to mention, we had a moment of affection outside so maybe we're a bit—"

"Frieda!" My face pales.

She gives me a rotten good wink as Edith's crying turns into laughter. It transforms into an ugly mess of crying and laughing all at the same time.

Ed stumbles in, eyes settling on me. He starts power walking forward to pat me on the back. "Dear Lord"—he thanks God and all his grace and scans me down—"thank Heavens! I was—"

"Worried sick? Everyone's been saying that."

"But I was!" he exclaims, gripping my hands tight. "I was shaking, Marshall! Shaking out of my own skin!"

"I'm here. I'm alive. We're all okay. I'm in dire need of a bath, though. I stink like a sewer rat."

"Oh, you're right." Ed turns away, jokingly disapproving. "You're an utter disgrace this afternoon, Sergeant Clark. Automatic disapproval from Robert Sallinger himself."

"Where is the man, anyway?" I ask.

"On the phone with the general, I presume, telling him all about the raid."

I itch behind my ear. "We'll be making the news by tomorrow, I'd say."

"I say we already have." Lester emerges with Sam on his tail, also covered in dust. "The Germans hurt like a stick up my—"

"Lester, you've said that almost ten times today, shut it. We get it, we all feel the same pain." Sam clears his throat. "Jesus, Marsh, you look like hell. What happened to you out there?"

"So do you." I stuff my hands in my pockets. "We were coming back from the range when the planes flew in. The one that was shot down went up in flames near where we were taking cover. The Germans, I must say, have improved their aim."

"Great, so now what? We've got a burning German plane *and* a German corpse on our side. Now what do we do?" Lester complains.

"We're in a war, Les. Anything could make for a good shield," I joke.

"Most certainly not!" Lester snarls.

I shrug with both my arms and shoulders. "I'm not wrong, admit it."

Sam presses his thumb and index to the space between his eyes in frustration, fatigue, or even a headache brought by Lester's whining. "All I want is to wash all this filth off me. It's so dry that it's flaking off in layers. What do you say, gentlemen?"

"Works for me," I agree, Lester nodding along.

"I can't," Ed says. "I have to stay inside the medic tent."

"We'll come back afterward," Lester answers. "Count yourself lucky that you don't have this muck all over you."

"I'll be with Alistair." When my lips part to speak, Ed interrupts me. "He's fine, by the way, Marshall. I knew you were going to ask one way or another."

As the three of us exit, Edith calls after us, Frieda standing beside her, "Where do you think you three are going?"

"Going for a bath, washing all this filth off." Lester waves a dirt-stained hand and winks. I swat him over the head at the sight. "Hey!"

"That's my *sister* and my *partner* you're talking to. I saw that. Wait until I drown you."

He cowers beside Sam. "Have mercy, sir."

"Just this once. Next time, you're getting your ass kicked."

Lester snickers as we set off through the land of death and destruction. More and more bodies pile up under white sheets, nurses and soldiers loading them onto the backs of military cars, wagons, and stretchers. They'll either be transported by boat back to their homeland or put in a mass grave somewhere in the fields nearby or suffer through cremation.

I almost throw up my breakfast at the thought of being a corpse: thrown in with the others, buried so suffocatingly close, the stench of decomposition, being trapped inside a dark hole underground. Lester himself pinches his nose. He's always been extremely sensitive to smells. I can't imagine how his gut is handling the stink only he can fully pick up.

In the sunset, soldiers sit on logs with their arms in slings, bending over themselves or sobbing away to the nurse advising them. One small group is listening intently as one of them leans over a bible, reading over a psalm or a prayer.

The line to the bathhouse is notably dwindling with less and less men bathing and more getting their injuries checked in the medic tents. I let out an exhausted sigh for Edith and Nathan, knowing they'll most likely be taking extra shifts to assist the wounded who squirm in pain in their cots, plus another bothered sigh for myself, since I have to walk three miles out to the docks near St Mihiel and Verdun, which are dangerously close to German territory; fortified towns, of course. I always get chills while walking through the streets, which are made of rubble, the bones of what it was before the war. The scenery is heavily saddening.

Sam's complaining to Lester about the reek of the cadavers nearby. Men who've just bathed stream past with their hair still freshly damp and washed. I envy them, being cleansed of dirt and grit, able to move without a layer of mud that's dried on their skin flaking away. I swear I've got some in my hair, and I know I'll have to make a ghastly attempt at washing it out.

* * *

The water is uncomfortably lukewarm in the large wooden tubs.

I don't complain as I dry my torso and my hair with a towel, checking my face for any stubble I've missed after shaving. It's become an undesirable habit to check the line of stitches going down my abdomen, a small depression in my skin from the bullet's entry hole. It's regressed merely to a white scar; a match to the one on my shoulder near my collarbone.

I curse myself when I gawk at my reflection in the steamed-over mirrors.

I've turned into a walking skeleton. My rib cage pokes out in disgusting angles under my skin. The tips of my clavicles jut out awkwardly where they meet my scapellas. It hurts to observe that some of the things I was proud of—my flat stomach and arm muscles—have atrophied over time with my service. My broad shoulders look far too wide compared to my shrunken limbs. A new, gagging disgust takes hold of me. My hands curl into fists at my sides. I let out a small noise of shock and horror.

"That's quite a scar you've got there," Lester remarks, toweling his hair. "Another one to add to your collection. Show it off to the ladies in the summer. They'll go mad for it."

"I'm ashamed, Lester." I slip on my thermal layer hurriedly, clipping my suspenders to my breeches. "I'm going to have these for eternity. Imagine me as an old man with all these scars on my saggy skin."

"At least you can tell your partner different stories about how you got them. Make yourself look like a war hero. Also, the picture of an eighty year old Marshall Clark is not as aesthetically pleasing as the handsome gentleman you claim yourself to be standing before me."

"That's what I told Frieda." I glance at Sam over Lester's shoulder, who's bending to wrap his puttees around his ankles, cursing as his sandy hair drips small droplets onto the floor. "Though, you never know what people would think of them."

431

"It's not like you're planning on strutting the streets half naked and yelling out 'hey, look! Come flock me, women!' Who would care? I bet in a year's time, people will look at those scars and thank you for serving their country. They're marks of survival, my friend."

I slide my arms through the sleeves of my tunic, buttoning it and slipping my coat on. "I have to go pick up some men from the docks now. I'll be back in likely one to two hours."

"You're walking the whole way? Couldn't they just lend you a horse or something?" Lester asks.

"I might need the fresh air to clear my head after all of this chaos just sprung up out of nowhere."

Sam's busy ferociously toweling his hair as he says, "Go on, it's getting dark. You don't want to be out too late. Especially with the Germans nipping at your heels."

"Yes, Mother. I'll be fine. They're probably sleeping or partying after the destruction they've caused us."

I set off along the dirt pathway to St Mihiel, the town where the boat and its men should be waiting. It's awfully cold this time of day, no trees here to obstruct the passing of the wind, either chopped down, burned to a crisp, or dead from the lack of healthy green fields growing.

As I set foot deeper into the clearing, the moon comes out in the sky. It's half full tonight, yellow through the clouds. My feet hurt with each step I take closer to St Mihiel.

* * *

The Western Front is quiet tonight with the exception of little jingles of news stations playing from radios at a low volume as I return with sore soles and heavy eyelids. The task of guiding the men was a hard one at most, but one that ran smoothly with no setbacks.

Another job well done, Sergeant Clark, I muse and imagine Sallinger speaking those exact words if he were by my side. *Why don't we just promote you to first class or drill sergeant? Would make your sheepdog business a little bit easier doing it full time, hm?*

"So, you had a nice stroll?"

Her voice has me flinching, catching me off guard and pulling me out of the warmth of my achievement that I'd love to bask in for a little longer. She's behind me, chuckling as I gather myself. "Edith! Don't sneak up on me like that!"

She hands me a new cloth mask, allowing me to pull the loops over my ears and fold it over the bridge of my nose. "I did, as a matter of fact. My feet are killing me. How is everything in the tents? Holding up okay?"

"We don't have as many wounded men as last time."

"Last time?"

"In August, we had a raid worse than this. I nearly passed out from exhaustion by staying up all night."

"Gosh, I'm sorry."

"Don't be. I'm alright." Looking at me head-on, she pushes a lock of black hair behind her ear. "Do you know how scared I was when the planes came?"

"Everyone was. I nearly became a bag of bones when I saw them."

"Literally, Marshall, I knew you were out in the field and I was scared that I lost my brother, and Frieda was out there with you. I was afraid I'd lose you both."

"Edith, I…" Trailing off, I'm unsure of how to reply. "…I was scared that I would lose you. Everyone else, too. I'm so glad you're still here."

"You should be glad we're both still here."

"I am. Hey, is something bothering you?"

"Tired." Her blue eyes—Father's eyes—are ringed by shadows that we all share. Her lips soften into a smile. "It's good to have you back, Marshall. Better go get your rations."

"Are you sure there's not something going on between you and Nathan? Do I need to shoot him for you?"

Edith laughs maliciously. "No, I'm the happiest I've ever been with him. Also, that would be considered a war crime if you were to shoot him."

"I know, I know, but if anything happens—"

"No need. Please, sometimes you're too overprotective."

"For good reason. You need to eat."

"So do you. I'll see you in a bit."

"As to you."

I watch her go, joining the line for rations, trying to catch a glimpse of anyone I know, stepping up to grab the dreaded beef and biscuits, plus a canteen and a blanket. They tell me it's from a donor, as the blanket was in the mail for me with my aunt's name on the return address. It's a fleece blanket; black and neatly folded. I make sure to handle it with care as I scan the men sitting around fires they've set up near the campsite, and I manage to catch Sam as he sits on a log in front of a fire with Lester and Nathan. There's no sign of Frieda. I take it she hasn't yet arrived.

"Gentlemen," I take off my cap and sit down, Nathan giving me a smile, Lester tipping his cap and a minute wave, "why are we all sitting out here?"

"The mess hall was bombed," Lester explains. "It's nothing but rubble now."

"Damn," I curse, setting myself up with the blanket on my lap.

Nathan eyes it. "What's that you've got there?"

"A blanket from my aunt." I glance behind me for any sign that Frieda may be coming any time soon. "Also, did you manage to find Frieda on your way here? I feel bad if I start without her."

"Last time I saw her, she was helping Alistair with measurements for his prosthesis," Sam informs me. "Don't worry, she'll show up soon. Did you have a good walk?"

"I did, but my feet are killing me." I take a swig from my canteen.

"Been awhile since you've walked a long distance, hm?" Sam opens his beef tin, readying his fork.

"I guess so." I too open my beef. "Alistair's getting a prosthesis?"

Nathan grins. "Indeed he is. Then he'll get used to it and learn to write with his right hand again. He's a spectacular patient."

"Peculiar of him." I settle on eating the biscuits first. Someone grabs my shoulders like a bird with hungry talons. "In the name of God, I will—"

"Hold your horses on that threat, Marshall. It's your friend," Lester sneers.

"Shut up, will you?" Frieda lowers her mask to kiss my temple—an admittedly risky move that gets me looking at my feet. "I'm sorry, did I scare you?"

"Well, duh." I raise a biscuit to my mouth, gagging before I take a bite out of it. "It's not every day that I get a surprise attack while I'm eating."

Frieda makes herself comfortable next to me, her hair noticeably the slightest bit damp. I'm guessing she finished bathing not long ago.

I still get flimsy and flustered whenever our shoulders brush. She sits by me, takes her mask off to eat, and gives me a snicker as she forces her food down, grimacing at the taste while staying content.

"You were helping Alistair?" I ask.

"Mmhm!" she replies confidently, swallowing. "He's rather excited. He smiled for the first time in days when I told him about it."

I take another sip from my canteen. "It doesn't take a lot to get him to smile, but it's probably the best news he's gotten in months."

"I'd say the best news he's gotten is his brother returning safely."

"That too." I shuffle closer, Lester clearing his throat, Nathan following along by moving, too. "Now Uncle Marshall can tell Kara about her father being a pirate. Alistair would love that."

She softens at the word, a flash of compassion twinkles in her eye. "You're horrible. I can't believe you're that excited over a baby."

"She's my niece! Of course I'd be excited."

"It's just"—the softness returns when she looks at me—"it's cute how you get so excited to tell her all these things and care for her."

"Duh," I dip another biscuit in my water, "what else would I be feeling?"

Frieda grins, knees tucked against her chest. "I wish I could see her."

"I could take you."

My heart skips a beat. Silence fills the air. Our eyes never leave each other's faces, a million thoughts going through my head.

I want to take you home, I want to say. *I want to take you away from here and keep you in my arms forever. I want to hold you tight and never let go.*

Her eye brightens and reflects the firelight, blinking back at me, seeming to get the message.

I do too, it seems to reply.

All is quiet until Lester clears his throat. "Alright, lovebirds, enough. You're making me sick."

"Let them have a moment." Nathan elbows him. "They haven't seen each other in months."

Lester *hmphs* and continues eating, shoving down his food, coughing. Frieda releases an amused snort as she takes another bite of beef, doing the same, giving Lester the excuse to chuckle. "If Eddie were here, he'd be dying on the floor, laughing."

"And teasing me so that I die of embarrassment? Sure." I put my finished rations aside, a chill biting into my bones. I untie the blanket from its coarse strings, pulling it around my shoulders.

"Where'd you get that from?" Lester asks.

"My aunt sent it." I wrap it tight, the heat of the fire making it warmer than it already is.

"I admit, that was nice of her," Nathan says. "A nice blanket, too."

"Indeed it was, and indeed it is," I agree.

"I heard from my good ol' pal Ricky that he scored some extra rum rations and is willing to share." Lester stands, brushing himself off. "Anyone up for doing shots?"

"Aye." Sam stands with Lester. "What about you three?"

"I have to get back to work. Duty calls." Nathan gets up to leave.

"Alright," Lester gathers his scraps, "what about you two? Are you going to start canoodling as soon as we leave? There's a bucket to douse the fire if you need it."

"I'm too tired to get drunk." Frieda rejects the offer with a flick of her wrist. "I have my morning patrol first thing tomorrow. I'd rather not risk working with a hangover."

"Ditto. I have to assist with tomorrow's drill," I reply.

"Suit yourselves." Lester winks, sending sparks down my back. Nathan shoots on ahead to the tents, waving goodbye. "Enjoy your time together."

"Lester!" Sam swats him on the back of the head, and they exit in an argument. As they leave, I keep my eyes on the flames in the silence.

"So," she breaks it, a thumb pressing against her lips, "did you have a good trip?"

"That's the third time someone's asked me today." I close my eyes and draw my knees inward, resting my forearms atop them. Someone's put a radio on, and a soft tune plays behind us. Men start jostling around and laughing. Two of them prance in a frenzied waltz against the tedious crooner. The tune is hauntingly familiar.

"*Moonlight Bay,* huh?" I point to the music. "I wouldn't think they'd be playing any Western music here, in Europe." Frieda shrugs as I inhale the wafting scent of smoking wood. "Did you know I danced to this song for a competition?"

"I don't think you told me."

"The more you know." I shuffle closer. "It was one of the last competitions I participated in before my dance partner quit."

"That's unfortunate." She's shivering, so I pull the blanket over her shoulders and let her head lean against mine. "I would ask you to dance, except I'm not sure how long you'd last."

"I would accept your offer if my feet weren't killing me," I retort.

"Then it would be best to let you rest." Her expression changes from calm to conflicted, her back straightening. "I was thinking about my mother again."

"Oh?"

"I still feel terrible, but not in a sense where I would cry over it." She swallows, tense. "I don't think I'm ready to go back to Seattle to help with packing up the house—you know, emptying it to put it on sale now that no one will be living there anymore."

I drape a comforting arm around her waist. "You could always rent it out. It's under your family name."

Frieda shrugs with a defeated slump of her shoulders. "I don't think I'd be prepared to live in a house with walls that hold so much pain. It's a big house, an empty one at that."

"It's your choice entirely." I stare once again into the fire.

"I'd rather start afresh, somewhere new...A fresh slate."

"And I wouldn't mind you moving in to live with my family and I."

"Huh?" She stiffens at my offer and pulls away from my arms to look at me. "I don't want to burden you."

"We'd get to see each other every day, I have a library full of books in the study we could read, and we could go for walks together. Alistair and Edith will be there, too. You wouldn't burden us in the slightest. It would be great to have some company."

"Sounds like fun." She looks away, rests her chin on her palm and stays silent.

"Is there something that I don't know about that's the matter?" I look down at her as her eyes close.

"I just...Like I said before," she yawns, "I don't think I'll ever be prepared to support myself. Who'd want someone with no parents?"

"You have your uncle's family, my family—hell, me, most importantly."

"Of course you would." She smiles tiredly. "I'll say it again: We make a great team."

That flutter reappears in my chest; the heat source that isn't the fire nor the blanket. I'm giddy all over, my heart beating faster and faster with each passing second.

"I agree," is all I can say.

"It's getting late." Frieda stands and adjusts her mask so it sits nicely across her face. "That was nice. I have a morning patrol first thing, so it's best for me to retire now."

"Of course." I douse the fire, putting my mask back on as I fan the smoke away. Before she leaves, I take the blanket off my shoulders and hand it to her in a bundle. "Take this."

Yet again, she draws back. "Your aunt—"

"She won't mind. I also don't want you going to sleep in the cold. Please take it. I already have Edith's to keep me warm."

Hesitantly, she takes the blanket and folds it with care, holding it under her arm. "I promise I'll keep it in the best condition. I'll see you after my patrol is done, right?"

"As always." I carefully lean forward and touch my forehead to hers, entwining her bare fingers in my gloved ones with the tiniest squeeze, breathing her in. I peel my mask away to press a chaste kiss in between her brows. All this behavior, I regret to say, is risky for the both of us, but I keep her close for a good two minutes and whisper, "Stay safe. Goodnight, cherished one."

She doesn't let go of my hand, whispering, pulling back her mask and kissing my cheek, "I love you."

The heat blooming inside my chest is more intense than before, threatening to turn my insides into mountains of soot and ash from its flames. I give her a smile and I pull my mask back on, dipping my head, returning her words to her.

"I love you more."

36

THE FINAL PUSH

FRIEDA

Since Marshall's return, the pandemic has gotten crazier and crazier with a dozen soldiers, nurses, and officials getting sicker each day. Millions are dying as the second wave of the disease hits, sending us all in a spiral. We rush for the nearest face mask, scramble for the earliest bath, the closest toiletries and sanitizers to help protect ourselves from the virus that's made our lives more of a living hell.

Amidst the chaos, I've received the news that I'm to be on the second line with Marshall, who received his pay, as Sallinger's crew are back in full swing. Sallinger had deemed the both of us suitable for battle, as on September 26th, the Germans pulled the strings of another offensive, grabbing us all by surprise. We once again prepared to push men over the line.

Our whole group started praying over Sam's bible and Lester's *Siddur*, held hands through gloves, squeezed each other's fingers tight as the machine guns peppered the air outside. We weighed ourselves down with our webbings, rifles, gas masks, and each other's grave words.

Sam and Lester are going west, Marshall and I are going east. Alistair stays in the medic tent with Ed, who lies asleep in his bed. He's been sleeping an awful lot recently, tossing and turning, screaming that his face was on fire, Alistair being there to comfort him as he battles his nightmares. Nathan says his wounds have become infected again and that he needs rest. Marshall broke into tears at first, getting a few waves of relief when Edith told him that the infection was minor and would be resolved quickly.

Tonight, we sit by the fire on the thirtieth of October, 1918. Sam pours the rum rations into shot glasses. Marshall's hands are shaking profusely. Lester's eyeing his glass with a vein jumping out of his forehead. I sit with my fingers intertwined in my lap and my eyes to the floor. No one dares break the silence, save the soft music playing on the radio nearby. Everyone is as pale as a sheet as Sam screws the lid back on the small rum bottle, setting it to the side and taking his shot glass, everyone copying him as if it's part of some tragic script.

The glass is cold in my hand, the alcohol's tang hitting my nostrils. Sam says another prayer: That God will light our way and keep us safe, Marshall nodding along, clenching his own glass, his jaw set, his sister's blanket around his shoulders. His other hand grips it tight, his knuckles white.

Once Sam finishes his prayer and closes his bible, everyone speaks a singular word.

Amen.

The alcohol goes down.

Lester is the first to shove the rum down his throat, wincing as he sets the glass back on the crate that serves as our table.

Sam is next, taking it head on, swallowing quickly and wiping his mouth, Marshall following close behind swiftly and licking his lips of excess rum.

Next, it's my turn, and the strong, sweet taste of the rum swamps my tongue. Swallowing fast, the fumes linger as I set my glass down.

Marshall's face blanches more than I ever thought was humanly possible as he chews away at his lower lip. He's in a state of a decline. He's plunged in a state of misery headfirst and is sinking closer to the bottom each day. He's been fraying at the edges since Ed's health has gradually worsened, occupied with the constant thought of losing a friend.

He found a way to the outside of my tent in the middle of the night, shaking and tripping over his own two feet, scaring the living daylights out of Fey when he fell to his knees.

He was having a sensory overload and a panic attack with fresh bandages lining his wrists, soaked through with blood. He kept chanting, *I've done it again, it's all my fault,* as he laid on the floor, coughing up his own saliva, stressing that he couldn't breathe and that his throat was closing up on him as Fey dressed his wounds with new gauze strips and reassuring words. He'd promised not to do *it* again, constantly and frantically, as he gained his breath back. His eyes were wild. He explained what had happened, that Ed was also declining back into a rough patch with his infection, and continued to bite back tears.

I was up with him all night, sitting outside in the cold as he fought away his urges, punched and kicked trees, snapped their twigs underneath his feet. He was distant, and yet again, fighting another war that stretched across a battlefield inside his own head.

"Let me go." His voice was hoarse, whimpering into my shoulder as I brought him close. "I don't deserve anyone. Please let me go."

I never felt so conflicted, so frightened for the boy who was crumbling away in my arms like sand. His fingers were clenched tight in my sleeves, holding me tight as he pleaded.

Gingerly, I laid kisses across his jaw, hushed him as he choked the words out, his grip growing exceedingly urgent. I ran my fingers through his hair. Each stroke caused him to soften and tense up all at the same time. He was a world I cared so much about, that shattered before my very eyes.

"You don't deserve anyone, Marshall," I said. He began to splutter before I quickly added, "You deserve everyone and everything."

"Everyone hates me. Everything I have is being ripped to shreds." He began to whine again.

I gripped him tighter, kissed his jugular; pulsating frantically. "And who's saying that?"

He shrunk against the question, fumbled for words, dove into the depths and came back to the surface, empty.

"Me. Because I know so." He chuckled bitterly. A metallic taste at the back of my throat formed at the sound. "Hell, you probably hate every fiber of my being and have been leaving subtle hints each time you see me. You hate my very presence."

My cheeks burned. My heart thrummed. He was taking a nosedive into the bottom of the deep black sea of illusions, conspiracies.

It was up to me to save him, to let him sink or swim. I wouldn't let him drown like I did.

"Let me ask you why you think that." It came out sharper than I wanted. I clenched my jaw momentarily. "Every compliment I've given you, every thought I let slip of you, every time I worried whether you'd be okay when another crisis appeared, every kiss painting your skin that's from me, everytime I wrapped my arms so tenderly around you, every letter I exchanged...How could you say that I hate you?"

His heart hammered in his chest, Adam's apple bobbing, as he broke into tears again. He was sobbing, throat ridden with the ugliest, most heart wrenching sound I ever heard.

His breath was chillingly warm against my skin, behind my ear, as he stamped down guilt-ridden kisses. A kiss to my lobe. Another to the back of my ear. Another to my temple.

My only response was to pull him closer, to reassure him as he apologized compulsively. I was terrified that I'd lost the man who stole my heart and held it in his bloodstained hands.

"I love you more than anything in this world," I murmured in his ear. His grip slackened with fatigue. "And that's a fact. Don't you dare think otherwise, because you're the very thing keeping me here today and holding me down."

After that incident, I barely saw him for the rest of the following week, as he isolated himself from us all.

It was a revelation for him to arrive in the medical tent with a cup of coffee in hand, his hair a mess, eyes shadowed over with exhaustion. They were hollow pits of peril, alight with fear, before I took him outside to talk. He apologized yet again for causing me anxiety, saying that he needed time alone to gather himself. I told him, despite my worries, despite my fear of what happened to him, I was glad that he took time away. As much as we enjoy the time we have side by side, we also need time away from each other.

441

"I need to ask, as I've been feeling a bit lost, and I hope this doesn't come off as offensive: What do you want me to do to help you?" I asked him before we went back inside for Nathan to tell Marshall what was going on with Ed.

He paused, staring at the horizon. He spoke in a tone so devoid of emotion as the tears dried upon his cheeks, bit his lip as his eyes remained glassy.

"Stay," he pleaded. "Stay. Be there for me."

His voice cracked. I took his hand and squeezed it tight; a silent affirmation that I would follow through. Then his second decline came.

Marshall's decline involved staring and talking to the walls, bringing up past memories, rocking himself back and forth, biting his nails and tapping his fingers against his knee or any other hard surface. He refused to read, for me to read to him, writing his feelings out, talking about his thoughts. He apologized many times, calling himself an inconvenience, saying over and over again the phrases:

"I should leave," as he rocked himself back and forth on a bench.

"No one wants me here," as he picked at his scabs.

"Why am I still here?" as he held his face in his hands.

"I'm a burden," as he tore his journal to shreds.

One day, I took him for a walk to the clearing nearby to clear our heads two days before we took our places on the second line. I told him to pick any book from his collection, anything he brought with him. He was reluctant to go at first, but agreed when he was in a better mood.

So we set out and sat on the grass in the outskirts of St Mihiel when all was quiet.

He was silent for almost the entirety of the walk, empty, a shell of his usual talkative self, so I didn't push him. I remained patient.

He brought *Jane Eyre* under his arm and situated his head in my lap. I read to him, ran my hands through his dark locks. I was reading to him for almost an hour when he fell asleep on me, finally relaxed and surrendered to rest.

He slept peacefully for almost a full hour, and I managed to coax a wan smile out of him when he awoke.

* * *

This morning is one of his worst days. He skipped breakfast, claiming that his uneasy stomach was wrecking his appetite. Lester forced him to eat, since he and I were setting off to the second line soon. He refused, and with Ed's words and supervision, ate only the slightest bit of burnt toast and beef to keep himself going, dry heaving half an hour later outside with nothing coming out.

He's silent as he grips his rifle, staring straight ahead as we enter the trenches, jaw clenched as he fixes his metal cap, webbings weighing him down. He greets the whistle blower and takes Edith's blanket, setting up a place for the both of us down in the burrows dug out of the walls for soldiers to sleep, to camp. He repeatedly checks his pocket watch.

Drinking out of his canteen, he boredly watches men pass by in the small and cramped walkways. The first few shots ring out, and the men's walking turns into sprinting from Point A to B. Visions of the last air raid come to mind as planes fly over, their pilots dropping bombs that make the ground shake. I start to shudder along with it and struggle for air as the panic sets in.

"Marshall?" His name is barely a whimper against my panicking breaths.

Still, he's able to pick up on it. "Yes?" he replies. I can see it in his eyes that he's equally as scared as I am.

"If they do send us over...what do we do?"

Marshall's fingers thrum against his folded knee in thought, shaking his head when he comes back empty-handed. "I don't know."

I sit hurriedly next to him, grabbing for his arm. Instead, he reaches for my hand and holds it tight against his chest. Under my own thrumming pulse, his is pulsating at a million miles per hour against my fingers.

"I'm still here." He pulls me in with his other arm, making a weak attempt to shield us from the danger outside. "Still here. Hold onto me."

"Mar—" I whimper before he cuts me off.

"Hold onto me!" he yelps over the gunfire hammering through the earth. His heart rate increases at the sound of it, dark eyes closing against the ruckus. With a terrified sob, my head buries itself into his chest. I forbid the tears to spill. I fear that if I start crying, I may never stop.

I shiver against him, fighting back another sob as Sallinger's lieutenant peers down at us.

"Sergeant Clark?" His voice booms over the gunfire; an omen of everything dark and horrible.

Underneath me, he freezes at the summoning, throat bobbing. Marshall's glare is made of steel. His grip around me tightens.

"You've been requested to be at the front line for the next assault."

The sinkhole inside my stomach only grows. Marshall nods, a robotic movement. "Yes, sir. Whenever you're ready."

443

I squeeze his hand, nails digging into his flesh. He pulls away and kneels before me, gripping both of my hands tight. His eyes have gone glassy, nose red from the cold. He turns into a mirror image of me with tears wetting my own cheeks. Despite every attempt at hiding and suppressing them, they're always able to come back.

"Marshall, please don't go."

"I'm afraid I can't disobey." His voice hardens with his answer. "I want to say something. Will you hear it?"

I nod hurriedly, taking him in. His nails dig into my knuckles. His grip grows even more taut, but I could care less.

Eyes alight with a courageous fire, he holds my gaze. "I don't know what's happening as of now, or what will happen after I leave you, but this war is going to come to a close soon. The gunfire is harsher than ever. The ground feels like it's going to collapse underneath us. I'm terrified like a little boy who has a bad dream. I'm scared that I'll die out there, and I don't want to do that. I confess, I want to live. I want to see the world. I want to get out of here and watch it all pass by as I grow old. I want to do that with you. I want to make it out of here with you and everyone else."

I'm unable to respond. The tears are clogging my throat far too fast.

"I just...I wanted to thank you for, you know...being the light of my life, and all," his voice shakes, turning into a sob, "for...uh...making me happy and keeping me going...for holding me close, even now, when I'm so far away. Every moment with you is like paradise to me and I wish I could hold onto that for a little while longer."

I grip his arms, holding him close. "You don't need to thank me. I will *always* hold you close. You're my equal, the dearest man to my heart. Don't think otherwise."

"I know." He nods, eyes red from crying. "You know what, Fred? I don't think I could be any happier with you by my side. I don't feel like I say this enough, and I don't think I ever will, but," his eyes dig into mine, full of light, full of determination, "I love you. I love you, I love you, I love you. I promise you, I always will, forever and always. You're my pride and joy, you know that? You've made me happier than anyone else ever has before. This war isn't fair, I know, but I'll try my hardest to survive. I'll pray extra hard, shoot at anything that moves, run as fast as I can just to make it home, back to you—my home. Freddy, *you're* my home."

"I promise I'll do the same if they ever throw me over."

"If I fail, which I pray won't happen," he gulps, "I want to thank you. Thank you for letting me die a happy man. Thank you for giving my life meaning, purpose, something to live for, something to look forward to every day. We've worked so hard to get here, and here we are. Remember this: If I don't make it out of this, find someone who makes you happy. Someone who will help you see life as this wondrous, beautiful miracle, who'll make you smile from dawn till dusk."

He stands and gives me one last look, a hug that lasts almost forever.

"Promise me you'll try to survive. For me. For everyone." I cup his face one last time.

Marshall wipes my eyes, nodding vigorously. "I'll try. I promise."

When we let go, another piece of my heart falls away with him as he vanishes around the corner.

His warmth is all gone. What remains of him is Edith's blanket, which I wrap tight over my shoulders, his scent—coffee, dirt, and all the things Marshall Clark would smell like—strong and caught in the wool. I hold it close, my fingers knotting in the crochets, mumbling his name, rocking back and forth, staring hard at the ground. The bombs going off startle me. I cover my ears against all the commotion.

Men yell. They scream, bellow out orders to each other, as the machine guns *pop-pop-pop* through the air. I put in a silent prayer that they shoot the enemy, wherever they're aiming.

* * *

It's the evening of the ninth of November. Every whistle that blows sets me on edge. Each time I think it's Marshall going over, another telegraph gets sent to me in his cursive and hurried handwriting. I ran the risk of sending him a telegram a day ago, and together, we started back up the old tradition of sending letters to each other daily.

Still here. Not sent over yet. Still have so many waves to go. Getting lonely. I love you.

Each day, the tension in the air tightens and pulls on all of us. Our anxiety grows. The men in the trenches become irritable: pacing back and forth to exercise, muttering old poems to themselves, playing card games that I always decline. My interest is close to nowhere at this point. I usually spend all day reading with Edith's blanket over my shoulders, sleeping away useless hours, even managing to finish *Anna Karenina* that Marshall left behind for the third time.

Now that the world is moving into the days of November, 1918, the days and nights grow colder longer, as the sun sets earlier and earlier. Candles in the trenches are lit in the walkways. Sometimes, the guns and bombs go off during the night. It all swerves back and forth as the Germans fire their never-ending rounds at the French, the Americans, even the Siamese, who've come to assist us.

When Sallinger appears to survey what's happening in this section of the trenches, I gave him a glare to send a message of all my hatred to him as he walks past, treating me as if I'm thin air or just another man, an empty space, another pawn in his dire game.

I once held a great admiration for Robert Sallinger. Now I can't stand his guts as he struts his way around the trenches and camps with gold bars decking his shoulders, the lanyard wrapped around his arm, badge above his heart. He's not a war hero, but an undeserving vermin who cares for nothing but himself: a bastard, a self-absorbed man praising his own preaches and ideals; an idiosyncratic at best.

To make matters worse, we may as well all just be pieces in one power's game, working and bending our backs to win, or else we'll face, like in a game of chess, checkmate, as they overthrow our king.

* * *

It's the morning of the tenth of November when I open my eyes. The sun hasn't risen yet. Rations are already being passed out. Another telegram awaits my viewing, so I unfold the piece of paper and read, once more, in his handwriting:

```
Good morning, goodnight, whenever you read this. Received word from Lester and Sam. All is
well in the west. Enemy seems to be weakening. Still not going over. Sunrise is lovely. Pink and
purple across the battlefield. Couldn't sleep last night. Too cold. Stay warm. Stay safe. I love
you. Will update soon.
```

I exhale a sigh of relief, knowing that Lester and Sam are doing okay. Marshall must've sent a telegraph during the night to check on them. With this much commotion, I'm honestly surprised it got through and that he got an answer back.

Rubbing the sleep out of my eyes, I get up and stretch, writing him a short and simple note.

Good morning. All is well on the second line. Gunshots kept going all night. It's too cold. Glad you're safe. Yes, the sunrise is beautiful. Finished *Anna Karenina*, by the way. Great re-read. I love you too.

Once I send the telegraph through, the gunfire goes off yet again and shakes the ground. I trip and fall from one of the shockwaves that hurl me off my feet and onto the floor. Men around me trample and yell at each other, snarling instructions and grabbing their gas masks, so I rush back to drag mine on.

Another whistle goes off, signalling another wave. Each time one of those blasted things sound, Marshall is still the first to come to my mind.

Two nights ago, I had a nightmare of him climbing up the grimy ladder with his rifle, sprinting into the enemy's range of fire, bullets ripping through his chest. I have to close my eyes and force the vision out of my head.

I often sit and stare into space, shuffling through visions in my mind's eye, cycling through the ones I need to forget, the ones I want to keep, which is hurts me inside, causes me pain that I need to endure, that yelps and screams to come alive, pulls me back into its many forms among my memories.

My head pangs from all the thoughts, the actions and feelings that're brought up as I let go of ones I'd rather forget. It passes the time, quietens the noise of both the war occurring outside and the one raging inside my head.

* * *

The morning of the eleventh is different to all other mornings.

The gunfire lasted all night. The planes flying over kept me on edge. A raging telegraph from Marshall in all capitals comes through at exactly ten fifty-seven.

SETTING UP WAVES. I'M TERRIFIED. I DON'T WANT TO GO OVER. I DON'T WANT TO DIE.

My grip tightens on the telegraph, crumpling the paper. I'm whimpering as if holding the paper itself hurts.

I'm frozen, unsure of what to do, where to go. His name is a flashing light—a street sign with multiple arrows pointing in varying, panicked directions.

I start to rock myself back and forth, shaking, my mind frazzled, wires fraying.

I can't save him.

"He's dead. He's going to die. He's going to die," I mumble to myself for long minutes at a time. "He's dead. He's dead. He's gone. It's all your fault, Frieda. All your fault, all your—"

The gunfire fades.

The lines go quiet.

The air is still.

No whistles are blown. No men are being sent over the top.

There's a yelp from Sallinger; indistinguishable, as he's yards away. Nevertheless, I cover my ears as men around me start to cheer. They rise, they hug, they scream, they chug alcohol.

Whatever celebrations these are, I can't take part. It can't be some sort of gathering during an assault. No, it can't possibly be.

"Frieda!" a voice calls my name, sending a shock shooting down my spine that jars me to my feet. I listen out for it as it cries out again and again, only a few feet away.

I follow the sound, kicking up mud and dirt as I sprint through the trenches, through men who dance, who continue to cheer for a reason I don't know of. It all feels like a dream, a terribly wrong dream, one which will take me back to the assault happening right now, the Germans shooting us all down one by one, killing us all.

"Frieda!" the voice calls again.

I stop dead in my tracks before a man who stands at the other near a ladder, webbings and rifle discarded. His hair is a mess, crusts of blood on his face, dirt on his hands and uniform.

Marshall Clark is alive. He's standing before me: healthy and strong, running towards me with his arms outstretched, gripping me in a ferocious hug, whipping his cap off and shaking me by the shoulders.

"Marshall—what—why are you—you said you were—What the hell is going on?"

"Didn't you hear?" He's breathless, panting, as if he's on the comedown after a marathon. "The war's over! We won!"

"The war's...over?" I gasp, gripping him hard. "You really mean it?"

"Yes, the war's finally over! We're free!"

I'm able to let one word escape. "How?"

"They were about to send me over, but then the Germans surrendered! God, I was terrified."

"You're not joking? Is it really you?"

"The men here wouldn't be celebrating for no reason, would they? Do I have to kiss you to show you it's truly me?"

"No, not here." I grip him tighter, making him flinch. "Do you know how worried you made me? I thought you were dead!"

I break into tears, hug him hard, and collapse in his arms, sobbing away and caressing his cheeks, his face, anything to tell me that he's here. He's real, alive, his pulse beating under his skin—a survivor, a veteran, a man by the name of Marshall Clark...*My* Marshall Clark.

"You're suffocating me," he wheezes. I loosen my grip on him with a tearful guffaw. "Come, let's go see the others. They'll be anxious to see us."

Grabbing our belongings, we step out of the trenches, the news of the war's end spreading like wildfire, the men around us hooting and celebrating as we wander past. There's a large party singing the national anthem—all out of key, of course—celebrating and spilling rum across the dead grass and mud under their feet. Lester and Sam are running towards us.

"Good God, you two! Thank God you're both safe!" Sam hugs us—or more rather, he constricts us with his strong arms. I catch a glimpse of Lester crying for the first time before he ducks his head. "Thank the Lord. Thank everything above us."

Marshall pats him on the back. "Sam, goodness me, you're a mess, but it's good to see you too, buddy."

"We received a telegraph from George earlier this morning. The war finished early in Italy because the Germans surrendered there too! Can you believe it? The vermin surrendered!"

"I know, and Lester, are you—"

"Marshall!" Edith's holding up her skirts as she sprints, Nathan tailing her. She catapults into Marshall's arms, hugging him tight and kissing his cheeks. "Thank God you're all still safe. I was so afraid, too terribly afraid!"

"I'm here, Eeddie." He hugs her with an equal amount of sibling love. "We're all here. Are the others alright?"

Edith nods enthusiastically. "Everyone's fine. Alistair and Edward are both okay."

Marshall lets out a sigh of relief, wiping his eyes, keeping his head held high. He gives her a smile—one of the first he's produced in weeks—while holding her tight as she dampens the front of his uniform with her tears. He's patting her on the back and muttering assuring words to her.

I stand back and watch as they mob him, ruffling his hair and cheering, Marshall groaning and peeling them off of him. He backs away and bends to whisper to me, quickly, "I'd like to see Ed and Alistair."

I let him go after I give his hand a small squeeze. "You'll be okay?"

Another beat of uncertainty. Then, he nods. "Yep. I'm feeling the best I can be in months."

His black hair recedes into the distance. Edith is rushing towards me in a sobbing mess to grip me tight, my exhausted body groaning where my bones have started to rust. "Too tight!"

"Sorry, sorry!" She gasps and loosens her ferocious grip. "Goodness gracious, I can't believe it! I thought...I thought I lost you."

I bring her closer and press a kiss to her forehead. "I'm still here. We did it, Edith."

She breaks into deeper tears and wails.

"Edith, dear..." Nathan comes up from behind as Edith pulls me closer. "She's a real hugger. You're going to have a hard time getting her off of you."

"Why, you—" she snarls, running toward Nathan and gripping him tight in another bearhug, tears still streaming down her face.

Sam and Lester cheer, "Let's get drunk!"

"You're joking," Nathan hisses, and wheezes, both from shock and his airways being crushed. "It's not even past noon!"

"Perfectly serious, my friend." Lester grins, pulling on Sam's shoulders. "Gather up the men! We're tearing down the house tonight! C'mon, Nathan! Let your wild side out!"

"We're getting drunk now?" Marshall returns with an upturned brow and his head inclined. "Are you sure?"

"We won't be needing the rations anymore, and I've got plenty to spare!" Sam beams, elbowing Marshall in the ribs. "C'mon, sucker, you know you want to."

"*Hmm...*" Marshall ponders mischievously. "I could chug down a few shots."

There's a hoot from Lester, who ruffles his hair.

His gaze settles on me, a sneaky grin taunting me from his lips. "Except I'm not getting drunk alone."

"Goddamnit, you arse! I'm in!" I cry. Everyone breaks into laughter.

As we set off, I tap Marshall on the shoulder. He looks down at me as we walk, holding my gaze. "Is everything okay?"

"Yes." He nods. "Ed's infection is getting better, and so is Alistair's arm. They both need to stay in hospital for a few more weeks to rehabilitate. I believe Ed's getting facial reformation surgery. They take some skin and reform your face back to the way it was before."

My face wrinkles at the mental image it provides. "Sounds painful."

"They do it with cleft palates, so it's not that bad. There's a high success rate, I believe."

"You seem to be feeling better. You look a lot happier."

"Honestly, I'm relieved. I was worried I was going to lose so many people to this war, but so many of them survived. It's absurd, too absurd, to believe that we're getting drunk to celebrate. Can you believe that? We're finally free to go home, to get out of here!"

"It truly is unbelievable," I echo.

We sit with the rest of our friends at a rickety, worn table. Sam plonks a large bottle of rum onto the wooden tabletop, a savage smirk crossing his face. He unscrews the top and brings out the shot glasses we took shots out of when preparing for our uncertain deaths just days before.

"Don't worry, I washed them. No one's getting each other's cooties." He winks, and lines the glasses up horizontally across the table and shakes the bottle for dramatic effect, Nathan shaking his head disapprovingly.

Nathan's hands settle on Edith's shoulders. "Come on, Sam. If you're going to be a bartender, do the job properly."

Sam sets the bottle down with a *clink*. "Sir, no complaining."

"If only we had club soda and some citrus," Marshall leans his elbows on the table, "then we'd have a mojito."

"And bigger glasses," Lester adds.

"Wow, you two finally agreed on something," Edith teases, which results in her receiving matching glares in response.

"We have a good taste in alcohol," Marshall quips. "You've never had any in your life. You're only seventeen and...what was it? Ah, four months."

"Old enough!" Edith snaps. "Let's see how long you can hold it, then."

"A challenge?" Marshall snickers as Sam pours out the rum in even amounts. "From my own sister?"

She goads, "See how long you can hold your alcohol, Brother."

He flicks his wrist calmly. "Last time I remember, I had four shots of vodka without getting too drunk."

"Four?" I gasp. "Did you feel at least the smallest bit faint?"

"A little light headed, yes, but I'm willing to get drunk," Marshall replies, "and see how long *she* can hold her drinks and embarrass her with my victory."

"Alright, alright. Enough banter." Sam pushes the glasses towards us, all full of dark liquid, looking like honey that's been mixed with water to thin it out. The strong fumes are back in my nostrils, reminding me of the night we all sat and prayed, reassuring each other it would all be okay in the end, that we'd make it out alive.

Here we are, sitting around a table with a bottle of rum, getting drunk like the teenagers we should've been, the war making us frightened to go out, to have fun—the complete opposite of the normal, carefree teenager. Now, we're all adults, and time has flown by too quickly.

I look over at Marshall, who grips his glass at the ready, glaring at Edith with a challenging sneer as she reaches for hers. "I'll see you at four."

He downs the shot all in one go, Edith hesitating before she follows in her brother's footsteps, screwing up her face.

"Jesus Christ," she curses. "How in the world do you even stand this?"

"Experience." He chuckles. "Junior year was wild."

"So, that's where you kept going in the middle of the night, huh? House parties?"

"Woah, woah, Edith! Just small house parties." He pushes his glass away, grinning. "No drugs, no smoking, no hookups. Just booze. I'm not letting my life go down the drain *that* far."

Edith groans. I give Marshall a challenging wink, downing mine almost as quickly as he did.

"Not you too," he chaffs playfully. "First time getting drunk?"

I straighten my back, grinning. "We'll see how long I can hold it."

He only winks back. "I'd like to see you try, darling."

Nathan coughs after downing his glass, cursing under his breath. "Be honest with me. How many parties did you go to?"

"Not many." He leans on his front atop the table, a relaxed smile sliding across his face. I nearly mistake it as a drunk one. "Only a few."

Exasperated, Nathan blanches. "Then how the hell do you down it so quickly?"

Marshall shrugs. "Pops has a great alcohol tolerance, same with spices. I have the gene."

Sam pours out the second round of shots, Lester downing his first. Marshall gives me a smirk before he follows behind, teasing me as he sets his glass down once more. "Go on, shoot your shot."

"Terrible pun, really." I raise the shot glass to my lips and wipe my mouth with the back of my hand once I swallow, Marshall watching intently. His eyes flicker with amusement as Edith holds back a cough next to me.

Upon my fourth shot, the world starts to slip away along with my senses. Everything blurs together, and I let out a snort of boisterous laughter, Marshall reaching for his fifth shot and glancing at me. His cheeks are a touch flushed. "Everything okay there?"

"I think I'm getting drunk." I lean on an elbow, giggling. "I dunno, I'm feeling a bit warm."

"Are you?" He leans towards me, the question coming out like a purr, and it jolts me. "How does it feel?"

I can't control the laughter that erupts from my mouth, and I'm embarrassed, being in such a vulnerable state in front of him, stepping out of my comfort zone.

He steadies me as I lean back, keeping a hand on my back to keep me from falling. "Should you stop?" Marshall whispers, his breath smothered with the strong smell of alcohol and the sweetness of rum, warm against the heat in my cheeks.

"One more?" I give him a lopsided grin. "Just one more?"

He gives me a sigh. "Fine, then all you're drinking is water."

"And what about you?" I poke him in the chest, giggling uncontrollably. "How come I stop drinking but you don't?"

"I'll stop when I feel I need to. For you, it's obvious you have a low tolerance."

"Shush!"

"Oi, Sam, we have a flirty drunk here." Marshall's hand remains on my back. "One more shot for my love. Only one. I don't want them getting too drunk. Attaboy."

Sam grins and pours more of the rum out for everyone. Edith snarls at Marshall, who takes on his fifth shot with ease, watching her as she pushes her glass away. "No more."

"Giving up so early?" Marshall taunts, tittering, dragging his words out in a sing-song lilt. "I win."

Edith rolls her eyes. Nathan takes another shot, leaning forward and wiping his hands on his thighs. "Jesus, how drunk can you get?"

Now, he guffaws. "I wouldn't want to see that side of me, Skipper, but oh well. Bartender! Another!"

Sam hands Marshall his sixth shot, which he takes, pushes his glass away and curses.

Lester grins. "Then, the alcoholist was finally defeated."

"Ey, hey, hey! You watch your mouth!" Marshall points at Lester across the table, leaning farther forward. "I never lose. That's for wimps."

"Even while drunk, they argue," Edith says.

"Same thing, you oaf!" Lester yells. "Losers are wimps, you wimp!"

"At least I'm not going to die without trying! Who's the wimp now?"

Lester slams his fist on the table. "You're terrible, y'know?"

Marshall slams his fist on the table in turn, even harder and louder. "I'm the bad guy? You better be scared!"

I break into laughter. Marshall's cheeks redden, and Sam joins me, Nathan shaking his head in disappointment.

"I think that's enough rum," he says.

"How are you still sober?" Marshall's head whips to Nathan, who shrugs.

"I gave up on my third or fourth shot. I can't remember."

"Wimp!" Marshall announces. "Sam, *amigo,* how about you?"

"Honestly, partner, partially drunk," Sam responds.

Marshall hands Sam back his shot glass. I chuckle behind my hand when he looks at me with sparkling eyes. "What're you laughing at?"

"I feel warm."

"You do?" Marshall scoots closer, his cheeks flushing darker as the alcohol hits him. As he leans in, the smell of the rum wavers on his breath again. "Is it because of me?"

"No," I make a lazy attempt to push him away, "booze. But other times, yeah."

Lester whistles. I can't stop the words from coming out. It frightens but excites me all at the same time. "Tell me, boy. How did you get such pretty eyes?"

"*Flirt,*" Marshall hiccups. "From my mama. What about that pretty face of yours?"

"I would tell your *mama* that she brought up a handsome colt." I'm still grinning without shame as I continue to flirt with him. "A face like mine comes rarely."

"The last of a dying breed, huh?" Marshall's voice lowers to a purr once more, his lids half-closing. His eyes never leave. A new aura appears in his dark hazel irises. "I'm glad I could see it, then."

Sam hoots at Marshall, who glares at him before the smirk reappears on his face. He licks his lips and straightens his back, puffing his chest out proudly. "If we were at the bar, I'd take your lovely-looking self to the dancefloor under the brass band. They better play our song, or I'll kill them for you."

I swoon a bit too loud. "You'd do that for me?"

"Anything for a delightful person such as yourself—my person, especially. It comes with a price for the others who want to lay their hands on me."

His smirk widens, and it riles me up inside, sends the heat rising with much more than just the rum humming in my veins. It makes me hot, sweaty, almost.

When he leans even closer, his breath plumes against my cheeks. "I made you even redder."

I give him a returning simper, giggling. "You did, didn't you?"

"Don't hide it from me." He titters drunkenly. "Come on, you know it."

"Yeah, you did. I'll admit it." He gazes at me leaning closer, yet still minding his boundaries. His fingers thrum against the table to a rhythm of his own, his fingertips inches away from mine as the rum warms the both of us.

"After we dance, we'll hit the dessert table for some snacks or something like that, do something fun." He hiccups yet again. "What d'ya say?"

Another wave of heat flows through my limbs. I lean on a fisted hand, looking up at him with a *hmph* of amusement. "Sure thing, *mon chéri*." I take his hand, batting my lashes, and knot my fingers with his. "When we find the time."

Sam whistles again. Marshall's smile quivers, becoming wider. He lets out an amused chortle. "You really *are* drunk, aren't you?"

"What do you mean? I feel great."

"That's the rum talking." His fingers close on mine; warm and scarred. "Let's get you some water."

Sam hands Marshall a canteen, holding it out towards me. "Here."

"Are you drunk, or is it just me?" I ask.

"Only a bit. I'm starting to sober up." He glances over his shoulder at a group of men who hoot and dance to music on the radio that comes out in a brass tune, echoing over the quiet battlefield. "Drink."

Groaning, I unscrew the lid and take a long sip of water. "We should dance with them. There's our dance floor."

"I was only trying to excite you," he takes his own canteen and takes a sip, "trying to make you laugh. Dance floors at parties are the very definition of claustrophobia to me."

"You succeeded greatly, and we should try going to a party together."

"Never again." He sets his canteen down abruptly, looking at me head on. "The last one I went to was utterly chaotic."

"You never struck me as a party person."

"Never was. I went to escape, to get out somewhere. It didn't help, but I don't know why I kept going."

"Something about them attracted you, maybe. The people, or something like that? Or was it something to do?"

"Always *something*," he says. "I don't think I'll be going to any college parties."

"But why? You're missing out on all the fun!"

"Fine, I'll think about it," he concedes. "If high school parties were that rowdy and college parties end up being any worse, I'm not going to any."

"Well said. When do you go to college again, anyway?"

"Next year, September," he replies. "If this whole pandemic hasn't cleared up by then, I'll have to keep studying from home...I haven't thought much about it yet, as I've been all over Europe, fighting in a war for the past year or so. I'll have to reread so many books, so many articles—"

"Hey, don't stress." I take another sip of water, the world becoming clearer to me. "You'll do fine. You're a smart man. You worked so hard to get to where you are now, and I'm sure it'll take you no time at all to get back to where you were right before college. You'll have me around to keep you company while you study."

"Ah, you've made up your mind? You're coming back to Philadelphia with me?"

"I can't think of a friendlier alternative, so…" I trail off, letting the pause excite him. "Yes."

This initiates a reaction where the smile that's vanished returns, his fingers tapping against the table with a heightened intensity. His happiness reminds me of a dog when its owner walks through the door: beaming, sparkling eyes, and a wagging tail.

"I'm glad. I'll have to show you the river and everything. We'll see what we can do in accordance with whatever the rules are back there."

"What happened to studying?"

"I'll do some in between." He gets more and more excited, clasping his hands together. "I'm glad. So very glad! We'll have to get a room ready for you."

"How many rooms do you even have?"

"Just one."

"If it's too much of an organization to follow through…"

"No, not at all," Marshall reassures me. "Nothing I can't do. My room would be just down the hall from you."

"Are you honestly suggesting I sneak into your room?"

"I mean, if you're willing. We could have a reading party on my window seat."

"You criminal." I expel a snort. "Please don't tell me you're one of those boys who leave a mess of things. My cousin is like that and it's dreadful."

"No, no, I'm a neatfreak. Where is Jay, anyways?"

"Probably working. The poor man's been so busy."

Lester clears his throat. "I see you two are done flirting?"

"Still drunk, are we?" Marshall retorts.

"Eh, not too shabby. Some good rum for once," Lester says. "By the way, Frieda, I saw Jay not long ago. As you said, he's working when he doesn't even need to anymore. We won the war! C'mon, time to let loose!"

"No, actually, we're still in the middle of a pandemic," Marshall argues. "There're still so many sick soldiers."

Lester points the rum bottle at him. "How come Edith and Nathan are here? Explain."

"Off their shift, most likely." Marshall cocks his head to his sister. "Hey, Edith?"

"Huh? You're going to tease me about how I can't get drunk?" she responds bluntly.

"As much as I'd like to, no." He takes another sip of water, licking his chapped lips. "I wanted to ask if you're coming back to Philly with me."

"With you? Yeah, I'm being dismissed since I'm just a volunteer, not an actual nurse. Most of the sickly are getting transferred, anyways, and guess what?" She pulls on Nathan's arm, making him jump. "He's coming with us!"

Marshall fights every urge to let his jaw fall agape. "When did you—"

"A few months ago! He agreed to come back to Philadelphia once the war was over. We even wrote to Father together about the whole thing so he doesn't think we're bringing a mystery man inside the house."

I guess Jay will be going back to Seattle, I think. Marshall stutters, arguing with Edith. *I'll have to say goodbye to him when I leave.*

"You and Nathan are *not* sharing a room," Marshall snarls.

Edith wags a hand in front of his face. "Of course not, of course not. Alistair moved out when he married Yvette, so we can move Nathan into his room."

Marshall's bottom lid twitches. "You'll have to ask *him* first, or he'll have to sleep in the study."

"I hope I didn't upset you," Nathan adds quietly.

"No, no, just a bit distressed," Marshall assures Nathan, grabbing his canteen again. "We'll find a way, but as your brother, *Edith,* I prohibit any sharing of rooms between you two whatsoever."

"No fair! You and Frieda may as well share—"

"She's taking the guest bedroom," Marshall interrupts sharply. "My bed wouldn't be big enough."

"But it's a double mattress—"

"No!" Marshall's cheeks turn red. "Edith, the main difference between you and me is I'm a grown man and you two are teenagers, not even eighteen—"

"Eighteen, actually," Nathan corrects, Edith nodding in encouragement. "I'm eighteen."

"You know where I'm going with this. Frieda and I are going into rooms, and you two should do the same. We'll talk to Father about it so he can deliver his verdict. I can already predict that he's going to say the same thing I did."

"You're no fun." Edith swats an annoyed hand at him, Marshall's arguing the equivalent to a lazy fly hovering above her. "Absolutely no fun. You're a buzzkill."

He hides his smile in another sip of water.

37

PHILADELPHIA

MARSHALL

The boat ride from Belgium to America was a wild one at best, with many parties and drinking games happening each night in the ship's cabins, getting rowdier and rowdier each time. Frieda managed to get herself in a bit of a pickle by taking too many shots of vodka and ended up hurling up her stomach the morning after. Edith and Nathan continued with—much to my dismay—the topic of sharing a room and their sleeping arrangements. I snapped one day and told Edith to quit asking until Father delivered his verdict on such an absurd request from his only daughter and a man he hasn't met yet. I'd feel every ounce of distrust if I were in my father's shoes.

After Frieda said goodbye to Jay, claiming he was indeed returning to Seattle, she'd gone to bid Colby, Catherine, Fey, and all the other nurses a farewell and a thank you. I myself said my goodbyes to Ed and Alistair, who were still asleep the morning we left—two days after the war ended.

Alistair gave Edith permission to move Nathan in, as he's planning to go back to Yvette and Kara once he's discharged. Ed held my hand tight for the longest time, wished me the best of luck on my travels back home, and promised he'd see me soon and do the best he could to recover. The two of us started crying when we said goodbye. It hurt me to turn away without looking back, promising to visit him when I could in the hospital, or write letters, one of the two.

Sam and Lester set off on their own travels. We gave out our addresses in case we wanted to write to each other. Upon departing, we were blessed with a last minute remark from Lester and a prayer from Sam.

Now, Frieda, Nathan, Edith, and I stand on the docks of Philadelphia.

All the memories of all the dire events of my life in this city come flooding back. The streets are eerily quiet, lacking the city's normal hustle and bustle, save for some of the ones waiting for their loved ones to return, breaking into tears once they do. The American flag ripples in the wind on its pole, welcoming us back to our homeland. The white stars and the red and blue stripes wink down at us, faded with time in the early sunrise.

Frieda takes my hand, letting out an audible whimper. Today she wears a high-collared spotted blouse with a navy skirt and heeled boots. A trench coat is over her shoulders. A dark gired beret tops her crown.

She grabs my arm like a scared child, eyes scanning the scenery of the early Philadelphian morning that comes with a cold that bites deep into our bones.

"Is everything okay, muffin?" I murmur.

"Cold and hungry."

"Once we get home, we'll get something to eat. How does that sound?"

She groans as we make our way to security. "I need sleep too."

The other couple follows close behind: Nathan in a straw hat, Edith in almost-matching clothes to Frieda, except for a fuller skirt. We made sure to buy some clothes on our stop in Ireland, converting our francs into euros to ditch our uniforms, folding them neatly in our cases. Despite how much they resembled a prison uniform of a war that held us captive, we couldn't bear to part with them.

"Oh, and perhaps some tea," she adds when we move farther up the queue.

"You'll get everything you want once we get home. My father should be waiting somewhere around here. We'll take the train to East Falls."

The security officer's call cracks amidst the cold air with a loud 'next!'

I step forward, holding my passport out. They pat me down and check my bag. He has to take two glimpses at me to make sure I match the grainy photo from four years ago. He asks me some security questions, and another officer rounds my thigh and pats down my trouser pockets with uncaring hands, going over symptoms and a quick temperature check.

"Any alcohol?" The officer sounds almost bored. He slams my passport back on the table.

"No."

"Any sharp objects?"

"No."

"Any weapons?"

"Heavens no." I left all my guns in France. I needed to be ridded of their blasted existence. They were one final restraint keeping me from leaving it all behind and moving on with my life.

"Any organic food products?"

"No," I repeat.

He unzips my satchel, sneering at the four books, my pen and inkwell, my soldier's uniform, another set of clothes, my cap, a fedora, toiletries, a bottle of cologne, and my leather gloves. The officer rummages through my bag with a white-gloved hand and closes it. "All clear. Thank you for your service."

He hands me back my passport. I step through, waiting for the others on a nearby bench.

Edith rants on and on to Nathan about the officer touching her and prohibiting their medical kits, including a scalpel, which had to be confiscated. Frieda comes out last with her patch in hand, her mask hanging off one ear, bag over her shoulder.

"Blasted git had me take these off to see me." She reties her patch and puts her mask back on. "Said something to me about women in the army. I wasn't really listening. I was more concentrated on food."

"As I've said, we'll get breakfast soon." I stand, stretching my tired legs, dipping my bowler hat which sits unevenly on my head of wind-tousled hair. I rub my hands together to keep them warm and offer an exhausted grin. "Now, let's go find Father."

"You're too excited in the mornings." Frieda grimaces, dusting off her skirt and folding her arms, rubbing her eyes. "Did you have coffee?"

"No, actually." I fall into step beside her. "I'm just happy to be home."

"Mmhm, and I'm hungry. I demand breakfast."

"Of course, my queen." I put on a horrendous English accent, teasing her shamelessly. "Would you like a hot cup of tea with that, too? On the menu, we have Earl Grey, English Breakfast, Lady Grey, Irish Breakfast, rose hip, peppermint, and chamomile, amongst many others. Pick your poison. For breakfast, would you like some waffles? Eggs on toast? Pancakes? Oatmeal? The chefs would be delighted to make *anything*."

At first, she frowns. Then, she fails to control her grin. "Shut up."

"Come on, admit it! You liked that!"

"Maybe I did. By the way, that was the worst English accent I've ever heard. I love it."

Satisfied, I hoist my satchel's straps higher over my shoulder. "I'm glad."

In the streets, a cold wind blasts past and numbs my cheeks. Edith clasps her hands together with a cry expelling itself breathlessly from her lips. "Father!"

It's too good to be true. Too far away to be real.

My father is standing on the sidewalk, arms outstretched, his graying dark hair blown back by the wind, his aging face smiling behind his face mask. He wraps Edith into a tight hug, swaying from side to side as the rest of us catch up to come close enough to know he's crying.

"Edith, my girl. Marshall, my boy." He reaches to pull me in. I can't stop the tears that escape. I break down in his familiar arms, hanging my head on his shoulder, gripping him close, sobbing into his pea coat. His hand curls around my nape and claps the back of my neck with recognition.

It all comes out in an ugly sob as he rubs my back. He grips me tighter, mumbling, 'my son, my child, my boy' over and over again with a fierce and fatherly love only he can show. He holds my cheeks in his hands, searches my face with his wide blue eyes that dart in all directions, taking me in. He's a full four inches shorter than me and has to look up to meet my eyes.

"I'm home, Father, I'm home."

He wipes away my tears with cold hands. I melt at a single wisp of his touch.

"Marshall! How hard I prayed you'd come back to me, my son. My beautiful, courageous son." His smile turns watery, stained with tears. "You're here, you're really back. My dear lord! Edith too!"

Edith wipes her own eyes, giving him a grin. "Alistair's on his way to the hospital. His boat left a few hours after ours, in case you're wondering."

"My boy! Is he alright?"

"Quite. He's healing nicely." Edith pats his shoulder confidently. "Yvette will be thrilled."

"Indeed she will be. She's been worried sick."

"Father?" I pipe up from under his arms.

"Yes, Marshall? What is it?"

"It's not just us. Ms Joyce and Mr Nelson are here, too." I step back to reveal Frieda and Nathan, who stand side by side, unsure and cowering. Frieda's tightly clutching the front of her trench coat. Nathan holds his briefcase even tighter with two pale hands.

"Oh! Frieda! How much you've grown!" Father gasps, stepping forward to greet her. "I haven't seen you in years! It's been so long! You look absolutely beautiful. You've grown into a wondrous young person."

"Thank you, Mr Clark." Frieda bows her head. Her voice possesses a nervous edge. "You look well yourself."

"I'm only forty-six, nothing special. I'm an old man now." He chuckles and turns to Nathan. "You must be Mr Nelson, yes?"

"Yes, sir. It's a pleasure to meet you." An added, intentionally heavy properness lies on his tongue, though his hands are visibly shaking. He shrinks back.

"No need for formalities, my boy." Father's grin widens, reciting the signature Clark family line. We hate any sort of formalities from friends, or friends of friends—the list goes on. "Please call me Cooper. Thank you for looking after Edith."

"Alright, Cooper. I'm Nathan." He fetches a smile, one that's both boyish and shy. "Also, no problem. I'm happy to help."

I turn back to Frieda as the both of them get acquainted, nudging her.

"What? Are we getting breakfast?" she asks.

"Not quite yet." I wrap my arm around her. Father shakes Nathan's gloved hands, nodding hard when Nathan says something inaudible. They both laugh. "Be careful. My father might adopt you as one of his own."

"Whatever is that supposed to mean?"

"When Alistair first introduced Yvette, he was all over her and asked Alistair when she'd come over next. He thought they were a good match and wanted them to interact as much as they possibly could. He means well and is no trouble for us."

"I see," she replies. "You have me shivering in my stockings."

I stifle a laugh. We make our way to the train station, hopping aboard. I sit by the window with Frieda while Nathan and Edith take their places next to my father in the seats across from us.

Father grins. "Now, Frieda, how is everything?"

Frieda hesitates, batting her eyelashes, stunned at his sudden question. "Where should I begin?"

"Anywhere, for that matter. You've just come home from a war, in the middle of a pandemic. I understand there's a lot to talk about."

"Well..." Frieda scratches the inside of her wrist; a nervous tick. I slide my arm back around her waist to comfort her, to give her the message to not be nervous. She takes a breath in—a shaky and long one. "My mother caught the Spanish Flu, and…"

"Didn't she remarry?" Father asks.

"She did, she did." Frieda looks down at her boots, lips trembling. "Except...she passed away a few weeks back. I'm not sure how my step-sister's doing either."

"Oh, no." Father sighs heavily. "My darling, I'm so, so sorry. I understand you feel a lot of grief as of now."

"I'll be okay, and thank you," Frieda responds, almost as if on autopilot. "Thank you for understanding."

"No need to thank me. I know how close you and your mother were."

My grip tightens on her. She stiffens and replies rigidly, "Yes, very. Thank you for letting me stay with you."

"Again, no need to thank me. It's the best I can do. We'll try to make you feel right at home for however long you'll be staying. *Mi casa, tu casa,* Alexandria always said. She would've loved to meet you. The last time I saw you, you were only fifteen! Nineteen now, aren't you?"

"Yes."

"My God, time flies. Four years." My father wipes his forehead, feigning exasperation. "You look just like your father."

Frieda nods a thanks. The train hits a bump in the tracks, making Nathan jump. She leans against me, letting out a pained whine.

I whisper against her ear, "Is something wrong?"

"Lightheaded," she whispers back. "My stomach hurts. I'm tired."

I pull her close, letting her slump against me. "Close your eyes for now. We'll be home soon."

"Did I do something wrong?" Father asks nervously. Frieda's eyelids flutter closed, leaning her head on my shoulder. Her arms wrap around mine.

"Just hungry. We haven't had any real food yet. Frieda hasn't eaten since last night due to nerves and seasickness."

"Poor doll. Once we get back, I'll fix something up for you while you put your feet up. You poor children must be starving. They don't give you much in the trenches either. Same old can of bully beef?"

"Mmhm. Biscuits included." I look over at Edith, who's asleep in Nathan's lap as he strokes her hair fondly. He's also nodding off to sleep himself, head ducked back against the pale green carriage seats of cracked leather.

"This might be a bit late, but I have your birthday present that I was going to send you in May. I wasn't going to risk it because it's a valuable one. It could've gotten lost."

"You're too kind, Father, there's no rush. We'll take things one step at a time."

"You're just like your mother: calm, collected, optimistic. I'm proud of you."

"What for, exactly?"

"For growing into such a wonderful young person—all three of you. I prayed and prayed every night for you—Frieda, Alistair, and Nathan included. Son, I'm so very relieved that you're back and that everyone is okay. I could never be a prouder father than what I am now."

"Thank you, Father." I bow my head, heart brimming with warmth. "It's good to be home."

The train chugs into a tunnel, the carriage going dark. The lights sway with the rhythm of the engine up ahead. I lay my head back against the seats, slumping.

Frieda groans, clutching her stomach.

I raise a hand to her hair and close my eyes. "Nearly there, *amor*," I yawn, smoothing out her curls. "I'll even do the English accent for you as we eat."

"You should sleep. Get a couple of minutes in." My father shuffles in his chair, leaning back. "You're as white as a sheet."

Staring at the roof of the carriage, my head leans against the window. The sky of orange and red from the American sunrise creeps in. Frieda's in my arms, nestled away under my coat, her fingers intertwined in mine, my other hand in her hair.

It's all too peaceful, too surreal, to be sitting in a train carriage with the one I love dearly in my arms. One I fought hard through blood and mud to be reunited with, to take home. To work on living our normal lives again, to rest and finally lay our weapons down. To start a new chapter and move on from the terrors of war that may as well circle inside our heads every passing hour of the night while we sleep.

* * *

The train's shrill whistle blasts in my ears, causing me to awaken, half of my body slumped against the window, crumpling the curtains underneath me with a crick in my neck and my arm half asleep. I blink back my drowsiness as a sign flies past the window, telling us we'll be arriving soon.

Welcome back to Philadelphia, Marshall, a voice chimes in my head. *Welcome home.*

Looking down, Frieda's made herself at home, her head leaning against my shoulder, our fingers lax but still resting on my thigh, her other hand draped over her belly. The train slows down as the whistle toots again, Edith and Nathan waking slowly, Frieda remaining fast asleep.

Jeesh. She must be exhausted.

Reluctantly, I lean in and mutter in her ear, "Good morning, Sleeping Beauty."

She stirs, her face contorting in disturbance. She shifts closer to me.

"Frieda, it's time to get up, please."

Frieda's eyes flutter open, and she covers her yawning mouth. "Are we there yet?"

"Almost. You were out cold."

"Was I? Did you sleep at all?"

"I did." I stretch my legs. "You obviously slept better than I did, though."

As she awakens, Edith and Nathan wake up beside my father, who watches the bustling city streets turn into suburban ones. The river passes us by through gaps in the road and houses, lamps that flicker bright in the early morning.

"Rather quiet," I remark.

"Yes." Father folds his legs at the knees. "The streets kept getting quieter and quieter since the flu spread. Those ladies who live just a few doors down and walk their dogs every day are staying inside. I haven't seen them in months. I hope they're okay."

"Pugsley and Rudolph? The terriers? We won't be seeing them anymore?" Edith whines from Nathan's lap, who continues to close his eyes and nod off to sleep.

"Not for a while, unfortunately, dear." He peers at Nathan. "Mr Nelson's tired out of his mind."

"He hasn't slept solid for a week." Edith runs a hand through his copper locks, him succumbing to her touch. Frieda's eyes are closing again as the train makes its arrival at the platform known with another hoot of its whistle. The doors open for passengers to clamber off.

"Frieda," I shake her lightly, jolting her out of her slumbering state, "we're getting off the train now."

Frieda stands and stretches, grabbing for her bag at her feet, thanking the conductor as she gets off with me flanking her closely.

My father eyes his wristwatch, nodding with newfound glee, as if there wasn't enough of it that came with our arrival. "You kids came at a good time. It's just after seven." He pops his coat collar up against the cold, waiting for all of us to gather around him like a flock of birds eager for crumbs. "Breakfast time."

"Finally," Frieda groans. "Thank the Lord for some real food."

"I did manage to find some pancake mix I bought a few months back—it's still good, don't worry. I was thinking we could have some pancakes to celebrate your return. How does that sound?"

"Mr Clark—Cooper—sorry," Nathan pipes up. "You don't have to go above and beyond for us."

"Don't you worry, chap!" Father claps his shoulder with a wide grin. "I'd be happy to. It's your first day back! You deserve to be celebrated."

Before Nathan can protest, we set off into the streets, everything coming back to me. More and more households awaken with the morning sun. One has their window open and is playing a saxophone to serenade the morning air, the man tipping his hat at us with a wink.

"Good morning, sirs and madams!" A huge beam appears on his round face. He clutches his saxophone. "Just returned home?"

"Indeed, Maurice!" Father calls back to him, waving. "Revving up the old sax, are we?"

The man, Maurice, grins. "Indeed I am, Sir Cooper! Who're you bringing along?"

"This is my son, Marshall, my daughter, Edith, and their accomplices, Frieda and Nathan. They'll be living with us for a little while as the world gets back on its feet."

"Good morning to you!" His happiness is contagious. He situates his sheet music in his lap while I hold back a grin. "I'll let you go. Don't want to be out in the cold for too long, do we?"

"Have a great day, Maurice. Keep going with that saxophone of yours. You're playing it wonderfully."

We walk past and turn down another street. I can't stop myself from asking, "Who was that?"

"I made a friend while you were away." Father has a skip in his step as a newspaper boy comes along on his bike, shouting about the end of the war, the Ottoman surrender. "He and I did some volunteer work at the hospital. We got along quite well."

We pass an intersection and turn onto our street. The walkway to the river is what I point out to Frieda, who nods tiredly when she sees it. Nathan is marveling at the oak trees that shelter the sidewalk. Father climbs up the steps of our house.

Father's obviously been keeping the herb garden fresh and the lawns trimmed while we were away, the empty house nice and clean. He digs through his pockets for the keys and inserts them into the door of the old Victorian style house that he and Mother always loved, the one we called home since we were infants. I help Edith and Frieda with their bags as they climb up the steps and past the open door. Inside, the air of the hallway is mildly cold.

"Let me turn the furnace up. I swear I left with it running," Father says, turning to a dial on the wall, poking at a knob, and turning a few switches.

The lamps that hang from the ceiling flicker on. He's put two rose bouquets in vases near the key bowl atop the front set of drawers, ushering us into the living room that holds Alistair's grand piano by the window, my favorite armchair that's of a matching plush red to the sofas, and an ottoman with a carpet that sprawls across the dark varnished floor. The fireplace is already decked with firewood. Small trinkets from Puerto Rico line the mantle along with a matchbox.

I hastily light a match and drop it into the fireplace, setting the firewood alight to warm the room, the smell of it catching in my nose. I stand on the hearth rug and watch the flames lick hungrily at the logs.

Edith sits on Alistair's light piano stool, tsking. "Father didn't take down the paintings yet."

"Which ones?" Frieda asks. She settles on the gray loveseat next to Nathan, surveying the room.

"The ones up there." Edith points to the portraits of the five of us lining the walls of the far right of the room. I had to be about seventeen in mine: head inclined with a dark satin bow around my neck and a winged collar, sat with my back straight in the plush chair of the artist's gallery. I almost cringe at how deadpan my face is compared to my siblings. Beside them, old pastel portraits of my parents line each side.

Frieda stands to observe them, her fingers to her chin. She points to the one on the right. "That's your mother?"

I look up at the one she's pointing at, the one of my mother with her soft, round, olive face. Her dimples are on full display in her tight grin, her deep brown ringlets cascading down her shoulders. She wears an elegant and square-necked cream white regency gown with a Swiss-dot pattern and bell sleeves, her collarbones and shoulders on show as she leans forward in the painting. Her hazel eyes—my hazel eyes— stare back at me from beneath thick, dark lashes.

"Yes, that's her." I smile up at the portrait. If you look just a little bit closer, you can make out the kohl lining her eyes. They're beautifully shaped, wide with adventure and a childish keenness to explore.

"Alexandria Clark was definitely a beautiful woman. You have her eyes," pinching my cheeks, she teases, "and her smile."

"I do?" I groan as she reaches to tip my hat over my eyes. Sitting in my armchair, that very grin becomes present. I get comfortable with the many cushions pressed against my back.

Edith rolls her eyes. Frieda settles on the armchair opposite mine. She's fidgeting with the cushions, burrowing deeper into the seat and folding her legs comfortably. I'm glad to see her getting used to the new environment. When Father enters the room, she merely turns her head to him and leans back.

"I've fixed the furnace." He wipes his hands free of soot with a tea towel. "It should be a little bit warmer now. Pancakes, everyone?"

"Thank you, Cooper," Nathan says from his seat, his copper locks shining red in the weak sunlight. "That would be great. Also, your house is lovely."

"I appreciate the compliment. It was all my wife's choosings. She had a knack for aesthetics. You two—" he points to Edith and I sternly—"why don't you show your guests their rooms, hm? Help them settle in. Alistair's and the guest bedroom should be ready. I put in fresh linens last night."

"Frieda," I hoist myself off my chair, offering my hand for her to take, "if we may?"

Her palms are warm against mine. She reaches for her bag, but I lightly push her away and give her a chaste kiss on her hand. "I'll take these."

I escort her up the polished stairs, hanging her bag over one of my shoulders, mine on the other, and wait for her, who takes her first steps up from the downstairs landing. I flick on the lightswitch, letting the lights buzz to life when she emerges. She follows close behind, and I take a left down the hall.

"I never saw this part of the house." She observes the walls and their many ornaments.

I stop at the door at the far end of the hallway. Fiddling with my hands, I crack it open.

The guest bedroom has always been one of my favorite rooms, with its bay windows and a cool blue color scheme. The walls are painted a cream white, adorned with floral paintings my mother enjoyed. A large oval, midnight blue rug with a white-patterned exterior cushions the dark floorboards. A four-poster bed sits on the far left with a charcoal duvet and pillows. On the duvet sits a black, white, and abalone woolen throw blanket folded neatly at the foot of the bed. The canopy is of a Prussian blue, matching curtains adorned with gold embroidering complimenting the large windows. A wooden vanity sits opposite an oak wardrobe in the corner.

"This is the guest bedroom, which is now yours for however long you'll be staying." I offer her a smile and set her bag down near the vanity. "My room is down the hall. It's the furthest one to the right. It should take you no trouble at all to find it."

"Marshall, this room is..." She hesitates as it all sinks in. "Wow, I...How do I thank you?"

"No need, my dear." I lean against the doorframe as she steps inside, the room stealing her breath away. "I'll leave you to make yourself at home and unpack. I have to do so myself."

"Of course. Marshall?"

"Yes, Frieda?"

She loops her arms around my shoulders. "I need to thank you."

"No need." I lower my voice. "What's mine is yours."

She reaches to cup my face and draws me in for a quick peck on the lips. "If you say so."

"It's good to have you here." I go for another kiss, one lasting only a few seconds longer, one that sends a flutter through my heart, already growing weak. "You know where to find me."

"If you're not careful, I'll sneak in." She winks.

"You're terrible." I chuckle and close the door with a small click behind me.

Making my way down the hall, I hesitate, gripping my doorknob.

It's been over a year since I've been in this room, let alone in this house. God knows what I've left behind, what I'll discover as I move back in.

Taking a deep breath, I push open the door and turn on the lights to see the room exactly how I left it the afternoon I set off for France. The bed on the left near the window is made, the black duvet tucked neatly over the mattress and underneath the pillows. The dark red curtains are closed, so I open them to let in some morning light and place my satchel on my desk, which possesses an unfinished entry in my other journal, lying open. The ink is beyond dry. My spare pen hides in the middle of the two open pages.

I'm about to go to war. I've seen what they did to the men who came home from France, heard

from the women who've volunteered as nurses.

I pity my past self. If only he knew what was coming in the following months.

I close the journal and place it carelessly in the bottom drawer of my dresser, eyeing the biology and anatomy manuals sitting on my desk, my acceptance letter crumpled at the top of the pile. Unpacking my satchel, I fold my clothes and put my coats upon their hangers, handling my uniform with care as I set it in the top drawer of my dresser, the trenchcoat in my closet, the cap hanging from a hook on the back of my door. I'm yet to burn it, to scorch away the bars of yet another cage chaining me to the war. Perhaps, like me, it'll grow thinner and older with time.

Sliding my shoes and coat off, I sit on the foot of my bed and look out the window. The river's dark, murky current churns and washes against the banks. The sun reaches its early morning peak. The city and its commotion is in the distance with many houses letting fires burn with the smoke going up their chimneys and their residents walking along the river's edge.

I get lost in the view before my father calls and announces that breakfast is ready. The clambering of feet down the stairs summons me to follow behind.

Stepping into the dining room, my father has set the table with five plates full of pancakes. He's just placed the teapot on the table with its matching cups and saucers. The windows are open, letting in a breeze. It truly feels like home again. I sit opposite Edith, Frieda on her left, Nathan to my right.

Father sits at the head of the table—his usual spot. "Yvette should be coming later to welcome you all back. I was on the line late last night telling her you all were coming in today."

"Is Kara coming?" I ask, almost too excitedly. Frieda snorts over the rim of her cup of steaming tea.

"Yes, Kara's coming. You'll love her, Marshall. She's the sweetest babe I've ever seen."

As we begin eating, I take a whiff of what tea my father's made—Earl Grey, judging by the scent. I nod in approval at the pancakes he's cooked and allow myself to go a little bit overboard with the syrup. When I peer over the rim of my cup, Frieda's tired face relaxes into a grin as my father rambles on and on about better days and what he did during the war. He wrote poems, tried a painting class, grew a lemon tree out in the backyard, and sold lemons to the neighborhood in the summer.

The scene is almost too perfect. I take the syrup and pour a little bit more on my pancakes.

Father turns to me. "Marshall, you'll be so very proud of me," he dabs at the corners of his mouth with a napkin, "I managed to get through that ghastly long reading pile you gave me."

"Wait," Frieda holds up a hand, "you gave your own father a reading pile?"

"During the war, there was nothing else to do. When I was in France, I asked him to give me a reading plan for when I came home. He gave me not five, not ten, but fifteen books to read. I managed to get through all of them, as I read compulsively when I returned."

"I'm glad. Did you enjoy them at least?" I inquire.

"You know it!" He cackles and takes another sip of tea. "You have a very profound taste in literature, my boy, and a very well read, imaginative mind. I didn't have any doubts at all. You kept me highly entertained with your recommendations."

I slice my second pancake in two, smiling without the tightening of a rope around my neck that I felt far too often on the battlefield pulling it taut. "I could recommend you some more."

"Have mercy! My eyes need a break!" He chuckles heartedly. "Don't trouble yourself. That reminds me! After breakfast, you could show Frieda the study. You'll have hours of fun."

"It's really up to her." When our eyes meet, a hopeful shine appears. "If she really does want to hear all of my bookish ramblings, I'll show her."

"I'd love to." She accepts the invitation with no hesitation, back straightening with her excitement.

Edith teases as she spreads more butter on top of her pancakes, "How romantic; bookworms bonding over fine art that they consume like lunatics."

Father tuts. "Edith, dear, go easy on them. They're going to have some bonding time."

Frieda giggles behind her hand—a flattering giggle. "I'd be glad to spend time with you. How about it?"

Her eyes stare into mine. A sheen of hope and joy reflects in both our irises. I dip my head, grinning from ear to ear. "Once we're both ready, I'll be happy to show you."

38

SANCTUARY

FRIEDA

After breakfast, Marshall leads me down the hall with an excited skip in his step; the walk of a man who's proud of his treasure. My own excitement bubbles and froths inside my chest. He giggles beside me, humming up a storm, a happy tune that vibrates on his lips as he smiles like a drunk, stopping at a pair of dark double doors with golden knobs.

"What're you smiling for?" I ask, watching his hands move to the doorknobs.

"I finally get to show you my sanctuary." He presses down on the knobs, grin widening. "I've been wanting to show you for so long. I sound like an absolute nerd saying it."

"You like books, I like books, so we're both nerds in this instance."

"Comforting. Then I'm sure you'll like this."

"Lay it on me."

He pushes the doors open and bows deeply in the doorway, putting on the god-awful accent once more. "This is Master Clark the Third's sanctuary and eutopia that he gladly permits his darling songbird, Frieda Joyce, to enter at any time. He asks me, his butler, to tell her not to thank him for his permission, as it is not needed."

"You're really addressing yourself as Master Clark the Third?"

"*Shush.* I'm the third Mr Clark of this household. It sounded fun."

He steps into the room, hurrying to open the dark green curtains that line the windows of the circular space and the wide desk that sits in the middle of it. Shelves upon shelves stand against the walls: varnished birch with beautiful patterns, decked with spines that shine in a myriad of colors against their pale wood.

"It isn't much." He sits himself down on the couch nearby, leaning back, at ease in his own little world, one that thrills me to be a part of. "But this is what kept me entertained for years upon years."

"'It isn't much,' he says." I scan the shelves, running my fingertips along the spines of many, many volumes. "'It isn't much,' he says, sitting in front of shelves and shelves of his beautiful books."

"Not just mine. *Ours.*" He holds a graceful arm out to me, leaning farther back on the couch, fully relaxed in this space of peace and quiet. I can see why he enjoys it here. Even the air itself has stilled and has become quiet. "I told you, what's mine is yours."

"I'm...I'm lost for words." I continue examining the shelves. "How long did it take you to get this many books?"

"They're not all mine. Some are my father's, my mother's, Alistair's...Edith doesn't read much, but I'm sure there's some in here provided by her."

"I'm astounded. Utterly astounded."

He leans forward, asking softly, teasing, "Did I take your breath away?"

My answer comes in a breathy laugh. "I feel like Belle from *La Belle et la Bête.*"

"Huh?" His grin wavers, a confused glaze in his eye.

"I have to read it to you." I settle next to him on the couch, facing him. "This whole thing reminds me of the scene where Beauty discovers the Beast's library, which is *massive,* I must add."

"I'm sorry, I'm the...beast here?" He lets out a whine. "Am I ugly?"

"If you were, you'd transform into a prince by the end. Beauty and the Beast fall in love."

"Garn, I'm royalty." He thumps a proud hand against his chest, leans closer and gazes at me, interested and taking me in. "It's French, I'm guessing?"

"It is. There should be a translation somewhere...You haven't read it, I presume?"

"I don't think so."

"I'll have to find an English version for you." I take a second sweep of the magnificent shelves. He moves closer, cautiously, closing the space between us. "Does this mean we can read together now?"

"A book club does sound fun." He angles the rest of his body toward me. Our feet touch. He's so close that the sun in his eyes allows me to make out every detail of his irises. "And to be sitting next to you, reading all day, would be even more fun."

"Flirt."

"Am I not allowed to flirt? I'm saddened, truly." He feigns sorrow, wiping his eyes. "A hopeless man who's not allowed to flirt with the lover of his dreams? What a tragedy! I've been wounded! Wounded!"

He slumps against the couch, letting out a cry that gets me laughing and reaching to grip him in a playful headlock, ruffling his hair, pinning him to the couch while he screams, laughing at the same time, the loser in a battle of aggressive, yet hilarious banter.

Once it settles down, I sit in his lap, in his arms, against his chest. Marshall's lips curve into yet another carefree grin as he takes my hand in his, drawing tickling, lazy circles on my palm. He puts his feet up, taking his time to release a long, relaxed exhale, chest heaving with the last of his laughter.

The thing is, we now have the time to show affection. On the battlefield, time was, as they say, of the essence. Now that we're finally alone together, time is no longer flying by, but slowing down for us to make room for memories.

His lips go to my hair, then behind my ear, stamping more and more kisses over and over again. My heart leaps with each one. His fingers find mine, and my stomach flips. His warmth merges with my own.

"You know," his breath plumes against my skin, his kisses cascade, "we could take a walk later this afternoon. We can get away from it all on the walkway that I told you about."

"That sounds fun, but don't feel so rushed." Another kiss. Another butterfly in my stomach flapping its wings. "We just got home from almost two weeks of traveling through Europe and the North Atlantic Ocean. We need rest, too. No need to overexert ourselves on the first day back."

His lips hover over my ear with the words, "I'm ready when you are."

"For what?"

"Anything," he replies, speaking softly. "Anything that comes our way. We'll take it on together."

"Even if it's just a walk in the park?"

"It's more than that when you're tired out of your mind. It's more like a walk through a valley at the moment."

"Sounds like life right now with everything going on."

"Mmhm," he agrees, pulling me closer, leaning his head back to expose his neck and under his chin. "We'll take it one step at a time. If it's two steps, two steps at a time. The list goes on."

I fiddle with his lapels, his left hand moving to the small of my back as he adds, "About the book club, I fear that it'll be just the two of us."

"We'll make the best of each other's company like we always do."

He leans in. A meaningful glint appears in his eyes. "Definitely. I look forward to spending more time with you, *cariño*."

"What does that mean?"

His right hand travels to my chin, tilting it upright. His fingers are cold against my skin. "It means *sweetheart* in Spanish. It's what you are to me."

"You never fail to back up my evidence that you are, in fact, a massive flirt."

"What's a guy gotta do to show his feelings, hm?" He laughs, lips inches away from mine.

The desiring glint in his eye doesn't go unnoticed. "Nevertheless, I'll allow it, dork."

"That stung." He sucks in a breath. "Calling me a dork now, are we?"

"I'm sorry, I hurt you. Do you want me to kiss it better?"

The glint glows brighter. He pulls me even closer. "Actually, if you don't mind, I would."

His hands cup my face as he presses his lips to mine, kissing me softly with all the love he can muster. The Earl Grey's bitter but pleasant taste is still present. I run my fingers through his hair; soft and curly beneath my hands. He lets out a guttural groan of satisfaction that sends my heart thumping, his thumb stroking my cheek.

The kiss continues, develops, and steals my breath away. All kinds of feelings fizz and bubble over the lid of its jar in the back of my mind, coming to life. He tests the waters farther and farther.

Elegant hands move from my face to my waist, his lips venturing to my jaw, kisses trailing slowly down my neck. They're tickling my skin as he handles me with care, his brow furrowing in concentration. His tongue grazes my pounding jugular vein. His stiff frame relaxes against mine as he gathers me in his lap, mindful, holding me like a delicate doll.

My breathing turns into pants, my hands gripping his shoulders, knotting themselves in the wool of his blazer. I mumble his name as he pulls away, leaving me open and vulnerable.

His boyish smile returns. His voice comes out in a rumble, one I was most certainly not prepared for. "You've healed me."

I swat at him playfully and rest against his front, closing my eyes. The grogginess of skipping through time zones and kissing a lovesick gentleman finally catches up to me.

As I close my eyes, his arm cradles me. He covers us with a black throw blanket. "Tired, huh?"

"Obviously."

"You could go rest in bed."

"I don't feel like moving." My eyelids weigh themselves down. His heart drums steadily on inside his chest.

His head leans back against the edge of the couch and closes his eyes. "You know," he drags on his words, tired and in an obvious state of elation, "we should do that more often."

"You're terrible!" I hiss at him. His chest convulses with a silent bout of laughter. "Absolutely terrible."

"I do it all for you." He shifts his weight beneath me, letting out a horrendously long yawn, slumping even farther against the cushions.

When I close my eyes again, the sun peeks through the curtains and warms my back, Marshall's breathing slows to become steadier, slower. If he dozes off with his head leaning back like that, he'll have terrible neck pain when he wakes up.

The world slips away. I put my feet up with his as his arms loosen their grip by the smallest portion, but I can't care any less. What I care more for is that he's here with me in the calm morning light of the study; his hideaway. I'm in his arms and safe: from the war, from sickness and injury, from death.

We may have met in a war. We may have fought and gone through Hell together, faced our fears and looked Death in the eye, told each other our secrets in words out loud or on sheets of parchment that traveled far and wide, but I wouldn't have it any other way. I would do it all again to stay here in this peace and quiet, to preserve this moment for as long as I can before time runs out.

* * *

When I wake, there's no steady rhythm of a second heartbeat or the warmth of another body, but a pillow against my cheek and a blanket wrapped around me, and I lie facedown on the couch.

My arm dangles over the edge and onto the carpet. I sit up to the sound of a gramophone playing the soft tune of one of Mozart's piano sonatas, the wind blowing through the open windows and curtains which have been parted even wider than before.

I stretch my arms free of aches and pains, and there's the scratching of a pen on paper. Methodic, square fingers on one hand lie relaxed on said parchment, the other roams freely upon a thick textbook, index pointing at words on pages. The sunlight rebounds off of his spectacles, thin metal, oval lenses, that perch on the bridge of his nose as he pores over his books. His dark vest is open at the top two buttons, adorned with a gray cravat. The sleeves of his shirt are folded up to his elbows, revealing the scars along his arms.

He's at peace, hard at work. His leg jogs under the table while he mumbles the words he writes under his breath. When I venture over to the desk, he sets a cup of coffee that wafts and battles the incoming autumn breeze from outside on a saucer, adding a bitter tinge to the air as steam blows from its murky surface.

"What's all this?" I lean over his shoulder to read the small print of what I gather is from a biology textbook and his even smaller font winking at me with a labeled diagram of a cell and all its parts. He's even filled out all their roles and all the different types of cells. *Prokaryote* and *eukaryote*, *unicellular* and *multicellular* poke out from under his arm.

"Biology recap." He picks up his coffee cup, taking a long sip as he waggles his pen in between his fingers. "I figured I'd start studying."

"Did you rest at least?"

"I did, I did. I slept for an hour." He pokes me on the nose, teasing me as he changes the disc on the gramophone to *Claire de Lune*. After he carefully places the needle down, he sits back down in his chair. "You, Sleeping Beauty, crashed for two. I should be asking if you even slept while we were traveling."

"I did, but not that much."

"Hm. Maybe you'll get more sleep tonight now that you have an actual bed? Trust me, the bed in the guest room is like sleeping on a cloud in Heaven. Once you get comfortable, you won't want to move. You'll become one with the bed."

He swivels on his chair when he hears the laughter of children outside, standing and opening the window a little farther, eyes lighting up at the sight of said children, a boy and a girl, who come by with kites and yellow gumboots.

"Thomas! Eleanor!" he calls, waving to them.

Their faces light up exactly like his as they call back.

"Marshall! Marshall! Mama! Marshall's home!" shrieks the boy, eyes shining under long, thick waves of blond hair, identical to who I'm guessing is his sister, who follows suit in chanting to their mother. A woman in long skirts and hair tied into a bun under her straw bonnet emerges, a hand lying on her bulging, pregnant belly.

"Mr Clark! You truly are back!" She waves. "Are you well?"

"I've come back in one piece, Mrs Mason. All in one piece," he jokes. "I'm bulletproof. I'm well, how about you? You're expecting another little one? Congrats!"

She laughs an airy and half-suppressed giggle, patting her swollen belly. "Thank you. All is well. The baby's due soon in December, right around the corner. It'll be here most likely by Christmas or even earlier. Is Edith or Alistair in?"

"Alistair's in hospital at the moment. His arm was shot and his hand was amputated. Edith's in, yes. I'll tell her you stopped by."

"I'm sorry to hear that. Send him my condolences." She tucks a stray hair behind her ear. Her children continue to wave up at Marshall. "They're so happy to see you. They missed their playdates with you dearly. Once they heard the war was over, they kept screaming, 'Cousin Marshall's coming home.' I didn't want to tell them yet if anything bad happened to you, but here you are, home safe and sound."

"I missed them. We'll have to catch up sometime soon. Did you finish building that fishing boat model I bought you two Christmases ago, Tom?"

"I did! It floats!" The boy, Tom, smiles wide, a gap in the middle of his two front teeth.

Marshall leans on the sill. "Brilliant, my boy. So the glue really is waterproof? Did the paint stick?"

"Yeah! Papa told me to put some varnish on it and it hasn't washed away yet."

"Great. Look, you two, I have someone I want you to meet." He takes my hand and gestures to me. "This is my partner, Ms Frieda Joyce. She's from Seattle and came with us after the war finished. She'll be staying for a little while, so, perhaps we could go for a walk later on this afternoon or tomorrow to meet each other and catch up? Frieda, this is Mrs Mason and her children, Eleanor and Thomas. They live next door."

I give them a wave and a smile, the children waving back with both of their hands. Ms Mason gives me a courteous wave with just her wrist. "Please, call me Marge. It's a pleasure to meet you, Frieda. Welcome to the neighborhood."

"Thank you." I lean on the sill next to Marshall, our elbows touching under the sunlight.

"It's best if we let you enjoy the rest of your walk. We'll arrange a stroll sometime soon, shan't we?" Marshall salutes playfully.

"Definitely." Mrs Mason waves goodbye. The children continue to chant Marshall's name as he closes the window, a beam adorning his face.

"They called you their cousin," I remark.

"Mrs Mason and my mother were close friends, almost like family. When Thomas and Eleanor were born, they were told to call me their cousin—family friend things. We're not blood related, obviously, but I find it simply adorable."

"It's sweet, I'll admit. You're an uncle and a cousin. The family only grows. You get so excited when you see children, as if you're a child yourself."

"I love children." He bookmarks his page and closes his notebook, sitting on the desk, closing his inkwell. "Paternally, obviously."

"I figured as much." I lean against the desk, beside him, as his lower legs rock back and forth over the edge. "You got so excited when you learned you were going to be an uncle."

"And until Alistair gets home, I'll make sure to help Yvette with Kara. I'm her uncle, after all, and my sister-in-law would appreciate the support."

"You're a brilliant uncle, then. All other uncles are unmatched against you. I can most certainly see you as a father one day."

"I'd like to be one," he shrugs, "but that conversation is for another time. About the boat: During Christmas, in 1916, I gifted Thomas a small wooden model of a fishing boat to build. His father told me he was gaining a developing interest in boats and how they operated, so I figured it would be nice to give him one to keep. We built it during the winter in the basement as I helped Eleanor with her English work, as she has the smallest bit of trouble reading and comprehending passages. I hope she's improved."

"Look at you; a good teacher *and* a babysitter. You're the whole pack in one." I elbow him.

He nudges me with an ink stained hand. "I wouldn't think so." Despite his rejection of my compliment, his smile doesn't fade. "I also invited them over one time to borrow books. We sat on the carpet all day as I read to them. Surprisingly, they enjoyed Jane Austen's works. Thomas was only seven at the time. Eleanor was five. Though she couldn't read so well, she loved hearing me read to her."

"That sounds fun."

"It was." He reaches for his cup, taking another sip. "It was summertime, too. School was out. We read all through the summer and went to the beach almost every other time. We had picnics with both families and everything—oh, that's when Alistair threw me in the water when I told him I couldn't swim. I went home covered in sand and seawater. I felt disgusting." He smiles at the memory as it flickers behind his eyes, coming and going. He grows distant, staring at the floor and holding his cup against his chest.

"Are you alright?"

"I...Just in thought." He takes another hurried sip of coffee, the cup almost empty. "I'm thankful Thomas wasn't as old as I was a few years back, or else he'd be as worn down and tired as I am now from the war. I wouldn't want him to see what I—we saw out there."

A lump develops in my throat. "He'd be traumatized."

"Exactly, and Thomas doesn't handle violence or agitation too gracefully. I wonder where his father is now. Is he home?" Marshall finishes his coffee, flashing me a smile, peering at the clock on the wall. "Say, Yvette should be here soon. It's almost one."

"She's coming with Kara?"

"Yes, yes, she is." He takes his biology textbook and places it back on its respective shelf, running his hands over the spines, turning back to me. "Also, did you have a look at these titles? I have nearly all of Jane Austen's books on one shelf and most of Charlotte Brontë's. There's some Doyle, some Leo Tolstoy somewhere, and H.P Lovecraft."

"You've got quite the selection."

"Who would we be without books?" His grin only widens. "They unlock passageways to imagination and a childlike joy even grownups can experience without feeling ashamed. They're a great pastime, too."

"I can't disagree." I scan the shelves, finding the Tolstoy section he mentioned. He's got *War and Peace,* his copy of *Anna Karenina* that I read during the war back on the shelf, and *Resurrection* all lined up and with cracked spines from age and usage. I find his Jane Austen shelf, which seems to be the largest collection. "Jane Austen's your favorite author, right?"

"One of my favorites."

"I'm not surprised. You have almost all of her books, as you've said."

"Because they're *good.* How many have you read?" He stands behind me, arms folded, marveling at his outstanding collection.

"Honestly, *Pride and Prejudice—"*

"Everyone's read that," he interrupts gruffly. "How basic can you get?"

"I know, but it's a classic. I've also read *Emma, Sense and Sensibility*...I'm not sure if I can remember any others."

"No *Northanger Abbey* or *Mansfield Park?"* He dramatically gasps. "Put them on your list at this moment!"

"Don't worry, it's already been done. I brought some books of my own. Let's see, have you read anything by Louisa May Alcott?"

"No, actually." He says it guiltily, as if he's committed a crime.

"What have you been doing with your life, Clark? Are you quite mad? You haven't read anything by Louisa May Alcott?" I raise my voice.

He quietens. "No..."

"Shame on you!" I jab a finger into his chest. "Alright, alright, let's make a deal: I read *Mansfield Park* and *Northanger Abbey* while you read *Little Women* and *Little Men,* deal?"

A challenging and excited glint shines in his eyes. "Deal."

"A warning for *Little Women:* You *will* cry. When you do, don't say I didn't warn you."

"I'll take your disclaimer. But here's mine: You'll be blown away by both my recommendations, I assure you. As my father says, I'm very well read."

When he chortles, the doorbell rings. There's the scampering of footsteps down the hall. Cooper calls, "Yvette! Yvette! I'm coming, I'm coming!"

Marshall takes his cup from his desk and skirts his hand over my waist as he walks me to the door. "That must be Yvette and Kara. Do you want to meet them?"

"I'd love to." I reach for his hand, his cup in his other.

We make our way down the hall. In the living room, a woman with wavy dark brown hair sits with a baby basket on the couch beside her, Cooper leaning over it and smiling as the baby coos at him and blabbers. Marshall squeezes my hand and clears his throat, his arm tensing. I can't help but laugh under my breath at his excitement.

"Yvette! How are you?" he yelps, voice oddly higher-pitched.

Yvette looks up, her soft, weepy eyes creasing. Her arm curtains the basket. "Marshall!" She gives him a tight grin. He stuffs his hands in his pockets, thumbs twitching nervously as they stick out. She speaks quietly, not to startle her baby. "How are things?"

"You're always so thoughtful. Things have been rather dull over the course of this month, but now that you're back safe and sound, it gives me hope. Is Alistair well?"

"He is. He should be in a nearby hospital. I presume he'll be sending you his location."

Yvette's gaze softens upon the basket. The baby inside it blabs on in gibberish, Marshall stepping forward with his hand on mine. "Yvette, I must introduce you to Frieda. We've been dating, to my calculations, for one year and one month up until now."

Dating.

The word strikes a chord I never knew I had. He's never said it before, at least from what I've heard from him, and it's obvious it brings him great pride to say it aloud. His eyes twinkle with an especially bright and adoring shine.

"Just look at you!" she swoons. Marshall draws me close. "You two are like lovebirds; so closely knit. Aren't you the woman who went to war as a man?"

"I'd rather say I went as myself, no other terms necessary," I answer, looping an arm around Marshall's waist, giving it a teasing pinch.

Yvette gasps. "My word! It's you! Your name was all over the streets for a straight week!"

"Look, Frieda, you're famous," Marshall jokes, replying with a returning pinch to my side.

I shove him lightly. "Wow, that's overwhelming. It's a pleasure to meet you, Yvette. Congratulations, by the way."

"You're too kind, and it's my pleasure to be meeting *you!* Would you like to see her?"

"I would," I say.

"I would love to. I'd love to finally see my beautiful niece." Marshall takes me with him to the basket to sit beside it.

Yvette stands to lift a small bundle wrapped in a pink blanket and beanie into her arms, Marshall covering his mouth at the sight of it. I grin wickedly in amusement.

"Oh, she's so small, *oh*!" He marvels as Yvette hands Kara to him. He practically melts as he gazes at her. She looks up at him, making him grin even wider—a watery grin—as the baby reaches for his face.

"Hi, Kara." He speaks to her softly, the baby babbling back at him. She presses down on his nose. "Yes, hi! Yvette, she's smiling at me!"

I giggle behind my hand as he continues cooing softly to Kara, Yvette grinning along. "It's me, your uncle Marshall—" she starts to blabber yet again as Marshall lets out an amused chuckle—"yes, hello!"

"Kara's quite the talkative baby, I've learned." Yvette sits on Marshall's other side. Kara reaches an arm out to push against his cheek, Yvette snorting as he scrunches up his nose at the force. "And she also does that from time to time. She likes to hold things."

"She's beautiful, just like her mother. I'm captivated. She's beautiful. How old is she now?"

"Ten months and three weeks. I keep a close count." Yvette peels back Kara's beanie a smidge to show an already thick, visible lock of black hair. "Look here; she's got Alistair's hair."

"I should warn you that our black hair gene is quite strong." He takes her small hand in his, her fingers wrapping around his pinky. "Wait and see whose eyes she'll have. I bet she'll grow to be a beautiful girl."

"She's adorable," I add.

"Thank you, Marshall, Frieda, we mean it." Yvette carefully takes Kara and sits her upon her lap. "Would you like to hold her, Frieda?"

"I'm alright." I lean against Marshall, who gazes lovingly at Kara while she plays with her mother's fingers.

She's content, blessing Kara when she sneezes. "That's fine, I won't force you."

"I must ask, Yvette, while Alistair's in hospital, would you like some help looking after Kara?" Marshall inquires.

"You're too kind. I would, yes. Father is already looking after her from time to time. Now she's got an uncle and an aunt to look after her."

At the words, Edith and Nathan clamber down the stairs, Nathan's hair and tie askew, Edith smoothing her skirt down. I can imagine roughly what they were up to, and I shake my head at them in disapproval, which is hypocritical, as Marshall and I got a taste of sweet romance ourselves not long ago.

Yvette looks up. Kara continues to blabber. "Welcome, Edith! Who's this dashing young man?"

"Greetings, Yvette." Edith plucks at her sleeve. "This is Nathan. He'll be staying with us for a little bit. Nathan, this is Yvette, my sister-in-law, and my niece, Kara."

"Hello." Nathan provides a shy wave and pulls his tie back in place. "Congratulations."

"Thank you, all of you." Yvette grins as Cooper stumbles in with more tea and tarts with, by the looks of it, strawberry, orange, and lemon jam in their centers.

"I've brought scones!" he cheerfully announces. "And tea! I've brewed up a light blend of white tea to accompany them. I hope I didn't overbake the tarts."

"Thanks, Cooper," I'm the first to respond, "you're too kind."

"I enjoy baking, so I figured I'd share my love of it with you all," he says, and sets the trays atop the coffee table in the center of the room.

"And his baking is *amazing*," Marshall whispers in my ear. He reaches to grab a scone with lemon jam, smiling as Kara reaches to grab it from him. I pour myself some tea, holding the bone china cup in my lap.

Marshall takes small bites of his tart, savoring the taste and nodding in satisfaction. "The tarts are great as always, Father." He gestures his tart towards his father.

"I'm glad. I put my heart and soul into my baking. Remember the apple crumble we had last week, Yvette?"

"That was splendid." Yvette nods. "I ended up eating the rest of it in the middle of the night. I was craving it."

"Your pancakes this morning were also amazing," I chime in, Cooper's smile growing wider.

"Thank you, Frieda." His cheeks flush boyishly from all our compliments. "Honestly, I'm glad you all enjoy it. It was my passion while I was a boy, and it still is. My grandmother got me hooked."

Marshall pours himself a steaming cup of tea after he finishes his tart, holding the cup graciously by the handle, raising it to his lips for a sip. Over our travels, he promised he'd hold back a little on the coffee and search for a healthier alternative. I'd say it's going quite well, just looking at him. When he had licorice tea for the first time, he'd sworn at how good it was, claiming that I had converted him.

"Say, shall we have crêpes one morning? We had some delicious ones in Le Havre." He takes another sip, leaning farther back in his place on the couch.

"I could keep that in mind." Cooper reaches for a tart.

"And perhaps I could cook dinner for a change? Help around the house?" Marshall asks as he grabs another tart.

"It's not going to be too much for you?" Cooper questions.

"No. I want to make myself useful." He says it proudly, puffing out his chest. "I could try to whip up *Mama*'s old recipe."

"Of course. We can't forget her *arroz a la cubanos* she used to make."

"I could try. It won't mean it'll be a success, though." A bout of laughter rings around the room. Marshall basks in it.

"Frieda, how did you like the study? Did Marshall show you?" Cooper takes another sip of tea.

"He did." I can't control the flashbacks I'm guilty of enjoying with his lips on mine, cascading across my skin, his hands caressing me. "You've got quite the collection."

"It's mainly Marshall's. He's the biggest reader of this household. He earned that title and has upheld it for a long, long time."

Marshall finishes sipping at his tea for the moment, relaxed, at ease. "What can I say? It's my passion."

"And I won't stop you, but now you can stop annoying me by quoting passages from your books and annoy someone else!" Cooper's brows waggle at me.

Marshall stifles a laugh. "I promise you, we'll both annoy the devil out of each other with our literature recitings."

Yvette pats Kara as she babbles. Marshall shifts in his seat, leaning on the arm of the couch. I was expecting him to claim the armchair by the window; a dark red piece of furniture, extremely Marshall-esque, something he'd pick out. But instead, it's his father perching himself on the chair.

Now, he takes another sip of tea. His eyes shine in the sunlight streaming in through the window. The green flecks are bold against the brown of his irises as he lazily scans the room, his hand in mine, his cup in his other, shaking his head at Kara, who reaches with her chubby arms for her mother's tart, gripping her hand with her fat fingers and drawing it to her.

"I see Kara's gotten more observant?" Cooper gazes at his granddaughter with pride.

"Yes, she has to look at every little thing." Yvette hoists Kara closer to her chest, placing her tart back on her plate and out of her grip. "Just like her father."

Marshall nods, as if affirming her remark, with a sly chuckle. Ever since he's been home, he's more relaxed, more tranquil than he ever was on the battlefield. His eyes close as he clutches his cup.

"Tired?" I ask.

"A bit." He rubs his eyes behind his spectacles that he hasn't thought to take off yet, setting his cup back on its saucer to uncuff his sleeves, setting them back to his elbows to reveal his scars.

He doesn't stiffen, doesn't hurriedly search his family or friend's faces, but stays calm, collected. They're white little lines on the inside and outside of his forearms. His revealing of his wounds makes my hand reach for my patch subconsciously, but I draw it back with a hidden gasp.

He feels me stiffen beside him, grasping my hand just a little bit tighter. "You can take it off if you want."

"I can't."

"No one's going to judge you, if that's what you're worried about," he replies, squeezing my fingers. Behind the lenses of his spectacles, he regards me closely and puts a hand on my forearm.

"I'll keep it on," is all I say back.

He leans against me and mutters in my ear, "Why don't you try a tart? They're amazing."

"What flavors are there? I saw strawberry, lemon, and some others."

"Definitely strawberry and lemon. He also made some orange jam ones. Here," he reaches for a lemon one, handing it out to me on a small plate, "try it."

Tasting the tart and its bittersweetness, I groan in satisfaction.

"I know, right?" He finishes off his own tart. "I'm not lying when I say that my father's a great baker."

Once Kara and Yvette depart, Marshall and I help wash the dishes, leading to a water fight in the kitchen. Cooper swears that we're 'bloody kids' and joins in.

Now, we sit in the study. Marshall reads a thick medical textbook with his arm draped over my shoulders as I make a start on *Northanger Abbey*. He occasionally sneaks in a few pecks here and there to rile me up, going in for another as the doors open.

"What're you lovebirds up to?" Edith's voice booms. She leans over the couch. "Reading?"

"Yup." Marshall turns to look at her with lazy amusement. "What've you two been up to? Canoodling in dark corners? How scandalous."

Nathan's eyes observe the study upon entry. Like always, he's cautious, checking his surroundings before he enters. "Edith's been showing me around the house, helping me unpack."

"Mmhm." Marshall snickers. "After dinner, you should show Nathan the trail by the river. Get some nightlife. I was thinking of taking you, Frieda."

"I would love to go," I say enthusiastically, offering him a content smile. "Night walks are always fun."

"You just need an excuse to tail and tease us," Edith snaps, Marshall huffing.

"No, no, you're as young and in love as we are, I get it. I'm not a stalker." He thumps his fingers in a soft rhythm against the arm of the couch. "If you want to be left alone so bad, why not go before dinner's ready?"

"Fine." Edith boxes her brother over the ears, causing him to titter. "Do you want to go, Nate?"

"Sure, let me just get a coat on. It's cold out."

When the couple exits, Marshall's chest heaves with short, sparse laughter.

"Clearly amused, huh?" I observe and turn a page.

"It's hilarious. She's such a teenager," he replies, bemused.

"You were one once. Where do you stand?"

"So were you, so where do we both stand?" he challenges.

"Why, you fox!" I jab him, provoking him to wince and slam his book against the coffee table, whipping off his spectacles.

"You're going to regret that." He pulls me in and tickles me. I shriek with laughter, my face turning red. Once I beg him breathlessly to stop, he removes his hands and lets me settle back down next to him.

Letting out a high-pitched sigh to expel the last of my laughter, I poke him on the cheek. "You're a bully."

"Shush." He pokes me back on the forehead.

I close my eyes and lay my head in his lap, his book back in his hand, perched against the arm of the couch. His other trails through my hair as I set *Northanger Abbey* on the table.

"Comfortable, are we?" He doesn't look up. "You look like you're getting ready for me to read you passages from a medical textbook as a bedtime story."

"As if. I probably wouldn't get half of it." I open my eyes and let them focus on his arms. "How did you show them?"

"Hm?" This gets him to look up from his book. "Show what?"

"Your scars." I can't stop the words from rolling out. "Today, at afternoon tea, you unrolled your sleeves like it was nothing."

"It's hard to gain enough courage. It wasn't the first time I did that. I had plenty of other wounds that are easy to explain because of the war. Honestly, that's the first time I did it in front of my father without sneaking foundation or concealer out of Edith's room to hide them. It felt good."

"Really?"

"Yes." His gaze softens under his thick eyelashes. He glances down at his arms with a curt sigh. "I don't have to squabble on the spot for a lie when I have a whole collection of stories from the war to tell. You know what they'd do to me if they ever found out what I did?"

Silence. I shake my head.

"They'd take me away." He shifts to face me, growing tense. "They'd label me as unstable. They'd inject insulin into me, make me go into a coma, drill a hole into my brain through my eyes, hook me up to wires and shock me until I'm deemed 'cured.' I wouldn't want to live with that."

I cringe at the thought. "That doesn't sound appealing at all."

"I know. It seems their methods are saying to me that I have to hide my pain, but I'm learning to not hold back in showing my feelings." He holds his gaze steadily on me. "I'm trying to embrace it, be my own person, and hell, if they think I'm too emotional, let them. I'm getting better, honestly. I'm working on it, working on articulating how I feel, you know?"

"How long have you…"

"How long have I…?" He cautiously watches me as I continue to eye them.

"How long has it been since you did it? I understand it's a delicate matter to discuss—"

"Not at all." His hand lies atop mine. "Not since the episode I had before we went to the lines."

"It breaks me, honestly." His eyes never leave my face. I ramble on. "You just…I don't know how to describe it. You went through so much pain, and I…" My hand tightens in his. My shoulders start to shake. "I just…I feel so sorry that you had to experience it. If I could, I'd take it all away. You don't deserve to live through such a back-bending agony."

"I'm still here, aren't I?" He draws me close, ducking to meet my eyes. "I got through it. I'm still here. I wouldn't want you to take it away, because that would only multiply your suffering and take away part of who I am."

"You'd be fine. You'd be happy for once."

"Who told you I wasn't happy?" My heart skips. His eyes don't break away. "I hate to say it, but pain is part of what shapes who we are. It's persistent, neverending, but it is what it is. If we didn't have pain, we wouldn't know what we're capable of as humans." His eyes are half closed, and he gives me a tight smile. "I'm not trying to be harsh when I say you can't ever wish for someone's pain to go away, because pain keeps coming. It doesn't care how much of it you have. Taking it away isn't taking it all away. It's only subtracting some from another's count and adding it to your own. It's a gracious, selfless move in the game of life, but it doesn't make you a winner."

"I feel bad."

"No, don't." His eyes dart across my face, looking for a way out. "Just a lesson to be learned—one I learned the hard way. I'm proud of you for caring, though. It shows that you're a good person."

I cast my gaze to the carpet.

"Don't dwell on it. That's the worst you can do." His hand reaches to brush the hair out of my face. He feathers a light kiss on my cheek, his voice a gentle rumble against my ear. "It's all in the past. Look at where we are now."

"Sitting in a study, reading books after a war, in the middle of a pandemic—" I offer before he cuts me off.

"Together, muffin." He prods me gently with his shoulder. "We're together. It's no use dwelling on the past when there's something happening right now, right in front of you."

"As I've said," I offer again, "sitting in a study full of books after the war, during a pandemic."

"Frieda, I love you, but sometimes, you're so *literal*." He cringes playfully. "You're such a left-brainist!"

"Am I?"

"You are," he jostles me, a lopsided grin appearing, "but I adore you for it."

"Says the one who denies the fact that he's a legitimate wordsmith and should work as a psychologist."

"Never in a million years." He spits out the words with venom, replacing his scorn with a boyish giggle. "But I appreciate the compliment."

There's a knock on the door. Cooper enters, interrupting the conversation with an apron still tied tight around his waist over his maroon vest. "I'm sorry to bother you and your alone time, kiddos. Dinner's just out of the oven."

"Great, I'm starving." Marshall stands, stretching his arms over his head. "What's for dinner?"

"You'll see. It smells delicious." He winks and turns away, leaving the door open. His footsteps fade down the hall.

I let out a squeak as Marshall's hand brushes against my waist. He holds me against him, putting on that *dreadful* persona of an English butler. "Shall I escort you to dinner?"

I reach for his hand. "You better shut up before I smack you over the head with one of your thickest hardbacks. You may."

39

COLD MORNINGS

MARSHALL

I escort Frieda down the hall. The events of the previous afternoon are stuck on replay inside my head. I have to swallow them down.

The taste of Earl Grey has never been so delectable.

I catch the idea by the tail, mentally cursing myself for thinking such impure thoughts. My shoulders ache at the memory of her fingers clutching them tight, massaging them, the pulsing of her passion zapping across my lips. A new sort of want warms my insides. I shrug it off as we enter the dining room.

Nathan admires the family photos on the wall (my grandmother and grandfather standing next to Alistair in his graduation gown framed right next to his wedding photos; a photoshoot of the three of us on chairs: Edith in a splendid—at the time—green gown, Alistair in a groom's tuxedo, and me in the dark groomsmen's uniform Alistair had me and a few of his friends wear as we stood by his side at the altar). It's the one photo I despise, as I don't look the slightest bit happy for such a joyous occasion.

Edith sits, smoothing her skirt. She beckons Nathan to sit next to her. He puts a hand up to stop her. "I'll sit if Cooper doesn't need help with setting out dinner."

"Such a gentleman, Nathan, why not?" Father beckons Nathan into the kitchen.

The smell of beef teases me as it wafts through the air. Edith watches as Nathan sets the bread rolls down in the center near the candelabras that are already lit and dripping with wax next to chilled bottles of rose lemonade, frost still on the glass.

Frieda heads into the kitchen to help with the salad, which consists of spinach, lettuce, feta cheese, carrots, and cucumbers and heads back for the other tray of roast potatoes, setting down sour cream with a spoon.

I marvel at her and pitch in by taking the roast beef out the oven and the bowl of peas. My father has also made a pot of chicken soup, still stirring it with his ladle.

"I hope you're hungry. I decided to treat you tonight," Father says as he adds a pinch of salt to the broth.

"You know already that we'll eat anything you make. It's that good," Edith says. She pours out the lemonade for everyone. "We haven't had real food for months, so be careful if you see one of us raiding the kitchen in the ungodly hours of the morning."

Father reaches to pat her on the shoulder and he finds his seat, winking at her, spooning broth into bowls for each of us. "I missed you and your quirkiness."

Father hands me some extra gravy he made especially for me to put over my roast. I scrape my knife over my plate, separating my food into different corners, cringing as everyone else mixes theirs together. Finishing my soup, Frieda's still eating hers, taking a break to drink the lemonade out of her glass. Nathan is hesitant, watching Edith as she tucks in, following behind with her unspoken reassurance. It almost makes me chuckle as I cut into my beef.

"So, Nathan," Father's voice breaks the silence, "where do you hail from?"

Nathan dabs at his mouth with a napkin before he tucks into his salad. "Lincoln."

"Nebraska? What're you doing in Pennsylvania? You're not back home?"

"My father was conscripted and my mother volunteered to work as a nurse overseas in France. I got correspondence telling me that I was able to come here and visit." He stabs a spinach leaf and a small block of feta with his fork. "They're both safe and sound, as far as I've heard."

Father reaches for his glass. "Next time you hear from either of them, send my regards."

Frieda's as quiet as a mouse while she eats, staring at the tablecloth.

"How is it?" I lean over to see she's finished the bowl quickly. There's almost not a single drop left behind besides some small amounts of residue.

"Brilliant," she answers, "how about yours?"

"Ditto. My belly is getting full for once." I reach for the bread rolls, handing her one with sesame seeds, spreading butter on mine, a whole grain one, asking Father, "Did you get these from Sally's?"

"I did." Father grins proudly. "She had a large bake sale, so I decided to purchase a few."

"Sally's a baker down the road," I tell Frieda as she tucks into the roast beef. "She makes amazing baked goods."

She lifts her fork, pierced through a piece of gravy-slicked beef as her only reply. Nathan starts on his peas after he finishes the soup entrée. He's quieter than Frieda while Edith beams by his side as she and Father discuss what's happened in the neighborhood while we've been away.

Taking a sip of rose lemonade, Frieda taps my shoulder. "Please tell your father that he makes amazing roasts."

"Why don't you tell him yourself?" I set my glass down. "You have the right to speak. There's no need to be nervous."

"What's this?" Father looks up when he's mentioned.

I nudge her. "Go on."

She stammers at first, Father grinning as he saws into his beef and potatoes. "I'm honestly glad you like my cooking. I pour all my heart and soul into it."

"I can tell," Frieda confirms. "I can taste it, even. Your cooking is just delectable."

"Nothing beats your cooking, Cooper. It's the best I've ever tasted," Nathan adds. "You'll have to teach me."

"A quarantine cooking class? I'm up for it." Edith claps her hands together, eyes sparkling. "I'd love to do it if you're in, Nathan!"

"I don't see why not." Nathan refills his glass and looks on eagerly. "Perhaps we'll learn something from the master?"

"You amuse me, young man." Father fans himself. "Me, the master? You have to be kidding! All I did was cook a big meal! Nothing special!"

"But it's the best *big meal*," I add. "Whoever tries to steal your thunder is going to get struck by your lightning in return for their crime."

"You kids, making my heart flush. I'm fainthearted. I might pass out from all your wonderful compliments. I'm truly flattered."

* * *

Dessert was wonderful, as expected. Father took his time to bake some apple crumble for us all to enjoy with cream in the living room. Frieda and I sit close together on the couch, compact, after we clean our plates and utensils, letting the food digest.

It's the fullest I've felt in months. The heaviness doesn't sit too agreeably in my stomach, which would've shrunk ten times smaller than its original size after being starved on dry rations, my bones cracking under my skin, my muscles eroding.

As the clock strikes nine, Frieda lets out a large yawn; a long, heavy yawn with an audible groan that escapes as she leans her cheek against the arm of the couch. The energy that bounced off the walls has died down as the night overtakes the day. Frieda's bound to pass out by ten.

"Everyone looks so tired." Father douses the fire and turns off the lamps. "I say we all go to bed, hm? You can sleep in as much as you want through tomorrow."

"But the night walk..." Frieda's eyes flicker to me. She struggles to keep them open. "You promised."

"We can go tomorrow night." I stand, kneeling before her. "I'll take you. I promised, and I don't break promises."

Frieda stands, yawning once more, leaning against me once we say goodnight to everyone, climbing up the stairs to the second floor of the house. "Say, why don't you come into bed, handsome? I'd let you slither in anytime."

"That sounds great, but I think I'll pass."

I keep walking, but she lets out a childish wail and stops in the middle of the hallway.

I wheel around to find her slumped forward at the waist, shoulders sagged. "Are you quite alright?"

"My legs...Everything hurts."

I roll my eyes, chuckling. "Come on, I'll carry you."

Her head nuzzles into my shoulder, arms taking their place around my neck. She closes her eyes while one of my arms goes to her waist, the other to the space behind her knees, holding her close. I nudge the door open with my foot, Frieda groaning as I turn the lights on.

"Too bright," she mumbles into my collar.

"I'll turn them off soon." I drop her on the bed gently, shaking my head, humored. She spreads her arms and legs out like a starfish, her heels sliding off her feet and plonking onto the floor. "Gosh, you look drunk."

"I'm tired." She sits up. "Do you think you could get my bag?"

Careful not to let the contents spill, I hand her the satchel that sits on the seat at the edge of the footboard. She rummages through it to pull out a nightgown, scowling at me. "Oi, pervert! Are you going to stay here and watch as I undress or what?"

"Oh—I'll be on my way." I cup her cheeks in my hands. "You'll be okay?"

"Mmhm," she replies. "I want to sleep forever."

"You can sleep as much as you want. If you need me, I'll be down the hall. Feel free to knock and come in at any time. It's not like I'll be half-dressed or doing something embarrassing." Frieda giggles dirtily, and I blabber on, embarrassed. "I would tell you if that were the case—that's beside the point. I think it's best you get ready for bed now. You look exhausted."

When I let go of her, her hands resume their grip on my shoulders and pull me back in for a hug. Her face buries itself into my neck, mumbling two simple words with an impossibly vast meaning. "Thank you, my love."

I don't even have to ask what she's thanking me for. I can feel it through the urgency of her arms, the soft whispering of the words.

My mouth curves into a smile. "Don't thank me, my dear. You already know that I'll always accept you with open arms."

I let the hug linger for a moment longer before I plant a soft kiss on her temple and back away. "Goodnight, Frieda. Sleep well."

"Goodnight," she replies with the beginning of a smile. "Sleep well."

I close the door with a soft *click* behind me, the hallway empty. Everyone else is in their rooms, getting ready for bed.

The quiet overwhelms me. I unpack my nightclothes back in my room, changing into them and turning off the lights, closing the curtains. A car blasts past the windows outside.

I peel back the dark comforter, Father's loud snoring booming from down the hall. It all feels so peculiar: the sounds, the sights, being back home. The room is too quiet for my liking, lacking the sounds of other men shuffling, talking in their sleep.

I open the window slightly and close the curtain before I slide back into bed, the weight and warmth of the blankets over my shoulders a comfort as I sink atop the mattress, my bones creaking. I adjust the pillows and occupy myself by staring at the wall until my eyes grow tired, fluttering shut in the peaceful silence.

* * *

"Marshall?" The voice is urgent, fingers poking my cheek, pestering me awake.

My eyes open to the sound, its quakes and quivers, and I find its owner in the darkness.

Frieda sits by my bedside, wrapped in a lace dressing gown with a cotton chemise that reaches her knees, arms folded across her waist to shield herself from the cold or the ties of the gown from coming undone. Her eyes and nose are puffy. Her teeth bite at her lips. The set of her shoulders remains tense.

"Frieda," I groan, letting out a yawn, turning on my side to face her, "what's the matter? Is something bothering you?"

There's a pause, then a small and anxious nod. "I can't sleep. I have, but I keep having bad dreams. I sound like a child, but I can't sleep alone. I can't be in there by myself with those dreams. Those *memories*."

"Do you want to talk about them?" I offer.

"I don't know." She twirls a loose lock of hair around her finger, voice strained with unease.

"Well," I shift back, making room, "there's always enough space here."

Hesitantly, she settles by my side, her eyes locking with mine. I reach to fix the blankets and fit them around her, tucking her in tight.

"What are you doing?" she asks, shaking against my touch.

"Making you comfortable." I lean on my elbow, rubbing my eyes, ridding them of sleep residue. "Now, say anything you want."

"I...I can't go back to sleep with the war happening over and over inside my head. It's painful. I can't do it. It's all so fast that I can't keep up."

"Is it the pace of the memories themselves or the contents?" I busy myself with picking at a piece of lint found on my duvet, ear cocked and listening intently to her worries and woes.

"There was so much blood. So much death and violence that I'd rather forget." She shakes a little harder, her limbs growing rigid, the bed shaking with her nervous tremors. "It's all coming back to me."

"I'm here." I reach to stroke her cheek with my knuckles. "You can stay the night with me."

Her expression goes from scared to lost, unsure of what to say.

"We've shared a bed before," I say, trying to be of comfort. "We can do it again."

"I can't sleep in there by myself." She moves closer, shaking against me. "I can't. I *can't*."

"That's why you have me. I'll defend you." I rub her back, kissing her between her brows. "I'll keep you safe. I'll be your knight in shining armor."

"Thank you," she mumbles, and nuzzles into the crook of my arm.

I hold her close by the waist. She lays her head against my chest, her ear over my heart.

Her tremors die down. The temperature under the blankets grows as our bodies melt into one. Her great green eye seeps into mine, terrified, in the darkness. She grips my shirtfront. "You won't leave me, will you?"

"No." I don't break her gaze, don't dare to look away for one second. "I left for too long—far too long. I'm not going anywhere." Her eyes struggle to keep open as she stares up at me, flickering with fear. "I'll stay right here until you wake up."

"Am I the only one getting nightmares, or are you, too?"

"I've been having strange dreams, but not nightmares." I shift closer, leaning my head closer to hers. "I'm not prone to bad dreams too often. Why don't you try going back to sleep?"

Frieda holds her gaze, her hands turning from fists to open palms, relaxing against my chest. "You promise you won't leave?"

I press a meaningful kiss to her freckled forehead, whispering tenderly, "I promise."

After a few flickering moments, she's slumped against my chest, safe and sound. I press a kiss on the top of her head, pulling the blankets atop the both of us to keep us warm and safe from the wicked world outside.

* * *

The cold sun creeps through the curtains, melting into the blanket of darkness shrouding the room.

I let out a groan and rub my eyes, the curtains blossoming from the wind pushing and pulling at them, having no mercy for if they fall or rip apart from their force. Frieda remains fast asleep. Her hair's come undone, down to the nape of her neck. She's turned away from me, one arm hugging a pillow. I can't help but watch as her chest rises and falls with each breath, expanding and relaxing. She's calm as the wind whistles against the windows.

Turning on my side, I roll closer, wrapping my arms around her delicately, leaning down to give her a small peck behind her ear.

"Marshall," she murmurs, groaning at my disturbance.

"That's me."

"What time is it?" Her eyes open halfway, blinking away the crust in the corners. She wraps a hand around my waist and burrows into my chest.

Squinting, I read the time off the clock on the wall. "After five."

"I don't want to get up just yet." She squirms deeper into the covers, a loud yawn escaping. "Not yet."

"Remember what Father said. Rest all you need," I murmur into her hair and press soft kisses behind her ear. "Any nightmares?"

"Not many, no. Very vague ones. You look like you slept well."

"I do?"

She turns onto her side and cups my face in her hands, her palms warm. "You do. You look more colorful than yesterday."

"I'll take that as a compliment," I answer.

Another pause. Her palms remain on my cheeks, face stretching into a grin.

495

And *oh, God*, she laughs.

"What're you laughing at?" I question, her chest convulsing wickedly.

"It's your hair!" she shrieks. "It's sticking up on one side."

I reach to smooth it down, indeed feeling the right side spiking under my hands, cursing. "I'm not a dashing prince in the mornings. I should've warned you."

"It just—it looks so..." She clutches her stomach, drawing her legs to her chest. Her laughs turn into breathless wheezes. "It has a mind of its own!"

"I know. Try battling it for twenty-one years. It's hated me all this time. Father told me that as soon as I was born, I had a full head of hair." I shake it out, cursing at it again and again. "Alright, is it better now?"

"Still looking like a rebel." She sits up, clutching her stomach. The sleeves of her nightgown have rolled up to her elbows to show the bruises and scars lining her wrists, the open neck of her chemise letting me view the small freckles and blemishes of her chest, still lined with cuts and knicks. Although she's covered in them, she's beautiful. "Was there ever a time where you could tame it?"

"You can't say much, looking like that." I tug lightly on one of her curls. She rolls her eyes as it springs back into place.

She pushes me onto my back, her eye sparkling with mischief. "Shut up."

"Are we flirting now?" I taunt her, speaking slowly. Her eye is now full of playfulness, to the brim with it, as she beams down at me. My head sinks back against the pillows. "I can do that."

"I—"

"I could do it all day." I reach for her cheek, pinching it playfully, her letting out an irritated groan. She pushes my hand to the side with a cheeky glare. "All, all day."

"You have been for the past year or so." Her hand reaches for mine, and I clutch it tight.

"You have to admit you like it." I gaze up at her, her knuckles grazing my lips as I bring them close. "You wouldn't change a thing. You'd do it all a thousand times over, even if my presence annoys you to the end of the earth, so much that you ultimately regret meeting me."

"You're kidding, right?" Her curls bounce as she adjusts herself and crosses her legs. I swear, those curls have as much liveliness as her. Maybe *my* hair reflects on how much of a mess I am. "How could I ever regret meeting you?"

Lost in thought, I fiddle with her fingers, making note of the small freckles that've somehow blossomed on her palms. It seems that every part of her is covered in sunspots; not a single patch left uncovered. "I was only joking."

I notice the question in her eyes, the way she looks at me when she suspects something. I take note of how her brows arch when she's concerned. She's stared me down with this very expression far too many times. She remains inquisitive, never letting me slide off the radar. She's too good to me, and yet, I still find myself incapable of accepting the fact that I deserve her.

So, I add, "I've had some people say they regretted meeting me. But that's beside the point. I was only kidding."

"I was going to say, who would regret meeting you?" She rests one bruised arm on her knee and snatches my hand in hers just as I pull it away. "Because I was also going to say I don't regret meeting you. Not for one second. So that's something, I guess."

"Oh, we *are* flirting!" I gasp, Frieda rolling her eyes when I poke her on the nose. "Thank you. Do you know what I believe?"

"What? What is it that the sharp-eyed Mr Clark The Third believes?"

"Honestly, it's a strange observation. We didn't come together just because we found each other attractive and decided we wanted to bed each other just like that. You've heard the term about how opposites attract, right?"

"You're saying you chose me because you saw me as fetching? I'm certainly *not* fetching in any fashion—"

"You are. It wasn't just that. You and I are two very different people. You," I point at her, "where would you most likely be found on a Friday night?"

"In my room, alone."

"And I'd be out somewhere, most likely for dinner or drinks. Hence, I'm more extroverted, you're more introverted. But that's all fine. Hot beverage of choice?"

"Tea."

"And I'd say coffee," I continue. "Also, you're more a listener than a talker—vice versa for me. See? We're opposites: sun and moon, day and night, North and South poles of a magnet, and *somehow,* we came together to attract at the center. That also applies to what we *want* from each other. I'm a raging storm of emotions in dire need of someone to tame me and be my center of gravity. I helped you climb out of your comfort zone, branch out and have more courage in yourself. We gave each other a little bit of ourselves...not to complete each other, but to help each other grow as people."

"Oh?" she ponders.

"No relationship is a solo project, and look at what we did: We came together. If you and I were the same, we'd be bored and wouldn't last a month. You think I'm out of my mind, don't you?"

"Woah," she breathes, letting out a chuckle. "Okay, smart guy, I see what strings you're pulling. I see it."

"You do? Oh, thank God."

"I see it all." She lays down beside me and shrugs. "We helped each other, didn't we?"

My heart swells. "Yes, *mi cielito*, we did."

I attach her focus to my lips. She bites her own, never failing to make me shiver in the uncanny heat of the moment; a fever that wrecks through my body with its cold sweat. My heart thuds as she moves closer, closing the space between us.

"How is it," she drags on her words, savoring the way they spill out, how they sound, "that you're so philosophical so early in the morning?"

"Should I shut up? I know it's a lot to take in," I fret.

The light creeps through the curtains, illuminating only half of her face. The other remains a shadow, a mystery. Her lips are upturned in a content, amused grin. One befitting for her, only her.

"Not at all," she replies. "That's one of the best things I like about you. You talk and talk, and honestly, I love people who *talk*. You could be explaining the most boring of topics and I'd still be interested with that voice of yours."

"Really? People get annoyed when I ramble."

"Those people don't know you, don't think of you as I do." She draws nearer, leering over me. I shiver in response. Her eyes are alight with admiration, pure love.

I let my smirk widen. My pulse quickens and roars in my ears. "Is that so?"

Frieda, after a moment, nods. "Very much so."

Inching closer, she pauses. She's waiting; waiting for me to give her the confirmation to grow even nearer.

"It's okay." I flash her a daring wink. My gaze doesn't break away. "I know. I look absolutely radiant in my nightclothes that you have to steal some more kisses from me."

Her laugh, rumbling inside her chest, is music to my ears as I press my lips against hers. Her eyes flutter closed at my touch. Before I can pull her in, she sinks into the pillows and pulls me by the shoulders down with her.

Cold hands are in my hair, teasing my locks, one straying to my clavicle, skidding against my skin. Her name escapes my lips through a gasp when one of my hands knots with hers.

Her curls are a spray of brown against the dark pillows, and I just can't stop myself from running my hand through them before it dips to her outer thigh, tracing the outline of her hips, her waist; sublime under my touch. Her breath hitches with each brush of skin, each exhale warming her neck when I attach my lips to the head of her mandible. A hand squeezes mine and her head tips back, allowing me to plant kisses beneath her jaw.

It's perfect. All too perfect as she sounds out my name in a breathless moan. I move to her collarbone, her other hand kneading into my shoulder. Her nails dully prick my skin.

"Frieda, my love, are you alright?"

Her fingernails trail down my back. A breathless 'uh-huh' is all the confirmation I need to carry on and guide my lips to the notch of her neck before I move to her chest, hovering just over the her sternum—

"*Marshall.*"

An unsteady twang obliterates the previous pleasure in her voice, causing me to halt all that I'm doing. Her jaw is clenched, body rigid beneath mine. The love in her eyes is replaced with fear and anxiety that widens them.

"What's the matter? Did I do something to startle you?" I search her face, removing my hand from her waist at once.

"P-please stop…" She whimpers, blinking rapidly to evade the possibility of spilled tears. "I'm…I'm scared…"

Guilt overrides the heat of my body in a pang as painful and quick as a whiplash.

To force her to do such a thing against her will is horrid. To force anyone to do something against their will is horrid. I could never push anyone that far.

Until she's ready, I'll wait. I'll give her all the time and space to consider it. I'll listen to every plea, every 'yes,' every 'no.' Every question she presents to me, I'll answer. Every issue, every verdict, every choice, I'll follow through.

Get off of her, the voice inside my head whines. I peel myself off of her.

"I'm sorry." I let her sit up and rearrange herself, wiping her eyes with a hurried hand. "I didn't mean to—"

"Don't. I should be the one saying sorry."

"What're you apologizing for, dearest?" I grab the throw blanket at the edge of the bed and drape it atop our shoulders.

"I don't know what was going through my head—I don't know what I was thinking." She rakes her hands through her hair, ripping off her patch, her steady breaths turning into gasps. Gasps turn into hyperventilations as she rambles on and on, rocking herself back and forth. "I don't know what I did. What did I do?"

When she knocks her knuckles against her wrist, I step in to help. I lean forward, trying desperately to get her to focus on me, "Frieda, let's talk it out, okay? Tell me what's wrong. I'm here for you. Right here."

I spread my arms for her, but she remains put, still mumbling to herself with big, fearful eyes.

"Frieda, please, look at me." I place a soft hand on hers, lowering my voice. "Do you want to get whatever it is you're feeling out first?"

She shakes her head, continuing to hammer her knuckles against the inside of her wrist.

"Frieda, it's okay, it's okay. I'm here. Breathe with me."

"I—I—" She takes in a large gasp, one that whistles through her lungs and through her teeth. "I'm sorry I led you on. I'm sorry I—"

"Hey, hey, hey, slow down. You did nothing of the sort. It's my fault for placing you in that position, for making you scared."

"N-no, it's all my fault."

"Love, nothing is your fault. Nothing that happened is your fault." I wipe a traveling tear away before she ducks against my touch. "It was all a misunderstanding, alright? It'll be okay."

"I shouldn't have done that."

"Everything's alright, Freddy." I reach for another pillow. "Let's get you comfortable—I'll put this under here—easy does it. There we go."

With two pillows under her head and the blanket on top of her body, I run my thumb over her knuckles. She quietens, sitting in silence, save for her whistling, wheezing breaths in and out.

I take to mumbling words of reassurance to her until she quietens. Once she's calmer, I speak. "Did I do something to scare you?"

She shakes her head, wipes her eyes. "No."

"Do you mind telling me what's bothering you?"

"I led you on," she breaks down further, "I ruined everything. I *don't know*. When I felt you on me, touching me, I wanted to run. You did nothing wrong, I promise. It's all on me. I'm just...not ready for that yet."

"You thought you were ready and had a change of mind. That's normal." I push her hair out of her face, wiping away the tears she missed. "There's nothing to be ashamed of. I'm honestly proud of you for saying something instead of keeping quiet and letting me continue to potentially hurt you. I see nothing wrong with choosing what's best for you."

"But why do I feel so guilty?"

"I don't know about that, but it's all okay. There's no need to feel that way."

Curling in on herself, she reaches out to me, our fingers brushing. "Wait for me."

"Don't worry." I draw her hand to my lips, pressing a chaste peck to her knuckles. "I'll be ready when you are. That's a promise."

"Thank you," she chokes out, reaching to kiss my chin.

"Please don't thank me for doing something that everyone should do: respect their partner's wishes and stop forcing things upon them. Common decency. But I respect your manners. You're welcome."

She's silent, her expression unreadable as I keep her close.

"Before you, I"—she pauses—"I had a thing with another man—this was years ago, by the way—when I was young and naive. His name was Henry...He was a...how do I describe him? A pompous ass with a collar stuffed with money? Yes, that sounds about right. He forced me into things I'd rather not talk about. He came into my mind and I just...I couldn't handle it."

"That's alright." I bring her closer to my chest, resting my cheek atop her head. "He won't hurt you anymore. I'll make sure of it. I'm so sorry you had to go through that."

"Save the apology. He deserves none of your mercy."

"Mercy for a man like him? Well, I never." I sniff. "My heart leaps for you and the fact that you had to suffer through such turmoil."

"It's all in the past. He and I will never cross paths ever again."

"I pray not. If you ever do, ring me and I'll shoot him. You know what? I somewhat understand your troubles."

"You do?"

Gravely, I nod. Here's the time to unhinge that loose floorboard. The first time I let the secret run loose. In times where she's showing vulnerability, I must shed some of my own. I pray that she'll hear me out.

"In my darkest times, upon the week of my fifteenth birthday, I met our good friend Edward. When he saved my life, I'd...he made me rethink who to love. I don't know what they call it—*bisexual*? I heard the terminology somewhere, I can't remember when. When he wed Alice, my heart ultimately shattered. I understand that heartbreak you felt for not being with the right person, having them use you, take advantage of you until they find something better. I'm past that stage, don't you worry. You're the best thing that's ever happened to me. I understand if...if you hate me for it, that part of me. You're free to go if you'd like."

The silence raises the alarms inside my head: to run, to hide in shame. But she raises her arms to loop them around my neck. She doesn't hiss, doesn't snarl out words of hatred. She smiles.

"I'm glad you told me, that you can be openly honest like I am to you." With eyes full of sorrowful determination, amorosity, she nods, as if to truly certify the truth of her words. "Regardless of who you are, regardless of who you decide to love, regardless of who you want to be, you'll still be my mysterious bookworm that won my heart with his magnificent self. You'll always be my Marshall, my special one. Don't ever think for a second that my words will ever change, because they're set in stone and will never be altered."

Choked, unsure of what to say, I press a kiss to her forehead, my eyes threatening to leak tears of gratitude.

"Thank you, Frieda," I mumble into her hair. "Thank you for accepting me."

"Don't thank me. I want to thank you for letting me be so honest, only to be honest in return."

"To lie to you would be my utmost sin. Why thank me for being truthful when I'd do it all again in a heartbeat?"

"I would, too. I really would."

"This is a lot to take in…" I mumble. "What usually helps me is to get some fresh air. What do you say to a walk together, hm? Maybe some fresh air will clear our minds? Or perhaps we'll go down to the study and read together?"

"A walk would be nice. Thanks, I guess, for respecting me."

"Again, no need to thank me. We'll take it one step at a time. I want to make you feel the best you possibly can."

"Me too." She sits up and meekly hugs me around the waist; a hug filled with a love that swallows me up. When she pulls away from my embrace, she asks, "Are we going now, or later?"

"If you'd like, the neighborhood in the mornings feels different...magical." When she gets up and out of bed, she tightens the strings of her dressing gown and wipes her eyes one last time. "I'll meet you at the door?"

"Sure," she replies before she opens the door into the dull and cold hallway. I stand to go after her, taking her hand before she leaves.

"I love you." I kiss her forehead. "Dress warm, it gets chilly out."

As the door closes, I swallow back a cry. Just the memory of her fearful whimper is sending me into madness and guilt for making her feel such a trivial emotion. The last thing I wanted to do was cause any harm to her, make her feel unsafe. It's the one thing I can't stop thinking about.

In anguish directed towards myself, I slam a fist against the door, setting off to get dressed and start the day.

This was just a setback, I repeat over and over in my head. *Everything is okay.*

I choose to dress in a gray vest with a blue silk bow around my collar. I pick lint off my trouser leg after I tie my oxfords tight, giving myself one last scan, making sure I've gelled my fringe down enough. I put on a dark trinity cap, grab my matching gray tweed ulster coat and hang it off my arm with brown leather gloves in my mouth.

With my gloves now on my hands, I reach for my key, mask, and a red woolen scarf, closing the door softly behind me. I make my way to the landing.

Frieda's in a black overcoat with a matching tweed skirt that reaches to her ankles. Around her neck is a bolo tie with a small jade pendant keeping the strings together and a dark cloche hat atop her head. Her hands are bare, her mask lying in them. Before opening the door, I write a note on the kitchen table to tell anyone who sees it where we've gone, tying my scarf around Frieda's neck.

"You'll get cold." I loop my mask over my ears. "Ready to go?"

"Yes. Please show me the river route you were talking about."

I smile behind my mask, her excitement that twinkles in her eyes mirroring mine. "Of course. I haven't forgotten. After you."

She steps onto the porch. I lock the door, breathing in the morning air, the sky a beautiful orange and pink as the sun continues its steady rise. I check the time on my pocket watch, seeing it's quarter to six.

"We could go into town. There's some shops nearby," I offer and slide my key and watch back inside my pocket, coming back with my arm for her to take. "If we have time, we can watch the sunrise."

Looping her arm through mine, we turn out into the street where a single car drives past, its engine droning in the quiet air.

"Is it usually this silent?" She surveys the empty road with a cock of the head, the houses with the lights still off and their residents still sleeping.

She's right. East Falls isn't generally this quiet in the mornings as men leave their homes and set off to work or stumble outside for a morning cigar.

"I know. It's weird, isn't it? It's much quieter than what it was back then." I direct her to the pathway leading to the river. She adjusts her scarf to sit closer to her neck. "It's chilly out. I was right."

Frieda tips her hat back and falls a little behind, either to take it all in or slowed by something else that's on her mind.

We venture to the river, which is a deep dark body of water early in the morning. The dull waters splash against the banks, and ducks perch themselves atop its surface like boats docked at a harbor. They paddle along: black with white bills, some others with their green feathers atop their heads and lining their wings. I'd be hunting them if I were out with my grandfather back in the day.

"Here's a fact for you." I point out to the river, the ducks quacking away. They dip their bills into the water. "Do you know the names of those ducks?"

Frieda arches a quizzical brow. "They're...ducks?"

"Not just *ducks*. They have names."

"What, like Gilbert? Jemima?"

"No, silly. Breeds." I bend down to her height and point to the ones with the black bills, who shimmy their tail feathers in the water when they stream past. "Those black ones are Coots. The green and brown ones are Mallards. Another fact: The ones with the green feathers on their heads are males, the brown are females."

"You know too much about ducks." She rolls her eyes and watches the ducks bob underwater, quickly chewing up whatever critter they've found.

"It's from hunting. From something I'll never do again." I pat her arm. "Hey, that was a pretty good idea, giving them names."

"Fine," she points to one of the Mallards, "that one's called Gary."

"Gary? How generic." I snort. "Okay, the one next to Gary is Yolanda."

"That has a Southern flair to it." She cracks a grin that's visible behind her mask. "But what if they already have names? Are we insulting them?"

"Try saying that to a Canadian goose. They're aggressive." I jump as one lands on the water with such an uncanny display of grace for a hostile bird. "When I was a kid, I was enough to try to feed one some bread on a hunting trip. I got too close. It saw me as a threat and chased after me for miles on end. It was hissing nonstop and pecking at my soles."

"You, being chased by a *goose*?" She struggles to hold in her laughter, her chest convulsing with a hidden glee that's all too visible to me. "That's a first. When is there ever a time you don't get yourself into trouble, hm?"

"Rarely." I scoff at the geese honking at the ducks paddling away. "I mean, look at them: menacing bastards. They'd bite your head off if they ever got the chance."

"You're not scared of them, are you?"

"Not anymore, but geese are just despicable."

"Reminds me of my aversion to cats." She sits on the bench by the banks.

"You don't like cats?" I gather some rocks lying in the dirt, collecting them in my palms.

"I never liked them. No matter how hard you try to like something, you just don't like it."

"Me, but with beer." I flex a rock in my hand, gripping it in my gloved fingers.

"Exactly. They're...how do I put it nicely...not my type of pet. Especially the ones with the scrunched up faces. Don't get me started on the hairless ones. They look like naked mole rats."

I skid the rock over the surface of the river. Droplets of water spray out of its path as it sails away. The sun glints in my eyes. I shield them under my hat's brim. "Either way, dogs are *evidently* better." I grab for another rock, aiming. A gust of wind blows. "The bigger the pooch, the better."

"I'd much rather have a slobbery friend who's happy to see me regardless of the situation than one that hates me and just wants food." She stands and holds her skirt down as another wind blows.

Once I throw all my rocks into the river, I check my watch, nodding at the time.

"It's quarter to seven. We should head back." I hold out my hand. A man walking his dogs comes by, giving us a scrutinizing look. "Shall we?"

"We may." Her bare fingers knot with mine, and we make our way back, the neighborhood becoming busier by the minute as the hours of the day increase.

"So, did you enjoy the walk?"

She has a skip in her step, replying with a cheerful and loud 'mhm!'

"Do you feel a little better?" I ask, her eyes dulling at the memory of earlier.

"Yes, actually, it worked."

"Good."

When we open the door, Nathan and Edith scamper downstairs in a laughing heap. Nathan shushes her, still in his dressing gown and bedclothes, Edith shushing him back in full dress.

"Good morning, family," I call in a singsong tone, pulling off my mask. "What on Earth is going on?"

"Good morning, sergeant, sir!" Nathan's posture snaps to become straight, saluting to me. He's in an eagerly good mood this morning. "Corporal, ma'am! I was going to teach Edith how to make scrambled eggs!"

"Scrambled eggs? Sounds brilliant." I slide my gloves off, scanning his attire. "You're cooking in...a dressing gown?"

"Wha—Ah! No! I was going to the laundry to grab my clothes for today and then make breakfast. I had to put some in the wash because they had stains on them."

"I'll make the coffee, if you'd like. I have to get some studying done, and perhaps I'll run to the market to get some necessities later this afternoon. Frieda, *cariño*, some tea?"

She flushes, sliding her hands across my shoulders with a tease. "English Breakfast, please. Make it strong, *mi amor*." She especially rolls her *r*'s, sending me reeling, my face scrunching up.

"Your accent is terrible." I lean in, winking. "'Make it strong,' I gotcha."

I slide off my coat, kiss the tip of her nose and squeeze her hands. Edith squeals as Nathan hugs her around the waist. With a kiss to her temple, he sets off to his room with his newly-laundered clothes tucked under his arm.

"Look at you," I tease her. "You've fallen desperately in love."

"Speak for yourself," Edith scoffs.

"I'm glad to see you happy after so much happening." I pat her shoulder and take off into the kitchen. "How does Mr Nelson like his coffee?"

"Black," she answers.

"Aw, you're so in love that you know how your man likes his coffee? That's so sweet!" I tease.

The tips of her ears turn red. "Just you wait until I—"

"Calm yourself!" I break into a hearty laugh. Edith grabs my collar, her blue eyes blazing. "I'm jesting! No need to get all protective!"

"You're horrible," her hands loosen on me, "out of control with your witty teases."

"I know. That's what everyone tells me." I pat her shoulder. "I'm just jerking your leg."

40

Clutching Tight to the Same String

Frieda

The first thing Marshall does before he gets the coffee out is whip his coat off his shoulders. Folding it over one of the wooden kitchen chairs, his hat perched atop its head, his hands then go to his cuffs, unbuttoning and pushing them back to his elbows, fixing his hair in a slow fashion where every action is equally measured to be taken in; obviously to rile me up, some sort of queer mating dance performed by the Clark family's eccentric middle child.

I have to roll my eyes at his effort, Edith scoffing at her brother as he fills the kettle with water and flicks the stove on at a low flame with a lopsided grin. He lines the mugs up on the counter, and Nathan steps into the kitchen in a cream waistcoat, his copper hair slicked back with gel. Edith whistles at the sight of him.

The phone near a tub full of spices and the salt and pepper shakers rings out.

"Frieda, darling, would you get the phone?" Marshall rummages through the pantry to find coffee beans and tea tisanes in tins, taking a whiff of the coffee beans, giving them a decided nod.

I do my best to get to the phone as soon as I can. Raising the receiver to my ear, I answer, "Hello?"

"Miss Frieda, is that you?" Marge Mason's sweet-as-honey voice booms straight in my ear as she speaks on her end of the line.

"Yes, yes. Good morning, Mrs Mason. I hope your morning's swell." I mirror her cheery tone and I turn my head to glare at Marshall, who yet again struts around the kitchen bench to place infusers into the mugs, smirking, eyes on me. I scrunch up my nose teasingly. He returns to the stove.

"Splendid. Now, I wanted to ask you if you and Marshall were willing to go for the walk we promised each other yesterday. The children haven't stopped pleading with me to follow up and ask if you wanted to go. We might go into town—we'll see where the path leads us."

"We'd love to! Thank you for the invitation! He's just here—I'll be a moment."

Lowering the phone, I whistle for Marshall's attention, his head whipping up as he gathers measuring cups for Nathan. "Who is it? Is it for me?"

"Partially. It's Mrs Mason. She's inviting us out for a walk today."

"Tell her that her invitation is accepted!" he exclaims, standing beside Nathan, who reads through a cookbook with Edith peering over his shoulder.

I raise the phone back up again. "We would love to. What time were you settling for?"

"Would twelve or twelve-thirty be fine for you? I have to go into town and do some shopping before the market closes, so it would be most convenient."

"Marshall, twelve-thirty?" I ask him again.

"Sure!" he calls. The kettle whistles. He races over to turn the stove off.

"Twelve-thirty would be brilliant," I reply.

"Amazing, we'll be waiting on your doorstep. See you then."

Hanging up, Marshall grabs hold of the kettle, letting out a gasp of pain, setting it back down on the stove hurriedly, drawing himself back.

"Are you okay?" Edith asks over her mixing bowl.

"Burned myself," he grumbles and sets his hand under the faucet, the knob turned to a mild cold. "Should've waited for it to cool down."

"Here, you sit, I'll do it," Nathan offers. "Where did you burn yourself?"

"My entire hand!" he cries. "My entire metacarpal—"

"No need to get so anatomical. Do you mean your knuckles?"

"Yes!" He bites back a sob.

"Keep it under for now," Nathan instructs, turning to Edith. "Once the kettle's cooled enough, we'll pour out the drinks."

I stroll over to Marshall, who leans against the sink with his hand lax under the streaming water. "How's it hanging?"

"Horribly." He gestures to his burn; red and inflamed. "It hurts. I was foolish enough to grab the kettle while it was still hot."

"It's fine. Just a mistake." I reach to massage his shoulders to get him to relax. "Keep it under for a little longer."

Nathan scolds Edith for swatting at him with a spatula when he offers to help her pour the egg mix into a pan on the stove. Marshall ducks his head on the edge of the sink, closing his eyes as his fingers prune. I turn the tap off and dry his hand, his knuckles already swelling. Another scar to overlay his older ones.

"Does it feel a little bit better?" I dab lightly at his hand with a towel. Nathan reaches to pour the water into the mugs, Marshall slumping against the counter. His frown fixes itself into a grin as he takes the towel from me.

"How much of a fool am I?" He folds it and puts it back on the oven rack, examining his hand.

"It happens," I reply. He folds his arms and watches Nathan guiding Edith while she stirs the eggs before he sets the mugs out. Marshall takes his gingerly in his unburnt hand, cursing the coffee, drinking it.

There's a clamber of feet on the stairs. Cooper descends in his pajamas and dressing robe.

"Good morning, children!" His voice is cheerful. It echoes through the kitchen. "All hustle and bustle this early in the morning? I expected you to still be fast asleep and overridden from your journey."

"Frieda and I went for a walk." Marshall kisses his father on the cheek and takes a long sip of coffee. "We'd be awake and alert right now if we were still in Europe."

"The war *did* want you to wake at ungodly hours of the morning, I'll give you that. Set your internal clocks to...let's say...wake up at eight-thirty and to go to bed at ten? That's a good ten hours or so for you to get back into shape."

"You know me. I don't sleep," Marshall argues.

"I'll make sure you do." I raise my tea to my lips. "Good tea, by the way."

The first few eggs are loaded onto plates; perfectly cooked. Cooper watches Edith and Nathan work at the stove.

"Edith made this?" he whispers to Marshall.

"With Nathan's help, yes." He glances back at his hand, the burn deepening further and further into an angry red. He winces at the sight as more eggs are loaded. Edith and Nathan clean the dishes. Cooper sets off to get ready.

By the time breakfast is over, Marshall bandages his hand, faded to an ugly dark pink, in a thin layer of gauze wrapped individually over four of his fingers, his thumb left untouched. The coffee table of the living room becomes covered in gauze rolls, tape, scissors, and a bottle of disinfectant. He gazes down at his handiwork and nods, satisfied.

"Now how's your hand?" I observe the bandages.

"It hurts like hell, but I'll get through it." He closes the door of the medical cabinet and flexes his fingers. "Another scar to add to my collection. If it's along my fingers, is it a scar, or scars?"

"I'd say a scar, just on different parts of your hand making it up."

"So, like a collage?" he retorts. "I'm a canvas; an art piece of scars."

"I wouldn't mind that."

He inclines his head, listening. "Huh?"

I sandwich his hand between mine, offering a smile. "I don't mind that you have scars, I really don't. They're just another blemish, like freckles or birthmarks. They tell a story only you can tell. Everyone has them."

"I can tell people I burned my hand on a steaming hot kettle while making hot drinks. It would be a bestseller."

As I break control of my laughter, Cooper rounds the corner.

"Marshall! I'm glad I found you. I have a list of things you need to buy if you go out today—just a small list—few necessities, nothing too grand."

Marshall takes the slip of folded paper in his other hand and turns back to me. "Remember to tell me to bring my wallet before we go."

"Noted."

He opens the piece of paper, scanning the list: milk, soap, flour, bread (multigrain specifically), detergent, and cooking oil. He pockets the list and shuffles past me as the doorbell rings. Clearing his throat, he opens it for the masked postman who dips his cap and hands him a stack of envelopes and a parcel. He files through the envelopes, mumbling 'bills' and 'taxes,' stopping to pull out three, putting the others in the letter basket. He yelps for Nathan to say he's got mail, which Nathan rushes up the stairs with, envelope in hand, Marshall staring down at one, handing me the other.

"What's this?" I peer at the envelope.

"You've also got mail." His brow inclines as he opens his, reading its contents. "Oh...no."

"What's wrong?" I peek over his shoulder.

"It's a revision list; a mighty long one." He curses in Spanish. I open my letter, reading my uncle's handwriting. "What does yours say?"

"Just my uncle checking in and saying he has a room at home if I ever need to come back."

I pocket the letter. Marshall files his back into its envelope. With a grimace, his lips purse. He pulls out his pocket watch, scratched, but still in one piece and ticking. The lid opens to reveal the clock face beneath it.

"Say, time flies." He carefully puts it back inside his pocket. "Ten to twelve."

He reaches for his thick ulster coat that he's placed on a hook by the door and slides it over his shoulders, buttoning it so it sits tight and snug around his frame. He dives into his pockets for his gloves.

"Would you like your scarf back?" I begin to unwind his thick scarf while he reaches for his hat.

"You keep it." He sets the hat over his brow. "It looks better on you, anyways. Here," in record time, he ties two knots through the scarf and pats down my coat, "this way is warmer. I don't want you getting cold."

"What about you?"

"I'm a man of steel." He flexes an arm, slapping his bicep. "I've survived mountains upon mountains of snow, hilly hikes, a virus, and a war. I'm invincible."

"With pneumonia, sure." I pat his arm. "It's best that you layer up, soldier."

"But I have. Look: I have gloves, a hat—"

"Not enough. You need a scarf."

"I'll be fine, I promise," he assures me. "I promise."

"You're not leaving until you put a scarf on. Let's not risk getting sick in times like these."

He takes my hand, laying his other atop it, kissing my knuckles. His lips flutter against them as the leather of his gloves sandwiches my hands, his eyes glittering.

"Where would I be without you to take care of me?" He squeezes my hand and starts up the stairs. "You win. I'll get a scarf."

"And your wallet."

"And my wallet." He titters and races upstairs, skipping steps and opening the door to his room. Almost tripping as he races downstairs, he slips a few notes into his wallet's pockets. He digs for his keys and his mask. I fix my own as the doorbell rings.

Before answering the door, he turns back to me with a confident simper, visible on the imprint that it draws on his mask. "Ready to go, *mi amor*?"

I take his side as he presses down on the handle, swinging the door open to show Mrs Mason with her two children beaming. They welcome us with all the excitement and energy of a dog welcoming its master back home. It takes a lot to not lose myself and melt at the sight of Eleanor and Thomas jumping up at Marshall as he greets them. Mrs Mason chortles and puts her hands on their shoulders to calm them, her pregnant belly sticking out beneath her thick coat.

"Mrs Mason, a pleasure to see you again!" Marshall gives her a small wave. I grip his arm, hiding behind his back, leaning on him. My heart fastens inside my chest. The dizziness returns.

Marshall ducks his head and speaks softly. "Is everything okay?"

My voice comes out shaky, strained. "A bit nervous, really."

"It'll be fine." He fixes my scarf and raises my chin in his hand. "You have me, and Marge is a wonderful woman. Deep breaths, my dear."

He closes the door. I reach back for his hand, catching him off guard.

When I flinch away, he reaches for mine and clutches it tight. "Come, we'll be fine. Again, deep breaths. Steady yourself."

"Marshall! Marshall!" Eleanor skips next to Marshall, who beams down at her as she pulls on the tail of his coat. "Thomas got the boat to float in the bathtub!"

"Did he?" Marshall listens. "Did it stay afloat?"

"I did! It did!" Thomas joins his sister at her side. "The glue worked."

"Good going, Skipper." Marshall ruffles the boy's pale locks, making him burst with childish glee.

Mrs Mason takes Eleanor's hand. "I hope they aren't bothering you two too much. They were up at the crack of dawn bursting with anticipation."

"Oh, to stay a child forever," Marshall sighs, a distant gleam in his eye.

"No matter how old we grow, the child in our heart never ages." She watches Thomas chase his sister, already miles ahead. "Frieda, was it? I forgot to ask, where are you from?"

Marshall steps back for Mrs Mason to get a clear view of me. My whole body stiffens. He squeezes my hand encouragingly, my mouth only able to muster one word. "Seattle."

"Gosh, all the way up in Washington? You're a long way away from home, aren't you?"

I shrink back, the lump in my throat growing. "I guess so. It never really occurred to me."

"She's a bit shy," Marshall adds.

"No worries, sweetheart." Mrs Mason's eyes crinkle with a warm smile. "I'm shy myself. I don't bite, don't you worry."

Marshall's eyes flicker from me to the children as Mrs Mason talks about her husband coming home and the telegraph he sent her the night before. I keep a tight hold of Marshall's hand. We follow the same trail Marshall and I did this morning, the pathway and its dense undergrowth in full view under the shining sun. The ducks are on the other side of the river, more of them than before, quacking away, hunting for their breakfast. The geese have long since vanished.

"So," Mrs Mason looks over at Marshall as Eleanor throws stones into the deep waters, "how did you two meet?"

"Buckle up." Marshall squares his shoulders against a cold breeze that wafts past. "I was walking around one of the towns in Belgium, then all of a sudden, this beautiful partner of mine comes up to me—"

"You weren't walking. You were reading while walking," I correct him.

He snorts. "Yes, sorry, I was. Anyway, we were in the same regiment and bonded from there. If I were to tell the full story, you'd be here longer than you'd like."

"My, it sounds like something out of a romance novel," she says. "By coincidence, you two were in the same space at the same time, and look where you are now."

"I never would've imagined it," I mutter, ducking my head.

Marshall fiddles with his lapels sheepishly. "What about your husband, Mrs Mason? He was in the war, too?"

"Yes, he was, since May of 1917, near Verdun. He's fine; unscathed, a little shell shocked, but he's coming home. All will be well."

"I'm glad for you, I truly am—for the both of you, of course." Marshall gazes at her. She replies in kind with, somehow, a smile that contains a maternal aura, and ruffles his hair.

As we stroll past the river, Marshall's head remains high, and my grip of his hand slackens. He's humming another soft tune that buzzes through my ears as the birds tweet in the trees. A heron flies over us, exposing its great wings against the cloudy gray sky. It's a mesmerizing sight to see such a majestic bird soaring up above.

"Look, Marshall, a heron." I point. Marshall shields his eyes against the sun as the water bird flies away and dissolves into a silhouette.

Once the bird is out of sight, his soles crunch against gravel. He halts and bends to inspect a nearby flower bush, picks one of the beautiful purple things by its stem, and fixes it behind my ear.

"What's this?" I gasp.

"This, my dear, is a morning glory," he explains. We're catching up to the Mason trio who amble on ahead. "You'll see them everywhere, but they look better on you."

"You, sir, are a massive flirt." I roll my eyes to the sky and beyond.

We stop at a road, waiting to cross. Workers yelp and snarl at each other while they fix a hole in the tar of the street. The policeman blows his whistle, and we do everything in our power to keep our distance from others around us. Leaning hard on Marshall's shoulder, my head low, I dare myself to look ahead rather than at my feet. He sets an arm around my waist, my arm circling his shoulders, dodging a pothole as we step over the curb and back on the pale sidewalk.

Even in the middle of a history-making pandemic, the city is full of life, full of sound, and crowds. His eyes sweep the buildings towering over us, seeming to cave in on the Philadelphian population with their brilliantly high structures. The high rises loom in the weak morning light, and Marshall's listing each one, admiring the new ones being built, the sun glinting off of their large glass windows. The businessmen held inside these buildings which somehow, to me, resemble cells, must feel powerful, overlooking the city at such a height. I almost grow envious of them, taking drags from a cigar by the window, watching life pass by.

Mrs Mason grips both her children's hands and slows to keep beside us. "I was thinking: There's a bagel place we could all dine at nearby. The last time I was there, they spaced out all the tables. Perhaps we can get two tables?"

"If they're open, and if it's alright with Freddy." His eyes find mine from under the brim of his hat; the color of dark roasted coffee in the early morning. They're sparkling with delight, livelihood. "If they don't have a certain item she'd like to savor on this fine day."

A laugh fights to escape my chest, and I have to swallow it down. His chivalry and affection are going straight to my brain like strong alcohol, making me giddy.

"It sounds lovely, Mrs Mason." I elbow Marshall, who holds down his hat against the wind that threatens to blow it away. "If the tables are all distanced, I don't see much risk in going."

"Brilliant! We'll head on over now." She jostles her children, Eleanor skipping over the cracks in the sidewalk, Thomas sticking by Marshall's side.

"Hello, Thomas! Enjoying your walk?" Marshall cranes his neck to peer at him.

"I love the fresh air." Thomas hums a tune identical to Marshall's. "It's better with you back home, with Frieda, too!"

"I'm glad, Skipper." He reaches to ruffle his hair under his newspaper boy cap.

"They don't talk much, do they?" Thomas inquires, peering up at Marshall with his boyish, blue eyes. He remains inquisitive, as a child should be.

Marshall stiffens at the question, eyes flitting between him and I.

"None taken," I mutter.

"People don't have to talk all the time, Tom." Marshall leans against me as we turn up a tight corner. "As I've said, they're shy. Give them time to open up. Why don't you get to know them?"

Thomas's eyes flick to me with an intrigued smile merging with his curiosity. "They *are* very pretty."

Shyly, I tuck a lock of hair behind my ear.

"They are. I agree with you one hundred percent." Marshall pulls me closer. "They're my pretty flower."

"Thank you, both of you." I pat the top of Thomas's head affectionately. My cheeks start to redden. "I'm deeply flattered."

"Here we are!" Mrs Mason stops in front of the bagel house, her hand hovering over the door handle, turning to me to explain, "I took Marshall and the kids here quite a lot when he was a boy." She turns to Marshall. "I'm sure Esmerelda remembers you, since you were pretty much the only one ordering all the poppy seed bagels."

"Esmerelda? Of course! I hope she does!" His posture straightens, hands clenching and unclenching, eyes glimmering brighter.

"Esmerelda?" I ask.

"The woman who owns this bagel house. Her bagels are godlike. She's another one of my mother's friends—they came to America together." He steps forward to clutch the handle with a gloved hand. "Should I go in and keep my face concealed like a mystery man or announce myself upon entry?"

Mrs Mason shrugs indifferently. "Do what you wish."

"In that case," he opens the door and lowers himself into a sweeping bow, "everyone, after you."

"Such a gentleman," I tease. He closes the door behind us, trapping the warm air inside.

With that warm air comes the wafting scent of freshly baked bagels, dough, and other baked goods. The cafe has a faded design with chairs of beech wood and matching tables, napkins and salt and pepper shakers atop their tabletops. Degas paintings line the walls in gold frames; little ballerinas highlighting little memories of my past: the lights of the stage, pointe shoes on my feet, the feeling of flying, light as a feather.

As the radio plays live music in the corner, Marshall pulls out a chair for me to sit. A waitress hands us a slip of paper to write our details—in case we come into contact with an infected person, she says—and Marshall gets into the habit of furiously washing his hands with the provided sanitizer.

"Got to stay clean," he talks to himself, eyes squinting at his palms. His burns have started to scab over in dull pink lines across the inside of his hands.

"Marshall," I lean forward, snapping him out of his hypochondriac state, "I think that's enough rubbing."

He lays his hands, spread open, atop his gloves, on the table. "I just...We're in a public space. How many people would've sat here? I don't want to get sick again. I don't want to get others sick again. I don't want to get sick at all."

"I'm sure you won't. They clean the tables afterward. They clean everything here. Breathe with me, Marshall."

"Frieda." His voice strains itself. A flicker of wild fear appears. A worried notch forms between his brows. "We're one of the worst cities in the United States to have been hit with this virus after the parade back in September. I wouldn't forgive myself if I got Eleanor, Thomas...those poor children—"

"You won't, I promise you. You've followed every precaution. Even if you got sick, you still looked after yourself. You continue to now, in the eye of the storm. It'll be okay. We'll be okay."

"I don't want to get them—" Pain surges behind his irises, his jaws gritting and gnashing.

"I understand that, I do." I reach to take his hands, but he backs away.

"Please, don't touch me."

"Alright, I won't." I pull my hands away, folding them in my lap. His retreat into fists, shaking. "Is there anything I can do to relieve some anxiety?"

He remains silent. I push forward with another subject.

"Tell me about what you're studying right now. What do you get to do at college?"

"Anatomy, biology, chemistry." His reply is curt.

"I understand what you'd be doing in bio and chem, but what about anatomy?"

"Dissections." His knee jogs beneath the table, knocking once or twice against its underside, a grunt of pain catching in his throat.

I choose to ignore it. "Of what? Like frogs back in high school? Rats?"

"Cadavers," his hands loosen themselves, "people who've donated their bodies to science."

"Woah." Truthfully, I'm astounded. "On actual dead people? I don't think I'd be able to handle that."

His only reply is to shrug, his posture relaxes, but the panic in his eyes still remains. He's building himself back together, slowly, as his fear subsides. "It's nothing special."

"But...how do you handle the smell?"

"I'm sure they clean them or something. There'd be a lot of chemicals in the works."

"No embalming?"

"I'm not sure about that, but I heard cutting them open, post mortem style, like in the movies, is just as fun as it looks."

"You sound like a murderer. The imagery!" I shiver. The waitress comes back around to take our orders, moving swiftly to Mrs Mason's table afterward.

Under the sunlight shining through the windows, Marshall's face is pale, still calming from his panic, his voice shaking and quivering as he chats with Thomas about his boat, sinking back into his regular, cheery persona.

Eleanor leans over in her seat to me, her eyes wide and questioning.

"Ms Frieda?" Her chair moans against the floor when she scratches it forward. I ready myself for her questions. "I hope I don't make you sad, but why do you wear that on your eye?"

"No, you didn't make me sad." I shift to face her. "I get a lot of people asking about it. When I was fighting in the war, some bad people threw poisonous gas at us, and the gas got into my eye. They had to remove it. Don't you worry, I can still see just fine. I've still got one left."

"You're still very pretty." Eleanor confidently flashes me a toothy smile. "Especially with your freckles."

"Thank you, Eleanor, really." I bow my head.

A shriek rises from the waitress serving us our drinks. Her dark flurry of curly hair is tied in a loose braid that trails down her back. She wears a long, dark skirt and a white blouse, all under a bright apron. She has brown skin and smile lines in the corners of her eyes.

"Marshall?" Her heavy accent rings in my ears. She takes in a gasp of shock.

"Esmerelda." Marshall waves to the waitress from our table, still shaken up from his earlier panic, quietly asking, "*¿Cómo estás?*"

"*Mi hijo!*" She sets his tea down in front of him with a boisterous grin, speaking in hurried Spanish. He nods along as she gushes all over him, holding her serving tray against her aproned chest to contain her excitement, and jumps up and down in her low-heeled shoes.

There are few words I understand. Judging by the conversation, she's asking him when he got home, asking loads and loads of questions, Marshall replying with ease. Esmerelda's middle-aged face glues on its smile.

She then points to me, Marshall's smile twitching ever so slightly. He listens with concentration, giving her an amused huff of laughter. '*Novia*,' he says, with his chest puffed out proudly, matched with '*cariño mio.*'

She squeals and claps her hands together, nearly dropping her tray, congratulating him.

He turns to me. "I'm sorry you didn't understand. English isn't Esmerelda's first language, but we're saying all good things." He reaches for his teacup with a proud look on his face. Mrs Mason and her children are grinning up at Esmerelda as her chatter continues. She tries her very best to battle the struggle of the English language, the Masons understanding her just fine. Their laughter echoes around the shop.

Marshall leans forward, eyes still twinkling. "This is where they sell real Spanish food. My mother lived in Spain for a while and showed her love for the country in her cooking."

"Can I ask what the *migas* are—is that how you say it?"

"That, my dear, is tortilla strips with scrambled egg and tomato."

"Interesting, but I'm not a huge fan of tomatoes."

"You could always get it without them, but I won't force you."

"I might get one of the bagels." I read the bagel menu and catch him staring at me over his own menu. "What?"

"Oh, nothing," he says. "Just observing the prettiest person in the world."

I roll my eyes at him. He releases a satisfied laugh and surveys Thomas, who's folded his napkin into a boat and is proudly showing Esmerelda his creation, who claps when he produces it to her with a squealed 'ta-da.'

Another couple enters the cafe and sits beside us, scoffing. Marshall's eyes narrow to produce a glare as sharp as a knife—a glare I wouldn't be caught dead under—before he goes back to Thomas's never-changing, wide smile as Esmerelda grabs their orders. Mrs Mason kindly points to the items for more clarity, thanking her in both English and Spanish before she returns to our table, unbothered by the audible scoffing of the couple next to us.

The woman sits with her hair high and pulled back tight. She's clothed in an expensive dark gown that hangs off of her shoulders with a faux fur shawl pulled over it. Her partner looks equally as uptight, his hair practically glued to his scalp. He sneers under his mustache.

Thomas hands Marshall his boat, explaining and loading him with information on how he learned to fold and build it. Marshall is forever gracious and patient, mirroring a Golden Retriever, with their smiling faces and large, loving eyes.

When I look over, the couple point and hiss at me, and I attempt to mimic Marshall's glare. I jut my jaw high; just like my father did to intimidate those around him when they tried to get under his skin.

No one, and I mean *no one,* will successfully attempt to discriminate against these people and their wondrous customs, their spectacular differences that make them themselves. Regardless of who they are, where they come from, what color their skin may be, all people are equal.

Marshall, Esmeralda, Alistair, Edith, Alexandria, Fey, among many more. These people hail from so many diverse backgrounds, so many brilliant cultures that they aren't afraid to embrace.

Whatever traditions a person follows, whatever past a person holds, whatever identity they chose to hold, all people are equal.And I'll stand by to death and beyond.

Esmerelda comes around a second time to take our orders. I resort to copying Mrs Mason and point to the items, Esmerelda hurriedly writing it down with little to no difficulty. I give her a cheery smile before

Marshall orders his lunch entirely in Spanish, Esmerelda taking both of our menus. Thomas continues to explain about the boats he saw in the harbor during Christmastime.

Eleanor creeps over to me again, and I prepare myself for another conversation. "Mama tells me you're from the West, near California."

"Indeed, I am." I take up my tea and sip it calmly. "But not right next to California. There's Oregon, Idaho, Nevada—"

"I know. My daddy's a geographer," she interrupts proudly. "He goes all over the world and everything. He's been all over America."

"Has he?"

"Yeah, but that doesn't matter." She watches me drink my tea. "Is Cousin Marshall telling the truth about when he met you? That he was walking and reading?"

"Somewhat. More like...reading while walking, bumping into me and falling to the ground."

"Silly Cousin Marshall." She giggles. "He's very clumsy."

"Oh, he is. I hate to admit it."

"I always told him to get a partner whenever he saw someone he liked, but he either said no and smiled like the goof he is or got all hot and bothered."

I wink. "Even with almost a whole friendship group made up of men, I still don't understand their ways."

Marshall peers over at us and says merrily, "Eleanor, fancy seeing you here."

"I was talking with Ms Frieda about how shy you are with crushes," she teases.

"Why, you little—" he hisses, jumping in his seat. She scampers back to her own, laughing away. He hides his embarrassed face behind his mug. Mrs Mason rubs her belly and watches, amused.

When the food comes, I peer at Marshall's plate over my sesame bagel, decked with cream cheese and salmon.

"What did you get again?" I cock my head questioningly. He grabs a knife and fork, cleaning them compulsively with a napkin before he places it on his lap, digging in.

"*Albondigas.*" He slices one of the many balls of what seems to be made of meat. "Spanish meatballs."

"Looks interesting." I reach for my bagel, which has been cut in half, taking a bite as he pokes his fork through one of his meatballs.

"They're good, too. I would give you one, but you said you didn't like tomatoes." He pops the slice in his mouth, nodding in satisfaction. "My mother made these all the time. I hate to admit it, Mother, but Esmerelda's are way, way better."

After swallowing my first bite of bagel, I ask, "How did your mother and Esmerelda meet, exactly?"

"Esmerelda's originally from Cuba and traveled with her family to Puerto Rico for better living. They went to school together, and once they graduated, they fought with every tooth and nail to go to college here in Philadelphia."

"Did they get in?"

"Unfortunately, no. They didn't, which I hope they're regretting, because my mother was a genius. They were housemates until Esmerelda met her other half, Rodriguez, a Latino man from Puerto Rico who moved with his own parents in hopes of better education. Good man, he is. A year later, Mother met Father at a gathering, and he was immediately head over heels for her, which caused an uproar with my grandparents. You probably know why. They learned the hard way that she was indeed a smart, witty woman and finally accepted her. Alexandria Diaz became Alexandria Clark, got busy, and your handsome man and his siblings were born."

"Remarkable." I take another bite of my bagel. Mrs Mason is served her tomato soup, continuing to rub her belly as she thanks Esmerelda once again while she gives Thomas and Eleanor their matching grilled cheese sandwiches. "You've got quite the family history."

"I know. That's what everyone says." He takes another bite of his meatballs and grins up at me from his plate. "How is it, by the way? Your bagel?"

"Oh, it's good, thanks. I see you're enjoying your...?"

"*Albondigas,*" he reminds me. "Yes, I admit, it's a tough name to wrap your head around."

"How is everything?" Mrs Mason peers over at our table and spoons her soup, giving us a wink. "Like you remember, Marshall? For your first time, Frieda?"

"Great," we reply in unison, and shoot each other chucklesome looks before Marshall adds, "Just like when I left. Esmerelda's cooking never changes."

"How often did you come here?" I poke fun at him. "Enough to try everything on the menu and remember exactly how each dish tastes?"

"No," with his fork, he stabs at another meatball, "it just has that nostalgic taste."

"Well, aren't I glad I took you two out today?" Mrs Mason watches Thomas set down the crusts of his grilled cheese while Eleanor eats it all. "How're you enjoying yourselves, children? Is everything tasting good?"

"Good, Mama." Eleanor's small hands cup her glass. Her grin doesn't vanish, Thomas joining her. "Are you enjoying your soup?"

"I am, Elle, I am." Though she's eating, she still holds her belly, protecting her unborn child from the unforgiving world outside of her mother's embrace.

Setting down my bagel, I look at the floor. Marshall leans to chatter with her about the baby, leaving me to my own thoughts.

Images flash through my head: Of my mother, the photographs I saw of her in long maternity gowns, her dark hair tied in a high bun as she posed and held her belly with those long, slender fingers. Papa always told me she rubbed her belly almost every day and sang to me, read to me, just as Mrs Mason is doing as Marshall teases her.

The memory leaves me hollow, my stomach turning into an endless pit—the same feeling I get every time I think of who my mother was: The one who I looked up to, who braided my hair for school when my father messed it up, and ironed my frocks for me until I learned how to do it myself.

It takes a lot to stop the sobs from escaping, to stop the ocean of grief from rocking my tiny sailboat, forever lost at sea, like the woman Rose South used to be.

* * *

"That was some fun we had!" Mrs Mason keeps hold of Eleanor and Thomas and says farewell to Esmerelda, who blows us all kisses and waves a dark hand. "We should do it again sometime, when the numbers settle down, yes?"

"We should, we should." I jolt at Marshall's arm, gliding across my waist as he works his mask back on with his free hand. He stuffs his gloves in his pocket in trade for his watch, checking the time. "My, it's after two. Frieda and I have to do some shopping for Father before the market closes."

"We'll let you take off, then. It was lovely seeing you both, and to meet you, Ms Frieda." She gestures an upturned, open palm to me in acknowledgement with a quiet giggle. "If he gives you any trouble, darling, call me, and I'll let you crash for as long as you need. He can be a troublesome little man; a true devil, he is. His madness can drive you to the end of the earth."

Marshall chortles. I dip into a shallow curtsey. "Don't thank me. Have a safe trip home."

The Masons depart. The waving party is over. I slump against Marshall, who tenses under my weight.

"Are you ill?" He grabs my shoulders and bends to look me in the eye.

I shake him off with the simple answer of 'tired,' his sigh warm against my ear. He bends to nuzzle his cheek momentarily in my hair.

"We'll be quick, I promise." He dips my hat over my eyes teasingly. "The market's down the road. When we get home, I'll turn the heater up, and we can rest."

Stuffing my hands in my coat pockets, I follow him down the street. A dash of light rain sprinkles down. He starts cursing that he should've brought an umbrella or looked at the forecast, and pulls his coat a little bit tighter around himself. My legs grow weary from walking for so long as we step inside a large supermarket with glass doors. With scarred hands, he takes a basket from one of the racks and accepts some sanitizer, pulling out his list.

"Why don't you wait there? There should be a bench nearby for you to sit. Wash your hands if you touch anything!"

After around twenty minutes, he emerges through the queue with a bag full of groceries, throwing the list in the trash, finding me and offering his hand. "You're very lucky you're sitting over here and not in the toiletry aisle."

"What's wrong with the toiletry aisle?"

"Panic buying. Men buying all the soaps and body wash. A throng of women had a basket full of sanitary products and were being aggressively selfish."

"Geesh." I stand, dusting off my skirt, following him out the store.

Now, it's bucketing down, and Marshall heaves a frustrated sigh.

"I'm not risking getting us sick today!" he yells over the din hammering down on the steel roof. "I'll call a cab."

Marching to the corner, pushing me out of the rain, it's humorous to watch him and many others try to holler at a cab to fetch them out of the rain. He resorts to jumping up and down, springing up and off his heels, even waving his hat around to drag up extra attention until he finally, after what seems like forever, gets a cab.

Beside me, as he tells the driver his address, rain drips from his hair and down his chin, getting caught in his lashes and down his neck. During the car ride, I start to shiver aggressively as the cold seeps through my clothes. He pulls me close to him and rubs my back to produce some sort of warmth. My hair grows heavy with rainwater.

"We'll be home soon," he whispers against my ear.

Once the cab parks on the side of the road and the driver is paid through the glass divider, Marshall helps me out of my seat with a damp hand. The taxi sets off down the road.

"Sweet Jesus, Marshall, you're as wet as a stray dog!" I wipe my hand on my skirt. He fishes for his keys, clutching the bag of groceries. "You need to have a bath as soon as you get inside."

"You should see yourself, then." He unlocks the front door, a gust of warm air hitting us both in the face.

Once he closes the door, he immediately puts the groceries near the letter bowl and whips off his hat, coat, and vest, leaving himself in his tie and suspenders and a rumpled, see-through shirt. He climbs the stairs, dashing into the bathroom, the door closing behind him.

In the hall, I'm alone, lured farther into the house. Laughter comes from the kitchen.

Poking my head around the corner, I spot Nathan with Edith at the kitchen counter. She's against his chest, listening to him guiding her hands over the chopping board decked with fruit: oranges, apples, and watermelon, his chin resting on her shoulder. He tells her something inaudible that makes her laugh and presses his lips against her jaw.

It feels rude, utterly perverse, to keep watching. I scamper upstairs to my room to change, setting my wet clothes on the chair, making a mental note to wash them later. Swapping them for a dry set of garments, I do up the last few buttons of my shirt and bend down to fix the tops of my socks.

There's a knock at the door.

"Come in," I answer.

"Please don't tell me I'm embarking on a dangerous journey of seeing something I shouldn't." Marshall enters the room, his back to me, taking a scared peek. He issues a sigh. "Good, you're dressed. *Anyway—*"

"You're not missing out on anything spicy, unless you find me putting on socks attractive," I retort, and tighten my other garter.

He squawks in shock. "So I *am* embarking on a dangerous journey of seeing something I shouldn't!" He covers his eyes with one hand, backing out slowly, saying before he closes the door, "Understandable, goodbye."

"No, come back! I was kidding!" I titter.

The door reopens. He pops his head of disorganized black hair back into the room. "Okay, good, because knock, knock, it's I, Mr Clark the Third."

"Oh my God, look at you! Let me get a comb or something—"

"It won't listen." He smooths a hand through his dark shag. "You didn't tell me that Edith and Nathan were canoodling in the kitchen."

"I couldn't. You were in the bath."

"I wasn't prepared to intrude on them! And good lord, they got a shock! Nathan backed into the counter behind him and gasped like he was in a horror film. Edith stammered that he was teaching her how to make fruit salad, Frieda. *Fruit salad!*" He accentuates the second 'fruit salad' in air quotes with a dramatic flair, his voice rising up several octaves. "I do *not* want to walk in and see my *sister* with her *boyfriend* making *fruit salad!*"

I slide my ballet flats on my feet, offering, good-naturedly, "Maybe they were just making afternoon tea? You never know."

"I'm mortified from just walking in and seeing that. I'm sure they are, too." He reaches for *Northanger Abbey,* which sits with a bookmark poking out of its pages, nodding at it. "When I asked where Father was, Edith said he went to the doctor for a health check. He hasn't been back as of late, apparently."

I pull back the curtains, confronted by the rain lashing against the window and the innocent victims on the sidewalk. One woman with her dog rushes past.

Marshall takes my side. "I would go into the study, but I'm too scared to even set foot downstairs after seeing them." He shakes his head like a wet dog, his hair still damp from his bath and the unforgiving storm outside, spraying water everywhere. I step back.

After a beat of silence, his voice drops to a murmur. "I got two phone calls while I was downstairs."

"You did?" I ask.

"I did." His eyes attach themselves to another dog walker rushing home. This time, the dog is yelping in her arms as the woman scoops it up to escape the thunderstorm. Thunder claps. Lightning lights the sky in electric, white streaks. "Both were from separate hospitals."

"Oh?"

"Don't worry, it was nothing bad. The first was for Alistair, who's been admitted for six weeks. The second was Ed, calling to tell me that he's in another hospital and that his infection has gone down. He's staying until he recovers."

"So they're both doing okay?"

"Yes, for now." He fiddles with his watch; a tic, I've observed, that he occupies himself with whenever he grows nervous. He plays with the lid, pressing the button so that it opens and closes, running his thumb over its engravings. "Right, I may as well study this afternoon after I put the groceries away. What do you think you'll be doing?"

"I'll explore the shelves and maybe get a few more pages of *Northanger Abbey* in."

"Do you like it so far?" He opens the door, holding it open for me with a coy grin. "I sure hope you do. I try my best to recommend some good literature."

"It's pretty good, I'll say. You chose well." I nod my head in thanks and step through to the hall with the book in my arms, following him down the steps, coming across the jolly laughter from the kitchen.

Marshall opens the door to the study, the lights flickering on when he flicks the switch. He grabs his spectacles from his inside pocket and perches them upon his nose. Off goes his blazer, folded over his arm when he bends to inspect his shelves of many tomes. He's already grinding down on his work, fingers pressed against his lips in thought before he sets on over to his desk. Sitting upon it is a crumpled sheet; a list of sorts.

"What're you studying this time?" I come over to inspect it. He grabs his pen and circles a few lines, threatening to attack the paper with its mighty nib.

His eyes narrow at the page. "Medical terminology. More cell theory."

"Seems interesting." I snatch his list, reading the many dot points printed on it: anatomy, medical terms, chemicals, dosages, and math, many more when I read farther down. "You're going to have the time of your life with this course."

"I'll try." He snaps his fingers, struck with a sudden thought. "I should get something to drink. I'm parched. Would you like something?"

"It is a bit stuffy here...Perhaps some water?"

"Water it is." He makes for the door. "I'll be right back."

When he returns, he holds two glasses stacked on top of each other and a plastic pewter filled with water. He's put in ice cubes and sets the items on the coffee table, leaning forward to pour both of us a glass, venturing back over to the shelves. His fingers travel over the titles' spines, fumbling through them until he finds the ones he needs.

It's interesting to watch Marshall work. He's like a machine, head ticking with equations and definitions. Even with his back to me, I can visualize the chewing of his lip, the glint in his eyes that appears when he slips into concentration. He travels back to the desk and plonks down a hefty pile of textbooks. The crackle of old pages and the musty scent of yellowing paper awakens my nose and ears.

I make my own adventure around the room and dive deeper into the wondrous shelves before me when the scratching of a pen against parchment begins. He pays me no mind as I sneak a peek at what he's noting down. Before him is an elaborate sketch of the human body. I take it he's testing the waters of anatomy today, too.

Peering at the shelves one last time, I make my way back and recline on the couch, continuing my reading, tucking my knees in tight. I sneak a few quick glances at him as he opens another book in front of him, muttering words I can't make out; long words. Long strings of them. He writes them with his fingers pressed against their pages.

My eyes get heavy from reading so much. Finishing the book in around two hours, I set it on the couch beside me. He's still going strong, four books opened and the pewter still half full, the ice completely melted.

When I close my eyes, there's the scrape of chair legs and the click of shoes against the floorboards. He's there beside me, the shifting of blankets heard. He lays them over my exhausted body.

"You've finished, huh?" Between my eyelids, his face is carved into soft angles, his spectacles hanging off the tip of his nose. The corners of his mouth are curved upward into a mellow grin. His eyes lie over my tired face.

"I did." I stare back at him as he adjusts the woolen blanket, tucking the corners in to fit snugly around my frame.

"Was it good?" A pillow is placed behind my head, his ink-stained fingers lingering over my cheek.

"It was."

A kiss to the forehead is planted with my answer. "That's good. I'm glad you enjoyed it. I'll leave you to rest. I'll be right here, studying."

"What're you studying this time?"

His smile only widens. "The cardiovascular system and bodily fluids."

"I'll miss you when you go to college."

"There's no need to say that. I don't even know when I'm going." He kisses the space between my brows, standing. "Get some rest. You need it."

I close my eyes.

The front door opens. Marshall's now out in the hall, talking with his father in a hushed conversation.

I slip in and out of a light sleep, not being able to stay put because of the nightmares that flash in monstrous scenes behind my eyelids. It's enough to constrict my chest and close up my throat, growing tighter. I try to swallow the horrid sensation away.

The next time my eyes snap open, the blast of a gunshot and a male scream is still fresh in my ears, the acrid stench of gunpowder billowing in my nostrils.

His hazel eyes lie wide and glassy, his body coiled in on itself. He remains dead at my feet. Blood oozes in a sickly red trail from a hole in his forehead.

I take in a sharp wheeze that hurts my throat. Hands lay themselves over mine. The metallic taste of blood is in my mouth. A cut from my lip is bleeding as I scream and jerk myself away.

"Frieda—hey! It's okay. It's just me, just me." Marshall's kneeling in front of me, hands creeping up my arms, stained with black ink. "It's okay. You were having a bad dream. Look at me."

When I do, his face is very much alive, his eyes all-seeing, wide—not from death, but from fear, love; the eyes that had minded me so anxiously on the battlefield.

I bite back another sob. His warm palm goes to my cheek, his gaze never breaking away. "You...you were shot...you died. Marshall, you—"

"*Shhh.*" He grips my other hand. Hard. "I'm still here. Right here. I'm breathing, speaking and holding your hand, holding *you*. Right where I should be: by your side." His voice is thick, small, tremulous against the rain and lightning that flashes streaks of light across the room. "I'm right here."

I struggle to reply without a wobble in my words. "Please don't leave me alone."

He brings his lips to my hand, pressing soft kisses across my knuckles, my palm, the inside of my wrist. All are soft, full of love, light as a feather. "I promise that wherever you are, I'll follow. We're planets orbiting the same sun, individuals clutching tight to the same string, pulling and pulling like our lives depend on it. To leave you alone, however, that wouldn't be possible."

Another kiss lands on my palm. He raises his head, declaring a loud promise, battling the harsh and unforgiving weather.

"We've already tied our hands so tight. It would be simply impossible to let go."

PART IV

FINALE

JUNE, 1920

FRIEDA AND MARSHALL

41

1920

FRIEDA

And just like that, a whole two years of strife and frustration have passed.

We walk under the clear summer sky in Philadelphia. The streets are crawling with people: women in the new drop-waist dresses of the decade (much comfier than the horrid, heavy dresses of last decade), men in summer suits tipping their hats against the heat of the sun.

Twenty-three year old Marshall clutches my hand in his. The scars have faded over the years into neat white lines that remain coarse against his soft skin under the sleeves of his own tan summer suit, snug against his fuller frame—I myself have a suit in a navy blue. He bops his head against the street band playing on the corner under his straw boat hat.

This time, no patch is there to obscure or smother the blind side of my face. I vowed to take no shame in showing my battle scars, letting them aid me in telling the story of my grand adventures.

I often get those familiar stares of men, women, and children alike as I pass through the streets, my burns on full display. The first time I did it was an unnerving experience, one on a date night Marshall and I organized as soon as the pandemic cleared up. I got so paranoid that after dinner, we skipped dessert and he took me home in a crying mess.

I pledged to never show my face without the patch in public ever again. I called myself ugly, sobbing in his arms, a disgusting creature with one eye. He held onto me so tight that I thought I might've collapsed and encouraged me not to care what anyone else thought. That I was me. No one could change me. I was fine just the way I was. Not bothering to sugarcoat his words, he broke into a cursing spell and a pep talk which knocked some serious sense into me.

He was right, in the end. I let my insecurities get the better of me. The next time I made an attempt to take the streets, I felt an obscene amount of courage and wanted to show people that I wasn't afraid of what they thought. It developed a confident kick in my step, my jaw lifted higher and higher with each outing.

Then came the prosthesis.

The eye, of course, was something strange for me to find whenever I ever so happened to stroll by a mirror. I'd grown so used to seeing myself with only the conformer in my socket. Now, I had both eyes back, blinking wondrously back in my reflection on the other side of the mirror pane.

Marshall was there, promising to come with me when I admitted my nervousness, when the doctor slipped it into my socket. He nearly fainted at the sight of it.

He shook madly, forcing his tears not to fall as I grew used to this new eye, this new look for myself. Outside the doctor's office, he even gathered my hands in his and commended me for being so strong and pushing through. I asked him what he thought of the whole affair, but he only shook his head at my question.

"Don't you ever think, for one split moment, that just because you have one eye means that I myself will see you as any different. Regardless of what you look like, I'll still see you for you. Forever and always."

Even in 1920, he still hums the same tune. His other hand clutches his suitcase, full of clothes and necessities he brought along on the trip to Seattle. He'd met my entire family and was reveling in the attention like a spoiled pooch with its tongue lolling out as someone scratches behind its ears.

In the ungodly hours of the morning, in the hotel room, I caught him feasting on the leftover apple pie Uncle Isaac baked. It led to an awkward, comedic silence for the both of us before I went back to bed. He showed no guilt the next morning, an evil, merciless glint in his eye when I mentioned the late-night occurrence.

The origin of the trip was to meet my family and help clean out my old house before it went on the market, a part of me lost as I re-explored the dead halls. Memories and footprints called back to me as I turned on my heel with the things I left behind in a small cardboard box. Irene and Fitzroy South were there, Irene apologizing for her taunts. As friends, we went out for the day before she announced she'd be moving back to England with her father, but made a hasty promise to write to me.

That night, Marshall took me into the city to get my mind off of the grief of my lost family—being someone with no immediate family at twenty-one was far too grueling for me to process at the time. He proceeded to find a nice restaurant to take each other in over dinner, which led to canoodling under the covers—the highlight of the night. The best bit was seeing him covered in red lipstick stains and hickeys.

Over our week of staying in Seattle and our trip back to Philadelphia, the hickeys have faded into dark splotches over his collarbone that he wears with stubborn pride.

"Nice day out," he remarks, a noticeable lilt playing on his tongue. "Would be a bit nicer if it wasn't so hot outside."

"It's not that bad, actually." I hoist my bag over my shoulder. The street band's brass echoes in the distance. We turn the corner onto Marshall's street. He lets go of my hand to wipe the sweat on his brow.

"It's like Mother Nature is having a cookout out here," he complains, whining and walking faster.

"Hey—slow down! You have much longer legs than I do!"

"I'm being incinerated!" His cheeks are bright red, eyes squinted against the sun. "The next thing you know, it won't be just your hickeys on the back of my neck, but a painful sunburn."

"Fair call." He walks even faster across the boiling sidewalk. "Marshall, I'm growing faint just from trying to keep up with you!"

"Run if you have to!" he shouts over his shoulder.

"Not in these heels! I'm practically a packhorse with this luggage!" I argue.

This doesn't break his fast-paced stride, so I bolt on ahead, *hmph*-ing. I fold my arms and march, straight as a pin. He slows down, growing tired, snapping out a loud, irritable string of curse words targeted at the weather—both in English and Spanish.

As he waits for me at the pathway to his house, I puff up at him, "Could you have waited?"

"I know, I should've." He ducks his head. "I'm sorry, *mi ángel*, but I despise the heat. It won't happen again."

"I'll forgive you." I take him by the arm. "Let's get you inside before you complain even more. I need food."

"Understood, Your Majesty." He winks and fetches his key.

"Please do *not* call me that. I'm not even close to royalty."

"You did not just say that when you're the queen of my heart," he whimpers.

"Am I really?" I break into a sob.

"Yes. Oh, no, I made you cry—"

I let out a squeal and wrap my arms tight around him, cupping his cheeks in my palms. "Come here, you precious *sweetie pie*. You're so cute that I could just eat you up, *mon doux petit bébé, mon petit homme—*"

"Frieda, sweetheart..." He tries to pull away, only to be pulled back in for a long kiss on the lips and several more peppered across his cheeks. "Okay, okay. Though I have no idea what you're saying, I love you too. Can we please go inside? I am *burning!*"

"Right." I flash him a cheeky grin and wipe away the pink lipstick stain on the side of his mouth, his eyes wide, left spellbound, in a trance. "You really meant that?"

He sneaks a mischievous peck below my ear and rummages through his pockets, clutching his key. "I do. I know that for a fact."

He slides the key inside the keyhole, holding the door open. Cold air blooms over us.

Inside, music booms through the floorboards as the crooner sings his song on the radio. There's twinkling chimes of laughter, the clinking of drinks and the light thumps of footsteps.

"We made it just in time. They're already here," he says.

He assists me upstairs, setting our bags in our rooms, reaching into the bathroom to wipe his face of sweat and spray on some cologne. I spritz on some perfume myself for good measure, Marshall hanging in the doorframe of my room, waiting patiently.

As I set the bottle down on the mantle—the perfume Marshall gifted me for my twenty-first—he tugs at the satin cream-colored scarf I left on the doorknob and sashays with it across his shoulders. "Say, would I look pretty with this scarf?"

"You'd look dashing," I take it off of him, brushing my hair, "but that's for my hair."

"It looks better on you, anyways." He tuts and places both hands around my waist. "How about I do your hair?"

"Can I trust you?"

"C'mon, of course you can. I used to braid Ed's hair when we were children."

His hands are delicate as he combs my hair back and over my shoulders. It's grown out from its bob down to my collarbone. I've been too lazy to trim it back. His fingers run through any remaining knots, and his touch is almost hypnotizing.

He's resumed his humming as he works peacefully with a grin softening his face. "We should put some flowers in your hair sometime. Perhaps some daisies?"

"Another time. I'm afraid I don't have any on hand."

"I'll buy you some." He braids my hair and ties the scarf in to keep it in place. His hands return to my waist, lips pressed against my ear. "I had to stick some of Edith's foundation on those hickeys you left on me, *Freddy*."

"Why're you blaming me?" I place my hands on his as he looks over my shoulder at his reflection. He's flawless, as always. "It was your idea to even let me do it in the first place."

"All part of the fun," he snorts. "Because I love you, I'll wear them with stubborn pride. If anyone decides to hit on me, I'll rip my shirt off to show them."

I wince at the idea. "That would be wasting a perfectly good shirt."

"Yes, but it would be worth it to show that I already belong to a deserving special someone. It's foolproof! Even Mr Darcy would do it if he had to with all the women looking to marry him."

"I highly doubt a rich aristocrat such as *Mr Darcy* would do such a thing." I squeeze his fingers with a stiff smile. "I'd rather you keep your shirt on to save you the embarrassment of walking home half-naked."

"*Touché.*" Letting go of me, he takes his place by the door, waiting. The chatter downstairs continues. "Ready to greet the guests?"

"Ready."

We set out into the hall, scampering down the stairs to the living room, where music plays softly in the corner. Food is lying atop the table in the dining room. The sun places the rooms in a blanket of light. Laughter bubbles in the air.

Marshall and I wander through the crowds, scanning them for familiar faces.

"Marshall! Frieda!" someone calls, darting towards us like a bull chasing a red flag.

Edward Surry stands bandage-free with a scar from his stitches running down his face and a bun keeping his magnificently long hair out of his way. With a ferociously gleeful flame in his eyes, Marshall spreads his arms for Ed to crash into him, nearly taking him off his feet. The two men squabble excitedly.

"Eddie! By God! I see the surgery went well!" Marshall claps him on the back. "You look as handsome as ever!"

"As do you, Marshall. Jesus, look at you! You've put on weight! You look a lot fuller." Ed pats his shoulder. "Don't look ever a day older, do you?"

"Ed, please, you're too kind." Marshall puts up a hand. "It's what I call *Post-War Glow.*"

Ed emits a nasally laugh and turns to me. "Frieda! Look at you! They did so well with your prosthesis! I think I'm going to cry."

"Don't break down on us now," Marshall sighs. "Are the rest of the boys here?"

"George is. Sam's ill with bronchitis. Lester couldn't make it because...You're going to go feral just from hearing what he said."

"Is it something bad?" I ask.

"It's out of this world!" Ed exclaims. "He told me he was seeing someone, as he called me on the phone and was going upstate with her family for the summer!"

"What?" Marshall and I gasp.

"I know! I know! It's so abnormal for Lester. I admit, though, I'm proud of him."

"Who's the lucky lady?" Marshall inquires and pours us each a glass of lemonade.

"A woman called Madeline. That's all the information I was able to coax out of him," Ed answers.

Marshall hands him and I a glass.

"*Madeline.*" Marshall teases the name on his tongue. "I'll have to hustle him for more information on this mystery maiden. *Madeline.*"

"Edward?" A blonde, plump woman calls Ed's name, a boy in her arms.

"Yes, Alice, dear?" Ed turns to who I presume is his wife. He gracefully holds his glass out in front of her. "Not for you, Joseph." He pulls it away as the boy grapples for it.

"Alice! Long time no see!" Marshall waves, not even scared of the woman who took his first love away from him. He was right when he said he was way past his heartbreak. "Who's this little one you've got?"

"Marshall, you look well. This is mine and Edward's three year old, Joseph."

"Joseph! Congratulations, by the way." His smile never fades. Joseph's eyes—Ed's eyes—lock on him, observing and silent.

Alice cradles him closer to her chest. "Thanks, Marshall, truly. And you, dear. You must be Frieda."

"Indeed. Congratulations, the both of you." I dip my head and wave at Joseph, who gives me a smile with his small mouth, Alice chortling.

"How was the trip, you two?" Ed takes a long sip of lemonade as Joseph and Alice chatter. "Did everything go as planned?"

I respond, "It was nice to return home."

"It was nice to spend time together; to help out and explore," Marshall adds.

"Good to know." Ed takes another sip. "Ah, here he is. The one and only Wellins."

"C'mon, Ed, you completely blew my cover." George appears from behind him in awkward disappointment. "You got me."

I grin up at him. "We're so glad you could make it."

"So glad I could see you." He swirls his glass, full of cranberry juice. Ever since January, alcohol has been strictly prohibited. "You too, Marshall. Don't think I forgot about you, Skipper."

"I'm good. Living in the moment." Marshall reaches to shake his hand. Nice and firm. "I missed you, *Skipper.*"

George's aged face crinkles with glee. "I missed you too—all of you. It feels so good to get the gang back together again. Well, most of us, really."

"How's Myrtle? Howard? Are they fine?" Marshall asks.

"Doing splendidly. Just fine."

Through the throng, another child scampers clumsily on their stubby little legs, gurgling. I recognize the child as Kara, streaming through at full speed.

"Kara Mary Clark, come back here!" Alistair tails her like the bloodhound, Rufus, that he has back home, when he chases a scent. With all the agility and quickness of a waterbird hunting for food, he scoops her back up in his arms and pinches her cheek with his prosthetic hand. "You rascal. Just like your uncle, always getting yourself into trouble."

Marshall shoots a glance at his brother. "Was that intentional? I'm standing right here."

Alistair returns the glance. Kara repeats the word 'Dadda' with a giggle. "Perhaps so. She really does. It's terrifying. She even did what you did when you were little."

Marshall smirks, busying himself by swilling his lemonade. "Oh, no."

"What was that?" I ask Alistair, who pulls Kara closer to his chest.

"Stole from the cookie jar, got into the pantry. It's terrifying how much she takes after you. She even stole the same raisin-oatmeal cookies you always did." He turns to me, a scowl worrying at his lips. "I remember catching him with them littering the floor."

Marshall, after a small swallow of lemonade, emits a concise and amused huff out through his nose. "History repeats itself."

"And you don't feel a shred of guilt years later?" I joke.

"Not at all. All worth the pantry burglaries. How do you think I was able to smuggle in all that extra food to you?"

"You bandit." I roll my eyes to the high heavens. His smirk only grows. "As a matter of fact, Alistair, while we were in Seattle, I found him breaking into the hotel room fridge to rob it of the leftover apple pie my uncle baked for us."

"Wow. Caught in the action too?" Alistair keeps his grip tight over Kara.

"Yes, caught in the action especially."

Ed elbows Marshall in the side. "Garn, Marshall, you should start up your own food smuggling business somewhere on the sidelines."

"What would he call it?" George teases. "What was everyone calling him in the trenches? The *Food Raccoon*?"

Ed and George break into conjoined laughter.

"Good times, gentlemen, good times." Marshall clears his throat. "Let's not forget when Ed fell through the roof while working. Or the time George tripped during a drill and got his entire front caked in mud."

"I remember that, actually," Ed recalls. "George falling, yes. The roof? Not so much."

"You were concussed, you doorknob," George sneers.

"Mighty loud crash, too. We thought it was the Germans letting out a ripper," Alistair says, causing the five of us to hoot.

Through almost-tears of laughter, Marshall waves a hand. "We heard a man had fallen through the roof and learned it was you. You got high off the painkillers and brought down the house with an utterly fantastic drunkard story of how you fell and everything."

"'The roof couldn't handle me,'" George recites, "'and it couldn't handle itself because it couldn't handle me.'"

"Merciful heavens." Ed's wiping his eyes. "The good old days, huh?"

"Indeed, indeed. Now, I'm starved. I haven't eaten yet. Who's up for some food?" Marshall asks.

"The Food Raccoon in action," George remarks.

"Oi," Marshall shoots George a glare, "it's my house. I get to do what I want."

"Still stealing food, *Raccoon*," George hisses in return.

"More like taking it and thanking my father for making it," he argues, stepping aside, clapping George on the shoulder. "My house, my rules."

"As defiant as ever," Ed teases under his breath. Marshall turns to him and rolls his eyes. "Even at twenty-three, you're still as cocky and stubborn as when you were seventeen. It's good to see you again."

Marshall's silent for a moment. He flashes Ed a toothy grin.

"As to you, Ed. Wise and as much as a fatherly friend as ever," he replies, vanishing into the mob of people who make way when he walks by. They start muttering his name, about his wartime experiences. The whole occasion looks like a celebrity herded by his paparazzi. And good grief, he handles it well.

"Am I really?" Ed gasps, starting after Marshall, calling out, "You better get back here before I squeeze you to death in my fatherly hug!"

Marshall wheels around, eyes wide, uttering a curse under his breath, and ducking back into the crowd. Ed charges after him, lemonade glass and all.

Alistair sighs. "When one goes, the other follows. Leave it to them. Marshall will be clobbered by the time he gets back."

"Watch: I bet he'll be rampaging back, screaming, with a plate full of food." George looks over his shoulder. The song on the record player changes, still light and airy, perfect for a gathering on a day such as this.

There's a groan from the crowd. Marshall and Ed come through, Ed's arms over Marshall's shoulders as he holds a small plate full of cheese and crackers.

"Ed, for the last time, I bought these!" Marshall pulls away from him, who only draws him back into his grip.

"Doesn't stop you from stealing them back, does it?" Ed snaps.

Marshall groans helplessly. He takes a bite out of the brie he's cut into a thin slice, nodding and observing its flavor. He takes his place next to me and pushes the plate forward.

"My family loves this stuff...prosciutto." He points to the pinkish red meat with white strips. "Italian ham. You could try some. Unless you don't eat ham, I'm making a grave mistake—"

"I do, if you remember the bacon you made three weeks ago."

"I don't think I've had you try prosciutto, though." He glares at the boys, who gossip childishly. "Why don't you try some?"

"Are you sure?"

"I didn't grab extra for nothing. I knew you'd be hungry."

I pick a sheath of thin meat off his plate, tearing off a small streak, chewing it thoughtfully. The salt hits my tongue. I let out an *mmm* of satisfaction.

"Good, isn't it?" He takes a piece of his own after he downs the last of his lemonade. "It's a rare type of meat."

"But it's good." I tear another chunk off. "It tastes so different."

"Saltier than most, yes." Marshall presses the plate closer to me. "Take some more. Take some cheese and crackers too."

Laughter rises from the groups of unfamiliar faces sitting on the sofas and couches, standing near the fireplace, turning to go into the kitchen, returning with plates of food.

Nathan comes through with a cup of tea in his clutches. Over the years, he's grown out of his boyish frame, turning lankier and lankier, taller and taller, battling me with more freckles to count without even standing in the sun. He's got a pretty nicely groomed goatee which Edith teases him relentlessly for. He went back to Lincoln after the pandemic and promised Edith he'd keep in touch, coming back to Philadelphia for the summer.

"Sharing food, are we?" Nathan takes a sip of tea. "Just get married already."

"On my to-do list, pal." Marshall points an accusing finger at him. "Hypocrite."

"I'm working on it," Nathan replies.

"Nate! The cream pie you made was delicious! It's all gone now." Edith follows him over to our group with a joyous beam on her face.

"I'm glad you liked it, Doll." His eyes light up, lips curling upward.

"Oh, it was too late for me to get any. My aunt and uncle were vultures, picking it apart."

"I'll make another one just for you, since it's such a hit," he replies and sits on a nearby chair, Edith settling on his lap.

Edith herself has grown into a beautiful young woman. Now nineteen, she's fuller, possessing the same gorgeous round, soft cheeks as her mother, and blue eyes that blaze like the ocean caught in the sunlight. She remains shorter than me by a full four inches, but is the perfect size for Nathan to carry around the house in his arms like a baby. She's grown into her magnificent curves that seem to ravish Nathan as he holds her by her hips with all the love that she and him share. Even I'm jealous of her figure and her hair that falls graciously down to the middle of her back. She's practically a living porcelain doll. That's how radiant her beauty is.

Now, Edith nuzzles against Nathan's cheek. She and him whisper and giggle. Ed and George have vanished, Alistair chasing Kara once he puts her down. I've set my lemonade glass on a nearby table.

Marshall sets the now-empty plate aside and whispers in my ear, "How about we go see my grandparents? They should be here."

I clasp my hands together. "Are you sure? I don't want to bother them."

He wrinkles his nose in denial. "Rubbish. They love meeting new people."

He guides me to the red couch by the window, where the elderly sit with cups full of tea.

"Marshall, who're these people?" I inquire, looping my arm in his.

"On the far right is my uncle Yosef. Next to him is my aunt Rachel. Next to them are my grandmother and grandfather."

"How do I address them?" I fret. "I don't want to be rude."

"Mr and Mrs Clark. Same as old." He steps forward, taking me with him with tender hands upon my bare, freckled shoulders. "Grandmama, Grandpapa, great to see you here!"

His grandmother, a witty and smart looking woman, has horn-rimmed glasses and matching black waves of hair tied into a tight bun. She's donning a high-collared blouse and pencil skirt. Her hand lies on her husband's.

Grandpa Clark is a man who owns thick square spectacles and high, gaunt cheekbones (I see now where Marshall got his facial structure). His hair is fair, eyes a pale gray. Their lips crack into matching smiles.

"Marshall, my grandson, you look splendid. Look at how healthy you are!" The man takes a sip of tea, adding, "I almost mistook you for your father. You look more like him day after day."

"Just look at him, Maurice! My word, have you gotten big!" The woman's smile grows. Marshall's hands tighten on my shoulders, giving them a light squeeze of reassurance.

"Thank you, the both of you," he replies with some unease. They both look upon us eagerly. Their eyes take me in and crawl under my skin. "Beside me blessing you with my company, I want you to meet someone very dear to me that I met during the war—well, she's more of a longtime family friend I ran into while serving—"

"A friend? How sweet!" Maurice interrupts.

"No, grandpapa, more than that." He lets out a short chuckle. "This is Ms Frieda Joyce. She's my everlastingly beautiful partner."

"Oh! Aren't you the cutest little muffin I've ever seen! Isn't she beautiful, Maurice? So young, so gorgeous! Look at all the pretty sunspots on her!" Marshall's grandmother grins, and I shrink back against his chest with a whimper. "Are you two courting?"

Marshall begins to blanch. I clench my jaw.

"She's pleased to meet you, but is a little shy." Marshall ignores the question, whispering in my ear, "Do you want to sit down?"

Upon my nod, he grabs one of the unused foldable chairs and pulls it out for me, retrieving a glass of water, placing it delicately in my hands, and standing by my side.

"It's a pleasure to meet you, Mrs and Mr Clark," I speak up, trying hard to control the wavering of my voice. Marshall rubs my back. "I'm sorry, I get anxious during gatherings and when I'm meeting new people."

"Don't apologize, dear. It's intimidating, meeting new people, I know. Don't stress. We're pleased to meet you too." The woman points to herself with a bony, wrinkled hand. "I'm Nora, and this is my husband, Maurice. Frieda, was it? Tell us, where are you from?"

"Seattle," I answer, with an encouraging nod from Marshall. "I lived with my father and mother before the war. He was from Lyon, she was from Brooklyn."

"American and French? Wow! Did he ever teach you?" Maurice presses forward.

A sense of dizzying relief sweeps over me. I don't have to explain what happened to my parents. I don't have to go deeper into my feelings than I already am. "He did."

"And you should listen to her speak it," Marshall adds. "Her accent is simply wonderful, as soft and beautiful as a nightingale's song and the person who harnesses it." He ends with a wink.

I look away to hide my scowl and curse him in my mind. *You flirt.*

"Maybe later, we'll get a chance to hear you speak it?" Maurice takes another sip of tea. "Do you read? Our dear Marshall loves books. He simply devours them."

"Of course." I let a smile slide onto my face, forcing myself to stop thinking of the many afternoons he and I shared on the couch. We often listen to the radio with his hands around my waist. Sometimes I sleep on him while he reads, other times he falls asleep mid-read with his body crumpled against me, book open in his lap. His mouth hangs open, snoring. "We often read together and discuss books; our little book club."

"He was in dire need of a reading buddy." Nora looks at her grandson, who continues to rub my back and stand by my side eagerly. "He's finally found one. How're you liking Philadelphia?"

"It's way, way different than Seattle, but I like it here. It's a change of scenery. The locals are nice. I'm enjoying my time here. Have you been here all your life, or did you live elsewhere?"

Marshall, from above, has a grin sliding subconsciously into existence, as if to say, *Good going.*

"I actually lived in Canada when my father had business up in Toronto. Nora lived in New Jersey. I met her while I was attending Princeton."

"I've never been to Canada. I'd like to go."

"You'd love it there, my dear. The air is so fresh! The Canadians are so nice, and their accents are so peculiar. I haven't been in a mighty long time. It would've changed during the war. Everywhere's changing: new nations are being founded, cities are being built, new machines are being revolutionized. The world is getting ready for another era, another decade. The cars, when I was a boy, were merely horse-drawn carriages. Now they're a set of wheels with one you can drive on your own without hiring anyone. How times have changed for the better, making life easier!"

"You'll have to excuse Maurice for his...excitement about machines. He was an engineer in the early days. He's been highly invested in the business since he was a boy."

"And a mighty fine engineer at that, Nora!" He takes a haughty sip of tea. Nora rolls her eyes. "You loved that music box I made you, the one with *Mary Had A Little Lamb* that played when you wound it up."

Nora pats his hand gingerly. "I still do, dear."

"You were an engineer, Maurice? What did you work on?" I ask, leaning forward in my chair.

"Trains, my dear. Glorious steam engines. I painted them, fixed their engines, cleaned their funnels...It was the time of my life. You remember when I took you on your first train ride, don't you, Marsh? When you were ten?"

"I do, Pa," Marshall answers, still standing, poised with his fingers spread along my back. "The train to South Philly?"

"That's the one. Gosh, you and your siblings have the memory of a dolphin. You never forget. Frieda, when your boy was ten, I took him down to the rails for his first ride with the conductor. My good friend William let him hoot the whistle each time we arrived at a new station, all the way to South Philadelphia. We had a picnic and stayed the night. He had the time of his life, the little man."

Nora grins. "We should go down to South Philly together one time, what do you say? We can show Frieda the wonders of the South."

"I'd like that. We can get to know each other a little bit better," I reply.

"You see, Marshall, I like her. She's optimistic, a real charmer; the best of the bunch." Nora nods affirmingly. Marshall clears his throat and bends to my eye level, his face next to mine.

"Thank you," I say, biting into my lip to hide my smile.

"She's just being her beautiful self." Marshall relaxes beside me, a hand still on my back. "I wouldn't imagine being with anyone else."

My heart swells. My smile hurts my cheeks. For once, the pain of holding it feels good. It's *brilliant* to feel this type of joy, to not hold up a false front, to not feel the pain of an emerging or hidden sadness, but the pain of happiness.

I let it take over, filling me from head to toe with warmth.

When Nora and Maurice excuse themselves to go fetch some of Nathan's newly-made pie, Marshall rushes to kneel before me and clasp my hands.

"You, my fair one, are a superstar." He caresses my hands in his, pressing a horrendous amount of affectionate kisses across my palms, the backs of my hands, my knuckles. "My most ardent, passionate love. You have no idea how proud I am of you."

"I just started up a conversation," I argue. "That's all."

"That's what's so good about it! Stop selling yourself short! Look at you! You went out of your comfort zone and talked, my love, you talked! How much improvement you've gone through!"

"I don't get it."

"Alright," he clasps my hands tight, "years ago, you'd remain silent, only talk up to a bare minimum until you were comfortable with that person. Me, for example: You only talked for so long when I met you, and now look at you! A chatterbox! I'm so proud of you for growing so much."

"It was you who made me."

"No, *mi amor*." He plants a soft kiss against the base of my thumb, grinning from ear to ear. "This is all you. I'm so devilishly excited to see the new you as it progresses."

"You're silly. I'm still the person I've always been. I never changed, I just grew stronger."

"Of course," he says, his grin widening more than I thought it ever could. "You have a heart of diamond, my dear. Like the most dazzling gem ever beheld, you're unbreakable."

* * *

Another nightmare.

Another night lying awake.

I told Marshall to stop worrying. To stop coming each time I cried out. To stop staying up all night and checking on me. I saw how it was drawing the energy out of him, making him too tired to stand from sleep deprivation, after so many nights catching up, only to lose it all again to another one of my nightmares.

I told him I could handle it. It all was a lie.

I'm rocking myself back and forth for the twelfth night in a row in a room blanketed in darkness. The memories keep coming back: Of the war from too long ago, the emptiness I felt while ill, the fear I felt with every waking hour making me want to throw up my entire gut. I draw my knees tighter to my chest. I've tried brushing it off, going back to sleep, reading, opening the windows and breathing in the summer air, full of flowers and the many other scents of life.

My fingers knot into my gown's sleeves. I wipe at the sweat that shines on my forehead for the thousandth time, taking in another gasp of air as the chills wreck through me.

He's in the other room.

Go to him.

Find him.

Find Marshall.

I push back the thoughts. I can do it on my own. I don't need him. I don't need his comfort.

I want to prove I'm strong. I want to prove I'm getting better, that I can handle myself and my thoughts, that I can—

A knock sounds at the door.

My jaw doesn't move, my eyes wide in the darkness. A pair of slippered feet cast a shadow under the doorframe. The knock comes a second time, and it takes everything for me to utter, "Come in."

The door opens just a smidge. A head full of black hair, untidy and mused by pillows, emerges, spectacles on the tip of his nose. Marshall carries the thick tome of *Les Misérables* under his arm, his other hand curled around the knob. He wears a pajama set consisting of a white nightshirt and pants under a navy blue plaid robe with its strings tied tight around his waist.

"You're awake?" His voice is a sleepless grate. "I thought I heard something."

"Why're you awake?" I try to smooth out my voice to mask my panic.

"I was reading. I couldn't sleep...I didn't feel tired. *Les Misérables* is some thick stuff." He makes his way inside the room. My heartbeat quickens. "Victor Hugo writes bricks instead of books."

He sets himself down on the bed, the book in his lap. "How come you're awake?"

"You know those times when your body goes from a deep to a light sleep? It was one of those." I'm quick to lie, him nodding, remaining unconvinced.

"Uh-*huh*." His eyes linger on the book's cover, picking at it. "I thought I heard someone crying. I presumed it was you, so I wanted to check on you to make sure you're okay, with your nightmares and all."

Does he still think of me as weak? Does he still think I cry out in my sleep?

His face is set, his expression unbarring of any obvious answer to my ponderings.

"Maybe it was a cat?" I offer.

"No neighbors have a cat." He leans forward, his concerned gaze magnifying itself upon me. "Are you sure it wasn't you? Edith? Nathan? Father?"

"I heard nothing." I speak too quickly, still far too uptight.

His eyes investigate my face. He's onto me, suspicious, the last thing I want. His hand snakes across the covers and reaches for my ankle. I flinch under his touch.

"Is everything okay?" Through the darkness, he watches my every move. He's desperately searching, chewing at his lip.

I forgot: Marshall's a human lie detector. He can read people like they're one of his books, leaving no word undefined, no page unturned.

My voice cracks with my answer. "Yep!"

There's no going back. He scoots closer, still searching me through his questioning stare. "What's the matter? Please tell me. Stop hiding from me. I'm here to help."

I shake my head. He's trying to crack me open and unlock what I'm keeping from him behind my wide eyes, my clenched jaw.

His tone becomes stern, but still patient. "Freddy, it's just me. I won't tell anyone."

"Everything's fine." I flop back down on the mattress, grumbling to hide my fear. "You don't need to help me. I swear it to you, I'm fine. It's quarter past two. You should get some sleep."

"But—"

I interrupt him. "I'm fine. Trust me."

His hands clench his book, tight and trembling. There returns the look of a puppy being kicked in the street, turned away from affection.

His hand moves to my back, to my shoulder. His thumb rubs into my flesh. "Alright. Seeing that I'm not needed, I'll leave you to rest. If everything's fine, I shouldn't be worried, right?"

His last words feel like an insult; salt in the wound. He reaches to kiss me behind my ear and murmurs a goodnight, departing. His hand brushes the doorknob as he turns it slowly, challenging me to call him back in.

A thousand mixed signals fire through my head at rapid speeds. A sudden tightening of my chest snaps my airways shut. A pit in my stomach forms and eats at my insides. As hard as I try to shove it down, I can't. I can't bear it. I can't get rid of it. Marshall's hurt face only probes it, feeds the beast and enables it more space to roam and tear me further apart.

Go after him, my nerves snap at me. *He's right there. Go after him.*

I bolt upright. His foot toes the hallway, stepping into the cold with his book under his arm, face solemn. The word comes out before I can even think of what to say.

"Wait!"

It's a feeble cry, but it's enough for him to wheel back around. His jaw is set, his unoccupied hand clenching by his side. His eyes dart across my face, searching me and my forever-confusing meanings and signs. If I were a storm, Marshall would have a hell of a time sheltering himself from all the mixed forecasts my moods transmit.

"I'm sorry." I hug myself and grip my shoulders tight, my nails digging into the lace sleeves of my nightgown.

I know my face is paling. I know I look ghastly in front of him.

I can't hide it. I can't run away.

I'm trapped in the middle of a boy's worried gaze and the nightmares that await my viewing as soon as I close my eyes. It's unbearable.

"I shouldn't have shut you out like that." I pick at my skin, rambling. "I shouldn't have—I shouldn't have—I shouldn't have said anything—"

Marshall's quick to go into action, seeing he is in fact needed when I start stuttering and repeating my own words. He knows when I start breaking down, when the hurricane warnings of another meltdown appear on the radar. It's an ugly feeling to be wrapped in your own chaos that you can't control, utter madness to be trapped inside your own head, paralyzed, unable to move as the world passes you by at the speed of light. It's a feeling I wouldn't wish upon my worst enemy.

"Frieda?" His words coax warmth into me, soft and caring. He doesn't hide from the trouble before him. He runs straight into the storm, not caring for what damage it does. "What's the matter, honey? You're pale."

I dip my head into my arms. The tears come, unstoppable. The nightmares flash behind my eyelids. Violent, graphic images swarm my head, Marshall's voice in the center of it all.

"Frieda, please. Talk to me. Are you ill?" His voice rises with panic. He stands, setting his book on the bed, coming to my side, inclining his head with worry. I swat him away. "My most cherished love, do you need to go to the doctor? The hospital? I can organize for an ambulance straight away. Let me get the landline, if that's what you want, what you need, I'll give it to you."

Once more, I shake my head. I'm growing blunt, more agitated than before.

"Did I do something to upset you?" he worries.

"No!" It's expelled with a whine. The words all spew out. I hyperventilate, gasp for air, lose control. I start begging him to not send me to the hospital, to not call an ambulance or a doctor.

He remains concerned, expression unchanging and watches me unravel, searching for a way out. "If you don't want medical attention, is there something I can do? Think for as long as you like. I'm here for you, for whatever you're going through."

"I—I had another...bad dream...Another nightmare. I...I didn't want to tell you because you were already sleep deprived and I didn't want to worry you. I wanted you to see I was getting better, that I could handle myself."

"Frieda," his reply comes in a sympathetic sigh, "you know you can get me at any time of the night, right? I told you that each time you had a nightmare. Don't think you bothered me. Don't think you worried me— I am now, that I know you've been putting yourself through so much pain. Coming to me doesn't make you weak. It means you're not afraid to ask for help, and that makes me proud. Please don't hide from me. I'm here. I love you. I'd do everything in my power to make you happy."

"I'm sorry." The apologies keep coming, unstoppable gushes and babbles. He pulls me to his chest, rocks me slowly, back and forth, strokes my fringe, and repeats a soft *shhh* sound. He doesn't say much, other than repetitions of 'it's okay,' 'I'm here,' and 'please don't apologize' until my cries have turned into sobs, hiccups. My stomach grows queasy and my head spins.

I cry even harder as more and more images flash behind my eyes, letting it all out, staring out into the vast ocean of darkness of the room. He continues to rock me, humming the same tune once more.

Once it resolves to me sitting with my legs tucked into my chest, Marshall still holding onto me, he bends down to kiss my forehead.

"Doing okay? You've calmed a bit." He doesn't stop stroking me, his palm warm against my forehead.

"I'm sorry," I sob for the millionth time. "I shouldn't have kept it from you."

"Tell me if you're struggling next time. It hurts me when you're in pain." He slows his breathing when he hears me start to hyperventilate again.

I take the hint, copying him. The world around me comes back to life with each deep breath. Once I'm calm, my muscles aching, he reaches for the tissue box on the nightstand and wipes my eyes, fetching me a glass of water and some painkillers for my head. "I think I should stay here tonight."

With some limits brought by my hesitation, some insistings and objections being tossed around before I concede to him and his reasoning, he stands to close the door. His head sticks out, muttering to Cooper, who's been awakened by the noise, that everything is under control. He says a goodnight before he closes the door and windows and draws the curtains, swallowed in an even deeper darkness. The *plonk* of *Les Misérables* and his spectacles on the nightstand, the shifting of him stripping himself of his robe, folding it neatly and setting it upon the vanity chair sets me on edge, my body still frozen with fear until my eyes meet his.

He makes his way to bed and halts with his hand clutching the duvet. "Are you sure? I don't want to frighten you or cause you to feel uncomfortable."

My agreement isn't spoken, but my affirmative nod is understandable.

Silently, he pulls back the duvet and climbs in bed. His shoulder brushes mine, and I'm quick to wrap him in my arms.

Safe.

My head turns off the sirens for now, the tremble of my legs and the soreness across my sinuses becoming the aftermath of yet again another ruthless hurricane.

"I mean to tell you..." He slumps his head against a pillow, eyes fighting to keep open. "Do you remember...during the war...how I was always the last one to fall asleep?"

"Mmhm?"

"It's become a habit." He strokes the comforter in thought. "Each night we sleep in the same bed, I keep watch until you fall asleep because I know you need me there. I know you need me to keep you safe. Once you're asleep, I tuck you in real tight and make you all comfortable so you look like you're inside a little bread roll. I sometimes sing to you, tell you stories, check your breathing, your heart rate—everything, to make sure you'll be okay before I go to sleep. You're adorable when you sleep, Frieda. Your hands turn into little fists when you're dreaming. You sometimes talk in your sleep, of random things. One time you were complaining that I hadn't washed the cat yet."

I'll save the discussion of my embarrassing sleeptalk for another time. "You don't have to do that."

"I do, and who's going to stop me when I want to?" he yawns. "It's all worth it in the end, isn't it? I feel it's my duty to watch over you and keep you safe because I'd feel horrible if I didn't. Tonight, I'd be sick if I left you alone." He pulls the duvet over our shoulders, adjusting the pillows. "I don't care how many nights it takes you to get better, to stop having these dreams. Keep coming. Move into my room—or don't. Come when you need me. I'll be right here, waiting. You're my light, my love, my *baby*. I'd die for you, fight for you. I'd cross the sea for you, anything to keep my love safe."

It feels almost blasphemous for me to mumble, "Perhaps you do it because you pity me."

"Pity you? Don't think I've sunk that low." He snorts bitterly. "You underestimate me, babe. My love doesn't stop, ever. This is my way of saying 'I love you.' I want to keep you safe, warm, as happy as can be. I don't do it out of pity; that wouldn't truly be love, would it?"

"I thank you, then. I was expecting you to give up."

"Heavens no. You have to learn, precious, that I do *not* give up so easily and am far too stubborn to give away something that is dear to me." He snuggles closer, clasping my hands in his. "You mean everything to me. How could I leave you behind? After all we've been through, after how long we fought in a war that nearly claimed our lives?"

"I wasn't accusing you of anything."

"I know," he yawns again, "but you may still accuse me of being absolutely enthralled by you up till now and onward."

"Quite a mighty pledge, don't you think?" I jab, my eyes fighting to stay open.

"For the most deserving person."

He lets out another yawn and shifts to place an arm around my waist, pausing for a sign that what he's doing is okay. I reach for him and move closer. When he envelopes me in his arms, his warmth comes in waves. He starts kissing my forehead and snuggling deep under the covers with me, holding me close, his eyes watching over us, his breathing slowing, body relaxed against mine.

"I was right when I said the guest bed was comfortable."

The weight from crying weighs on me, pulling me down, dragging me further and further into sleep. He murmurs a goodnight, pecking me on the lips, brushing the hair out of my face, committing to his nightly ritual, guarding me from danger as I fall safely to sleep.

42

JULY PLANS

MARSHALL

The night is long.

Tragically long.

Frieda dances in and out of sleep. She manages to crunch in a few hours, but ends up waking up, screaming and shaking like someone's tearing her apart. Each time, I'm here beside her, rubbing her back, wiping the sweat off her forehead, and doing plenty of breathing exercises. Each apology, I repeat the line 'it's okay,' and 'please don't apologize' while she hyperventilates in my arms. It seems the nights alone made her worse, sicker. She feels skinnier, where she was two years ago.

The tiredness that aches in my bones threatens to pull me under and sleep alongside her, but all this drowsiness is worth it. I've slept in intervals; a light sleep awakened frequently by the slightest whimper, any potential jump into a new panic.

It's five in the morning, a few hours after the last nightmare. My eyes open to Frieda, swaddled in blankets, on my chest. Her hands remain clenched in my nightshirt's sleeves, her face slumped in sleep against the pillow. Her hair's come undone, the dark brown curls falling down to her shoulders—there's her fists forming again, her eyelids twitching.

Finally, she's at peace, getting the slumber she very much is in need of. Though her face is pale, color has returned to her cheeks. Her chest rises and falls with each sleeping breath. I never told her this because she'd disagree with me, but she looks so beautiful in the mornings that I'm driven to think compulsively of how blessed I am to bear witness to her beauty. It wasn't too often until now, since she told me she was getting better and that she could handle herself. If I were to tell her this, she'd most likely sit me down and present to me an hour long essay on why she disagrees. The thought of it jolts laughter alight inside me. She's always quick to clap back and defend her opinions.

The hollowness comes back each time I think of going to college and leaving her here alone. Sure, she has the study, Edith to bother her, Nathan too, if he ever comes around. But as I sit in a classroom taking hurried notes off a blackboard, she'll be alone, truly alone, until I return. Although she managed to do without me in the war, she can do it again.

A whimper escapes her lips. She burrows deeper into my chest, another bad dream flitting behind her eyelids. Her fingers knot tighter into my nightshirt, a pained sob escaping her. I'm quick to rub her back, muttering words of reassurance. Her nails claw into me, and I let out a gasp of pain against their sharp edges pinching me through the fabric.

Her eyes fly open. Her chest heaves, breaths wheezing in and out, her face ashen with panic.

"Frie—" I gasp.

"You're still here?" Her eyes search my face, wide, scanning my tired eyes. "Awake?"

"I woke up on my own." Which is a lie. I woke up to her legs spasming and kicking my shins while she dreamed. I don't have the heart to tell her that.

The slope of her shoulders is rigid, her whole body alert. "I had another one."

"I know."

"They don't go away." She covers her eyes with her hands, digging the heels of her palms into her sockets, rubbing furiously. "They'll never go away."

"They will, I promise." I speak through a yawn. My arms curve back over her waist. "Do you want to talk about them?"

"More shots, bombs—everything happening over and over again." She begins to whine. "I can't deal with this anymore!"

She bolts upright and swings herself out of bed. She opens the blinds hurriedly, opens all the windows, paces frantically, tapping her knuckles against her wrist in a repetitive beat, a sort of nervous tic to calm herself down

I hop out of bed and slide my robe on, sitting on the chair of the vanity by the bed.

"I can't deal with this anymore." She slams her hands against the vanity table, her fingers curling into fists. She grows distant, paler.

"Frieda," I start, but she stops me, eyes wild, impaling my own concerned gaze.

"How're you not having bad dreams? How're you not tossing and turning every night?"

"I don't know if it'll help if I say this, but I still have them, very much so. They're vivid—very vivid— and full of death. What I do before bed is I lie flat on my back, close my eyes and work through my body—"

She swears through her teeth, too distracted to take in any of my advice. "I don't want to do this anymore."

She's caught me off guard, perplexed. "Do what?"

"Have nightmares, have memories. Two years, Marshall. *Two years,* and it hasn't stopped!" She continues to hammer at her wrist, moving to scratch at her arms, letting out an audible curse when blood wells from her skin.

Without hesitation, I stand and grip her hand as the blood runs down her arm, reaching into the vanity to retrieve a handkerchief to press on the wound.

She's waiting for me to snap, to scream, lips trembling.

"Frieda, darling. Please look at me." I keep my hand and the kerchief pressed on her arm, leveling myself with her line of sight. "I understand, I really do. I understand the pain you're in, the turmoil you're facing. The last thing I want is for you to suppress it and make it worse. It gets you nowhere. You shutting me out this entire time has made it relapse into what it was two years ago—one of your worst states of mind. Please, Frieda. Let me in again. Let me help you. We made a promise, remember?"

"I broke it."

"You didn't." I reach for a gauze roll that sits on the top of the vanity after I clean away the thin drops of blood. "You were scared. I don't blame you. I'd be terrified if I were in your position. Please don't feel afraid to let me help you. I'm here for you. I well and truly am."

While I wrap the gauze around her wound (a small red line on the inside of her wrist from her nails), she slumps her shoulders and knocks her head against my collarbone.

"I thought you'd leave me." Her words are almost incoherent, a whisper, a breath of chilling, warm air against my skin.

"Heavens no." I grab some gauze tape and seal the bandage over the wound. "Boys do that, as insensitive as they can get. I'm a man. I don't leave those I love. Plus, it's not in my genetic makeup to leave anyone behind. Gosh, if you remember how many friends I made, I never left anyone alone. I never left you alone. I never will."

Her arms pull me in tight, patting me on the back. She ducks her head against my chest. "I'm sorry...for shutting you out."

"You thought you could handle it. You tried, which is brilliant, but you might need a little bit more support." I kiss her hair. "You're brave for trying to fight it."

"I let it get the best of me. That's not being brave."

"We'll work on it. One step at a time; how I got over things that held me back." She leans farther on me, growing weak. "You must be exhausted. Let's get you back into bed."

"Where are you going?" she asks.

I hoist her gently over my shoulder. "Nowhere. Just to make you some tea to help you fall back asleep."

I lower her back into bed, careful to remain quiet downstairs, sneaking into the study to scan the shelves that loom over me like monsters in the dark. In the lamplight, I reach for the faint gold lettering on the spine of *Emma* and nod in satisfaction. I pour lavender tea into a small mug and make my way back upstairs with the flowery scent tickling my nose.

She's lying on her stomach, her cheek resting on her hand. "You've come prepared." The remark is empty, tired. "You're going to read to me?"

"No, I'm going to smack you on the head until you fall asleep," I retort, and set the mug on the nightstand. She bristles, rising. "I'm kidding. Yes, I am."

I slide back into bed, carrying the book with me. She reaches for the mug, taking small sips. I prop *Emma* against my knee as she lies next to me. I read word after word, watching her eyes close on their own, the cup empty, on the bedside. I lightly snap the book shut, brushing the hair out of her face.

"Lavender tea works like a charm." I chuckle, turning to face her. "I'll have to remember that."

With a kiss to the forehead, my eyes closing, the book on my nightstand the day is spent catching up on lost sleep.

* * *

The next night, she suffers another blow.

Another cup of tea is swallowed.

Another chapter is read.

The night after that, a knock sounds at my door at three in the morning, Frieda clutching her throw blanket like an innocent child. I let her steal my teddy bear, Fenton, the little brown bear sitting on my nightstand that I've had ever since I was a newborn, for the night. The next thing I knew, Fenton was sporting his own new purple bow as he sat on my nightstand and watched the days go by.

The next night, I was wandering the halls after my late night studying and heard Frieda pacing. She was muttering to herself, incoherent, repeated words. Her feet padded lightly against the floor. I was so proud of her when the whole affair was put to a stop by her and herself alone. She was finally gaining some control.

Night after night, another scoop of lavender tea is ingested.

Frieda's nightmares cease.

* * *

Tonight is July ninth when Frieda knocks on my door upon the twelfth hour. She stands in my doorway, wrapped in her dressing gown.

My sidestep is enough to let her know that she's welcome inside. She comes as she pleases, and so do I.

"Midnight studying?" She peers over at the books that sit wide open on my desk, reading the titles of their chapters. "I thought you'd be asleep."

"College is fast approaching." I slump against the wall, my entire body aching, wrists stained blue. "I need to study harder than ever now."

"At least tomorrow, you can catch a break. I've missed grabbing time with you."

"As have I." My head spins from sleep deprivation. The coffee is wearing off. It must've been a weak brew of some sort.

I'm so sluggish that I don't even notice her reaching for my spectacles until her fingers brush my cheek. "What're you doing?"

"Getting these off." She takes them by the arms and folds them delicately back into their case. I'll be forever thankful to her for having the thought of not touching the lenses.

In the moonlight, she's radiant, sitting at the foot of my bed. I push any unholy thoughts to the back of my head when she pats the blankets.

"Well, aren't you coming?" she asks.

"Of course." My brain is too slow to reply with anything else. I settle beside her in the comfortable silence, flat on my back.

She slinks closer, poking me on the tip of my nose. "You have an ink stain there."

"Do I? I'll have to wash it off later."

She huffs her amusement. "Is there ever a time when you're not afflicted by ink stains? They appear like freckles on you."

"Speak for yourself."

Silence again.

Frieda's the first to break it. "What're you thinking?"

"Nothing of the immoral type." I get comfortable in bed, flopping onto my stomach. "About tomorrow."

"What about tomorrow, exactly?"

"How much fun we're going to have."

"You seem quite confident. Perhaps it's the sleep deprivation talking?" Her eyes flutter shut. She reaches to loop her pinky finger around mine. The gesture is minimal, yet it expresses a thousand words in so many ways.

"Perhaps so." My eyes close, surrendering to sleep, my senses growing faint. "I have a gut feeling."

"Of course you do." She releases a good-humored sigh. "You always do, one way or another. It either gets you in or out of trouble."

I open one eye and look at her, side on. "In trouble? Are you calling me a rascal?"

She bats her lashes innocently. "When did I ever say that?"

I sit up, lightning fast, smirking at her playfully. "I bet you like that type of thing."

"You better shut up before I—"

"Before you *what?*" I challenge her. She rises to meet my glare. "Before you what, *mi amor*? Are you threatening me?"

"I may as well irk you a bit. It's fun to watch you grow cross."

"Ah, so you *are* threatening me?" I bite my lip with a chuckle. "You better stop before something happens."

"Make me," she sneers, flashing her teeth with a cheeky grin.

It's enough to send a rush through me, for my cheeks to plume, to become a rosy pink. She's guffawing at my expression, my red cheeks.

It isn't long before I dare her with my lips against hers, swatting at each other playfully, tumbling around the bed with a bout of laughter, bidding each other goodnight within each other's arms.

* * *

On the tenth of July, Father is hanging lanterns, bright, flickering bulbs inside their glass houses, on the doorstep, planting cosmos flowers in the front garden to be seen by guests and family members upon entry to the house: pink and delicate petals, yellow centers, highlighting the well-kept grass.

There's to be a family gathering going on, as we hold one every summer. Our house was the chosen location for this year's party, and upon the announcement, everyone is taking great pride in cultivating food, drinks, decorations, and many other surprises for tonight. It'll be the perfect time to introduce Frieda and Nathan to the family, for them to branch out.

It's a hot day today. The air conditioning is on at full blast as Edith and I go over the plan, Nathan assisting and cracking jokes to keep my nerves from frying as he whips the cream for tonight's desserts. "Please tell me you didn't lose it. I swear to God, if you broke it—" Edith worries.

"I didn't. Calm yourself, Edith." I lean against the kitchen counter.

"Broke what?" Frieda takes cautious steps into the kitchen, poking her head around the corner. Edith turns swiftly on her heel to grab the strawberries out of the refrigerator, but more likely, she doesn't want to raise any suspicion.

"Nothing, my dear. Just the—the window. Yes, the window. I had to fix the hinges on Edith's window this morning. A couple of screws were loose." My face heats up, and my hands grip the corner of the tabletop for support.

She doesn't inquire further, much to my relief. Her eyes scan the kitchen bench, the delicacies being prepared.

"Marshall, you're sweating through your shirt," Edith remarks, slicing the tops off of the strawberries. Her cutting board is stained in an array of reds and pinks, various shades and chunks of the berries and their juices wetting the wood.

"Am I? Jesus, Mary and Joseph, I am," I scoff and slide off my vest and set it aside, groaning at the sweat that moistens my now unbuttoned collar. Frieda whistles. I roll my eyes.

"I expected you to be studying." She steals one of the uncut strawberries, picking off the stem, popping it in her mouth.

"Too hot in there. I deserve a day off." I take the punnet away from her, putting it in between Edith and Nathan. "And those are for dessert."

She whines, "But I'm starved!"

"Your loss for sleeping through breakfast."

She pokes her tongue out at me, only to resume her smirk. "Your fault for keeping me up past midnight tying cherry stems with that tongue of yours!"

Nathan snorts behind his hand. Frieda sits atop the kitchen counter. Edith bursts into an unashamed bout of laughter.

I'm at a loss, struggling for words. "Wait a moment—"

Edith bends forward, gripping the counter as she hoots. Frieda joins in with a smug giggle. "God, Frieda. Actually?"

"Just a little bedtime smooch, right, Marshall?" She mischievously steals another strawberry.

As I lean back against the counter, I sneer, "I'll do it again if you want me to."

"I don't know if I like being associated with this," Nathan says over his chopping board. "Let's just say whatever happened in the bedroom stays in the bedroom, *please*."

"Children!" Father pokes his head into the kitchen, sweat sprinkled on his brow. "The flag's been set up. I thought I'd come inside and see how you're all doing. Edith, Nathan, brilliant job on the desserts so far."

"Thanks, Cooper." Nathan grins and scrapes the strawberry slices into a bowl, continuing to mix the cream before he pours it in. "Thanks for letting us make it. Edith was so keen on making strawberries and cream for tonight, so I thought, why not?"

"Polite as ever, my boy." Father pats him on the shoulder and turns to me with a secretive wink. "Marshall, my boy, you're *drenched*! Change your clothes before tonight."

"I've got you, don't worry. That's already managed." I return the wink and duck away when he reaches to ruffle my hair. Frieda's busy chattering away with Edith, who pokes fun at her for her abnormally rosy and blushing cheeks.

As Father digs into the tool bag for a hammer and nails, he gives me a nod of the head and angles it to the front door, recommending my assistance. "Why don't you help with dusting the house, Marsh? You look bored, not having anything to do."

"Sure." I roll back the sleeves of my sweaty shirt, wiping a whole sheen of sweat off my forehead.

When I step into the laundry to get out the feather duster, I catch a glimpse outside: Father stands with his arms crossed and laughs along with the neighbors, who seem to be complimenting him on his gardening skills, specially utilized for tonight's gathering, on show more than any other time of year.

He waves goodbye, jumps up the steps—two at a time—and bounds into the laundry to pester me about tonight.

"So, do you have the ring?" He picks up the vacuum in the corner. "The living room needs extra dusting—especially Alexandria's ornaments. You can do that, can't you?"

Of course. I should've expected it. He dragged me here with the excuse of chores to chat me up about the plans for tonight; the plans we've been organizing for the past month or two.

"It's in my tie drawer. She never goes through it, so I thought it would be a good spot to hide my surprise."

"I'd highly doubt she would be going through your drawers, anyhow." He plays with turning the vacuum on, and it coughs in response. "Is the ring pretty?"

"Sterling silver with diamonds. Edith helped pick it out." I make a grand step over the machine's wire that snakes across the floor. Even with my great attempt to avoid it, I almost trip. "I must say, she has some taste."

A truth: I became indecisive at the jeweler's when I narrowed down the choices to two rings: one, the ring that Edith picked out, the other an older design with a smaller diamond. I started pacing when Edith told me to 'feel which one was right.' The sterling silver immediately felt like Frieda. My pacing stopped, a check was paid for. The secret mission was a success.

"She does. I'm glad my girl has a good sense of fashion." He bends to a crouch to examine the vacuum, which he finds has a full container. No wonder it wasn't starting. "Do you remember the signal? The song that'll play before you make the proposal?"

"*Let Me Call You Sweetheart.* I chose it myself."

"Good, good. Don't forget when the time arises."

"Father, we've rehearsed it a bazillion times. I'm not going to forget it. I followed Robert Sallinger's orders for nearly two years and I've never gotten in trouble."

"You will, if you mess this up." He winks. "I'll lick that flank of yours."

My smile is shaky. "I swear it to you, I won't. This is the last thing I want to mess up. Ever."

"Make me proud, son. Make us proud."

"I will."

I step back inside, bombarded by horrendously loud laughter and cold water splashed viciously on my face. "What the hell is going on in—Edith!"

Both Edith and Frieda are giggling with shot glasses full of water, now empty and leaking through my clothes, dampening my hair which allows sopping drops to run down my face, cool against my neck.

"That was meant for Nathan! We're so sorry!" Frieda pats my hair down with a damp hand and hands me a towel. "He spritzed us, so we have to get him back once he comes downstairs."

"You're truly horrible." I wipe the water that drips down my face and stings my sockets. "You have me waiting to get revenge."

They squeal and scamper away from me. Nathan comes downstairs and steps right into the commotion.

"Dodged a bullet, Nate." I bump him on the shoulder and shuffle past, up the stairs to my room, shrugging out of my wet clothes in exchange for new ones..

Downstairs, Nathan screeches. Edith and Frieda hoot aloud their victory, their sworn revenge finally carried out.

43

LIGHTS AND LAUGHTER

FRIEDA

The lights and laughter fizz through tonight's celebrations. Music blasts from the radio. People are dancing

in the backyard in the summer air, grabbing drinks at the kitchen counter, food at the dining room table. I'm

caught in the thick of it, watching as friends and relatives of Alistair, Marshall, and Edith file past, hoping

to find Nathan to know I'm not the only outsider here.

The chatter is loud and full of energy. The urge to eavesdrop is contagious. I pour myself a glass of

carbonated water, observing Nora and Maurice's faces, creasing into elderly smiles as they converse. It's

ridiculous to try to count the amount of shaggy black hair on people's heads here. Marshall wasn't wrong

when he said the gene traveled down the line like a wildfire. In almost every corner, it swallows the room.

"Found you," a voice whispers in my ear. A hand brushes over the hip of my plum purple dress. I jump at

the sudden warm breath against my ear. "It's just me. I didn't mean to scare you."

"I knew it was you from that singular gesture. Can you be more creative?" I tease.

"Apologies." Marshall curtseys, accentuating his hands far too much for it to be taken seriously. "Shall I

curtsey each time I see you, then?"

"No, please don't." I raise my glass to my lips. "Where were you?"

"Getting ready, of course." He puffs out his chest. "Don't I look swell?"

"It usually takes you twenty minutes to get ready, and it took you almost a full hour tonight." I scan his

suit—a white coat, a dark vest and tie with matching gray slacks—before I drag him in by the lapel. "But,

I'll let it slide. You're practically eye candy."

He runs a hand over an escaping strand of hair from his combover, gelled and slicked to the side. A smirk

spills on his lips. His laugh comes in a suppressed chuckle, a rumble that makes my heart flutter. "Aw,

shucks. My apologies, I wanted to look nice for tonight. And you, looking beautiful, as always."

"Always one for compliments." I set my glass down on the counter. He reaches for the bottle of mineral

water, pouring some for himself in another glass.

He takes a shallow sip, leaning on the edge of the counter. "Did I leave you alone for too long? I hope I

didn't."

"No, actually. I was able to strike up another conversation with your grandparents."

"Brilliant. I'm glad you're coming out of your shell." He gives me a content smile and adds, "I'm proud of you."

Once again, he catches me off guard. "Proud of me?"

"I'm proud of you because you're relaxing more in public. You're more at ease, less tense."

"Thanks to you. As you said, we benefit from each other, right?"

He takes a long sip of his water. "You still remember me saying that from, what, two years ago? Good memory."

"I remember it because it's true. It stuck with me all this time. It feels good."

"Let me say it was all you with me pushing you along in support. You toughened up all on your own, buttercup."

"What I've noticed from you is you seem a lot happier. You don't feel down at all?"

"I'm *livid*," he sighs heavily. "Kidding! I'm having the time of my life. I rarely feel sad."

"That's all on your own." I offer a smile. "I'm proud of you too. You've matured a lot."

"You and I both." He gestures his glass to me, the carbonated water sloshing against its walls. "On a lighter and less philosophical note: You're enjoying yourself?"

"Very much. Nathan amused me by trying pure lemon juice on a dare. His face screwed up like a raisin when he complained about how acidic it was and proceeded to exit the room to grab some water. Edith was doubled over, laughing in her chair."

"Nathan doesn't strike me as one with much of a taste for citric acid." Marshall's eyes survey the party in front of him. He checks his pocket watch. It still ticks, after all this time, after all the war, death, and destruction it's seen, it still ticks to this day. It's counting down something only its bearer knows.

I loop his arm through mine. "Are you waiting for something? Someone?"

"Fireworks," he replies, and folds the watch neatly back in his pocket. A dark haired man appears before him. "Cousin Greggory! A pleasure to see you."

"Marshall!" the man replies, sloshing the liquid in his glass. "Look at you, a wallflower, sitting by the bar."

"Just enjoying my companion's company." He straightens, taking a shallow sip of water. "Gregg, this is Frieda. Frieda, this is Gregg, my cousin."

"A pleasure to meet you." Gregg gives me a short bow, only for me to curtsey in return, as if on autopilot, still programmed by the code of my mother's old teachings of common and correct social etiquette.

"And you, Gregg." I flash another smile before I sip my water to give myself something to do.

After a long chat about the party and the card games going on in the living room, he excuses himself. Marshall and I move onward to the parlor, where it's alive with action, cheering and hooting. One of his family members draws out a set of cards and points to them on the table: a royal straight flush, it looks like. He's won the game, whatever they're playing. The men at the table applaud.

In the backyard sit Edith and Alistair with Kara and Yvette, on lawn chairs. Nathan sits with Thomas and Eleanor in front of Mrs Mason with a chubby little boy in her lap. Rupert, she calls him, as she strokes back his growing, thin baby hairs. He clenches and unclenches his fists, sharing all the same bouts of excitement as his older siblings, blabbering and watching them play.

"We should join them." I take Marshall's hand and sit, Eleanor and Thomas's arms circling his waist in a group hug before he drags a chair over and folds his legs. He's rigid, only half-listening to our conversation as he eyes his watch's face, rubbing his thumb over its lid in anticipation. He's waiting for something, growing fidgety as the deadline draws near.

That's when the dancing starts, and the festivities come to life in full swing on the grass in the backyard, the crickets chirping along with the slow waltz that plays on the small radio someone's set up out here. People are caressing each other closely, hand in hand, enchanted and enamored with each other. One couple, who I presume are some of Marshall, Alistair, and Edith's aunts and uncles—the side of the family indiscernible—are swaying, hands held, fingers entwined, foreheads pressed together tenderly. The man is saying something to the woman—something humorous, because she laughs and kisses his cheek before he sneaks in a peck on her mouth.

My eyes surf the crowds for one fact amongst the others, that white suit that stands out so starkly, yet so beautifully, from the rest, the one that said he'd be going to get refreshments and is taking an awfully long time. He's nowhere to be seen, but the cackle that cracks through the air like a whiplash is enough to tell me where he is. I'd know that laugh even in a crowd of thousands, if the challenge reveals itself.

I slink past without uttering a word to those who are already busy in conversation, choosing to entertain themselves with words rather than the closeness felt when waltzing away to a faraway tune. There's more laughter, the swishing of drinks in glasses, an array of both English and Spanish being exclaimed all around. I can't help but catch wind of Edith giggling at something an older woman, graying hair at her temples, smile lines mapping her face, says and pats her shoulder, eyes creasing with her smile.

My hands begin to shake, begin to grow clammy, but nonetheless, I prevail and venture further into the crowds, spectators of the lively dance floor. I fill my lungs with a deep inhale, one that slows my erratic heart rate and grounds me, even amidst all the chaos this party is creating. His laugh sounds again; loud and lively, and I train my ears to follow it. Closer and closer I get. Further away from where the action is the most ecstatic.

Marshall has quite a paparazzi circled around himself, but remains at ease, that interested, entertained grin reaching his lips, the intrigued sparkle in his eye on full display. His arms are folded across his chest, the slope of his shoulders relaxed.

Though, his expression changes when I come into view. He's no longer looking at the person talking to him—a young man in a crimson suit—but right at me, that twinkle in his eye shining ten times brighter. He gives me a shy wave, cheeks flushing, most likely remembering the errand he had to run.

"Apologies, Jose, but I have some important matters to attend to," he interupts, and turns away once the man finds a new listener to entertain.

Marshall bounds towards me, and before he can say anything, I poke an accusing finger at his buttonhole. "You were supposed to get the drinks."

"But, you see, once Cousin Jose starts talking, there's no way out," Marshall groans.

"You seemed to be having a jolly good time," I argue.

"Look, I'm sorry," he bows his head in shame, "I know I got sidetracked. I promise you, I'll never do it again."

"You better not," I threaten, but playfully, and rustle his hair. "I could've died of dehydration by the time you got back."

"I'd best be there to save you then," he says, with a wink. "What's happening over there?" He points in the direction of where the waltzing is. "It seems action packed."

"Dancing," I say.

At the word, his arm hooks itself along my waist. He leans in, planting his mouth to my ear to whisper, "I think we should join in."

"What makes you say that?" I ask, turning to face him.

His hands become more secure, his lips moving from my ear to my neck. "I miss the close contact."

A snort expels itself from my nose. "Really? The *close contact*?"

He shrugs, and sighs, his breath warm on my skin. His arm drags me closer to him. "More than that. Perhaps there's something perfectly magical about it, being so close to the one you love. It's almost as if you fit together into one perfect mold."

The smile that forms on my face excites him even more. The laugh that erupts in his throat can't be ignored.

With a burst of energy, he takes both my hands and pulls me through the crowds, shushing me when I squeal, but breaks into another bout of chuckles all the way to the dance floor.

In a huffing mess, grinning away, cheeks flushed to the extreme, not just from the heat, Marshall bows and retakes my hand and presses a kiss to my knuckles. Once he regains his composure, he asks in a low, gentlemanlike voice, eyes locking with mine.

"My most exquisite love." He carries on with the flattery, even when I burst into bubbly laughter. "Will you take this dance?"

Through my giggles, I nod. "I will."

It's not until he rises back to full height that the world slows against the soft, lilting tune playing, just reaching my ears. Marshall hears it too, and something inside of him snaps into place. But it doesn't prevent him from guiding me into the thick of the bustle, his forever-careful hands returning to their places on my shoulder blade, my open palm, dutifully arranging themselves, their owner leaning forward, every freckle donning his cheeks able to be seen, stardust in its own galaxy.

He says something, but I'm too distracted to make out the words. "Pardon?"

"I said this is slower than what we danced to," he repeats, "in Le Havre."

"It is, isn't it."

He gazes up ahead at the lanterns hanging above us on the wires Cooper set up outside as some kind of makeshift arch way, and he's done a fantastic job at it. "I think I know who added this one in."

"Who?" I ask.

Marshall's grin widens, feet starting to move along with the music. I follow his lead. "The person is a real charmer, often described as 'lovesick,' or—"

"You truly are enamored." The words come out in a sigh, and I lean into his warmth. Despite the heat, it's welcoming all the same. "I wouldn't have it any other way."

"I love when you appreciate the smaller things," he says, soft, so only I can hear it. "It makes me grow all warm and fuzzy, knowing that all the little things I do are appreciated."

"Don't go all mushy on me," I tease. "This is supposed to be romantic."

"Oh, sorry," he leans farther forward. "I shall become the stoic hero of your dreams."

I swallow down my laughter. He and I sway back and forth, slowly, from side to side. It's not one of those electrifying, exhausting waltzes seen often at parties, with fast strokes of bows across string instruments, the brass section booming away, but a sobering, quiet dance that only requires intimacy and the willingness to come closer.

It's beautiful, in a way, feeling yourself in your partner's arms, their hands holding yours, holding *you*. I never thought I'd experience this type of happiness, with this boy, at this party, right here, but all dreams will become a reality if you really put your foot in the door and *try*, no matter how many bruises or scrapes you get, or slams in the face. You keep going. You keep pushing forward.

Marshall, usually watching over me, the hazel in his eyes forever bright, is resigning from his post, hand relaxed in mine, his other keeping me close to him. The cologne he put on earlier wafts past my nose: strong, biting into the sweetness of the summer night air. He withdraws himself even further with a kiss to my forehead and his head nuzzling into my shoulder. He's humming, but not his own tune, along with the song floating above us, singing us a soft melody of love and tenderness.

The song fades, but it's still Marshall and I, trapped in this moment, wandering further into it, refusing to let the serenity of it go. But it leaves once Marshall clears his throat, brings my hands into his, and squeezes them. The whole backyard has gone quiet, expecting him to speak, to do something only known to him.

"Frieda, I.. uh…" He racks his brain, lost in thought.

"Yes? Take your time."

"O-oh, well, for once, I'm not trying to come up with a comeback about my coat or anything embarrassing like that. I've actually been wanting to ask this for an extremely long time. Gosh, time flies when you're living life with the person of your dreams."

A prickle of nervous excitement flutters in my stomach. "What're you trying to say?"

"What I'm trying to say, dear, is that you're remarkable—truly astounding. There are so many adjectives to describe you: gorgeous, strong, selfless, and you simply take my breath away. You've brought so much light, so much joy, that my heart might just explode inside my chest from all the admiration I feel for you. Everyday is golden and will always be golden with you. I love you so much, and every time I look at you, I always feel a sense of warmth and hope that this will never end, that you'll stay mine forever."

I bite my lip, eyes widening. I let in a gasp, my body tensing at the boyish grin that twitches at his lips.

"Every exchange of love lingers. We've become better people, and how glad am I to be standing where we are today after experiencing so much turmoil, so much that kept us apart. It tried to separate us, but only made our special bond stronger, one that only you and I can feel. I remember the string analogy I told you a couple years ago. I'd like to revisit that."

He pats my trembling hands, squeezes them to tell me that we're okay. What he's trying to say is okay.

"We're still two individuals holding tight to the same red string. Each moment lets us pull each other closer. As I've said before, we've already tied ourselves so tight that it would be impossible to let go, to simply cut the string. Today, tomorrow, and each day after that, I'd like to make that knot even tighter."

It only occurs to me now that the crowd around us is silent, listening and intent. He clutches my hands tighter, his glittering gaze never faltering. Each passing second, he's growing softer, sticky with the sugary-sweet taste of the love his heart bleeds out.

"I want to spend the rest of my life with you. Every day, every night...I want to spend it with you. Every rise, every fall, whatever the tide may bring, I want to experience it all with you..."

A shriek of shock that I didn't even know I could muster escapes my lips as he lowers himself to one knee on the lawn, gracefully reaching into his pocket for a small box. My hands fly to my lips and tears sting at the back of my eyes.

"Every push and pull, every twist and turn, I want to ride with you. I want to ask you, right here and now." He carefully opens the box, unveiling a beautiful silver and diamond ring. "Frieda Joyce: my love, my light, my most beautiful and gracious darling, will you take the pleasure of making me the happiest man to ever live? Take my side as my eternal joy? Will you marry me?"

A gasp erupts through the crowd. The weight of more than a dozen eyes is upon us. The suspense hangs in the air.

After a long, gleeful sob, I nod hurriedly. "My love...Yes! A thousand times yes!"

He wipes his own tears away, takes the ring from its box, and places it on my finger. His lips brush my knuckles, charged with delight before he stands and lets me gather him in my arms for a heartfelt, tender kiss.

His family and friends cheer. There's a round of applause, a choir of men singing a frenzied, off-key tune of *Here Comes The Bride.* He pulls away, only to dive in for another tearful kiss before he pulls away again and cries into my shoulder.

"My poor baby, you're shaking!" I rub his back before he grips my hands again and holds them tight, ducking to meet my eyes. "Thank you, God bless you—thank you!"

"Please, thank *you* for sharing the same dream as me." He hurriedly wipes his eyes and kisses my ring finger again. "The boy inside me is hooting and screaming with joy."

"Hold on, you have lipstick here." I wipe at the pink stain on the side of his mouth with my thumb and kiss his cheek. "That's better."

"Anything is better with you," he says, the flirty, loving essence of his personality showing at its fullest flair. He wipes his eyes, a watery chuckle breaking through his sobbing breaths. "I can't stop crying!"

I envelope him into another hug, patting him on the back. He stamps meaningful kisses along my forehead, my nose, my cheeks. Last but not least, my lips.

If I could choose one way to live my life with no going back, it would be with him. With the man who's blubbering and laughing through his tears in my arms. I'd give my soul, my entire being, to be by his side for as long as we live and nurture our foundation as we grow old. I'd offer my everything to clasp his hands through the depths of Hell.

Most importantly, I'll save him from drowning when he doesn't know how to swim.

When he crumbles, I'll put him back together as he's done with me for so long.

He's nursed every cut, every scrape, every fall. Glued each fragment of fragile glass together when need be.

I'd travel to infinity to have the mystery bookworm I happened to fall head over heels for to remain by my side for the rest of my days.

* * *

For the rest of the night, after washing the dishes and helping tidy up, Cooper and Edith can't stop gushing about the newly engaged couple in the room. My boyfriend's—now my *fiancé*'s—cheeks gush each time the word is spoken, a boyish, impish excitement sending that heartstring-pulling smile to his lips. His eyes never leave me, shamelessly winking.

Later, gazing at me over the blankets in his room, he rests beside me, worn out from tonight's extravagant festivities. He's in his fleece pajama bottoms, shirt off, his scars, a map drawn on his torso on full display; forever a wondrous exhibition of strength. The room was too hot to sleep in the heavy nightshirt, he'd complained. I highly doubt this was the truth, as it was obvious he was trying to flex the set of his shoulders, his defined stomach and chest.

"At our wedding, we *have* to have a chocolate fountain. Chocolate makes everyone happy," he says.

My finger traces the white line of scar tissue on his bare shoulder. "No objections here. Put it on the wedding plans."

"I mean it, Frieda! A chocolate fountain would be just amazing!" he exclaims.

"Alright, alright! We'll have a chocolate fountain!" I exclaim louder.

"Gosh, I sound like a child arranging a birthday party. This feels like a dream."

"You do, as a matter of fact," I tease, both of us erupting in a hearty laugh.

Our laughter rings around the room until Nathan knocks harshly on the door. His hair is a mess, his eyes are stained with shadows, squinting and still half asleep. "Look, I understand you're newly engaged and all, but Edith and I can hear you two down the hall and we're both exhausted. Please tone it down."

With apologies as the door closes, our laughter drops to a chuckle before it dies all together. Letting out an amused sigh, he relaxes. I resume my tracing of his scars.

"Frieda, *cariño*," he purrs after a few moments of silence, "you have no idea how excited I am to spend the next chapter of my life with you, to see what adventures we'll go on." His body slumps against mine, pressing against my chest. Hands on my hips, he lies flat on his stomach, resting his head upon my heart. His hazel eyes flutter shut, the blankets lying across his waist, his hair bedraggled, just how I like it: young, wild and free. "I'm beyond ecstatic."

"I feel the same as you, Marshall." I rest my head against the pillows, closing my eyes, beaming, overjoyed. My fingers trace more and more scars on his shoulder blades. "All the same feelings." After he reaches to turn off the oil lamp and settles back down in his spot, I kiss his forehead and whisper excitedly, "I simply can't wait."

PART IV

THE ENCORE

MAY, 1924

FRIEDA AND MARSHALL

44

ENCORE

And so, the next chapter begins. A new page is turned. A photo album stocking memories and hardships of the years before is filed away.

In the following months since our engagement, Marshall stationed himself at his desk, continuing to prop open textbooks and large medical manuals to help him finalize his studies for college. In September, we saw him off at Jefferson Medical College on his first day, which was a whole lot of nerves for him and his father. Cooper cried and cried as Marshall repeatedly patted his back with all the reassurance he could muster. He wanted me there specifically to witness the entire episode. It was my duty to calm him until his son came home for the day, which resulted in even more tears.

On December 7th, 1921, Marshall and I were wed at the Cathedral Basilica of Saints Peter and Paul, followed by an amazing after party filled with delights of dancing, speeches from both families and the promised chocolate fountain on display before we set off on our honeymoon in New York in late January. This included plenty of cold nights out and even some on Broadway, Marshall managing to run to the box office in the unforgiving New Yorken blizzard to purchase two lucky tickets for *Shuffle Along.* He spoiled me with bagels from the nearby deli for breakfast in the hotel room the morning after.

We were beyond excited to move into a large house in Spruce Hill, nearly twenty minutes away from East Falls. We became ecstatic once Marshall graduated from college and landed a fair-paying job as a nurse at the Pennsylvania Hospital on Spruce Street. All those hard hours of studying, internships, and missed hours of sleep handed him his ninety-three percent on his thesis. He spent a week writing about the Spanish Flu pandemic which landed him his degree and a new chapter to turn the page over, deeper waters to swim.

Each morning, his alarm rings on his nightstand at exactly five-fifteen. At first, he groans into the pillow, digging deeper to evade the shrill ringing before his hand slams atop it to shut it up. He makes the time to kiss me good morning and gets up quietly to shower, pick out his clothes for the day, and make himself look presentable.

The kitchen grows thick with the scent of coffee. He departs with his medical kit over his shoulder. One hand clutches a warm travel cup of dark, roasted coffee, the other handles a slice of buttered toast. With his spectacles on his nose, he kisses me goodbye and sets off into the dark dawn as I rise to start the day.

There's a pleasant train ride waiting for him at five forty-five, and he tries to be home by six if he isn't required on the night shift. He uses the hospital phone to call me to say he'll be late to diffuse predicted anxiety and comes home the next day to rest, exhausted. He doesn't work on Sundays and spends the day catching up on overtime and on walks in the park with me.

Though work carries him on a relentless and unforgiving current, he makes time for the both of us. One of our first fights flamed into existence when I brought up that I wasn't seeing enough of him, and that I missed him far too much for my own good. The house was growing lonely without his presence, except on Sundays.

Out of stress, he yelped back at me that he was trying, *trying* to make time, and asked if I could 'just wait.' That snarl sent me slamming the bedroom door shut, crying on the floor. He rushed in to apologize straight away for lashing out and that he didn't mean for those words to come out the way they did. He'd admitted to getting lost in his work, even though he'd only been in it for a few months, and felt absolutely horrible for doing so, and that he missed me. He made up for it, making sure to get as much time with me as possible after work with a date night booked for the following Sunday.

That's the thing about Marshall: He doesn't make false promises. He's probably the most trustworthy man I've ever known and one that actually keeps his word.

In 1922, Edith got engaged to Nathan. Soon to become Edith Nelson, their wedding was to happen in Florida in late August when the weather warmed.

Marshall started crying and pulled his sister into the most ferocious, brotherly bear hug I ever saw. Alistair joined them and became a sprawled disaster of Clark siblings on the floor, like squirming puppies just learning to walk. The whole affair was highly amusing to watch when you had a thirty-one, twenty-eight, and twenty-two year old squiggling around on the floor. Kara, now nearly five, chuckled away as her father became knitted in the chaotic mess.

In the meantime, after several questions and queries, several 'are you sure's,' 'are you certain's,' and preparations, Marshall and I tried for children. To this day, he keeps bringing up that the 'third time's a charm,' a remark that sends me reeling. His face lit up like a Christmas tree when I brought the subject up one afternoon. He was practically glowing with joy when I announced I was pregnant with our first child three months later.

That following April, it wasn't one child that was born, but two. Fraternal twins. Marshall almost fainted when he stepped into the delivery room a few minutes after their birth. As soon as they were in his arms, his paternal instincts took over and had him crying.

When they were only a few hours old, he spoke softly to them, telling them stories and humming them off to sleep when they started crying. He kept making the same heartfelt pledge that he, their father, would always be there to protect and nurture them, as they were two gracious little stars that two magnificent bodies of the universe created. His words, not mine.

The first and eldest is Anastasia Alexandria Clark. She quickly became quite a mouthful for a small girl with eyes that could carry the entire galaxy. She has, of course, Marshall's hair, which crossed another genetic border to reach her, paired with my green eyes. She was the loudest of the two, the record holder for the most nights keeping us up, even snagging a spot between Marshall and I in bed until she calmed down.

The second and the youngest of the two is William Victor Clark. Marshall slotted in his middle name to reference his great grandfather, mooning over William as his first name. He got, humorously, my hair and Marshall's eyes, a brilliant combination of brown on hazel, with a birthmark over his left eye. He possesses more of my personality; more laid back but anxious in social situations. His sister is like her father, getting up to so much chaos with him that you could fill a whole book on how many adventures they went on together with their mischief.

Of course, Marshall's a brilliant father that our children truly need and look up to. His smile grows ten times brighter when he comes home from work while Anna and Will are all over him, waddling on their chubby, three year old legs, calling 'Papa' from across the room with all the excitement in the world.

Each Sunday, he stays home and plays with them. One time, I walked in on them sprawled out in the Florida room under his arms as he read Lewis Carrol to them in a soft, narrative voice, also often reading them bedtime stories, tucking them both in bed. It breaks my heart when I watch over him saying goodnight. He tucks them in extra tight, making sure they're both comfortably asleep before he retires himself. During the flu season, he sat in their room all night and watched over them for a solid week before he grew ill himself.

In the early days of 1924, Nathan and Edith brought Timothy Nelson into the world with his father's glorious red hair and pale eyes. Cooper was all over him, Marshall and Alistair the happiest pair of uncles anyone could see.

Other than external family life, all's been well.

Living with Marshall could never be better. He's a caring and perceptive husband, one to take both our feelings into a count and work to provide the best outcome for all of us. He carries the role with grace, one to keep the nest and pecking order in line and remind everyone who's boss. He's never hit or screamed at anyone out of anger or punishment, simply stating that he needs 'alone time' to cool off when he does happen to suffer from the common swings of irritation or annoyance. He sometimes still goes through funks of depression, often when memories of the war are brought up, getting caught up in flashbacks during nights lying on the floor, curled in on himself. He's taken to writing his feelings out, seeming to help him filter out his bad thoughts and ideations. In summary, he's been in a better mental state than ever before, old coping mechanisms working greatly for him.

I still get nightmares; ones that aren't so vivid, but still send me spiraling into a panic and a cold sweat, only to wake in Marshall's arms and be welcomed back to reality with his snores.

Over the years, the scars have faded, both inside and out. Reparations are made. Each day, more and more weight lifts off my shoulders. The days of the war grow further and further away. More light shines in my eyes. I'm a new person, no longer a shell of who I used to be.

The war, in all honesty, has changed me. It made me grow thicker skin and harden up against the cruelty of the world and whatever Hell may bring to my doorstep. I'm an entirely new person, one that saw every terror the Devil gave me and made it out alive. My heart still beats. I still smile. I press on and step farther through life. Each day and every hour is a new experience.

Even with so much strife, so much destruction blocking the roads, I wouldn't have it any other way.

* * *

It's a week after Marshall's 29th birthday when he comes home from work.

His key fumbles in the lock, the methodic *click* of the teeth echoing in the front hallway as he unlocks the door and swings it open against the still-cold winds outside in the autumn weather. There's the familiar *thump* of his bag being set on the floor and the rustle of his overcoat, probably revealing the white lab coat he wears at work.

Snapping *Crome Yellow* shut, placing it on the desk in the library, I open the great double doors and proceed into the hallway. The thudding of Will and Anna's tiny feet clamber down the stairs.

"Papa! Papa!" they call and compete to reach him first.

He bends down onto one knee with outstretched arms set to hug them tight. His laughter is contagious as he bends to kiss them both on the forehead. His chortle only grows louder when they start yelling over each other to talk to him.

"My children," he giggles, "my children, one at a time! I can only hear one of you! I don't have four ears. Ladies first. Anna, what would you like to say?"

571

"Did you find that pretty flower I was telling you about, Papa? The one I drew yesterday?" She looks up at him hopefully, her hands clenching and unclenching with excitement.

Marshall's face softens, even softer than it already is. "Of course I did, little one. You know your father never forgets these types of things! Not when it's a request from his daughter! Now, where did I put that pretty flower?"

I watch him from down the hall. He fiddles with his pockets, humming a tune of concentration. "If I remember correctly..." He gives Anna a raised brow. "It should be right...here!"

He presents her a yellow rose from his pocket, Anna letting out a squeal of delight which causes him to beam. Will shares her delight, jumping up and down while flapping his hands.

Marshall turns to talk to him. "What about you, my boy? I heard you had Show and Tell today. Did you treat my medals well?"

He releases a laugh. "Yeah! Mrs Abbott even said you were a hero!"

"I'm merely an old man getting older." He ducks his head with a sigh. "I'll take it as a compliment, though. Tell her tomorrow that I said thank you. Now, did you put them back in their case?"

"Yeah, I even wiped them down after everyone touched them. It went super well!"

"I'm proud of you, Will, I really am." He reaches to hug him once more, kissing his cheek, which sends him giggling with childish glee.

The kids chatter and play. Marshall sets his coat on one of the hooks by the door, eyes set on me with the greatest smile I'll ever know, full of light and joy that he's carried for so many years. It never seems to expire, even when he donates it to guests and family members. He still looks at me as if I'm the most dazzling thing in the room, a painting with brushstrokes creating a masterpiece of perfection.

"Hello, *mi preciosa bebe*." He wraps me close, pecking my lips before he bends down to place a kiss on my bulging belly, his hands patting the bump and shaping it under his palms. "Hello, my child. How're the light of my life and the little one doing? Feeling better than yesterday?"

"A lot better, actually. I've been sleeping all day." I give him another peck on the lips when he jumps back up to full height. "Little Elijah or Virgina hasn't given me much trouble. I've been craving a lot of chocolate as of now. How about you, *mon amour*? Work was okay?"

"Good, as always." His eyes venture from the bump to my face. "Better when I come home and get to see my family. It truly brings a smile to my face." He looks down at the bump again, tutting and rubbing it. "Gosh, you're getting bigger and bigger each day. You better not give Ma too much trouble, or else you're in for a conversation with your father, tough guy—or girl—or person. However you want to be addressed, little one, I will call you whatever you please."

"Oh, don't scare them!" I put my hands on my belly, Marshall snickering.

I'm merely teasing." His hazel irises are soft and warm with love, with admiration. "Now, Edith's dinner party is at seven. I'm starved."

"Oh—of course, I forgot!" I run my hands through my hair, cursing.

"Not in front of the children!" Marshall exclaims. "Especially when they're young and impressionable! No rush, my dear. Take your time. We have an hour or so to get ready, anyway, unless you're thinking of rocking a satin dressing gown and chemise at dinner. I'd love to see that. It would be most enjoyable."

I roll my eyes. "After all this time, you're still a flirt."

"Come on, you know you enjoy it."

"I suppose I do." I give him a smirk and rush as fast as I can back to the bedroom to get ready, my pregnant belly weighing me down. Changing out of my bedclothes, swapping them for a Charleston dress of baby blue, I rejoin Marshall and the children downstairs. He's put on a dark trench coat and gloves, grinning up at me from under a straw boater hat.

"That was quick." He grabs his keys, opening the door back into the cold air outside.

Once I make my way to the door, he stops me and tells me to wait, clambering back upstairs, returning with one of my winter coats, pulling it upon my shoulders.

I give him a look, eyes narrowing, an accusing hitch in my brows. "Seriously?"

"I don't want you getting cold. Especially with another little one on the way." He presses a chaste kiss to my cheek. "Please accept my act of consideration."

"You're my husband and the father of my children. Of course I will." I poke him on his nose, grinning. "Gosh, you're so darn cute."

He steps outside with a proud *hmph* and reaches for my hand, helping me out the door. His eyes are like an eagle's as he supervises Anna and Will. They wait for us out in the lawn, throwing fallen leaves at each other and screaming with laughter. His hand remains around my waist as he locks the door.

"You know, I really do hope they've put that roast lamb with extra gravy on the menu like last time. Nathan cooks like a world class chef."

"Only you would wish that." I jostle him playfully in the ribs, a chortle rumbling from deep in his chest.

"But come *on*! His roasts are absolutely amazing! Edith is so lucky to have a chef in the house who could make her as many roasts as she wants whenever she requires. I'd die if I were her. Every night would be a roast beef night."

"Keep praying. Maybe he'll answer you if you say 'pretty please.'"

"I would hope so. His chicken breast is quite good, too. I'll settle for that if it's not beef."

He jingles his keys in his hand, unlocking the car, and buckling the kids in the backseats, nodding along as William tells him more about his Show and Tell at school and how many questions the kids want Marshall to answer, making him giggle sheepishly out of embarrassment. He settles into the driver's seat while I buckle myself in the passenger side. He slides his keys into the engine start up, the car coming to life, his hand on the wheel, his other sticking the gear shift in reverse, backing out of the driveway and into the street.

"Ma?" Will calls for me.

"Yes, Will?" I lean over the corner of the seat, gazing at him, his smile only expanding when he's acknowledged.

"I also told Mrs Abbott about you—how you fought with Papa in the war and how you met. They called you...I dunno the word...That's it! Rem...ark...able. Yes! That's it!"

Hesitantly, I let a smile unfold. "Really? I'm glad they enjoyed my story."

Marshall relaxes in the driver's seat, humming the same tune he's been humming for years. Like his soul, it never grows old. It never changes.

"Son, let me tell you that your mother is honestly the most extraordinary person I've ever met. She's brilliant; an extremely strong brilliance that set my world on fire. Her flames are addictive. Their burns don't harm you. It rather keeps the excitement in your heart warm."

"Poetic as always," I remark.

He squeezes my hand momentarily. "Only for you. You see, children, the world is changing. I can feel it every day, in every moment I spend here. Soon, women will have a fairer share, better outcomes than when Ma and I were young. The whole world will brighten up to you as soon as you flick the switch of those magnificent minds and send those currents gushing out. Just like your mother, you all share that flare, those flames. I'd be happy to have them dancing at my feet over and over again."

He turns onto the main road and brakes when the police officer standing in the middle of the intersection holds up a hand, fingers splayed to indicate that he should halt.

"As I've said, we're living in a pivotal time of change. You're lucky to experience it." His fingers thrum against the wheel in a staccato beat. His eyes brighten. "The gears are shifting. The sparks are starting to fly. Get ready, everyone. Rev up your engines. Floor the accelerator. The world is starting to wake up!"

THE END

ACKNOWLEDGEMENTS

When I was thirteen, I sat down one day and said to myself, "Hey, let's write a book," and on I went.

Little did I know, it would take five years to actually get, as I called it throughout its later years of writing, editing, and sending it out to countless agents, *The Leviathan* into its final form that is being distributed today.

During the process of writing this absolutely massive project, I was going through a rough patch in my personal life, struggling with dysthymia, anxiety, some not-so-great influences and environments, and later, the acceptance of my Autism diagnosis. Throughout, I feel as though I've sprinkled little specks of myself that I've chosen to leave embedded in my stories, learning to love myself more and more throughout. Hopefully, this makes them more human, and you, the reader, more at home.

I have a heapton of thank you's to give out:

To my mother, Jennifer Richards, for going with me to every poetry slam, writer's workshop, every bookstore, and introducing me to the magic of books.

To my father, Simon Richards, for being the critical eye in the center of the storm, reading through and enduring the ultimate cringe that were my rough drafts and my inconsistent ramblings of subplots and ideas I had.

To my grandmother, Barbara Letzer, for being my number one fan. Your bragging over the years has been much appreciated, and I hope I've made you proud.

To my best friend—or as we like to say, my sister from another mister, Nikita Kaitler. Thank you for accepting me for who I am ever since the day you told me off for feeding the chickens by our primary school chicken coop. I knew it would spark a crazy tale of adventure between us.

To my brothers, Liam and Jackson Richards, for driving me insane through the entire writing process, and being my confidantes with my stories and plans.

To my many friends, both online and in person, for tagging along, listening to my silly little excerpts I enjoy showing you way too much.

And to you, the reader, for giving me a chance to make your day. Your support is immeasurably incredible.

ABOUT THE AUTHOR

T.G Richards is an Australian-American, non-binary author that resides in Michigan, USA. From a young age, they have been telling stories ever since they were little and believes that their world is encompassed by magic and stories worth telling.

They're happiest with a warm cup of bitter tea in their favorite armchair, on a dark, rainy day, curled up with a good book and their bearded dragon, Horatio.

You can find more fresh updates and shenanigans from T.G Richards from their social media, @theo.on.mars_.

Made in the USA
Middletown, DE
05 August 2022